4

THE
STRANGER
YOU
KNOW

THE
STRANGER
YOU
KNOW

Jane Casey

EBURY
PRESS

1 3 5 7 9 10 8 6 4 2

Published in 2013 by Ebury Press, an imprint of Ebury Publishing
A Random House Group Company

The Random House Group Limited Reg. No. 954009

Addresses for companies within the Random House Group can be found at:
www.randomhouse.co.uk

A CIP catalogue record for this book is
available from the British Library

The Random House Group Limited supports The Forest Stewardship
Council® (FSC®), the leading international forest certification organisation.
Our books carrying the FSC label are printed on FSC® certified paper. FSC is
the only forest certification scheme supported by the leading environmental
organisations, including Greenpeace. Our paper procurement policy
can be found at: www.randomhouse.co.uk/environment

Printed in the UK by Clays Ltd, St Ives PLC

Hardback ISBN 9780091948337
Trade paperback ISBN 9780091948344

To buy books by your favourite authors and register for offers visit:
www.randomhouse.co.uk

For Kerry Holland

Some flying from the thing they feared, and some
Seeking the object of another's fear . . .
. . . And others mournfully within the gloom
Of their own shadow walked, and called it death . . .

'The Triumph of Life', Percy Bysshe Shelley

1992

The garden was quiet, the air still. As still as the girl who lay under the tree.

So still.

Her eyes were closed. Her hands lay by her sides, palms up. Her hair spread across the grass like yellow silk. And the flowers under her were like the stars above her.

He put out his hand and felt the heat radiating from her skin, even now. Even in the moonlight he could see the blood on her face, and the bruises around her neck, and the way her eyelids sagged, empty. Her eyes – her forget-me-not blue eyes – were gone. Her lip was split. Her face was swollen.

She was beautiful. No one would ever be as beautiful. She was perfect.

It surprised him, but he didn't mind that she was dead. He could look at her, really look at her, without being interrupted. Without being afraid that she would say something, or do something, that might hurt him.

He could touch her. He reached out, but stopped himself.

He could never touch her again.

His breath came faster. He wanted to touch himself but he couldn't do that either. Not here.

It was just because he loved her so much. More than anyone. More than anything.

Forget-me-not.
'I won't forget,' he promised. 'I'll never forget.'
He almost thought she smiled.

THURSDAY

Chapter 1

I'd seen enough dead bodies to know they can look peaceful. Calm, even. At rest.

Princess Gordon was not that sort of corpse.

It wasn't her fault. Anyone would have struggled to look serene when they had been battered to death, then shoved into the boot of a Nissan Micra and left to stiffen into full rigor mortis.

'I'm going to need to get her out to give you a proper cause of death, but from a preliminary examination she was beaten with something hard but rounded, like a pole, sometime within the last twenty-four hours.' The pathologist stood back, touching the back of one gloved hand to her forehead. 'I can't narrow it down for you yet, but I'll have a look at stomach contents during the post-mortem and make an educated guess.'

'I can make an educated guess for you now. It was her husband.' The voice came from beside me, where Detective Inspector Josh Derwent was taking up more than his fair share of room in the little ring of officers and crime-scene technicians that had gathered around the back of the car. The garage door was open but it still felt claustrophobic to me to be in that small, cluttered space. The air was dusty and the lighting cast long, dark shadows. I felt as if the piled-up junk was reaching out to grab me. Derwent had his hands in his pockets, with his elbows jutting out on either side. I had already inched away twice, to get out of range, but there was nowhere left to go.

'She wasn't married,' I said.

'Partner, then. Whoever that bloke is in the house.'

'Adam Olesugwe.'

'Him.'

'What makes you say that?' The pathologist was new, earnest and heavily pregnant. I wished she would just ignore Derwent. She had no idea what she was dealing with.

'Bound to be him.'

'If you're basing that on statistical probability—'

Derwent cut her off. 'I'm not.'

One of the response officers cleared his throat. I thought he was going to raise his hand and ask for permission to speak. 'He said he came back and she was missing. He said someone must have come into the house and attacked her.'

'Yeah, he'd know. He was the one who did it.' Derwent waved a hand at the body. 'Say this wasn't a domestic. Say it was a burglary gone wrong or a random murder. Why bother putting her in the car? Why not leave her in the house?'

'To hide her,' the response officer suggested.

'Why, though? It's hard work, moving a body. And she's a big girl, too. Look at that arse.'

'Sir.' I didn't usually try to manage Derwent's stream of consciousness but I had seen the look of shock on the pathologist's face. Dr Early, who had arrived late and made a joke about it. Derwent hadn't laughed.

'What is it, Kerrigan?' He glared at me.

I didn't dare say why I'd actually interrupted. It would only provoke worse behaviour. 'Just – why would Olesugwe move the body?'

'He was planning to get rid of the body but then her sister came round.'

It was Princess's sister, Blessed, who'd found the body and called 999. Last seen in hysterics being comforted by a female officer at the kitchen table, she'd been too incoherent to interview.

4

'Why would he want to kill her?' Early asked.

'Your guess is as good as mine. She was having an affair, or he was, or she didn't do the ironing.' He looked down at the pathologist's rounded belly. 'She was four months pregnant, according to Olesugwe. Women are more likely to be victims of domestic violence when they're up the duff.'

'That's a myth.' Dr Early put a protective hand on her stomach, as if she was trying to shield her unborn child from Derwent's toxic personality. I personally felt lead-lined hazard suits should have been standard issue for anyone who came into contact with him, pregnant or not.

Derwent shook his head. 'They did a study in the States. Murder is the third most common reason of violent death for pregnant women.'

'What else kills them?' I asked.

'Car accidents and suicide. Women drivers, eh?'

'Well, this lady didn't die in a car accident and she certainly didn't beat herself to death.' Dr Early folded her arms, resting them on top of her bump.

'That's my point. He killed her,' Derwent said. 'He gets angry about something, he beats her up, it goes too far, he dumps her in the car, starts to clean up, gets interrupted by the sister and all bets are off.'

'There was a smell of bleach in the kitchen,' I remarked.

'And no sign of a break-in. Wherever she died should look like an abattoir but I didn't see a speck of blood in the house.' Derwent pushed past a couple of officers and peered into the back seat of the car. 'Bags. If you forensic boys would like to do your jobs and get them out for us, I bet we'll find blood-stained clothes in Olesugwe's size.'

Dr Early looked down at Princess's body. 'I'll need some help to get her out of the boot.'

'Nice to hear a woman admit she needs some help,' Derwent said, and walked out without waiting to hear what Dr Early had to say in response, or, indeed, offering any assistance.

The doctor's lips were pressed together and her eyes were bright. I recognised the signs of someone trying not to cry. I'd been there, many times. 'Is he always like that?' she asked me.

'Not always. Sometimes he's worse.'

'I don't know how you can stand it.'

'Neither do I,' I said.

The reason I could stand it was because in addition to his numerous personality defects, Derwent was a brilliant copper. He left the SOCOs to their work and took both Olesugwe and Blessed to the nearest police station, Great Portland Street, where Blessed confessed to the affair she'd been having with Olesugwe, and Olesugwe admitted that Princess had found out about it. The murder weapon – a metal pole that had been used as a clothes rail in the couple's wardrobe – turned up in a shed in the garden of the small house, stuffed in a bag behind a lawnmower. Olesugwe had the key to the shed's padlock on his key ring, as well as the only set of keys for the Nissan. When I pointed out that neither the padlock nor the car boot was damaged in any way, he admitted moving the body and hiding the weapon.

'But he still won't admit that he killed her,' I said to Derwent as we left the police station, heading back to the office to get the paperwork underway. I shivered as the cold hit my face. We were on foot because Derwent had flatly refused to drive through central London to Somers Town, where Princess had breathed her last, when our new offices were in Westminster and it was twice as fast to go by public transport.

'He's still looking for a way out. I bet he'll say it was Blessed who attacked her and he was just trying to help her.'

'Do you think that's what happened?'

'Nope. Doesn't matter, though. He'll still lie about it.'

'I don't think Blessed would have called the cops before they were finished tidying up if she'd been involved.'

'She might have. She might be thick. Most criminals are.'

'I've noticed,' I said. I was only a detective constable but I had seven years of experience behind me. Derwent tended to forget that.

Instead of answering me, he sighed. 'What a waste of fucking time.' It wasn't my imagination: Derwent's mood was darker than usual.

'We got a result,' I pointed out.

'Anyone could have got it. Even you.'

'We did a good job.'

'The local murder team could have handled it.'

'They were too busy.'

'Is that what the boss told you?' He shoved his hands deeper into his pockets and walked faster. I lengthened my stride to keep up.

'Why else would he send us up there?'

'Why indeed?'

I realised I wasn't going to get an answer out of Derwent. Besides, I wasn't sure I wanted one. There was a chance he was referring to the fact that I was out of favour with the boss, and I couldn't imagine that Derwent would be pleased if he knew about it. Especially if he knew why.

I'd have been sensible to keep my mouth shut and walk in silence, but there was something I wanted to know. 'You were a bit off with Dr Early. What was the problem?'

Derwent's jaw clenched. 'She shouldn't be doing that job in her condition.'

'She's more than capable of doing it.'

'If you say so. She probably won't even be able to reach the table to do the PM.'

'I'm sure she'll manage.'

'She shouldn't have to.' Derwent flipped up the collar of his coat, hunching his shoulders as a scattering of rain spat in our faces. 'It's no job for a woman anyway. But when she's got a baby on board, she shouldn't be near dead bodies.'

'You are so old-fashioned it's untrue. Are you worried her unborn child will see the corpses and be upset? Wombs don't come with much of a view.'

'It's just not right.' His voice was flat. No more arguing.

I held my tongue until we got to the tube station and discovered that two lines were closed, just in time for the evening rush hour. We forced our way onto a packed Metropolitan line train to Baker Street, switched to the Bakerloo line and suffered as far as Charing Cross. It was a positive pleasure to resurface from the super-heated, stale depths of the Underground, even though the cold autumn air made my head ring as if I'd just been slapped.

Even with the inspector as a companion it wasn't a hardship to walk through Trafalgar Square and on down Whitehall as the lights came on. It had rained properly while we were on the tube, a short but sharp cloudburst, and the pavement had a glassy sheen. Fallen leaves were scattered across the ground, flattened against it by the rain, looking as if they had been varnished to it. The going was slick and my shoes weren't designed for it. Opposite the Cenotaph I slid sideways and collided with Derwent, clutching his arm for support. He bent his arm so his biceps bulged under my fingers. I snatched my hand away.

'Steady on,' Derwent said.

'It's the leaves.'

'I know you, Kerrigan. Any excuse to cop a feel.' He crooked his arm again. 'Come on. Hang on to Uncle Josh. I'll look after you.'

'I can manage, thank you.'

'It's not a sign of weakness, if that's what you're thinking. It's good to recognise your shortcomings. Look at Dr Early. She knew she couldn't shift that body on her own so she asked for help. You could take a lesson from that. Accept help when it's offered.'

'Is that what you do?'

He laughed. 'I don't *need* any help.'

'Of course not. The very idea.'

'Seriously, if you need to hold on to my arm, do it.'

'I would if I did, but I don't.' I would rather take off my shoes and walk barefoot than reinforce Derwent's ideas of chivalry. He would see it as proof of what he'd always thought – women need looking after. And I was junior to him, as well as being female, so he was totally comfortable with patronising me.

It made me want to scream.

We turned the corner into Parliament Square and I gazed across at the Houses of Parliament, not yet tired of staring at them even though I saw them every day on my way to work. They were a Victorian idea of medieval grandeur and there was something fantastic about them, something unreal about the delicate tracery, the honey-coloured stone, the soaring gilt-topped towers. From here, Britain had ruled the world, temporarily, and the buildings remembered. They were a physical manifestation of the superiority complex that was bred into the British, my father had said once. He had little time for the Empire and less sympathy for the country he lived in. I didn't think you could characterise a whole nation that way, but then I wasn't in the comfortable position of being foreign. Nor could I count myself as British. I was born in London of Irish parents, bred and raised as an Irish girl, despite the fact that we lived in Carshalton rather than Killybegs. I'd learned to dance the Walls of Limerick and played 'Down by the Sally Gardens' on the tin whistle and struggled into thick, sheep-smelling Aran jumpers knitted by relations and swapped the soda bread in my packed lunches for my friends' white crustless sandwiches. I'd played camogie, badly, at weekends, and played hockey equally badly at school. I was Irish by blood and English by accident and I didn't belong to either tradition, or anywhere else. I'd grown up feeling as if I'd lost something and it was only now I was starting to wonder if it mattered.

Derwent threw out an arm. 'Look at that. What a disgrace.'

'The Houses of Parliament?' I asked, surprised. I should have known Derwent was unlikely to be experiencing post-colonial guilt.

'Those fuckers. Shouldn't be allowed.' He was referring to the protesters camping on the grass in the middle of Parliament Square, occupying the space where the anti-war crowd had maintained their vigil, and where the demonstrations against globalisation had raged. There were regular police operations to clear the lawn, but somehow the campaigners came back in ones and twos, and it was rare to see it empty.

I tried to read the banners but it was hard to see them in the dusk, especially since they were rain-sodden. 'Capitalism is evil?'

'Dads Matter.'

'Oh, them.' The Dads Matter group was the militant alternative to Fathers for Justice, a pressure group for men who felt they had been victimised by the family courts. Dads Matter was small but growing and prone to extravagant publicity seeking. Its leader was Philip Pace, a handsome, charismatic forty-year-old with a background in PR. He was a smooth talker, a regular interviewee on news and current affairs programmes and had made the Top Ten Most Eligible Males list in *Tatler* the previous year. I didn't see the attraction myself, but then I wasn't all that keen on zealots. As the public face of Dads Matter, he made it his business to be reasonable and moderate, but as a group they were neither. 'What's their new campaign? Twenty-Twenty?'

'Someone hasn't been paying attention to briefings,' Derwent said. 'It's Fifty-Fifty. They want the courts to split custody of children equally between parents. No exceptions.'

'Oh, that sounds reasonable. What about abusers? What about protecting children from that?'

'Dads don't harm their children. They love them.' For once, Derwent's ultra-sarcasm had a decent target.

'What bullshit.'

'You don't think fathers have rights?' Derwent's eyebrows were hovering around his hairline. 'I thought you were a liberal, Kerrigan. If I said feminism was wank, you'd report me.'

'You say that frequently, and I haven't yet. Anyway, it's not the same thing. The courts make their decisions on a case-by-case basis. Sometimes the mothers get full custody because the dads aren't fit to be involved with their families. These men are just sore losers.'

'Doesn't mean they're not dangerous. You know they've been sharing tactics with extremist anti-abortion activists in the States, don't you?'

'I didn't, actually.' I was amazed that Derwent did. He generally didn't bother with reading briefings. In fact, I wasn't aware of him having read anything properly since we'd been working together.

'Pace was over in Washington recently, trying to get a US branch up and running. He appeared on a platform with the pro-lifers at a massive rally, though he doesn't want that to get out in this country in case it puts people off. They've got a lot in common, though. It's all about the sanctity of the family, isn't it? Two-parent happy families with hundreds of smiling, cheerful children. Fucking fantasyland. If you didn't read the briefing notes you'll have missed this too: they found a Dads Matter-affiliated messageboard on the Internet with a list of names and addresses for family court judges and their staff. Everyone is very jumpy about it. They're expecting parcel bombs and anthrax and God knows what.'

'How did I miss all of this?' I felt as if I hadn't done my homework and I'd been caught by my least favourite teacher – which was basically what had happened.

'Dunno. Maybe you're too busy concentrating on what's right in front of you to get a decent idea of the big picture. That's why you're a DC. You do all right at the small stuff, but you need a bit of a flair for strategy at my level.'

Maybe if you didn't leave all the paperwork and form filling to me I'd have time to read about the big picture. 'Thanks for the advice.'

'Freely given,' he said. 'Listen and learn.'

'I do. Every day.' It was true. If I wanted to know about misogyny, right-wing conspiracy theories or competition-grade swearing, working with Derwent was roughly equivalent to a third-level education.

Our route took us close to where the protesters stood, rain-blasted and pathetic, huddled in their anoraks like penguins in nylon hoods. Most were middle-aged and a touch overweight. They didn't look dangerous.

'They can't all be evil, and they must miss their children,' I said.

'Pack of whingers. If they loved their kids so much they wouldn't have left them in the first place.' He glowered at them. 'Anyone who's got the nerve to sit under the statue of the greatest Englishman who ever lived and make it look like a gypsy camp has got no principles and no soul.'

'Winston Churchill?'

'Who else?' He looked at me as if he was waiting for me to argue, but I knew better than to try. Derwent needed a fight occasionally, to do something with the aggression he seemed to generate just by breathing. But I was not going to be his punchbag today.

I could have sworn his ears drooped.

Chapter 2

Back at the office, Derwent threw himself into his chair and waved at me imperiously.

'Go and find the boss and tell him where we are with the case.'

I felt a thud of dismay. 'Don't you want to do it?'

'I've got things to do.'

'So have I.'

'Mine are more important.'

'How do you know?'

'Because I'm senior to you so whatever I have to do is bound to be more important.' As he said it he was reaching over to pick up a copy of the *Standard* that someone had left on a nearby desk.

'Look, I'd really rather not—' I started to say.

'Not interested. Tell someone who cares.' He glanced up at me. 'Why are you still here?'

I turned on my heel and stalked across the room towards the only enclosed office, where Chief Superintendent Charles Godley was usually to be found. I rapped on the door and it opened as I did so, Godley stepping towards me so that we almost collided. I apologised at the same time as he did. My face had been flaming already because I was livid with Derwent, but embarrassment added an extra touch of heat to my cheeks. I was aware of Derwent grinning at his desk on the other side of the room, and the speculative

13

glances from my other colleagues across the tops of their monitors. I knew, even if Godley didn't, that there was frequent, ribald speculation he had brought me on to his team because he wanted to sleep with me. I knew that Godley attracted rumours of that sort like roses attract greenflies; he was head-turningly handsome with ice-blue eyes and prematurely silver hair, and I was the first woman he had recruited in a long time, though not the last. I also knew that people had picked up on the fact that I was extremely awkward around him all of a sudden. The general theory was that we had had an affair and I had ended it, or he had ended it, or his wife had found out and *she* had ended it.

They couldn't have been more wrong.

'Did you want something, Maeve?'

'DI Derwent asked me to update you about the Somers Town murder – Princess Gordon. We've got one in custody.'

'Her husband?'

'Partner.'

'Give me the details.' Instead of inviting me into his office he stayed where he was, standing in the doorway, in plain sight of everyone on the team. Maybe he did know about the rumours after all.

Briefly, I explained what we had found out. Godley listened, his blue eyes trained on my face. He had a gift for total concentration on whatever was in front of him, and it was a large part of his charm that he made you feel as if you were the only person in the world when he was listening to you. I could have done without the rapt attention, all the same. It made me too aware of my voice, my face, my tendency to wave my hands around while I was explaining things, my suspicion that my hair had gone frizzy in the damp evening air.

Not that he cared about any of that. He cared about the fact that I had worked out, beyond any doubt, that he was utterly, totally corrupt. He was paid by one of London's biggest drug dealers, a ruthless gangster with an appalling record of violence, and I wasn't sure exactly what Godley did for him in return. I didn't want to know. I had worshipped the superintendent, blindly, and finding out that he was a fake made me more sad than angry. And for all that he was on the take, he was still a supremely gifted police officer.

I'd promised him I wouldn't give him away, because it was none of my business and I couldn't throw him to the wolves. He'd promised me it made no difference to how he did his job, and he'd also promised not to treat me any differently. But he had lied about that, and I was starting to change my mind about interfering. I still couldn't reconcile the two facts: he was a boss who inspired total loyalty in everyone who worked with him, and he gave away inside information for money. He'd said it was more complicated than I knew, and I wanted to believe him, I really did.

I just couldn't trust him.

'And the sister?' Godley asked.

'DI Derwent wants to interview her again, but he doesn't think she was involved.'

'Unless she's a fuckwit.' Derwent crossed the room, folding his stolen newspaper as he approached, and sat down at a desk that was currently unoccupied. He started casually, carelessly ransacking the desk, opening and closing drawers. 'Who sits here?'

'I don't know,' I said. I did know, in fact, but I didn't want to tell him. The desk belonged to DCI Una Burt, his superior and emphatically not a member of the very select group of colleagues that Derwent could stand. Nor was she one of the even smaller group who liked him. 'I know they don't want you to go through their things.'

'That's a nice stapler.' He clicked it a couple of times, very fast. 'That's better than the one I've got.'

'Josh. Concentrate.' Godley's tone was mild but Derwent dropped the stapler and turned around to face the boss.

'The CPS were happy for us to charge Olesugwe but they

15

agreed with me that we need to know more about Blessed before we decide what to do about her. I think Olesugwe will plead eventually but at the moment he's still hoping for a miracle. Which he's not going to get, because he's fucked. Did Kerrigan tell you about the keys?'

'What about them?'

'Kerrigan had a look through his personal effects before we interviewed him. She spotted that he had the key to the shed and the car, and she just happened to ask him if there was a spare set of car keys anywhere.'

'The car was fifteen years old,' I explained. 'I thought it was probably second-hand or third-hand and there was a good chance it was down to one set of keys.'

'Well done,' Godley said, without enthusiasm, and I blushed, wishing that Derwent had just said nothing.

Apparently oblivious, he grinned at me. 'You see, you look vague, but you're actually not all that stupid when you try.'

'Thanks.' *For nothing*, I added silently.

'Makes me wonder why you're being left out of the big investigation.'

'What investigation?' I looked at Godley, whose face was like stone.

'Josh. That's enough.'

'It just doesn't seem fair of you to shut out Kerrigan. She hasn't done anything wrong.'

'That's not what's going on and you know it.' Godley stepped back into his office. 'Come in here and shut the door, Josh.'

Derwent was flipping through the newspaper again. He flattened it out on a double-page spread near the centre and with a flick of his wrist sent it spinning towards me. It landed by my feet. 'Have a read of that, Kerrigan. It's as close as you're going to get.'

I picked it up. The headline screamed: SERIAL KILLER TARGETING LONDON'S SINGLES. Most of the space below was taken up with pictures of two young women. One had red hair to her shoulders; the other was dark and had short hair. She was huge-eyed and delicate, while the red-head was a stunner with a full mouth and slanting green eyes. Both were slim, both attractive. And dead. My eye fell on a pull quote in bold type: 'They lived alone. No one heard their cries for help.' And then, on the opposite page: 'Mutilated and murdered'.

'It's not our case,' Godley said, to me. 'I've been asked to put together a task force in case they turn out to be connected, but I'm working with the local murder teams and they're still officially investigating them. The victims didn't know one another. They lived in different areas. The first woman died in January. The second was two months ago. This article is just speculation.'

I appreciated the explanation but it wasn't really aimed at me. Nor was Derwent really complaining about me being left out. He wasn't the type to care. He was absolutely the type to make use of a subordinate to get at his boss, though, and he wasn't finished.

'Oh, come on. Of course they're connected.' Derwent leaned over and snatched the paper back, flattening it out so he could read aloud: '"Both Kirsty Campbell and Maxine Willoughby lived alone. They worked within two miles of one another in central London. Friends describe both of them as bubbly and outgoing, but unlucky in love – Maxine had never found the right person, while Kirsty had recently broken off her engagement to her fiancé, Stephen Reeves (28). He describes himself as 'heartbroken' on the Facebook page set up in memory of Kirsty, but declined to comment for this article. Police have cleared Mr Reeves of any involvement in Kirsty's death."'

'He declined to comment but they scavenged a quote from him anyway,' I said. 'I bet the lawyers made them put in the bit about him not being a suspect.'

Derwent read on, this time with more emphasis.

'"And the similarities don't end with how they lived. Kirsty and Maxine were strangled in their homes. There was no sign of a break-in at either address, suggesting that in each case they may have known their killer. Most shocking of all is the anonymous tip-off we received that both women were horribly mutilated, their bodies desecrated, their eyes gouged out. Police had not revealed this grisly detail to the public, but more than anything else it seems to suggest that Kirsty and Maxine were killed by the same person."'

I shuddered. 'That's horrible. I'm not surprised they didn't want that detail revealed. But if no one knew, it can't be a copycat.'

'It's not proof of any connection between the two deaths,' Godley said. Derwent slammed his hands down on the desk.

'Like *fuck* it isn't.'

'I wanted to talk to you about that article, but not out here, Josh.'

'Nothing to do with me.'

'Someone tipped them off. Someone who wants there to be a connection between the murders. Someone not particularly well informed. I don't have to look too far to find someone who fits the bill.' I'd never heard Godley sound so stern. He turned and walked around his desk. Derwent jumped up and followed him. He didn't even glance in my direction as he went past, his face set and pale, his hands clenched. He slammed the door after him, to make it absolutely clear, as if I hadn't known it already, that my presence wasn't required. The newspaper had fallen to the floor, forgotten, and I picked it up. Back at my desk, with one eye on Godley's door to watch for Derwent's return, I read through the rest of the article, and discovered two things. One: I knew the senior investigating officer in the Maxine Willoughby investigation all too well. Two: I had no idea whatsoever why Derwent was so angry.

But I would make it my business to find out.

Chapter 3

'What are you doing tonight?'

I didn't even look up. 'Going home early.'

'Wrong answer.' Liv began tidying my desk around me, humming under her breath.

'Can you stop doing that?'

'It's so untidy.' Liv was the only other female detective constable on Godley's team. She was as elegant and lovely as a Japanese ink drawing; I had never seen a strand of her long dark hair out of place. Her own desk was arranged as neatly as if she'd used a ruler to organise it.

I was basically her exact opposite in every way.

'It's creative mess. I work best like this.' I slammed my hand down on a pile of papers that was beginning to slide sideways. 'That was fine before you started messing with it.'

'If they ever bring in a clean-desk policy—'

'I'll change jobs.' I took the file she was holding and stuck it back in the middle of the muddle.

'It hurts me,' she said.

'Don't look, then.'

'I can't stop myself.'

'It's not that bad.' I rolled back a few inches so I could see what she was talking about. 'Okay. It looks like an explosion in an origami exhibition.'

'Worse than that.' She picked up my pen pot and tipped

the contents out over the desk. 'There. I think that's how it was when I found it.'

I brushed paperclips off the page I had been reading. 'Thanks, that's much better. Why were you asking me about my plans?'

'Come for a drink.'

'I shouldn't.'

'Why not?'

'Rob's going away tomorrow morning. Two weeks in the good old US of A.'

Her eyebrows went up. 'Holiday?'

'An FBI course in Virginia. His boss arranged it.' His predatory, female boss, who had almost caused me to break up with him over the summer, so heavily had she been leaning on him to sleep with her. I'd known he was hiding something and assumed the worst. I'd been absolutely sure he was cheating on me, when the opposite was true. It was like that, with Rob. I kept waiting for everything to go wrong because no one was that perfect, and I couldn't believe he felt the way he said he did about me. To my constant surprise, we were far beyond my usual cut-off for relationships. Most of mine had lasted weeks, not months, but here we were, still together after almost a year.

The course was too good an opportunity for him to turn down, as I'd told him when I encouraged him to go. But I hated that he was going to be gone for so long, and so far away. And I hated that DI Deborah Ormond was going too.

'Two weeks in the States. Nice work if you can get it.' Liv settled down on the chair next to mine, getting comfortable. 'And how do you feel about that?'

'Stop using your relationship-counsellor voice. I'm looking forward to it.'

'Bullshit.'

'No, I am. I'll be able to do whatever I want, when I want. It'll be like being on my own again. Being free.'

Liv raised an eyebrow. 'Still working on the commit-ment issues?'

'No, because I don't see them as a problem.' I shuffled pages, trying to look busy. 'I just like having options, that's all.'

'How does Rob feel about it?'

'Oh, who knows. He acts as if we've mated for life.'

'What a bastard.'

I glared at her. 'We can't all settle down and get a dog on the second date.'

'It was our fourth,' Liv said, ultra-dignified. 'And not a dog. Goldie is a goldfish.'

'Well, that's totally different.'

She grinned. 'Seriously, though. Is two weeks the long-est the two of you have spent apart?'

'Yes, but I haven't seen all that much of him since he left the team.' That was another sore point. He'd had to leave a job he loved because of me. Godley had a rule about rela-tionships within the team and we'd been found out. One of us had had to go. Being Rob, he'd netted a promotion and a slot on the Flying Squad, but it had complicated his life and I knew he missed the old team. I sighed. 'We just never seem to be on the same schedule.'

'It gets a bit like that, doesn't it? Especially in the job.'

'So it seems. If they're not job, they don't understand the hours and stress and bad pay. If they are, you don't get to see them. What's the point?'

'There isn't one. You have to become a nun.'

'I would, but the veil wouldn't suit me.' I checked the time, suddenly aware of the ache in my shoulders and neck from hunching over my desk. 'Where are you going for this drink and who else has signed up?'

'The local, and it's just me and Joanne, and Christine. Please note, I'm not offended by you wanting to know who else is going.'

'Joanne as in your girlfriend? I haven't seen her in ages.'

I'd only met her a couple of times but I liked her a lot. 'Okay, I'm in. Who is Christine?'

Liv shushed me, leaning across so she could mutter. 'Civilian analyst. She's been working for Godley since before I joined the team. Please don't tell me you didn't know who she was.'

'Oh, her. I'd forgotten her name.' I was aware of her, but I hadn't paid much attention. She was young and giggly, addicted to shopping for clothes in her lunch hour and flirting with the male detectives.

Liv tilted her head to one side, like a bird about to peck. 'Don't judge her. You don't know her.'

'Okay. I don't know her. But I don't think we're going to get on.'

'She's sweet. And she's terrified of you.'

'Of *me*?' I glanced over to where she was working, facing away from me so all I could see was light brown hair in a messy up-do and a narrow back. 'But I'm not scary at all. How is that possible?'

Liv sighed. 'You have no idea, do you?' She counted her points off on her fingers. 'You never speak to her. You aren't afraid to snap at the boys if they get out of line with sexist remarks. You're a workaholic and you take your job very seriously. Plus you have a habit of solving our shittiest cases. Most of the team think you're the mutt's nuts and would sacrifice a body part for the chance to sleep with you, which you don't seem to care about. Then again, you do have the finest bloke ever to work here warming your bed, so why would you? She worships you from afar. I made her day by telling her I'd ask you to come with us.'

'You are kidding.' I was feeling deeply uncomfortable.

'Not in the least.'

'She'll be so disappointed when she finds out the truth.'

'What did I say that wasn't true?' Liv patted my head. 'Especially the part about being a workaholic. You really need to have a break now and then.'

I considered that for a moment. By the evening I was usually exhausted, fit for nothing but half an hour in front of the television and then bed. That was on ordinary days, when I wasn't in the middle of a nightmare, headline-grabbing case. I'd been tired for so long, it passed for normal. I only really noticed when I was so fatigued I could neither eat nor sleep.

Now that I thought about it, none of that sounded healthy.

'All right. You've persuaded me.' Liv looked triumphant and I held up my hand to forestall her. 'But just for one drink. Then I really have to go home.'

It was simply amazing how quickly one drink turned to three when you were having fun. I beamed across the table at Liv and Joanne, who were holding hands. Joanne was tall and dark-haired, with clear, freckled skin and high cheekbones. She looked like a model, spoke with a Scouse lilt, and had a high-flying job in the Counter Terrorism Command. Liv had met her when they both worked in Special Branch. The contrast between them was striking. Both were exceedingly attractive, but in very different ways. And they were obviously, transparently in love.

The gin loosened my tongue. 'You know, you two make a lovely couple.'

'Oh, we know.' Joanne smiled at Liv, then back at me. 'Poster girls for Metropolitan Police inclusiveness.'

'The friendly face of lesbianism.' Liv untangled her fingers from her girlfriend's to lift her glass. 'Here's to being a dyke.'

We all clinked glasses, Christine giggling nervously. That was more or less all she had done so far. Sitting beside me, she was facing the bar and therefore had a view, as I did, of most of the team propping it up, drinking as if it was a competition. From where I was sitting it looked as if DS Chris Pettifer was winning. As I watched, he took three goes to get his pint glass back on the bar, then stared at it blearily as if daring it to move again.

'Not a pretty sight,' I said. 'I think Chris needs to call it a night.'

'Poor DS Pettifer. His wife's left him.'

I looked at Christine curiously. 'How did you find that out?'

She shrugged. 'I get to know things about the people on the team. They were having IVF and it didn't work out. They can't afford any more and they're not entitled to another round on the NHS. She's gone off travelling on her own, so I suppose I shouldn't say she's left him, because she might be back and they haven't exactly split up.'

'Why didn't I know any of this?' I asked Liv.

'Because you don't really have time to gossip. You're too busy.'

'That's so sad.' I knocked back the end of my drink. There was another lined up in front of me, fizzing gently. I'd drink it quickly, I thought, checking the time with a twinge of guilt.

'Pettifer?' Liv asked.

'Me. I'm so boring. It's not that I don't like gossip. I absolutely do. It's just that I'm too scared of getting in trouble with Derwent to be caught having fun at work.'

'What's it like?' Christine asked. 'Working with DI Derwent, I mean?'

'A laugh a minute.' I was trying to get at the slice of lemon in the bottom of my glass. Ice slid past my hand on to the table, and I swore.

'Really? It's fun?' Christine had pale blue eyes that were very large, surrounded by a lot of eyeliner and set far apart in a heart-shaped face. She was too pretty to dislike, or take seriously. She had already confided in us that she had always dreamed of being a police officer but having worked for Godley, she wasn't so sure she wanted to be one any more. I imagined myself watching other people do my job while I spent all day reading and colour coding Excel spreadsheets of phone data that meant nothing to me. Hell on earth, I concluded.

I also concluded that Christine and I did not have a lot in common.

I tried to explain what I meant. 'Well, it's sort of fun. In a way. You have to ignore a lot of what he says, and he likes to test me.'

'Test you?'

'Challenge me. I don't know. I can't really describe it.' It was a working dynamic that was as close to dysfunctional as you could get, but we got results. 'I make suggestions and he shoots them down. Or he gives me a hard time for being too good at the job. Or for being a woman.'

'Sounds like a charmer,' Joanne observed.

'I'm used to him,' I said simply.

'I'd rather work with anyone on the team than him. He's a bigoted prick.' Liv sounded extra-fierce and I grinned at her.

'Tell us how you really feel.'

'He hates me because I'm not interested in men.'

'Oh, he hates everyone. Don't take it to heart.' It wasn't often that I found myself defending Derwent, but I knew him better than Liv did. He really wasn't picking on her specifically. There were very few people he liked in the world, and it happened that the majority of that select group were straight white men, just like him.

Christine leaned her chin on her hand and stared dreamily into the middle distance. 'He doesn't have a girlfriend, does he? What do you think he's like in bed?'

'I don't think about that.' I was hoping to stop her before she got too far with that line of conversation.

'But if you did think about it . . .' She sighed. 'I bet he's dominant.'

I pulled a face, appalled at the very idea.

'Energetic,' Liv suggested.

'Go on, Maeve,' Joanne said. 'It's your turn. In a word.'
'Quick.'

The burst of laughter turned heads at the bar. They were wondering what we were talking about, with that prickly suspicion born of being self-conscious. Because of course the four of us had to be talking about the men we worked with.

They were right, as it happened. But we might not have been.

Liv grinned. 'I know, let's play Shag, Marry, Kill. Maeve, who would you pick if you had to choose between Derwent, Godley and . . . Belcott.'

'Too easy. You'd kill Belcott straight away *then* you'd have the party to celebrate. You'd have quite a while before you had to choose between Derwent and Godley.' Belcott was a nasty little man, the same rank as me but going nowhere. I'd seen him in action, taking credit for things he hadn't done and sucking up to anyone who might put in a good word for him with the boss. He'd taken pleasure in the fact that I'd had a stalker who had invaded my privacy, gloating about the fact that he'd seen footage of me with Rob, during private moments. And that was only the beginning of what he'd done to piss me off.

'And?' Liv demanded. 'Marry Godley, shag Derwent?'

'Not so fast.' I was considering it. 'I bet Derwent would worship his wife, in a patronising way, obviously. You'd never hear a word about his cases but he'd bring you flowers every Friday night.'

'And perfume on your birthday,' Joanne agreed.

'Always the same brand . . .' I said.

'The same as his mum used to wear.' Joanne grinned at me.

Liv's jaw had dropped. 'You're not turning down Godley as a marriage prospect, are you? For *Derwent*?'

'I don't know how happy Mrs Godley is. He's married to the job, isn't he? More than any of us. And you'd have to put up with people staring at him as you walked down the street, because the man is beautiful.'

'I'd turn for him. He's on my freebie list,' Liv said. 'Near the top.'

Joanne nodded. 'I wouldn't mind as long as you told me all the details.'

I ran my finger down the side of my glass. 'I don't really want to have sex with him, though.'

'Because you love Rob.' Liv sing-songed the words and I glowered at her.

'Thank you, Disney Princess. It's not that.'

'But you do love Rob, don't you?' Christine sighed. 'I had such a crush on him when I started working here.'

'Who wouldn't?' I made it sound wry, but I kind of meant it.

'Me,' Liv said promptly. 'But only because I love Jo, and he has boy bits, and I knew he was totally head over heels for you the first time I saw you together.' She narrowed her eyes. 'Anyway, get back to Godley. I'm intrigued.'

Even on the wrong side of three drinks I wasn't going to tell them what I knew about Godley, but knowing it had changed the way I saw him. He had been my hero. I had worked my arse off to impress him. I'd been determined to prove he'd been right to whisk me away from Borough CID to work for his specialist murder squad. Then I'd found out the truth about him, and suddenly I couldn't see him any other way.

All three of them were looking at me, waiting for an explanation. Liv and Joanne were too good at interrogations for me to hope they'd drop it. 'I just don't go for older men.'

'Everyone says you've slept with him already.' Three drinks down, Christine had gone far beyond the point where she was capable of being discreet. I'd known about the gossip, but it was irritating to hear it parroted back to me as if saying it would make it true.

'Never. And I never will. Make sure that gets around the squad room when you're passing on things you know about the team.' There had been an edge to my voice, but I was still surprised to see Christine's face crumple. 'Oh, shit.'

'Sorry . . .' Two perfect tears slid down her cheeks.

Liv drew Christine's glass away from her. 'That's quite enough gin for you, dear.'

'I didn't mean to say anything wrong,' she wailed, hunting through her bag for a tissue. Even when she was crying she looked adorable, a fact that wasn't lost on the guys at the bar. Ben Dornton won the race to our table and handed Christine a paper napkin.

'What are they doing to you, Christine? Why do you want to go out drinking with these miserable cows?' He scowled at the three of us. 'Fuck me, it's proper bubble, bubble, toil and trouble over here. Is it Halloween or something?'

'Not for days,' I said.

He seemed genuinely cross. 'Well, you lot are all set for costumes.'

I looked around, noticing that Liv, Jo and I were all in black suits. Christine was wearing a purple cardigan with a butterfly embroidered on the shoulder. *Spot the difference.* I had been too harsh, I knew.

'I didn't mean to upset you, Christine.'

'Don't worry, I always cry when I'm drunk,' floated out from behind the napkin.

'Come and have a drink with us,' Dornton suggested. 'We'll look after you.'

'It's a girls' night out, though.' Christine emerged, looking tragic, as if that was an insurmountable obstacle. The very phrase made me wince.

'I wouldn't say that. Colleagues' night out.'

'Well, that includes us. We're your colleagues too.' Ben gave a little laugh, shooting for casual. It occurred to me that he was trying hard. I glanced up and saw the expression on his face as he stared at Christine: pure yearning. Over at the bar, Dave Kemp was watching us, turning his beer bottle around and around as he brooded. And the brooding wasn't aimed at me. Kemp I didn't know at all, but he was cute if you liked blue eyes, fair hair and a boyish manner. Dornton was all close-cropped hair and attitude, older than Kemp and usually cynical about everything. I'd never seen him look quite so vulnerable before and I hope Christine had the sense not to play them off against one another because I wasn't at all sure Dornton would cope. It reminded me of Rob, all of a sudden, and how he had looked at me before we got together – knowing what he wanted, not at all sure he was going to get it – and all of a sudden I missed him like mad.

'Okay, then.' I stood up. 'I need to get going. We can carry on another time.'

'Oh, what?' Liv began, and Joanne grabbed her knee.

'She's right. We should get going too.' She caught my eye and gave me a wink and I knew she'd seen the same thing I had on Dornton's face. 'Down in one, Maeve.'

It was such a bad idea to knock back my drink, but I didn't even consider leaving it; I did as I'd been told. Slightly high from the gin burning in my stomach, I turned to Dornton under cover of pulling on my jacket and murmured, 'I'm trusting you to look after Christine. Make sure she doesn't get too drunk, and make sure she gets home all right.'

He looked wounded. 'You know I will.'

'I *think* you will, but I'm still making it your job. She needs looking after.' I poked him in the chest. 'And no taking advantage.'

'As if I would.'

'Make sure you don't.' I gave Dave Kemp a long stare to convey the same message, and saw it hit home.

As I stalked to the door, I found myself thinking I could get to like being scary.

Chapter 4

By the time I got home, I'd slid all the way down the helter-skelter from the tough detective who doesn't let anyone intimidate her to the usual version of me, second-guessing every decision I'd made that day and wincing as my feet complained about hours of punishment in heels. It didn't help that I had to take a long route back. Rob and I had moved to a flat in Dalston, in a purpose-built block of no charm whatsoever. It was an easy enough commute to work for both of us, but I was still getting used to the area. I hated the fact that we'd had to leave our flat in Battersea, where we'd been happy, because the stalker I tried not to think about had found out where I lived.

My usual inclination was to stand up to being bullied, but I was scared enough of Chris Swain to follow elaborate precautions in order to avoid being traced. He was a rapist and a coward, a peeping Tom and a technological genius who ran password-protected websites in shady corners of the Internet where like-minded creeps could share their fantasies – and memories. I'd been the one who uncovered the truth about him, and I was his ultimate target, or so he told me. He'd found me before; he could find me again. But I wasn't going to make it easy for him this time. Our land-line was ex-directory and all of our post was redirected to work; I had no magazine subscriptions and wasn't a member of any organisations that might put me on a mailing list. None of the bills were in my name. I took different methods of public transport home, when I had to rely on it rather than getting a lift. I hadn't replaced my car when it died; Rob parked his anywhere but in front of our flat. I checked, always and methodically, that no one was following me on my walk home, and I never went the same way twice.

Chris Swain had affected every decision we'd made in moving. The area was a busy one, well served by public transport but with a shifting population who wouldn't pay any attention to us. The flat was on the second floor in a modern building with good security and CCTV. It had low ceilings and small, bland rooms: a sitting room that did double duty as a dining room by virtue of the table in the corner, a galley kitchen, a poky bathroom that got no natural light, one bedroom with built-in cupboards and a bed and no room for anything else. We kept the blinds down in the bedroom almost all the time, more aware than most that privacy was an illusion in urban areas. It was a six-month lease and there was nothing to make us leave at the end of those months, but nothing to make us want to stay either. Functional was one word that occurred to me about it. Bleak was another.

It took me three goes to get my key in the door and the first thing I did was fall over the suitcase in the middle of the hall. I landed on my knees with a bang.

'Jesus. Fuck.'

'If that's a request, Jesus is busy. He told me I should stand in.' Rob came out of the bathroom, toothbrush in hand. 'Are you okay?'

'The booze is taking the edge off the pain.'

'Where have you been?'

'I fell among thieves.' Since I was down there anyway, I sat on the floor and pulled off my shoes while Rob finished brushing his teeth. 'Liv made me go for a drink.'

'Twisted your arm, did she?' He said it lightly, but I felt

guilty anyway. When he came back to the hall he put out a hand to me and I allowed myself to be lifted to my feet, smelling mint.

'I hadn't been out for ages. Joanne was there too. And Christine. Do you remember her?'

'The analyst? Yeah, she was sweet.'

'She remembers you, let me tell you.'

He grinned. 'I deny everything.'

'She said she fancied you rotten.'

'That's nice.' It wasn't an unusual event in Rob's life, and not just because he was tall and lean and broad-shouldered, or because of the black-hair-blue-eyes colouring, or the quiet, understated commitment to doing the right thing that had landed him in harm's way once or twice. It was because when he listened to people he seemed to hear more than what they actually said. It gave him an unnerving ability to read minds, which I found inconvenient at times. Like now. He reached out and touched my cheek. 'Don't worry. I only had eyes for you.'

'Who said anything about being worried? I think she fancies Derwent too, so it's not all that flattering.'

'What gives you that idea?'

'She was speculating about what it would be like to sleep with him.'

'And?'

'We speculated.' I blinked up at him. 'Don't make me think about it again. I've been trying to forget.'

'I've heard you talking about him in your sleep.' He imitated me. '"Ooh, Josh, again. Like that. Harder. Don't stop." I think that was it.'

'Yuck. That's a horrible suggestion.'

His eyes were wide with innocence. 'Imagine how I felt having to listen to it.'

'I've never had a dream about Derwent. My subconscious mind is above that sort of thing.'

'I know what I heard.'

'You're making it up.' I looked at him doubtfully. 'Aren't you?'

He laughed at me. 'How is Derwent, anyway?'

'Rude. Horrible. Oh, and weird.' I hadn't noticed him come out of Godley's office; the next time I'd seen the superintendent he'd been alone. Derwent, for once, had gone home early. I told Rob about it and he listened, frowning.

'You know and I know he doesn't give two shits about my career progression. He was using me to get at Godley for leaving him out of the task force he's setting up and I don't know why he would be left out. Or why he'd care, particularly.'

'Maybe because DCI Burt is involved?' Rob suggested.

'Maybe. She does make him crazy.' I sighed. 'He was so angry with Godley, though.'

'He's an angry man.' Rob stretched and yawned. 'I can't believe I'm talking about him rather than sleeping. I'm shattered.'

'Are you going to bed? What time is it?'

'Late. I've got to be up in six hours.'

'I missed your last night.' I rubbed my eyes. 'I am such a crap girlfriend.'

'You have your good points.' Rob looked thoughtful. 'I may need a reminder of what they are.'

I slid my jacket off and leaned back against the wall. 'Where would you like to start?'

'With you taking your make-up off. If you go to bed like that, you'll wake up looking like the saddest clown in the world.' He was standing very close to me, and he started unbuttoning my shirt.

'That is not motivating me to get out the cleanser.'

'What? I'm just helping.' He leaned in for a kiss and I let him do what he wanted with me as his hands roved. The effect he had on me was not wearing off – quite the opposite. He only had to look at me a certain way to make me catch my breath, and when he touched me, I was lost.

33

'I have been thinking about this all night,' I whispered, the plaster cold against my back as Rob slid the last of my clothes to the floor. His hand slipped between my thighs and I clung to him and shivered, wanting him to keep doing what he was doing. Wanting more.

'It was on my mind too.'

'Oh really?' I pressed against him. 'What were you thinking?'

'I would really rather show you than tell you.' He stepped back, moving towards the bedroom. 'Hurry up, though.'

I came down to earth with a bump as soon as I saw myself in the bathroom mirror. The gin-euphoria had worn off. I was blotchy, with mascara streaked under each eye and my hair was tragic. Sobering up, I scrubbed my face and brushed my teeth until I could no longer taste alcohol. All of the things I was worried about came and stood around me as I wearily, savagely rubbed moisturiser into my face. Why was I so crap? I only had to manage two things: my job and my relationship. Sometimes I felt I was failing at both.

And in the kitchen, as I drank half a litre of water, I saw that he had made dinner for both of us, which made my guilt bite down even harder. It was like him not to mention it. It was like him to say he didn't mind. Sometimes I would have given all I had to know how he really felt.

I found Rob sitting up in bed with his eyes closed, his arms folded across his bare chest, fast asleep. He looked tired too, with dark smudges like thumbprints under his eyes. As usual he was sleeping in a self-contained, composed way, not sprawling or snoring. He was just too perfect.

Too good for me.

I shied away from thinking about it, knowing that I'd touched on the truth but absolutely not wanting to consider it any further because I knew, logically, where it would end: with a break-up. And I didn't want to lose him, even if I didn't deserve him. I turned off his light as quietly as I could and edged around to my side of the bed, intending to get in without waking him.

Some hope. He slept as lightly as a cat. As I slid under the covers, he reached for me.

'Where were we?'

'You don't have to. You're tired.'

'I'll find the energy, believe me.'

I turned over, burrowing into the pillow.

'Don't you want to?' Rob sounded puzzled.

'I'm really, really sorry I missed dinner,' I whispered. 'I'm sorry I missed your last night.'

'Not my last night on the planet, hopefully.' He put on his light. 'Maeve, look at me. If I really minded, I'd have phoned you. I could have gone to bed hours ago. I was watching TV until five minutes before you showed up. I don't mind you going out and having a good time with your mates. I don't expect you to be here if you're not working.'

'But you're going away.'

'And I'll be back.'

'You don't hate me for being selfish?'

He looked startled. 'Who said you were selfish? You're terrible at managing your time, but I knew that before we started going out.'

'And you still find me attractive even when my make-up is smudged and I smell of alcohol.'

The corner of his mouth lifted. 'Then more than ever.'

The thing about Rob was that he had an unerring instinct for the right thing to say, and do. I felt all of my worries slip away as he made me absolutely sure he loved me, despite all of my flaws. Maybe because of some of them. I showed him, because it was true, that I loved him, even though I still hadn't said it, and couldn't, and it turned out to be the sort of sex that makes you smile to yourself when you think about it afterwards, and you think about it a *lot*.

I was almost asleep when I remembered to ask him if he thought I was intimidating, and had to listen to him laughing on and off for the next five minutes, so much that the bed shook, until I turned over and went to sleep in a proper temper.

Some time in the small hours, around the time I usually got a phone call about a dead body, I woke up and reached for him again, curling against him, my knees tucked behind his, my arm around his waist. He held my hand and said my name, and I was almost sure he was asleep but I didn't dare say out loud what I was thinking. *I love you*. It shouldn't have been difficult.

I forgave him everything all over again when I woke early but not quite early enough the next morning to find a glass of water and a couple of Alka-Seltzer on the bedside table, along with a note telling me he loved me and he'd see me in two weeks and of course I could be intimidating if I wanted to be, if that mattered to me.

The flat was tidy, and too quiet, and I wandered around feeling suddenly unmoored. I hadn't lied to Liv. I really did like the idea of being on my own. The reality just seemed a bit brutal.

What I wanted, I realised, was to be on my own with Rob for two weeks. I missed him already.

I hadn't even said goodbye.

FRIDAY

Chapter 5

In the interests of making the best of things, I got into work early. I had a filthy headache, which I refused to admit was a hangover. All I wanted was to sit quietly at my desk, sipping the vat of coffee I'd bought on the way in. I had yet to find a route that meant I *didn't* pass a Starbucks on my journey to the office and sometimes I succumbed, even though I preferred to think of myself as the sort of person who would support small businesses rather than global coffee-pushers. When it came down to it, I just wanted caffeine, and lots of it, with absolutely no conversation on the side, to the point where I couldn't even be bothered to correct the baristas when they mangled my name. That was why I was clutching a cup with 'Maisy' scrawled down the side. I had been 'Midge' and 'May' before, but 'Maisy' was a new one.

The office was practically empty and I sat down at my desk, glad that I had a chance to get through some work before the phone started ringing and people – Derwent, mainly – started to make claims on my attention. His cutting little remark about not reading briefings had stayed with me. I resented it without being able to deny it, which made it worse.

I didn't get very far.

'Maeve, could you come in here, please?' Godley was standing in the doorway of his office, his expression stern.

I jumped up and crossed the room on legs that were suddenly not quite steady. I didn't know whether to be relieved or nervous to discover that Godley wasn't alone. DCI Burt sat in one chair, and DS Harry Maitland in another. Burt looked exactly as normal: plain, abstracted, intense. Maitland's usually cheerful face was serious.

'What's going on?'

'Bad news, I'm afraid.' Godley picked up his coat and began to put it on. 'Another dead woman. Tottenham, this time. It looks as if Josh was right and we are looking for a serial killer. The Commissioner has asked me to get a task force up and running and I want you to be on it, Maeve. I'm not taking most of my team because I'll be in overall command of the two current investigations and I'll have about a hundred officers altogether. No sense in dragging everyone along.' He picked up a folder. 'Ready?'

I was still processing the news that there was another murder. 'How do we know this latest victim is connected? I mean, the timescale—'

'Una can give you the details on the way. You can drive her. Harry, you're coming with me.'

I shot back to my desk and gathered up my things as the others headed for the lift. The four of us crowded in and I fought back a wave of claustrophobia, quickly succeeded by nausea. Maitland was wearing an ancient waxed jacket and it stank of dogs, cigarettes and its own linseed odour. I turned my head away and encountered DCI Burt, who was staring at me with keen interest. Her clever, pale face was scrubbed clean, and she smelled of nothing more glamorous than Pears soap. She was square, mid-forties and sweating slightly in a synthetic blouse she must have had for decades.

'Are you all right?'

'Fine.' I tried to look alert, wishing I could think of something intelligent to say. 'Same MO as the other two?'

'So it seems,' Godley said. 'Glenn is meeting us there.

He did the PMs on the other women, so he should be able to give us a better idea of what happened to her.'

Fantastic, I thought. Glenn Hanshaw was prickly at the best of times. Being under pressure made him less helpful, not more. Godley got on with him well enough, but he was the only one who did. And Hanshaw seemed, for no reason that I could think of, to despise me.

The lift doors slid open on the underground garage. It reeked of exhaust fumes. Godley's Mercedes, sleek and black, was in pride of place nearest the lift. Maitland didn't even try to hide how pleased he was about getting to ride in it.

I picked up a set of keys to one of the pool cars and found the bay where it sat. It was a navy Ford Focus that looked unloved, with mud around its back wheels and dust on the windscreen. DCI Burt stood back, writing something in her notebook, while Godley and Maitland got into the Mercedes. It took off up the ramp with a low, throaty rumble. The car was a high-end tank, indestructible and fast, and I'd been Godley's passenger more than a few times, basking on the leather upholstery in climate-controlled comfort. I had very little prospect of ever sitting in that seat again, though. It was pool cars all the way, with their soft brakes and total lack of poke and breathy heaters that only worked on the highest setting.

So, Maeve, how good does it feel to be right today?

Burt snapped her notebook shut. 'Right. Give me those keys. I don't know why Charles Godley thinks I can't drive myself. You can do the navigating.' She unlocked the car, flung herself into the driver's seat and started adjusting mirrors, frowning with concentration.

'I don't know where we're going,' I pointed out.

'Tottenham. Green Lanes, really.'

'It's not an area I'm familiar with, and I really don't mind driving.'

She bounced up and down, trying to get her seat to slide

forward. 'Do you want me to be blunt? You were obviously out last night, you clearly don't feel the best this morning, and I don't want you driving me in that condition.'

'I'm fine to drive.'

'Legally. But your reaction times will be off. You'll struggle to concentrate on the road as well as what I need to tell you about the case, since you missed the briefing.'

A briefing I hadn't known was going to happen. I opened my mouth to say so, then shut it again. I didn't know Una Burt very well, but I did know she wasn't the type to be moved by self-pity. I got in, wedging the coffee cup between my legs because the car didn't have any cup-holders, unlike Godley's. I just hoped DCI Burt wasn't heavy on the brakes.

'There's the address.' She pushed the notebook at me, open at the correct page. 'Carrington Road.'

The sat nav was out of order, spilling wiring through cracks in the sides where someone had tried, and failed, to tape it together. I pulled out the *A–Z*, grateful for once for Derwent's prejudice against modern technology. He liked to drive and drove too fast. I was capable of plotting routes on blues at the same time as giving a commentary over the radio to the controller and hanging on for dear life. I was fairly sure I could cope with whatever DCI Burt threw at me. Fate and my colleagues often conspired to make me work with Derwent. It was the exact equivalent of altitude training: I felt like vomiting at the time, but he gave me an edge that I'd otherwise have lacked. Just at that moment I needed anything that might impress Una Burt.

I risked a glance sideways. She had flung her jacket into the back seat where it lay in a crumpled heap, tangled up with her coat. Neither was going to look the better for it. Her light brown hair was collar-length and copious. It never seemed longer or shorter, which gave rise to suspicion that it was a wig. No make-up today or ever. No jewellery. She gave not a single shit about what anyone thought of how she looked or what she wore. She had a reputation for being blisteringly clever, mildly eccentric and totally absorbed in her work. The drive would be the longest time I'd ever spent with her, but I was already quite sure I wouldn't know her any better after it. She wore her concentration like armour.

'Better catch up or Charlie will be wondering where we've got to,' she said. *Charlie*. I wondered if she called him that to his face. It was just possible that she did. I couldn't imagine her flirting with him, or anyone, but I could believe she revered him for his professional achievements.

The car eased up the ramp and paused for a bare half-second at the top before it slid into a gap in the traffic. I was still reading the map, working back from the address, but I had enough spare capacity to notice that she was an excellent driver, smooth but unshowy. The car was purring.

We actually made good progress until we landed on the Euston Road. It was moving at its usual rush-hour crawl: eight lanes of traffic going precisely nowhere. Burt tucked the car in behind a red bus that had an ad for its cleaner emissions plastered all over its rear end. Bathed in diesel fumes, I couldn't actually tell that there was much improvement. I hit the button to recirculate the air in the car, and listened resignedly as the fan made a horrible grinding noise.

'You'll have to bear it, I'm afraid,' Burt said.

'I'll survive. At least I'm not in the same car as Maitland and his coat of many odours.'

She half-smiled, then her face went blank again as she returned to her own thoughts. When she eventually looked at me, I could see the effort that went into returning to here and now. Like a diver resurfacing, it took her a second to orientate herself.

'What were we talking about? I was supposed to be briefing you, wasn't I?'

'If you don't mind.'

'Do you know about the other two cases? Maxine and Kirsty?'

The way she said their names made it sound as if she knew them personally. There was nothing like investigating someone's murder to get to know them. None of them would have any secrets left by the time we were finished – no shadows in the corners of their lives. It was what I was trained to do and it still felt, at times, like a violation of the victims themselves.

'I only know what I've read in the papers. Both were single women who lived alone, found strangled. No sign of a break-in in either case. No apparent links between them. Apart from the fact that they were killed by someone they trusted.'

'Exactly. And the killer's signature.'

'The eyes.'

She nodded, satisfied. 'That's what makes us concerned that this latest murder is the next in the series.'

'But that detail was in the *Standard*. Everyone in London read it. It could be a copycat.'

'What it said in the *Standard* was that he gouged out their eyes. Not true.'

'Oh, really?' I didn't know why I was surprised. Journalists rarely got stories absolutely right, especially given the Chinese-whispers effect of secret tip-offs.

'He removes them with a knife. He does it quite carefully.'

'Are they trophies? Does he take them away?'

'No. He positions the bodies in a distinctive way, as you're about to see. In all three cases, they've been found with one eye in each hand. If it was a copycat killer working off the *Standard* article, I think he'd have used his hands to remove the eyes, don't you? Given that they used the word "gouge"?'

'Right. Yes.' My stomach was flipping over and over.

The bus accelerated through the lights in front of us, on the amber. Derwent would have gunned it through on red and ended up squatting on the intersection, causing traffic chaos. Una Burt stopped sedately, well behind the white line.

'Charlie had mentioned to me that we might be involved, so I've already familiarised myself with the files. It helps to be prepared.'

No kidding. It would be nice to know what that felt like. I was distracted by *Charlie*. And people thought I was the one who was over the side with Godley. Una Burt's greatest asset, it turned out, was looking like the back of a bus. They *couldn't* be having an affair. Godley wouldn't. Would he?

Burt was continuing, oblivious. 'And of course we were fairly sure there would be a third. Just not so soon.'

Three was the magic number. Three tipped us into serial-killer territory, with all the hysteria and hype that would bring to the media's reports. And three was what it had taken for the Commissioner to become seriously agitated about the safety of London's young women.

'He's bringing the SIOs to the new crime scene, after we've had a look at this girl, so we have as much information as we can share with them. We're working with them, not taking over. At least, that's the official line.'

'They're not going to be happy,' I predicted.

'Would you be?' She glanced at me. 'Didn't think so.'

I was following my own train of thought. 'Is that why I'm involved? Because I've met Andy Bradbury before?'

'Who's he?' The question came immediately at machine-gun speed: DCI Burt didn't like being uninformed.

'He's a DI. Just been promoted. He's in charge of the Maxine Willoughby investigation.'

'How do you know him?'

'I met him a few months ago at a crime scene.' *And I have absolutely no happy memories from that encounter.*

'Charlie wanted you to be involved because you have more in common with the victims than the rest of us do.'

'Oh.' I looked out of the window, waiting for the sting of disappointment to fade. I was there because of what I was rather than who I was. All the old insecurities about making up the numbers came rushing back.

'Don't take it amiss. You have to know what's normal to see what's not.'

'Fine, but you don't have to be the same as a victim to know what was normal for them.'

'It might help.' She looked across at me again, for longer. 'You know, most people your age and rank would be pleased to be involved with an investigation such as this, especially at such an early stage.'

'I am pleased.' It came out sullen and DCI Burt sighed.

'I don't give advice and I'm certainly not going to pretend to be a mentor to you. But you can waste a lot of time worrying about why you're here, or you can use the time wisely. You should be asking me what we know about what happened last night at number eight, Carrington Road.'

I managed to stop myself from squirming. A headmistress tone came easily to DCI Burt and it was far more effective than any of Derwent's sarcasm. 'That was my next question.'

'I thought it might have been.' She had her notebook open on her lap but she didn't even glance at it as she recited the facts. 'The property is a self-contained two-bedroom ground-floor maisonette with its own front door and side access to the rear of the building. It's owned by Anna Melville, aged twenty-nine, who lives there alone. She works in HR at a bank in the Square Mile. A neighbour heard a disturbance at her home last night at about ten thirty and thought about it for a couple of hours before he called it in as a possible burglary.'

'You wouldn't want to rush into anything,' I said.

'Exactly. Much better to wait until there's absolutely no chance of us catching anyone in the act. A response team was dispatched to the address and found it was secure – no lights on, no answer when they knocked at the door. They spoke to the neighbour and he said he hadn't heard anything since he'd phoned, so they left. The lads on early turn picked up on it in the briefing and decided to check it out in daylight to make sure there was nothing amiss. I gather they've been getting hammered on domestic burglaries so it's a high priority for them.'

'That'll be the recession. Burglary stats always go through the roof when people are skint.'

Una Burt nodded. 'The premises looked fine from the front, but the response officers were thorough. One of the PCs went around to the rear of the property and looked through the windows. Everything seemed to be in order until he reached the main bedroom. It was in a state of considerable disarray, and on the bed he could see what he thought was a body. And so it proved to be.'

'Anna Melville?'

'Yet to be confirmed but we're working on that assumption.'

'And she was laid out as the others had been?'

'More or less. We'll see when we get there.' She frowned to herself and I fell silent too, looking out of the window at the pedestrians who were making better time than us, seeing the young women walking on their own. They were heading to work, for the most part, striding in high heels or scuttling in flat shoes. It was cold, thanks to a stiff easterly wind that came straight off the North Sea, and their hair flew behind them like flags. What they wore and the way they wore it told me so much about them: the ones who dressed for themselves, but with care; the ones who wanted to be looked at; the ones who wanted to hide. What would I look for, if I was hunting? Who would I choose?

Anne Melville had shared something with Maxine Willoughby and Kirsty Campbell, apart from the manner of their deaths. The killer had seen that something, and had known it, and had used it to destroy her. At the moment, he was a stranger to me, a black hole at the centre of the picture. But if I could see what he had seen, I might know enough about him to find him. Una Burt was right. It was far better to be on the team than left out, no matter why I was there in the first place. Every case was another chance to prove I deserved to be there because I was good at what I did – and I *was* good, and I could do it. I sat up a little bit straighter. My hangover slunk away, defeated. I had better things to do than feel sorry for myself.

Like answer my phone. It hummed in my bag and I dug for it, knowing I had six and a half rings before it cut to voicemail. *Two . . . Three . . .* It came out wrapped in an old receipt and I had to waste a second untangling it. *Four . . .* Beside me, DCI Burt's voice was cold.

'Who is that?'

'DI Derwent.' *Of course.*

'Don't answer it.'

I stopped with my thumb poised to accept the call, obedient to the tone of pure command without having the least idea why she'd forbidden it. The ringer cut off and I waited for the beep of a new voicemail. I wasn't actually all that keen to listen to it. A disappointed Derwent was an angry Derwent, and an angry Derwent was even less charming than the usual kind.

'Why can't I speak to him?'

'Because it's not a good idea.'

Which wasn't actually an answer. 'Okay, but he'll be livid. He'll be wondering where I am, for starters.'

'He doesn't own you.' The road ahead was suddenly, miraculously clear – one of those freak moments in heavy traffic when the lights all go your way and no one else does. We were actually making some progress towards the crime scene.

'Of course he doesn't.' *He thinks he does, though . . .* 'Is he meeting us at the house? Or—'

'DI Derwent will not be involved in this investigation.'

I stared at her profile. 'But he was asking about it yesterday. He was insistent.'

'He will not be involved in this investigation,' she repeated, and I didn't know her well enough to be able to tell if she was pleased.

I listened to half of the voicemail before I deleted it: Derwent, ranting about my absence from the office when there was work to be done on the Olesugwe case. It was certain to be the first of many messages. I couldn't imagine why Derwent was shut out, but I knew it was going to be bad news for me.

Chapter 6

When we arrived at the crime scene Godley was standing outside, a still point in the organised mayhem, impossibly glamorous as the low autumn sunlight struck a silver gleam off his hair. The SOCOs were at work already, sealing off the property, and the superintendent was watching from a safe distance. Something about him suggested he was impatient to get into the house, and that he had that impatience under control, but only barely. I felt the same pull myself. There was nothing like seeing a body as the killer had left it, in the place where the victim died. Photographs didn't do the job. Every sense had to be engaged, I had learned. Where a normal person would shy away we leaned in, absorbing every detail. To understand what had happened, you had to allow yourself to relive it, and I was keen to get it over with in Anna Melville's case. I had known what it was like to be afraid for my life, but I had always been lucky, so far. Anna Melville's luck had very definitely run out.

The house wasn't the only focus for the SOCOs' attentions. They had identified her car. It would be taken away for detailed examination, in case she had given the killer a lift, or in case he had opened the door for her, or in case he had so much as leaned against it while they spoke. Like her home it would be ripped apart. There was so much mud to pan for one tiny fleck of DNA gold that could incriminate a killer. Technology meant we needed less and less to prove our cases, but that made it harder on the technicians who had to search for evidence that was literally invisible. There was still a place for good old-fashioned police work to narrow the focus to one person, one man with a dark heart, one killer. Jurors treated forensic evidence with reverence, but more often than not we were the ones who had put the defendant in the dock, and the forensics were just part of the picture.

All of which made me sound like any other copper, I thought. It was a commonplace to complain about not being appreciated, across all ranks, in all branches of the service, across all the different forces. It wasn't a job to do if you liked being praised or if you wanted to earn a lot of money. It was a job to choose if you couldn't see the value in doing anything else. It was a fundamental part of what made me who I was: without it, I wouldn't know myself.

And the reason why I put up with the terrible hours and disappointing pay and sometimes miserable working conditions was staring out of the windows on either side of the road. The neighbours were starting to realise what had happened, staring at the news come to life in their very own street. Later some of them – the more sensitive ones – would think about the fact that a murderer had walked past their doors not long before, on his way to kill. Somehow it was worse to think about him leaving after he had finished, dragging his slaked desire behind him. It made *me* shiver and I didn't have to sleep on Carrington Road. It wasn't my home that had been defiled.

DCI Burt parked the car, humming under her breath. Godley heard the engine and turned to glance in our direction. I saw his eyebrows twitch together in a frown, but I couldn't tell why.

I let her walk across to him on her own as I took a detour to drop my coffee cup in a bin. The wind stung my face and I huddled inside my coat, dropping my chin down to hide behind my collar. Carrington Street was lined with maple trees, which were shedding their leaves as if foliage was going out of fashion. The gutters were clogged and the air had that vinous smell of decay that I associated with autumn. A mordant technician in wellies and a boiler suit was working his way along the road, raking through the piles of leaves, filmed by the handful of news cameras that had made it to the latest crime scene. Someone had tipped them off that it was a murder but so far, judging by the questions they were shouting at me, they didn't know there was anything to connect it to the other deaths. And they wouldn't find out from me. I turned to walk back to the house and my bag vibrated against my hip.

Shit.

I don't know why I looked at the screen because I knew who it was going to be, and why. The ringing was somehow more insistent, the vibration stronger, because it was Derwent on the other end of the line, hating me for making him call back. I simply didn't dare answer it when DCI Burt had specifically told me not to. I looked up and saw she was watching me, as was Godley. I made it very clear that I was rejecting the call, dropping the phone back into my bag with a flourish so they couldn't miss what I had done. The part of me that rebelled against authority and hated working in a hierarchical organisation was outraged that I was obeying orders blindly, without being offered any explanation as to why it was necessary.

If it had been pissing off anyone other than Josh Derwent, I might even have said so.

'I spoke to the uniforms. They'll be around later if you want to ask them anything,' Godley said. 'We shouldn't have too long to wait now.'

On cue Kev Cox appeared at his elbow, a small balding man with a pot belly his boiler suit did nothing to hide and a sweet nature that survived routine exposure to the worst things people could do to one another.

'Two more minutes, folks. Thanks for the patience. You might like to get ready.'

'Gloves and shoe covers?' Godley checked.

'Suits too, please. Got to be careful here.' Kev knew as well as any of us that there would be ferocious interest in Anna Melville's murder. No one wanted to get it wrong.

'Glenn's just been in touch. He's stuck in traffic, but he's on his way.' Godley set off towards the house. Over his shoulder, he threw, 'Keep it in mind, you two. He won't want anyone to touch the body before he sees it.'

I wouldn't have dreamed of it. I went out of my way to avoid it, usually. The loose, yielding feel of dead flesh, especially through rubber gloves, was developing into a phobia. Never a great cook, I had abandoned cooking meat altogether since I'd started working on murders. The raw-meat aisle at the supermarket was the stuff of nightmares, even if it was sanitised in cling-film.

They had set up a tent in front of the door and it functioned as an airlock between the real world and the crime scene. I hurried to get dressed in the protective gear Kev had specified. Beside me, Godley was doing the same. Burt had been about to get changed when her phone rang and she stepped back out to answer it. I wondered if Derwent had started calling her instead. Then I wondered what she didn't want to say in front of me. Then I decided that was pure paranoia, and self-absorbed to boot.

'Where's Harry Maitland?'

'Coordinating the house-to-house. I've got plenty of uniformed officers at my disposal to cover the area but I want them asking the right questions. Maitland's putting the fear of God in them for me.'

I found myself hiding a smile at the unconscious pun. Godley was nicknamed 'God' in the Met not just for his name but also because of his looks and his perfect, untouchable record. It wasn't something he encouraged, and it was used mainly by people who hadn't worked with him. There was nothing grand about the way he did his job – nothing showy – and he had time for the youngest, the least experienced, sometimes the least promising officers he encountered. In turn, he got undying respect and dedication, and very often results no one else would have. And yet he was as dirty as they came. The thought wiped the smile off my face, and when I looked up Godley was watching me. I had the uncomfortable feeling that he knew exactly what I had been thinking.

'Do you want to wait for DCI Burt?' I asked.

'She knows where we're going.' Courteously he held the door open for me, letting me walk into the flat first, and I scanned the hall as I passed through it, starting to form an opinion of Anna Melville from the things she had chosen to keep around her. The hall was painted a faded green and a collection of twelve vintage mirrors hung on one wall, spaced out exactly in rows of four. The floor was polished wood and the cream runner that lay on it was pristine. It wasn't even rumpled. I looked for – and found – the shoe rack by the door. No one was allowed across the threshold without taking their shoes off. If she had let him in, the killer had been in his socks or barefoot, so we wouldn't get shoe treads or soil fragments to match against an eventual suspect. The rack was neatly arranged with shoes that were predominantly pretty rather than functional – delicate, spindly high heels on everyday court shoes, embellished ballet flats for casual wear. Even her wellies were pale pink with silver stars. A girly girl.

'No blood,' I observed to Godley, who nodded. He moved past me into the sitting room.

'Let's start in here. Una will be in soon.'

The room wasn't large but the furniture was expensive. The grey velvet upholstery on the two-seater sofa and armchair looked as if no one had ever sat on it. There was a fireplace, with candles sitting in the grate, and the alcoves on either side of the chimneybreast were shelved. They were filled with vases and ornaments rather than the books or DVDs that might have told us something about her personality. The fact that there weren't *any* books or discs made me think she worked long hours and didn't have time for entertainment. The giant grey wicker heart above the sofa made me suspect she was a romantic. The armfuls of cushions arranged on the sofa itself were impossibly feminine and dainty; I couldn't imagine a man sitting there to watch television. And on another wall, there was a framed poster: the word 'Beauty' in elaborate writing. Pin your colours to the mast, I thought. If that's what matters to you, why not frame it? And what harm was there in any of it? Still, something made me feel I wouldn't have got on with Miss Melville. The array of photographs on the shelves gave me one reason.

'What is it?' Godley was watching me instead of looking around, which made me feel like a canary in a mine. 'You're frowning.'

'Is this her?' There were probably thirty pictures on the shelves and the same dark-haired woman appeared in almost all of them.

'I believe so.'

'She must have been massively insecure, then. Who has framed pictures of themselves when they live alone?' I picked up one which was of a group of girls ready to go out, dressed to the nines. Two of them were talking, their mouths twisted halfway through a word, and one wasn't even looking at the camera. The dark-haired girl was looking right at the lens with a dazzling smile. 'And look at this. She's the only one who looks good in this picture. Why would you choose to frame that?'

'Being insecure isn't a crime.'

'But it makes you susceptible to flattery. The three women lived alone. They were all heading towards thirty and not in a relationship. That has to be one way he could have got in. Do we know if any of them did online dating?'

'I'll ask the other SIOs this afternoon.'

'He's seeing something vulnerable in them. This woman was hyper-feminine and very conscious of how she was perceived. What do you look for in a man if you are like that?'

'Someone who comes across as traditionally masculine,' Godley suggested. 'Someone strong.'

'And forceful. Someone who would take control. Sweep you off your feet. Someone confident.'

'Confidence fits in with murdering them in their own home. He's comfortable in their environment. He takes his time, too.'

'What makes you say that?' I asked.

'How the bodies are left.'

I was staring at the only thing that was out of place in the room: a vase half-filled with greenish water and a few bits of leaves. 'Where are the flowers?'

'I think we're about to find out.' Godley checked his watch. 'Come on, Una. Wind it up.'

She came through the door as if she'd been waiting for the invitation, rustling importantly in her boiler suit. 'Sorry. All done.'

'Are we finished in here?' Godley asked me and I nodded, watching Una Burt scan the room.

'Lead on,' Godley said to her, and I followed her through the hall, past a small bedroom that was primrose yellow and obviously for guests, past a tiny bathroom where the SOCOs were climbing over each other to collect swabs and empty U-bends, past a kitchen with red tulips in a vase on the table and the washing-up neatly stacked on the draining board. No secrets here – nothing that Anna would have been ashamed for us to see. It reminded me of a flat that had been tidied for viewing, down to the matching tea towels hanging neatly on their rail and the cutesy blackboard with 'Nearly the weekend!' written on it, above a shopping list. Organised, careful, feminine, self-conscious. And there was nothing wrong with being like that – I wished I was more like that myself – but I felt it had marked her as a victim and I wondered how he'd seen it, and known her, and calculated how he could have her.

How he had had her was laid out for our inspection in the main bedroom, as neatly and obsessively as everything else in Anna Melville's home. I stopped short in the doorway despite myself and Godley collided with me, then leapt away as if I was burning to the touch.

'Sorry. I just—'

'Don't worry,' he said shortly. 'Take your time.'

Burt had gone ahead and was leaning over the bed, peering intently at the body that lay on it. I skirted the bed, not quite looking at what lay on it. The floor was wood, painted white, and Kev was lying down shining a torch through the cracks between the boards. On the other side of the room another SOCO was doing the same, crawling on hands and knees. I recognised her – Caitriona Bennett, the pretty, soft-spoken technician whose work had led us to a killer during the summer. It was a slight comfort to me to know that Anna Melville was getting the best of everything in death. It gave us a chance to get something like justice for her.

Godley stepped over Kev's prone body. 'Found anything?'

'Dust.' He didn't even look up, working his way along the gap inch by inch. 'Stuff. We'll have these up later to collect anything that seems interesting.'

I stopped beside the window, which was draped in gauzy voile panels. There was a hand-span gap between them where I assumed the uniformed officer had peered. Turning, I saw that the room showed the same feminine attention to detail as the rest of the flat, with a white-painted carved wooden beam nailed to the wall above the bed. Curtains hung down from it, draping the bed head. The bedclothes were white and embroidered with tiny stars, also white, but they had been drawn down to the end of the bed and folded over, out of the way, leaving a clean white sheet underneath the body. A mirrored bedside table had a carafe of water on it, an old-fashioned alarm clock and an iPad that I knew we would be taking away with us. I itched to start looking through it but there were protocols to observe. And a body, I reminded myself, forcing my eyes to where she was waiting.

She lay with her head pointing towards the foot of the bed, her feet together on the pillow. She wore white – a silk nightdress so fine I could see a dark shadow at the top of her thighs and the two faint smudges of her nipples through the fabric. She was small and slim, her bones fragile, her kneecaps sticking up like a child's. Her hands were by her sides, palms up, loosely holding what he had cut out of her head. Her face was horrendous – dark with blood, her tongue protruding – but mercifully for me he had closed her eyelids over the empty sockets. The marks on her neck stood out like splashes of paint on snow. Her hair – her long, glossy dark hair – was gone. He had cut it off close to her head. She looked more vulnerable with her collaborator's crop, and young, and I wondered if he'd cut it before she died or after. Was it to torment her? For his own gratification? Or something more complicated?

'Did he take the hair away with him?'

'Nope. Found it in the bathroom. He dumped it in the bath,' Kev said cheerily. 'But he cut it in here. We found a lot of loose hairs over here in this corner.'

Two candles stood on either side of her head and on either side of her feet – fat ones, about eight inches high.

'Did he bring these, do we think?' Godley asked, pointing at them.

'They're the same as the ones in the living room,' I said, my voice metallic in my ears. Robotic. Emotionless.

'Were they burning when the uniforms got here?' Una Burt asked.

'No. He seems to have put them out when he was leaving,' Godley said.

'Never leave a naked flame unattended,' floated up from the floor where Kev was approaching Godley's feet.

'I'm not sure that was his priority.'

'There were candles at Maxine's house as well. None at Kirsty's,' Burt said. 'So he makes do with what he can find.'

'It makes her look like a sacrifice,' I said. A memory drifted to the surface: helping one of the nuns to prepare the altar for an early-morning Mass. White linen altar cloth. Pure white candles in their low holders. And flowers, rammed by me into a brass container too small for them, because I was bored and wanted to be finished. The nun had taken them from me, tutting under her breath, and cut away the bruised stems with a short, stubby knife she'd produced from the folds of her habit, until the arrangement looked perfect. I moved forward to stand just behind Anna's savaged head and looked down at her. From this angle I could see what I'd missed before: she was lying on a handful of lilies. Their heavy scent drifted up, mingling with the bitter smell of the burnt candles.

'These will be the flowers from the living room.'

'Probably,' Godley said, leaning over beside me. His sleeve brushed mine and again I was aware of him flinching away. Not the way to convince people we weren't having an affair, I thought sourly. Since I had no way of actually saying that to him without stepping a long way outside what was appropriate for my rank, and his, I affected not to notice.

'What do you think the flowers signify?'

'No idea. Part of the ritual, I suppose, along with the candles.'

'Being outside?' Burt suggested.

'Did he do this with the others?'

Godley nodded.

'With lilies? Or other flowers?'

59

'Other flowers, I think.' He frowned. 'I have crime scene photos in the car.'

'We should have a look,' Burt said. 'With the other SIOs.'

'How did he know there would be flowers here?' I bent down: from what I could see of the petals they didn't look fresh. One or two were brown and coming away from the flower. Even allowing for them being crushed under the victim, they weren't in the best condition. 'Did he deliver these, maybe, earlier in the week? Is that how he saw her first?'

Una Burt didn't hide her scepticism. 'Why would she let him in again, though? There was no sign of a break-in. Even if she recognised him, she'd never let a delivery man into her house.'

'Unless he was carrying something heavy.'

'Like what?'

There was no evidence of anything having been delivered and I subsided, feeling squashed. But Una Burt was right, and she wasn't trying to put me down, unlike Derwent. She was just saying what she thought.

'What did he use to cut her hair? Scissors?'

'Not that we found.' Kev surfaced beside the bed. 'If you ask me, looking at the way he left it, he used a knife.'

'The same knife he used on her eyes?' Burt suggested.

'It's possible.'

'Did she fight?' I asked. 'What did the neighbour hear?'

'Unusual noises, he said. Moving furniture. Thumps and bumps.' Godley scanned the room. 'Not that you'd know.'

'If he made a mess, he took the time to tidy up afterwards. This was important to him – making this image.' I stepped back to look at it as he might have, wondering what he wanted us to see. 'He took the hair out of this room. He could have left it.'

Godley was using his torch to examine the woman's face, peering at it from a distance of a couple of inches.

He looked disturbingly like Prince Charming leaning over Sleeping Beauty, ready to wake her with a kiss.

'Stop. Go back.' Something had caught my attention. 'Where you had the torch before – I saw something.'

He turned it back to the side, shining it across her bloodless skin, and again I saw a glint.

'There's something under her neck. A hair.'

'Not surprising,' Godley said, disappointment colouring his tone very slightly. 'You'd expect him to miss a few.'

I reached over and took the torch out of his hand, shining it directly on what I had seen. Caitriona swooped in with tweezers and drew the hair out, holding it up so she could slip it into an evidence collection envelope. Now that I could see it properly, I could tell it was maybe fourteen inches long. It hung in an elongated 'S', the bottom curling out and up as if it had been styled to flick up. It was pure gold in colour.

'Not one of hers,' Kev said happily. 'Where did that come from?'

'Him?' I said, dubious. My mental image of a serial killer didn't really include styled, shoulder-length hair.

'One of the other victims?' Burt suggested.

'They weren't blondes either,' Godley said. 'Let's hope it's relevant.'

'We'd have got it on the bedclothes,' Caitriona pointed out, as defensive as if someone had told her she'd failed. 'We were going to take the sheets away once the body was moved.'

'No one is moving anything without my say-so.' Glenn Hanshaw's voice was grating as it cut through the room. We scattered away from the bed like cockroaches surprised by a light going on. 'I'm sorry I'm late.'

He didn't sound sorry. He sounded livid. I edged back, towards the door, as he folded his tall, bony frame into a crouch beside the bed and began unpacking his equipment. I appreciated that he was good at his job, but the snap of his rubber gloves going on and the rattle of the thermometer as he took it out of its case made me clench. He was exceptionally professional but his patients were beyond feeling and he was businesslike about the way he examined them, quick and somehow brutal. I felt it was uncomfortably close to a violation and as I watched him lever Anna Melville's legs apart – moving quickly because he was late, and angry, and she was beyond caring if he was gentle – I felt a wave of unease that was close to distress. I went and stood in a corner of the hall, taking deep breaths, waiting for my heart rate to drop.

'Are you okay?' Una Burt's face was close to mine when I looked up.

'I hate that bit.'

'So do I. But it's not Hanshaw's fault. He's not the one who put her there.'

'I know.' And I did know it. 'I don't blame him. It's just – this case feels a bit close to home. You were right. I do feel something for these victims. Not that it could be me.' Although it nearly had been me when I'd thought my stalker Chris Swain was just a friendly neighbour. He had got closer than I liked to recall. 'It could be someone I know. One of my friends. Someone more trusting than me.'

'You think he gains their trust.'

'She wasn't tied up. She wasn't beaten up. She was killed. How did he control her before that? The only thing I can think is that he had some authority over her. She did what he said because he asked her to.'

'You could be right.' She looked away from me, into the room where Anna Melville still lay, and the next thing she said proved I wasn't following her train of thought at all, because I couldn't tell why it had occurred to her. 'If DI Derwent attempts to talk to you about this case, refer him to me.'

She was gone before I could ask why.

Chapter 7

I was just about to go back in to confront the body and whatever Glenn Hanshaw was doing to it when I heard voices outside the front door. I scooted down the hall to see four men pulling on protective suits, watched by a crime-scene technician who had his arms folded. His name was Pierce, I recalled, and his voice was both camp and carrying.

'It's even more important for you guys to be careful about what you're walking into the property, given who you are. One of you brings in some material from another crime scene and we are screwed, do you know what I'm saying?'

'Yes, I think we have the idea.' The testy response reminded me how uncharming I found Andrew Bradbury. He was thin and unsmiling behind glasses with heavy frames. Some men made going bald look good: Bradbury was not one of them.

'I'm sorry if you don't like it. I'm just doing my job. I'd be skinned alive if I let you in.' If anything, Pierce sounded rather pleased to have a reason to tell the detectives what to do. I cleared my throat and he twisted around. 'Oh, here's DC Kerrigan. She'll look after you.'

I was expecting some glimmer of recognition from Bradbury but it seemed I had made no impression on him at all. Since I encountered him he had been promoted, though he'd been one of the least impressive detective sergeants I'd ever met. Getting him out of harm's way by pushing him up the ladder, Derwent had suggested. Derwent had given him quite a hard time, and Bradbury had conceded in a hurry to the alpha male. If Derwent had been there, Bradbury would have thought twice about pushing past me. As it was, he didn't even say hello.

'Where's Superintendent Godley?'

'The bedroom at the back, on the left.'

He barrelled past me and down the hall. I let him go, addressing the three who remained outside the door.

'Thanks for coming. I'm Maeve Kerrigan – I work with Superintendent Godley.'

'Nice to meet you.' The speaker was lugubrious, sallow and in his mid-forties. 'DI Carl Groves. This is DS Burns. Frank by name and nature,' he added.

The sergeant waved a gloved hand at me instead of shaking mine. 'Thanks for laughing at the boss's little joke. I did too, the first thousand times I heard it.'

I grinned at the pair of them. They were a double act – one fat, one thin, around the same age, old in their very souls and as cynical as murder detectives are supposed to be. The third man introduced himself as James Peake, a detective from the East End where Andy Bradbury worked and where Maxine Willoughby had died. He was about my age, a big handsome redhead.

'Did you want to speak to Superintendent Godley first, or . . .'

'Probably more use to have a look round, isn't it?' Groves said. 'That's why we're meeting here, after all.'

I agreed with Groves. Only Bradbury, it seemed, had missed the point.

They were quiet as soon as they entered the flat, taking in everything it could tell us about poor Anna and her aspirations. DI Burt appeared in the kitchen, dispatched by Godley, and there was another round of introductions.

'Are you seeing similarities?' she demanded, and all three nodded with varying degrees of enthusiasm.

'Same type of victim, definitely.' Burns lifted a fold of curtain material and weighed it. 'Better off than Kirsty, I'd say.'

'Didn't she live in Blackheath?' I had noticed it in the *Standard* article because it was a nice part of south-east London, close to the river at Greenwich and rich in green open spaces. It was on my list if I ever managed to save enough money for a deposit for a place of my own, assuming – as I tended to – that I was buying it alone, Rob having gone the way of all men. It was emphatically not the sort of place where you expected to be strangled in your bed.

'It was Blackheath in estate-agent speak. It was more like Lewisham.'

'Lewisham's all right,' Groves said. 'What's wrong with Lewisham?'

'Where do I start?' Burns rolled his eyes. They'd be doing a music-hall number next. Una Burt could see the warning signs as well as I could and cut in.

'What about Maxine Willoughby? Where did she live?'

'She had a one-bed flat in Whitechapel,' Peake said. 'This place is a big step up from what she could afford.'

'Anna was in HR in the City,' I said. 'I'd imagine she was earning a fair bit.'

'Living simply, though,' Una Burt said. 'Quietly.'

'Not attracting attention to herself,' I agreed.

'Whether she wanted attention or not, she attracted the wrong kind,' Groves said.

'The worst.' Burt looked around. 'Shouldn't DI Bradbury be in here too? I thought he was following me. Where's he got to?'

'Have a look in the superintendent's arse,' Peake suggested, very quietly, so that only I could hear, and I smothered a laugh, converting it into a cough that made everyone stare at me. To do something worthy of everyone's attention since it was on me anyway, I asked about the vase. Kev Cox had made sure it was removed since Godley and I had noticed it, but I described it.

'Did you have anything like this in either of the other flats?'

'Flowers, yeah.' Groves's face was twisted in thought. 'Don't know if we ever worked out where they came from.'

Peake was flicking back through a folder of photos he'd been carrying under one arm: pictures from Maxine's flat. I looked over his shoulder, seeing rooms that were neat but IKEA-unimaginative, and all painted the same shade of cream.

'There. On the draining board.' I put out a hand to stop him as he flipped past the kitchen. 'That's a vase, isn't it?'

It was turned upside down, as if it had been washed out.

'Do you think he left it like that?'

'Could be. He definitely cleaned up after he'd finished with Maxine. He wasn't in a hurry to leave. He even vacuumed the place, we think, and took the bag away with him. He must have been feeling very confident. If there was more noise here – didn't you say a neighbour called 999? – maybe he didn't feel it was worth his while to tidy up after himself.'

'You could be right.'

Groves and Burns were conferring in low tones, and concluded that there might have been a vase. They couldn't remember.

'What's your theory?' Peake asked.

I squirmed. 'I don't really have one yet. Maybe he delivers them and that's how he gets to check out the victims and their homes. Or maybe he brings them flowers to get them to trust him.'

'Well, he must be fucking charming is all I can say. They let him in. They don't fight back.' Groves shook his head. 'Maybe he buys them chocolates too.'

'And offers to fix a few things around the house,' Burns suggested. 'And tells them he hates football.'

'But he loves shopping.' Peake was grinning.

Burt looked as entertained as I was, which is to say not very. *Poor silly women, pinning their hopes on Prince Charming, trusting the wrong man.* 'I hate to interrupt, but I think we'd better move on. Dr Hanshaw is going to want to move the body, so if you want to see it in position . . .'

The three of them fell into line and we toured the rest of the flat, including the small bathroom, now SOCO-free, where I noticed the shower curtain was decorated with tiny yellow ducks. It was the kind of detail that reminded me why we were there. The person who had chosen it and hung it up and looked at it every morning was now stiff and dead and lying exposed to anyone's view in her own bedroom, because someone else had decided she should be.

The bedroom itself was getting crowded and I hung back, watching Caitriona extract herself from the room with the urgency and purpose of a cross wasp fighting its way out of a bottle. Glenn Hanshaw had finished and Godley was listening, patiently, to Andy Bradshaw's self-important account of the Maxine Willoughby crime scene and how it had been different.

'I thought we'd discuss this at the local police station. I've asked them to let us have a room,' he said when he could get a word in. 'We need to see your crime-scene photos. And I'd like everyone to hear what you have to say, not just me.'

'Of course.' Bradshaw sounded as if that was only natural, not appreciating perhaps that it was meant to apply to everyone.

'Then, Kev, I think we're finished here. Can you let them know they can take the body?'

Kev nodded cheerfully. 'We'll finish up.'

As I followed the others out of Anna Melville's flat I felt

bleak. Someone would come and tidy it up, once we'd taken all of the evidence we required. Someone would decide to throw out or sell or keep the things Anna had chosen. The flat would be sold to a buyer who wasn't squeamish or didn't know what had happened there. Someone would take Anna's job. She had no children to mourn her. She had been an only child and her parents were dead: the next-of-kin contact we had been given for her was a godmother who hadn't seen her for five or six years. Anna's life would be undone and she would be gone.

It just didn't seem fair.

Chapter 8

The room at the local police station was on the small side but it had a projector and, importantly, blinds to cover the windows and the glass in the door. It would be a very bad idea indeed to let anyone else see or hear what we were discussing. We sat around the table like well-behaved children at a party. The heating was on full and the room was stuffy even before we'd begun. I started to undo the buttons on my jacket but changed my mind halfway through, when I noticed Peake looking at me with a little bit too much interest. I would have to swelter.

'Right. I think it would be useful to go through what we know from the beginning,' Godley said, taking charge. 'Carl?'

Groves flipped open the file in front of him. 'Kirsty Campbell. Lovely girl. She was twenty-eight. Broke up with her fiancé a few months before she died but it was because they'd grown apart, not because he was cheating or she was or anything of that sort. We considered him as a suspect, obviously, but he had an alibi and a new girlfriend and he wasn't the type to do something like that.'

Burns was nodding. 'Stephen Reeves, his name was. We interviewed him twice, just to make sure. Never got a bad feeling from him. Honest and straight down the line.'

'What about Kirsty? Had she found anyone else?' Burt asked.

'That's the question, isn't it? We asked, believe me. Some friends said yes, others not. She'd said she didn't want to date for a while – she was hurt that the ex had moved on as quickly as he did. She broke up with him, but it seemed like it was worse for her than for him.'

'Biological clock ticking,' Burns said wisely.

His boss carried on as if he hadn't spoken. 'According to her colleagues, she cried at work sometimes.'

'Which was where?' Godley asked.

'Westminster Council. She was a planning officer.'

Being a planning officer meant she had to see people face to face. 'Did you manage to trace all of the applicants she'd been dealing with at work?' I asked.

'We went back twelve months,' Burns replied. 'Didn't find anyone with a grudge against her, or anyone who acted weird when her name was mentioned. A few had criminal records, but for fighting and fraud, not stalking or anything sexual. We did follow them up.'

Godley smiled. 'No one is suggesting that you missed anything, Frank. I want to make that clear to you too, Andy. This isn't about going over old cases to see what you didn't do. It's about finding common ground for the victims.'

'What was Kirsty like as a person?' I asked.

'Gentle. Soft-spoken,' Groves said. 'She was from Edinburgh originally. Not a strong accent, though. One of her colleagues said she had the most beautiful speaking voice he'd ever heard.'

'Bit of an odd remark,' Bradbury said.

'Do you think so?' Groves's face wrinkled as he thought about it. 'He was an older man, her boss. Married. Nothing dodgy going on with her. And I think he was actually out of the country when she died.'

We had so little to go on, we were chasing the slightest hint of a lead. Godley drew Groves back to the point. 'Was she popular at work?'

'Very. No one had a bad word to say about her. She was

very attractive.' Groves held up a picture of her, not one I'd seen before, and proved his point. The main impression was of tumbling red hair and a smile that was shy but endearing. 'She worked hard. She volunteered for a charity that works with inner-city kids on improving their reading.'

'And we traced everyone else who was involved with it, and the teachers she met, and the parents of the kids she worked with,' Burns added.

'Her parents said she was always a credit to them. Very stable background. We spoke to all her ex-boyfriends and there weren't that many of them. They all said the same thing: gentle, fair-minded, a perfectionist. Much harder on herself than anyone else.'

'Any history of depression or mental health issues?' I asked.

'Why do you ask, Maeve?' Godley said.

'Being a perfectionist, crying at work, being hard on herself – that all sounds as if she was quite fragile. She broke up with her fiancé, but then she took it harder than him. Maybe she thought she wasn't good enough for him.' *I wonder how that feels.*

'That's what her mum said,' Groves agreed.

'They were planning to get married and then suddenly they weren't. That changed how her life was going to be, completely. Maybe she needed counselling. Or a support group,' I suggested.

'She wouldn't necessarily have told anyone she was doing that kind of thing,' Peake said. 'She might have hidden it.'

'We didn't think of that,' Groves said.

'Look into it,' Godley said to me. 'Check out the area near to her home. Local churches and the library.'

'Can we look at the pictures from her flat?' Una Burt asked.

Burns got up and fiddled with his laptop, which he had

linked to the projector. 'I hope this thing works.'

'It was easier in the old days,' Grove said. 'When we were young. Stick some pictures up on the wall and no one had to worry about technology. I've yet to see anything that's actually improved by computers.'

The screen flickered and a desktop appeared. We watched as Burns slowly, painfully tracked the cursor across to the folder of pictures on the desktop. He was breathing heavily, concentrating as if he was doing something exceptionally difficult. There was a universal sigh of relief when he succeeded in double-clicking it.

'Ground-floor flat in a purpose-built block,' Groves said, as the first picture in the slideshow appeared. 'She'd lived there for six months.'

'Since the break-up?' Burt asked.

'Exactly.'

The block was red brick and rather nice, with grey-framed windows and some low shrubs around it.

'Communal hallway. The front door was supposed to be locked, but the lock wasn't working.'

'Suspicious,' Peake commented.

'Yeah, it was. The contacts were damaged so it didn't engage the magnetic lock when the door was closed. It broke a couple of days before the murder. The managing agent had been told, but they hadn't actually done anything about getting it fixed. Wasn't the first time it had gone wrong, so no one was too bothered. Each flat has a front door and they weren't allowed to keep personal belongings or bikes in the stairwells anyway.'

'How big is the building? How many other residents were there?'

'There were six flats, nine other residents. All checked out. No one heard anything. No one made it on to the suspects' list.'

The image on screen was a front door, green-painted but inlaid with frosted glass. 'This is Kirsty's.'

'CCTV?' Bradbury asked.

'No.'

'Shame.'

'Yeah, it was.' Groves waited for the next image, a close-up of the door locks. 'No damage here. No damage to any of the windows.'

'She let him in.' Godley sounded grim.

'Indeed she did.'

'Do we know where she'd been the evening before she died?' I asked. 'What day of the week was it?'

'A Friday. She went for a drink after work with a colleague who was celebrating her birthday. Didn't stay long, apparently. Wasn't drunk. Got the train back. We have her on CCTV walking through the station and later passing her local pub. No one seems to be following, for what it's worth.'

A living room. Bookshelves. A huge collection of DVDs and maybe twenty novels.

'Was she in a book club?' I asked.

'Don't know.' Groves looked at Burns, who shrugged.

'Try and find out, Maeve,' Godley ordered. 'What else did she do?'

'Went to the gym – one in Blackheath. She didn't have a car, so she walked everywhere. She'd joined a knitting group, believe it or not, in a local pub, but she'd only been to a couple of sessions and no one really remembered much about her.'

'Knitting?' Peake rolled his eyes.

'It's very trendy, apparently,' I told him.

'Not the sort of thing you do if you want to meet blokes.'

'I thought we'd established she didn't.'

'Settle down, you two,' Bradbury said. 'She liked knitting.'

'Didn't travel much,' Burns said. 'She went to Edinburgh to see her folks when she had time off. Liked baking.' The picture on screen was the kitchen, a bland pine one accessorised with red tea towels, a red teapot and red storage jars.

'Anna was very feminine too,' I observed.

'That plays into them doing what they're told,' Una Burt said. 'Used to taking orders from men.'

The next picture was the bedroom door, left ajar, a glimpse of the bed beyond offering a clue to the horror that was the reason for our knowing anything at all about Kirsty. There was a vacuum cleaner on the floor outside the door, tipped over, and a bucket with cleaning products in it.

'It was her cleaner that found her. She was actually one of the other residents in the block who was looking for a bit of cash because she was a single mum and Christmas had cost a lot. Kirsty got her to do her ironing and cleaning. Bit of charity, I reckon. She said the place was always spotless.'

'Had she cleaned the rest of the place before she got to the bedroom?' Godley checked.

'Yeah.'

There was a groan around the room and Groves nodded. 'We didn't have much luck with this one. We got nothing on the forensics, even in the bedroom itself. What she didn't clean, the killer did.'

'And on the body?'

'Nothing. He didn't have sex with her, either with a condom or without, with permission or without. He only touched her to kill her.'

The next few pictures were of the bedroom and the body, both from a distance and in close-up. Her bedclothes had been blue, but he had piled them in the corner of the room and spread a white sheet on the mattress. She wore white too, something that looked like a sundress, with ties on the shoulders and a tiered, mid-calf skirt. Her head had been roughly cropped, as in Anna's case. It was pillowed on roses, white ones, the petals splayed and the leaves brown at the tips.

'Those flowers aren't fresh,' I observed. 'Do we know where they came from?'

'No. It was the thirtieth of January and all the florists were on a post-Christmas comedown. They'd have remembered someone buying roses, but no one did.'

'Where did he leave her hair?' Burt asked.

'In the bin in the kitchen. In a bag. Neat, like.' DS Burns sounded sour.

Her injuries were very similar to Anna's. I asked Bradbury, 'How does this compare to how Maxine was found?'

'She was dead too.'

You arse. 'I mean the level of violence he used.'

Peake answered for his boss. 'Bruising to the neck, where she was strangled, and he cut her around the eyes but we think that was while he was removing the eyeballs and it was after she died.' He held up a picture from his file, one from the post-mortem, a close-up of the woman's face. I wouldn't have recognised her as the same person I'd seen in the newspaper. Her skin had a pearly quality, like the bloom on a plum. Dark hair, like Anna.

'That's pretty minimal violence,' I pointed out. 'No defence wounds. No bruises or scrapes. He's very controlled.'

'Nothing that will ruin the image in his head.' Burt picked up the photograph Peake had been holding and looked at it, then at the screen. 'That's what he's doing, isn't it? Painting a picture but with dead bodies.'

'I don't want any talk about him being an artist, or anything else that glorifies what he does.' Godley's voice was hard. 'He kills women because he gets a thrill out of it. He does it because he likes it. If we start taking him at his own estimation, he's won.'

'We need to understand why he's doing this,' Burt objected.

'We need to know how, and who. Not why.' I'd never heard Godley speak so abruptly to Una Burt. He was

75

courteous as a rule anyway, and particularly towards his brilliant but difficult chief inspector since it set a good example to the rest of the team. But I had noticed before what little patience he had for the idea of a killer with a mission, a serial murderer acting out an elaborate game. He was a realist. The people he hunted were indulging their darkest desires, but that didn't mean he was going to play along. A killer was a killer and that was that.

'Did he cut Maxine's hair?' I asked.

'No, she did. She wore it short. Started getting it cut that way about six months ago and liked it, according to her best friend.' Bradbury sounded as if that was just about the most outlandish idea he'd ever heard. But she'd had fine, small features, like the other two women, and short hair had suited her.

'So he didn't bother cutting her hair for the sake of it. That must mean there's a practical reason for him to do it,' I said. 'He didn't need to, with Maxine.'

'Maybe the short hair attracted him to her in the first place,' Peake suggested.

'That's the trouble, isn't it? We don't know what attracted him.' Godley sighed. 'You've had less time than this lot to look into your victim's life, Andy, but tell us what you know anyway.'

The inspector's ears coloured slightly as everyone turned to look at him. He liked being important but not being put on the spot, I thought. Power but not pressure.

'Maxine Willoughby was twenty-nine. She was Australian, from some tiny town in the middle of absolutely nowhere, and she'd been living in London for nine months. She worked near Covent Garden, in the marketing department of an insurance company. She didn't have anything to do with clients or the public – it was more of a backroom job. Her colleagues liked her. She worked hard, and long hours. No boyfriend and it became a standing joke with her colleagues that she needed to find a good Englishman. She didn't seem to be trying to meet anyone. The word her colleague used was "asexual". When she joined the company, the single men all tried it on with her but she wasn't interested or didn't notice.'

'Maybe she wasn't interested in men,' I suggested.

'Not a lesbian. I asked. One of her colleagues was, and Maxine found the whole subject agonising in case she said the wrong thing.'

'Both Kirsty and Maxine had accents,' Burns said.

'Everyone has an accent. You have an accent. There's no such thing as a neutral voice.' Una Burt didn't even look to see if the sergeant minded being corrected. I was starting to realise that she wouldn't have been upset to be told she was wrong so she assumed everyone else felt the same way. The important thing to her was being accurate.

Burns cleared his throat. 'I mean, they were both from places with distinctive accents. Maybe he spoke to them on the phone.'

'Does anyone know about Anna? No?' Godley turned to me. 'Make sure you ask her friends and colleagues about the way she spoke. We can get the phone records for all three and see if there are any common numbers.'

That sounded like a fun job. I didn't mind asking the question but I would rather poach my eyes in lighter fluid than spend days reading reams of numbers.

Bradbury continued. 'Maxine wasn't your stereotypical Aussie. She was shy and reserved, young for her age. The big city intimidated her. She picked Whitechapel as a place to live without knowing very much about it and she found it hard to settle in.' I thought of the street stalls that lined the main road in Whitechapel, the market sellers shouting in hundreds of languages, the sense that thousands of lives were being lived all around you. Coming from a quiet rural community, Maxine must have been dazed.

'Why did she stay there?' Godley asked.

Bradbury shrugged. 'She could afford it.'

'I think she was too proud to admit to her folks she'd made a mistake in moving there,' Peake said gently. It was a sensitive reading of Maxine's decision to stay where she was. I knew people who loved Whitechapel, who wouldn't live anywhere else, but I still thought she'd have been happier elsewhere.

'I don't have this on a PowerPoint display, but these are the crime-scene pictures.' Bradbury skimmed them across the table, laying them out so we could all see them. 'Carnations underneath the body. White, of course. But she was naked.'

She was covered with a sheet, not exposed. The bed was surrounded with tea lights this time, ten or twelve of them, all burnt out. The carpet was cream and not new, marked in various places with stains that didn't look recent. Her room was neat but the furniture was as cheap as it gets.

'Any DNA?'

'Nothing.' Bradbury corrected himself. 'Nothing fresh.'

'They could at least have replaced that carpet between tenants,' Groves muttered.

'No sign of a break-in. No mention to friends or family that she'd recently met someone, as far as we can tell. Unlike Kirsty, she didn't seem to have any hobbies. She wasn't the kind to go out and join clubs.'

There was something desperately pathetic about the girl who'd travelled to the other side of the world to live in a grotty flat in Whitechapel, alone, and work hard at a job where her colleagues thought her awkward and immature. It was a rite of passage for young people from Australia, New Zealand and South Africa, but they tended to flock together, taking over whole neighbourhoods and creating their own version of London. Maxine hadn't made it to her own group. And lone animals were more vulnerable outside the herd.

'Okay. Wait.' Burns was snapping his fingers. 'I'm getting an idea.'

'Brace yourselves,' Groves said.

'Colours. Places.'

'What are you talking about?'

'*Black*heath. *White*chapel. *Green* Lanes.' He looked triumphant. 'What do you think?'

'I think there are a lot of places in London with colours in their names,' Groves said. 'A hell of a lot.'

'And it was Lewisham, you said, not Blackheath.' Una Burt was flipping back through her notes to check, her forehead puckered.

'Greenwich. Redbridge. Limehouse. Blackfriars. Bethnal Green. Wood Green. White City.' Groves sounded as if he was going to go on all night, and Godley spoke over him.

'Is there anything else anyone would like to share? Any ideas?'

'Plenty of ideas, but they don't lead anywhere,' Peake said. 'Every time we come up with a way to find him, he's already thought of it and avoided it. Everywhere we look, he's missing. No DNA. No CCTV. No parking tickets. Nothing that links the victims. Nothing that tells us why he chose them and not someone else. He hasn't left us anything but dead women. It's like he knows how we think.' I could hear the bitterness in his voice, the frustration at two months of getting nowhere. 'It's like he's better at this than we are.'

We were all thinking it, but Bradbury said it.

'It's like he's one of us. A police officer.'

Godley shuffled his papers, looking down so I couldn't catch his eye. I switched my attention to Burt, who had a bland, inscrutable expression on her face. The smallest suspicion was starting to form in my mind.

But it was clearly ridiculous.

'He could be a copper,' Groves said. 'We thought of that. He could have got in by pretending he needed to ask them questions.'

'It would fit in with them doing what they were told,' Una Burt said.

'He'd be used to ordering people around.' Burns was looking bleak.

We contemplated the idea in silence, until Groves spoke again.

'The gaps are getting shorter. Seven months to two months. He's getting more confident. You know what that means.' We all did, but he said it anyway. 'We don't have long before he does it again.'

Chapter 9

Having wimped out at the house when Dr Hanshaw was doing his worst, I made a point of attending Anna Melville's post-mortem and managed not to disgrace myself by fainting or throwing up or acting as if it bothered me to see her turned inside out. I found it was easier in the morgue, where she was out of her own context. It turned her body into an object of scientific interest rather than something that had once lived and felt and breathed. And Hanshaw was on better form in his own environment as he methodically unravelled all of Anna Melville's secrets. I stood beside Godley, my hands in the pockets of my coat, well back from the action but with a grandstand view nonetheless. I had been at enough post-mortems to know what to expect, so none of it came as a surprise.

Except for one part.

'Your victim was *virgo intacta*. No sign of sexual assault, no sign of sexual activity at all.'

'At her age? Seriously?' I was struggling to believe it.

'So it seems. Maybe she was saving herself for the right man,' Hanshaw suggested.

I batted it back. 'But she found Mr Wrong.'

'Please, don't. All we need is for the papers to start calling him that.' Godley was looking pained, as well he might. The news had got out that there was another death, which meant there was a serial killer stalking single women. That was a headline-grabbing development in itself, but then, at the press conference Godley had reluctantly given, a tabloid reporter had christened him the Gentleman Killer.

Godley *hated* it.

Now he shook his head. 'I don't get it. We know he doesn't interfere with his victims but there has to be a sexual element to it – dressing them up like that, cutting the hair. He gets a kick out of what he does.'

'Maybe he can't have sex with them,' I said. 'Or maybe he isn't prepared to risk leaving body fluid and skin cells on the victims, if he's scared we'll find his DNA. He was extra-careful about cleaning up, which suggests we have him on file somewhere. When I'm back in the office, I'll have a look through the CRIS reports for anything that sounds similar in any respect – strangulation and not necessarily to death, cutting hair, removing eyes – all the combinations.'

'You'll be swamped. There'll be too much for you to review alone.'

'I can get someone to help me. Colin Vale would be good.' It was the sort of task that was pure grinding tedium. That made Colin light up with excitement.

'Colin's busy.'

And I decide who does what on my team, I filled in silently.

'He must be very controlled,' Dr Hanshaw said, and I was grateful to him for breaking the awkward silence that had fallen. 'This would be the high point of his sexual gratification, if that's why he does it. Not touching them, not touching himself – doesn't that spoil it for him?'

'The crime scenes suggest someone in command of the situation, someone prepared to take their time to achieve what they imagined. I don't pretend to understand the psychology but I know there's a kind of killer who gets off on reliving the thrill afterwards, like Ted Bundy. Killing is the risky part, with the highest likelihood of being caught. Once he's done it and got away, he can indulge himself at his leisure.' Godley sighed. 'Maybe fiddling with them isn't the point of what he's doing. But I would dearly love to know what is.'

'It might just be killing them. And leaving them for us to find as he wants us to find them,' I risked.

'Controlling how we see them.' Godley nodded. 'The hair depersonalises them. Maybe that's what he wants. It's a pretty powerful signifier of femininity. Cutting it off, dressing them in white, lighting candles, women who have sworn off men – what does that say to you?'

'Becoming a novice.'

'A bride of Christ,' Godley said.

'You know, He wasn't on my list of suspects up to now.'

It was a joke, but Godley didn't laugh. 'That's rather the trouble. There doesn't seem to be a list. These three women – nothing overlaps.'

'There'll be something,' Hanshaw said, lifting a glistening object out of her chest and placing it into a bowl to be weighed. 'He's not picking them at random.'

'What makes you say that?' Godley asked.

'I saw how he left the others. He's a perfectionist. He wants conformity. So they'll have something in common that attracted his attention, even if you can't see it yet.'

'I never thought I'd wish for a common-or-garden murderous rapist,' Godley said. 'At least it's easy to understand what motivates them.'

'But if we can understand what he's trying to do with the way he leaves the bodies, we should be a lot closer to finding him,' I pointed out. 'It's the common-or-garden murderous rapists who go undetected for years because they just do their straightforward raping and killing and fade away into the night. This guy is making it complicated, which gives us more to go on.'

'How do you know he hasn't been killing for years? Decades, even?' Godley's voice was cold. 'Kirsty Campbell is the first one we can link to him directly, but she won't be the first of his victims. He'll have done something to someone before that, even if it wasn't murder. And you should know that, Maeve.'

Out of the corner of my eye I saw Hanshaw glance at us, then share a look with his assistant. *Not you too . . .*

I kept the hurt out of my voice. 'That's why I wanted to look at the CRIS reports. He's specialised in his MO to the point where we should be able to find a pattern and watch him escalate. He's making that easy for us.'

Godley's jaw was tight. 'He's making it a hell of a lot more complicated. If you knew—' He stopped.

'If I knew what?'

'Not now. Not here.'

I knew better than to argue with a superior officer so I shut up and watched the completely routine remainder of the post-mortem while I tried to think of a polite way to tell him everyone thought we were shagging and could he please stop making cryptic remarks all the time as it was making a bad situation worse.

I failed.

When the PM was over, Godley went back to the office but sent me in the opposite direction to Anna Melville's place of work in the City, so I was alone with my thoughts and several hundred strangers on the Underground. It was a long, dull journey. The train was slow, held up by signal problems way up the line, and we stopped between stations. I tested how much I could find out just by looking at my fellow passengers. What they read, and what they carried, and what they wore. Work ID cards were a gift: name, job title, office address . . . what more could you need? It was the perfect environment for hunting, proximity allowing fleeting intimacy. And it was so easy to follow someone without being noticed in the surge of people coming and going through the maze of corridors and escalators at every station. I wondered if that was all the killer had needed to do – sit on the train and wait. Look for the feminine, submissive kind of woman, the sort who stood back to let others get on first. The ones who blushed if you stood beside them. The ones who read books about falling in love. The ones who couldn't help staring at kissing couples wistfully, when everyone else in their immediate environment was trying not to yak. The ones who would make ideal, obedient victims.

I got off the train at Bank and came out into the fresh air in the shadow of the venerable Bank of England itself. I noticed, as always, the sudden upsurge in wealth that distinguished the Square Mile from the rest of central London. The bars advertised twenty types of champagne, the women wore immaculate suits and carried bags worth multiples of my salary, everyone walked fast and talked loudly in acronyms that were meaningless to me. The City was all about money, making it for other people and for yourself, and it was so far removed from my world that I felt as if I'd landed in another country. Disorientating too was the sense that the glass-and-steel modernity was just the latest layer of development. The history of the place lived in the street names and the idiosyncratic angles they took along medieval byways. Pudding Lane, where the Great Fire had started in 1666. Cheapside. Tokenhouse Yard. Threadneedle Street. The old thriving life of the city seemed to stir in the shadows, the names a reminder of a time when trade was in the things that kept you alive, like bread and poultry, not futures and securities.

I walked towards the Monument, thinking about Anna Melville and how she had journeyed to work, and the other women and how they had lived. Kirsty had been a planning officer with Westminster Council. Maxine was in an insurance company just off Long Acre. It wasn't surprising that they worked near one another given that central London was quite compact and, during the working day, densely populated. It was a truism to say Londoners tended to know small areas in minute detail but have the haziest idea of the rest of the city. My frequent changes of address made me more conscious than most that London was still a collection of villages, as it had been in the dim and distant past, and you could live in your village quite happily without ever needing to go much further afield. Covent Garden was within walking distance of the City and Westminster, but it would be unusual for someone to be familiar with all three areas, unless they were a taxi driver.

He could be a taxi driver. I made a note to mention it to Godley. Assuming, of course, that the superintendent was willing to listen to anything I had to say. I'd been determined to do my job, regardless of what I knew about him. I knew he was a good police officer and I loved working on his team. But I hadn't allowed for how awkward it was going to be.

Kirsty Campbell had loved her job too. Maxine Willoughby had lived for hers. If Anna Melville had been dedicated to her work too, that was practically the first and only thing I'd found they had in common. The more I looked, the less I found that they shared.

Except for being dead, of course.

I found Anna's office and asked for Vanessa Knight. The receptionist stared at me covertly while I waited for Anna's boss to meet me.

The lift doors opened and a blonde woman shot out, her heels skidding a little on the polished floor. She rushed over to me.

'You're the policewoman. Come with me.'

When the lift doors closed, she looked at me. 'I'm sorry. I'm nervous. I've never spoken to the police before about anything.'

'I just have a few questions about Anna.'

'How did it happen?'

'I'd rather not talk about it in the lift.'

'No. Of course not. Of course.' She jabbed at the buttons. 'Oh God.'

'Are you all right?'

She leaned against the side of the lift with one hand pressed against her chest. Her rings sparkled in the lights as she took deep, quivery breaths. 'I just get very nervous. I'm being so rude. Oh help.'

'Mrs Knight, there's nothing to be nervous about. Just try to calm down.'

'Okay. Yes. You're right.' She looked at me piteously. 'I'm going to be lost without her, you know. Anna. I don't know how I'm going to cope.'

Which was very different from, 'I'm going to miss her.'

When the lift doors opened she hurled herself out. 'This way.'

She led me to a small conference room and spent ages fiddling with the blinds, trying to block out the low sun that was shining across the table and making me screw up my eyes. I clenched my jaw to stop myself from telling her to hurry up, waiting until she was seated opposite me to start asking questions.

'Did you know Anna well? Had she worked here for long?'

'About five years.' She tilted her head from side to side, thinking. 'Yes. Five.'

'Would you say you were friends?'

'Close colleagues. We had a good working relationship.' Vanessa laid a slight emphasis on the word 'working'.

'Would you know what was happening in her personal life? Any boyfriends?'

She shook her head. 'She went on a couple of dates but nothing serious. She wanted to get married, not have a boyfriend, and it was a bit hard to have one without the other. She was quite well off, you know, and someone had told her she'd be a target for gold-diggers.'

'What about her social life? Friends? Classes or groups that she went to after work?'

Vanessa's face was blank. 'I really don't think so. She watched television a lot. And she shopped.'

I'd looked through Anna's wardrobe before leaving the flat and it was all colour-coded and neat and dry-clean only. None of it was showy, though. If anything, she'd dressed so subtly as to be almost invisible, and the clothes seemed to be made for someone older than she was. Looking at Vanessa, languid in grey cashmere with a pencil skirt, I thought Anna had been dressing to impress her boss.

'How did she travel to work?'

'No idea.'

'Was she popular at work?'

'Of course.'

'Did she ever make people redundant?'

'She helped to process redundancies, but it wasn't her responsibility to do it alone.'

'Was she involved in disciplinary proceedings?'

'Sometimes.'

'Did she have any enemies that you know of?'

'Of course not.'

'What sort of person was she?'

'Efficient. Competent. Dedicated.' The words came without prior thought and I realised I was getting the short form of the eulogy that would be emailed around the office along with confirmation that the rumours were true, it really was Anna Melville from the sixth floor who had been murdered . . . 'She was liked by everyone who knew her,' Vanessa finished, as if that was the last word on the subject.

'Would you describe her as attractive?'

'Yes. Of course. I mean, I never thought about it.'

'Did she ever have meetings with anyone from outside the company?'

'Not that I can recall.'

'What was her speaking voice like?'

Vanessa stared at me, floored.

'Did she have a regional accent?'

'No. She sounded normal. Totally normal.' Vanessa herself sounded extremely posh, nay for no and yah for yeah. I was getting more nays than yahs, I thought.

'There were two other murders in London in the last twelve months that we're looking into. There may be a connection with Anna's – it's one of our lines of inquiry. Did Anna ever mention knowing anyone who'd been murdered? Did she ever mention the names Kirsty Campbell or Maxine Willoughby?'

A slow headshake.

'Did she ever spend time south of the river, or in the East End?'

'I have no idea.'

'Did she ever say she was scared of anyone?'

'No.'

'When was the last time you saw her?'

'Yesterday, around four. I had to leave early. I'm supposed to be going on holiday tomorrow. Anna was going to look after things while I was gone. I just don't know how I'm going to manage to get away now.'

I wrapped things up pretty quickly, asking if I could have a look at Anna's desk. Without enthusiasm, Vanessa led me through a corridor of glass-walled offices to an area filled with cubicles, where every head was bent over a desk and every single person was aware of every move I made. Vanessa stood beside the cubicle, watching me, which didn't really help my concentration either. I thanked her for her time and told her I would be in touch if I had any other questions.

'You need a widget to make the lift work and I don't have a spare one I can give you. When you want to leave, just mention it to . . .' She looked down at the cubicle on her right.

'Penny,' a voice supplied from within the cubicle.

'Yes. Penny. Of course. She'll show you out.'

I nodded my thanks and waited until she was out of

sight before starting to go through Anna's work station. She had decorated the wall of her cubicle like a hermit crab, sticking random bits and pieces on it as they took her fancy. A sample of Chanel Mademoiselle from a magazine. A pair of dangly pearl earrings – costume jewellery, but pretty. A postcard from the Maldives seemed to be from a friend and I pocketed it so I could pass it on to Harry Maitland. He was working through her address book and email contacts. I hoped he was having more luck than me.

I sat in her chair to go through the drawers of the desk, finding neat stationery, an empty notebook, a zipped make-up bag and hairbrush, dry shampoo, a toothbrush, high heels, flat shoes . . . all the essentials for someone who spent long hours at work. Or someone who went out after work on dates. I swivelled on the chair, swinging from side to side. It wasn't completely professional, but it always helped me to think. I spun around 180 degrees and looked straight at an interested face that was peering over the side of the cubicle. She was young and fair-haired and had a wide mouth that made her look sulky and a little bit cheeky.

'Penny?'

'Just checking you didn't need anything.'

'Not at the moment.'

'Okay. Let me know if you do.'

I watched her disappear. 'Penny.'

'Yep.' She bounced back as if she was on a spring.

'Do you know the password Anna used for her computer?'

Instead of answering, she disappeared again and I heard scuffling before she arrived beside me, holding out a crumpled Post-it. 'I had this stuck to my monitor. She gave it to me the last time she was on leave in case I needed to look at her files. I don't know if she's changed it since, but the IT department creates them and we're not supposed to change them.'

I took it from her. 'Thanks.'

'Do you need anything else?'

'I don't think so.' Lowering my voice, I added, 'Unless there's anything you know that you think might be useful for us to know.'

'About who killed her?'

'Ideally. Or about her life. Anything strange or out of character she did.'

Penny shook her head regretfully. 'She was so straight it was unbelievable. She never did anything strange or unexpected.'

'Did you know her well?'

'Yeah, I suppose. I worked with her for two and a half years.'

'Did you like her?'

Penny had been speaking quietly too, but now her voice dropped to something close to a whisper. 'I couldn't stand her. She was so self-centred. Really precious and self-absorbed. She used to suck up to Vanessa but she'd never even talk to anyone else. She never so much as asked me if I'd had a nice weekend.'

That was the base level of in-office communication; it was what you said to the receptionist, the post-boy, your boss, the managing director when you bumped into them on a Monday morning. Even Derwent had been known to ask me that question, though I always felt it was in the hope of getting some salacious details about what Rob and I had been up to. Not saying it was pretty much a mortal sin.

'What about her love life? Do you know if she was seeing anyone recently?'

'I presume so.'

'Why?'

'Because she made enough of a fuss about the flowers he sent her last week. White lilies.' Penny wrinkled her nose. 'That's a funeral flower, I always think. And the smell. They stank the office out.'

'I quite like them,' I said.

She shuddered. 'Not for me, thanks. But Anna was delighted.'

'When did the flowers arrive?'

'Umm . . . Thursday?'

'Was there a card with them?'

'I don't know.'

'Did she know who they were from?'

'I think so. She wouldn't say, though. Someone said—' Penny laughed, then looked guilty and a little scared.

'What did someone say?'

'That she might have sent them to herself.' She looked edgy. 'Sorry. That was mean.'

'Well, she might have. But I think she probably didn't.' *I think they were a prop disguised as a gift. I think they were window-dressing for her corpse, a present from her killer.* 'What sort of a person was she? What words would you use to describe her?'

'Cold. Manipulative.' Penny thought some more. 'But sweet too, in a fake way. Needy.'

I asked Penny a few more questions but got no further and let her go, clutching one of my business cards. She might remember something, or she might not. I hoped she would try, even though she hadn't liked Anna.

I turned to the computer and looked at the Post-it Penny had supplied. A_Melville, with Xanna0Melv underneath. I put them in the required fields and lo, my brilliant detective work was rewarded with access to all of Anna's files. I worked through folder after folder looking for anything personal and finding nothing remarkable. In some cases, finding literally nothing. The Internet history had been wiped, which made me curious. Everyone used the Internet for something, whether it was work-related or personal. I checked with Penny, who confirmed that it was Anna's habit to wipe her history every day 'in case her identity was stolen or something'. On a hunch I checked the preferences and found that she had forgotten or not known about the cookies that tracked visits to websites. I scrolled through at speed, seeing lots of shopping websites and fashion blogs. Internet banking. A couple of newspapers featured. YouTube. Amazon. Ebay. It was like a greatest hits of the Internet, and nothing I saw was remarkable.

Except.

I had scrolled past it before I registered that I'd seen it, because it was so familiar to me. Familiar to me, but I didn't know why it would be on Anna's computer. Without the Internet history I was missing the whole story and I didn't know enough to be able to track it back any further, but alarm bells were ringing loud enough to deafen me.

Three days before she died, starting at 5.53 p.m., Anna Melville had spent twelve minutes looking at the website for the Metropolitan Police.

Chapter 10

I didn't go back to the office after my trip to the City, though I'd planned to. I called Una Burt first.

'I don't think she was all that popular in the office. A bit self-absorbed and cold. She was more focused on work than interested in her colleagues.' Too late I realised I could have been describing DCI Burt herself, who was legendary for her lack of interest in other people's lives, unless they were dead. If she noticed, she didn't mention it.

'Sounds quite different to the others, then. Kirsty was gentle and sociable. Maxine was reclusive and immature.'

'Anna was stuck-up and self-centred. Mind you, none of them was having much luck with men.'

'Don't assume that's why they let him in,' she said sharply. 'Everyone in that room this morning thought they were desperate old maids, but it's got us nowhere with this investigation so far. Think of the other things they had in common.'

Desperate old maids . . . I wondered if this was all a bit too close to home for the chief inspector, who was single and had apparently been so for ever. I felt I was letting her down even by just thinking that. There were plenty of police officers her age who were unmarried but it wasn't worthy of comment if they were men.

Besides, the victims had more in common with me than with Burt. I was their age, more or less. I could have walked into Kirsty's place and set up home without changing a thing, from what I'd seen in the crime-scene pictures. Usually the crime scenes I visited were the places no one wants to go – the festering one-bed flats in bleak, poverty-stricken areas, the sad, dated homes of forgotten pensioners, the back alleys and abandoned buildings and bits of secluded waste ground where bodies were dumped. Murder was a great leveller and I had been to lavish, multi-million-pound properties as well as the dives where you didn't want to touch anything, where you knew if you sat down you'd stand up with fleas. But I had never been so conscious of the hair's-breadth difference between me and the victims as on this case. I was luckier, and hopefully wiser, and I was very definitely not single any more, but I didn't have to work too hard to know these girls.

'Did you get the results from the technical examination? Did they find anything on Anna's iPad?'

'It was wiped. The history was cleared.' I could hear the frustration she was feeling. 'They're trying to retrieve data from it but they told me there wasn't likely to be much. It was almost new, apparently.'

'Do you think it was the killer who cleared the history?'

'We can't speculate about that. We'll never know.'

I felt reproved. She was right, of course. Unless we found the murderer and he was cooperative enough to tell us if he'd done it. 'It could have been Anna. It was her habit to clear it at the end of a session. Her computer at work was the same.'

'Was it? Damn.'

'Yes, but it's still worth recovering and examining. I've told Anna's colleagues not to touch it until someone comes to collect it. Because guess what Anna had been looking at before she died.'

Burt listened as I outlined what I had found, the trail that led to the Met website. Without seeing her face I couldn't even guess what she thought about it. There was something massive about her silence, something more than concentration. But her only comment when I had finished was, 'Where are you going now?'

'Back to the office. I've got some paperwork to do, and—'

'What about following up those leads in Lewisham? The book club and support groups.'

'Oh,' I said lamely. 'I could.'

'It may seem insignificant to you but it's the sort of leg-work that can make a case. And it was your idea.'

'No, I think it's definitely worthwhile. It's just that I wasn't planning—'

'You might think it's not time-sensitive given that Kirsty has been dead for almost a year, but we have an active serial killer at work in the city and I don't need to remind you that the intervals between murders are getting shorter. Make no mistake about it, this needs a prompt response.'

'Yes. Of course. I understand that. But I thought it was a bit of a long shot.'

'This late in the day, they're all long shots.' Burt sounded tired. 'Get it done. And Maeve?'

'Yep.'

'I thought the others did a good job, from their pres-entation, even though they didn't make this particular connection. They were thorough. Make sure you don't tread on any toes while you're on their patch.'

I rolled my eyes. Being lectured on politeness by Una Burt was like taking make-up advice from Barbara Cartland. 'I'll keep it in mind. But I think if we have problems with anyone it will be Andy Bradbury.'

'Why do you say that?'

Because he's a dickhead. 'Because he's recently promoted and he seemed defensive at the meeting earlier.'

'So he did. Was he like that when you met him before?'

'Pretty much.'

She made a noise that after a moment of sheer disbe-lief I identified as a chuckle. 'Rest assured I will take great pleasure in going through his work on this case and finding out what he has done wrong.'

'Without treading on his toes.'

'Some toes deserve it.' She hung up without saying goodbye.

I'd armed myself with a few pictures of Kirsty Campbell, given that she'd been dead for nine months, but I didn't need to remind anyone in Blackheath about her. The article in the evening paper had brought her right to the forefront of most people's minds. Anna's death had led the news all day and there was a strange, unseemly excitement in the air, a kind of suppressed thrill that something was actually happening, right there and then, something potentially historic in a Jack the Ripper sort of way. I was too close to the reality of violent death to see why it was exciting.

I walked from the station to the flat where she'd died, following in her footsteps, seeing what she had seen. More than ever I found myself identifying with her as I walked along the busy main street and into the quieter residential roads where the lights were starting to come on in the houses. I recognised the block of flats from some way off and walked around the outside of the building. There was no value in demanding to see the flat where she'd died. I was too late to see it as she'd arranged it, and I had the crime-scene photos to study. But I noted that Kirsty's flat was at the front, and not overlooked. The security on the building wasn't all that impressive either. I wondered if the killer had started with where she lived when he was thinking of choosing a victim. It had been pretty much perfect for his purposes.

I made some progress once I started talking to people, finding the place where she had her dry-cleaning done and the shop where she always bought the paper on Saturdays. A smart, newly painted pub with squashy leather sofas and a huge collection of board games was the venue for the knitting club Kirsty had briefly attended, though the landlord couldn't remember her.

'We get so many in, you see.' He eyed me, as much on edge as if I was going to blame him for what had happened, and take away his licence.

'Do you have any other groups that meet here?'

'Rugby club on a Tuesday night. Bitching Stitching on Wednesday, which is the quilting group – their name for it, not mine,' he said, noticing the look on my face. 'Knitwits is on Mondays. Thursday to Sunday we're too busy to spare the space.'

'No book clubs?'

He shook his head. 'The library might.'

I thanked him but not effusively. Derwent would have said something sarcastic to him about joining the Met with brilliant ideas of that sort. He hadn't been much help. Kirsty was a pretty, nicely spoken woman and it bothered me that he couldn't recall her, probably because she'd been gentle and polite and hadn't made a fuss about anything.

Maybe that was what the victims had in common, I thought, walking on down the street as a double-decker bus tore past, swaying as it went, apparently seconds from overturning. They were the kind of women who could be overlooked, despite being conventionally attractive and reasonably successful. They were introverts and being singled out for attention was such a change for them it made them drop their guard. Because they had to have done that to let their killer in. I couldn't escape the conclusion that he'd made them trust him.

Or they were too scared to do anything but follow his orders. I shivered, imagining myself in their shoes. I couldn't fool myself that they had been anything other than terrified at the end, when they knew they had no way out. I'd have bargained, and fought, and begged, and done anything at all to save my life, but maybe they had done all that and more. Or maybe they had abandoned hope in the face of implacable evil. Only the killer knew now.

At some level I had decided I would find what I was looking for at the library, so it was a disappointment to discover that there wasn't a book group there, at least not for young women. They had a group for the pensioners, and a club for schoolchildren.

'We've been forced to reduce our opening hours to save money so we can't offer any evening sessions,' the librarian explained. 'That means we're not really able to reach the younger professionals who might be interested in that sort of thing.'

'Do you know if there is a book group locally? The sort of place Kirsty might have wanted to go?'

The librarian tilted his head to one side. He seemed fearsomely competent, and had been brisk in dealing with the large queue. I was holding things up. There were about twenty people standing behind me, and it was five minutes to closing time. The library was intensely hot, too, and I wished I'd taken off my coat when I went in.

'I'm not aware of a book group. Leave me your contact details though, and I'll check with my colleagues.'

'What about a support group? For bereavement, or eating disorders, or—'

He was shaking his head.

I gave him my card and went to stand outside, the cool air a pleasant shock after the tropical heat. They could save on some costs if they turned the thermostat down, I thought. I was tired, and frustrated. This whole trip had been a huge waste of time.

'Excuse me. Sorry. I was in the queue behind you and I couldn't help overhearing . . .' The girl was standing about two feet away from me and I hadn't noticed her at all. She was wearing a hand-knitted scarf with long tassels, and a matching hat that she had pulled down over her eyebrows. 'You're the police, aren't you?'

'That's right.'

'Investigating Kirsty Campbell's death?'

'Among others.'

'I heard about the others. That one in Tottenham, today.' She plaited the tassels and undid them again, her fingers flying. She was tall and slender, slightly ungainly, and young in a way that had nothing to do with her actual age.

'Can I help you with something?' I didn't sound encouraging. She would want advice on staying safe, reassurance that there was no reason to be afraid. My patience for that sort of thing was not infinite, and I was tired.

'I knew her. Kirsty.'

'Really?'

She nodded. 'From church.'

I tried to remember if we'd known Kirsty was religious. 'I didn't know Kirsty went to church.'

'She didn't. Not really. Neither do I. But the vicar at St Mary's did a series of lectures that we both went to.'

'What were the lectures about?'

'Personal empowerment.' She flushed a little. 'It was about taking control of your life. Not depending on anyone else for fulfilment. I think the idea was that we were supposed to start depending on Jesus or something, but that didn't really happen.'

She'd just gone from potential nuisance to potential lead, and I felt my heart rate pick up. 'What did you say your name was?'

'I didn't. I'm Ruth Johnson. But everyone calls me Jonty.'

'Has anyone spoken to you about your friendship with Kirsty since she died? Anyone from the police, I mean?'

'No.' She squirmed. 'I didn't think anyone would be interested. We weren't friends really. I mean, I only met her three times.'

'It all helps. Especially if there's something that's been bothering you.'

'Well. Maybe. I don't know. It's probably not important.'

I'll be the judge of that. 'Look, is there anywhere around here that we could talk?'

'Bon Café is nice.'

I didn't care about nice. I cared about whatever Jonty Johnson had been suppressing for nine months because she didn't have the nerve or the notion to go into the police station and ask to speak to whoever was handling Kirsty Campbell's murder investigation. I wasn't going to let her out of my sight until I'd found out what it was.

Bon Café turned out to be devoted to ultra-organic vegetarian food – pulses and quinoa – and was painted green in a fairly literal-minded way. I sat on a bench that was just the wrong height for me and backless so I couldn't even slouch. The muddy liquid they called coffee came in a thick earthenware mug that was rough to the touch and quite startlingly unpleasant to drink out of.

Jonty had chosen a herbal tea that came in a glass, which was an improvement on what I had. It smelled, however, like tomcats' bottoms. That didn't seem to put her off. If it was the reason her skin glowed, it would almost be worth drinking it, because she had the radiance of someone who habitually washed in melted snow. Under the hat she had thick fair hair that she'd plaited and twisted and attached to her head somehow. She had narrow eyes that she'd made smaller with black liner, and her eyebrows were straight and thick. Her teeth were very white, and small, and spaced out like milk teeth. I was aware of the guy behind the counter staring across at her, admiring the effect. Jonty herself seemed oblivious. She was looking everywhere but at me, fidgeting in her seat, checking her phone and her watch. Now that we were indoors and face to face, her confessional urge had sputtered and died. I started with an easy one.

'Tell me about the lectures.'

'Um – it was a three-week programme. Once a week,

fifty minutes long. Non-denominational, but I think you were supposed to want to go on to do the Alpha Course and become a fully fledged Christian.'

'When was it?'

'January. It started right after Christmas. For everyone who'd resolved to get their lives in order, I suppose.' She sounded ironic.

'Was that why you did it?'

'Oh yeah. Time to stand on my own two feet and stop depending on other people. My parents, specifically. I needed to cut the apron strings.'

I thought of my own parents with a qualm. My life choices were so clearly not what they had wanted for me, from my job to my unmarried status. I went my own way and I made my own decisions, but basically I was still trying to make it up to them that I hadn't done what they expected. I was still hoping that they might one day be proud of me. Most of my friends didn't seem to have this problem. I had a feeling it was an Irish thing.

'Did you manage it?'

'Not really. My parents are very controlling. They're rich. They bought my flat. I just can't afford to walk away from them yet.'

'What job do you do?'

'I'm a singer. I write songs for other people too.' She sipped her tea, then anticipated my next question. 'I don't make a living out of it or anything. I keep going because it's what I want to do.'

'How did you find out about the lectures?'

'I saw the course advertised outside the church and it just seemed like it might be interesting, you know? It was one of those "Keep Calm" posters, like the wartime information ones.' She laughed a little. 'Typical – they're not exactly trendsetting at that church. Like, those posters are so overplayed. But this one was "Keep Calm and Find Happiness". And then underneath it said, "You can be everything you need". It just spoke to me. I was feeling really frazzled and stressed out and down and like I should just give up, and all I wanted was to take a moment for myself. I wanted to find myself without having to go off and travel the Far East for a year.' The tea slopped over the side of her glass as she turned it on the saucer. 'Again, I mean. Anyway, it was free.'

'How many people signed up?'

'About fifteen. There was this little circle of chairs and I was just so embarrassed to even be there that I sat down in the first one I got to and it happened to be beside Kirsty.'

'And the two of you got talking?'

'Not then. Afterwards. We came out and I didn't feel like going home straight away, because all these ideas were just buzzing around in my head and I didn't want to be on my own staring at the walls, you know? And I suppose Kirsty felt the same way because she came over and asked if I wanted to get a drink and talk about why we were there and what we wanted to get out of it.'

'What did Kirsty want?'

'She was trying to put her life back together after breaking up with her fiancé.' Jonty sighed. 'It was really hard on her. She was so brave to break it off. They were all involved in planning the wedding and inside she was just like . . .' She dragged her fingers down her cheeks, her mouth open in a silent scream.

'Why?'

'She didn't love him enough, she said. She felt smothered. She felt like he was going to run her life for her, or try to. It made her uncomfortable. She wanted to be on her own for a while to work out what she actually wanted to do.'

I'd had that smothering sensation myself. I knew exactly the chord of guilt, frustration and resentment that it struck, and it was the death knell for relationships. Rob was very careful to back off when he noticed I was getting claustrophobic. He was almost too good at backing off. Hence the paranoia.

I dragged my mind back to Kirsty. 'So, she wanted to be on her own. She wasn't trying to meet men.'

'No. Well, not then.' Jonty looked down at her tea. 'This is disgusting. I wonder if it would be better with sugar.'

She reached to take a packet from the jar on the table and I put out my hand and stopped her. 'Okay, firstly, no, it wouldn't help. Secondly, what do you mean by "not then"?'

'Because of the guy.'

'What guy?' I was leaning forward.

'The guy she said she was meeting the last time I saw her.' Jonty drew one leg up onto the chair and retied the laces on her Doc Marten. I bit the inside of my cheek hard enough to taste blood, fighting the urge to tell her to hurry up. 'The third week she couldn't come for a drink. She said she had to meet someone afterwards, and she was really sorry but it was the only day he could do.'

'A date?'

'I don't think so. I said "ooooh", you know, as you do, when she said she had to meet someone and she was really short with me. She just said, "Not like that" and then she gave me her number and told me to give her a call if I was at a loose end and wanted to meet up. Look.' She flicked through her contacts until she came to Kirsty's name and showed it to me, like a child proud of her homework.

'When was this?'

'Towards the end of January. The twenty-sixth.'

'And she died—'

'On the thirtieth.' Jonty nodded. 'I saw it in the paper. I couldn't get my head around it. I almost texted her – can you believe that? Even though I knew she was dead? Crazy.'

'It's not that unusual. People call their loved ones' phones after they're gone. They leave messages for them to say the things they didn't get the chance to say.'

'That makes me feel a bit better. I thought I was mental.' She gave me a rueful grin.

'Can we get back to the man? Had she mentioned him before?'

'Definitely not.'

'Did you see him? Did she tell you anything about him? A name? How they met?' I made myself stop. I could see the barrage of questions was confusing her.

'I didn't see him. She was meeting him somewhere else. She didn't tell me why they were meeting but it seemed more like something she had to do than something she was excited by. Like he was a chimney sweep or a plumber or something and she had to let him in.'

'To her flat?'

'I don't know.' Jonty frowned. 'That was just the impression I had. When she said he couldn't do any other night she sounded a bit irritated but business-like.'

The flats' management company was supposed to sort out tradesmen for the tenants. I made a note to check with them to see if she had made any complaints in the couple of months before her death.

'And you're sure she didn't use a name.'

'She might have, but I'm crap with names.' Jonty gave a tiny, panicky laugh, knowing that it was a terrible name to have forgotten. 'It was something short and simple. Not a foreign name. Geoff or John or something. But it wasn't Geoff or John.'

I wrote them down anyway. Not foreign, one syllable, possibly with a 'J' sound. 'Jack. James. Jim.'

'None of those.' She shook her head. 'I can't remember. I've tried and tried.'

'It doesn't matter.' I succeeded in keeping the frustration out of my voice. Mostly. 'One of those things. Just let me know if it comes back to you. You've been really helpful.'

'Have I?' She looked piteous. 'I wanted to help but I thought it would just be a waste of everyone's time.'

'Far from it,' I said. 'Would you be willing to give a statement to the local detectives who investigated Kirsty's death?'

'I don't mind.' She looked terrified.

'They're nice. Nothing to be frightened of. Let me call and check when they'd like to see you.' I rang Groves, who was pleased to hear from me but went quiet when I explained what I'd found out. He wanted to speak to Jonty immediately, he said. At the police station, if she could present herself there. He'd try not to keep her too long.

I passed it on to Jonty who agreed without any difficulty, being the good girl she was. Her eyes were troubled, though, and she drained her glass of tea without apparently remembering it was disgusting.

She was winding her scarf around her neck again in long, misshapen loops when she asked the question I'd been dreading.

'Do you think the man she mentioned was the one who – you know.'

'Killed her?'

A nod.

Yes. 'I don't know.'

She swallowed. 'Do you think I should have come forward earlier? When they were appealing for witnesses?'

'You're not responsible,' I said, seeing where this was going. 'You didn't make him kill anyone else. You could have come forward earlier, but I don't think it would have made any difference.'

In the overall scheme of things, a small lie sometimes made more sense than the truth. It might have made a huge difference, but she didn't need to know that.

Chapter 11

It was late by the time I got back to my desk, getting on for nine. The office was emptying out after a busy day. It smelled stale, despite the air conditioning, and the large windows were filled with dark skies and bright lights like sequins on velvet. Nightfall changed the atmosphere in the office. The desk lamps – so much better than fluorescent overhead lighting – marooned each of us who remained on our own individual island, and the noise level had dropped to a murmur of a few phone conversations, most of them winding up.

The door to Godley's office stood open. His desk was vacant, but his coat still hung on its hook and his computer was on. Una Burt's desk was similarly unoccupied, and she wasn't answering her mobile. I hoped I would see them before I left for the day, so I could share what I'd found out in Lewisham. There was no reason to dash home, anyway. I had had the best of intentions about how I would live while Rob was away: eating properly, going to bed early, painting my nails and writing emails to friends I hadn't seen in ages, catching up on reading books that had sat beside my bed for months. It was the first day and already I could tell my intentions were going to fall by the wayside. I would eat when I could and work as much as was humanly possible and the books would remain unread.

Too bad. There were more important things than manicures.

Being out of the office all day meant that I had to deal with what seemed like thousands of emails. I skimmed through them, trying to keep track of cases that had no press attention, no clamour for a result. Princess Gordon's death had passed almost unnoticed, and not just because it had been solved so quickly. There was no media interest in a young black woman being beaten to death by her partner, even if she had been pregnant. But she was just as dead as the Gentleman Killer's victims.

DS Burns had come up trumps with the number for Method Management, the company that looked after Kirsty Campbell's apartment building. I was gratified to discover that they had an emergency hotline number and I rang them straight away, even as I was reading through the rest of my emails, to ask about Kirsty's property. I explained who I was to the bored-sounding man who answered the phone.

'Is it possible to check if Kirsty had any issues with her flat, or the building? Any complaints?'

'In what period?'

'Let's start with December and January.'

'I'll have to look it up. Do you want me to call you back?'

'I'll hold on.'

He put the phone down beside his keyboard and I listened to the tapping, hoping he was doing what I'd asked rather than updating his Facebook status.

'I've just got to go and check something.' He didn't wait for me to reply, dropping the phone again with a clatter. His chair squeaked as he pushed it away from his desk and I imagined him walking across the office, giving him a crumpled white shirt that was pulling out of the waistband of wrinkled trousers and scuffed shoes. My version of him needed a haircut and had a weakness for pies. He was probably whippet thin and bandbox neat in real life.

While I waited I dealt with the remaining emails. Just as I was getting to the end, a new one popped into my inbox. It was from James Peake, the DS on the Maxine Willoughby case, which in itself wasn't that odd; I had given him my card when I was distributing them to all and sundry after the meeting. The bit that made my heart sink was the subject line. *Drink?*

'You still there?'

'Yep,' I said, dragging my mind back to Kirsty.

'Just to say, I've had to speak to my boss about releasing this information and he wants me to make sure you realise that we aren't liable for anything.' *Anyfing.*

'That's not why I'm ringing. I just want to know her concerns.' I wiggled my pen between my fingers, tapping the end on the desk. The tapping was getting faster the longer he delayed.

'He wants to speak to you.'

'Fine. Give me his number.' I would speak to anyone if they could just tell me something helpful.

The phone didn't even ring before he picked up with a sharp-sounding 'Hello?'

'This is Detective Constable Maeve Kerrigan.'

'I'm Kevin Montrose, the owner of Method Management.' *Good for you.* 'I'm investigating the murder of Kirsty Campbell.'

'So I'm told. Just so you know, there was no damage to the property and no sign of forced entry.' He sounded anxious as well as sharp. Something was up.

'I'm aware of the lack of damage.'

'There was going to be an investigation of Miss Campbell's concerns and we were actively engaged in organising that at the time she died.'

'I see. And what were those concerns?'

'According to the file, Miss Campbell raised some issues about the quality of the locks used on the external doors and the internal front doors in the building. She was also concerned about the window locks and the provision for escape from the property in the event of a fire. Obviously we are very careful to maintain smoke alarms and carbon monoxide monitors in the properties we manage, as I informed her.'

'When did she contact you about this?'

'Twenty-seven one.'

It took me a second. 'The twenty-seventh of January? Three days before she died?'

'I believe so.'

'Was there anything else?'

'She said she had been advised we should have CCTV fitted on the outside of the property, to cover the front and rear exits and the car park area. There is a bike rack at the flats too and she was worried about bikes being stolen from there. I told her a determined thief won't be put off by locks or CCTV but she wasn't impressed.' He gave a thin laugh. 'And she wanted us to install a video entryphone so the residents could see who they were buzzing in to the building.'

'That's recommended on the Metropolitan Police website.'

'Well, they can come up with the money, then. I told her it would cost a fortune and I also told her she'd have no chance of persuading everyone else in the building to pay their share. The landlords don't want to be bothered with that sort of thing and the owner-occupiers have enough to worry about with the basic charges.' He sounded smug as he said it, and since his company set the charges, I could see why he might.

'Anything else?'

'Letterbox shields on the back of the door to stop people fishing through the letterbox. Security lighting outside. And she wanted the doorframe reinforced on her flat.'

'It sounds as if she was desperately concerned about her security.'

'Something had made her aware of potential security issues.' Montrose's version was a much blander, safer one than mine.

'Did you speak to her yourself?'

'The call was transferred to me at Miss Campbell's request.'

'How did she seem? Was she upset?'

'No. It wasn't an unpleasant call. She was calm. It was as if someone had given her a list and she was just working through it. She didn't seem to know or care if it would be expensive to make those changes.'

'Maybe she thought it was worth any money to be safe in her own home,' I said. 'But she wasn't safe. And you had no intention of making any of the changes she requested.'

'That's not so. We listed them as I've just proved since it was all in the file, and we were working on a costing when her body was found.'

'Do you have the costing on file?'

'I think we didn't complete it. Under the circumstances—'

'I would have thought the circumstances would have made it more urgent, not less.' *And it's 'in the circumstances', you greasy little twerp.* 'I was at the flats today, Mr Montrose. Do you know what I saw? No CCTV. No security lighting. No video intercom at the front door. I didn't examine the locks but I bet they're the same ones that were in use when Kirsty Campbell was alive.'

His silence told me I was right.

'If you were taking her seriously, you would have gone ahead with the changes the tenants agreed to make. You would have done a proper costing and circulated it to all the residents and it is possible that not all of the security measures would have been adopted but some of them would have gone ahead. You heard she was dead and as far as you were concerned the problem had gone away.'

'She didn't die because the locks weren't adequate,' he blustered. 'There was no sign of a break-in at the address.

111

We were in close contact with the officers who were investigating the murder back in January and they were absolutely clear that there was no damage to the building, the locks, the doors or the windows.'

'What about the fact that the front door lock was broken?'

'What about it?'

'That had been reported to you, hadn't it? Not just by Kirsty. By the other residents. You'd had complaints, I gather, before the murder.'

'A couple.'

'When was the first one logged?'

'Four days before the murder.'

'Four days,' I repeated. 'And you hadn't got it repaired.'

'We were bringing in a technician.'

'From where? China? While the door was broken, the tenants were at risk of burglary or worse. And Kirsty *died*.' My voice had risen and I glanced around, suddenly self-conscious. The room had emptied out while I was talking. With the exception of the new detective, Dave Kemp, I was on my own. 'What was the hold-up?'

'I'm not sure.'

'Pretty standard, was it?'

'I'm not sure I should answer that.'

'This isn't a civil court, Mr Montrose, and you're not in the witness box. I'm just trying to find out the facts. I'm not going to sue you on Kirsty's behalf.'

'There are no grounds for suing us.' The reply came too quickly. I really doubted Kevin Montrose slept well at night.

'Did Kirsty mention being afraid of anyone or anything in particular?'

'No.'

'Did she mention where she'd got this list of security measures?'

'No.'

'Did she mention anyone else at all? Other residents?

Friends? A boyfriend?'

'No. The police asked me all this at the time.'

'Well, I'm asking you about it again.'

'Is that because of the other girls?'

I didn't answer him straight away, wondering how to play it, and he went on.

'I saw it in the paper. Now there are three of them. Terrible, isn't it? You know, you're giving me shit about not having sorted out the security measures, but it seems to me the Met are more at fault than anyone.' He was angry, and getting more confident by the second. 'If you'd caught him back in January, two women would be alive who aren't now. That's a lot worse than being a bit slack about fixing a door.' He hung up almost before he'd finished saying 'door', afraid that I'd find some way of hitting back so he wouldn't get the last word.

'Pillock,' I said under my breath anyway and put the phone down so I could click on James Peake's email. I'd been putting it off while I was on the phone but I hadn't forgotten it; I'd seen it out of the corner of my eye the whole time I was enduring my conversation with Kevin Montrose. It didn't take long to read it.

> *Thought we should meet up to discuss the case.*
> *Might be useful to talk about it one-to-one.*
> *JP*

I felt less tense. Just a friendly invitation to go for a drink. And perhaps an indication that he felt as enthusiastic about Andy Bradbury as I did. Maybe there was something he wanted me to know about how the new inspector had been handling the investigation and he couldn't say so directly on his work email. He'd never grass Bradbury up to a senior officer like Una Burt or God himself, no matter how annoying Bradbury was to work for. I was low enough to the bottom of the pole to be unthreatening, yet I could pass the word on to the bosses that Bradbury was out of his depth. It all made perfect sense. I rattled off a reply suggesting that we meet the following night and leaving the venue up to him. It meant we would be meeting on a Saturday, which made me slightly uneasy, but I would be working all weekend and so would he. He would know it was strictly business.

I sent the email without another thought about it, except the vague relief that I wouldn't be left to my own company. So much for wanting to enjoy spending time alone. I checked my phone again, hoping for a message from Rob, but there was nothing. I'd had a text to say he'd arrived, but that was it so far. Punitive roaming charges meant he was unlikely to use his mobile. I couldn't help looking, though.

'What are you doing?'

I must have jumped a foot in the air. 'N–nothing.'

Derwent was standing directly behind my chair. I hadn't heard him coming; the carpet had made his footsteps completely silent. His face was shadowed, his expression equally dark, and I twisted awkwardly in my chair to keep him in view. He was looking at my desk, and the notes I had written while I was on the phone with Kevin Montrose. Kirsty's name straggled in capitals across the top of the page, and the rest was a tangle of dates and phrases. It made sense to me, but I doubted anyone else could follow it. Nonetheless, I pulled a file across the page to hide it from Derwent's view.

It was like snapping my fingers to wake a sleepwalker. His attention jumped to me, and his face hardened. 'Covering up your work? Afraid I'll copy you? Don't tell the teacher, will you?'

'What's up?' I said calmly, ignoring his tone. My heart was racing.

'I was going to ask you the same thing. You've been avoiding me. Screening my calls.'

'No, I haven't.'

He leaned across me and snatched my phone off the desk. 'Voicemail. No new messages, no saved messages.' He showed me. 'But I've called you eight times and left messages every time. That means you've been deleting them.'

'It was an oversight.'

'It was a big fucking mistake, I'll tell you that for nothing.' He leaned in and I could smell the doublemint chewing gum he liked, and something else that was sour underneath it, as if he hadn't eaten for a while. 'Don't ignore me.'

'I was busy. DCI Burt—'

'Don't give me that. Don't mention her name.' He was still leaning over me and now he knocked the file to one side so he could see my notebook again. 'Kirsty Campbell. The girl who died in Lewisham in January. Are we investigating this now?'

'*We* aren't.'

He straightened up as if I'd pushed him, staring down at me with surprise and enough hurt for me to feel sorry for him, and guilty, and unsure of myself.

'What are you saying? You are but I'm not, is that it?'

'The boss asked me to work with Burt on it. She's had me running around today. I didn't have time to call you.' And I hadn't wanted to face his anger. It was like standing at the door of a blast furnace. The heat of it was withering. He stared at me for what felt like endless seconds.

'Whose idea was it? Who cut me out?' He grabbed the arms of my chair and turned it around so he was right in my face. 'Who told you not to talk to me?'

'I did.'

I had never, ever been so pleased to hear Una Burt's voice. She was at the door to the office, quite far away, but there was something reassuringly calm about the way she said it.

'You.' Derwent had turned to see her but he was still

leaning towards me, his face inches from mine. I pressed my head back against the seat, trying to make more space between us.

'That's right. If you want to intimidate anyone, try me.' She stomped in and across to her desk, putting her handbag down on it with a thud. She wasn't even looking at Derwent any more. She'd turned her back on him, which was more than I'd risk when his eyes were so wild. At long last, he straightened up and I sucked air into aching lungs, realising I'd been unable to breathe while he was in my face. Behind her, Dave Kemp shrugged into his coat and headed for the door, careful not to look at any of us as he mumbled a goodbye. Sensible not to want a ringside seat. I wished I could do the same.

'What gave *you* the right to tell *her* not to answer my calls?'

'She's engaged with a sensitive case. It wouldn't be appropriate for her to speak to you about it.'

'I work with Kerrigan. We've got cases together. And I know all about sensitive cases. I know all about this one.'

'I'm sure you do.'

'What's that supposed to mean?' He came out from behind my desk and started moving towards her with that faltering sleepwalker step that told me he was blinded by rage. The red mist. A killing fury. Call it what you wanted, but it was controlling Derwent now, making the decisions for him. His rational mind had stepped out of the building, along with Una Burt's sense of danger, apparently. I stood up too, not really sure what I could do. Clobber him with something, maybe. I started to look around for a suitably heavy object and came up short. The stapler wasn't going to do it. I really wished I had my Asp, the extendable baton that I'd used to win friends and influence people while I was on the street. Twenty-one inches of steel tended to end arguments pretty quickly.

'Was this your idea?' Derwent demanded, still getting

closer to Una Burt, who was reading a file, completely unconcerned, as if nothing was going on. 'Was it your suggestion to shut me out?'

'It was Godley, if you must know.'

'No, it wasn't.' Derwent stopped.

'It was.' She twisted around to look at him and I felt even more uncomfortable when I saw how much she was enjoying this. 'He was quite clear about it. You're to be kept well away from this investigation.'

'Why?' The way he said it was almost plaintive.

'I think you know.'

I heard footsteps in the corridor and Godley appeared in the doorway. He stopped dead. 'What's going on?'

'Just finding out why I'm not in the gang, boss.' The bitterness in Derwent's voice was searing.

'It's not like that.'

'It is,' Derwent insisted.

'I have a small team working on this inquiry. I don't need another DI.'

'But you need Kerrigan. And *her*.' He pointed at Una Burt.

'And Harry Maitland. And one or two others.' Godley moved a little closer to Derwent. 'I've got officers coming out of my ears on this one. I don't want to take people like you away from the other cases that are going on. They matter too.'

'I've asked you. I've *begged* you.'

'Not going to happen. And you need to leave now, before you make a serious mistake.' Godley took another step forward. Because he was so civilised, I tended to overlook the fact that he was tall and physically fit. He'd done his time on the street too, back in the day. Standing near Derwent, his eyes watchful, Godley looked as if he could handle himself in a fight. I saw him shift his feet to adjust his balance and I suddenly felt sorry for Derwent – sorry and scared.

'It's all right,' I said, not really knowing what I was going to say next.

Godley's attention switched to me for a second before he focused again on Derwent. 'Go into my office, Maeve.'

'Sir, I hadn't returned DI Derwent's calls. I hadn't been communicating with him. He needed to talk to me about the Gordon case, urgently.' Derwent was staring at me as if he'd never seen me before or heard the name Gordon. 'I'm sorry,' I said, tailing off. *Please take the hint. Take the exit strategy I'm giving you. Everyone knows what I just said is total bullshit, but it means you can keep your dignity at the very least.*

Derwent looked back to Godley and it was as if something in him had died. Not the anger. More like his pride. His voice was dull. 'That's right. I needed to talk to her about the Gordon case. Follow things up.'

'Another time.' Godley's face was unreadable. 'Maeve, go and wait in my office and shut the door. DCI Burt and I want a word with you before you go home.'

I took the long way round rather than walk past Derwent. When I'd closed the door I sank into a chair, feeling like I wanted to cry. I didn't understand what was going on. I didn't know why Derwent was behaving that way, or what they were saying to him. Through a gap in the blinds I could see the three of them standing in a tight little triangle as Godley talked to Derwent. He was looking at the floor, not at the superintendent. While the boss was still speaking, Derwent turned and walked out of the room. Burt and Godley stood together, watching him go. By the time they turned back and started to walk towards the office, I was far away from the gap in the blinds, leafing through the newspaper from the day before as if I was completely engrossed. I doubted I was fooling anyone.

'Right, Maeve. Tell me about Anna's workplace. What did you find out?' Godley was aiming for a normal tone of voice but it came out too hearty, too honest and direct. *You can trust me . . .* Except, of course, I couldn't.

I explained again about the trail of cookies on her computer leading to the Met website. A meaningful look passed between Burt and Godley so quickly that I almost missed it. But I didn't.

'The tech guys have already recovered the computer. They're talking to the IT department at the office to see if there's any other record of what people have been browsing on their work computers,' Burt added.

'There's bound to be in a place like that, I should think.' Godley nodded. 'Good. What else? You went to Lewisham, didn't you? Anything new?'

'Nothing on the book club, but I did find out that Kirsty Campbell was planning to meet a man a few days before she died and she was worried about her home security.' I told them about meeting Jonty, and the conversation I'd had with Montrose.

'Do we think she was being stalked?' Burt's eyebrows were drawn down in a thick, bristling line. I found I couldn't quite look at her. No one had mentioned Derwent, but I couldn't get his shattered demeanour out of my mind.

'It's possible. But according to Montrose, she was calm on the phone.'

'Check with Groves. See if her friends and colleagues had picked up on anything. I'm sure they've asked the question already.'

'Even if they've done nothing else.' Burt sniffed. 'Maeve's been following up leads for half a day and she's already found out more than they have in nine months.'

'You're doing well,' Godley said to me, and I forced myself to smile. They were both watching me. They were both trying to see if I was on their side, I thought. I could play this game. I could cooperate and get another inch or two up the ladder.

I could lose my self-respect.

'About DI Derwent.'

Twin expressions that were the opposite of encouraging.

'I think it's time you told me what's going on.'

Silence.

'Okay then.' I stood up. 'See you tomorrow.'

'Where are you going?' Una Burt demanded.

I gave the pair of them my best sunshiny smile. 'If neither of you is prepared to start talking, I'll just have to go and ask him myself.'

Chapter 12

I'll say this for Godley and Burt: they were realists. They knew I wasn't joking and they knew the only thing they could use to stop me was the truth. If they'd been in my place, they'd have done the same. So they came clean.

Not, however, without a warning from Godley.

'There was a reason we were trying to keep this from you, Maeve. This sort of thing – you can't unknow it. You have been working with DI Derwent; you may have to work with him in the future. You must not reveal to him what you know, if he asks you about it. Can you do that?'

'I have quite a lot of practice at being discreet.' And let Godley take that however he pleased.

'It's vital that you keep this to yourself, as well. I don't want this being talked about. The more people discussing it, the more problems we're going to have.'

'I understand. And I don't gossip.'

'Everyone gossips,' Godley said flatly. 'This is the main reason why I'm keeping the team's involvement in the serial killer investigation to a minimum. I want to know exactly what's going on with it but I don't need everyone else to know about Josh. Do you understand?'

'Sort of.' I had remained standing by the door, but now I came back and sat down. 'I can't really say I understand when I don't know what the issue is.'

'It's pretty straightforward. When Josh was a teenager,

his girlfriend was murdered. He was the number-one suspect but he was never charged.'

'No evidence,' Una Burt chipped in. 'I've read the file.'

'He had an alibi.' Godley glared at her. 'There was no question of him being responsible for her death. It didn't stop him from being accepted when he applied to the Met, and they wouldn't have considered him for a moment if he was a potential murderer.'

'So you say.' She didn't sound convinced.

'I know you don't like him, but—' Godley seemed to remember I was there and broke off. 'Where was I?'

'Murder. His girlfriend.'

'Right. Well, there are some . . . similarities between the girlfriend's murder and the recent deaths.'

'Such as?'

'Angela Poole was strangled. Had her eyes gouged out. But it happened in her back garden, not her bedroom.' Burt's voice was matter-of-fact, even when she added the last detail, the one that made me wince. 'She was fifteen years old.'

'Did they get whoever did it?'

'No one was ever charged,' Godley said. 'And Josh has spent the last twenty years trying to find out who killed her.'

'So Derwent is obsessed with his dead girlfriend, and the case is superficially similar to the current killings.' I still wasn't seeing the problem.

'The killings aren't similar. They are identical in many respects,' Burt said.

'I didn't want Josh involved from the start,' Godley said. 'There's a good chance he'd say or do something inappropriate – you saw him just now. He's not himself.'

Burt snorted. 'I think that was the real him, Charlie.'

'I know him better than you do.'

'I'd rather not know him at all.'

They were bickering like an old married couple. I

cleared my throat. 'So is that it? That's the reason why he's not allowed to know what's going on? Why I'm not even allowed to *talk* to him?'

Godley looked down, not meeting my eyes. 'At the meeting today, there was speculation about the character of our killer. And about his job.'

'He could be a police officer. Or pretending to be one,' I added.

'It makes sense, doesn't it?'

'Yes, but it doesn't have to be Derwent.'

'Tell her about the profile,' Burt said.

'What profile?'

Godley started to leaf through his in tray. 'I had Dr Chen profile the killer a couple of weeks ago. Obviously she based it on the information we had, which was from two murders. It's worrying, Maeve.'

'I don't believe it. You're hanging Derwent out to dry because of a forensic psychologist's profile?' Forget diplomacy; I was outraged. God knows, I didn't like Derwent, but he was a committed police officer and loyal in his own way to those he chose to care about, which included Godley. Moreover, I didn't believe he could be responsible for the crime scene I'd seen that day. Killer was possible – cold-blooded was not.

'Just listen before you make up your mind,' Godley said, and started to read aloud. 'The subject is aged between thirty and forty-five and has a dominant personality. He is confident with women and probably works in a position of authority. He is single and lives alone. He is obsessive about detail and a perfectionist. He can be manipulative and has sadistic traits but he is controlled in his behaviour, able to suppress this aspect of his personality much of the time. He could have a military background or experience of being in a highly controlled environment such as a strict boarding school, young offenders' institution or prison. He is employed in a job where he has considerable personal freedom and may work for himself rather than a private company. He may have spent time outside the UK. He is well-spoken, middle-class and superficially attractive but he has serious sociopathic traits.'

I snorted. 'Derwent is an arsehole. That may not be what the psychologists would call him, but it's true. He's not a sociopath.'

'It's more common than you'd think. One per cent of the population, they estimate. No ability to empathise. No guilt about committing violent acts. No morality,' Burt said.

'Derwent is one of the most moral people I know.' By his own standards, obviously; he wasn't winning any prizes for equality campaigning.

'If he is a sociopath, he's an expert at disguising it,' Burt said. 'And you know very well he's bright enough to look up the traits that distinguish a sociopath so he can create the opposite impression. Weren't you listening, Maeve? Most of that profile might as well have his picture beside it.'

'I don't know that a profile is the best way to find a killer. I prefer to rely on the evidence. And there isn't any.'

'No, there isn't,' Godley said. 'But you see why I can't take the risk of letting him know too much. I shared my initial concerns with Una when Josh first raised the possible connection with Angela Poole's death—'

'And it was my idea to consider him a possible suspect,' she finished.

Godley winced. 'I don't like to suggest it's a possibility but I can't just defend him because I like him. I've got to keep it in mind. He's on leave for the next two weeks and I've warned him not to come near the office, or you, or anyone else who's working on the investigation.'

'So if he does approach you, tell us.' Burt ran her tongue over her upper lip and I turned away again, sickened at the look of anticipation on her face. She hated Derwent almost as much as he hated her. She must have noticed that I was upset. 'Look at what you've found out just today, Maeve, that points at Josh Derwent. Anna was looking at the Met website. Miss Johnson thought the man who Kirsty was meeting had a name that could have been Josh.'

'She didn't say that.'

'She suggested it.'

'I think you're seeing what you want to see. With respect,' I added, recalling that she was a DCI.

'He is obsessed with this case. He is obsessed with being involved in the investigation. Angela's murder changed the course of his life – you know his parents kicked him out, don't you, before he joined the army? It was because they were so ashamed of him. Imagine how they must have felt to cut him off like that. *They* thought he did it.'

'That's just speculation,' I protested.

'It's a theory but it makes sense.' Burt leaned towards me. 'I heard about what happened yesterday. Derwent lost his temper because he wanted to know about the investigation into Kirsty and Maxine's deaths. A few hours later, Anna was dead. Why then? Why so soon after Maxine? He was angry last night and today we have a murder. It's possible that he was angry in January, and in August, before the other two women died.'

'This is Derwent we're talking about,' I said. 'He's angry all the time.'

'Has he ever spoken to you about Angela?' Godley was watching me.

'We don't really have that kind of relationship.' By which I meant I would rather crawl over broken glass than talk to him about my private life and he didn't volunteer much about his, except stories about his sexual exploits that he knew would make me edgy. Sadistic tendencies? Well, maybe.

Godley pushed the file across the table towards me. 'This is a copy of the case file. Take it. Read it. Get familiar with the facts of the case and draw your own conclusions.'

'You cannot believe that he is a killer. You wouldn't have him anywhere near your team if that was the case.' I held Godley's gaze, challenging him.

'Honestly, I don't know what to think. He's been obsessed with this murder for as long as I've known him – talking about it, talking about her.'

'I've never noticed anything.' But even as I said it, I was remembering incidents from other cases – his prud-ishness, unusual among cops, where young girls were concerned. I remembered him throwing up at a crime scene where the victim was a teenager and blaming it on food poisoning. I remembered him being surprisingly tender when it came to persuading a troubled young woman not to set herself on fire. I remembered him say-ing he wasn't in touch with his parents, and not wanting to talk about it. I remembered him taking a positive and wistful delight in my so-close-it's-claustrophobic family. All of the times Derwent had surprised me, it seemed, could be traced back to this. He walked around with it like a shadow.

'You know Josh.' Godley's voice was quiet, the effect hypnotic. 'You know what he's like. He gets an idea in his head and he has to carry it through, no matter who he hurts or what goes wrong in the process. It could be him, Maeve. And even if it's not – and I hope and trust it's not – I can't have him rampaging through this case causing mayhem. Now read the file. Take it home. I don't want you to look at it in the office, for obvious reasons.'

I stood up and took it from Godley. The file was thin for a murder investigation, even one that had happened twenty years ago. Too thin to be a reason to sabotage some-one's career.

'Give it back to me tomorrow. Come and see me at ten. You too, Una.'

I couldn't get out of Godley's office quickly enough. The file fitted in my shoulder bag but there wasn't any room for my notes from the current case. I switched off my computer and light, grabbed my coat and headed for the door. DCI Burt was back at her own desk and I was aware of her watching me as I strode across the room.

'You were the one who wanted to know.'

'I don't mind knowing.' *I mind the way you're enjoying all of this.*

'I'm glad you do know now. For your own sake. And safety.'

I laughed. 'I'm hardly in danger from Derwent.'

'You don't know that. Just be on your guard.'

She reminded me of the people who'd mobbed public hangings for entertainment in the nineteenth century. I wasn't yet on Derwent's side but I was also very far from being on Burt's. I would make up my own mind.

I set off down the stairs, hurrying, because I was madly curious to read about what had happened to Angela Poole. It was the best way to find out what had made Derwent the man he was. A normal, happy upbringing didn't produce anything as complicated as him. The building was hushed, so quiet I could hear the lift shuttling up and down beside the stairwell. My heels echoed on the tiled steps, a quick staccato. I was already planning my route home. I'd get a bus, I thought, at least some of the way. Changing methods of transport was a good way to check I wasn't being followed. Thank God for free travel, one of my perks as a police officer. I had my ID in my hand as I nodded goodnight to the security guard and pushed through the revolving door onto the street. Force of habit made me take the measure of the people passing, the cars on the street, the safety or otherwise of my surroundings. No vehicles I had seen before. No one giving me a second look. Nothing suspicious. I paused to wrap my scarf around my neck, tucking it in under the collar of the expensive coat that had been a Christmas present from the well-heeled boyfriend before

Rob. Behind me, the revolving door made a noise like a quick intake of breath as someone else emerged. I barely registered it.

So it was a shock to be grabbed from behind, one arm held in a way that suggested the person who had taken hold of me wasn't going to let go for anything – not tears, not swearing, not violence. For one brief moment I still considered trying all three. I had known who it was the moment he touched me, without even looking; it was surprise and outrage that made my heart pound, not fear. He steered me down the street, walking beside me, so close that most people wouldn't have noticed the way he was grasping my arm. It was expertly done.

He guided me down a one-way street not far from the office, one of the little forgotten lanes of Westminster, too narrow to allow cars to park on it, a cut-through for taxis, a breathing space between buildings more than a street in its own right. And it was deserted. We walked halfway along it before Derwent stopped. He was wearing his dark over-coat buttoned, the collar turned up as usual to ward off the sharp east wind that was ruffling his hair and whipping colour into his cheeks.

I found my voice. 'What the hell do you think you're doing?'

'Bit of kidnapping. Nothing fancy.'

'Get off.' I leaned away from him, or tried to. All the feminism in the world couldn't give me enough heft to move an inch.

'Where are you going in such a hurry?' He sounded jittery, the nerves masked by a horribly unsuccessful attempt at being jocular.

'Home.'

'Home,' he repeated. 'And what's this? Taking work with you? Little bit of extra reading?' He twanged the strap of my bag and I couldn't stop myself from clenching my arm against it.

'It's just some stuff I wanted to go through. You know I never have time to read the briefings properly.'

His eyes glittered in the streetlight, the half-smile less convincing by the minute. 'Was that why you stayed late, Kerrigan? Printing them off like a good girl? Showing Burt and Godley you're more dedicated than the average detective?'

'If you like.'

'It's not about what *I* like. *I* don't matter any more. You've got someone else to suck up to now.'

It wasn't the first time I'd been scared by Derwent, but I knew him better now than on the last occasion, and this time I was angry too. 'Spare me the self-pity. And I'm not like that. I've never tried to suck up to you or Chief Inspector Burt. You wish I would so you could enjoy upsetting me when you put me down.'

He looked surprised. 'Why would I want to put you down?'

'I wish I knew.' I took the opportunity to try to pull my arm away again, and failed. 'Look, what do you want?'

'To talk to you.'

'You don't have to behave like a thug.'

'I did try calling you.' His jaw was clenched.

'Is that what this is about? You want to have another go at me for not returning your calls? You really need to work on how you handle rejection.'

'Shut up.' A black cab turned into the street, its orange light on. The throaty diesel engine sounded loud in the narrow street. Derwent leaned into the road and held up his hand. The driver slid to a stop within inches of us and Derwent yanked open the door. He pushed me forward. 'In there.'

'I'm not going anywhere with you.' I meant it, too.

'Why not? Don't you trust me?'

I looked up at him, about to say something cutting, but the words faded out of my mind as I realised he actually meant it. His face was set, the strain showing around his eyes and his mouth.

'What do you want from me?' I asked, very quietly. 'What do you think *I* can do?'

'I don't know. It's just – I don't know what else to do.' No attitude. No belligerence. Derwent was actually asking me for help, in his own awkward way.

'Look, mate, what's the problem?' The driver was staring at us with frank interest. 'Everything all right, love? Want me to get this gentleman to leave you be?'

I was aware that Derwent was silent beside me, waiting for me to answer. 'No,' I said. 'It's fine.'

'Are you getting in or not, then? Only I've got a living to make.'

Derwent let go of me completely and stepped back. 'Up to you. Are you in or out?'

I would have liked the time to read the file first. I wasn't sure I could trust him. I'd been specifically warned against talking to him. The cautious approach would have been to put him off.

I'd never been a great one for caution.

I got into the cab.

Chapter 13

The address Derwent gave to the driver was in London Fields, which was actually not all that far from where I lived, though I didn't feel like starting a conversation about it. He sat on the fold-down seat opposite mine and looked at me with puppy-dog eyes.

'Do you understand why I had to do it this way?'

'Not really.'

'Godley warned me to stay away from you,' Derwent said.

'And yet here we are.'

'I want to know what's going on with the case.'

'I'm not supposed to talk to you about it.' I folded my arms over my bag. 'You know you're a suspect, don't you?'

He glanced over his shoulder at the back of the driver's head. 'Keep your voice down.'

'You targeted me because you thought you could bully me. You knew Burt and Godley would shut you down as soon as you started asking questions, but I'm not in a position to tell you to get stuffed.'

'Well, I'm on leave. At this moment I'm not your supervisor. You can say what you like as long as you're honest with me.'

'I'm not going to talk to you about it.'

'Because you agree with them.'

'I don't know enough about it yet.' I looked at him. He

filled most of the other side of the taxi, bracing himself with the grab handles as the driver took corners at speed. His shoulders were wide and he was all muscle; it took a lot of determination to move that kind of bulk over 26.2 miles, as he did for fun. He was ruthless in fighting the softening that came from too much time in cars eating junk food, his stomach flat and his jawline firm. And as he'd just proved, he was stronger than me. Physically, he was intimidating. His personality was controlling. He was unpredictable and brutal when it suited him. I was more wary of him than I wanted him to know. The possibility that he was a killer made my stomach flip every time I thought of it, as if I'd missed a step and was halfway to falling. I didn't believe it – I didn't want to believe it – but that didn't mean I was sure of him. The one thing I knew about the killer we were hunting was that he was good at making women trust him. So despite the way he was looking at me, I wasn't going to let my guard down.

'Why are we going to your place?'

'Because I didn't think you'd let me come to yours.'

'One hundred per cent correct.'

He grinned, a flash of the old Derwent appearing for a moment. 'I like feisty. You can keep that going.'

'You haven't even seen feisty, mate.'

The grin widened. 'I almost wish your pal Burt was here to see you. She thinks you're made of sugar and spice.'

'Did she stick up for me?'

'Told me to fuck off. In those words.' Derwent shook his head. 'I didn't think she had it in her. I thought she'd *never* had it in her.'

'Is that a sexual reference?' I pulled a face. 'I've changed my mind. I'm going home.'

'Don't.' The appeal was instant, unpremeditated.

'Una Burt was using me to get at you. She doesn't actually think I'm all that fragile.'

'What did I ever do to her?'

132

'Where should I start? You've been undermining her since she arrived on the team. The real question is what you've done to piss Godley off. I'd never have expected him to take his cue from her.'

'He's not pissed off with me. He's just trying to avoid trouble. And I'm trouble.' He looked lost, bereft. For someone so used to knowing their place in the wolf pack, being an outcast was torture. And he was still defending Godley, still loyal even if the superintendent wasn't. 'Look, I don't want to drop you in the shit because you're talking to me. I do need to know what's going on. They've told you about Angela, haven't they?'

I nodded.

'Right.' He took a deep breath and blew it out, looking away from me for a moment. Struggling for composure or pretending to be? 'Well, I've always wanted to find whoever did that to her. That's why I became a copper.'

'Then you should be working cold cases, not murder.'

'No one is ever going to reopen Angela's case.' He sounded definite. 'There was nothing to go on.'

'Forensics?'

'Not here.' He rubbed a hand over his face. 'I'll tell you about it, but not here. All you need to know is that this is the first chance there's been to find out what happened to her.'

'Do you really think it's the same killer?'

'I don't know. Because I've been shut out, haven't I?' He thumped the door with a fist and the driver slowed for a moment, looking back to see what had made the noise. 'It's driving me mad, Kerrigan. I've waited for this for twenty years. Everything I've done in my adult life has been about this. And now I can't get close enough to know what's going on.'

'It's not the same guy.'

'Why do you say that?'

'It's been twenty years. Why would the killer start again now?'

'He could have been in prison. He could have been abroad.'

'It could be someone else.'

'How can it be? I'm only going on what I've read in the paper and heard on the news, but it sounds like her. The eyes.' His voice broke on the last word and he cleared his throat, annoyed with himself. 'Look, if I was working this case, I'd want to compare it to the original murder. It feeds back to that. Crack Angela's case and you find this guy.'

'If there's a connection.'

'There has to be.' He held my gaze. He had everything staked on me. I could get him in a world of trouble if I told anyone what he'd done. I could get him fired.

'So you want me to tell you what I know.'

'Please. Like I said, I don't know what else to do.' He was hunched in his coat, the picture of misery.

I made up my mind. 'Okay. Here's the deal. You tell me about what happened to Angela. Everything.'

A nod.

'I'll share with you what I know about the other murders. But there's no guarantee I'll know what you want to know.'

'I appreciate that.'

'And this stays between us. Godley would have me back on Borough CID before I had time to say I was sorry if he found out about this.'

'Strictly off the books.' He was looking better already, the tension easing a little. Give Derwent what he wanted and he always cheered up.

I hoped like hell I was doing the right thing.

One of the compelling reasons for wanting to help Derwent was the chance to see where he lived. From the outside, it was a neat enough place, an end-of-terrace Victorian house in a street where most of the properties were in good condition. It wasn't the best in the street and it wasn't the worst.

He had his own front door to one side of the building, where there was a small hallway before a steep flight of stairs led up to his flat. Slinging his coat on a hook, he stood back to let me go up the stairs.

'You know where you're going,' I said, and stayed where I was. Now that we were alone together, I was seriously doubting I'd made the right decision. He was volatile, and I knew he had a temper, and the army had trained him to kill people. I couldn't make myself believe he was the Gentleman Killer but I was staking a lot on that, and I definitely didn't feel safe. It was too late to back out now, though, so I'd carry on, but I didn't want him behind me on the stairs. Nor did I want to take off my coat. He didn't comment, beyond flicking on the lights above us, and I followed him up the narrow stairs with no very clear idea of what to expect.

'Living room.' He pointed. 'Have a seat.'

It was small and not showy, but incredibly neat. He'd been in the army and it showed: everything was spotless. One sofa, one armchair. A vast television, all the better to watch endless hours of sport. A complicated music system. A coffee table with remote controls lined up like soldiers. No cushions or rugs; blinds at the windows rather than curtains. No ornaments. No pictures. It could have been bleak but it wasn't, somehow: it was comfortable and everything was chosen to be functional. The central heating was on and I felt my feet thawing for the first time that day. I perched on the edge of the sofa, my bag leaning against my legs, and went as far as loosening my scarf.

He came back into the room having shed his jacket and tie, rolling up his shirtsleeves. 'Drink?'

'This isn't a social occasion. You don't have to play the host.'

He shrugged. 'I'm not cooking dinner. But a drink's easy enough.'

'What have you got?'

'Beer.'

'And?'

'Whisky.'

'And?'

'Beer,' he repeated, giving me the widest version of his grin. In his own environment, Derwent was a lot calmer. I just hoped he wasn't going to take off any more clothes.

'Glass of water,' I said.

'Boring.'

'Again, not here to have fun.'

He came back with a bottle of beer for himself and a pint glass of water for me. The glass was wet and he fussed over finding a coaster.

'God forbid I should leave a mark on your coffee table.'

'Just try not to.' There was an edge to his voice. So we had got to the end of Derwent being nice, I diagnosed, and felt obscurely reassured. I even went as far as to take off my coat. I caught the whiff of alcohol on his breath as he moved the table closer to me. A shot of whisky in the kitchen to give him Dutch courage? Two shots? More?

'Where do you want to start?' He turned off the main light, leaving only a single lamp on beside me. He sat in the armchair. 'I feel like I'm talking to a therapist.'

'Have you ever spoken to one?'

He squirmed. 'A couple of times. When I was ordered to. Waste of time.'

I could imagine he was impervious to guidance from others, especially if they weren't superior officers. 'Why do you think they think you're a suspect?'

'Fucked if I know.' He drank from his beer.

'That's not an answer.'

'Because of what happened to Angela.'

'But you were never charged.'

'Exactly. I was just a bystander.' He put the bottle on a table beside him, placing it carefully on another coaster. 'They'd have stuck me on for it if they could. And I've no doubt they'd do the same now, for this, if they had the evidence.'

'Godley wouldn't.'

'Godley absolutely would. In a heartbeat.'

He was right, I thought. For the sake of solving the case. Or maybe he wanted to get rid of Derwent because he knew him better than anyone and might spot that Godley was on the take. You couldn't appeal to Derwent for mercy if you'd done wrong. He was a lot tougher than me. For a moment I considered telling him what I knew, tempted to share the burden with someone who would act on what I'd found out, but I stopped myself. Now was not the time to tell Derwent what I knew about Godley, if there ever was a time for that conversation.

'I can tell you this. It's fucking weird being a suspect again. Makes me feel like I'm seventeen. And not in a good way.' He tried for a laugh but it didn't quite work.

I sat back on the sofa. 'Okay. Tell me about the last time.'

'Where do I start?'

'Tell me about Angela,' I said patiently. 'Whatever you can remember.'

'I remember everything.'

'Then tell me everything.'

Rather to my surprise, he did just that.

In the summer of 1992, Angela Poole was fifteen. If anyone had ever deserved the name Angela, it was her, because she was as close as you could get to an angel on earth. She had heavy, honey-blonde hair and eyes the colour of a summer sky. She was small, and slim, and giggly. She wasn't the best academically but she wasn't stupid either, and she worked hard. She was a good girl, a sweet girl, and the only thing she ever lied to her parents about was her boyfriend.

*

'Me, obviously.' Derwent looked sheepish.

'Bad influence,' I commented.

'Always.'

Everyone in Bromley knew who Josh Derwent was. He was a troublemaker, cheeky – a cocky little shit. He was always hanging out around the shops giving backchat to anyone who tried to tell him what to do. He went to school because he liked it and he was bright enough to be top of the class or thereabouts without making too much effort. He liked that he never got grief for being a swot because he was good at football – good enough to have a trial for Arsenal's youth team.

'Which didn't go anywhere, as you might have noticed.'

'Imagine if you'd become a footballer instead of a copper. This would be a mansion.'

'And I'd be retired by now.'

'But your knees would be knackered. No marathons for you.'

He raised an eyebrow. 'I'd survive.'

How Josh had persuaded Angela to go out with him was no mystery. He was best mates with her brother Shane, and Angela had worshipped him for years. He was good-looking, funny and good at fighting. She was not the only girl who wanted him to notice her, but she was special. He'd watched her grow up without thinking anything of it – she was just a kid – until suddenly the day came when she wasn't a kid any more. She walked into a room wearing tight jeans and a clinging top and he just about lost his mind. Couldn't speak. Couldn't think. He spent a year trying to convince himself she was too young for him, too sweet, too innocent, but no matter how many other girls he snogged, even when he was allowed to play with their tits, even if he was allowed the confusing and exciting treat of fingering them, he couldn't stop thinking about her.

'This is so romantic.'

'This is how seventeen-year-old boys think. I'm sure you encountered your share of them, Kerrigan.'

'I wasn't allowed to know that sort of boy.'

'Neither was Angela.'

Shane and Josh hung around with Vinny Naylor, and Vinny's sister Claire. Vinny was the wise one, the one who called a halt when things were going too far. He had a good head on his shoulders and a genius for fixing things that were broken. Claire was a tomboy, one of the lads. Flat as a board, hard as nails. She and Vinny were born eleven months apart and did everything together, always; if Vinny was in the gang, so was Claire. Shane wasn't all that thrilled about Angela coming along too, but there wasn't much he could do about it. Josh was the one who called the shots. Shane went as far as warning him not to take advantage of his sister, and Josh thumped him for suggesting she might be prepared to have sex with him.

'But you were hoping she would.'

'I wasn't trying to persuade her,' Derwent snapped. 'Fuck, I had this at the time. I didn't want to corrupt her. I was in love with her. I wanted to wait. She was the one who—' He broke off. 'I'm getting ahead of myself.'

'Get on with it.'

All that summer, during the long days when they weren't at school, the five of them wandered around getting into trouble, having a laugh. During the nights, Angela and Josh spent every moment they could together, aching for each other. They had no money and nowhere to go. Josh had a part-time job washing dishes in a café in town. The only reason he kept it was because the owner was mates with his mum and he didn't dare play up too much. The only reason he wanted it was to have enough cash to take Angela out now and then, to the cinema or into London to wander around. They couldn't go to a pub because even if Josh could pass for over eighteen, Angela didn't have a hope of fooling anyone. They couldn't go to Josh's house because his mum didn't approve of him having a serious girlfriend at his age and she'd have flayed him alive if she thought they were even thinking about kissing, let alone having sex. Then there was Josh's little sister, Naomi. Five years younger, she was a pain in the balls. She never left him alone when he was at home, and when he wasn't there, she was always in his stuff. He got in trouble for shouting at her too. They couldn't go to Angela's because Shane would be there, glaring at him. Besides, Angela's parents weren't all that keen on him as a mate for Shane, let alone a boyfriend for their beautiful daughter. Claire and Vinny were two of the eight children in the Naylor family.

'They were Catholics, as you might imagine. Irish background. Same as you.'

'I'm one of two,' I pointed out.

'So your mum's frigid or your dad couldn't get it up more than twice. That wasn't Mr Naylor's problem.'

'It sounds more like Mrs Naylor's problem. Eight pregnancies is hard work.'

'More that that. She had hundreds of miscarriages too. It was a four-bedroom house so God knows where they got the privacy to have sex.'

'Or the time.'

'Anyway, it was a madhouse, so we couldn't go there.'

'Where did you go?'

He had the grace to look shamefaced. 'The cemetery.'

It was a good summer that year, no hardship to be outside.

And the cemetery was easy to climb into, and had secluded corners where the trees and bushes grew close together, and had benches in it where you could sit for hours, staring at the stars. It was, by definition, quiet. They could be alone together which was more than you could say for any of the local parks. They were full of teenagers drinking and carousing once the sun went down. Josh didn't really want an audience when he was with Angela. It might damage his reputation if people saw him handling her like she was bone china.

She was the one who made all the running. She was the one who whispered the things she'd like to do to him. She was the one who stroked his cock through his jeans, who went out with no bra on so he could see her nipples through her top, who bit his lip when they kissed and left purple love bites on his neck. She was the one who sat on his lap, straddling him, and ground her pelvis against him until he came in his pants.

I blinked. 'You're really not holding back, are you?'

'You need to understand how it was.' He picked up his beer but stopped before he drank from it. 'That hasn't happened since, obviously.'

'Obviously.'

Josh got in the habit of bringing a rug and a bottle of wine when they went to the cemetery. He was careful not to let Angela drink too much because she wasn't used to it and it made her silly. She had to face her parents when she got home and they were wary enough of her being out at all hours without her being blind drunk when she came back. She always left the house looking modest, with a cardigan hiding whatever skimpy top she was wearing to excite him, and her hair in a little-girl ponytail. Somewhere along the way she shed the cardigan, the hair-tie and her inhibitions. It scared him, sometimes, the way she was. It worried him.

He was the one who tried to slow things down. But Angela had other ideas.

'She wanted to pop her cherry before we went back to school. She had a thing about it. One of the reasons she was with me was because everyone knew I'd shagged around a lot.' A long swallow of beer. 'Which was a total lie. I'd never done it. I didn't mind, obviously, because it was a lot better for my reputation. And the girls didn't mind because it was a status thing to have shagged me – no one wanted to admit I hadn't done it with them.'

'Why didn't you?'

'I don't know.' He started peeling the label. 'I couldn't admit that I hadn't. I couldn't take the risk that when I lost it, whoever I did it with would tell everyone I was crap. I was scared, basically. Vinny had done it a few times, with a few different girls. Shane had a girlfriend called Mags and she was into all sorts. She had a copy of the Kama Sutra and she was making him work through it.' He grinned suddenly. 'Poor bloke. She wouldn't let him skip anything. I still remember him saying, "Sometimes I just want a hand shandy and a nice lie-down".'

I laughed with him. 'Are you still in touch with Shane?'

'No.' The answer was quick, the change in his mood instant. The room felt colder and darker.

'Back to the story,' I said.

Josh wasn't going to tell Angela he was a virgin too. There was plenty of time to confess when they were older. He'd already decided he was going to propose to her on her eighteenth birthday. If he trained as an electrician, he'd have to do an apprenticeship but then he'd be earning good money. There was always a demand for sparks in the building trade. His uncle was an electrician; he'd told him about it. The careers teacher at school shook her head over it because she wanted him to go to university, but he told her he'd made up his mind.

'I thought the sun shone out of Angela. I'd have done anything for her.' He sounded bemused. 'Never felt that way about anyone before or since.'

'The first time you fall in love is special.'

'It was going to be the only time,' he said coldly.

'You were very young.'

'I knew what I wanted. It was her.'

I nodded, thinking of my first serious boyfriend, Gerard, and how very glad I was that we hadn't got engaged. He had cried every time we had sex.

Every. Time.

The charm of that kind of thing wore off after a while.

'Anyway,' Derwent said. 'We were serious about each other is what I'm saying. And I'd have killed myself rather than hurt her.'

'So what happened?'

'I'm going to need another beer.' He stood up and bolted out of the room and I could only wonder what was so bad that he wasn't prepared to share it with me, given everything else he'd said without turning a hair. He came back with two bottles and handed me one.

'I know you said you didn't want one—'

'But now I do.'

He opened his, then threw me his keys so I could use the bottle opener on his key ring. It was in the shape of a pair of handcuffs.

'Cute,' I observed.

'It was a present.'

'From someone who knows you well?'

'Someone I was going out with a while back. She liked shagging a copper.'

'Did you have to use your cuffs on her? Wear your uniform?'

143

He smirked so I knew he had, and I concentrated on swapping the bottle for the glass on the precious coffee table. *Never ask a question if you don't want the answer.*

'I appreciate you doing this, you know,' Derwent said.

'Noted.'

'Do you need to call Rob to tell him where you are?'

'No. He's not my keeper.' No need to tell Derwent he was thousands of miles away, I thought. 'Where were we?'

'Young. Happy. In love.' He sighed. 'Then everything turned to shit.'

I sat and listened while Derwent told me about the end of Angela Poole's short life. I kept my mouth shut this time and let him tell it his way. And after the first couple of minutes, I think he'd even forgotten I was there.

1992

The mirror in the bathroom was steamed up, which wasn't all that surprising after the – Josh checked – twenty-three minutes he had spent in the shower. The bathroom was tropical and he'd used all the hot water. He swiped at the glass with a towel and succeeded only in smearing it. He still couldn't see himself clearly enough to risk shaving.

'Fuck my luck.' He ran a hand over his chin, feeling the velvety fuzz of a day's growth. It wasn't so bad that he had to shave, not really. But he had a bit of a thing about showing respect for Angela. When they spent as long snogging as the two of them tended to, any stubble at all made her skin go blotchy, which made her folks suspicious, and made him feel guilty.

So. Shaving.

He grabbed a towel and wrapped it around his hips, as low as he could sling it without it sliding off altogether. Then he leaned over and opened the bathroom window wide, resting his elbows on the sill. A lawnmower whined in the distance and some kids played on a trampoline in the garden behind, singing pop songs at the tops of their voices. Summer made him happy.

Angela made him happy.

The mirror was drying off and he could see himself in it again. He looked at his torso critically, wondering if it was his imagination that his chest and shoulders were bigger.

He'd worked on them enough. He curled his arm, staring at the bulge of his biceps. Not bad.

He shaved quickly, without cutting himself, pulling faces in the mirror for his own amusement. God, it was boring. A lifetime of this, unless he grew a beard, but Angela wouldn't like a beard. So no beard. He finished off with a handful of Cool Water, the aftershave she loved. It stung like a bastard on his skin and he swore, his eyes swimming in sudden tears. It was good pain, though. Part of the ritual, like wearing a clean T-shirt or checking the condoms were in the side pocket of his backpack.

The condoms. If she'd known they were there, they'd have done it the previous week. He didn't know why he hadn't said they were in the bag. He wanted to do it – God, he wanted it so much the anticipation sat in the middle of his brain, blocking all logical thought. He had to think around the sides of it as best he could. But when it came to it, he couldn't just *say* it to her. Now, in the bathroom, he couldn't understand why he hadn't. She wanted to as much as he did, if not more. She'd have been delighted.

But tonight was the night. At last. He gave a shiver of anticipation and stared at himself again, wondering afterwards if he would look different or just feel different.

He was looking good, he decided. He was tanned. His hair hung down from a centre parting as far as his eyebrows. From the nape of his neck to halfway up his head he had a blade two cut. Mrs Beale at school had told him he looked like he should be in a boy band with a haircut like that, and he'd just looked at her without saying anything until she went red and walked off. It was common knowledge that she fancied him, undoing an extra button on her blouse before his class came in for their geography lesson. He didn't mind. He never minded when women liked him. He liked saying things to see if he got a reaction from them – a catch in their breath, the blood coming to their cheeks, their pupils dilating. And it was so easy.

He tilted his head back to give his tough-guy stare, his come-and-have-a-go-if-you-think-you're-hard-enough look. It looked good, he decided. It wasn't a shock that he was popular with the girls, when all was said and done. But he was still young. No hair on his chest to speak of. He ran his finger down the trail that went from his belly button to beneath the towel, imagining Angela stroking the hair with her small, perfect fingers. His cock sprang to life instantly and he held it, thinking about later. Thinking about what she'd said to him the previous week, her hand sliding up and down on it the way he'd shown her.

'I want to suck it.'

He hadn't allowed her to. She'd be disgusted with herself afterwards, he thought. And he didn't want her doing that kind of thing, not at her age. Fifteen was too young to be giving blowjobs. But the *idea* of it – her tongue flickering around the tip, her pretty mouth stretched wide to accommodate him as he thrust, his hand on her head, pushing her down on it . . .

Fucking hell. He groaned, checking his watch. He had time, he thought, for a wank before he finished getting ready. It was a good idea to relieve some of the pressure.

And it wouldn't take long.

He felt ten feet tall, walking along her street with his backpack slung over one shoulder. He'd got a bottle of wine from a mate who worked at an off-licence in town and the bag was heavy. She was outside her house already, sitting on the brick pillar beside the gate. Her father had grown a massive hedge in front of the house, for privacy, and it needed cutting back. All he could see of her at first were her feet, crossed at the ankle, neat in white Converse. He liked that about her – that she didn't feel the need to mince around in stupid heels when they had walls to scale and grass to trudge through. She was brave, he thought, and steady. Not a squealer. She was like him.

He got right up close to her before she realised he was there. 'All right, babe.'

'Josh!' She went to slide down off the pillar but he got there in time to stop her, sliding between her knees and reaching up for a long, greedy kiss. She wrapped her legs around his waist, laughing a little as her denim miniskirt edged up towards her hips.

'This is risky.'

'Is he in?'

'Yeah. Getting ready to go.'

'He' was her dad. He drove buses, and this week it was the night bus. He worshipped Angela. If he knew the truth about what they'd been doing together he'd castrate Josh with rusty scissors and smile while he did it. Then he'd never speak to her again.

Josh didn't give a fuck at that precise moment. She was so warm, so real in his arms. He kissed her again, her tongue teasing his and he remembered what she'd said, and how he imagined her running that tongue over his bell end, and he was rock hard, which she could feel, which made her laugh, again. He turned his head to let her nuzzle his neck – she had a thing about it, especially when he'd just shaved – and his eyes wandered to the house next door, and up to the front bedroom, where a figure was standing in the window, watching them. Fat Stu. Fifteen, like Angela, but that was all they had in common. He was short and podgy with a feathered fringe, like Princess Diana, and buck teeth that would pay for an orthodontist's five-star beach holiday if his parents weren't too mean to get them fixed. He wore black at weekends and listened to the Smiths, very loud, which was enough for Josh to be sure he was gay. He looked like a beaver, Josh thought, and that was what he called him – beaver boy. Or Fat Stu. Or dickhead. Or gaylord. Or anything else that came to mind.

Josh held Fat Stu's gaze while he took a good handful of Angela's arse and squeezed it, his fingers sliding towards the cleft of her buttocks. He ran the other hand up her back, the middle finger extended. *Go fuck yourself, beaver boy.* Even at that distance he could see the colour rushing into Stu's cheeks before he turned away and disappeared. What was he doing, anyway, standing there in his mother's bedroom? Probably trying on her clothes. Josh had a vision of him wearing high heels and stockings with suspenders on his invisible bottom half, and had to turn his head to bury his face in Angela's hair so she wouldn't notice him grinning and ask why. He didn't want to talk about Fat Stu.

The distraction had at least taken his mind off sex so his erection had subsided enough to allow him to walk down the street.

'Are you ready?'

She nodded.

'Sure about this?'

Another emphatic nod.

'Let's go.'

It was nine by the time they got to the cemetery and the sun had set but only just, the sky still streaked with pink and purple clouds. *Red sky at night, shepherd's delight.* August was a funny month: hot, but the nights were getting longer, and the trees were starting to turn here and there. Summer wasn't going to last much longer. Josh didn't want to think about that, though. Didn't want to think about A levels and university versus apprenticeships and homework and stress from his folks and not seeing Angela. They'd have to abandon their cemetery soon and he couldn't think where else to go. Keeping the gloom to himself, Josh helped Angela climb the wall, her skirt riding high as she scrambled over. He swung himself up and over, landing on the grass beside her with a thud.

'Usual place?'

'Where else?'

The usual place was the far side of the graveyard, away

from the houses, in an area that was mainly old grave-stones. They were mossy, broken, the inscriptions faded away by years of polluted rain. Long ago, grieving families had planted trees around their loved ones' graves, and they had grown tangled and unkempt, draped in ivy, climb-ing roses blossoming on briars that threaded through the branches. Sensibly, the council hadn't attempted to fix it. The health and safety types had stuck a notice up warning about entry at your own risk and someone had donated a bench to go under the largest tree, and there was a patch of flat ground in front of it that was just right for the rug. It didn't *feel* like they were in a graveyard, there.

The hardest part was getting across the graveyard in the gathering dusk. Josh had eyes like a cat and didn't mind it, but Angela often stumbled. They had to go fast in case any-one saw them. He didn't fancy explaining what they were doing to a nosy groundsman, or a neighbour, or even the police. This time, they made it without difficulty, though his heart was thudding in his chest like a heavy bass beat.

That would be excitement, a detached part of his brain observed. He looked at Angela, whose chest was rising and falling rapidly, and grinned at her.

'So here we are.'

'Yeah.'

'Drink?'

'Yeah.' She smiled, sliding the bag off his shoulder and unzipping it, taking out the rug and unfolding it.

She was complicit in her own downfall.

She was happy.

Later, much later, and the sky had darkened to a brilliant blue that was as clear as glass. Angela's knickers were on the ground beside them, her top pushed up, her skirt around her waist. She smiled up at him, her eyes hazy with lust and alcohol, and let her knees fall apart.

'Do it.'

'Ange.' He was breathing hard.

'Go on.' She propped herself up on one elbow and ran a hand up his chest to stroke his face, then down again to his cock. 'I want you in me.'

He'd never moved so fast. He leaned across to the bag and dug around for the condoms which he knew were in there, which had now disappeared. He'd taken them out of the box so he could get at them quickly. Nothing he touched felt like foil and it was too dark to see where they were.

'What's wrong?'

'I can't find the condoms.'

'It doesn't matter.' Her voice was soft, beseeching. She held on to him. 'I don't care. I want to feel *you*, not some rubber.'

He felt light-headed but there was still some reason in him, something detached from the maelstrom of desire that was making him shake like he had a fever. 'You could get pregnant.'

'It's fine. It's not the right time.' She took his hand and put it between her legs. 'Feel how much I want you. *Now*, Josh.'

He assumed she knew what she was talking about and it was all right. He was a virgin and so was she, so he didn't have to worry about STDs. If he didn't get inside her soon . . .

As he was thinking it she moved his hand away and lifted her hips, offering herself to him and he lost all his reason as he lowered himself onto her, into her, finding the right place by luck rather than skill. It was more difficult than he'd expected to get into her and he pushed, pressing against her until something gave. He stopped moving when she gave a gasp that was definitely pain, not pleasure, but she dug her nails into his arse.

'Go on. Do it.'

So he kept pushing, and suddenly all of him was in her, and she was wet and warm and tight around him and he fucked her, his breath coming in gasps, thrusting hard as she pulled him towards her, scratching his back, moving to let him get even deeper though her face was twisted like it hurt, a lot. He didn't care. He couldn't. He was almost coming and then he was coming and he made a noise he'd never made before, a sound that was like choking and then he collapsed down to one side of her, bruising his cheek on the hard ground.

The euphoria lasted for about as long as it took him to get the power of speech back. Then the fear kicked in.

'Oh Jesus. Angela. Are you okay? Did I hurt you?'

'It's fine.' She wasn't looking at him. She was staring up at the trees above them, with a strange little smile on her face.

'Are you sure? Ange, if I hurt you . . .'

'Don't be stupid.' She wrapped an arm around his neck and patted his shoulder. 'It's okay.'

He was used to being the one in charge, but suddenly he felt as if she was older than him. Decades older. Centuries.

'Was it not—' *Good*, he was going to say, but she stopped him with a kiss.

'It was lovely.'

'Are you sore?'

'I'll survive.' That smile again. Then, 'Did you bring any tissues?'

He hadn't. It hadn't occurred to him. He'd thought all the mess would be in a condom, tied up neatly and thrown away. He gave her his socks, in the end, and she did her best to tidy herself up while he turned away, pretending he needed to do something important with the bag, with what was in the bag, until she'd finished and put her knickers back on.

She stood up and again he had the feeling that things had changed between them. She was in charge now, even though he'd had her. He couldn't understand it. 'It's time to go.'

'Sure. Of course. I'll walk you home.'

'Thanks.'

They walked to the place where they'd climbed in. Usually they stopped to snog before they went over the wall again, back to reality. This time, Angela shinned up the brickwork without even waiting for him to help her, let alone a kiss. He followed in silence, his trainers loose on his bare feet. He was on the point of asking what was wrong but he couldn't, afraid to hear the answer. It hadn't been good. *He* hadn't been good. The buzz from the wine was gone. He felt sober, and tired, and he really wanted to be back at home, in bed, asleep, instead of walking along a pavement on the other side of town beside the girl he adored but somehow didn't know any more.

They came to the point where Josh would have turned off if he was going straight home, and Angela stopped.

'You might as well go. There's no need to walk me all the way.'

'I will, though.'

'Come on. It's ten minutes.'

'Exactly.'

'But that's twenty minutes for you, there and back.' She was looking away from him, down the street. She hadn't looked at him since, he realised.

'Do you want me to go?'

'*I* don't care.' The way she said it made it sound as if he'd asked something so unreasonable, so outrageous, that the only possible response was mockery.

'Ange . . .'

'What?' She looked at him then, with that pitying half-smile. 'What is it, Josh?'

'Are you all right?'

'I told you, I'm fine.'

'You're acting like you're pissed off.'

She looked away again and sighed. 'I'm not.'

'I thought it was what you wanted.'

'It was.' She slid a hand around him, leaning against him, her head under his chin. 'I'm tired.'

'If that's all.'

'Of course.'

'When will I see you again?'

'I don't know.' She did sound tired, he thought. 'I'll see you tomorrow, maybe. Are you working?'

'Breakfast and lunch.' He had to be up at half past five to do the morning rush, the builders and scaffolders and taxi-drivers. They put away vast quantities of food in short order. Clearing away plates, up to his elbows in hot water, the muscles in his arms complaining as he hefted trays of mugs around. 'I'll be finished at two.'

'I'll come and find you.'

'Don't come to the café. I'll go home and change.' He was sensitive about the smell of the place, the grease that made his skin and hair reek. He didn't want her associating it with him.

'Three o'clock at your house, then.'

'Yeah.' He turned her face up to his and kissed her, but it was a chaste kiss, no tongues. Her lips were pursed against his. 'Look, let me walk you home.'

She shook her head. 'We've already said goodbye.'

'Angela.'

'Tomorrow, Josh.' She slipped out of his grasp and walked away from him, down the street, moving carefully as if something hurt. But she'd said she was fine, he thought. His own legs were quivering as if he'd just done a fast four miles. Maybe that was the problem.

He waited until she'd gone out of sight before he turned to lope away. He would never forget that. He would never get over the guilt about the main thing he felt, watching her walk away from him.

Relief.

Chapter 14

It was one in the morning when Derwent ran out of words, around the same time Angela had run out of luck in his story. His voice was raw from talking, his eyes red from fatigue. I wouldn't have dared suggest it was emotion. At some point he had switched from beer to whisky, pouring a glass for me. Scotch was not my usual drink but I drank it slowly, feeling the warmth spreading down to my toes with every sip. He knocked it back in gulps, not noticeably affected by it. Practice, I presumed, and added that to my list of things to worry about. An alcohol-dependent Derwent was not going to be an easier colleague.

After he fell silent he stared into space, lost in memories that were two decades old, and I felt my jaw creak with the effort of not yawning. It was a lost cause. My mouth sprang open as if it had been spring-loaded and I covered it with the hand I wasn't using to take sketchy notes.

'Tell me if I'm boring you, won't you.' Heavy on the sarcasm. Back to the Derwent I knew and loved.

'Sorry. It's late.'

'I'm fucking pouring my heart out here and you're yawning.' He shook his head. 'I thought better of you, Kerrigan.'

'What happened after that?'

'She was strangled to death.'

'I know that. To you, I mean.'

He shrugged. 'I went home. I slept. I went to work the

155

next day. Didn't hear from her and didn't think anything of it. This was before teenagers had mobile phones, you realise. We're going that far back. I hoped I'd see her at my house around three, and she never turned up. But two fat detectives did.'

'And interviewed you?'

'Arrested me. Took me to the local nick and interviewed me. Gave me a hard time.' He sipped his drink meditatively. 'Course, I was lying my arse off at that stage. They said she was dead and I thought it had to be a set-up. Her dad's way of finding out what we'd been up to. One of the coppers was a mate of his, going way back, so I didn't really believe him. Besides, I was petrified to say what we'd done. She was fifteen so it was statutory rape. Took me a long time to believe what they were telling me was true.'

'How did they convince you?'

Another gulp and a wince as he swallowed. 'Showed me pictures from the scene.'

'Her body?'

He nodded, looking down into his glass, his face bleak.

'Did they really think you'd killed her?'

'Definitely. No question about it. Longest twenty-four hours of my life.'

'But you weren't charged.'

'Nope.'

'Why not?'

'I had an alibi. Someone saw me walking through town on my way home. Again, there wasn't a lot of CCTV around back then, so I was bloody lucky there was a witness to back up my story.'

'Whoever saw you must have been absolutely definite about the ID.'

'He was. Believe me, he'd have liked to say different, but he was a fair man.'

'Who was it?'

'Angela's father.'

'Wow.'

'Poor bloke. I was on my way home through the town centre. Typical teenager, thinking I was immortal. I walked out into the road right in front of his bus. He had to stand on the brakes in a hurry. One of the passengers fell over and cut his head. The guy was too pissed to hold on properly but it was still Charlie Poole's responsibility. He made a note of the time it happened, as he was required to do, and since I'd been that far away from him,' – he held up his hands about two feet apart – 'and waved at him, cheeky little fucker that I was, there was no doubt about the ID. It happened at two minutes to midnight and that was right about the time she died.'

'Don't tell me the pathologist was prepared to give an exact TOD.'

'They didn't need the pathologist for that.' Derwent smiled bitterly. 'They had a witness.'

'Who?'

'Stuart Sinclair. Fat Stu from next door. A noise woke him at 11.56 p.m., which he noted because his clock radio was beside his bed. He looked out and saw nothing. A few minutes later he got up again to make sure there was nothing wrong, and saw a male walking through the gate of the garden next door and down the road. That was at one minute past midnight.'

'Did he give a description?'

'Yeah. Me. Down to the colour of my T-shirt.'

'But it couldn't have been you.'

'That's what I said. And they had to accept it, after a while.'

'Didn't Stu retract his statement?'

A slow headshake.

'But he had to admit it was nonsense.'

'He was adamant about it.'

'Not your biggest fan,' I suggested.

'No. He had a thing about Angela. Not that she'd have dreamed of looking at him. And he hated me because I was a shit to him.'

'Poor Stu.'

'He was a twat,' Derwent said, outraged. 'Poor Stu tried to fit me up for murder.'

'I take it he wasn't a suspect.'

'No. His hands were too small to have left the marks on her neck. Mine would have done, but I was already getting towards six foot. He really was just a kid. Still waiting for puberty to kick in.' He laughed. 'I think he was even a vegetarian, just like Morrissey. He sang in the school choir. Definitely not murderer material.'

'Okay. But he was muddying the waters for the investigation.'

'The waters were muddy enough as it was. They didn't get much further with it once they ruled me out. I've looked it up. In the five years before and after there were plenty of deaths by manual asphyxiation in the greater London area but nothing with those distinctive elements.'

'The eyes.'

'Specifically.' He rubbed a hand over his face. 'Where were we?'

'How you went from golden boy to chief suspect to being ruled out.'

'By the police. Not by public opinion. Everyone knew I'd been picked up and that someone had seen me nearby. They assumed the police had just fucked up. Our house was vandalised. Then a gang of girls thumped my sister on her way home from school because they thought she was sticking up for me too much. That was it. By then I'd come clean about the sex, because they'd found semen in Angela and told me they could match it to me, which would have taken weeks, probably – but by then I was cooperating with everything they asked me. Proper broken by it. So everyone knew what we'd done too. My parents were disgusted with me for it, and scared for my sister. I don't really blame them for what they did.'

'Which was kick you out.'

He nodded. 'Vinny's parents let me stay with them for a bit, but they didn't have room for me really and I didn't want to be a nuisance. I was under eighteen so I was entitled to go into care and I ended up in a home.'

'Not known for being pleasant.'

'It was all right.' His face was shuttered and I knew he wasn't going to tell me what it had really been like. I also knew that meant it had been bad. 'I was in a bit of a state because of what had happened to Angela. Vinny and Claire were still talking to me but Shane couldn't stand the sight of me. He threw up when I tried to tell him I was sorry about what had happened – literally chucked up, right in front of me. I stopped going to school. Then someone told me I was old enough to join the army. I didn't think about it. I just did it. My way out. I rang home to tell them and my dad put the phone down on me and I haven't spoken to them since.' He drained his glass then refilled it with a practised swoop. 'The army took me in and fed me, housed me, clothed me and paid me for years. It was my family. Better than my family.'

'But you still left.'

'I realised what I wanted to do with my life. I quit, studied for A levels, got my exams, got into the Met and the rest is what you know. Brilliant career, inspector by thirty-six. All-round sex symbol and winner of popularity contests.'

'Sorry, who are we talking about now?'

He grinned. 'Watch it, Kerrigan.'

'Have you got a picture of her?'

'Yeah, I do.'

'Can I see it?'

He was reluctant to say yes, I could tell, but he knew he would have asked the same thing if he'd been in my place. 'Wait there.'

He disappeared into the room next door and I heard a drawer open and close. He didn't keep it where he could see it, but not because he didn't care. I doubted there was a day he didn't think about Angela.

When he came back he handed me a framed photograph and stood beside me, looming. 'Ange. Me. Vinny. Claire. And that's Shane. It was his girlfriend who took it.'

It wasn't a great picture; the focus was a bit off and the colours muddy. They had been at a barbecue, in a back garden, the background an anonymous fence. An impossibly young Derwent sat on a white plastic garden chair, leaning back so the front legs were off the ground. He looked innocent and cheeky and I stared at him for a long time, trying to match it up with the present-day version. A girl sat on his lap, petite and pretty, her head leaning against his, her arms around his neck. Possessive was the word that sprang to mind. Insecure, maybe. They all wanted him and she had him, even though he was two years older and her brother's friend. I bet she couldn't believe her luck, which was a strange thought in connection with Derwent. Her brother was darker than her, and built like a brick shithouse. He stared at the camera as if he was daring it to capture his image. Claire sat beside him on another chair, one leg pulled up, drinking from a can so I could hardly see her face. She was long-limbed and very slender, with short dark hair she had tucked behind her ears. One arm had a collection of leather cuffs on it and she was wearing the Nirvana Nevermind T-shirt.

Vinny was at the back, standing, his arms spread wide, his mouth open as if he was cheering. He and Shane and Derwent were dressed identically in layered T-shirts, baggy jeans and Vans trainers, and Vinny had the same haircut as Derwent.

'It wasn't a good era for fashion, was it?'

'You can say that again. Seen enough?'

I nodded, letting him take it out of my hands. 'Is that the only one you've got?'

'Do you need to see another?' He glowered at me and I shook my head. The thing with Derwent was to know when you should stop pushing your luck. I got it right some of the time. He left the room and the drawer opened and closed again. Everything in its place. The words from Dr Chen's profile repeated in my head in Godley's voice. *He is obsessive about detail and a perfectionist . . .*

I stuffed the thought to the back of my mind in case Derwent could tell what I was thinking. While he was gone I stood up and put my coat back on. It went down predictably well.

'Where do you think you're going?'

'It's late.'

'And?'

'And I have to be in the office early.'

'You owe me. Time to start talking, Kerrigan.' He folded his arms. 'We had a deal.'

'And I'm going to honour my part in it.' I pulled my bag onto my shoulder. 'Look, I don't have the file on the murders with me and I'm still getting my head around it myself. I'm meeting up with Bradbury's DS tomorrow to hear about what they've found out. I can come here after that and give you the whole picture.'

He stared at me, trying to decide if I meant it. 'Do you promise?'

'I promise. And no need for any kidnapping shenanigans this time.'

'Do you believe me?'

'Would I volunteer to come back if I didn't?'

He was too clever not to pick up on the fact that I hadn't answered him. He nodded, as if I'd proved something to him.

'How are you getting home?'

'It's not far,' I said.

161

'Where do you live?'

'Dalston,' I admitted.

'Seriously? How did I not know that?'

'I keep it to myself.'

'What else are you hiding?'

Not as much as you, I thought. He hadn't told me every-thing, not by a long shot.

He went down the stairs in front of me and took his coat off the hook. I stopped two steps from the bottom.

'What are you doing?'

'How are you getting home?'

'I'll get a cab. There's an office near here, isn't there? I saw it from the taxi.'

He shrugged his coat on. 'Right. I'll walk you there.'

'There's absolutely no need.'

'Fuck's sake, Kerrigan. Did you listen to *anything* I said?'

'I don't need you to protect me.'

'Yes, you do.' He came towards me, the little hallway suddenly feeling very small indeed. 'Do you think you're invincible or something just because you're a cop? If some-one wanted to attack you – a man – what would you do? Fight him off?'

'I've had combat training.'

'Didn't do you a lot of good this evening, did it?' He took another step and it was with difficulty that I resisted the urge to flee back up the stairs. 'This is why I hate women's lib. You're not equal. You're not independent. The minute you walk out there, you're prey, pure and simple.'

'You're overreacting.'

'I don't give a fuck.' Massive in his coat, he was stand-ing between me and the door. His face softened. 'Look, Kerrigan, I have to do this.'

'I'm not Angela.'

'I know that.'

'What happened to her wasn't your fault.'

'I don't agree.'

162

'Someone killed her. *You* didn't. Someone chose to end her life and that's on them.' I was arguing against two decades of conditioning and I could tell from his face I was getting absolutely nowhere. I sighed. 'Okay. Walk me to the cab office.'

'Finally.' He headed for the door, happy again. 'I thought I was going to have to follow you.'

'You say that like it would be a reasonable course of action.' I saw the look on his face. 'Please tell me you don't follow women around.'

'When they're on their own and it's late. Just to make sure they're safe.'

'Christ almighty.' I followed him out. 'I mean, really.'

He locked the door after me, not one little bit abashed. 'So what? Most of the time they don't even know I'm there.'

Chapter 15

It was a short run back to the flat but it felt endless. The driver had taken offence at Derwent asking him his name, checking his licence and ostentatiously noting the number of his car. I sat in the back, fuming, as Derwent lectured him on maintenance of his tyres and cross-examined him about whether his MOT was up to date. By the time he got back in the car, the driver's mood matched mine. He turned up the radio as he accelerated away from where Derwent was standing, watching, and I was blasted with bhangra music all the way home. I over-tipped, despite the surliness and the soundtrack, and was rewarded with a tirade of hurt, semi-comprehensible English about how he was a good driver and trustworthy and he had daughters himself.

The taxi drove away eventually, the street quiet as the noise of the engine receded into the distance. There was no one around, no noise in the building as I trudged up the stairs to the flat. I felt the tension of the day hit home, leaving me exhausted. I wanted to sleep more than anything, but I had to look at the Angela Poole file while Derwent's account of what had happened was still fresh in my mind. I felt hollowed out. Today had taken all I had to give, and more. Alcohol on an empty stomach had left me with a headache and heartburn. I needed food and caffeine. I would spend an hour reading through the file and no more. Four hours' sleep – that was a complete cycle. Into the office, to face Godley and Burt. To defend Derwent, maybe, if I had the nerve, and if I could do it without revealing I'd spoken to him. If nothing else, the evening's adventures had confirmed one thing: he was just as deranged as I'd always suspected. But not, I thought, a murderer.

Probably.

The stairs made me breathless but the reason I ground to a halt on the landing by my front door was not so I could catch my breath. Leaning against the door was a fat bunch of red roses, a tied bouquet with a little reservoir of water inside the cellophane to keep them alive while they waited for me to return.

It was all kinds of sad that my first reaction was fear. My second reaction was anger. *Not this again.* Flowers by the front door made me think instantly of Chris Swain. It was just the sort of romantic gesture he knew would terrify me.

I pulled on the blue latex gloves I carried in my bag and approached the flowers as warily as if they were hiding a fully grown tiger. There was a little white envelope taped to the plastic and I ripped it off carefully to preserve the tape. SOCOs loved tape. It was good for trace evidence and fingerprints and matching the ends to a roll if you ever tracked down a suspect. The envelope wasn't stuck down and I edged the card out, trying not to touch it. A hastily written message in biro, presumably dictated over the phone to the florist who'd made up the bunch, because I didn't recognise the writing.

'I'll miss you. Be good while I'm gone. Love, Rob.'

Relief made me irritable. 'Be good'? That was unusually patronising of him. And having flowers delivered to the flat was against the rules, especially when they were addressed to me by name. I picked them up and sniffed the one nearest me. They'd been bred for looks, not scent, but it was still faintly sweet, and my irritation faded. He missed me. I missed him. He must have known coming back to the empty flat was going to be hard. I was smiling as I carried them in and ripped off the cellophane, then shoved them in a vase, still tied with the straw-like twine. It was good that he'd chosen an arrangement that didn't need much input from me because I was not the type to spend hours fluffing a flower arrangement. But then, he knew that.

I made toast and a pot of coffee, then set my phone to ring at three thirty to remind me to go to bed. Already in pyjamas, I sat down on the sofa with the file and spread out its contents on the table in front of me. I put the news on to check the headlines: we were still the lead story. They had found some file footage of Anna Melville presenting a bunch of flowers to Princess Anne. It was strange to see a younger version of the victim walking and smiling – strange and unsettling. Godley looked as film-star perfect as ever in his press conference. And of course, the Gentleman Killer name got full play. After the report was over, the newsreader went through the morning editions of the papers: front page after front page featured the case. We didn't know if the publicity would encourage our man or put him off, but there was nothing we could do about it anyway.

The second story after Anna Melville's death was a Dads Matter demonstration in Liverpool where a police officer had been hit over the head and concussed. Philip Pace gave a smooth statement managing not to apologise and suggesting it was the officer's fault. I switched the television off rather than listen to any more of it and turned my attention to the file.

First up was the MG5, the summary of the case written by the officer in charge, the OIC for short. Inspector Lionel Orpen was his name. I set the pages to one side, looking for witness statements and piling them up. Stuart Sinclair would be Fat Stu's real name. His statement matched Derwent's story, as I glanced through it, and the timings did rule Derwent out. Charles Poole's statement, complete with an alibi for Derwent. Josh Derwent's own statement where I found the story he'd told me but in official language. 'I last saw the victim at 11.39 p.m. on AUDERLY Road, proceeding in the direction of KIMLETT Road.' Disappearing from him for ever. The Orpheus and Eurydice of Bromley. It was the statement agreed after hours of interviews, after all the suggestions and insinuations and repeated questions had battered their way to the truth. The tale was told without emotion, without comment. I was glad I'd heard Derwent's story first. I could read exhaustion in every line of the statement. Broken was the word he'd used himself. And he'd rebuilt himself in the army, in an environment that was comfortably intolerant of difference, whether it was difference of race, sexuality or gender. Why was I surprised he was a twat?

I put the rest of the witness statements to one side and found what I really wanted: the forensics from the scene and a sheaf of colour-photocopied pictures, recent copies of the originals, which had held up well enough themselves to the passage of time. A house, taken from the other side of the road: a small 1930s semi-detached one, four-square like a child's drawing, with two windows above a door and a bay window on the ground floor, visible through the gate that made a gap in the hedge. The hedge, as Derwent had described it, towering ten feet. It was dense and spilled over the front wall. Moving forward, the path to the front door. The photographer had worked around the house, tracking along the path made in grass that was helpfully overlong and showed the dragging struggle that had taken Angela to her death. To the right of the front garden, by the hedge that ran between it and the Sinclair house next door, there was a small beech tree. Underneath it there was a sweep of greenery dotted with tiny white flowers on delicate stems. And in the middle of the flowers, under the tree, lay Angela Poole, in a denim mini and a white low-cut vest top. Her hair was tangled in the grass, blonde locks gleaming in the light of the flash. Her pale pink cardigan was balled up nearby. Her legs were apart, but as she had fallen rather than in a deliberate attempt to display her. What was deliberate was the removal of her eyes. This was gouging, I thought, staring at the gelatinous mess that had been left to one side of her head rather than in her palms. No knife. He improvised.

The photographer had included a few generous close-ups of Angela's face. I had no personal involvement with her; I'd seen one picture of her and heard Derwent's highly coloured account of how perfect she had been and neither had made me feel like I should care about her. But there was something unspeakably dreadful about the purple bruises on her throat, the red flecks on her skin caused by blood vessels bursting as she struggled for air. Her mouth was open, her teeth white. Her lips looked bruised but I thought of teenagers kissing for endless hours and remembered my own mouth tingling as I crept into the house, unable to stop smiling, after getting off with Brian O'Neill at the Krystal disco when I was fifteen. Without eyes, her eyelids sat oddly, puckered and deflated. The lashes were still clotted with mascara. I wished for the crime-scene pictures from Kirsty, Maxine and Anna so I could compare them, but I knew what I would see. There were differences – he worked inside, not in the open air. He had moved on from this death, making it his own with the candles, the dying flowers, the white sheet under the body. But Derwent was right. This was where it started. This was the beginning. And it demanded that someone take another look at Angela Poole's murder.

The next pictures made me jump: seventeen-year-old Derwent looking back at me with the flawless skin and lean features of youth. His hair was ridiculous, hanging down on either side of his forehead like curtains, and he hadn't mentioned the double line he'd shaved in one eyebrow.

'Vanilla bloody Ice,' I said aloud, grinning. If I had the nerve I'd give him a hard time about it when I saw him next.

In the first picture he stared down the camera like it was a gun. His eyes looked angry and wary, with the dangerous bewilderment of a cornered animal, and the skin around them was puffy, as if he had been crying. Next, the photographer had got in close with the camera to focus on a scuff on one cheek and I remembered what he'd said about bruising his face. Another shot was his neck, with a yellowing mark just under one ear: an old love bite, healing now. The next picture was of his back and a handful of long, deep scratches raked across his tanned skin. You could see where they were going with this. It was hard to tell, sometimes, if they were love marks or wounds made by the victim. In Derwent's version, there was an innocent explanation for every injury. It was as if he'd tailored his story to account for them.

Or it was the truth. That was the other possible explanation.

The next picture was an A4 blow-up of Angela alive, unmade-up and very pretty in school uniform, posing for her picture as if butter wouldn't melt. Innocent. Virginal. Reluctantly virginal, as it turned out. Assuming that the sex had been consensual, and I hadn't seen anything yet to say it wasn't. I flipped through the remainder of the shots: exhibits such as Derwent's bag, the unused condoms, the cardigan spread out on a table with a close-up of a tear in one sleeve. There was a list of items removed from Derwent's house: the bag and its contents, notes from victim, tape made by victim, pictures . . . the whole history of their relationship, everything that she had touched. They'd taken her away from him all over again. And a set of photocopied pages from Angela's diary showed that she had been a typical teenage girl. She wrote a lot about Derwent, usually in the kind of code that takes no time at all to crack. She sounded very enthusiastic about what they'd got up to, I noticed.

I was grateful for a map of the area and returned to Derwent's statement to plot his journey, and Angela's. If there was time the next day I'd do them on an overlay so I could see where they had been together, and where they had parted.

More interesting still was the floor plan of the house and the one next door, with Stuart Sinclair's room marked on it. I went back to the pictures which showed the side of the house with the hedge and tried to imagine what Stuart Sinclair could have seen. I'd have to go there and imagine the hedge was still at the height it had reached in the summer of 1992. It would be worth checking whether the Pooles still lived there. I didn't want to disturb them unless I really had to.

I was too tired to plough through the fine detail of the post-mortem report though I did get the gist: manual strangulation. The removal of the eyes had taken place before she died, which made me stop reading for a moment. Her vaginal area was abraded and there was a trace of blood on the anterior vaginal wall. The pathologist noted the presence of a quantity of semen inside her and on her underwear, but her underwear had been in the correct position and it was the pathologist's view that the injuries were consistent with consensual sexual activity. As usual, everything came with a hefty dose of prevarication.

My eyes were closing. The last pages got the quickest glance, just so I knew what I was skipping. A report on scrapings from under the victim's fingernails. A statement from the bus passenger who had fallen. A statement from Shane Poole and one from his mother about when they'd last seen Angela. A statement from Derwent's mother, who had washed his clothes early the following morning. It was her habit to get the wash on before breakfast, she had explained, outrage in every line of her statement. He hadn't asked her. She'd picked his clothes off the bedroom floor, as usual.

It didn't look good for him that she'd done the laundry but there was nothing to find on the clothes; his alibi was sound. So said Lionel Orpen in his summary, listing the many ways they'd tried and failed to prove Derwent's guilt. They had looked for other suspects, of course. Sex offenders. Murderers on parole. Men the local prostitutes identified as liking to choke them during sex. They'd done the rounds looking for their man, and hadn't found him.

My phone burst into life, playing the jaunty little tune that made me want to fling it against the wall most mornings. I flicked through the statements, seeing names I recognised, longing to keep reading. I was out on my feet, and tomorrow would be a big day. I shovelled everything back into the folder and headed for my cold, empty bed, glad that I was too tired to think, too tired to be aware of being alone.

In spite of my unsettling evening, or maybe because of it, I slept like the dead.

SATURDAY

Chapter 16

'The killer does not see his victims as human beings. Their role is to assist him in creating a scene that has some personal significance, either a memory or a fantasy that he wants to make real.' Dr Chen was sitting in a corner of Godley's office, her legs crossed neatly at the ankle, her hands folded in her lap. She had a soft speaking voice and the three of us – Godley, Burt and I – were all leaning forward, trying not to miss anything. It created a strange atmosphere in the room, I thought. An intimacy, as if we were listening to a prophecy about our futures instead of a scientific analysis of a criminal's likely background and status. Usually, she would have been addressing a larger group, but Godley's policy of keeping the Derwent angle confidential meant that there were just the four of us in the room.

'Is it likely to be something he's experienced himself? Or could it be something he's seen, like a photograph or a film?' Una Burt, making sure that Derwent could still fit this profile, even if she couldn't bend time to make him a suspect for Angela Poole's murder.

'It could be. It would be something of enormous importance to him though. This is an experience that has defined him. He wants to relive it, or recreate it.' Dr Chen was wearing her usual red lipstick and a cherry-red cardigan over a white shirt; she looked immaculate. 'You can look for similarities between the women but it's possible that they are only connected by the fact that he was able to convince them to trust him.'

'What if he's pretending to be a police officer?' I said. Emphasis on *pretending*.

'That would work. It would fit in with how he presents himself too. Trustworthy but able to control their behaviour. I find it interesting that none of them seem to have mentioned him to their friends or family. He managed to persuade them to keep him a secret. Or they didn't want to talk about him for other reasons. They were embarrassed, perhaps, or they didn't want to jinx a potential romantic partner.'

'They were all waiting for their happy ever after. Only it didn't work out that way.' Godley shook his head.

'There was no sexual assault in any of these cases. Is that significant?' Burt asked.

'I should say so, yes. There is a sexual component to this, even though there is no sexual assault. The strangulation can be very arousing to killers of this nature.'

'Is this something that girlfriends or partners would be aware of?' I asked. 'The choking, specifically?'

'Possibly. But it's extremely likely he is impotent with women in ordinary sexual encounters. Or you may find he has been able to maintain medium-term relationships with women that include a healthy sex life. But he will most likely have been using pornographic material or encounters with prostitutes as an outlet for his less mainstream desires.'

'So he could be impotent, or perverted, or into porn, or normal.' *Not exactly narrowing it down for us.*

Dr Chen picked up on my implication and she flushed. 'Killers share characteristics and we can make educated guesses about this one, but when you find him you will find some parts of the profile are exact and others less applicable. This is designed to help you rule suspects out.

A profile on its own won't find you a killer, no matter how accurate it is.'

Which is why the police still have jobs instead of handing the hunt over to the psychologists.

'So strangling them is arousing but he can control himself. He doesn't touch them,' Burt said. 'Knows too much about forensic investigation to risk it.'

'More than likely he waits until after the body is arranged and masturbates. He may take photographs so he can revisit the scene in his own time.'

'But he's cleaned up too well for the SOCOs to find anything.' Burt made a note. 'We'll keep it in mind for the next one.'

'Una.' Godley's tone was a reproof.

'Well, there's going to be another one. He's not going to stop now.' She turned over another page. 'Unless he gets spooked and runs. But I'd say there's time for another.'

Godley ignored her and went back to Dr Chen. 'What about the way he leaves them? The white clothes, the flowers, the candles?'

'The way these victims are left is very deliberate but it's not designed to shock those who see them. A lot of killers will humiliate their victims by leaving their genitals and breasts exposed.'

'This is the opposite,' I said, thinking of Maxine draped in a sheet, covered from neck to knee.

'Yes. His fantasy involves them being pure. The bodies are clean. There's no blood. The cut hair is tidied away.'

'And the mutilation?' I said. 'It's the only damage he does, aside from killing them. Why?'

'Ah, that's interesting,' Dr Chen said. 'The fact that it's post-mortem means it's not to torture them. The Victorians believed that the last image a dead person saw remained imprinted on their retina after death. In this case, that would be their killer. They took it seriously – they tried to photograph the eyes of one of Jack the Ripper's victims.

That's what I thought of straight away when I heard about the eyes.'

'Don't mention Jack the Ripper in connection with these crimes, please,' Godley said. 'A serial killer operating in London with a victim in Whitechapel – the ghouls will be circling anyway.'

Dr Chen's mouth became a scarlet line: she did not enjoy being told off. Hastily, I said, 'What about the hair?'

'Traditionally, cropping the hair is a punishment. It's possible he tempts them into what he would consider indecent behaviour – maybe they offer him sex as a way of placating him, but it has the opposite effect. Then he cuts their hair to make them atone for their sin. Or he could do it after they're dead.'

'It makes them look like mannequins. Dehumanises them.' Burt tapped her pen on her teeth. 'Or it could be that it makes them unfeminine.'

'It makes them look younger,' I pointed out. 'They're all quite short and very slim. Anna looked like a child.'

Dr Chen looked at her watch. 'I'm sorry to break this up but I need to go.'

'Of course.' Godley stood up. 'Is there anything else we need to know?'

'Chief Inspector Burt is right. He will continue killing unless he feels threatened. He's not a risk-taker. At the moment, the odds are heavily in his favour. But if you can reduce those odds, you might find he stops, or moves on. If he stops killing in London, it will be worth keeping an eye on murders in other parts of the UK or even other jurisdictions within Europe and the US.'

'That won't happen,' Godley said. 'We'll get him before he moves on.'

You won't if you can't look past Josh Derwent, I thought.

Ever the gentleman, Godley walked Dr Chen out. I went over to the noticeboard and looked at the pictures of the three dead women that Godley had pinned there.

'You look tired,' Burt said.

'I am. I was up late.'

'Reading the Angela Poole file. What did you make of it?'

I shrugged. 'I'm not sure yet.'

'Do you think it's relevant to this case?'

I opened my mouth to say yes, then changed my mind. 'I don't know. It could be a wild goose chase.'

'What makes you say that?'

'Look at the differences. She died out of doors. These women are killed in their homes. Our victims are in their late twenties and she was fifteen. They're left lying on beds, not the ground. She wasn't wearing white and her hair wasn't cut. Someone followed her and killed her – that didn't take a lot of planning or ritual, and these deaths did. There's a twenty-year gap with no deaths. We can't be looking for the same killer. It doesn't make any sense.' I rubbed my eyes, suddenly exhausted. 'Derwent is obsessed with Angela and he sees similarities with every murder of a female by manual strangulation. He wants there to be a connection and you're going along with it, but that doesn't make it true.'

'What about the eyes?'

'What about them? You heard Dr Chen. Maybe the killer is superstitious. Anyway, Angela's eyes were gouged out while she was alive and left to one side. The three victims in our case have them removed after their deaths with a knife and are positioned holding them. That's a Masonic symbol, isn't it – the eye on the palm of a hand. Maybe we should be looking for a Freemason.'

'Maybe we should.' Godley had come in behind me while I was talking. He was leaning against the doorframe with his arms folded. 'You think we're seeing what we want to see, Maeve.'

'I do. And I think you're being unfair to Derwent to let him think there's a connection. He's losing his mind over this. Probably,' I remembered to add. *Because I haven't seen him since you told him to leave me alone.*

'What do you think, Una?' Godley asked.

'I can't agree.' She glared at me. 'You're just as wrong to try to make the facts fit your theory that he's not guilty.'

'If there were any facts, that might be true.' She looked furious. I reminded myself I was speaking to a senior officer and carried on in a more measured tone. 'If you're right and there is a connection between these deaths and Angela Poole's, why are you assuming Derwent is responsible? Angela's killer was never found.'

'Angela's killer is probably dead. We're looking for someone who has spent his life thinking about her.'

'You're narrowing the search down too quickly.'

She slammed her hand down on the desk. 'You're making excuses for someone who wouldn't do the same for you.'

'It doesn't matter what he would do or not do. This isn't about a personality. It's about the truth.' My voice had risen too. Heads were turning outside Godley's office.

'That's enough.' Godley stepped between us. 'Una, you had somewhere else to be, I think.'

'Whitechapel. I'm reinterviewing Maxine's neighbours.' She shut her notebook with a snap and stared at me. 'Want to come?'

No.

'No.' Godley gave her a bland look. 'Maeve has other things to do. Take Belcott with you.'

She didn't look thrilled, but I didn't blame her. Belcott was not a lot of fun at the best of times. I was annoyed with Una Burt but I wouldn't have wished Belcott on her. She stumped out of the office with a frown and Godley shut the door behind her.

'What do you really think?'

'I don't know. At all. But I don't think Derwent can be involved.'

'I never thought I'd see the day when you'd be sticking up for him.' He sat down behind his desk.

'And I never thought I'd see the day when you'd be trying to drop him in it. This is Derwent we're talking about. His one quality, the one thing that makes him decent, is that he is totally loyal. He'd literally die for you. And you're trying to tie him into a serial murder.'

Godley's jaw was tight. 'At the very least I don't want my case interfered with by someone who is a stranger to doing things by the book.'

'I didn't know doing things by the book was so important to you.'

'What does that mean?'

'You know what it means.'

He stood up, his face white. 'I will not be blackmailed by a member of my team. If you have a specific complaint to make about me, there are official channels for handling that.'

'I don't want to make a complaint and I am not blackmailing you. I just feel you're not being fair to Derwent.'

'I would think very carefully about whether you want to use your undeniable advantage for Derwent's benefit.'

I could feel my hands shaking, partly from anger, partly from tension. Get this wrong and I'd be back to local CID if I was lucky. Get it really wrong and I'd be in a traffic car writing tickets for bald tyres. 'This isn't about me. Or you. I still don't understand why you would risk your reputation and your career for money but I meant what I said when we spoke about it before – it's none of my business. And I am not the sort of person to try and turn that knowledge to my advantage. So please, stop assuming that I'm two seconds away from threatening you with disgrace.'

Godley fiddled with his pen, still on edge.

'Look, I'm just pointing out that nobody is perfect. I can understand why you don't want Derwent involved but I can't see why he has to be sent away in disgrace. And you know DCI Burt can't stand him. You know she's taking every opportunity to make him suffer. Neither of you seriously believes he's guilty, do you?'

'I don't know. Did you read the file?'

'Yes.'

'All of it?'

I thought about it. 'I – yes. Not in detail. I didn't have time. I didn't get in until after midnight.'

His eyebrows shot up. 'You must have taken a long way home.'

Shit. I'd forgotten he knew when I'd left. 'What was it you think I missed in the file?' I asked quickly.

'He was a different person then.'

'He was seventeen years old. Anyone is entitled to change in twenty years. And he's been in the army. He was shot at.'

'Exactly my point. He hasn't had an easy time of it. You know him well enough now, Maeve. You know he's not stable.'

'He's not always *pleasant*.'

'You don't want to believe the worst of him. Neither do I.'

'I'll believe it when I see the evidence.'

'All right,' Godley said. 'All right. You know, I like Josh and I like working with him. I take your point about Una – she is enjoying this. But she is a professional, as am I. We both think there is enough of an issue here to be concerned about him. He is off-balance at the moment, and these murders are pushing him in the wrong direction.'

I thought of him jumping on me the night before. 'I agree.'

'You seem to think I'm trying to harm him, but I'm not. If anything, I'm trying to protect him. I want to sit on the Angela Poole thing until we're sure that it is connected, or sure that it's not. If we start investigating it alongside the three current murders, people will talk. It needs to be done quietly.'

182

'May I look into Angela Poole's death?'

'Are you able to be objective about him?' Godley asked.

'Of course.'

'Do you consider him a friend?'

'No.'

'An enemy?'

'No.'

'Do you consider yourself to be neutral?'

It was hard to be neutral about Derwent. 'He's a colleague. I admire some things about him. I dislike others. I don't need him to be my friend to work with him.'

'All right. Keep it quiet. Report to me. I'm bringing some other members of the team on to the investigation into the current murders, but I'd rather keep the details of the Poole murder between us. Josh still works here, and as I said before, I don't want gossip about him.'

'What about Chief Inspector Burt?'

'She's liaison with Bradbury and Groves. She's busy with the current cases. She's read the file and formed her own opinion and she thinks we'll get our man if we start at this end, not in the archives of an unsolved.'

'Do I talk to Derwent?'

'Stay away from him.'

'He might be able to help.'

'He might be dangerous.' Godley gave me a warning look. 'Don't even think about it, Maeve.'

'I have his statement anyway,' I said, which was true, but not actually relevant.

'Talk to the witnesses. See where she died. Keep it quiet. Report to me. I can tell Josh we're looking into it and mean it.' Godley sighed. 'You don't think there's a connection between the two cases, and you don't think we should be worried about Derwent. I hope you prove yourself right on both counts.'

Chapter 17

I spent the day reading the Angela Poole file in detail and dealing with paperwork, and my head was aching by the evening. I was glad to have a reason to leave the office, and besides that I was looking forward to seeing James Peake again. He was a lot more charming than his boss, though that wasn't difficult. I also liked the idea of getting the inside track on Maxine Willoughby without having to ask Una Burt about it. I thought less of her for being vindictive towards Derwent. It was ironic that Derwent was the prince of vindictiveness. In her position, he'd have done the same and worse. Still, I had my standards, and Una Burt was not meeting them, currently.

Peake had picked a hotel bar in Kensington, a place with lots of mirrors and glass and low-slung designer armchairs and dim lighting. It was busy but the noise level was pleasantly muted, the conversations pitched to a murmur. He was sitting at a table at the end of the room when I got there and he waved, looking exactly like a DS who'd just come off duty in his suit and woeful tie. I hoped I was looking a bit better than him. I was wearing a Liv-approved charcoal-grey trouser suit, low heels, hair down but more or less under control. Businesslike. Not flirtatious in the least. But I couldn't quite suppress a small, guilty glow of pleasure when Peake watched me walk all the way to the table, his expression telling me that he liked what he saw. The glow faded as I contemplated exactly how awkward it would be to encourage him to think of me as anything other than a colleague. And of course I had no interest in him, beyond finding out what he knew about Maxine Willoughby. No interest at all. The old me, before Rob, would have been quivering with lust, but I was totally unmoved.

'Thanks for coming.' He stood up and pulled out a chair for me. 'What'll you have?'

'Tonic water, please.'

'With gin or vodka?'

I smiled. 'Not when I'm still working.'

'Yeah. Of course. Maybe later.'

He headed over to the bar and leaned against it, taller by inches than the men on either side and a good deal broader. He looked as if he'd expect to win an arm-wrestling competition with anyone there. His hair was really properly red, which I happened to like. From the looks Peake was getting from ladies – and quite a few men – all around the bar, I wasn't alone in noticing that he wore it well.

He came back juggling a beer, a bottle of tonic water, a glass for me with ice and a plate of nuts and crisps.

'Brain food. Here you go.'

I crunched a pretzel, suddenly ravenous. 'Do they know you here? How come we've got this and no one else has?'

'I was nice to Magda.' He looked back at the girl who was working our end of the bar and grinned at her, getting a lopsided smile in return. 'She's from Krakow.'

'I think you made her night.' She was now polishing a spot on the bar that probably hadn't needed a two-minute shine but it allowed her an unimpeded view of Peake. It wasn't altogether surprising, I thought. He was pleasant, handsome, and I found him attractive. I reminded myself firmly that my boyfriend possessed all three characteristics in truckloads, and concentrated on sipping my drink.

'So what did you do to annoy my boss?' Peake raised one eyebrow slowly. 'Anything I should know about?'

'I didn't think he remembered meeting me. Why, what did he say?'

'He said you were arrogant.'

'Just arrogant?'

'An arrogant bitch.'

I nodded. 'Nice.'

'Sorry.' He drank his lager. 'I hadn't planned to say so much.'

'Christ, don't ever commit a crime. The interview would be pitiful.'

'What can I say? I can't lie to you.'

I looked away, smiling politely.

He moved on without further comment. 'So I thought we should get together and have a chat about this case minus my twat of a boss and your . . . Chief Inspector Burt.'

I wondered what choice phrases he had decided not to use. It was wise of him not to slag her off, as he didn't know how I felt about her. The funny part was that I didn't know either.

'What's been going on? How did Bradbury get this case when he's only just been promoted?'

'No one else wanted it. Everyone assumed it was a domestic gone bad, an easy one that Bradbury could handle. They didn't make the connection with the other woman until after the post-mortem, when Dr Hanshaw said he'd seen something similar. And then Groves and his fat friend came along and looked over our shoulders.'

'They're quite the double act,' I observed.

'They've been dying to take over. Not that I blame them.' He finished his beer in one long swallow and caught Magda's eye, holding up the glass. 'Changed your mind?'

I'd barely touched my drink. 'I'm fine. What's been the problem with the investigation? Why do they want to take over?'

'Bradbury doesn't want to listen to anyone. I mean,

186

anyone. He took some convincing to admit it was the same killer.'

'Hadn't he seen the crime-scene pictures?'

'Yeah. He wasn't prepared to admit they were identical straight away. I think he was afraid the case would get taken away from him.'

'He must be just delighted at how things have worked out, now that Godley's taken over the lot.'

'Actually, I think he is. He's glad to have an opportunity to impress your boss.'

'Please, God, don't let him impress Godley so much that he gets him to join the team.'

'Godley's got to know better than that.'

'You'd think, but he doesn't filter out the tossers.' I stirred my tonic water with the totally unnecessary swizzle stick, jabbing the ice viciously. 'As long as they're good coppers, they can join the team.'

'Rest easy. That leaves Bradbury out.'

'Is he actually fucking it up or is he just dragging his heels?'

'Fucking up. He put everyone's backs up at Maxine's work, asking questions about her sex life and everyone else's in the office. He upset her parents – did a video link interview with them and they were so steamed up about what he was suggesting that they complained to our boss.'

'What was he saying, for God's sake?'

'He got it into his head that she was working as a hooker to make some extra cash. Don't ask me what gave him that idea, because there was no evidence that I saw. A hunch, apparently. Gut instinct.'

'Always reliable.'

'I think it was the address that made him think that.' He went quiet while Magda put a fresh coaster and glass in front of him, with a flourish. She got a smile for her trouble and looked thrilled. Once she was out of earshot he went on, 'It's flats, right, and the one upstairs was being used by a part-time prossie for work. Prearranged meet-ups only. She didn't solicit on the street and bring unknown punters back and she didn't live there herself. We found her when we were tracing the tenants to do interviews.'

'How did she advertise her services?'

'Escort websites. She waited to give the address until she was sure she was willing to go ahead with that particular client. Said she's good at picking out the wrong ones.'

'Until the time she doesn't,' I said. 'Did she ever arrange to meet someone there but get stood up?'

'All the time.' Peake grinned. 'Apparently a lot of men lose their nerve the first time. When they've been once, they tend to go back. This is what she told me,' he added. 'I'm not speaking from personal experience.'

'I'm just wondering if someone got the address by pretending to be a client and then got the flat numbers confused.'

'That was something we looked into, but we didn't get very far with it. Bradbury decided that Maxine got the idea to be a hooker from her and started working the streets without having the local knowledge or the smarts to stay safe.'

I thought of the crime-scene pictures. 'She really doesn't seem to have been that kind of girl.'

'That's what her parents said. Anyway, the girl said she'd never even seen Maxine, let alone advised her on a career in prostitution. She only saw regulars in the time Maxine was living there. She's a student, by the way. This is how she's paying her tuition fees. She'll probably end up being a lawyer and earning five times what I do.'

'She could probably earn that now if she wasn't so picky about her clientele.' I frowned. 'If the killer thought Maxine was a prostitute, maybe he was trying to redeem her from her life of sin. Maybe that's what he's doing.'

'Cutting off the hair. Dressing them in white. It's possible.'

'Any link with prostitution in Kirsty's case?'

'None that I know of.'

'Did Groves and Burns look into it?'

'You'd have to ask them.' Peake looked pained. 'Bradbury insisted that all queries go through him. I hadn't been allowed five minutes to talk to them on my own until we got to Anna Melville's house.'

'I should always bring Godley along. He's the highest-ranking officer Bradbury is likely to meet. He made for him like a dog finding the only lamppost for miles.'

'Bradbury would absolutely piss on his leg if he thought Godley would like it.'

'Not having much fun working with him?'

'You know when someone is wrong, and you tell them they're wrong, and just being told they're wrong makes them determined to stick to what they said?'

'All too well,' I said, thinking of Derwent.

'He's a twat.' Peake took a handful of peanuts and started working through them. 'I hate coming to work with him. If he'd been more open-minded and less shitty about Maxine, we wouldn't have to reinterview everyone now. Your chief inspector has got him where she wants him – he's actually terrified of her. So that's something.'

'No better woman.'

'She worked out that Bradbury was out of his depth about two seconds after she started dealing with him.' He shook his head. 'Godley has a good eye for female talent.'

'She'd made her reputation long before Godley took her on,' I said calmly, ignoring the implicit compliment.

'I bet you're glad she's there. It's proof he doesn't just go on looks.' He looked down, then up again, pretending to be awkward when he was nothing of the sort. 'Sorry. But you know, you're very attractive. You must have had people saying that you got where you are because of that.'

'Oh, they said it. And then they took it back.'

'I'm sure they did.' He leaned forward. 'I'm glad you

were able to come out tonight. I've been wanting to get to know more about you since I saw you.'

It wasn't often that I was aware of the significance of choosing one course of action over another. The images clicked through my head like a slideshow. Option A: go home, be glad you have a nice boyfriend, be grateful that you have the sense to know when you're in danger of trampling all over the things you care about. Option B: keep talking, keep drinking, allow yourself to flirt just a little bit, here and there. End up getting to know the dashing DS Peake better. Do something you regret just to prove to yourself that you're still free to make mistakes, even if you are in a serious relationship. Dispel the feeling of being trapped. Behave like the old Maeve. Be the person you used to be.

Option A was safe. Option B had its dangerous attractions. The risk-taking part of me yearned for it. The rest of me was terrified at the prospect.

I picked up my bag. 'It'll have to wait for another time, I'm afraid. I've got to go.'

He looked genuinely surprised. 'You've only just arrived.'

'I've got to meet someone now.'

'A date?'

'No. Work. Like this.'

His face darkened, then cleared. Peake had too much pride to admit he was annoyed, or disappointed. 'Another time, then. Somewhere a bit less formal, maybe.'

'This is nice.' I stood up. 'Quiet.'

'And there are rooms upstairs if you don't feel like heading home.' His eyes held mine, then dropped to my mouth, then skimmed over my body. My cheeks burned.

It was my cue to say, *Actually, I have a boyfriend, so . . .* I couldn't bring myself to do it. I hated excusing myself like that – *I'm the property of another man, so I can't stay in spite of how much I want to.* It wasn't the only reason I wasn't going to stay for another drink, so why mention it?

I smiled, composed again. 'That is convenient. If you find out when Magda finishes work, you might get to try one.'

'I don't think so,' he said softly, and I hoped he didn't think I was jealous. 'You pick a place next time. I'll leave it up to you. Let me know when you're free again and I'll be there.'

It was too awkward to say something about Rob now, or make a weak excuse about working late a lot. I hesitated, left it too long to reply, stammered a goodbye that sounded breathy rather than decisive and walked out, wondering why it was so damn hard to tell men to back off when they couldn't or wouldn't notice the not-interested signs. Be too brutal and they called you a bitch. Be too nice and you ended up giving them your phone number or agreeing to see them again.

And then there was the one who wouldn't take no for an answer, who persuaded you to trust him. The one you let into your home so he could murder you and dress you up for kicks.

Suddenly I missed Rob, a lot. I rang his mobile, knowing that it probably wouldn't work. It clicked through to voice-mail which I wasn't sure he could pick up in the US. I left a message anyway, thanking him for the flowers, telling him I was busy but looking after myself. Coping fine without him. Missing him a bit.

Half-truths.

He knew me well enough to know better.

I hung up and had no regrets at all about leaving handsome, charming James Peake sitting on his own in the bar. He wouldn't be alone for long, I thought, and he was free to get up to mischief with whomever he liked.

But not me.

Chapter 18

Derwent opened the door with the positive mental attitude of a boxer heading into the last round of a must-win prize fight. His first shot was a haymaker. 'What time do you call this?'

'I had to work. Then I had to meet someone. Then I had to go back to the office to collect these.' I was standing on one leg, my arms full of files, one knee supporting them as they threatened to slide out of my grasp. 'Can you take these? Or let me come in?'

He grabbed the top two files and started flicking through them. I was still standing on the doorstep.

'Excuse me.'

'What is it?' He hadn't even looked up.

'I'm still out here. On the street. And it's cold.' I shivered as the wind cut at my ankles. 'Let me in, for God's sake.'

'The choice was between taking the files and allowing you into my flat again.' Still reading. 'I have made my choice.'

Seething, I dumped the rest of the files at his feet. 'Fine. Enjoy. I want them back in the morning.'

I was ten yards down the street when he caught up with me. 'I was joking. Come on, Kerrigan. I didn't mean it.'

'I was going to tell you about everything that's *not* in the file,' I said coldly. 'But you don't deserve it.'

'I know. I'm an arsehole. But you love me anyway.'

'You're half right.'

'Come on.' He took my arm. 'Don't make me kidnap you again.'

I pulled away from him. 'Don't touch me. I'm here because I choose to be and I can choose to go home just as easily.'

'I know. I'm sorry.' He tilted his head to one side, considering me. 'Why are you choosing to be here?'

'Because you're not getting a fair deal.'

'Lucky for me you love an underdog.'

'Yeah, it is. And it's also good for my career if you're right about Angela's murder being connected to the three killings this year.'

'That's more like it.' He looked relieved. 'Ambitious as ever, Kerrigan.'

'You'd be the same if you were in my position.'

'Very possibly.'

The wind blew my hair around my face and I pushed it back, shivering. 'Are we going inside or what?'

'Of course.' He hesitated. 'You know I was only taking the piss.'

'I know. But I can't understand why when you also want me to help you.'

'I'm my own worst enemy.'

'Despite considerable competition.'

He stared at me, deciding how he was going to react, before he threw his head back and laughed. 'You know, Kerrigan, I'm starting to see the point of you.'

'Then I can die happy.' But I muttered it as I followed him to the flat, and I was pretty sure he didn't hear me. I'd gone just about as far as I could go with Derwent and the next smart remark would earn me a snarl.

It was warm in Derwent's flat and this time I let him hang up my coat downstairs, as a token of something – what, I wasn't sure. Trust wasn't quite the word. I wasn't feeling at home, exactly, but I was getting used to being around him.

We were halfway up the stairs, both carrying files, when Derwent stopped without warning. I almost collided with him. 'Who else is on this investigation?'

'Generally? Burt, Maitland, Colin Vale, me . . . oh, Peter Belcott was out with Burt today. Then there are the teams in Whitechapel and Lewisham.' I propped the files I was carrying on the step nearest me, since Derwent didn't seem to be moving any time soon.

'And they all know about Angela? And me?'

'No!' I suddenly understood what he was getting at. 'Absolutely not. Godley wants to keep it quiet to protect your reputation in the team.'

'So who knows? Burt does.'

'Yes, but she's senior to you.' It was the simple truth but I saw him flinch; he hated that it was true and I quite liked reminding him. 'I'm the only other person who's seen the file. I don't think anyone else has even heard Angela's name.'

'The file?'

Belatedly, I realised the trap I had dug for myself, and also realised that I was peering up from the bottom of it.

'You've got Angela's file?' He was staring at me.

'I've seen it.'

'Read it?'

I nodded.

'Can I see it?'

'Why would you want to do that?'

'Don't.' He shook his head, warning me. 'You know better than that.'

'Okay. All right.' He was leaning over me, looming, and I took a step back, flustered. 'I'll have to ask Godley.'

'He'll say no.'

'Not necessarily.'

Derwent hit the banister with the side of his hand, thinking. I know he could tell that I was spooked enough to take the files I'd been carrying and go. And he wanted to know about the other victims too. He had enough control to weigh it up and make the right choice.

'Okay. Run it by him first. That's how I've been training you to behave. No independent thinking. Chain of command.' He punctuated the last three words with a forefinger poking my head.

'I'm not going to show it to you just to prove I'm capable of making up my own mind.'

'Exactly what I'm saying. I'd be disappointed if you did.'

I followed him into the sitting room, still very much on my guard.

Derwent lined up the files he'd been carrying, two inches from the edge of the coffee table, in a straight line. 'Drink?'

'Ever the perfect host. Tea, if you're making it.' I stacked mine on the sofa to watch his face work as he tried to quell his OCD. No chance.

'Gimme those.' He put them beside the others, nudging them into position like a sheepdog coaxing recalcitrant ewes. 'And I'm not making tea. No milk, for starters. You can have instant coffee.'

'You spoil me. Coffee's fine.' *Anything hot*, I almost said, but stopped myself. That was the sort of open statement he was likely to punish.

He left and I heard him opening and closing cupboard doors down the hall. I followed the sounds to a small, tidy kitchen – white units on two sides, with a fold-out table under the window and two chairs stacked beside it.

'That's nifty.'

'What? The table? I made it.'

'Really?'

'Yep.' He wiped some non-existent drips off the counter. 'Can't stand eating in the living room.'

'A place for everything and everything in its place.'

'What's wrong with that? First rule of life is don't eat where you shit.'

'Please tell me you don't shit in your living room.'

195

'Obviously not. But I've extended it to cover sleeping and watching TV too. No crumbs in the bed, no marks on the upholstery.'

'I guess it depends on how messy you are.'

'No, it doesn't. Food belongs in the kitchen and that's where you should eat it.'

'But TV snacks are surely exempt.'

He looked me up and down. 'Yeah. That's how you'll get fat.'

'Excuse me?'

'You've got the height advantage and your metabolism is ticking over now, but you hit your mid-thirties and it's all going to go. Sitting on your arse watching telly eating crisps is the quick way to becoming obese. Mindless consumption.'

I folded my arms, feeling the familiar slow burn of rage that Derwent usually provoked. 'I am a long way from obese.'

'Now, maybe. But give it some time.' He picked up the mugs. 'Finished snooping?'

'We were having a conversation,' I pointed out.

'You were nosing around.'

I opened my mouth to argue, then closed it again. He was right, basically. Busted. Taking a leaf out of his book, I went on the attack. 'Takes one to know one.'

'Occupational hazard. Coppers don't do casual chats.' He grinned, then thrust one mug at me. 'Come on. I'm not your slave. Carry it yourself.'

Back in the living room, he sat down. 'How do you want to do this? Stay while I read, or pick them up tomorrow?'

'I thought we could go through them together. See what jumps out.' I opened the nearest one, which was Maxine's. 'You know, everyone's been looking at them to see the similarities. I think we need to look at the differences too.'

'Floor?'

'Floor.' I helped to move the coffee table out of the way,

and then joined Derwent in taking the files apart. The space filled up quickly: victim pictures I hadn't seen before with the three women full-face and smiling, crime-scene photographs, maps, floor plans, diagrams of the victims' injuries, post-mortem close-ups, forensic reports. Witness statements. Interviews. Phone records. Bank statements. Paper, and lots of it. Three dead women generated a lot of words.

'These are just the edited highlights,' I said. 'I left most of it at work.'

'It's a start.' Derwent was scanning the post-mortem report on Anna Melville, scrawling notes as he went. 'Let's see how far we can get.'

For the next couple of hours, we read. I hadn't had time to go through the paperwork for Maxine and Kirsty in detail and I was glad to have the chance to familiarise myself with it. Derwent talked to himself as he worked, which I had never noticed before. I found it strangely endearing.

I was sitting on the floor on the opposite side of the room, looking at a floor plan of Maxine's flat, when Derwent stretched. 'This is doing my head in.'

'Problem?'

'Just trying to get it all straight in my head.'

I put down the plan, realising that I'd ended up in a very uncomfortable position. My neck was aching. 'Do you want to have a break? Talk it through?'

'Yeah. What did you say? Focus on the differences?' He flipped to a new page in his notebook. 'Go for it.'

'Right. Well, I don't think there's any doubt they were killed by the same man.'

'*Differences*, Kerrigan.'

'I'm getting to that,' I said, with dignity. 'From what I can tell, they each had very different personalities. Their jobs were completely different and none of them worked or lived near any of the others. No connection between their backgrounds – Kirsty grew up in Scotland, Anna in

Hampshire, Maxine in Australia. So we really don't know where our man found them or why he chose them.'

'Something made his psycho radar ping,' Derwent said. 'Something they did, or said, or the way they looked.'

From where I was kneeling the three pictures of the victims were upside down. I glanced at them and then looked again. 'Hold on.'

'What?'

I grabbed three pieces of paper and made a frame that I laid over Kirsty's head, hiding her hair. 'One.' I made another and put it on Maxine's picture. 'Two.'

'What is this, kindergarten?'

'Bear with me.' I covered Anna's hair. 'They look alike now. That's the same smile.'

'You think they smile at him.' Derwent did not sound convinced.

'That could be enough.' I frowned, remembering, then scrambled across to the forensic report on Anna Melville, which I hadn't had time to read yet. 'Bingo. We found a hair on Anna's body. This report says it was a synthetic one. From a wig. He crops their hair so they can wear the wig.'

'What colour?'

'Fair.'

'Like Angela?'

I really wanted to compare them too. I had to make a quick decision. Instead of answering Derwent I got up and found my bag, pulling out Angela's file. 'Don't go mental.'

He was up on his knees, trying to see what I was holding. 'What's that?'

I laid the school photograph of her beside the other three. 'Perfect match, I'd have said.'

'Is that Angela's file?'

'Yes, but concentrate on this. This is important. He sees them – doesn't matter where. He makes a connection. They were all about the same height – five two, five three – with a physical resemblance to Angela. The wig makes them identical. You're right. This is all about her.'

'Give me the file.' Derwent's eyes were fixed on it.

'You're not listening.'

'Give it.'

I held it against me, my arms folded across it. 'Not yet. What did you pick up? I heard you mumbling.'

Derwent glowered. 'Enjoy this moment, Kerrigan, because you're not going to be in charge for much longer. When things get back to normal, you're going to get a reminder that you're a very junior detective.' He picked up the crime-scene pictures from Maxine's flat and Anna's bedroom. 'Right. Look at these. Why is Anna Melville lying with her head at the end of the bed?'

'Don't know. So you can see her through the window?'

He made a buzzer sound. 'Good answer but wrong. Why did the killer move Maxine's bed?'

'Did he?'

'Definitely.' Derwent pointed. 'That's the bedside table over there. That's the line from the headboard on the wall. That mark in the carpet is from the castors on the bed. This isn't where the bed was supposed to be.'

I checked Kirsty's pictures. 'This one wasn't moved.'

'No need. Do me a favour. Look up the crime-scene pictures from Angela's file.'

I did as I was told. 'And?'

'He leaves them with their heads to the east. I bet Angela's the same.'

He was right. I chewed my lip, thinking. 'So he's making them into Angela all over again. That suggests he killed her, too. Why the twenty-year gap?'

'No idea. You'll have to ask him.' He looked pointedly at the file. 'You know, it would be a good idea to compare the original crime-scene pictures with these.'

I slid them out of the file and hesitated, weighing them in one hand. 'Are you okay to look at these?'

'It was a long time ago, Kerrigan.'

'Even so.'

He held out his hand. 'Come on. I've seen them before, anyway.'

'When was that?'

'When Leonard Bastard Orpen was interviewing me.' He fanned them out, his hands steady. 'Right. What have we got?'

'The flowers and greenery match our new victims.' I looked across the images. 'Candles, though. There weren't any at the Poole crime scene.'

'It would have been dark there, at that hour of night. The less light he has in the room, the more it resembles Angela's death. A few candles give him enough light to see his victims. He can't open the curtains or blinds in case someone sees him, and electric light isn't going to make it seem real for him.'

'Candlelight flickers,' I said. 'The light might make it seem like they're moving. If he's acting out a scene, I mean.'

We sat for a moment, imagining our killer and his conversations with the dead. Because dead women can't answer back. Out of nowhere, I recalled Derwent telling a joke at a domestic murder scene, the victim lying on her kitchen floor in a pool of blood.

What do you say to a woman with two black eyes?

Nothing. You've already told her twice.

'And the eyes,' Derwent said. 'What about them?'

I told him Dr Chen's theory about the retinal image.

'Jack the fucking Ripper.' He shook his head. 'I don't think so.'

'He does it differently now. I don't know if that's relevant. Knife rather than by hand.'

'More squeamish.' He tapped the recent crime-scene pictures. 'This is all more tentative, isn't it? He doesn't have the nerve to do them outside. Angela's death was quick and dirty. He took a big risk, killing her beside the house.'

'Why did he kill her in the first place? She wasn't sexually assaulted, according to the file.'

'Maybe he didn't have time. Got interrupted.' Derwent blew out a lungful of air. 'I'm not imagining the connection, am I?'

'I don't think so. Are we looking for the same killer?'

'Fuck knows. Maybe.'

'A twenty-year gap and it's not quite the same MO, is it? But he's using the same signature as Angela's killer. Reliving it.'

'We could be looking for a twenty-something killer in 1992 who's been in prison or abroad and now that he's forty-something he doesn't have the stomach for killing out of doors, or gouging out eyes with his hands. Or back then he *wanted* to use a knife on Angela and he didn't have one. He'd have *preferred* to be indoors but had to go with being outside when the opportunity presented itself. Works both ways. Maybe he's perfecting his technique, not imitating what happened in 1992.' Derwent was pacing back and forth along a narrow strip of carpet that was all that remained uncovered by the drifts of paper.

'I'll go through the files again. See if anyone who was sent down for a long stretch in the year after Angela's death has been released recently.'

'Or if anyone's just come off probation. That might be making him cocky, now that no one's looking over his shoulder.' He snapped his fingers. 'Speak to probation officers too. See if there's anyone they're worried about for these killings.'

It would take roughly a million hours to cover all of the paperwork. 'The geographical spread doesn't help,' I said tentatively. 'We have no way of knowing where he actually lives. He seems happy to operate wherever the victims live.'

'I like him for being ex-army. He adapts according to the territory. That's a military mindset.'

'It could equally apply to a chess player.'

'We're not looking for a fucking geek, Kerrigan. Nerd boy who loves chess isn't going to be out there strangling and mutilating women. He's an alpha male, this guy. He takes control. He knows what he wants and he makes it possible to get it.'

'You sound as if you admire him.'

He shook his head. 'Admiration is not what I feel for this turd. But you have to admit, he's doing a good job. Three murders and we've got nothing. There isn't one credible suspect in that pile of interviews, just like last time. I was the only one they had and I was just lucky to have an alibi because otherwise I'd have gone down for it.'

'What about this time round?'

'What do you mean?'

'Have you got alibis for the nights the murders took place?'

He glared. 'Probably. I haven't checked.'

'Maybe you should.'

'Why?'

'In case someone makes the same connection as us and comes asking. Andy Bradbury would love the chance to make you sweat in an interview room.'

'That tosser.'

'Yeah. That increasingly senior tosser.' I started to sort out the pile of pages nearest me. 'Someone has already suggested we might be looking for a police officer.'

'We might. But it's not me.'

I glanced up at him and found that he was staring at me with the peculiarly intense blue gaze that meant he was irritated. 'Of course not,' I said, a little too late.

'So what happens now? You said Godley's keeping it quiet. Are you and Una Burt the only people actually working on comparing Angela's case with the three recent deaths?'

'That's not quite right,' I said cautiously. 'Una Burt is tied up with organising liaison between the different teams.'

'So it's just you.'

'And you know you can trust me.' *Look on the bright side . . .*

'For fuck's sake.' Derwent paced back and forth again. 'I'm going to have to get involved.'

'No, Josh, you have to stay out of it.' I stopped for a second, surprised that I'd used his first name, but he didn't notice.

'I'm not staying out of it. I'm in it. It's my story, for fuck's sake. This is about me.'

'It's about three dead women. Four, including Angela. And you can't be involved because Godley would sack us both, and he'd be right. Look, I'll tell you everything I find out. I'll discuss interview strategies with you and let you know who I'm talking to. You just can't be there.'

'Kerrigan . . .'

'No.' I put Angela's file down on the sofa. 'It's late. I'm going to go home. I'll leave you this because I think you should read it, no matter what Godley says. You need to stay in the background but you can absolutely advise me, and between us, I think we might be able to get somewhere.'

He was shaking his head. 'You can't buy me off with the file.'

'Okay, then I'll take it away and you can talk Godley into letting you be officially involved.' *Which will never happen.* His shoulders slumped and I knew I'd won, though it didn't give me all that much pleasure. 'I'm trying to help you, you know.'

'I know.'

'I want to find out what happened too.'

'Yeah.' He looked out the window at the street below. It was deserted, except for a rangy fox scavenging on the other side of the road. He watched it until it disappeared. Almost to himself, he said, 'I'd just like to know.'

SUNDAY

Chapter 19

I don't know if I'd have recognised him in the street, but when I saw him in the bar he owned, my first thought was that Shane Poole hadn't changed all that much since he was seventeen. He was broader in the shoulder and softer around the middle, and his hair had a startling amount of grey in it considering he wasn't yet forty, but the basic elements were the same: a tall, hefty guy with big hands and a serious expression. He reminded me of Derwent, but I couldn't have said why – his voice, maybe, and his demeanour, and a little bit his appearance. I wondered if it was just growing up in the same place or if Poole had been so influenced by Derwent's example that it was still, after all these years, how he chose to carry himself.

His business, the Rest Bar, was in a side street off Brick Lane, something that had pinged my radar when I tracked him down. Brick Lane was curry-house central, popular for office outings, open until late and the very definition of vibrant. It was close to the City where Anna had worked, closer still to Whitechapel where Maxine had lived. It was a place where my victims might plausibly have gone, where they might have met their killer. A killer who was obsessed, it seemed, with Shane Poole's sister and how she died. I went to meet him with a long list of questions and the uncomfortable feeling that Derwent was standing right behind me, looking over my shoulder, watching my every move.

At nine on a Sunday morning the Rest Bar was empty except for a man slowly sweeping the wooden floor. It was a bleak place at that time of day – too quiet without the hum of conversation and music, too bright when the sun was shining through the windows on grey leather seats that looked unpleasantly sticky. Everything would look a lot better at night when the great copper pendant lights over the bar were switched on. As it was, nothing could make up for the smell of spilled wine, stale beer and bleach. I'd expected Shane Poole to speak to me in a back office but he sat down in one of the booths, stretching out an arm along the top of the banquette as if he was relaxed. He was anything but, I thought, noticing the tremor in his right eyelid and the rapid tapping of one finger that he couldn't seem to suppress.

'Thanks for agreeing to see me.'

'You said it was about Angela.' He had a raw-edged voice, throaty and pitched a little too loud. The cleaner looked up when he spoke, then quickly bent his head over what he was doing. I thought the man looked scared and wondered if it was because he was scared of Shane or because he thought I was there to check the employees' visas and send him straight back to Lagos on the first available plane.

'We're trying to work out if there's a connection between Angela's death and three murders that we're currently investigating. Kirsty Campbell, Maxine Willoughby and Anna Melville.'

He pulled the corners of his mouth down and shrugged, as if to say the names meant nothing to him.

'They were strangled in their homes in the last nine months.'

'Sorry to hear it.'

'There are . . . circumstances that made us want to compare them with Angela's death.'

'Do you think it's the same guy?'

'It's possible.'

He leaned forward with his elbows on his knees, staring at the floor instead of at me. 'I thought I'd left all this behind. It's years since we've heard anything from you. Years.'

'You' in this context meant the police, I understood. 'Sometimes there's nothing to tell the families in unsolved cases. Sometimes it's better to wait until a proper case review instead of bothering you for no reason.'

'It would have been nice to know someone still cared.'

Someone had cared. Someone named Josh Derwent had cared, a lot. I wasn't ready to mention his name, though.

'There were no new developments. Solving a murder can be a waiting game but I understand it's hard to be patient if you feel nothing is being done.'

'My mother waited. My mother was patient with you. She's dead now. She died three years ago come December.' He rubbed a hand over his face, rasping stubble. 'She never got over it, as you might expect. Never forgave herself for not stopping it. Never could rest, knowing you hadn't caught him.'

'It wasn't an easy case,' I said quietly. 'There wasn't a lot to go on.'

'There was an obvious suspect and they let him go.' Shane looked at me, his eyes watery but defiant. 'Now he's one of you lot.'

'He had an alibi. Your father—'

'My father. Do you know where he is?'

I shook my head.

'In a home – not far from where we used to live, though he doesn't know it. He's got dementia. Doesn't know what day it is. He was probably going that way back in 1992 – he had to retire two years later. Mum tried to look after him but it was hopeless. We sold the house to pay for his nursing home and she had to move in with her sister.'

Shane pointed a finger at me, a little too close for comfort. 'Don't tell me he couldn't have made a mistake. Got confused. Mixed up one young lad with another. One person was responsible for what happened to Ange. One. And he walked away from it.'

'He was ruled out as a possible suspect early in the investigation.'

'He was my *friend*. He raped my sister.'

I squirmed. 'I am the last person to be an apologist for a rapist, believe me, but if it was rape it was only in a technical sense. From what I understand there was consensual intercourse.'

'She was fifteen. He was older than her. It was rape.'

'The Crown Prosecution considered it at the time and decided prosecution wasn't in the public interest.' I hesitated, wondering if I should go on. *In for a penny* . . . 'I read the file. Statements from her friends. Transcripts from her diary. There was a lot of evidence that she was a willing participant in whatever sexual activity took place up to the night in question. Obviously she was killed before she could talk to anyone about what had happened, or write about it, but—'

His nostrils flared. 'He took advantage of her and then he killed her, and as if that wasn't enough he *mutilated* her.'

I wasn't going to argue with him any more; he'd had twenty years to resent Derwent and I couldn't change his mind in twenty minutes. 'What happened to Angela was horrible. As I say, I've read the file. I am more sorry than I can say that the murderer wasn't caught. I'm not discounting what you've told me about who was responsible, but I think it's worth investigating other angles too.'

'If you can't or won't see the truth there's nothing I can do to help you.' His tone was final and I was afraid he was going to get up and walk away.

Quickly, I took out three pictures and laid them on the

table in front of Shane. 'Can you look at these and tell me if you recognise any of them?'

He glanced at them. 'Who are they?'

'The recent victims.' I didn't identify them beyond that. Let him try to put a name to a face if he recognised some-one. He leaned over and stared at them for another few seconds.

'Did any of them drink here?' I tried.

'You'd have to ask my staff. I don't spend a lot of time talking to the customers.'

'But you're here when the bar is open.'

He spread his arms out. 'I live here. I've got a flat upstairs.'

And he hadn't invited me to see it, preferring the public space of the bar. I could almost have felt hurt. Except that I would have wanted to do the same thing, if the police had been interviewing me.

'You might have seen these women even if you didn't talk to them. Look again.'

When he reached out and picked up Maxine's picture, I felt a brief flutter of excitement, but he laid it down without making any comment.

'No one ringing any bells?'

He shook his head. 'Leave them here if you like. I'll show them round the regulars and the staff. See if I can find someone who knows any of them.'

I was surprised. 'That's very helpful of you.'

'I have a personal interest in making sure killers get caught. Seems to me you need all the help you can get from the general public.'

I dug out a stack of business cards and handed them to him. 'If anyone thinks they remember any of the women, they can get in touch with me.'

He put them to one side and raised his eyebrows. 'Anything else?'

'Going back to 1992. Angela's death. Do you mind

talking about it a little? I don't want to bring back unhappy memories but if there is a connection with the recent killings, we need to find out as much as we can.'

'What do you want to know?'

'Before Angela died – do you remember anything strange happening? Someone you didn't know hanging around, or a strange car driving by the house more than once?'

'Nope.'

'Do you recall anyone behaving oddly around the time Angela died? And afterwards – did anyone's behaviour change? Did you think anyone was particularly affected by her death?'

'Everyone was. It knocked a fair few people for six.'

'But no one stands out?'

'I told you who killed her,' he said heavily. 'I don't know why you're bothering with these questions.'

'Bear with me, please.' I changed tack. 'What do you remember about the night she died?'

He sighed, looking away from me again. 'I don't know. Bits. I was out that night with some mates and I'd been smoking a bit of weed. When I got home I saw police cars outside the house and I got it into my head that they were there to arrest me. I tried to hide between two parked cars, if you can believe that. What a twat.'

'When did you realise the police weren't there for you?'

'There was an ambulance too, which I thought was weird. The paramedics were talking about Mum, giving her a sedative and stuff. I thought something had happened to Dad. And then one of the coppers spotted me so I gave myself up. I was all sweaty and shaky and paranoid, but I think Mum and Dad were too upset to notice. The cops weren't interested in arresting me for smoking marijuana given what was actually going on, but one of them had a quiet word a week or two later. Recommended that I knock the smoking on the head. Which didn't quite work out, but he was doing his best.'

'Did you see Angela?'

'Then? No. I went with Dad to identify the body later. Mum couldn't do it. I didn't want him to go on his own.'

'Where was that?'

'The local hospital. In the morgue.' He shuddered. 'Horrible place.'

'Did you ever see pictures from the crime scene?'

'No.'

'Do you know if there were press photographs of Angela's body, either in the garden or in the morgue?'

'Don't think so. Why do you ask?'

'I'm just trying to narrow down the number of people who saw her body at any stage. Sometimes photographs like that get passed around – at school, for instance.'

He flexed the muscles in his chest and shoulders. 'No fucking way would I have allowed that. Not for a second.'

'What else do you remember?'

'The funeral. All the girls in her year crying, holding on to one another. They were supposed to be doing an honour guard but they were a fucking embarrassment to the school and themselves.' He shook his head and I was suddenly reminded of Derwent again: the disapproval, the scorn for weakness of any kind when there was a duty to be performed.

'It must have been very upsetting for everyone.'

'Last funeral I went to. Never again.' He looked at me again, briefly. 'You'll be able to find this out easily enough, so I'll tell you. Josh came to speak to us at the funeral. Tried to shake my dad's hand, and mine. I threw up. All over the floor of the church. It fucking stank. That's what I remember from Angela's funeral. This massive arrangement of lilies on the coffin that reeked, mixed up with the smell of sick.' He almost gagged at the thought and I didn't blame him. He stood up, looking green. 'I need some water. Do you want a drink?'

'I'm fine.'

When he sat down he had more colour in his face and he gave a wry smile. 'I remember the next time I saw Josh too, at school. I punched him in the face. I really regret it.'

'Oh,' I started to say, 'I'm sure he doesn't remember—'

'I should have hit him harder,' Shane interrupted. 'That's what I regret.'

I could see how you might feel that way about Derwent. 'And then he stopped coming to school.'

'That's right. Joined the army. Disappeared off to drink and fuck and wave guns around in Cyprus or Germany or wherever. Playing soldiers and calling himself a hero.'

'What happened to everyone else?'

'Everything went out of control. There was a little group of us – Josh, Ange, me, our mate Vinny and his sister. It affected each of us differently. I started doing a lot of drugs – pills and coke, everything except smack because I didn't like needles, thank fuck. Claire, Vinny's sister – she disappeared for a couple of years. Went to live with their aunt in Birmingham. I think she wanted to get away, so she could get over it in her own time.' He shrugged. 'Dunno. When she came back she'd been engaged to some Brummie, but he'd broken it off. She had a little kid by him. The kid took up all her time so we never saw her. She was only young but she was determined to be a good mum. I think she got pregnant on purpose. I think she had something to prove. She wanted to get a lot of living in because Ange didn't get the chance.' His eyes were wet suddenly and he looked at the corner of the ceiling fixedly until he'd got himself under control again. I pretended not to notice.

'What about Vinny?'

He half-laughed, then coughed, still fighting for composure. 'Vinny and me finished in school, and then he went travelling. I couldn't go because Mum and Dad needed me around. Good thing too because I'd have OD'd somewhere along the way. Vinny went around Thailand, Cambodia,

Laos, Vietnam – just wandered through Asia, basically, living on rice and sleeping in cheap dosshouses. He did a bit of kickboxing in Thailand, fought a few bouts. He thought about staying there and turning pro but he came back instead. He couldn't keep a job here – got bored too easily. He had no patience for authority, so it was a big joke when he went into the army too.'

'To be like Josh?'

'It was a different regiment.'

I wanted to say *same difference* but I knew better. 'Okay. But it seems quite similar to how Josh dealt with Angela's death.'

'Maybe. I dunno. I never lost touch with Vinny, though. Josh disappeared, much to my relief. Vinny was always there for me, even if he was on the other side of the world.'

'How can I get in touch with him?' I asked, and saw him flinch.

'You can't.' I somehow knew what he was going to say but I let him say it anyway. 'He's dead.'

'When did he die?'

'Last November. Almost a year ago. Afghanistan. Stepped on an IED. A car battery wired to some leftover Russian plastic explosives by a fucking goatherd in the worst country on earth.'

'How awful.' I meant it.

Shane nodded. 'He was my best friend.'

'I didn't realise. I'm sorry for your loss.'

'I miss him a lot,' he admitted. 'There. That's Vinny.' He had taken a picture out of his wallet and he showed it to me: a formal portrait, full dress uniform. Vinny had been handsome, in a square-jawed, tough way. His neck was wider than his head.

'And that was in November,' I double-checked.

'As I said.' The photograph went back where it belonged and he tucked his wallet away.

'Who else should I speak to? Your father . . .'

215

'Don't waste your time. He doesn't remember me or Angela, let alone what happened to her.'

'Who else?'

'Claire, I suppose. She's back in Bromley. Not married – she's still Claire Naylor. Manages a card shop.'

'I'll find her.'

'She'll tell you the same as me, but you might as well hear it from her too.' He stood up, making it clear that he'd said all he had to say and our interview was over. 'Yeah. Talk to Claire.'

Chapter 20

I tracked Claire Naylor down by calling the four card shops in Bromley. As luck would have it, she was the manager of the fourth, and was off sick. I insisted on getting an address out of the very hassled deputy manager. The reduced Sunday opening hours were a nice idea in theory, but it just made the shops busier for a shorter space of time. It was, the deputy manager told me bitterly, the run-up to Christmas. Already.

I decided it was worth a trip to see Claire in person rather than a phone call. I drove a pool car that had an iffy clutch, got stuck in traffic on the way and spent an hour touring Bromley before I spoke with her, by which time I was in the blackest of moods.

I found Derwent's old home, now inhabited by an Asian family, and the cemetery where he and Angela had shagged, though I didn't make a pilgrimage to the exact spot. There was unlikely to be a plaque, I thought. I drove from there to Kimlett Road and the Pooles' old house. From what Shane Poole had told me, it had changed hands years earlier so there was no need to worry about upsetting family members. Even so, I kept a low profile, standing near the gate and looking into the garden to see where Angela had met her end. The tree was gone, the hedge between the houses had been replaced by a high wooden fence and the house had acquired a large conservatory that took up most of the garden. The house next door, however, looked much the same as it had in the pictures. Stuart Sinclair's house. It was worth ringing the doorbell, I thought, and did so. A child opened the door, a girl aged nine or ten whose face fell when she saw me. Her mother came hurrying towards me down the dark hallway. She was stocky, with heavy features and very dark straight eyebrows that made her look fierce.

'Sorry. She thought it was her friend.' To the girl, she said, 'Into the sitting room, Milly, quick. I've told you before not to answer the door.'

She waited until the girl had gone out of sight before she said, 'I don't buy at the door.'

'I'm not selling anything,' I said quickly, showing her my ID as she started to close the door. 'I'm a police officer. DC Kerrigan is my name. I just wanted to ask you if Stuart Sinclair still lived here, or if you had an address for him or his family.'

'He's the landlord. Dunno where he lives.'

'How do you contact him then?'

'I don't.' She sighed. 'Look, I can ask my husband. He's the one who handles all that.'

'Is he here?'

'He's away. A stag weekend.' She rolled her eyes. 'At his age.'

I gave her a business card. 'It's really important that I get in touch with him. If you could get your husband to call or email me, I'd appreciate it.'

'I'll see what we can do.' No enthusiasm.

'Can I just make a note of your name?'

'Sharon Parsons. My husband's name is David.' She watched me write the names down, peering as if she was suspicious I'd write something else or spell them wrong.

I started to turn away, then changed my mind. 'Would it be possible for me to have a look upstairs? I just want to see the view from the windows, not anything in your house.'

She was already shaking her head. 'Absolutely not. It's private.'

'I understand. I only ask because I'm involved in a murder investigation, and—'

The word 'murder' usually provoked a reaction of some kind. Not here. Her expression didn't waver. 'I can't help, I'm afraid.'

There was nothing else I could do; I couldn't compel her to let me into her house. I left with more questions than ever and very little hope her husband would be in touch.

It took a further twenty minutes to locate Claire's house. She lived on an ex-council estate that was constructed around long, winding cul-de-sacs and I got more than enough practice at three-point turns before I found it. I rang the doorbell and while I waited, I turned to look at the immaculate strip of lawn, the clean but elderly Fiat on the driveway. A perfectionist.

'Can I help you?'

There was no doubting that Claire deserved to be off sick: her eyes were glassy, her skin pale and the end of her nose was scarlet. Unlike Shane she looked a good twenty years older than the photograph Derwent had kept, if not more, with lines across her forehead and her hair dyed a harsh blue-black. She was huddled in a dressing gown and looked as if the last thing she wanted was a long chat.

'Claire Naylor? I'm Detective Constable Maeve Kerrigan. I was hoping to ask you a few questions about Angela Poole.'

'Angela?' She wrapped one hand around her waist, the other clutching the neck of her dressing gown. 'Why do you want to ask about her?'

'Angela's death may be relevant to an ongoing investigation.' The woman didn't move. I took a leaf out of Derwent's book and put my foot across the threshold so she couldn't shut the door on me. 'Can I come in? I'll try not to take up too much of your time.'

'I don't . . . Oh God.' She rubbed her forehead. 'I've got the flu.'

'I'll keep it short.' *And I'm not going anywhere so you might as well let me in.*

She must have seen the resolve on my face because she stepped back and I went past her into the hall. It was as spotless as the front garden, so tidy that it was almost bleak. I moved towards the door to the living room, assuming that's where we would talk.

'Wait! I want to tidy up first. Give me a second.'

She pushed past, closing the living room door behind her, and I listened to sounds of drawers opening and closing as she moved quickly around the room. After less than a minute she opened the door again.

'You can come in.'

I walked into a room that had never been untidy as long as Claire Naylor had lived there. She seemed obsessively house-proud, because the walls and shelves were practically bare. One drawer of the sideboard in the corner of the room was sticking out a little, as if it had been closed in a hurry, and I would have given a lot to see what was in it. As if she knew what I was thinking, she stood between me and the sideboard, holding on to the back of an armchair.

'Please, sit down.'

I did as I was told, getting out a notebook.

'Would you like anything to drink? Tea? Water?' She coughed, a rattling sound that shook her narrow frame.

'No, thank you.' I waited until she sat down too, perching on the edge of the armchair, ready to flee at any moment.

'You said it's about Angela. I don't understand. Why do you want to talk to me?'

'We're looking into Angela's death because it seems to be connected to a series of murders that have taken place in the last few months.' I showed her the pictures, naming each of the women in turn, and she nodded.

'I read about them in the paper. Strangled, like Angela.' She looked up at me. 'Just like Angela?'

'There are similarities.'

She shuddered. 'Don't tell me any more. Do you think it's the same murderer?'

I hesitated. 'We don't have any definite suspects at the moment. That's one reason why I've come to talk to you. I know it must seem unlikely but we need to see if there's anything you can tell us that might send us in the right direction.'

'I don't think I can help,' she said flatly. 'I don't really know why you're here.'

'It was Shane Poole who suggested I speak with you.'

'Shane? I haven't seen him for years.'

'Your brother was in touch with him, I understand.'

'Vinny was.' She sniffed and I couldn't tell if it was because she was upset or because of the flu. 'I moved away, after what happened. Shane and Vinny stayed close but I didn't want to. It just felt as if I was reliving it all the time.'

'You were friends with Angela.'

'We were all friends. Vinny and Shane and Angela and me.'

'And?' I prompted.

'Josh Derwent.' She said his name in a toneless voice and I couldn't tell how she felt about him. She looked at me sharply. 'He's a policeman now. Do you know him?'

There was no reason to pretend I didn't. 'I work with him. But he's not involved with this investigation.'

'Does he know where I live? Have you told him you're speaking to me?'

'No, no. I won't, either, if you'd prefer me not to.'

'Don't tell him. Please.' She started to smooth the skirt of her dressing gown over her knees, fidgeting. 'I don't want to see him. I haven't since that year and there's no reason to start now.'

'He was the main suspect in Angela's death, but he was

ruled out during the original inquiry,' I said gently. 'He had an alibi.'

'I know *that*.'

'So it's not that you're scared of him.'

'Of *Josh*?' She laughed. 'No. I just don't want to go back there.'

'When was the last time you saw him?'

'A few months after it happened.' She paused to cough again. 'I stuck by him afterwards. I didn't believe what everyone was saying about him. I knew Angela was the one who'd wanted them to sleep together. It wasn't Josh's idea. And he worshipped the ground she walked on. He'd never have hurt her. He'd never hurt a woman.'

'Does that mean he didn't hesitate when it came to hurting a man?'

'If you know Josh, you'll know it was his solution to fight his way through anyone who said he was guilty, which was everyone. And his family kicked him out. He was a lost soul.'

'It sounds as if you really felt for him.'

'I did.' She'd been gazing into the middle distance, her expression wry, but now it snapped back to serious. 'That doesn't mean I want to bring him back into my life. I'm happy with things the way they are. I supported him when he needed me, and I'm glad I didn't let him down. We were just kids, though, and he'll be different now. I know I am.'

'I gather you became a mum. You must have had to grow up fast.'

'Who told you that? Shane?' She coughed again. 'I met someone in Birmingham – Mark, his name was – but the relationship was never going to last. I got Luke out of it and that was enough for me.'

'Does Luke live here with you?' The living room was so pristine I couldn't imagine a teenager sprawling on the sofa watching television, but there was a PlayStation behind the TV, the leads unplugged and wound in neat loops.

'He's away. He's a student. At Cambridge,' she added. 'Studying engineering.'

'He must be bright.'

'Very.' She looked proud.

'Does he take after you? Did you go to university?'

'Not once I was pregnant. They had crèches and my mum would have helped look after him but I was too wrapped up in him to think about studying.'

'That's a shame.'

'It was a lot more important to concentrate on Luke than to indulge myself. I wanted to be a lawyer but I gave up on the idea of having a career.'

'You work, though.'

'Just to put food on the table. I don't love it. No one cares if I run the best card shop in Bromley. They don't think about whether I'm a good manager or not. I can miss a day or two and nothing bad will happen to the shop, prob-ably – I'll pick up where I left off and no one will notice I was gone. But Luke needed me to be there every second of every day, and I did it, and I don't regret it.'

She was self-possessed in a way that I thought was rare – prepared to defend her decisions, devoted to doing the right thing no matter what it cost her.

Claire frowned. 'How is this relevant to what happened to Angela?'

'It's not. Sorry. I just have a habit of asking questions.' I'd been trying to set her at her ease by talking about gen-eralities. And I had my mother's need to put people into context, analysing every twig in their family tree until the subject was exhausted.

'Well, that's your job, isn't it?' She tightened the belt of her dressing gown again. 'I don't mean to be rude, but you did say you'd be quick.'

'Can you tell me what you remember about Angela's death? How did you find out what had happened to her?'

'Shane rang our house at four in the morning to talk to

Vinny. None of us had a mobile phone – funny, isn't it? It doesn't seem like that long ago, but they were still a rarity. So he called up on the house phone and woke half the family.' She paused, remembering. 'You know when you hear a phone ring and you know, even before anyone's answered it, that it's bad news? Yeah. It was like that. No reason for anyone to be calling us then unless it was that someone had died. But I never thought it would be Angela.'

'Did you see her body?'

'No. Of course not.' She looked affronted. 'It was a closed coffin.'

'Did you have any suspicions about who was responsible?'

'I knew it wasn't Josh. Beyond that, no.'

'How did you know?'

'I told you, it couldn't have been him.' She sounded definite. 'He was . . . sweet. Not the brooding type. He had a temper but it was the sort of thing where he'd shout or punch someone and then spend half an hour apologising. If he was upset it blew over quickly. He'd never have strangled her, even if she'd provoked him.'

Something in her voice made me ask, 'Were you and Angela close?'

'Not exactly.'

'But you all hung around together.'

'Vinny and I were like that.' She held up crossed fingers. 'I got on well with Josh and Shane, but they were Vinny's friends first and it took them a while to accept me. I was a tomboy. We were like a bunch of lads together – same sense of humour, same interests. Angela wasn't really part of the gang. Well, she was because Josh wanted her there.'

'But no one else did.'

'Vinny didn't like her. He thought she wasn't right for Josh. He told me she was always trying to flirt with him when Josh wasn't there. She just needed boys to fancy her, I think, so she'd know she was attractive.'

'Did anything happen between them?'

'No. He'd never have touched her because his first loyalty was to Josh. Anyway, he really didn't like her, but we
were stuck with her. Shane was seriously fed up to have
his little sister following us around and I ended up spending more time with him and Vinny while Josh and Angela
went off together. Shane didn't want to see them kissing.
He was the big protective older brother, but then he adored
Josh, so he couldn't really get his head around how he felt
about them being together. Conflicted, you'd have to say.'

'He's not a fan of Josh, even now.'

'Yeah. Well, Shane wasn't the brightest.' She sniffed.
'Vinny was the only one who could really talk to him. Do
you know about Vinny? Do you know he's dead?'

'Shane told me.'

'Such a waste.' Her eyes filled with tears. 'He should
have had kids. He should have been around for a lot longer
than thirty-eight years.'

'He must have liked the army, though, to stay in for so
long. If he died doing what he loved—'

'It's still a waste. Anyway, Vinny was just a creature of
habit. He stayed in the army because he couldn't think of
anything better to do. They fed him and housed him and
sent him to the ends of the earth and he never had to make
any decisions for himself once he'd chosen to join up.'

'But he did choose that life. He'd travelled, hadn't he?
He'd had a chance to see the alternative.'

'He was never going to do anything else once Josh did it.
All he ever wanted was to be like Josh. Shane too.'

'Like *Derwent*?' I couldn't keep the surprise out of my
voice.

'You don't know what he was like.' She shrugged.
'Maybe he's different now. He was . . . he was funny and
mad and everyone wanted to be him, or be with him. There
were people who didn't like him, but all he had to do was
snap his fingers and they'd change their tune. They didn't

like him because he had no time for them, but they wanted him to notice them. He had a real gift for making anyone and everyone fall for him.'

'Did you?' I asked and got a glower.

'We were friends. That's all.'

'And you never thought he was guilty.'

'Never.'

'Did Vinny?'

'No.'

'Did you have any idea who might have been responsible?'

She sighed. 'I thought about it a lot. I talked about it with Vinny. Not Shane – he was too raw about the whole thing. You couldn't say her name or he'd fly off the handle. But Vinny and I – we tried to work out what had happened, and we came up with nothing. I always assumed it was a stranger who happened to see her walking home and followed her, and did whatever he wanted to do.'

'Had you noticed anyone hanging around? Any cars you didn't recognise that you saw more than once, or anyone on foot?'

She shook her head, but then stopped for a moment, staring at the ground. 'There was a guy who got talking to us in the park one night. He said his name was Craig and he was older than us – twenty-eight, he said, but I thought he was shaving a few years off, even though he was wearing pretty trendy clothes. He was trying too hard to look like one of us. You know how teenagers think everyone is ancient, though, so I wouldn't put too much faith in my opinion.'

I was inclined to believe her, all the same. She'd been seventeen, not a child, and if she had thought he was in his thirties she'd probably been right.

Almost to herself, she said, 'Funny – I didn't think anything of it at the time, but now I'm wondering why he wanted to hang out with a bunch of teenagers.'

I was writing it down, knowing that it was probably going to be a dead end. At least it was new information. 'Can you remember anything else about him?'

'He had really good gear.' She grinned and I saw a flash of the tomboy who'd been best friends with Derwent. It was only for an instant, though, and then her expression turned serious. 'Not much else. He was really interested in us – the girls, that is. He sat between me and Angela and asked us about school and boyfriends. He seemed nice, not creepy. That was about ten days before it happened.'

'And did you see him again before Angela died?'

'Around town, once. Not to talk to. He waved.'

'And after?'

'Never. He said he was just passing through. He was heading south.'

'To where?'

'France, he said. On from there. He wasn't planning on settling anywhere.'

'Could you describe him?'

'Tall. Long neck – he had a really prominent Adam's apple. White. Brown hair.' She shrugged. 'That's really all I remember. I don't think I could describe him in more detail.'

'What about a photofit?'

'No. I don't remember the shape of his face, even.'

'If I showed you some pictures, would you be able to pick him out?'

'I really doubt it.' She saw the look on my face. 'It's not that I don't want to help. It was a long time ago, and it was dark, and we were high. I'd forgotten it, you know?'

'Did you mention him to the police at the time?'

'No. I'd never have said anything to an adult about smoking drugs.' She shifted her position. 'I wouldn't get too excited about it. He was probably lying about his name and his age, if he was the killer. And if he wasn't he was just some sad sack who you'll never trace.'

'You could be right, but it's a start. Can you remember if he told you anything else about himself?'

'He said he'd been up north but it was too cold for him there. He said he could speak French but it was rubbish – he just knew a few phrases and busked the rest. Angela and I took the piss out of him all evening. But he didn't talk about himself all that much. He was more interested in us. And we were flattered, I suppose, and young enough to talk about ourselves a lot and think that was all right.' She coughed for a long time. 'Speaking of talking a lot, this is killing my voice.'

'I know. I'm sorry. I'll go soon.' I hesitated. 'Is it all right to come back if I think of anything else?'

'Sure. But alone. Not with Josh.'

'I'll respect your wishes, I promise.'

'Thanks.' She rammed a knuckle under one eye, catching a tear before it spilled over. 'I don't expect you to understand but I left that part of my life behind a long time ago. And I wouldn't want him to see me like this. Not having achieved anything with my life except turning into a hag.'

'I don't think that's what he'd see, for what it's worth.' But I could hear Derwent's voice in my head. *Shit, she's got old. How hard is it to slap on a bit of moisturiser now and then?*

'Is he married?'

I shook my head.

'Girlfriend?'

'Not this week, as far as I know.'

She sighed. 'Do you know him well?'

'I work with him a lot. I wouldn't say I know him well. He's senior to me.' *And he's a wanker, so . . .* 'We're not really friends. It's a working relationship.'

'Is he good at his job?'

'Very,' I said, without having to think about it.

'Is he still funny?' She sounded wistful.

'He has a unique sense of humour,' I said truthfully. 'He's not like anyone else I know.' *Thank God.*

She nodded. 'Sorry for asking you about him. I'm just curious. I don't want to see him but I'd like to know how he turned out. Don't tell him I asked.'

'I won't.'

She followed me to the door and watched me walk to my car. Her expression was worried and I knew she didn't trust me.

Over the time I'd spent in Bromley my bad mood had faded to mild melancholy. There was no one else to hear, so I tuned the radio to a Golden Oldies station and crooned along to love songs all the traffic-clogged way back.

MONDAY

Chapter 21

I'd done the Parsons an injustice. My mobile rang before I'd even left the flat the following morning. In contrast to his wife, David Parsons couldn't have sounded more eager to be helpful.

'Sorry for calling you so early but the wife said it was urgent. I've got a number for Stu Sinclair but it's not a landline and I don't know where he lives.'

'Mobile will do,' I said, scrambling for a pen. He read out the numbers slowly, checking that I'd got it right by making me read it back to him.

'You'll probably have to leave a message because he never answers it but he's pretty quick to get in touch usually.'

'Thanks for your help.'

'He's not in trouble, is he? Only we were wondering. The wife said it was a murder investigation you were looking into.' Curiosity, raw and undisguised. I kept the smile out of my voice.

'It's an old case and he was a key witness, that's all. I do need to speak to him, though, so I'm very grateful.'

'Any time.' He sounded as if he meant it too.

I hung up wondering how two people could have such different personalities and yet be married. As he had promised, there was no answer from Stuart Sinclair's number but I left a message on his voicemail. The office was where I needed to be anyway; the paperwork had been piling up and I had a few phone calls to make. Once again, I found myself thinking about Derwent's criticism of my failure to keep up with briefings. I wished I could point out to him that my current problem was investigating his girlfriend's death in my spare time.

Before I left the flat I hesitated over the window in the sitting room, which was open a few inches. With Rob gone, and since I was out all the time, I'd noticed the flat was developing a stale smell. I'd checked the fridge for horrors and emptied the kitchen bin but there was still an unpleasant undertone to the atmosphere. We were too high up to be afraid of burglars but I still didn't want to take the risk and leave it open – locking all the doors and windows was part of the security routine that left me able to sleep at night. I slammed it in the end and double-locked it. Smells I could deal with; my own fears were not so easy to tolerate.

I got my head down to work once I got into the office. It was after eleven before Stuart Sinclair got back to me and it took me a second to change gears when the phone rang. I sounded vague rather than competent.

'Oh. Right. Yes, it was regarding—'

He interrupted. 'You rang me, originally. I hope you know what it was about because I haven't got a clue.'

I was used to Derwent; Stu Sinclair didn't stand a chance of flustering me. 'As I was saying, I would like to interview you regarding the witness statement you made in 1992 about the murder of Angela Poole.'

I heard him blow out a lungful of breath. 'Going back a bit. I was just a kid then. Any particular reason why this is urgent now?'

If he had been more pleasant I might have told him it was connected to the recent murders. 'I've been carrying out a review of the case file and there are some anomalies. I'd like to speak with you in person. Today, preferably.'

He sounded borderline scared when he replied, which was good: it was the reaction a normal person should have to being involved in a murder investigation. Something had told me the hard-arse routine was a fake. 'Oh, okay. It was a long time ago and I don't remember everything in as much detail as I did then, obviously, but if you think it would help, I'll try. I'm actually looking after my kid this afternoon so if you don't mind interviewing me with a toddler running around, you could come to my house.'

'That's fine. What's the address?'

'Eighty-two Danbury Road, West Norwood. That's SE27.'

'I know the area,' I said, writing it down. 'Two o'clock?'

He hesitated. 'Make it half past. And I can't let you stay for long, I'm afraid. If it's going to take longer than half an hour or so, we'll have to rearrange it.'

'I'll be quick,' I said, meaning it. I had a short list of questions for Stuart Sinclair, but they were important, and I'd have promised him the moon and stars if it meant I could see him sooner rather than later.

Danbury Road was a terrace of Victorian houses, but not the grand, four-storey kind – the narrow ones built by the hundreds and thousands for high-ranking clerks and managers with small families. Roads like it snaked through London's outer suburbs, the late Victorian middle-class desire for a bathroom and garden manifested in red brick. Norwood had never been fashionable and Danbury Road was indefinably shabby, but quiet. Lots of families with small children, I thought, noticing pushchairs parked in the bay windows of several houses as I walked to number 82.

Without giving it too much thought I was expecting to see a grown-up version of Fat Stu, the buck-toothed unfortunate Derwent had described to me, so when a dark-haired, well-built man opened the door I immediately assumed I'd got the wrong address. His first words made it clear that I was in the right place.

'Bang on time. I'm impressed, DC Kerrigan.'

'Mr Sinclair?'

'None other. Come in.' He stood back and I hurried into the narrow, dark hallway where a jumble of wellies and tiny shoes told me the house was run for and by the child who lived there.

'He's still having his nap,' Sinclair explained in a low voice. 'We might be able to talk uninterrupted.'

I nodded and followed him into a heroically untidy sitting room, with wall-to-wall toys littering the floor and a pile of sofa cushions in the corner.

'Sorry. We were playing hide and seek after lunch.' He started dismantling the stack and I muttered something about there being no need to tidy up, distracted by his appearance. It wasn't the muscles flexing in his forearms or his lean, gym-honed torso that made me stare as he rearranged the room. It was more the fact that, like Shane Poole, he had conformed to the Derwent template as he grew into adulthood. I tried to work out what made them look similar. He was better-looking than Derwent but his hair was cut the same way and his clothes were the sort Derwent wore off duty, as I now knew. He had a very white, very perfect smile, an ad for his orthodontist if what Derwent had said was true. Despite the resemblance to Derwent I thought he was attractive – a handsome face with blue eyes, a square jaw and a straight nose. He turned around at just the wrong moment and caught me staring: I deserved the smirk I got. I sat down on the restored sofa and took my time over getting my notebook out, spending ages looking for my pen although I knew exactly where it was. Derwent would never let me live it down if I let Stuart Sinclair get the upper hand, I thought, and sat up a little bit straighter.

'Thank you for agreeing to see me at such short notice.'

'Glad to help,' he said, sitting down in an armchair and propping his right ankle on top of his left knee. I could hear Derwent's opinion of that: *only a total plonker sits like that, Kerrigan, no matter how pretty he may be.* He wore thick-soled boots and I wondered if he was sensitive about his height. He was a shade shorter than me – five nine to my five eleven, a difference that was negligible when he was wearing such heavy boots. Far from small, anyway, but I remembered Derwent's description of him and while diet and exercise could put manners on your genetic heritage, height was pretty difficult to change. Being tall myself I couldn't quite understand why anyone would care; it wasn't all that amazing to be leggy.

Quickly, I filled him in on the possible connection between Angela Poole and the three current murders. Each victim got a two-second look from under eyebrows twisted with pity, but no reaction beyond that.

'And what makes you think there's a connection?' He handed the three pictures back to me.

'The MO. That's modus operandi.'

'I know. I watch a lot of crime dramas.' A big grin. 'Bet you avoid them.'

'Like the plague. I don't know how much you remember about Angela's death—'

'More than I thought,' he said promptly. 'I've been thinking about it since you called. It's all coming back.'

'Great. Because you're one of the only people who might have seen Angela's killer, and I was wondering if you'd managed to recall anything that you didn't tell the police at the time.'

He shook his head. 'I told them, and I'm telling you now, I saw her boyfriend walking off, just after midnight. Something woke me up a few minutes before that – must have been the poor girl screaming, I suppose.'

There was something dispassionate about how he spoke about her, especially compared to Derwent's raw grief.

It had been a long time since she died, though. 'Did you know her? Angela?'

'She was the girl next door. I knew about her more than I knew her.'

'Did you have a crush on her?' I saw him look surprised for the first time and explained what I'd meant. 'Because she was the girl next door. That's what's supposed to happen, isn't it?'

'I don't remember that.' He smiled. 'Anyway, she wouldn't have looked twice at me. I was short and fat and ugly. And as I said, she had her boyfriend. The one the police wouldn't arrest for killing her.'

'He had an alibi.'

'That must have been wrong. He did it. I saw him.' His eyes were unwavering. He sounded sure and I had to resist the urge to argue with him, to defend Derwent.

'What exactly did you see? When you got up, before twelve – did you see anything in the garden?'

'No. Or hear anything. It was summer and my window was open. I leaned out, didn't hear anything, gave up. That's why I went back to bed.'

'And then . . .'

'I got worried. I thought I'd go and look out of another window.'

'At the front.'

'Yeah.'

'That's the main bedroom, isn't it? Your parents' room?'

'My mum's. My dad had left us.' A flash of the white teeth. 'I've got over it now, but I missed him at the time.'

'So you went in and looked out.'

'Yeah.'

'And she was in bed, asleep, or . . .'

'I don't remember.' He raised his eyebrows. 'You're very interested in the details, aren't you?'

There was no easy way to say it. 'I don't believe you really did look out of the window upstairs at the front.'

'Are you calling me a liar?' His voice was still pleasant but his fingers were digging into the uppermost leg, his knuckles white.

'I think you've told the story so often you almost believe it yourself, but you didn't see anyone walking away at a minute after twelve. You didn't like Angela's boyfriend and you wanted him to get into trouble, so you said you'd seen him. You didn't know about his alibi, and once you'd said it, you had to keep saying it.'

He was shaking his head. 'No. Wrong.'

'He was mean to you, wasn't he? He bullied you. Called you names. You had a massive grudge against him but you were scared of him and this was your chance to get him into trouble like you couldn't believe. You were fifteen – you probably didn't even realise how serious it was and that the last thing you should do was lie.'

'Oh, spare me the psychology.' His face was red now. 'I saw someone and I thought it was Josh Derwent. It looked like Josh Derwent.'

'In what way?'

'He was tall. Moved fast. He – I don't know. I was expecting it to be Josh. I thought it was him.' He looked at me again, back to the wide-eyed sincerity. 'I really thought it was him.'

'Thinking again, can you add anything to the description that you didn't say before?'

'Nope.'

'You'd seen Der— Josh Derwent earlier in the evening. Did you describe the clothes you'd seen him wearing? Or was the person you saw really wearing the same colour T-shirt as Josh Derwent and similar jeans? Could you tell, in the streetlight, when he was walking away from you at speed?'

'Okay. Okay. You're right. I just saw a silhouette, really. He might have been wearing black. Dark colours, anyway.' Stuart touched a hand to his upper lip and looked at it. 'I'm actually sweating. You're pretty good at this, aren't you?'

'I do all right.'

'But you gave something away. You started to call him by his surname. You know him, don't you? Josh Derwent? He's a copper, I know that much. Are you mates?' He waited a beat. 'Lovers?'

'I know him. I work with him sometimes. But I'm here because my guv'nor wanted me to find out about Angela's death, not because of Derwent.'

'You must get asked that a lot. If you're in a relationship with him, I mean.'

'Surprisingly often,' I agreed. 'Especially since he's not my type.' The understatement of the decade.

'I'll do you the courtesy of believing you if you'll do the same for me. I really did think I saw him. I wouldn't have been able to keep lying about it.' He shuddered. 'I'd almost forgotten that guy – Orpen, his name was. He was a beast. A real old-fashioned copper. I was terrified every time he spoke to me. He always seemed to be trying to stop himself from lashing out. Met him?'

'A pleasure that awaits me,' I said with a smile.

'You're in for a treat.' He checked his watch. 'Wow. Time marches on. Is there anything else?'

I ran through my usual questions about seeing strangers or strange cars, to which he replied in the negative.

'Do you recall anything else from that night? Even after the body was discovered? The noise and lights must have disturbed you.'

'They must have. I don't really remember.'

I found that very hard to believe, but then I had been fascinated by the police and their work since I was about five. A murder next door would have been more entertaining than the best soap opera. 'Did you see the police? The ambulance?'

'Yeah. I did.'

'What about Angela's body?'

'No.' He looked edgy. 'Why do you ask?'

'There are similarities in the crime scenes we've been processing. It looks as if someone familiar with how Angela's body was left is perpetrating these crimes. I'm just trying to work out how many people could have seen her there. But you said you couldn't see anything from the window.'

'No.' He pulled at his lip. 'Is this important?'

'Very. Do you know if there were photographs circulating in school, or outside it? Were you aware of people talking about it, even?'

'No. But . . .' He went into the hall and came back with a brown leather messenger bag, an expensive man bag that Derwent would have described, instantly and implacably, as gay, and would not have meant that as a compliment. He took out a battered iPad and tapped at the screen before handing it to me. 'If you want to know who's seen Angela's body, you'd better see this.'

I stared at it, not understanding for a second. There, filling the entire screen, was the close-up of Angela's face that I'd seen in the file, her hair caught up in flowers, her eyelids drawn down over empty sockets. 'What the *fuck*?'

Instead of an answer a long, miserable wail cut through the air and I jumped.

'It's the monitor. Oliver's up.' Stuart picked up a white handset and poked at it until the noise stopped. 'Thank God for mute.'

In the distance there was a faint shadow of a scream, coming from the top of the house.

'Do you think you should go and get him?' I asked.

'Probably.' He was still staring at me, trying to read me. 'You know what that is, don't you?'

'A crime-scene picture of Angela Poole.'

'Scroll down. There's more. I could not believe it when I saw it. I'm sure you feel the same way.'

I did as he suggested, distracted by the crying from

241

upstairs. It was getting louder and more high-pitched by the second. 'How did you find this? What is this website?'

'It's a blog called Crime-scene Shots. I'd never heard of it. After we spoke I was thinking about Angela and I don't know, I just thought I should search for her name online to see if there had been any developments I didn't know about, and *that* came up.'

I swore under my breath as pictures slipped down the screen, images I hadn't even seen in the file. 'Anyone could have seen this.'

'Anyone with access to the Internet,' Stuart agreed. Reluctantly, he edged towards the door. 'Better go up.'

'Yeah, I'll wait.'

'Well.' He checked his watch again. 'It's just that my wife will be coming back, and I didn't tell her you were going to be here.'

'I'm good at explaining things,' I said, not moving.

'I don't want to have to tell her about Angela. It's history. Nothing to do with who I am now.'

'I'll be gone in five minutes,' I promised and he looked as if he was about to say something else, but then changed his mind and left. I heard him taking the stairs two at a time.

He was back quickly, holding a red-headed boy of about fourteen months with his thumb lodged in his mouth. The child was wearing a vest and nappy and still had tears on his cheeks, which were flushed. *Teething,* I thought, remembering my nieces and their misery as the incredibly sharp baby teeth cut through their gums.

'Is he all right?'

'Fine.'

'Is it his molars? They're awfully sore when they're coming through.'

Stuart shrugged. 'Could be. It's always something.' The boy was leaning away from him and he bent down to let him stand on the floor. 'There you go, Oliver. Find a toy. Plenty of them about.'

Oliver looked at me, then turned around to check the rest of the room. Finding no one else, he collapsed to the floor and gave an anguished howl.

'Missing Mummy,' Stuart said over the noise. 'I definitely come second compared to her. Was there anything else?'

'Do you remember anyone behaving differently after Angela's death? Erratic behaviour, seeming upset, or changing their routine?'

'Yeah. One person. Josh Derwent.' He shook his head. 'I know you don't want to hear this, but I still think he was guilty.'

'If he was, there would have been some evidence to prove it.'

'He had an answer for everything. He made up a story and got away with it, but he killed her.' On the floor, Oliver was coughing and crying alternately, snot running down his upper lip in two grey-green rivers. Stuart bent down to him and ruffled his hair. 'Come on, Oliver. Belt up. She'll be back soon.'

'If you think of anything else—'

'I'll call.' He snatched the card I held out to him and shoved it in his back pocket. 'Right. I'll show you out.'

He left Oliver in his puddle of misery and disappeared into the hall. I couldn't just walk past him. I crouched down beside the boy.

'It's all right. Your mummy will be back soon. Daddy will play with you once I'm gone.'

Oliver stared at me, his face blank. I dug in my bag for a tissue and swiped it across his face, heaving slightly as I folded the soggy tissue up. There was no bin in sight so I had to put it back in my bag and I hoped like hell I'd remember it was there before I went looking for something and put my hand in it.

Stuart was standing in the hall, impatience obvious on his face. When he saw me emerge from the sitting room he opened the door. No long goodbyes, then.

As I stepped onto the doorstep, a small dark-haired woman was striding up the front path, neat in a grey suit and carrying a briefcase. She stared at me, then looked past me to Stuart.

'What's going on?'

'She's just leaving.'

'Who are you?' There was a cry from inside the house and her attention switched to Stuart before I could answer. She was already moving past me. 'Was that Oliver? Is he okay? When did he wake up?'

'Just now.'

'Shit. I thought he'd sleep for another half-hour at least.' She turned and glowered at me again. 'Who are you? Did you say?'

'Jehovah's Witness,' came from behind her and I saw Stuart pulling a face, like *what could I do?* 'I did try to discourage her.'

'I don't do God,' the woman said to me. 'Stu, honestly. I leave you alone for an hour and you let random people into the house. You're hopeless.'

'You know me. I can't be rude.' Over her head he widened his eyes at me. *Go away.*

I walked off without saying anything to back him up or undermine him. Behind me, I heard Stuart ask, 'How was the interview?' The door closed before I could hear a reply. It made sense that he wasn't usually left in sole charge of Oliver. He really didn't seem used to the messy end of parenting. Typical dad, loving the toys and games, hating the snot and nappies, I thought, and couldn't suppress the thought that the fair-weather dads had the right idea. Wiping snotty noses was not my idea of fun.

I hoped Stuart didn't get into too much trouble. If I'd been his wife I would have known he was lying, and I'd have been going through him for a short cut at that very moment. Maybe it was easier to pretend she believed him, given that they had a child. Maybe she didn't even care that he'd been alone with a relatively nice-looking woman, or that he was prepared to try to mislead her about it.

Or maybe I was vastly overrating my personal attractiveness. It wasn't my favourite option, but it was probably the most likely.

TUESDAY

Chapter 22

I sat in the car waiting for a traffic light to change to green and wished myself absolutely elsewhere. I'd have been nervous enough about interviewing Lionel Orpen, Detective Inspector (retired) on my own. Having to take Derwent along was positively the last straw.

'Tell me again what he said.'

'He told me to bring you with me. He said he wanted to see how you'd turned out, and he wanted to tell you some things about the investigation that he'd never told anyone else.' I was beyond bored now with repeating my phone conversation with the retired police officer. Gruff wasn't the word for his phone manner. Once I'd explained who I was, all he wanted to know was whether I knew Derwent.

'And then?' Derwent prompted.

'And then he said he wouldn't talk to me at all unless you came with me.' I shot a glance at him. 'Happy now?'

'Intrigued.' He grinned. 'Glad to be back in the saddle.'

'You're not. That's why you're not driving.' The car tore away from the lights and I braked, then bit my lip. The accelerator needed to be practically on the floor before the car would move and it was easy to misjudge it. Easy for me, as Derwent had said two minutes after I picked him up. A *normal* driver would have been fine, apparently.

'Remember, you mustn't tell anyone you were with me. I'm supposed to be doing this on my own.'

'You need someone to hold your hand, Kerrigan. Firstly, because Lionel is fucking scary. Secondly, because you let Fat Stu run rings around you. *And* Shaney.'

I hadn't told him I'd seen Claire; I hadn't even mentioned her name. Undoubtedly I would have got that interview wrong too, somehow. Derwent was the worst kind of back-seat driver and not just in the car. I was glad to have him along if it made Lionel Orpen more forthcoming but I was seriously considering dumping him by the side of the nearest main road on my way back.

'Remember, I'm not telling Godley you came with me today. If you let it slip, I'll get in a ton of trouble.'

'Relax,' Derwent said, opening the window and sticking his elbow out. Icy wind blasted across my face, blowing my hair into my eyes.

'Hey! Shut it.'

'I need air.'

'It's like having a dog. Do I need to take you for a walk before the interview or do you think you can wait until afterwards?'

'Very funny,' he said, without shutting it. I gritted my teeth and concentrated on getting to Kensal Rise, where Lionel Orpen was living out his retirement in a small ter-raced house.

There was nowhere to park on Orpen's street so I drove around the corner and left the car beside a small park with a playground. The day was cool but bright and the park was busy with mothers and small children, who were running around shouting at top volume. I thought of Oliver Sinclair and wondered if Stuart would be allowed to look after him on his own again after letting a strange woman into the house.

Derwent squinted across the top of the car looking pained. 'Do they have to make so much noise?'

'It's a key part of having a good time when you're little.'

Two small boys ran past us on the other side of the railings, scuffling with one another.

'Give them fifteen years and they'll be being arrested for fighting outside pubs after closing time.'

'Well, that won't be your problem any more. You'll be retired by then,' I said.

He pulled a face. 'Not quite. Anyway, they'll have extended retirement age to seventy to save on pensions. Or I'll keep working for free. I'm not exactly thrilled at the thought of doing fuck all every day for the rest of my life.'

'I don't think fuck all is obligatory. You could find something worthwhile to do.'

'What sort of thing could I do? What else would I want to do? The crossword?' He snorted. 'Come on. Let's go and see how it's done.'

Good policeman or not, Lionel Orpen was no poster boy for retirement. He opened his door and peered out at us suspiciously, two days of stubble frosting flabby thread-veined cheeks. He'd been a big man in his time but now his clothes hung off his body, apart from where a substantial gut pushed against the thin wool of his jumper. Even before I smelled the alcohol on his breath I knew he was a drinker. It was half past ten and he was weaving as he led us into a living room piled high with newspapers and books.

'Excuse the mess. I'm writing my memoirs. This lot is the raw material. Sources, and such.' He sat down in a threadbare armchair by the gas fire, leaving us to find somewhere to put ourselves. Derwent perched on the arm of the sofa, which was loaded with yellowing magazines and otherwise unusable. I stood near the door, not wanting to touch anything. The house smelled of mildew and I was afraid to disturb any of the piles in case something jumped out at me. A movement at the back of the room made me whirl around, my heart thumping.

'Gave you a fright, did he?' Orpen patted his lap and

a cat threaded his way through the stacks of books, uttering low cries. It was a round-faced tom with tattered ears and a scarred nose. It jumped up on Orpen's knee and he scratched it under the chin. 'Poor old Rudolf.'

'As in the reindeer?' Derwent asked.

'As in Hess.'

Derwent glanced at me and I could see what he was thinking. *Oh, here we go . . .*

'You're wondering why I named him after a Nazi. Well, he reminded me of him. He used to be free – I fed him now and then, when he came into the garden. He had a great life, fighting and screwing and chasing rats. Then he got picked up by the do-gooders next door and taken to a rehoming centre, as if anyone would want him. He was on death row when I found out where he'd gone. I got there in time to save him but he'd been de-balled. The way he looked at me, through the bars of the cage – it was Hess at Spandau all over again.'

'Oh. That's—'

Orpen interrupted Derwent. 'You didn't come here to talk about Rudy. You came to talk about Angela. Don't bullshit me. I spent long enough doing the job you're trying to pretend you're capable of doing.'

'All right.' Derwent shifted position on the arm of the sofa. 'Tell us about Angela.'

'You first. What made you join the Met?'

'It seemed like a good career.'

'Bollocks. The truth.'

'I wanted to help people.'

'You're wasting my time.'

'I wanted to fuck up the people who think they can do what they want with other people's lives.'

Orpen's eyes lit up. 'That's what I liked about you, Joshua. You understood what we were trying to do.'

'You were trying to fit me up for murdering Angela,' Derwent said with commendable restraint.

'It was obviously you. All the evidence pointed to you. Except that you couldn't have done it.' He gave a rattling, wet cough. 'We put Charlie Poole under plenty of pressure to take back his statement but he wouldn't. Said it wasn't fair. He wanted justice, not revenge on you for putting his darling daughter in the wrong place at the wrong time.'

'He was a good man.'

'Oh, do you think so?' Orpen leaned back in his chair to let the cat surge up his chest and lie against his shoulder. 'He had no love for you.'

'Not surprising. Men tend to have trouble with their daughters' boyfriends.'

'He thought you were a fool.'

'He was probably right.' Derwent smiled. 'I was a teenager.'

'You weren't the worst. Not as clever as you thought you were, but cleverer than most.' Another cough. 'I knew you joined the army, you know. I kept in touch with your social worker. Found out when you left and decided to become a police officer.'

'I'm flattered.' Sarcasm was so much a habit with Derwent that I couldn't tell if he meant it or not.

'Don't be. I kept track of a few lads. The ones I couldn't lock up, for whatever reason. Some of them turned into killers and rapists, just as I'd thought, and got sent down. Some of them got on the straight and narrow. You're the only one who joined the Met, I'll tell you that much.'

'I'm not surprised. You weren't the best example I could have had.'

'I. Did. My. Job.' He slammed his hand down on the arm of his chair, his face livid with rage, and I actually stepped back even though he wasn't speaking to me. The cat took offence and jumped off, sliding under the chair instead. Orpen was depleted now, a shadow of what he had been in his prime. It must have been truly terrifying to be interviewed by him when he was in the full vigour of middle age.

Derwent folded his arms, outwardly unmoved. 'Yeah, but you didn't. Because you never locked anyone up for Angela's death. Who did you like for it, apart from me?'

'The dad, initially. That went nowhere. The two of you cancelled each other out, didn't you? Alibied each other.' Orpen burped, loudly, and went on as if he hadn't. 'The local troublemakers. We had a couple of sex offenders who were living nearby who seemed right, but then there wasn't a sexual assault.'

'Why do you think that was?' I asked, too interested to stay silent.

'Dunno. Maybe he lost his nerve. Couldn't get it up. Got disturbed and ran off.' He looked at Derwent with a glint in his eye. 'Didn't fancy sloppy seconds.'

I saw it hit home. It was only the smallest shift in his posture but it was a giveaway nonetheless and Orpen didn't miss it either.

'Still sad about her, aren't you? Still wish you'd walked her home.'

Derwent was the last person to need rescuing, usually, but in this instance he seemed defenceless and I found myself stepping forward to stand beside him.

'Mr Orpen, I spoke to Stuart Sinclair yesterday. He admitted he'd lied to you in his original witness statements.'

'About seeing this fellow?' Orpen pointed a long, wrinkled finger at Derwent. 'I knew that. He was a real mummy's boy. His mother kept her door locked at night to stop him from coming into her room.'

'Fucking hell,' Derwent said. 'You mean—'

'Not like that.' Orpen raised a hand to stop Derwent from going on. 'Don't get too excited. The Sinclair marriage had split up earlier that year. Stuart was going through a bad time and he'd stopped sleeping. He wandered around the house all night. Drove his mother mad. She didn't want him bothering her.'

'So he didn't see anything from the front window,' I said. 'No.'

'And you knew he was lying at the time.'

'Yeah, but he wouldn't budge. Said he'd seen what he'd seen.'

'Did you go into his bedroom?' I asked. 'What sort of view did he have of the garden next door?'

Orpen's face went slack and he gazed into the corner of the room, trying to remember. 'He could see a bit, I think. His room was on the left at the back.'

'Could he have seen Angela with her killer from his bedroom?'

'He said he didn't.'

'He lied about seeing Derwent,' I pointed out.

'There was a tree in that corner of the garden. It was in full leaf. He wouldn't have been able to see much, if anything.'

I thought about it, trying to imagine myself there. A sleepless fifteen-year-old, attracted by the noise of a scuffle, seeing movement under the trees. Assuming it was the girl next door and her boyfriend. Assuming they were having sex, there and then, only feet from him. And he hated Derwent. Certainly enough to want to disturb them.

'You know who didn't have an alibi?' Orpen was watching Derwent again, his expression wry. 'Your mate. What was his name? Vinny. He said he was with Shane, but it was bullshit.'

'Why didn't you arrest them?' I asked.

'No evidence.' He sucked his teeth. 'And Shane *did* have an alibi in the end. Some girl he wasn't supposed to be seeing. That's why he lied. He dragged Vinny into it to back him up – that was their story.'

'So Shane was out. But why didn't you arrest Vinny?' I asked.

'I wanted to. It was just a hunch, though. No evidence. I interviewed him twice and didn't get anywhere. Got told to back off by my boss because he was a juvenile and his parents were getting antsy.'

'Who was the girl?' Derwent demanded.

'Now you're asking me.' He went looking through a stack of papers by his chair, wetting his thumb the better to flick through them. 'Here we are. Claire Naylor. You should talk to that Vinny again. Find out if he knows anything about these killings you're investigating.'

Derwent didn't say anything. He was staring into space. I assumed it was too hard for him to tell Orpen what had happened to Vinny, in the end. He had walked away from me when I told him – just turned and left before I could say I was sorry.

'Vinny died, Mr Orpen. In Afghanistan,' I said.

'So he's probably not your killer, then.'

'Probably not.'

'He wouldn't have hurt Angela.' Derwent had recovered. 'No way.'

'Well, someone did. And you asked me what I thought, and that's what I thought.'

'Do you remember if you showed the crime-scene pictures to many people when you were doing interviews? Do you recall who saw them?'

Orpen winced. 'Bit of a sore point, the pictures. We lost a set.'

'What do you mean, lost them?' Derwent demanded.

'They went missing. They were in the police station, on a desk, and someone misplaced them.'

'Or they were stolen,' I said.

'Who'd want to do that?' Orpen asked. 'Anyway, why are you asking me about them?'

I explained about the website Stuart had shown me, and the relevance to our murders. Orpen shrugged.

'Can't help you. Didn't know who nicked them at the

time and I'm certainly not going to be able to tell you now. Any more questions?'

'Just one,' I said quickly. 'Do you recall any intel coming in on a guy called Craig? He was passing through the area around the time of Angela's death.'

'First name or last name?'

'No idea.'

'Description?'

I told him what Claire had told me and he shook his head. 'Where did you get that?'

'I came across the name,' I said vaguely.

'Never heard of him before. And good luck with tracking him down twenty years on.'

'Thanks.'

Orpen nodded at me. 'She's a bright one, Joshua.'

'Never thought you'd fall for a pretty face,' Derwent said, dismissing me as usual.

'Not my type. Too tall. But she's got something.'

'Yeah. Ears.' I glared at the pair of them. 'Can you stop talking about me as if I'm not here?'

'Take it as a compliment, lovely.' The old police officer gave a wheezing laugh that degenerated into a cough.

Derwent turned so Orpen couldn't see his face and looked from me to the door. I took the hint and said goodbye, leaving Derwent behind. He joined me on the doorstep a few minutes later and blew his nose.

'Good to go?' I asked.

'Yeah. I am.' He set off towards the car and I hurried after him.

'Are you okay?'

'Of course. Got dust in my sinuses. That place is a health hazard.' He blew his nose again, and took the opportunity to wipe his eyes. 'Oh, fuck it. I must be getting soft.'

A lorry with a skip on the back of it blasted past, taking the speed bumps along the road far too fast. The skip flew into the air and thumped back down after every bump. I waited until it had gone by, with a thud and a crack that sounded like a gunshot, before I tried to ask anything else.

'What did he say to you?'

'He told me he was proud of how I'd turned out.'

'Aw. That's nice.'

'Don't,' Derwent said, shaking his head. 'Just don't.'

'I knew you were sentimental but that's astonishing. I bet he never made you cry when he was interrogating you.'

'You're right, he didn't.' Derwent sniffed. 'Don't tell anyone about this. Ever.'

'You're not here, remember?' I took out the car keys. 'So no one will ever know.'

We turned the corner so the park came into view. The children were still screaming, sounding shriller than ever. I glanced across at the playground, about to make some remark to Derwent about it, and stopped. I was aware of him pausing too, looking in the same direction. Something was wrong, I thought, trying to work out what it could be. I couldn't see any of the children or mothers at first, just a lot of abandoned prams and buggies, but I could see a man standing in the middle of the park, all in black.

And as he turned towards us I saw the gun in his hand.

Derwent and I started running at the same time. Towards, not away.

It didn't occur to either of us to do anything else.

Chapter 23

Being fitter and quicker, Derwent got ahead of me, but not by much. I sank down behind the car nearest the park gate, a couple of seconds after he had done the same thing.

'Stay here. Call it in. Tell them to send SO19.'

'I won't need to tell them to do that,' I said, not unreasonably. A gunman in a playground would get every resource available to the Met. I had my phone out and was dialling already. Derwent turned and prepared to move.

'Hey,' I hissed. 'Where do you think you're going?'

'I'm not going to stay here and wait for him to start killing kids.'

'And what do you propose to do about it? Talk him to death? You're not armed.' I got through to the police control room before I could say anything else to Derwent and he took advantage of that to dart out from behind the car and slide through the gate. I moved along a bit further, still crouching, still on the phone, so I could keep him in view, see the gunman, and monitor the distance between the two of them. It was not enough and narrowing all the time.

And then Derwent whistled, a jaunty two notes to attract the man's attention.

'All right, fella? Lovely day for it.'

The gunman turned, his free hand stretched out towards Derwent as a warning. 'Go away.'

He was older than I'd thought – forty, at a guess. White.

Fair hair, thinning a bit. Deep lines scored his forehead and bracketed his mouth. Staring eyes: I could see white all around the irises even from where I was lurking. The gun was rock-steady in his right hand, though.

'Come on, mate. You don't want to wave one of those around.' Hands in his pockets, Derwent was walking towards him, slowly but inexorably. The gunman stepped back a pace.

'Fuck off, *mate*. This is none of your business.'

'What's the problem? What's going on?'

Through his teeth, the man hissed, 'I was looking for my bitch wife and my little boy.'

In my ear, the operator was repeating all I'd told her and checking the address, her voice calm and nasal. I was riveted to the scene in front of me.

'We'll get backup to you ASAP. Trojans are on the way. ASU is lifting. Stay on the line.'

I wasn't going to argue with her but I needed both hands. I put the phone in my jacket pocket, still on so she could hear what was happening, and moved forward to the gate. Derwent was about thirty feet away from me, getting closer to the gunman and, crucially, his weapon. Beyond him, I could see a group of about ten women and maybe fifteen children, huddled together in a tight group. They were looking at Derwent as if he was their only hope.

'The two of you not getting on?'

'We split up. A couple of months ago. She threw me out.'

Derwent tutted. 'What's your name, fella?'

'Lee.'

'This isn't going to help, is it, Lee? You don't want your little boy seeing you with a gun, do you? Not for real.'

'I don't know where he is.' Lee swung back to face the group of children and women, waving the gun in their direction. 'They won't tell me.'

'Maybe he's not here. Maybe he's gone home.'

'Not without his mother.' A ghastly grin. 'She's not going anywhere.'

I saw it at the same time as Derwent: a body lying on the ground. From my angle, all I could see was a pair of legs in skinny jeans and flat brown leather boots. They weren't moving. She was lying on her front, just beside a brightly coloured climbing frame in the shape of a giraffe.

'What did you do, Lee?' Derwent's voice was sharp. 'Did you shoot her?'

'Sometimes you've got to stop talking and start doing. She never listened. I warned her about it and she never changed. Anyway, what do you care?' He held up the gun again, pointing it straight at Derwent's chest. 'Fucking stop moving or I'll shoot you too. I told you before, go away.'

'Not going to happen, mate.' But Derwent had stopped. 'I'm not going anywhere. She needs help and you need to put the gun down.'

'I want my son. That bitch took him away from me. She poisoned his mind against me. She made him say he didn't want to see me. Me! His daddy.' Lee was shaking his head, incredulous. 'It broke my heart. If no one's going to listen to me, and people like me, it's time to take control. It's time to do something that can't be ignored.'

'This isn't the right way to go about getting him back,' Derwent said. 'This is going to fuck up your chances some-thing chronic unless you stop shooting and start thinking. Give me the gun and let's get an ambulance for the lady.'

'She's a whore and she deserved what she got.'

I was close enough now to see that the weapon was not a handgun, which made sense because they were illegal and hard to come by on the street. It was a modified starter's pistol – still illegal but much cheaper and easier to get hold of. It would be unpredictable even in an expert's hands, and risky to use. His aim would be rotten. There was a very good chance he'd have bent the firing pin with his first shot, making the gun useless. Then again, he might not. I doubted he was using heavy ammunition, but at close range a small projectile could kill. I wished I could see more of the woman on the ground. I took out my phone and murmured a report to the operator, telling the paramedics to expect at least one gunshot victim.

'This isn't going to help,' Derwent said again. 'This was a bad idea and you need to start thinking about how you're going to walk away from it.'

'This is what I was driven to do. The courts don't listen to men. They don't listen to honest, straight-talking people. They don't value fathers, except as a source of income for lazy sluts like Marianne.'

Marianne, I assumed, was the woman lying on the ground.

'You sound like Philip Pace,' Derwent said. 'That Dads Matter guy.'

'Philip Pace is the only person willing to stand up to the feminazi left-wing cunts who are running this country.'

I tried to think of a woman of any political persuasion with real power, currently, and failed. Somehow, I didn't think Lee was in the mood for a discussion about it.

Proving that he was the worst negotiator possible, Derwent was getting annoyed. He dropped the all-in-it-together matey tone and spoke in his usual trenchant way. 'Pace is an egomaniac. He's in it for the attention and the fame. He doesn't care about you.'

'He's the only one who cares. The only one.'

'Mate, you are fucking deluded. But then again, you must be if you're standing in the middle of a playground waving a gun around.'

'Have you got kids?' Lee asked. 'Do you even understand what I'm trying to do here?'

'I don't think you even know what you're trying to do. This was never going to go well, was it?'

'I don't care what you think. It's none of your business.'

'You've made it my business. I don't give a flying fuck through a rolling doughnut about your marriage problems, but I do want to see everyone make it home in one piece.'

'It's a bit late for that now.'

'It's not too late. It will be when the firearms officers turn up and shoot you because you're armed and dangerous. They don't mess about. They will kill you.'

'I don't care.'

'Course you do. You want to see your little boy grow up. That's what this is all about, according to you. You can do that if you put the gun down and give yourself up.' The thud-thud-thud of a helicopter sounded overhead, approaching fast. Derwent spoke louder to be heard over it. 'You're about to get into a world of shit, mate. I reckon you've got about three minutes to get this sorted. The thing about firearms officers is that they spend their lives training for this moment, and they're trained to shoot to kill. Head, chest, boom. You know they're going to take the shot if you give them the opportunity. Be smart about it.'

'Are you a copper?'

'Yeah.'

'Why aren't you in uniform?'

'I'm CID. An inspector. So I know what I'm talking about.'

I decided that was my cue and moved forward. 'These women and children have nothing to do with you. It's time to let them leave.' They would have to walk past him to get to the gate, unfortunately. The railings around the park were designed to keep people out. They were high and not climbable.

The gunman looked at me for the first time, then swung around to check on the group huddled behind him. The screaming had stopped but someone was sobbing, a dry and terrible sound that made my stomach contract. 'They're not going anywhere.'

Derwent shook his head. 'Not helping anyone, my friend. Buy yourself some time. Let them go.'

'No.'

'You don't need them. They're just one more thing to think about.'

I risked a look over my shoulder and saw that the promised backup had arrived, though I couldn't yet see the distinctive blue boiler suits and body armour of the Met's firearms unit, SO19. I could see three officers from where I was standing, all more or less camouflaged behind cars, which meant there were a lot more I couldn't see, but they would have tasers at best. Too far away to help at the moment.

And the only consolation was that if they had been armed, I'd have been standing in the middle of their field of fire.

'I want to take a hostage,' the man said. 'One of them has to stay.'

'Not a chance. Move towards them and I'll have to stop you.' Derwent sounded very sure of himself. The helicopter hovered overhead, not so low that we could feel the wind from the rotors, but low enough that it was necessary to shout.

'You wouldn't dare.'

'I'd have to.'

'I'll shoot you,' Lee promised, pointing the gun at Derwent again. 'You know I will.'

Derwent took a step closer, getting into position. 'Get them moving, Kerrigan.'

I went past the two of them quickly, not even acknowledging the possibility that it might be dangerous, though fear was a heavy weight in the pit of my stomach. I was less afraid for myself than for the children. And Derwent, who hadn't the sense he was born with, who lived to be a hero.

I chose an older woman who looked calmer than the rest and had two little girls by the hand. 'Walk, don't run, and small groups. You three first.'

She nodded and led them across the playground towards the gate, not running but not dawdling either. I sent another two after her, and then four, watching to make sure they made it. The first woman crossed the road and disappeared around the corner and I knew the officers were directing them from their hiding places behind the cars, sending them out of sight to safety. Another four. Three. Five together, taking a chance but they were all holding hands, two women and three children. The group was dwindling now and as I got down to the last few they were getting more agitated. One of them was holding a squirming little boy. She was on the verge of hysterics.

'I can't do it. I can't.'

'Calm down.' I put a hand on her shoulder and held on while I sent another two women to safety, carrying their children. 'You'll walk with me.'

'Don't make me. Please.'

'It'll be all right.' Her panic was starting to affect the others who were left: two women who looked like a mother and daughter and a little girl who was clinging to the younger woman like a koala. 'You've seen everyone else do it. It'll be fine.'

Derwent was talking to the gunman all the time, his voice low and calm. I knew he wanted me to hurry up: I could practically hear him thinking it. I made myself be patient.

'All right, ladies. We'll all go together. No crying, no screaming, no running. Let's not frighten the children.'

'But I'm scared,' the panicking woman wailed, and I saw Lee turn around. Derwent leaned forward, still talking, trying to get his attention back, but he was focused on us now.

'Walk,' I said through gritted teeth and took her by the arm, marching her towards the gate as if I was taking her into custody. I took the side closer to Lee, shielding her from him as I strode past, but he leaned forward and saw her.

'Izzy, you cow. This is all your fault.' He grabbed my arm and pulled me back so he could reach her, lifting the gun to point it straight at her head.

I still had a firm hold on Izzy and I dragged her with me, turning away from the gun so I was between the two of them, staring at her terrified face and the small head of the boy she was holding against her, his face buried in her shoulder. I was glad I couldn't see the gun any more and I was glad I wouldn't have any warning when he fired. Everything seemed to have gone quiet and I felt detached from gravity, floating in the moment.

Out of the corner of my eye I saw a movement: Derwent charging the last few feet to grab for the gun. Too slow. Too late.

When it came, the shot sounded like the end of the world. Izzy dropped to the ground and I went with her, sprawling on the rubberised surface. Behind me, Derwent staggered, off balance. I could see his lips moving but I couldn't hear anything because my ears were ringing from the shot, and I couldn't tell if I was hurt or Izzy was or God forbid if the boy was injured. I checked them both and found they weren't shot after all and the sound was starting to come back as if someone was turning up the volume, the low tones of the helicopter first, and screaming, and a voice shouting instructions to the gunman.

I looked around and saw Derwent still on his feet but only just, stepping back and back, trying to remain upright and failing. Falling. It seemed to happen in slow motion, and I'd never thought I'd see him defeated but his face showed it: resignation. He hit the ground hard, falling back onto one shoulder, his head smacking a paving slab that was concrete, not the soft, yielding surface of the playground. I had no time to think about him because I was still turning and saw Lee, his face the colour of ice, and he lifted the gun again even as I looked up at him, pointing it at my face. He'd swapped hands, I saw. Blood was dripping from his right hand. Even money the gun had misfired that time. It was probably wrecked. Useless. He'd be right-handed, at a guess, and his reactions would be slower when he was using his left. I could rush him. Grab the gun. Disable him, as Derwent had intended to.

I couldn't move.

Behind me, Izzy scrambled to her feet and ran, holding her boy. I counted her steps, visualising the path to the gate, to the pavement outside, the sanctuary of the police cordon. They would help them.

No one could help me.

'No shot, no shot.' Pure frustration: between the playground equipment and the civilian coming through the gate with her child, the armed officers were at the wrong angle to take Lee out. A shout came in response, and a bit of basic training resurfaced at just the right moment. I got low, wrapped my arms around my head and waited as something rushed past me quicker than any human being could move, flying through the air with one intention. To kill.

And I heard Lee scream as he hit the ground with eighty pounds of Belgian Malinois on top of him.

It was moments before the handler caught up with his dog, followed by what seemed to be the entire SO19 team, but it felt like for ever. I uncurled myself and remained wary, remembering the question one of my fellow recruits had asked of the dog handler the day we got our training in working with canines.

'How do they know not to bite police officers?'

'They don't. They've got a high prey drive. To them, we all look like legitimate targets.'

'Can't you train them not to bite people in uniform?'

He had shrugged. 'Why bother? Keep your distance. They like doing their jobs. They get excited. Get in their way and they'll bite you.'

Lee was the ultimate legitimate target and on this occasion the dog was taking great pleasure in teaching him a lesson. One of the firearms officers retrieved the gun as the rest of them kept a respectful distance. The handler tried, not very hard, to persuade the dog to let go of Lee's arm.

'Come on, Bruiser. Good lad.'

Bruiser wagged his tail ecstatically. His jaws remained

clamped on Lee's biceps. Lee was still making a fair amount of noise, but it was terrified moaning now, not screaming or invective. It made a nice change.

I didn't stay to watch the show. I was more worried about Lee's victims. The paramedics were crouching around the woman who was now on her side in the recovery position. The ground where she'd been lying was saturated with blood but she was talking to the paramedics and it was her left shoulder that was injured rather than any vital organs. I ran over.

'Marianne? Where's your son? Where's your little boy? Is he all right?'

She looked up at me, huge-eyed. 'I told him to hide. I didn't want him to see Lee like that.'

'Where is he?'

'In the ladybird.'

I looked around wildly, then saw what she meant: a big red plastic ladybird with steps up the back and a slide down the front. It was hollow and there was an opening in the side to a space underneath.

'What's his name?'

'Alfie.'

I went over and crouched beside the ladybird. 'Alfie? You can come out now.'

'I'm playing hidey seek. Wiv Mummy.'

'That game's over. It's time to come out. Mummy's waiting.'

'You have to *count*.' A furious face appeared at the opening: his mother's eyes, his father's mouth, white-blond hair. He was three or four and he was livid. 'I been waiting for *her*. For *ages*. If you want to play, you have to *count*.'

One of the paramedics came and crouched down beside me. He was a fatherly type, mid-forties and he winked at Alfie before muttering to me, 'I'll take care of this. I think you're needed over there.'

I looked where he was pointing and went cold. Derwent

was still on the ground, with another team of paramedics gathered around him, and uniformed officers standing behind them, looking grave. I flew across the playground and shouldered my way through the sightseers, dropping to my knees beside Derwent's head. He was awake, sheet-white and quivering with pain.

'What happened? Where did he get you?'

'He's been shot in the thigh,' a young woman replied. She was a doctor, according to her high-visibility jacket, and she was preparing a syringe. 'This will help, Josh.'

'What is it?' he ground out between gritted teeth. 'Morphine? I don't want it.'

'It will help with the pain.'

'I can cope with the pain.' Typical macho Derwent. He was sweating.

'You don't have to cope with it. We can take it away.'

He waved a hand at her, very definitely saying no, and looked at me. 'What a fuck-up.'

'You took one for the team,' I said.

'It fucking hurts.' He grabbed my hand and held on to it, digging his fingers in. 'Sorry. It helps.'

'I don't mind.'

'I can't believe he shot me.'

'He did warn you.'

'Yeah, but I thought he was faking.' He looked up at the sky. 'You win some, you lose some. How does it look?'

I glanced down at his leg. They were holding a pad over the entrance wound and had slipped another under his thigh, so I couldn't see how bad the damage was, but it looked nasty. I kept my voice light. 'I think your trousers have had it. You'll probably keep the leg, though.'

'Of course he will.' The doctor glowered at me. 'It's a through and through. I think the bullet grazed the bone which is why he's in so much pain.'

'Did you get that?' I asked Derwent, who had shut his eyes.

'Every word.' He squeezed my hand again. 'Sorry I didn't do a better job.'

'You were amazing.'

'If I had a pound for every time a woman's said that to me . . .'

'You'd have a pound,' I finished.

'Got it in one.' Derwent winced. 'Jesus God.'

'Just have the morphine. You've done enough heroics for one day.'

'One lifetime.' He shook his head. 'No, thanks. I don't like morphine. It makes me say what I really think.'

I regarded him with awe. 'You mean there's usually a filter? I can't imagine what you stop yourself from saying given the stuff you come out with.'

'Just as well.' He lifted his head up and eyeballed the doctor. 'I mean it. Put the needle down. I'll survive.'

'Yes, you will,' the doctor said crisply. 'But we need to move you now.'

I let go of Derwent's hand.

'Hey,' he said, protesting. 'Come back, Maeve.'

'There's no room in the ambulance,' one of the paramedics told him.

'I'll see you at the hospital,' I promised.

'You'd better.'

I watched them lift him onto a stretcher and wheel him to the waiting ambulance, and I was so busy staring at that I completely missed the black Mercedes stopping beside the park. Godley was standing beside me before I registered he had arrived.

'What's going on? What happened? What was Josh even doing here?'

I looked up at Godley. 'He called me Maeve. He never calls me Maeve.'

Then, to my eternal shame, I burst into tears.

WEDNESDAY

Chapter 24

'Christ, you look worse than I do.'

'That's debatable,' I said, dropping my bag on the end of Derwent's bed and perching beside it. 'Anyway, why wouldn't you look well rested? All you've had to do for the last twenty-four hours is lie in bed.'

'I was shot,' he protested. 'I'm injured. I had to have a blood transfusion.' He looked seedy, as it happened, with untidy hair and a greyish tinge to his skin. He needed a shower, a shave and a juicy steak, in that order. A lunch tray on the table told its own story: untouched macaroni cheese congealing on a plate, and a bowl full of something covered in custard. Two slices of white bread sat on a side plate, the edges curling up in the dry, over-heated hospital air. It was pale food that was plainly not going to do the job, and I didn't blame Derwent for not trying it.

'Never mind. You're well on the mend, according to the doctors.'

'What happened to patient confidentiality?'

'Don't blame them. They had to make a statement.' I bent down to retrieve the other bag I'd brought with me and took out a stack of newspapers. 'Have you seen these?'

'Just what's on the TV.' Derwent struggled to sit up and I went to rearrange his pillows. 'Oh, give it a rest, Florence. I can manage.'

'Fine.' I retreated. 'You'll find your picture on the first five pages of every tabloid and most of the broadsheets, but they don't really do you justice. They're mainly ultra-fuzzy long-distance shots from yesterday or old pictures. The *Guardian* is running a special poll on whether the police should be armed, but you don't need me to tell you the answer will be no. The *Mail* is campaigning for us to be given tasers as standard kit. And *The Times* has dug up your military background as well as your achievements in the Met. I didn't know you were a sniper.'

He flinched. 'I don't talk about that.'

'You might have to in future. Everyone wants to interview you. You're quite the star.'

He was staring at the front page of the *Sun*, which was a dramatic but blurry shot in which he was falling backwards. Izzy and her son were in the foreground, running for cover. She looked terrified and her son was crying. It was a still from a video one of the neighbours had taken with a phone, and the film had been running on every news bulletin, along with footage from the police helicopter's camera. Derwent had the TV on with the sound turned down; he must have seen it. But there was something compelling about the single instant they had selected. High drama, caught in colour.

'Where were you?' Derwent asked.

'Behind the gate. Not shown, anyway.'

'That's not on.' He shook his head. 'You were there too.'

'Oh, please. I'm more than happy for you to get the credit for tackling Lee.'

'You should be on the front page, not relegated to page . . .' He flicked on. 'Nine. Jesus, look at your hair. Was that the best you could do?'

The picture was a formal uniformed portrait taken when I passed out of Hendon. I did not look my best. Mad hair was about the least of it.

'I don't need the attention.'

'Your mum will be furious if there's nothing for her scrapbook.'

'She'll be furious anyway. With me.' I shuddered. 'I dread to think what she'll say about us blundering in to confront a gunman. She might blame you for leading me astray.'

He looked genuinely upset at that prospect. Derwent liked my mother, for reasons he had yet to explain to me. The home cooking helped. And, it occurred to me for the first time, he probably missed his own mum. It was awful to think that she was the one who'd cut off contact. He'd deserved better than that. Another tiny bit of my dislike of Derwent crumbled and fell away, much to my own surprise.

'I can't believe you haven't spoken to her yet,' Derwent said. 'Don't you call her every day?'

'Not if I can help it. Anyway, I haven't been home. The answering machine is probably full already, just from her calls.'

'She must have your mobile number.'

I groaned. 'Yes, but I dropped it in the playground and some jobsworth SOCO bagged it and tagged it as evidence. I spent hours trying to get it back yesterday. Even the SIM card would have done. But no luck.'

'Butterfingers. Why haven't you been home? Did you go clubbing or something?'

'I've been a bit busy being debriefed by everyone you can think of.' He probably hadn't noticed but I was still wearing the same clothes as the previous day, now creased and limp with added blood on one knee from tending to the fallen warrior.

'Who debriefed you?'

'Godley. The commander of SO19. The heavies from the DPS to make sure we did things by the book.'

Derwent rolled his eyes. No one liked to attract the attention of the Department of Professional Standards, the bogeymen of the Met. 'Hope you told them to fuck themselves.'

'Not in so many words.' I knew he'd like the next bit. 'The Independent Police Complaints Commission sent a team round, just in case Lee makes a complaint.'

'I'd like to see him try.'

'Some lawyer is probably talking him into it at this very moment.' A yawn threatened to crack my jaw.

'Bored? You've only just got here. Imagine what it's like for me.' He rolled his head from side to side. 'I'm climbing the walls. How come it took you so long to visit me?'

'You're supposed to be recuperating. We were leaving you alone to rest. Anyway, the investigating officers have been letting me read the witness statements for the last few hours.' I yawned again. 'I'm shattered.'

'Anything interesting?'

'What you'd expect. Lee and Marianne had a stormy relationship – lots of arguments, a history of domestic violence on both sides. Izzy was the one who persuaded Marianne to leave him, which is why he had such a massive reaction to seeing her walk past him. The break-up turned nasty when Lee was months late paying his child support. Marianne went to court and stopped his visits to Alfie back in August. It took Lee this long to set up his little stunt, but he was planning it for a while. Marianne knew Lee was looking for her because his brother warned her. She wasn't expecting the gun, though.'

'A starter's pistol. Not a real gun.'

'It fired real bullets,' I pointed out. 'Luckily, Lee only had four, so he didn't do any practice shots. He was aiming for Marianne's heart, she said, but the shot was high and to the left.'

'Too close for comfort. Where did he get it?'

'He bought it in a pub car park in Gravesend, he says. He got a tip-off from a friend of a friend of a friend and we're never going to be able to trace it back to the armourer if you ask me. Anyway, it wasn't much good. According to the ballistics report, by the time he shot you the gun was practically falling apart. It was about half as effective as it might have been and it seriously damaged Lee's hand when he fired it. He probably wouldn't have got another shot off.'

'Lucky for you.'

'And lucky for you he didn't shoot you before Marianne, or aim a bit better. If he'd hit your femur and the gun had been in full working order you'd be walking with a limp for rest of your life and living off a disability pension.'

'Instead of being released later on today.'

'Already?'

Derwent grinned. 'I'm talking them into it.'

'I bet they can't wait to get rid of you.'

'What are you talking about? The nurses love me.'

The door opened behind me and Godley walked in, carrying an elaborate flower arrangement in one hand and a bag of grapes in the other. 'They said you were ready for visitors.'

'Not flowers, please. Makes me feel as if I'm dead or gay or something.'

'I think it takes more than a couple of flower arrangements to change your sexual orientation,' I said.

'I'm not taking any chances. Go and find the prettiest nurse you can see and give them to her instead, boss.'

Godley dumped the grapes on the bedside locker and took the flowers back out to the hall.

'This is why you're popular with the nurses,' I said.

'That and the friendly banter.'

'God help them.'

'Just because you don't appreciate it, Kerrigan.'

'It's growing on me,' I admitted, and Derwent looked smug.

'They all fall for it eventually.'

Godley came back. 'The nurses' station looks like a florist's shop. All your doing, apparently.'

'I don't want them. I told them to give anything that came in to people who didn't have any.' He shifted against the pillows, obviously in pain. 'I don't know why anyone would send flowers.'

'Well, I didn't. They're from Marianne Grimes.' Godley sat in the single armchair by the bed. 'She's very grateful.'

'So she should be. She had the sense to play dead but that wasn't going to work for ever. How's the kid?'

'Confused,' Godley said. 'He doesn't know what happened except that his mum is a bit unwell and staying in hospital. He didn't see Lee so for the time being everyone is keeping their mouths shut about it. He's too young to understand.'

'That's something, anyway,' I said. He'd find out eventually, though.

'Speaking of not understanding things.' All the warmth had left Godley's voice. 'Josh, would you like to explain what you were doing there in the first place?'

'Kerrigan needed me.'

'For my interview with Lionel Orpen,' I clarified. I'd told Godley this already. And the DPS. I had yet to work out how much trouble we were both in, though.

'He wanted to talk to me,' Derwent said.

'He insisted.'

'It wasn't Kerrigan's idea.'

'It was just for that one interview.'

'No one else was ever supposed to know I was there.'

'I thought it would be all right,' I said. 'It was all about Angela, not about the current murders.'

'That wasn't your call to make.' Godley looked at Derwent. 'And you. Where do I begin? You should have said no. You were on leave. I warned you.'

'Yeah, but—'

'I don't want to hear it.'

'If I hadn't been there,' Derwent said, ignoring the interruption, 'Kerrigan would have had to deal with Lee on her own. Someone would have died – a kid, or Marianne. Kerrigan, even.'

'So we were really lucky that you both disobeyed direct orders and you were both prepared to lie about it, is that it?' The sarcasm in Godley's voice made me wince.

'It was the right thing to do.' Derwent wasn't backing down.

'You should have asked me for permission.'

'You'd have said no.'

'If you think that argument is persuasive, being shot in the leg has affected your brain.'

'Look, boss, we needed to talk to Orpen. He's a miserable old git. He would have said no to Kerrigan.'

'He *did* say no,' I interjected.

'Leaving Lee aside, it was a good morning's work. I'm sorry it happened that way but it was worth it.'

Godley raised his eyebrows. 'The end justifies the means? Really, Josh?'

'What do you want me to say?'

'An apology would be a good start.'

'I'm very, very sorry.'

'Sorry you got caught,' Godley said, and Derwent grinned at him.

'You can't stay angry, can you?'

'If it ever happens again, Josh, you're out. No more second chances. I mean it.'

'Understood.' A look passed between the two of them that was, on Derwent's part, an acknowledgement that he'd been wrong, and on Godley's that he wasn't going to stand for being messed around any more.

'And as for you, Maeve—' Godley began.

Derwent lunged for the remote control, his attention fixed on the TV screen. 'This is us. Look. We're on again.'

I half-glanced at it then turned away. I had seen that particular report more than once.

'Come on, Kerrigan. Watch it. Your big moment is

coming up.' Derwent turned up the volume so we could listen to the commentary. The reporter's voice was solemn.

'The moment a father lashed out against society . . . and the brave police officers who stopped his murderous rampage. Lee Grimes had a grudge against his ex-wife – and an illegally held firearm. The modified weapon was unreliable, but it had the potential to be lethal.'

In order to spin out the visuals for longer they had slowed it down so every frame of the blurry footage got full value and I had seen myself trying to block Izzy from Lee, and watched Derwent fall to the ground too many times. Knowing how it ended didn't make it easier viewing.

'Wait for it. This is my favourite bit.' Derwent was grinning. I glanced back at the screen in time to see myself dissolving into tears while Godley supported me.

'I was in shock.'

'You were worried about me. I made you cry.'

'I had just come very close to being shot. I think I was entitled to get a bit upset.'

'Now, now,' Godley said. 'Settle down, you two.'

The report was now dealing with the emotional scenes as parents clung to their mostly uncomprehending children.

'I hate this,' Godley said, wincing. 'As soon as you have children, the thought of them being injured or even upset is unbearable. You hold them a bit closer for a while.'

'Do you feel sorry for him?' I asked. 'Lee, I mean?'

'A bit. I hope I wouldn't behave the same way, but he sounded desperate to see his son.'

'They should have been safe in a playground on a sunny autumn afternoon, but only chance – and two unarmed police officers – stood between them and a potential massacre,' the reporter intoned.

I snorted. 'Again, he had four bullets. Four. And he'd used one on Marianne already.'

'He could have finished her off, killed Alfie and turned the gun on himself. He could have killed Izzy for interfering.

He could have shot at random and killed some of those children.' Godley shook his head. 'Four bullets could have done plenty of harm.'

'I didn't exactly come out of it unscathed,' Derwent pointed out. 'I don't know when I'll be able to run again.'

'Or work.' Godley stood up. 'I came to tell you, you'll need to be passed as medically fit to return to work. It'll be weeks, not days. Make some plans for your time off if you get bored in here.'

Derwent, predictably, exploded. 'Fuck that. I don't need my leg to solve cases. Look at Ironsides. He was in a bloody wheelchair.'

'You know that was a TV programme, don't you?' I said.

'I know I've wasted enough time on the sidelines recently and I want to get back to what I do best.' Derwent's attention was caught by the news again. 'That bastard.'

The screen was filled with a face that was instantly familiar, even without the banner on the bottom of the screen. Philip Pace looked tense but still handsome in a slick way. His tan was too deep, his hair too groomed for my liking. He was wearing a dark suit and a cobalt tie, which he touched while the newsreader was introducing him.

'That's a giveaway. He's nervous,' I said.

'So he should be.' Derwent threw a grape at the screen and missed. 'This is his fault. Whipping people up. Telling them they're victims.' Another grape hit the target and bounced off onto the bed. 'If Lee Grimes had really cared about Alfie he'd have paid the child support on time instead of pissing off his wife and making her play hardball in the family courts.'

'This just goes to show the desperate situation of men in an uncaring society, one that doesn't recognise their rights as fathers and as *people*.' Philip Pace's eyes glistened with sincerity.

'*People* who are still paid more for doing the same job as women,' I said.

'Right and proper,' Derwent said. 'They don't go off and take a year's paid leave any time they like to have babies.'

'Which they do by themselves, of course. No men are involved in the process.'

'Don't rise to the bait, Maeve. He's teasing you.' Godley stretched. 'I wish I could stay longer, Josh, but I have to get going.'

'So does Kerrigan.' Derwent threw another grape, this time at me. 'Don't you have work to do?'

'I was just leaving.' I gathered up my bags.

'I think as a society,' Philip Pace said, 'we need to understand why we're demonising a loving, caring father because he missed his little boy.'

'I can't watch this.' I reached over and switched the sound off. 'Most loving, caring fathers don't try to kill the mothers of their little boys.'

'Most fathers would die for their children,' Godley agreed.

'Not all,' Derwent said. 'Some people shouldn't be allowed to breed. You should have to get a licence.'

Godley had got as far as the door, and was just raising a hand to salute Derwent when his phone rang.

'Don't tell me someone's gone and killed someone,' Derwent muttered to me. 'Don't they know I'm off work?'

I half-smiled, but I was watching Godley's face and trying to work out what he was being told. He checked his watch. His side of the conversation was mostly yes and no so I couldn't make much of it.

'Text me the address. I'll be there in half an hour. Yes. She is. I will.' He hung up and looked at me. 'I know you've had a tough twenty-four hours but you should probably come with me.'

'What is it?'

'Another woman. Strangled.'

'When did that happen?' Derwent demanded. He was

trying to sit up again, and his face had lost the colour it had gained during our conversation.

'The last time anyone spoke to the victim was ten thirty last night, and she was found at lunchtime.'

'Which puts you in the clear,' I said to Derwent. 'You were here, surrounded by adoring nurses.'

'Talk about your silver linings.' Derwent still looked ashen.

'We need to go,' Godley said to me. Something had happened to flip the switch in him; he'd gone from total composure to simmering excitement and I couldn't work out why news of another dead woman was making him giddy. 'Get better soon, Josh.'

'Yeah.' He sounded distracted and I knew he wasn't paying much attention as I said goodbye. For all three of us, the only thing that mattered now was the new victim, and what her death could tell us about the man who killed her.

Godley set off down the corridor at a blistering pace, leaving me to try to keep up while dodging around patients and trolleys. He was whistling under his breath, though I doubted he was aware of it.

'What's her name, guv?'

'Deena Prescott.'

I thought hard, but it didn't ring any bells for me.

'I can't believe it's happened again. And so soon after the last one.' I was doing my best to keep my voice down because the last thing we wanted was an entourage of reporters. 'Are we sure it's the same guy? Is it the same MO?'

'More or less.' Godley pressed the button for the lift, then changed his mind and headed for the stairs, as if he had to keep moving. I went through the door after him and grabbed his arm. It was something I would never have done normally, but I was tired, and confused, and deeply unsettled.

'Stop! Just for a second.'

I waited for a couple of visitors to trudge past us. I could hear footsteps approaching from the floor below, and someone was talking on the floor above, so we didn't have long. I half-whispered, 'I don't understand. He's killed again in the space of days, not weeks or months. Why are you pleased?'

Godley leaned close to me so his words didn't carry through the echoing, busy stairwell, his mouth almost grazing my ear. 'Because this time, we've got a lead.'

It was my turn to feel the adrenalin rush, so intense that it made me dizzy. As I followed Godley down the stairs, I wondered if the killer felt the same thrill when he knew he'd found a victim – if it was as addictive for him as it was for me. There were times I felt almost too close to the criminals I was hunting. He was born to be a killer. I liked to think I was born to catch him.

Chapter 25

There was an element of déjà vu about our arrival at Deena Prescott's tiny modern townhouse in Walthamstow. As at Anna Melville's home the street was clogged with police vehicles. The media were pressing against hastily erected barriers a hundred yards in either direction from the house, and as Godley's car was waved through a hundred camera flashes went off, half-blinding me. I put my hand up to shield my eyes.

'Jesus. Can you see enough to drive?'

'I'm used to it.' He parked and headed for the crime scene, not hanging around. I scrambled to follow. Godley started up the steps to the front door, which had already been screened off. Before he reached the top, the canvas screen parted and Una Burt appeared, rotund in a protective boiler suit. She pushed the hood back and her hair was flat against her head, damp with sweat. It was quite amazing to me that she had no personal vanity, but it seemed that she really didn't care.

What she did care about was her job. Without preamble, she said, 'I think he panicked.'

'Our killer?'

'Yes.'

'Are we sure it's the same guy?'

'Yes and no.'

'Explain,' Godley said.

'Not yet.' She didn't say it in an argumentative way, but you could tell there was absolutely no chance of persuading her to change her mind. She looked at me and her expression darkened. 'I want a word with you.'

'Not now, Una,' Godley said. 'Let her view the crime scene.'

'That's not why she's here. She needs to explain why Josh Derwent was with her yesterday.'

'I've already spoken to her. And Josh, indeed.'

Burt wasn't going to be put off so easily. 'I suppose we'd never have known about it if you hadn't run into trouble.'

'Probably not,' I admitted.

'You were specifically told not to allow him access to any part of this investigation.'

'With respect, I wouldn't have been able to conduct that interview without him. And he's got an alibi for this murder, so your concerns about him were unfounded anyway.'

'Some of them may have been unfounded. Not all.' She was still glowering. 'Was it useful? The interview?'

'Oh. I think so.' I struggled to think back to what Orpen had told us. There were things to follow up, if I ever got the chance, but I couldn't tell yet if they would help.

Godley was getting impatient. 'This isn't the time or the place, Una. Can you drop it for now?'

'For now.' She stood aside to let him go past her and then moved to block me. 'Don't think I'm going to forget about it, though. You deliberately disobeyed an order and you were prepared to lie about it. I thought you were better than that.'

I felt the colour rise in my cheeks. 'Look, I didn't have a choice. I—'

'You did. You chose Josh Derwent. I hope you won't regret it, but I can't see how you won't.'

'I don't see that there's a need to take sides.'

'Then your judgement is even more unreliable than I thought.'

I followed her into the house, shaking my head when her back was turned. It was a first for anyone to make me more annoyed than Derwent, but she was getting there.

'You need a suit, please, Maeve-y, and shoe covers,' said Pierce, Kev Cox's assistant, who was in charge of supervising access again. He handed me the protective gear I needed. 'Kev is pretty twitchy about this scene.'

I put the suit on, hurrying to catch up with Godley and Burt. I could hear them talking in the first room off the hall on the left, a sitting room, and I strained to hear the conversation. It was about the crime scene, not me, for which I was truly grateful. I couldn't have endured Godley standing up for me, or – worse – damning me as Burt had.

'No staging,' Godley said.

'Not this time.'

'Any sign of forced entry?'

'No. She let him in. Or at least she opened the door – he may have forced his way in.'

'And they came in here. Were the curtains open or closed when the body was found?'

'Closed. Lights on.'

'Which explains how he was able to kill her in here without being seen. And suggests she was killed last night, not this morning.'

I passed Pierce's inspection and rustled into the sitting room, where the first thing I saw was an overturned table, and the second a body on the floor, Godley crouching by the head. She was lying at an awkward angle, one arm thrown up over her face, and her torso twisted so her hips were flat on the floor but her right shoulder was supporting the weight of her upper body. She was dressed in pyjamas but the top was unbuttoned, the bottoms halfway down her hips, exposing most of her torso, which was bruised and scratched, as if he had lost control and ripped at it with his bare hands. It made her look pathetic and I had to resist the urge to pull her clothes back into place. I couldn't work out if the killer had left her like that to demean her or because he couldn't be bothered to dress her as he had the others. She was small but busty and her hair was henna-red. He had cut it off, as he had done with the others, but it lay in tangles around her body, scattered all over it. I wondered about that too.

Godley was peering at her face, which was bruised and bloodied. 'He lost it, didn't he? He stabbed her in the eyes rather than removing them.'

'That's not the only difference.' Burt leaned across to point. 'There's blood all over that wall and the floor. He beat her first. Slammed her against any hard surface he could find.'

'Angry because just killing them isn't enough any more?' I asked.

'Good question,' Burt said. 'But I think I know why Deena's death was different. When I got here, I had a very interesting conversation with Elaine Bridlow, her best friend. She's the one who found the body. She'd been try-ing to get in touch with Deena all morning and was worried enough to dash here during her lunch hour to check on her.'

'This is the lead you were talking about.'

She nodded. 'She was pretty hysterical, but from what I can gather, Deena rang her last night, quite late. She was sounding confused, but she said she'd just seen the news and she thought someone she knew was in hospital and she didn't know what to do.'

'Did she explain?'

'She'd seen the footage from the playground. Derwent's little adventure. According to Elaine, she said, "I think it's the same guy, but I'm not sure. I only saw him once."'

'*What?*' Godley and I said it at the same time.

Burt nodded. 'She told Elaine she'd met someone who said they were a Met inspector called Josh, and he'd said he worked on homicide investigations. He followed her home, she said, one night last month, when she came back late from work, and she noticed it and challenged him. He told her there was a dangerous criminal operating in the area and he wanted to make sure she got home all right. He asked her not to tell anyone about him because he could get in trouble for warning her and he wanted to keep it between the two of them.'

I was recalling what Derwent had said about shadowing women to safety, with or without their knowledge, and a prickle of unease ran down my spine.

'Did she say anything else?'

'He'd been in touch with her, calling and emailing. He was supposed to be coming around to check her security arrangements. She thought he'd been flirting but she wasn't sure if he was just being friendly.'

'Kirsty Campbell made a list for her building's management company,' I said. 'Maybe that's how he gains their trust. He tells them he's a police officer and they need to let him into their homes so he can advise them on their safety. But really, he's just stringing them along while he gets to scope the place out from the inside.'

'Elaine asked why Deena hadn't told her about him before and she said she hadn't had any reason to mention it. It was a chance encounter and so far it hadn't come to anything. Deena was a real romance addict, according to Elaine. She said she hadn't wanted to jinx a possible relationship by talking about it.'

'He has a real gift for finding the right women,' I said.

'It couldn't have been our Josh,' Godley said firmly. 'He was in hospital when she died.'

'It could have been someone covering for him,' Burt said.

'No way,' I said. 'It's not Derwent.'

She whipped around. 'You are hopelessly biased. You won't admit the evidence in front of your own eyes. There are major, striking differences between this killing and the others, and one explanation is that it was not the same person but it was supposed to look like the same person.'

'Because it's so easy to find someone to do your killing for you if you need to establish an alibi.' I didn't even bother trying to hide my disbelief. 'You can't be serious about this.'

'I've never been more serious. And Andy Bradbury agrees with me.'

'That should be your first clue that you're completely wrong,' I said, my voice pure ice. 'Bradbury is a moron.'

'And how does he know about it, anyway?' Godley asked.

'I told him.'

'You did *what*?'

'He's put in a lot of time on this investigation and he deserved to have the full picture. It was wrong to keep something back, especially when it could be the most important element in the case.'

'Does no one listen to me any more?' Godley was livid. 'I ordered you to keep it to yourself, Una. You're as bad as Derwent.'

'That's grossly unfair. I felt you were exhibiting an unusual lack of judgement and I stepped in.'

'Look, keep it down,' I said, noticing that the conversation was attracting some interest from the SOCOs working in the hall. Pierce's ears were flapping.

'This discussion is not over,' Godley said. 'But I am not going to talk about it over this poor woman's body.' He glared at Burt. 'You need to reconsider your tone, too.'

'I'm just saying what I think.'

'I noticed.'

'What are the differences between this murder and the others?' I asked, partly to keep the peace but also because I really wanted to know. 'He cut her hair but threw it on top of her. He didn't arrange the body. He beat her. He killed her quickly. What else?'

'He put her clothes in the bath and poured bleach on them.'

Now that Burt mentioned it, I noticed a strong chemical smell. I looked around at the room. It was smeared with fingerprint powder that had highlighted swirls and sweeps and smears and smudges but no actual fingerprints. 'Did he wipe the place down?'

Kev Cox answered me, leaning in from the hall. 'He cleaned up in here, the hall and the kitchen. Didn't bother with her bedroom upstairs, which suggests he wasn't in there, except to get her clothes. The bathroom is like an operating theatre – spotless.'

'What does this say to you?' Godley asked, looking at me.

'Damage control. He must have been scared she was going to give the game away. This one wasn't about living out his fantasies. He wanted her dead.' I stared at Una Burt. 'That doesn't mean it wasn't the same killer as for the other three.'

'This is a pale imitation of the others.'

'He likes to control the women and the crime scenes,' I pointed out. 'He likes to use minimal violence. There's something almost artistic about the way he leaves the bodies. Now, if Deena challenged him – if she argued, or fought with him, or if he wasn't prepared as he wanted to be for her death – he might have killed her differently. I think he sees it as an honour to be selected by him. She didn't deserve the treatment the other victims got. She betrayed his trust.'

'He probably didn't know about her phone call to Elaine. He might have thought he could come here and kill her before she spoke to anyone,' Godley said.

Burt looked stubborn. 'It was someone acting on Josh Derwent's behalf.'

'Who? Who would?'

'A friend. Someone he met through work – someone he arrested, maybe.'

'Because that's the best way to make friends.' I turned to Godley. 'This is insane. Isn't it?'

'I respect Una's opinion,' Godley said slowly. 'I don't agree with her, but I'm not writing it off just yet. I can't be sure my objectivity isn't affected by my friendship with Josh.'

Lack of sleep was making me slow-witted. I felt as if I was lost in a fog. 'Derwent was in hospital. How would he arrange for this mythical person to come and kill Deena for him?'

'He wasn't unconscious. He had his phone. I'm going to get a list of all the calls from and to that number over the last twenty-four hours, and all the calls to and from his hospital room, and I'm going to prove that Derwent was able to make contact with someone who, for love or money, was prepared to kill at his request. He could have briefed them over the phone – not in detail, maybe, which explains the differences.' She looked at Godley. 'You've known him for a long time. You know he's capable of killing. He did it in the army. He shot people—'

'That's different,' I objected.

'Yes, it is.' She didn't even turn her head. 'He doesn't have a girlfriend. He lives alone. Who knows what's in his flat? We need to get a search warrant while he's still in hospital and go through it.'

I snapped. 'Okay, first of all, I've been in his flat recently and I doubt there's anything to find. Do you really think if he was a killer Derwent wouldn't have the sense to keep everything relating to that in a different location? A storage unit or a lock-up garage? He's seen enough practical examples of what not to do, hasn't he? And anyway, he's not going to be in hospital for long. He might be out already. Do you really want to tell him you think he's a killer?'

'Absolutely not,' Godley said. 'Una, this needs to stay between us for now. If you're right, I want Josh to think he's free and clear. We'll check his phone and bank accounts and get surveillance on him.'

'What about the other investigators?'

'We'll have a conference with them in the next couple of hours. Set it up. I don't mind talking to them behind closed doors because it's worth considering every possibility, but I don't want you talking to Bradbury or anyone else about it when I'm not there. Not a word.' He turned to me. 'Maeve, I know you don't agree with this approach to the investigation. I'm not going to insist you come to the conference. You have other work to do on this case, don't you? Leads from the Orpen interview to run down.'

I struggled to think. It all seemed very remote and irrelevant. I knew I was being moved sideways so I didn't get in the way and I would have resented it if I'd been able to muster enough energy.

'There were some phone calls I should make,' I said. 'But shouldn't I be at the conference?'

'Better not.' In a flash I realised that he was thinking the same way as Una Burt: I couldn't be trusted. 'This goes double for you. Not a word about Josh's potential involvement, to him or anyone else.'

'I wouldn't,' I said, wounded.

'He's very persuasive. He's manipulated you quite a bit over the course of this investigation, hasn't he? You've even been in his flat and what you were doing there I don't want to know, but I hope it was personal rather than relating to this investigation.'

'I'm not *sleeping* with him, if that's what you're suggesting.'

'It wouldn't be the first time you slept with a colleague.' The words seemed to come out despite his best efforts not to say them.

'I would *never*—'

'It's none of my business.' He sighed. 'I can't pretend

I'm not disappointed in you, Maeve. You've done the exact opposite of what you were told to do, because of Josh.'

'I just wanted to find out the truth,' I whispered. 'I did what had to be done.'

'You did what you wanted. You went against specific orders and the consequences of that have yet to be seen.' Godley looked down at Deena's body. 'If you'd handled things differently, Derwent wouldn't have been with you yesterday to get his face all over the news. Whether he is responsible for this death or not, it seems clear that his sudden elevation to public notice is likely to be the reason Deena is dead.'

'That's not fair.'

'Even so. I can't take the risk of letting you remain involved with this end of the investigation. You might as well follow up the leads on the cold case, but report back to Harry Maitland. Brief him when you get to the office. I'll get him to read your notes. He can take over from you.'

'If you don't trust me, you shouldn't have me on your team,' I said, because I had to.

'If you leave it will be your choice.' He shook his head slowly. 'I don't know why everyone finds it so hard to follow orders, but we're standing beside proof that it's important to do so.'

Una Burt was watching me intently, her expression showing that she agreed with Godley.

The thing was, I couldn't say he was wrong. I had done the opposite of what I'd been told. I had let Derwent order me around. And somehow I'd set off the chain of events that had led to Deena's death.

My vision blurred as I turned away, stumbling to the door. Crying at work for the second time in twenty-four hours. That was really the sort of thing that shouldn't become a habit, I thought, trying to distract myself.

I held myself together while I took off the crime-scene coveralls, even chatting with Pierce about his plans for the weekend. I walked out to a darkening sky as the rain closed in. The wind cut through my clothes, making me shiver. One of the police vans was getting ready to leave and I begged a lift, flipping up my coat collar as I sat in a seat near the back, out of reach of the cameras.

A young female PC leaned across the aisle. 'Aren't you the detective who was shot at yesterday?'

I shook my head and sort of smiled at her to take the sting out of it. It was technically true – Lee Grimes hadn't shot at me. She blushed, knowing that she was right but too polite to persist.

'Leave her be. She doesn't want to talk about it.' I could hear the whisper from where I was sitting, but I affected not to. They were right, I didn't want to talk. I wanted to sleep. I wanted to make sense of the chaotic thoughts that were spiralling around my head. I wanted to work out what was bothering me about what I'd heard in the previous days. I wanted to prove Una Burt wrong and prove Derwent wasn't involved. I wanted to make Godley eat his words.

Most of all, I wanted to stop feeling like I'd blundered, time and time again, because I hadn't the least idea how to make it right.

Chapter 26

By the time I got to the office I was in control of myself. I found Maitland, who looked wary when he saw me. Godley had been in touch, apparently, to tell him to expect me, and to familiarise him with Derwent's background. I was miserably conscious that he would have warned Maitland I might be emotional. He needn't have worried. I was icily calm as I ran through the details of the Angela Poole murder and told him what I was planning to do next. He made absolutely no fuss about letting me make follow-up inquiries before I handed the lot over to him, though I was prepared for a fight. He was a good police officer and I trusted him to do his job well, but this was my case and my investigation and I had questions that I needed to ask, by myself.

'Sure. Of course. That's fine.' Maitland ran a hand up and down his shirt front, fiddling with the buttons. 'Tell me what you find out, obviously, and then maybe we can have a final handover in an hour.' *At which time you will be out of this case for ever and I will be taking your place, but I don't have to tell you that's what's going on because you know.*

'One hour,' I repeated, and headed for my desk. I could work to a deadline, if I had to. And it didn't look as if I was being given any choice. So I had an hour to find someone who was not Derwent but seemed to be pretending to be Derwent.

Or someone who was following Derwent, killing the women he tried to help.

Or Derwent.

Which I was not going to think about because it was impossible. I picked up the phone.

My first calls were to all the care homes I could find in Bromley, working through them in search of a resident named Charles or Charlie Poole. It took five tries before I struck gold at the Tall Pines Care Home. The woman who answered the phone was Eastern European and had a strong accent but her speech was fluent, rapid even.

'Charlie? Yes, he is here. You are a relative?'

I explained who I was and that I wanted to come and see him.'

'Oh dear. This is not a problem, you understand, for us, but for you. Charlie is a long-term sufferer from dementia. He is not capable of conversation. He is not even able to say yes or no.'

'If I showed him some pictures—'

'No. The only thing he responds to is music and only sometimes. We do try, but . . .' The shrug travelled down the telephone line.

'Does he get many visitors?'

'His son, sometimes. He comes to sit with him.'

'Does Charlie still recognise him?'

'Not for a year or more.'

Poor Shane. I thanked her for talking to me and she sighed.

'I have great respect for the residents in our home but I feel sometimes that they are just waiting, waiting, waiting. The ones like Charlie – they are the ones death forgot. It makes me sad.'

I thanked her and said goodbye. She'd been helpful, but if there was a spate of sudden deaths at Tall Pines, I knew where I'd start the investigation.

The next person on my list was Claire Naylor, now back

at work and not pleased to be phoned. She became even frostier when I asked her why she'd given Shane an alibi for his sister's death.

'I don't remember. We must have been together.'

'I don't think so,' I said quietly. 'You told me you found out Angela was dead when Shane rang your house at four in the morning and woke everyone up. You were in bed, asleep.'

She didn't answer and I wished I could see her face.

'Shane told me he was out with some mates smoking weed before he came home and found the police were already there. You wouldn't happen to know who the friends were, would you?'

'No.'

'You told me you liked smoking weed, didn't you? But you weren't there that night.'

No answer. I waited, and as so often, silence did my job for me. She sighed, irritated, and I heard a door close, cutting off the background noise from the shop.

'All right. I said he was with me. What's the big deal?'

'It was a murder case and you lied.'

'Only because he was terrified of the policeman.'

'Lionel Orpen?'

'Him. He'd been giving Vinny a shocking time – he'd got it into his head that Vinny might have killed her. Only he absolutely didn't and there was no evidence. He thought he could get Vinny to confess if he leaned on him hard enough, but there was no way that was going to happen. Vinny had too much spirit.' She sounded proud of her brother, and a little sad.

'So Shane was scared.'

'Yes. Especially since he'd been doing drugs that night. I mean, it was nothing. It was just some weed. In ordinary circumstances the police wouldn't have bothered with it but Orpen was looking for an angle all the time. He was starting to look beyond Vinny and he'd have got to Shane sooner or later. Shane was bricking it.'

'And you weren't suspicious when he asked you to provide him with a fake alibi?'

'Absolutely not. He was a very scary guy, that police officer. None of us trusted him.'

Fine work, Orpen. It was no wonder the case had never been solved.

'And you don't know who Shane was actually with.'

'You'd have to ask him.'

'I will.'

'And don't call me again, please. I don't want to be bothered about Angela's death any more.' Her voice was vibrating with tension.

'I'm sorry. It's just—'

'Just leave me alone.' The phone went dead.

I frowned. It was a bit of an overreaction to a phone call. Again, I had the feeling that I'd missed something. Something Claire was trying, quite desperately, to hide.

Shane was the next person I rang, naturally enough, but his phone went straight to voicemail. I doodled a star next to his name to remind me to call him back and went on to dial Stuart Sinclair's number. The same impersonal voice instructed me to leave a message and I did, hoping he'd get back to me as quickly as he had the previous time. I added another star beside his name as I left a message. He seemed to be the kind of person who never took the risk of answering his phone, preferring to know who was calling him, and why, before he actually engaged with them.

I checked the time. Twenty minutes left. Maitland was unlikely to hold me to a strict sixty minutes but there was no doubt I was up against it. No Shane. No Stuart. I dearly wanted to ring Derwent and ask him if he'd ever prowled the streets of Walthamstow looking for women to rescue, but I knew better than to try to contact him. They would be watching everything he did already. They would be checking the calls in and out of his hospital room. It would be useless to say I hadn't told him anything about the case, and it would have been a lie, because Derwent would have known why I was asking straight away. I put out my hand to the phone and took it back again, irresolute.

Better to play it safe. *Sorry, Derwent.*

I filled in the remaining minutes by going through my notes from the various interviews, making sure there was nothing else I'd meant to follow up. I even checked that Claire's son really was at Cambridge, scouting around the Internet for references to him. Whatever else she was lying about, it wasn't that. I found his college, his Twitter account and a Facebook page in seconds. The college was large and prestigious, with extensive grounds and a rowing tradition, and I thought he was lucky. Wondering if Luke had any pictures of Claire, or Vinny, I had a look at Facebook. No privacy settings: perfect. His profile picture was a bottle of beer. I clicked through to his albums and was two pictures in before I'd identified him, and identified a whole new set of problems. I sat and stared at his face, and the sound of things falling into place in my head was deafening.

Oh, *fuck*.

'Your last few words on the subject, then, Kerrigan? Get anywhere with your calls?' Maitland, trying to be amiable and missing by a nervous mile. He started to lean around my computer, looking at what I had in front of me. The only clear thought in my head was that he shouldn't see it until I'd worked out what I was going to do about it. I closed the window and told him I hadn't got very far.

'What about this?' One fat finger descended and pointed at the star beside Shane's name.

'A reminder to try him again. There was no answer from his phone.'

'Who's he again?'

'Angela's brother. He gave a false alibi in the original investigation. The SIO missed it at the time. Apparently he was afraid of getting into trouble for smoking marijuana.'

'Shocking.'

'Well, he was only a teenager. And not outstandingly clever.' Unlike Derwent, apparently. The mind boggled. I made myself think about the case again. 'You know, he was out that night with some people who've never been traced. It would be worth talking to him to find out who they were and whether they might have seen anything.'

'Fine by me,' Maitland said. 'Anything else?'

'Stuart Sinclair. He was the only witness. Except . . .'

'Except what?'

'He lied.'

Maitland shrugged. 'Didn't everybody?'

'Pretty much. But Sinclair lied about what he'd seen. Or maybe he lied about where he was when he saw it. Either way, I think he needs to come clean.'

'You wouldn't think, twenty years on, that they'd even remember to lie, would you?'

'Depends on why they did in the first place, I suppose. If they had a good enough reason – or thought they did – maybe they remember the lie first and the truth second.'

'Well, it's time to jog some memories.' Maitland ran a finger along the desk, looking down. 'Where can I find this Shane Poole?'

'He lives above his bar near Brick Lane.' I wrote down the name and contact details on a loose sheet of paper and handed it to him. 'Go easy with him. He's a bit edgy.'

Instead of going away as I'd expected, Maitland turned my phone around and began to dial. I appreciated the gesture. It meant that I could hear enough of both sides of the conversation to follow it. He was a good DS and he loved Godley but that didn't mean he thought the boss was right to punish me, and I liked him for that.

'Can I speak to Shane Poole, please.'

'. . . not here.'

'Do you know where he is?'

'. . . wish I did. He was supposed to open up, but . . . an hour late . . . *still* hasn't come.'

'Is that unusual for him?'

'First time in six years . . . always reliable.'

'Have you tried ringing his phone?'

'. . . doesn't have it with him.'

'How do you know?' Maitland asked.

'I can hear it ringing upstairs.' The voice had suddenly got a lot louder and more distinct. The fringe benefits of irritating someone.

'Are you sure he's not upstairs too?'

'Well, I haven't seen him.'

Maitland put a hand over the mouthpiece of the receiver. 'Did you get that?'

'Not there but his phone is.'

'That's odd, isn't it?'

'Exceptionally. I'm concerned he may be there and unable to answer his phone. I'm concerned he may be in danger.' I raised my eyebrows. 'Aren't you?'

'Very much so.' It was our passkey to get into the flat without going to the bother and delay of getting a court order. He returned to the call. 'Right. I'll be with you in half an hour. Do you have a key to get into the flat?'

A squawk that I interpreted as a 'yes'.

'Well, don't do it until I get there. And try not to worry.' He hung up. 'Looks as if I'm off to Brick Lane.'

'Good luck.'

He turned around, then turned back. 'You could come. You've met him. You know what to ask him when we find him.'

'I'm not supposed to—'

'It's part of the handover. You'd be helping me.'

'You're being very kind, but I don't want to get you in trouble.'

'What trouble?' Maitland spread his hands wide. 'Who could possibly object?'

I hadn't the heart to list the names but they started with Charles Godley and ended with Una Burt, and I didn't feel like getting shouted at any more that day. I was about to say as much when I checked myself. It was pathetic to ignore the old familiar pull of curiosity that made me a good police officer just because I was scared of getting in trouble. Derwent would have wasted no time even considering saying no, and while his career trajectory was levelling out drastically there were still things he could teach me. And one was being single-minded despite the possible consequences.

'All right. If you insist.'

'I do insist,' Maitland said firmly, hauling his trousers up to rest just under his paunch and setting off. I shut down my computer and followed, shelving all thoughts of Luke Naylor for the moment. *One problem at a time* . . .

Chapter 27

The bar was open already and a few tables were occupied with people having an early lunch. Behind the bar, a woman was serving drinks. She was a bit older than the rest of the staff – mid-forties, I guessed – and something about the set of her shoulders and the droop of her mouth conveyed that she was upset even before she looked up and spotted us. With a mutter to the barman she came out from behind the bar and hurried towards us.

'Are you the man who phoned about Shane?'

Maitland nodded. 'And you are?'

'Ginny Miles. I'm the assistant manager here.'

'No sign of him, I take it?'

'Nothing. I called his phone again, just in case.' Her breathing was shallow and I wondered if she was asthmatic.

'It might be a false alarm,' I said. 'He might have gone out and forgotten it. But we'd still like to check.'

'When was the last time you saw him, again?'

'Yesterday afternoon. He went off for a break before the evening rush. He does lunch and then it goes quiet in the afternoon so he goes upstairs for a lie-down or does some errands then. This place is open until one and he needs to be wide awake.'

'I'm sure.' Maitland scanned the room, then turned back. 'All right, Ginny. Lead the way.'

She took us out through the kitchen where I dodged a rubber-aproned man lifting a huge tray of glasses out of a dishwasher, enveloped in clouds of steam. Two chefs were working, heads down, barely aware of our presence as we passed through to an alley behind the pub where there was a blue door. Her hands were shaking when she produced the key that unlocked it.

'He has a separate entrance to his flat because it's easier when the place is shut up and the alarm is on. And he can come and go as he pleases without getting caught up in work stuff.'

'But you said it was out of character for him not to be there,' Maitland objected.

'It is. He still comes and goes a fair bit. It was strange he didn't come in at all today. I can't remember him doing that before. Ever.'

'Go ahead,' I said, and watched her struggle with the lock. 'Have you been in the flat before?'

'A couple of times.'

'Would you know if anything was missing?'

'I couldn't swear to it.' She held the door open for us, revealing a grey-carpeted flight of stairs rising steeply from just inside the door. It was narrow and claustrophobic and I went up as quickly as I could without stepping on Maitland's heels. In deference to seniority, I let him go first and he checked for signs of life – or death – before coming back to Ginny and me at the top of the stairs.

'Nothing. I found his phone, though, in the kitchen area.' To Ginny, he said, 'I think we should walk through and make sure we're not missing a clue to where he might be.'

She nodded, her arms folded tightly, her expression pure misery. 'It's not to do with those girls, is it? He showed us the pictures. The Gentleman Killer. You don't think it's him, do you?'

'Don't worry about it,' Maitland said easily. 'We're just having a look around.'

I was already getting a feel for the layout. The main room was at the top of the stairs, open plan, with a leather suite of furniture and a table taking up most of the room and the kitchen filling the space on the opposite wall. There was a large bedroom on the left, with a wall of built-in cupboards and an en suite, and a smaller bedroom on the right with a sofa bed and a desk. The furniture was functional but not cheap, and the kitchen looked as if it had been quite expensive to put in, all high-gloss units and granite work surfaces. The overall effect, though, was impersonal and it was cold, as if the heating had been off for a while. I was shivering. It wasn't the kind of place I felt at home. Nor did it tell me a lot about Shane, except that he hadn't stinted on money. There were no personal items on display in the main room, and the smaller bedroom was fitted out as an office. I flicked through the material on the desk, seeing invoices for the bar and accounts. A folder full of bank statements caught my attention but there was nothing particularly exciting about it – bill payments by direct debit, and large sums of cash withdrawn regularly. There were people who preferred to use cash rather than cards to avoid fraud – a lot of police did it, I happened to know – but it was a bugger from an investigative point of view. I circled back to the living room where Ginny was still waiting.

'Was this here? Before?'

'He had it gutted and redesigned,' Ginny said. 'When he had the bar refurbished. He thought this was a good investment but I dunno. Who wants to live above a pub?'

'Handy for last orders,' Maitland said, coming back from the bedroom. 'I've found his passport.'

I held up a card wallet I'd just come across between two stacks of magazines on the coffee table. 'Is this the one he usually carries?'

'Yeah,' Ginny confirmed. I'd thought it was familiar

myself. I opened it and checked, finding bank cards and the picture of Vinny he'd shown me but no cash.

'Who's that?' Maitland asked.

'His friend. He's dead.'

'There's a few pictures of him in the bedroom.'

I went in and looked where Maitland was pointing, at a small collection framed on one wall. His parents on their wedding day, an unposed shot that was a little out of focus. Angela at eight or nine, eating ice cream, her brother's arm around her neck. Claire and Vinny, teenagers, sneering and giving the finger to the camera. And the one Derwent had – all of them together – except that Derwent's face had been coloured in with black marker. I took it down off the wall and stared at it, at the friends together, before the fall, wondering if they had really been as happy as all that, despite the sunshine and the wide smiles.

Behind me, Maitland was getting rid of Ginny, promising to lock up and assuring her he'd call if we found anything that might locate her boss. It took some doing, but she left eventually and he came to find me.

'So he hasn't done a runner. He's just disappeared from one minute to the next. What do you think? Kidnap? Wandered off?'

'No sign of violence if it was a kidnapping. This place is immaculate.' I looked around. 'My hunch is he planned it so carefully he didn't need this stuff. Leave the phone because it acts like a transmitter so we can pinpoint where you are. Leave the bank cards so there are no recorded transactions – he runs a cash business so it's not all that hard to get hold of a lot of money in a hurry. He's probably got a safe full of cash around here somewhere. Leave the passport because you want to come back once you've done what you left to do.'

'And what was that, exactly?'

'I don't know,' I admitted. 'But he disappeared not all that long before Deena Prescott died.'

Maitland gave a sigh that came all the way up from his boots. 'Bloody marvellous. However you cut it, he should be here and he's not, and we've got a big problem.'

My problems were made a lot worse because I wasn't supposed to be anywhere near the Rest Bar. Maitland gave me the option of running away but I turned it down. I wanted to stick around for as long as possible, the urge to know what was going on drowning out the small voice that advocated caution. Godley was taking no chances: a possible lead in the investigation was going to get every resource available. They came in force: SOCOs led by Kev Cox who was as imperturbable and good-tempered as ever, and a spaniel trained as a cadaver dog who might catch a scent of blood or a speck of human remains that we would otherwise miss. Una Burt arrived with Andrew Bradbury and James Peake, fresh from the conference where they'd been discussing Derwent's likely status as a suspect. I didn't doubt that Burt was annoyed I had interrupted it, especially since it was to draw their attention to the fact that there was someone else to consider. Peake was the only one of the three who looked pleased to see me, but in enthusiasm he more than made up for the others. His eyes lit up when he saw me standing outside. He made a beeline for me and I was glad to have him to talk to, if it meant I didn't have to acknowledge the disapproving looks I was getting from his boss and Burt.

'Found a suspect for us, have you?'

'Possibly. We've found a lot of nothing so far.'

'Did you search the place?'

'We gave it the once over, but Maitland wanted to get the SOCOs in before we trampled all over the place.'

'Is this guy really a serious contender? How did you find him?'

I answered the second question first. 'He was involved

in a cold case that had possible relevance to the current inquiry. And I don't know if he's a proper lead or not, but he's the closest thing we've found.'

'You're telling me.' A helicopter hovered overhead and Peake looked up, shading his eyes. 'Not ours. That'll be a news crew.'

'Already?'

'We passed a load of them setting up down the street when we were driving here. There are five or six satellite vans parked up.'

'For God's sake. One of the bar staff must have tipped them off. That's not going to help us if he's on the run. If he knows we're chasing him, it's not going to make him easier to catch.'

Peake shrugged. 'Big news, isn't it. Everyone wants a breakthrough in this case. And speaking of big news, you've had an exciting week of it, haven't you?'

I half-smiled, reluctant to talk about it. Leaning sideways, I saw Burns and Groves making their way up the alley and I went to meet them. We had almost an identical conversation, except that their side of it was full of the double-act banter that came naturally to them.

'Give you a week and you've got a suspect for us. We had months to track him down.' Groves was twinkling at me, obviously delighted.

Burns sniffed. 'Tell you now, I never heard of this bloke before we got the call, but if you're right about him that's all that matters.'

Godley was the last to get there, unusually. Maitland had come to join the group outside in the alley, kicked out by Kev who needed the space.

'Sorry, Harry. I got held up by the press at the cordon.'

'What did you tell them?'

'That I would make a full statement later. But it took a while.' He grinned, then turned to me. 'Maeve. Why am I not surprised to find you here?'

'I asked her to come along,' Maitland said. 'It was my idea.'

'I'm sure it was.' I thought he was going to have a go at me but instead he looked back at Maitland. 'Please tell me you got a search warrant before all this started.'

'We were lawfully on the premises, boss. We were concerned for Mr Poole's safety.'

Godley held up a hand. 'I'm not blaming you, Harry. You have to take the opportunities when they come. But I want the rest of this search to be completely unquestionable in court. If he is our killer, we want to throw everything we can at it.'

'Right you are.'

'What stage are we at?'

'Kev is going through the place at the moment. We gave it a quick look before he started, but we didn't find anything suspicious except his phone and his wallet.' Maitland glanced at me. 'We thought that was potentially his choice, to avoid being tracked.'

'It's possible.' Godley looked up at the building. 'How big is the flat?'

'Not very.' I described it for him and he nodded. 'I don't want everyone tramping around in there when Kev lets us back in. I want a thorough, proper search done. Harry, you can do it, and Colin Vale. I'd like him to do the office to go through the paperwork.'

'Who else?' Maitland asked. 'Just us two? Might take a while.'

Godley turned. 'What about you, Maeve? Searching is your speciality, isn't it?'

I blushed to the roots of my hair. It was a reference to the first time I'd come to his attention a few years before, and I had assumed he would have forgotten it long ago. I hadn't but that was because it was a decisive event in my life. I hadn't expected him to recall a two-minute chat with a uniformed officer on a case that had just blown wide open, even if it was the reason I was working for him now.

Behind him, Una Burt's eyebrows drew together. From his tone, and the fact he was offering me a chance to get involved, it was clear that I was back in his good books. It would burn her, too, if she didn't know the background to his comment.

'I'll do it.'

'Good.' Godley turned around to address the rest of the officers gathered in the alley. 'The rest of us had better find somewhere to wait, I'm afraid. Once we know all we can about Shane Poole, we can start making some plans. Until then—'

'The pub's closed,' Groves observed. 'That might make a good place to wait.'

'Trust you,' Burns said affectionately, then added, 'Not a bad idea, mind.'

'Indeed not.' Godley nodded to Maitland. 'Keep me informed, Harry. We'll wait down here.'

Knowing that the pub below us was full of police officers who would have traded places with us in a heartbeat made me a little bit edgy as I searched Shane Poole's home. Maitland allocated me his bedroom and I spent a long time going through the pockets of everything in his wardrobe. I searched inside shoes and drawers, turning them upside down to make sure there was nothing taped to the underside. I looked inside the cistern of the lavatory in the en suite, and checked that the panelling on the side of the bath didn't come off. I cleared shelves, unfolded jumpers and socks, shook out bedclothes and lay on the floor to check under the bed.

'Anything?'

I looked up at Maitland and shook my head. 'You?'

'We found the safe.'

I'd heard the drilling. 'And?'

'Should have had the week's cash takings in there, but

the notes were gone. He hasn't been to the bank with them, either.'

Unmarked, untraceable, non-consecutive notes. I swore quietly. 'Whatever he needs money for, he's got it.'

'Yeah. Are you almost done?'

'Almost. Give me a hand to lift the mattress, would you?'

He went to the other end of the bed and helped me lever it off the base. There was nothing shoved underneath it, and the mattress itself was as it had come from the manufacturers. The divan, on the other hand, had a hole in it, as we both spotted immediately. Maitland adjusted his gloves and stuck a hand in, retrieving a small envelope.

'Kev,' he yelled. 'You probably want to have a look at this.'

Kev arrived and spread paper on the divan so he could tip out what was in the envelope. A pair of earrings came out first, little silver bows tarnished black. Then came two rings that looked like they had been much worn.

'A wedding band and engagement ring.' I leaned over. 'Quite old-fashioned. His mother's, maybe?'

'Maybe. But the earrings?'

'Angela Poole was wearing them when she died,' I said. 'I recognise them from the crime-scene pictures.'

'What about this?' Kev shook the envelope again, coaxing out the last items. A curl of honey-blonde hair, dry and slightly faded, tied with a scrap of black ribbon. A photograph, passport-picture size, cut from a strip of them – Angela Poole laughing as she sat on the young Derwent's lap. He had his face in her hair, nuzzling her neck. Someone had scraped Derwent's face away with short, angry jabs. And the last thing: a cutting from a newspaper that was some years old, covering the sentencing at the end of a murder trial. An elderly woman, mugged for her handbag, had died of head injuries sustained in the attack and two seventeen-year-olds had been convicted. Highlighted in yellow, near the bottom, a quote from DS Josh Derwent:

'For Beryl's family, this conviction doesn't make up for her loss. She was in good health before the attack and might have had many years ahead of her. Although the people who committed this despicable act are young, they must take responsibility for their actions and I'm glad the court has recognised the serious nature of their crime.'

In the margin beside it, someone – Shane, presumably – had inked an exclamation mark.

I looked at the little pile of things and felt a creeping sense of unease about Shane Poole, and where he might be, and what he might be planning to do.

Chapter 28

It was probably inevitable that I'd be the focus of attention at the conference in the pub. Out of all the police officers in the room, I was the only one who had actually met Shane Poole. I wasn't altogether comfortable with being the main attraction but there was nothing I could do about it. I got a coffee from the bar before the last member of staff was asked to leave, and took a seat near the back, which just meant that everyone turned around to look at me every time my name was mentioned. Godley had got hold of Dr Chen. She was sitting at the front, arms folded, slight but formidable in a navy suit.

The bar staff had drawn the blinds to give us some privacy and the place had the feel of a lock-in, albeit with no booze on offer. The big television in one corner was on with the sound muted, showing a rolling news programme that intermittently displayed live footage of nothing happening outside the pub. Groves was near a window. Now and then he twitched one of the blinds, trying to tempt the cameraman to zoom in on it.

Godley stood by the bar with Maitland and filled in the blanks for those who didn't know. He started with who Shane Poole was. What had happened to his sister. How the current crimes resembled the death twenty years before. Why DI Derwent had come up as a suspect, and why he might be a target for Shane.

'Or,' Una Burt said, 'they could still be friends. Shane could have killed Deena on Derwent's instructions.'

'Shane hates Derwent,' I said, unable to stay quiet. 'He blames him for what happened to Angela. He wanted me to arrest him for statutory rape.'

'A smokescreen.'

'No. He meant it.' I told them about the photograph, coloured in to hide Derwent, and the other picture that was scratched.

'Let's leave Josh Derwent to one side for now,' Godley said. 'What about Shane? He was a teenager when his sister died. Was he a suspect?'

'He had an alibi but it was faked.' A murmur ran around the room. I went on: 'It's worth considering one feature of Angela's death that we've seen in the current series of murders. No obvious sexual element.'

'That doesn't mean that there isn't a sexual thrill involved for the perpetrator,' Dr Chen said.

'I know, but if it was Shane who killed her, that could explain it. Instead of him killing her because he wanted to have sex with her, maybe he wanted to punish her for sleeping with her boyfriend. He was obviously disgusted by the thought of her having sex with Derwent when he spoke to me about it.'

'Okay. Let's look at that,' Godley said. 'He kills his sister. Then what?'

'Then he spent some years taking an awful lot of drugs,' I said. 'And then he got clean, got some money together and started this bar, which is doing very nicely according to the paperwork in his study.'

'A success story. He'd left his past behind him. So why would he risk everything by starting to kill women in the last twelve months?'

'There could have been a triggering event,' Dr Chen said. 'Something that reminded him of what happened twenty years ago. Something that brought him back to the state of mind that made him want to kill.'

'His best friend died,' I said. 'In Afghanistan, about two months before Kirsty's death. He was a big influence on Shane, and he knew Derwent too.'

Dr Chen was nodding. 'That sounds like a possible source of trauma.'

'So what?' Bradbury had folded his arms and his face was stony. 'We're supposed to ignore the evidence pointing us towards a police officer so we can chase a missing bar owner? Was there anything upstairs that connected Shane Poole to the current killings, or did I miss something?'

'Nothing so far,' Maitland admitted. 'But all the forensic work might throw something up.'

'That could take months,' Bradbury pointed out. 'We've got a good suspect already, and we know where he is. I say we stick with the original plan – covert surveillance on Derwent and quietly investigate every single thing we can think of that might prove he's our guy. And if that doesn't work, arrest him and sweat it out of him.'

I couldn't help myself: I laughed. 'Do you really think Derwent would confess because *you* put him under pressure? Good luck.'

Bradbury glared. 'We know where you stand.'

Burt leaned across and whispered something in his ear, shielding her mouth so no one else could hear. He nodded in response. I burned to know what it was while being quite sure it was better not to. If Burt was throwing in her lot with Bradbury, I didn't feel quite the same need to impress her.

Godley cleared his throat, drawing everyone's attention back to the front of the room. 'Some of you know Josh Derwent personally and most of you know him by reputation. I will be extremely relieved if we can rule him out of any involvement with these murders, but I am not going to make the mistake of moving on to a new suspect

316

without investigating him properly. So there's no need to worry, Andy.'

'Isn't that him on the news?' Groves said from his position by the window. 'What's he done now?'

As one, every head in the room turned to the television screen, where a Breaking News banner ran along the bottom of the screen. By the time I looked, the video clip they'd been playing had come to an end, and the screen was filled with a newsreader. Her mouth was moving, the studio lights gleaming on her lipgloss.

'Turn it up,' Godley said tightly.

'. . . we're going to stick with the story and speak to our reporter, who was there when this incident actually happened. Tom, are you there?'

'Yes, hello, Carly.' Tom was young, easy on the eye and wryly amused by whatever had taken place. For a journalist, there was nothing better than being in the right place at the right time, and he was looking more than happy to tell the world what he'd seen. He was standing on a street corner that looked faintly familiar and I frowned, trying to place it. He was in front of the sign, so all I could read was the word 'Street'. Not helpful.

'What can you tell us about what happened this afternoon?'

'Well, extraordinary scenes at St Luke's hospital in London, where Detective Inspector Josh Derwent was recuperating after being shot in the leg yesterday in that incident in a playground. Today he was well enough to be able to discharge himself from hospital, so obviously making a good recovery. We were here around three o'clock this afternoon at the invitation of Philip Pace, the leader of the Dads Matter pressure group, who were of course blamed in some quarters for the actions of the playground gunman, Lee Grimes. Philip Pace was hoping to see DI Derwent to thank him for resolving the situation safely.'

And hoping to use Derwent as a means to getting some

much-needed good publicity. I had a feeling of impending doom.

'But things didn't go according to plan,' the newsreader prompted, a tiny smile hovering around her mouth.

'Indeed they did not. DI Derwent was not keen to speak to Mr Pace, and refused to see him inside the hospital. Philip Pace is not someone who likes taking no for an answer, as we know, and he managed to find out which door the policeman was going to use when leaving the hospital. He approached him and I think our footage probably tells the story better than I can.'

The screen flickered and showed a hospital doorway, with Philip Pace standing to one side of it. The door opened and Derwent hobbled through, on crutches, as unshaven and unkempt as he had been that morning. He glared at the assembled press.

'What are you lot doing here?'

Philip Pace reached out and put a hand on Derwent's left arm. 'On behalf of Dads Matter, I wanted to—'

'I told you, I'm not interested.' He shook the restraining hand off.

A quick glance from Pace to the journalists: you could see him calculating the damage to his reputation, the wheels whirring as he tried to come up with a graceful way out of it. 'Oh, ha ha ha, DI Derwent. It's nice that you still have such a good sense of humour.'

'Who's laughing?' Derwent gave him the most intimidating glower in his repertoire.

Pace misjudged things to the extent that he dropped a chummy arm around Derwent's shoulders before he replied. Derwent was injured, but not incapacitated. He dropped his left shoulder and swung with his right hand, pivoting as the crutches fell to the floor. His fist connected with Pace's nose, making an obscene crunching sound that was followed by a shriek from Pace and a murmur from the journalists off-camera. The leader of Dads

Matter slid to the ground, screaming, both hands to his face where blood was seeping through his fingers, and the camera followed him. In the corner of the screen, someone retrieved one fallen crutch, and Derwent was heard to limp off, refusing all questions. The cameraman turned from Pace at the last minute and caught the back of Derwent's head as he disappeared into a police car. Pace was altogether better box-office, writhing in agony and moaning inarticulately.

Someone in the bar – I couldn't see who – began to applaud, and soon the entire room was cheering. Godley was grinning, I was relieved to see. The police officers quietened down as the newsreader appeared again.

'What's going to happen now? Is DI Derwent under arrest?'

Tom looked amused. 'You may have noticed him getting into a police car. That was actually his lift home, but he delayed his return to his house to speak with officers who were on duty nearby and made a statement to them about what had happened. He wasn't arrested. My understanding is that Philip Pace is unlikely to press charges. He seems rather embarrassed by the whole affair and has refused to take any calls from members of the media, or issue a statement.'

'How bad were his injuries, Tom?'

'I believe he had a broken nose and some severe bruising, Carly. He received immediate treatment in St Luke's accident and emergency department.'

'Has DI Derwent had anything to say, Tom?'

'Well, we dared to ask him about it when he returned home, and this happened.'

The screen again switched to the shaky handheld camera, which was now focusing on a police car drawing up on the street outside Derwent's flat.

'Inspector Derwent, sir, hello. Could you come and speak to us about the incident with Philip Pace, please?'

Derwent was extracting himself from the car. He turned, looking exhausted, and shook his head.

'Did you want to say anything at all?' Tom appeared in the frame, microphone extended to Derwent with the sort of timidity I'd associate with someone hand-feeding a tiger.

'Plenty,' Derwent said. 'But not on camera.'

The screen flickered and went back to Tom on his street corner. He laughed. 'That was all we got, I'm afraid, but at least no one got hurt.'

'Oh, Josh,' Godley said, shaking his head. 'You do have a knack for getting into trouble. I imagine I'll be getting some calls about that before long. Mute it again, please.'

I watched the screen as the reporter signed off. There was a buzz of conversation in the room, most of it approving but some of it very disapproving indeed. No prizes for guessing who was complaining about Derwent's behaviour. Godley clapped his hands.

'Okay. That's enough. Does anyone have any suggestions?'

James Peake raised a hand. 'Release Shane Poole's picture to the media and tell them to report that we want to question him as we think he might have useful information for us. He wasn't planning to go too far, I'd say, especially if he left his passport and didn't clear out his bank accounts.'

'Worth a try. Anyone else?' Godley looked around the room. 'Right. I've asked for details of Shane and his car to be added to briefings across the South-East. All ANPR cameras will be looking for his plates, but he's been canny about other things that might draw our attention so I'd expect him to be using fake ones. We'll keep Derwent on our list and keep digging into their backgrounds. Harry is taking over the cold case, by the way, so address any questions to him.'

Maitland looked terrified. I gathered my things together. Forgiveness only went so far, I could see. I had proved myself to be a useful member of the team but Godley was a long way from reinstating me.

'Where are you going?' Peake strolled over, hands in his pockets.

'Home. Bed. Maybe a bath first.' I wound my scarf around my neck. 'I need a rest.'

'Sounds like fun.'

I wasn't in the mood. 'No fun. Just sleep. And plenty of it.'

'I didn't mean—'

'Yeah, you did.'

In spite of myself I smiled: he was looking at me from under worried eyebrows, biting his lip, overselling the anxiety just a tad but damn cute with it. 'Good luck. I'll see you when Shane lands in custody.'

'If not before,' Peake said, and stood back to let me go. I nodded to Godley as I went, and he nodded back, as if to say: *yes, that's the first sensible thing I've seen you do today.*

I wouldn't have admitted it, but I thought the same.

Chapter 29

It was dark outside, and raining hard, and the air was raw. I reeled, feeling as if I'd walked into a wall of pure exhaustion. I took a roundabout route to the tube, dodging news cameras. It was unlikely that I'd do a Derwent but not impossible.

I had to battle delayed and crowded trains and edgy fellow commuters. I took the shortest possible route from the station to the flat, checking behind me in a cursory way, but far more focused on getting some sleep than on my personal safety. My hair was soaking, the rain seeping down between my coat collar and my neck. It had saturated my shoulders already and the cold struck up through the thin soles of my shoes.

Things didn't get a lot better when I got home. The air in the flat chilled me and something definitely smelled off. I squeezed rainwater out of my hair and tied it back, then went through the kitchen while the kettle boiled and the heat came on, finding nothing in the fridge or cupboards or even the bin that might be responsible. I moved on, searching every other room in the flat, winding up in the sitting room. The light was blinking on the answering machine and I pressed play, letting it squawk in the background while I kept looking. There had to be something. A plate with leftover food under a chair. A mug growing exciting mould. God knows, I wasn't the best housekeeper in the world but just forgetting I'd abandoned food somewhere was a new low.

'Maeve, it's your mother. I was just wondering if you'd had a chance to write to your aunt Niamh. I—'

I cut her off. Next message.

'Maeve. You're not back yet. I was just ringing to see if you'd got my earlier mess—'

I stabbed at it irritably. My mother's refusal to come to terms with the modern world meant she hated ringing me on my mobile. It suited me fine – otherwise my voicemail would have been solid with calls about nothing much that I would never, ever return. But on this occasion, it would have been vibrating on its own, wherever it had ended up, lonely in its evidence bag, and I would have been wonderfully out of range.

'Maeve Áine Kerrigan, what have I just seen on the news? Call me when you get this, please. At once.'

She sounded really cross. I winced and let the next message play in full.

'You could have been killed. I don't know what possessed you to go in there with no gun or anything. And they say your nice boss was shot. Well, it's no more than he deserves, dragging you into a dangerous situation like that and you with no more sense than a day-old chick. Call me as soon as you get this message.'

She was less angry, more scared in the next message, and then in the next one said she'd tried my mobile number but had got no answer, and then in the one after that I got the full, cold, 'Of course, we're the last people who matter but it would be nice if you'd acknowledge our existence now and then.'

I put out my hand for the phone and then stopped as the answering machine beeped again. I put my finger on the delete button, but pulled back when I realised it was Rob. He sounded tense. 'Maeve, I got your message. I've been trying to call you on your phone but you're not picking up

– I don't know why. I've left a message for you at work, too, so maybe you'll get that first. Maeve, don't be scared, but get a bag – now – and go somewhere safe.' He was striving for calm but the urgency kept breaking through, and I stopped lifting sofa cushions, looking for the rogue prawn sandwich that had to be the source of the stench. I stared at the machine as if it could tell me in advance where this was going.

'Your message – you thanked me for the flowers, but I didn't send you any and I don't know who did. I know you'll want to find out who it was, but don't waste any time, please. Just go.'

It was all very well for Rob to tell me to leave without further delay, but it was human nature to examine the flowers to see if there were any clues, and I was only human. The smell was far stronger as I bent over them. The roses had opened fully now, and they were packed so tightly together it was hard to see what was going on – until the overhead light struck a gleam of something that was clearly, obviously flesh. Not needing to put on a brave face since I was alone, I screamed and dropped the vase. It shattered, sending little bits of glass everywhere. In among the glass shards and leaves I saw white, squirming things. Maggots. The smell was strong enough to make me gag. With gloves on, the kitchen scissors in hand and a wooden spoon for poking purposes I managed to pull the bouquet apart so I could see what was at the heart of it: a piece of meat wedged in tightly, surrounded by stems. It was chicken, I thought, or pork, but green with decomposition and alive with maggots. I turned my head away, convinced I was going to be sick. It wasn't just that the meat smelled revolting. Someone had pretended to be Rob to send me a message. They knew where I was. They knew I was alone. And they wanted me to know that they knew.

It didn't take a genius to leap to the same conclusion as Rob. Chris Swain, the guy who had seemed so harmless when he was just my neighbour, had an uncanny ability to track me down, no matter how hard I tried to stay hidden. Up to now, he'd been happy to play games with me. He got his kicks from taking me to the edge of terror and letting me see just how powerless I was to stop myself from falling over. He had marked me out as a victim and I couldn't seem to shake off the role, no matter how much I hated it, and him. He was a sneak, a voyeur, a rapist whose style was to drug his victims to avoid the possibility of them fighting back. A coward.

Dangerous.

And the thing that really bothered me about the game he was playing was that I had no idea what constituted a win. Humiliation? Aggravation?

Death?

I went into the bedroom and changed into jeans, boots and a thick sweatshirt, all too aware of the possibility that I was being watched or filmed with the sort of secret camera Swain had used before. I put a change of clothes and some toiletries in a backpack, then got ready for the hard work: two layers of gloves and the dustpan and brush. I got a bag from the kitchen and shovelled the whole pile into it: the oozing meat and broken glass and bent stems and every last one of the maggots. I excavated the cellophane and tissue paper that had been wrapped around the bouquet from the kitchen bin and folded them into a brown-paper parcel. I got an envelope and went through the recycling to find the florists' card, aware that I had missed a collection the previous day. If I had just been a little bit more efficient, the evidence would have been long gone.

'Score one for me,' I said aloud, trying to keep my spirits up. Trying to keep the fear at bay because I had things to do before I could leave and every instinct for self-preservation I possessed was pushing me towards the door.

I needed the evidence, because I was reporting this as a crime. I wanted it on record. Swain was on the Met's wanted list already because of video evidence we'd seized of him sexually assaulting dozens of unconscious women, but when we caught him – and we would – I wanted him charged with the crimes he'd committed against me. He owed me that much, even if I wasn't going to be first on the indictment. Others had suffered more than me, but I had endured quite enough from Swain. I would have my day in court, and he would hopefully have a decade or so in prison when we finally caught up with him.

I put the bag inside another bag and left it in the hall, hoping it wouldn't stink too badly the next day. There was no point in calling it in now. The response team would never consider it a priority at that time of night; I'd be in a queue behind every domestic and suspected burglary and bar fight in east London, and I wasn't inclined to wait around in the flat for hours, wondering when or if I was going to be attacked. Better to wait until early turn started for the local CID and hand it over to a nice, friendly detective who could take a statement and file a report. I wanted to be free to leave as soon as I was ready to go. Just being in the flat was close to unbearable. My jaw ached and I realised I was clenching it, and my fists, as the adrenalin played on my nerves. What else did I need to do?

Oh yes. That was it. Find somewhere to go. Which was where I ground to a halt for the second time. I didn't know anyone nearby: Rob and I had chosen Dalston in part because we never socialised around there so we could keep a low profile. I had no mobile phone so no numbers for anyone I could trust not to panic, which would teach me to learn some off by heart. I only knew Rob's, my parents' and my brother's. I was not going to involve my parents in this particular flap; I couldn't go to my brother either, because someone – a niece or his wife or even Dec himself – would be bound to let it slip to Mum and then I would be in even more trouble for not having told them in the first place. The rain rattled as the wind caught the drops and flung them against the windows. I couldn't stay in the flat; it wasn't safe. I didn't want to leave without knowing where I was going.

I stood in the middle of the living room, shivering, and considered my options, none of which were appealing. Back to the office, where there was nowhere to sleep at all. Stay where I was and hope Swain had sent the flowers because he couldn't get past our security arrangements. But I already felt I was being watched, and I'd never sleep. Trek to Liv's house, though she lived in Guildford, miles outside London, and it would take me an age to get there. I didn't want to risk it without knowing she'd be in. Call the office, get put through to Godley and let him take over – but he was fully occupied and I couldn't divert him from a murder investigation for the sake of a sick prank, even if it had me terrified. Stay in a hotel – somewhere cheap and soulless but with decent locks on the doors. It wasn't an appealing option. I didn't want to be on my own with my fears, even if it was somewhere other than the flat. I would never relax enough to close my eyes, let alone sleep. But it looked as if I was out of luck.

Except that I knew one person who was nearby, and at home, and would be more than pleased to help. In fact, he would be angry if I didn't call on him. And he owed me a favour. It was a terrible idea, but it was a better option than anything else I'd thought of.

I just hoped the surveillance team wouldn't have started yet.

Chapter 30

'Go. Away.'

'Sir, it's me.' I was crouching by the letterbox, trying not to let the skirt of my coat get wet, the wind tugging at my hair and clothes until it felt as if someone was pulling at me, trying to get my attention. I was half-whispering because I really didn't want to attract the interest of passers-by, the media or even Derwent's neighbours. There was only one person I was trying to reach, and he was having none of it.

'Fuck off. I'm not telling you again.'

'It's Maeve. Kerrigan,' I added, then rolled my eyes. He only knew one Maeve, I was fairly sure. I checked over my shoulder – no one – and levered open the letterbox again. I could see his feet, and realised he was sitting at the top of the stairs. Forgetting about speaking softly, I snarled, 'I'm only here because I need help. Now if you're not going to man up and let me in, I'm going, but I want you to know I think you're a— a—'

'A what?' He sounded interested.

'A twat. Sir.'

'That must be you, Kerrigan. Only you would take so long to come up with the word "twat". I was expecting something really good.' He got to his feet slowly, with some difficulty, balancing on one leg as he turned to reach his crutches. 'I'll let you in but it'll be a while before I can get to the door.'

'Take your time,' I said, shuddering with the cold. I couldn't feel my hands any more, or my ears.

Instead of coming down towards the door, Derwent levered himself up, out of sight.

'Where are you going?'

'I was making tea. It'll be stewed if I don't get the bag out of the mug sharpish.'

I fumed on the doorstep for another five minutes while Derwent did whatever he had to do and then came down the stairs with roughly as much fuss and as many dramatic pauses as an elderly diva making her Vegas debut. When he finally opened the door I pushed in past him.

'Wait until you're invited, missy.'

'That's vampires, not house guests.' I turned. 'When are they coming round with your heavyweight belt?'

'Oh, you saw that?'

'I think the world's seen it by now. It was a hell of a shot.'

'You're telling me. I bruised my hand, look.' He showed me his fist, which was red and swollen and had a gash on top of one finger.

'Is that a fight bite?'

'Yeah. If he didn't have such big horse teeth I'd have been fine because it was a direct hit on his nose. Knowing my luck, he'll have rabies.'

'You got a round of applause from the coppers I was with when they saw it.'

'Really?' He looked pleased. 'The guys at the hospital didn't even consider arresting me. They talked Pace into letting it drop. Nice of them.'

'I think a lot of people were hoping something like that might happen to him.'

'You know me. Being a hero comes natural.'

'I'm sure.' It was freezing in the hall and I made for the stairs. 'I'm going up to get warm.'

'You're not going to wait for me?'

'I've done a lot of waiting for you this evening already.'

I ran up and into the living room, which was warm and softly lit. He had drawn the blinds, shutting the world out, and I started to feel I could relax for the first time in hours. I took off my boots and coat, and held my hands over the radiator, wincing as the warmth started to bring them back to life.

Derwent made it up to the top of the stairs eventually and abandoned the crutches with a clatter. He limped in to the sitting room.

'Make yourself at home.'

'I knew you'd want me to be comfortable.'

He ignored that. 'To what do I owe the pleasure? If you've had a fight with your boyfriend, I'm not providing a sympathetic ear.'

'You wouldn't be the first port of call for that,' I agreed. I was still shivering. At this stage I was starting to think it was because I was ill or in shock. The flat was boiling. Derwent was wearing a T-shirt with his tracksuit bottoms. I tried, very hard, to send a message to my nervous system that it could calm down for the time being. 'I couldn't stay in my flat.'

'Why not?'

'Because of a bunch of flowers, would you believe.'

Derwent listened, asking the occasional question, as I faltered through the story. He had dropped the attitude. I was talking to the police officer version of Derwent, focused on the facts and their implications. I wished I had the luxury of a cool-headed assessment of the situation, but I was far too involved for that.

'First thing: who knew Rob was going to be away?'

'No one.' I got a look for that and tried again. 'Okay. I did, obviously. I mentioned it to Liv, who might have told Joanna, I suppose. People Rob works with. I didn't tell you.'

'No, you didn't.'

'I didn't tell my parents or any of our friends.' I chewed my lip. 'That's it, as far as I know.'

330

'Did you talk to anyone about it over the phone? Could your landline be bugged?'

'I only use the landline to pick up messages, mainly from Mum. I always use my mobile.'

'What about email?'

'No.'

'Facebook?'

'I'm not on Facebook.' Like I wanted to share details of my personal life with the world. Derwent should have known better.

'Any other social websites?'

I shook my head. 'Nothing.'

'Is your place bugged?'

'I don't know. That's what Swain did before.' I was starting to shake again.

'Get that checked out.' Derwent had sat down on the arm of a chair while we were talking and now he jumped up and started to pace. He got two steps before his leg went from under him and he collapsed inelegantly into the chair. 'Oh, fuck-a-doodle-do.'

'Are you okay?'

'Fine.' He righted himself. 'What about Boyband? Does he keep his mouth shut?'

I ignored the jibe. 'As a rule.'

'And you thought the flowers were from him.'

'Yes, but I didn't think the message sounded like him. It was patronising.'

'Could you imagine Chris Swain saying it?'

'I try not to imagine Chris Swain saying anything at all.' I sighed. 'Look, I don't think we're going to get to the bottom of this tonight. It was creepy as hell and I generally assume that means Swain was involved. I hope you can understand why I ended up here.'

'Yeah, I know why you're here. Let Uncle Josh look after everything.'

I tried not to look repelled but it was a struggle.

'Drink?' Derwent said.

'I don't need anything.'

'I was telling you to get me one.'

'Oh.' I bit back *get it yourself*. Being on crutches, he couldn't carry a drink easily, and it was the least I could do. 'What do you want?'

'Beer. In the fridge. You know where the kitchen is.'

I did. I was on my way back, bottle in hand, when a thought struck me. I doubled back to make sure, then went and stood in the doorway of the sitting room until Derwent looked up.

'Over here, love. Don't ever quit and become a waitress, will you? You're rubbish.'

'You lied to me.'

He raised his eyebrows.

'You said you were making tea, but the kettle's cold and there are no mugs in the sink or the dishwasher or in here. You have no milk in your fridge and I couldn't find a single tea bag in your kitchen. You don't even drink tea. You told me that before. What were you doing? Tidying up? Hiding the evidence?'

He gave me his widest, whitest smile, the one that reminded me of a hunting dog grinning. 'Give me the beer.'

'Not before I get an explanation.'

'Come on.' He held out his hand. 'If you need me to say it, I'm impressed, Kerrigan. You put it all together.'

'Yay for me. I still want to know what you were doing.'

'Tidying.'

'You never tidy because you never make a mess.'

'What does it matter?'

'It matters because I don't like being lied to.'

He stretched. 'Well, I've never lied to you about any-thing important. You know that, don't you?'

'I thought I did.'

'It's true.' He looked straight at me, his eyes limpid. 'You can trust me. But you can also trust me to be a bit of a lad.

332

I thought you were coming round to tick me off for punching Pace on camera. I wanted to make you wait.'

'Thanks very much.'

'Any time.' He looked as ashamed of himself as it was possible for Derwent to look, which was not very. 'You should get to bed. Get some rest. You look like death.'

'Where am I going?'

'In there.' He indicated the room next to the living room.

I picked up my bag and went in, flicking the light on. I stopped for a second, then reversed.

'That's your room.'

'So?'

'So you seem to have misunderstood.' My face was flaming.

'No, you have. This is a one-bedroom flat. I am letting you have the bedroom. I do not propose to sleep with you and that phrase includes any possible meaning you like, from sharing a room to shagging. And don't flatter yourself.'

He was amused, not angry, but I was still mortally embarrassed. It put an edge in my voice when I replied. 'And what about you? Where are you going to sleep?'

'The sofa.'

'No. You're injured. I should sleep there.'

'It's not on offer.'

'I am not sleeping in your bed when you were shot a day and a half ago and you should still be in hospital.'

'Who told you that?'

'It's obvious,' I said. 'You look dreadful.'

'Said the woman with bright red eyes and crazy hair. Fuck me, it's like getting a lecture from Coco the Clown.'

I put a hand up, encountered frizz and decided not to fight that particular battle. 'Never mind how I look. You are recuperating and you shouldn't be doing it on a sofa.'

He rubbed both hands over his face. 'Give me strength. Listen, Kerrigan, I'm going to let you in on a little secret.

This leg? Hurts like buggery. I'm not going to be getting much sleep tonight even if I'm in my own bed.'

'Didn't they give you painkillers to take home?'

'Yeah.'

'And?'

'I don't like them. I'm not taking them.'

'You are so stubborn.'

He levered himself to his feet. 'I know. But it's my body. I don't like drugs and I don't mind pain. I just don't think there's any point pretending I'm going to sleep tonight. And you look as if you could sleep for a week.'

'Two.'

'There you go.' He limped past me, holding on to the wall for support. 'I'll get a spare duvet out and nick a pillow and I'll be fine.'

There was no arguing with him, ever. I was too tired for a fight anyway. The thought of sinking into a real bed at long last was enough to make me give in. I brushed my teeth in a bathroom that was antiseptically clean and male from the toiletries to the towels. When I came out, Derwent was leaning against the wall in the hall.

'Need anything else?'

'No. Thanks.' I hesitated. 'And thanks for this. Letting me stay.'

'It's a pleasure,' he said, as if he meant it.

I said goodnight and shut the door firmly behind me, wishing I could lock it. I trusted Derwent but I wanted the security of being behind an unopenable door. He'd stripped the bed while I was in the bathroom and I spent a few minutes making it again, wrestling with the duvet. It was strange to be doing a domestic task in Derwent's home, his private space, a place I had never imagined being. I could only imagine what Godley would make of it if he knew.

'Mind out of the gutter, boss,' I murmured and climbed into Derwent's bed before switching off the light. I pulled the covers up and huddled, relieved. I was glad that

Derwent had trusted me enough to let me stay. I was glad I had stuck by him when Godley and Burt told me to be wary. I was starting to think we might become friends.

Friends with Derwent? Stranger things had happened. But not many.

Despite everything, I went to sleep with a smile on my face.

At ten to four, I woke up, with no idea where I was or what had disturbed me. I didn't know anything, except that I was scared. It took a couple of seconds for me to remember where I was and why, relief sweeping over me as I reminded myself that I was safe and everything was all right.

A couple of seconds after that, something moved in the room, passing in front of the shaded window so I saw a silhouette for a second. A man.

'Derwent?' I said, my voice blurry with sleep. I assumed, I thought that he had forgotten something, or that he'd forgotten I was there. I thought it was an honest mistake.

I thought that until, without warning, he landed on top of me with his full weight, pinned my arms to my sides with his knees, wrapped his hands around my neck and began to squeeze the life out of me. It wasn't fear I felt, or despair, but anger. I was angry with myself. I'd believed Derwent, and I'd been wrong, and whatever happened was my fault. God, I hated being wrong.

White and red lights burst in the blackness and I couldn't fight, or scream, or do anything at all.

Anything, that is, except die.

THURSDAY

Chapter 31

I'd love to pretend that I found superhuman strength from somewhere and kicked my way free. I'd love to say that I saved my own life by being quick and clever and instinctively good at fighting. The reality was that I was in serious trouble, as close to dying as I had ever been. I was aware of almost nothing as my brain became starved of oxygen, nothing but a bright light and the dreadful weight on top of me that was crushing my ribs, and the impossibility of taking a breath when my body was crying out for it. And then, suddenly, the weight was gone and I could breathe again, dragging air into my lungs as my knees came up to my chest. My throat was on fire, my eyes full of tears, and the sound of my own heart thumping filled my ears. I rolled onto my side in a tight little ball and wheezed piteously.

It was probably a minute – not more than that – before I came round enough to start making sense of my surroundings. The bright light was the main bedroom light. A scuffling sound interspersed with dull thuds and grunts of pain was a fight happening somewhere nearby. The thumping sound was someone trying to batter the front door in. The urgency of doing something galvanised me: I sat up and saw Derwent on the floor, on the wrong side of a fight that was the definition of nasty. The man struggling with him, anonymous in dark clothes and a beanie hat, was big and angry, and while I was still trying to get my head around what was going on he hit Derwent with a short, nasty jab in the stomach that made Derwent groan. He retaliated by forcing the man's head back, pressing against his throat, fingers digging for the pressure point that would – in theory – reduce his assailant to a quivering wreck. The guy retaliated by kneeing him in the crotch, missing his target by a matter of inches as Derwent twisted sideways.

It was time to stop watching and start helping, I realised, and looked around for something to use. The bedside light was metal and surprisingly heavy when I hefted it. I unplugged it and struggled off the bed, ready to hit—

I stopped. I had no idea who I should want to win. I couldn't tell who had attacked me and who had come to the rescue. Derwent caught sight of me and glared, for the split second he could spare, and I could translate it easily enough: *what are you doing, standing there? Get stuck in, Kerrigan.*

Instead, I moved around so I could see his opponent's face. Derwent pushed his head back again, the muscles standing out in his arm as he stretched his fingers towards the man's eyes, and I recognised him at last: the Met's most wanted, Shane Poole. I lifted the lamp and brought it down on the back of his neck, and he collapsed over Derwent like a tower block disintegrating in a controlled explosion.

'Thank fuck.' Derwent pushed at Shane's shoulder, trying to lever him off. 'You took your time. Were you waiting for an invitation?'

'Is he still alive?'

'Yeah. Out cold. Nice job.' Derwent wriggled out and sat up, leaning his arms on his knees as he tried to get his breathing back under control. He looked past me. 'This must be my night for unwanted guests.'

Two men were standing in the doorway when I looked round, one small and one big, both in leather bomber jackets, both so obviously policemen that they might as well not have bothered being in plain clothes.

'We saw him break in. We were waiting for backup to come, but then we heard the fight so we opened your door.'

'Do much damage?' Derwent asked.

'Just a bit.' The larger one lifted up the battering ram he'd used. 'You might need to get the hinges fixed.'

'Fucking marvellous.'

The smaller policeman lifted his radio. 'One in custody. We'll need an ambulance, please. Two ambulances,' he said, looking at me, and I put a hand to my neck, suddenly aware that it was throbbing.

His big friend bent over Shane Poole and put him in the recovery position, then cuffed him, hands in front. 'Not to take any chances,' he said to me. 'Amazing how quickly they recover when they want to.'

'What was he doing here?' I asked Derwent.

'What are these two doing here?' he shot back. 'Were you watching me?' He looked at me. 'Did you know about this?'

'I knew there was going to be surveillance on you. I didn't know they were here.'

'Why the fuck didn't you tell me?' He looked utterly incensed.

'Because I still owe some loyalty to my boss and he told me not to. My career is already in tatters. What do you think Godley would have done if I'd warned you about the surveillance?'

'Sacked you.' Derwent shrugged. 'Not my problem. My problem is being lied to.'

'Get over yourself.' I turned to the plain-clothes guys. 'What did you see?'

'We were parked on the corner. We saw matey here having a look at the place a couple of hours ago and then wander off. He didn't look dodgy enough to stop – all he did was look. We didn't know who he was, obviously, or we'd have had him. He went over the wall at the back about ten minutes ago and in through the bathroom window.'

'Damn it,' Derwent said. 'I bet he's broken it.'

'Sounded like it.'

'Ten minutes ago?' I was stuck on the timings. 'Was that all?'

'He was only in here for a minute before I put the light on,' Derwent said. 'I heard him in the hall. Knew it wasn't you because you don't make that much noise, walking around. He came in to the sitting room first but I wasn't in a position to tackle him then.'

'Where were you?'

'Behind the sofa.'

I tried not to laugh, and failed.

'I wasn't *hiding*. I was trying to sleep there.'

'Oh, sure,' I said. 'I believe you. You thought you'd wait until he was distracted and then take him down.'

'I am just out of hospital,' Derwent said, hurt. 'I'm not at my best.'

'You did all right,' the larger of the two policemen said. 'Not a bad effort.'

Derwent's chest expanded a couple of inches. 'My trouble is I don't know when I'm beaten. I keep fighting even when the odds are against me.' He looked at me. 'That's the definition of a winner, Kerrigan.'

'Sounds like the definition of a moron to me.' I was sailing very close to the edge of what Derwent considered acceptable repartee. I rushed to change the subject. 'So why was he trying to kill me?'

'That's what we'll have to find out.' Derwent looked down at the body at his feet. Shane groaned, but kept his eyes closed. Derwent stuck a toe in his ribcage experimentally and got no response. 'If he ever comes round. Bloody hell, Kerrigan, how hard did you hit him?'

'Very. I imagined it was you.'

Although the paramedics tutted over Shane's head and took him to hospital where he was scanned, tested, prodded and poked, he was concussion-free when he woke up, and passed as fit to be interviewed later that afternoon. I sat in the nearest police station to Derwent's house in a room that was too small for comfort, with Derwent, Maitland, Godley and Una Burt. Derwent was in an edgy mood, inclined to bicker, and more than once Godley had to tell him off for being rude.

'Sorry, guv. This is pissing me off, though. I don't understand why you won't let me speak to him.'

'Because you are far too involved. Maitland and I will handle this and you can watch the video link.'

'Don't do me any favours,' Derwent said under his breath.

'If you want, you can give us some idea of how you would handle the interview. We might find it useful.'

'Ask him why he wanted to find me in the first place. Ask him what all of this has to do with Angela. Ask him if he killed her and the other women. Ask him why he started killing last year.'

'This is revelatory,' Burt said, borrowing Derwent's trademark sarcasm and making it work for her. 'No one would have thought of asking such comprehensive questions without your input.'

'Okay, so maybe I'm not coming up with anything you haven't thought of, but you can't ask it the way I can. You walk into the room and he'll be . . . I want to say *appalled*, but it won't be because he's intimidated by you. He'll laugh at you.'

'*Josh*,' Godley snapped. 'I'm *warning* you.'

Derwent ignored the interruption. 'When it comes to me, on the other hand, he's scared shitless. I go in there and ask him these questions and he'll give up. I can make him angry. Get under his skin. I *know* him.'

'You used to know him,' Godley said, glancing up as Colin Vale came in holding a file. 'You haven't spoken to him for twenty years. You knew him when he was a teenager and now he's a successful businessman.'

'You're talking about Poole?' Colin checked. 'Well, if now's a good time, I can tell you exactly how successful he is.'

'Go on.'

'He's turned the bar from a seedy local to one of the reliable earners in that street. Talking to the neighbouring businesses, it's all his hard work. He works insane hours, lives for the business, spent a long time putting any profit back into the bar rather than living it up. He's meticulous about his records, which is useful for me, and as a business the place is on the up. It's also on the market.'

'Since when?'

'January. Not a good time to sell, unfortunately, with the downturn in the economy. He's got a high price tag on it, but he's right, according to those who know. He's prepared to wait until someone comes along who'll pay him what he deserves and in the meantime he's keeping back more of the profit to divert into savings and investments. Or he was.'

'What do you mean?' Godley asked.

'Well, it's a funny thing. You noticed the cash thing, Maeve, didn't you?'

I nodded. 'He doesn't seem to use his bank card for personal purchases; everything is in cash, in-person transactions that we can't trace.'

'That's a relatively recent development,' Colin said. 'He started that last year too. So something made him start hiding what he was doing then.'

'Getting ready to start killing,' Burt said.

'Or putting the business on the market,' I pointed out, playing devil's advocate. 'If it sold, the due diligence would have involved all of his records. Maybe he wanted to keep a few things to himself.'

'But this is his personal account we're dealing with,' Burt snapped. 'Nothing to do with the business.'

'You don't know he wasn't paying some casual

employees cash in hand to keep down the staff costs and make the place look more appealing to an investor,' Colin said. 'Staff are the curse of catering because even on the minimum wage they cost a lot, and you have to cover their National Insurance contributions. If you're just taking some money out of the till, on the other hand, they don't have to pay income tax and you can make your overheads a lot smaller.'

'That sounds possible,' I said, remembering the Nigerian cleaner who had looked scared of me.

'He's trying to hide something to do with the killings,' Derwent said, sounding bored. 'Do we really have to fanny about providing him with innocent reasons for using cash all the time?'

'I hate to agree but I feel the same way.' Burt turned to Godley. 'You must think he's a credible suspect.'

'Must I?' Godley looked amused. 'He could be. I'm going to wait until I've spoken to him to see.'

'I want to sit in on the interview.' Burt didn't look at Derwent as she said it, but it was her loss because his face was a picture. It was an obvious power play – a reminder that she was senior, and closer to Godley than him as well. To give him his due, Godley saw it a mile off.

'I don't want anyone there who doesn't have to be. I want to speak to him. I want Harry with me because he's a trained interrogator and the best I have on my team.'

Maitland looked pleased. 'Too kind, boss.'

'Please, both of you – all of you – watch the interview. We'll take breaks so you can give us a steer if we miss something. I do value your input but I don't want you in there.'

Burt got up, muttering something about having to make some calls, and stumped out of the room. Godley and Maitland followed, heading for the interview room to set it up as they wanted it. Derwent laughed and stood up, wobbling as he found out the hard way his leg wasn't working well enough to pace about.

'He doesn't want Burt in there because she'd frighten the wits out of Shane. She's mentioned specifically in the UN mandate against torture, you know. Cruel and unusual punishment, just looking at her.'

'She's all right.'

'She doesn't like *you*.'

'What makes you say that?'

'Gave you evils when you were speaking. Shot down your point about the bar records being up for inspection. That wasn't altogether stupid, I thought. Well done you.'

'I live for your praise,' I said drily.

Derwent sat down again, this time beside me. 'Answer me one thing. It's been bothering me.'

'What?'

'Do you always sleep fully clothed?'

'I didn't pack pyjamas.'

'I'd have lent you something.'

'There was no need. I don't mind sleeping in clothes.'

'Seems a bit extreme. Must save on wear and tear on your hangers, I suppose. But I thought it might be because you didn't trust me. I meant what I said. You are flattering yourself if you think you're my type, Kerrigan.'

I was saved from answering by the video link flickering into life. Beside me, Derwent fell silent, thinking his own thoughts as Godley and Maitland got ready for Shane to be brought in.

It took the usual age for the cast to be assembled – the solicitor was taking a call in the corridor and Shane elected not to enter the room without her – but when they were finally seated around the table, Maitland began, and his technique was a joy to behold. Gentle, persistent, friendly, he was a world away from the table-thumping rhetoric that was popularly supposed to be effective. He persuaded Shane to trust him inside the first three minutes just by talking to him like a human being, and I could sense Shane's confidence growing as his brief became more and more uneasy.

It didn't take long to get to the events of the previous night.

'You broke in.'

'Yes, I did.' Shane seemed relieved to agree.

'What were you planning to do when you broke in?'

The solicitor was a large woman with spiky hair and long, red nails. She leaned over and spoke softly to her client, who shrugged and answered in a matter-of-fact way.

'I wanted to find Josh Derwent and kill him.'

Derwent didn't so much as blink.

'Why?' Maitland asked.

'Because he was responsible for murdering my sister and no one would listen to me when I told them. Because there's a fucking conspiracy of silence just because he's a copper.'

Godley sounded infinitely reasonable when he replied. 'If there was evidence of him having committed a crime, we would take that very seriously. More seriously than if it was a civilian, not less.'

'Tell me another fairy tale.' The bitterness on Shane's face was clear even on the smudgy video.

Maitland took over. 'Why did you attack DC Kerrigan?'

'She was in his bed,' he said, as if that explained everything. I really wished I could explain, for the benefit of the transcript, that I'd been alone, and fully dressed, and not expecting him to join me.

'Was that a good enough reason to try to kill her?'

'No.' He swallowed. 'Is she okay?'

'She's very shaken,' Godley said, his voice cold.

Derwent leaned over and patted my hand. 'Poor dear.'

'Save it.' I touched the scarf around my neck that was hiding a technicolour display of bruises. 'This is all your fault.'

On the screen, Shane put his hands over his face. 'I'm sorry. I shouldn't have done it. It was dark in the bedroom and I didn't know it wasn't Josh until I felt that it was a woman. She'd woken up – I thought she'd scream – and I panicked. I was trying to work out what to do even when I knew I was going to kill her. Then I thought, "Well, what does it matter? He'll find out what it's like to lose someone he loves."'

'You decided to kill her.'

'I didn't know what I was doing.'

The solicitor wrote something on her notepad.

'Have you ever killed anyone?'

'No.'

'Did you kill your sister?'

'No! Of course not.' His voice had risen, the veins standing out in his neck. Godley put a hand flat on the table, a signal to Maitland to let him take the lead again.

'Let's come back to that. I want to know why you disappeared the day before yesterday, Shane.'

'I saw him on the news. Josh, I mean. Being shot in the playground. I realised he was in hospital and I could get at him. I stayed in a hotel near the hospital while I was working out what to do, how to get in to his room. But when I saw the footage of him leaving the next day I thought I'd missed my chance, and I would have if it wasn't for him punching that Pace guy.'

'How did that help?'

'The reporter who followed him filmed his house and then I saw a street name and checked it on Google Maps, and it looked right. I couldn't believe my luck.'

'Nor can I,' Derwent said darkly. 'You get on the news a couple of times and you're a sitting duck. How fair is that?'

'Maybe this will teach you to stop punching people on camera,' Burt observed.

'Name one person I hit who didn't deserve it,' Derwent demanded, and was rewarded with silence.

They took a break before they asked Shane about his switch to cash ('to avoid getting ripped off'), about why the business was on the market ('I've had enough of this country. I want to live somewhere warm') and about the timing of both. He denied any knowledge of the murders beyond the conversation he'd had with me about them.

'Were they in your bar? The women?'

'I don't know. I don't think so.'

'DC Kerrigan said you told her you'd show their images to your staff. Did you?'

'Yeah. No one knew them.' He shook his head. 'I don't know what you're trying to pin on me. I'm admitting what I did last night but that's it. I have nothing else to tell you.'

'Do you have alibis for the nights of the murders?' Maitland reeled off the dates.

Shane put one hand up to his face and rubbed his eyes. 'I don't know. I'd have to check my diary.'

'We'll need you to do that.'

'You have trouble with alibis, don't you?' Godley observed. 'You had to invent one for Angela's death.'

'What? How did you know that?' His face darkened. 'Did Claire tell you—?'

'Did you kill Angela?'

'No, I didn't.'

'Angela wasn't sexually assaulted. That always makes us think it could be a family member who did the killing. You. Your father. Someone who wanted to punish her, not rape her.'

'Please. My dad was on the other side of town and I wasn't even there until after the police came.'

'Why did you need to lie?' Godley asked, intent.

'I was terrified of the copper who was investigating – I thought he'd crucify me for smoking dope. And I didn't want my parents to know I'd been doing drugs instead of looking after Angela. They'd have been mortified, and they'd have hated me for it. I hated myself.'

'Very moving,' Una Burt said in a voice that indicated she thought the exact opposite.

Derwent glared at her. 'You don't know him. He means

it.' Shane could hate Derwent all he wanted, but Derwent was still loyal to him, even after so long.

'When did you decide to lie?' Godley asked.

'It was Vinny's idea. The policeman had been giving Vinny a hard time and he knew I wouldn't be able to cope.'

The story matched Claire's version of events, at least. I was starting to think we had got through all the murky lies to the solid truth, or at least an approximation of it.

'Tell us about Vinny,' Godley said. 'He was in the army, I understand. When did you hear about his death?'

It was an easy question but Shane looked wary. He turned to his lawyer. 'Can we take a break?'

'We've just had a break,' Maitland said quickly.

'My head hurts. I want some painkillers. I need to see the doctor.' He squeezed his eyes shut, then opened them. 'I'm getting double vision.'

Godley reached out to the tape recorder. 'Interview suspended at 16.22.'

'He didn't like that,' Derwent said. 'He didn't like that at all.'

'Why not?' Burt asked. 'You're the one who knows him, after all.'

'I don't want to speculate.' Derwent got up, found his crutches and limped out of the room, banging against most of the furniture on the way. He was clearly heading for Godley and Maitland so he could talk it over with them, and I wasn't surprised Una Burt looked put out, or that she made an excuse to go after him a few seconds later.

Colin Vale was still working through the numbers, shuffling paper behind me, as happy as a child in a sandpit. I was silent. It was nice to have some time to think. I thought about the little group, the relationships, the complicated dynamics of it all. And about Vinny, who'd also had no alibi but held up to Orpen's questioning. Vinny, who'd run away, first to travel and then to join the army. Vinny, whose death came before the current run of murders. Shane, and his cash-based lifestyle. The hospitality industry and its hidden workers. A face I had seen and not recognised at the time, because it was out of context and impossible and wrong.

'I've just got to make a phone call,' I said to an oblivious Colin, and left.

It took a long time to get the information I needed – longer than I'd expected. One phone call became two, and then I had a long wait for someone to get back to me, swivelling on a chair at a borrowed desk and fielding questions from the local CID. It was torture but I made myself wait until I knew the story, or as much of it as I was likely to find out from third parties. I hung up the phone for the last time and gave myself a second to process what I'd found out. Then I headed back to our little room, where the atmosphere was pure poison and Colin Vale looked desperate for someone to referee the Burt/Derwent bitch-off that was in progress. On screen, the interview was continuing.

'We need to interrupt them,' I said.

'Absolutely not,' Burt snapped. 'They've only just started again, and it's going really well.'

'There's something they need to know.'

'Give her a chance,' Derwent said. I'd been sure he would take my side once Burt was against me. 'What is it?'

'Vinny didn't die in Afghanistan. He got an honourable discharge in November last year, and came home. He's in London.'

'Motherfucker,' Derwent whispered. Una Burt looked as if she was thinking the same thing.

In case they hadn't worked out where this was going, I wrapped it up for them. 'And six weeks after Vinny got back to the UK, Kirsty Campbell was killed.'

Chapter 32

There was no need to argue with anyone after that. Burt herself went and knocked on the interview-room door. Maitland and Godley came down the corridor at a run to hear what I'd found out, crowding into the little room with Burt behind them.

'Are you serious?' Maitland demanded.

'Never more so. He's alive and pretending not to be.'

'Why did he leave the army?' Godley asked.

'There are two versions to that. I only know the truth because I managed to speak to his commanding officer, who is now based in Essex. The official story was that he put in his papers because he'd had enough. I leaned on the guy a bit and he told me, off the record, that Vinny got in serious trouble in Helmand. He attacked a teenage boy and almost killed him. They hushed it up – said the guy was Taliban and Vinny had been acting in self-defence – but according to his CO, he beat him half to death and left him with life-changing injuries.'

'What does that mean?' Derwent demanded.

'He ripped his balls off.' Every man in the room looked sick, Derwent most of all. 'You asked,' I pointed out.

'Any idea of a motive?'

'A row about a local girl.'

'Huh,' Derwent said. 'A crime of passion. He was bloody lucky they didn't do him for it.'

'Vinny was very popular, very well respected. No one wanted to see him in a court martial. There was a ton of evidence against him – he didn't bother trying to hide what he was doing or why – so he was looking at considerable jail time and a dishonourable discharge. His CO advised him to put in his papers instead and go home.'

'And they let him?' Maitland was incredulous.

'It's not as if he did this in Warrington or somewhere. Afghanistan is a long way from the UK, and an eye for an eye isn't such a big deal there,' Derwent said.

'The CO actually said to me, "What happens in Helmand stays in Helmand",' I added.

Godley folded his arms. 'Let the army sort out its own mess. If the Red Caps were prepared to let him go, I'm not going to make a case against him for that. But given the timings, I want to find out more about Vinny, and I want to know what Shane knows about him.'

'Start off by asking him where Vinny's been living. Not with him, not in that flat.' I was absolutely sure of it, having searched it.

'Find out if he's been giving him money. That could explain the switch to cash,' Colin said.

'If Vinny's folks think he's dead, he must be sending them his pension,' Burt suggested. 'That'd leave him short.'

'Shane has been giving him money, but not as a hand-out. Vinny's been working for him in the bar.' I was getting used to being the one who dropped the bombshells but that got almost as good a reaction as the news that Vinny wasn't dead after all.

'What the actual f—' Derwent started to say and Godley cut him off.

'How do you know that?'

'I saw him.' I turned to Maitland. 'You saw him too. Remember when we cut through the kitchen at the bar? The guy unloading a dishwasher? Tattoos up both arms? Muscles?'

'Vaguely.'

'He was wearing a blue T-shirt,' I said. Maitland shook his head. I gave up and went on. 'I saw his face but I didn't make the connection until just now because I thought Vinny was dead.'

'So you think he got back, got in touch with Shane and got a job,' Godley said.

'And Shane switched to cash as far as he could to hide whatever money he was sending Vinny's way. I bet he was being paid more than your average kitchen hand,' I said.

'We need to get him picked up,' Burt said.

I shook my head. 'Once I found out he was alive, I did some checking. I had time on my hands while I was waiting to hear from the CO. No one at the bar knows where he lives and no one has seen him since we found out Shane was missing. He's gone.'

'Let's get in there and hit Shane with what we know.' Godley was fidgeting, unusually for him. He wanted this case solved, and not just because of the media interest or the pressure from his bosses. He wanted the person who killed those four women to be stopped.

'If you can't find out anything else, try to get him to tell you if anyone else knows Vinny's alive,' I suggested. 'He's going to need help to get out of sight. It's a place for us to start looking.'

You could have heard a pin drop in the little room where we were waiting. Everyone was staring at the screen, where Maitland and Godley were pulling out their chairs and sitting down.

'All right, Shane? How's the head?' Maitland asked.

'Yeah. Fine.'

'All right for water? Do you want a tea or coffee?'

'No thanks.' Shane was looking suspicious but he didn't have the experience to know what Maitland was doing:

closing off the options for him so he had no legitimate excuse to stop the interview.

'Sorry for the interruption,' Godley said easily. 'This is an active inquiry and we're getting more information all the time that helps us to work out what's been going on.'

'Yeah, but the last bit was a shock, wasn't it?' Maitland said to him, grinning. 'Not every day you find out someone's made a full recovery from being dead.'

Shane's eyes went from Maitland to Godley and back again, trying to read their expressions. Godley leaned forward.

'Vinny Naylor. Rumours of his death have been greatly exaggerated.'

'I don't know what you're talking about.'

'Oh, come on. Course you do. Big lad, works in your kitchen in the bar. Not chatty but nice to the others.'

'That's Jimmy. He's got learning disabilities. No education. Nice guy but all I can give him to do is menial stuff.'

Godley tapped the table. '*Jimmy*'s disappeared. Around the same time your bar filled up with policemen. Where do you think he went?'

'I don't know.'

'By your own account you headed off to punish Josh Derwent. Did Vinny try to stop you? Was Vinny looking for you while you were holed up in your hotel? Or did Vinny have problems of his own?' Godley was hitting him hard, not even giving him time to answer. Shane's expression was pained.

'We know about what happened in Afghanistan. We know he came home and didn't want anyone to know he was back. We know he came home just before Kirsty Campbell was killed. Are you saying that timing is a coincidence?'

'Yes. It has to be.'

Godley pounced. 'So you're admitting that Jimmy is really your friend Vinny.'

He didn't want to say yes. In the end, he gave a tiny, infinitesimal nod, which Godley described for the benefit of the transcript.

Beside me, Derwent sighed. 'Poor old Shane. Never the sharpest knife in the drawer. Almost makes me feel as if we're taking advantage of him.'

With no such pangs of conscience, Godley went on: 'And you've been giving him cash from the business to cover his costs and pay his family.'

'I've been paying him for working.'

'Why in cash?'

'He doesn't have a bank account,' Shane admitted. 'Cash is easier.'

'Where does he live?'

'I don't know.'

Maitland snorted. 'Come off it.'

'I *don't*. Some sort of hostel in the East End. I asked him about it a couple of times and he told me I was better off not knowing, that it wasn't the sort of place you'd have your mates round for curry anyway.'

Vinny, knowing that Shane was unreliable, taking steps to protect himself in the event that someone came looking for him. It rang alarm bells for me in a big way. Burt and Derwent obviously felt the same way because they were busy exchanging meaningful glances when I looked. Maybe what simmered between them wasn't animosity, but sexual tension. I made a note to suggest it the next time I was alone with Derwent and felt the need to be shouted at.

'Where did he go, Shane?' Maitland asked.

'I don't know. I've been a bit tied up.'

'Have you been in touch with him?'

'No.'

'Got a mobile number for him?'

'No.'

Godley was going through the file in front of him,

looking for something. 'Here's a printout showing all the contacts on your phone. Are you sure Vinny isn't on here?'

'Yeah.'

'Who's Jimmy Vincent?'

'A bloke.'

'Not "Jimmy" whose real name is Vincent?'

Shane looked mortified. 'No comment.'

'It's too late for that. You can't give a no comment interview now.' Godley's voice deepened, sounding more authoritative. 'He's gone underground, Shane, and we need to find him. For his sake and for the safety of others. Why do you think he disappeared?'

'Dunno. Probably because he doesn't like coppers.' Shane shrugged. 'I'm beginning to see his point.'

'We can't let him kill again.'

'He's not a killer.'

'Beating up that boy in Afghanistan – what if it reminded him of Angela? It made him want to hurt someone. It set off the chain of events that have left four young women dead. Four. Do you really want to add to the tally?'

'It's not him.' Shane looked close to desperate. 'I don't know how to explain it to you so you'll understand me. He's not a murderer. He's just not.'

'Sometimes it's the people you think you know best who have the darkest secrets,' Godley said. 'Nothing to be ashamed of. Think of all the wives who defended their husbands until they were proved wrong.'

Maitland stirred. 'You're not married, Shane, are you? How would you describe your relationship with Vinny? Friends? Or more than friends?'

'What are you trying to say?' Shane demanded, his face dark.

'He's not going to like that,' Derwent predicted.

'Someone needs to look into possible addresses for Vinny,' Una Burt said abruptly. 'Maeve, you've been doing well today. Do you want to make some calls?'

No, thanks. I'd like to stay and watch us get within touching distance of London's most wanted killer. She wasn't looking for a proper answer. I got up slowly, reluctantly, and headed for the door.

'And when you come back, bring coffee,' Derwent commanded, not even looking away from the screen.

'I might be a while,' I said.

'That's okay. I can wait.'

'You'll have to,' I said through gritted teeth as I shut the door. I might miss out on the interview, but I was absolutely not going to hurry back.

Allocated the same spare desk in the detectives' room I spent the next two hours doing Internet searches, checking phone books and ringing people. I called hostels, working men's clubs, cheap rented accommodation, charities, churches. I rang the places people went when they had nowhere else to go. I rang anyone who offered cheap, medium- to long-term accommodation in the East End and beyond, prioritising places that could be described as hostels. I described Vincent Naylor, AKA Jimmy, until the words ceased to have any meaning for me, until my voice was hoarse and my hand ached from writing notes. I listed the possibles, passing them on to Colin Vale, who contacted the local police stations and asked for neighbourhood officers to make calls in person as a matter of priority to interview our candidates.

It was a pleasant, slightly vague voice on the other end of the phone that put me out of my misery, a voice belonging to Father Gordon from St Philip's Catholic Church in Bethnal Green. He was responsible for running their hostel. ('Which is a grand name for a house left to us by a parishioner. We house the homeless and others who are down on their luck. They each get a room and share the bathroom and kitchen.')

I explained who I was and where I was calling from,

then described Vinny without saying why I was looking for him.

'Oh, yes. Jimmy has been with us for a while. He's very helpful – I don't know how we'd keep the place running without him. He's already fixed a hole in the roof and a bit of loose guttering and mended the gate where someone reversed into it. Worth his weight in gold.'

'Do you know where he is?'

'He's not here now, I'm afraid.'

'When was the last time you saw him, Father?'

'This morning.' He sounded puzzled. 'Is everything all right?'

'We just want to talk to him about the bar where he works.'

'Oh, I see. But it's closed at the moment.'

'Yes, I know,' I said patiently.

'I'll tell him you were looking for him.'

I got in quickly. 'There's no need. Really. It's not urgent and I was just really making sure we knew where to find him.'

'But if you leave me your name and number, I'm sure he'll get back to you.'

'I wouldn't put you to the trouble,' I said, which was a phrase my mother used when she absolutely didn't want to let someone do something. It was surprisingly effective and worked as well as ever on the priest.

Colin had been hanging over my shoulder and as soon as he got the nod he hurried off to let Godley know we had an address. The superintendent would send a team to arrest him, and in the meantime there was a force-wide alert to keep looking for him, just in case he'd heard of Shane's arrest, just in case he was running now for real. I leaned back in my borrowed chair, fuzzy with tiredness. Now that the chase was almost over I felt as if I'd slipped into neutral. I had nothing left to give. I picked up the phone and rang Rob, just to listen to his voicemail message, just to feel that he wasn't all that far away on the other side of the Atlantic. When the bleep came, I told him I was fine and work was exciting and I'd hardly been in the flat since he left so the danger had been minimal. I made myself sound cheerful and carefree and as if I wasn't missing him at all.

There was no chance he'd be taken in by it, but it made me feel better, and that was more or less the point.

Ninety minutes later I was still at the police station, still exhausted and very bored. From being at the centre of the investigation, the Shane Poole line of inquiry had turned into a bit of a sideshow. Godley had left, accompanied by Colin Vale. Harry Maitland and Una Burt were still asking Shane endless questions about his sister, Vinny and the murdered women. I was there to mind Derwent and make sure he behaved himself, on Godley's instructions. How I was supposed to do that, I didn't know. I'd noted the location of the nearest fire extinguisher and I was prepared to use it on him if need be.

The interview with Shane was staggering to a close. It was late and everyone in the room was exhausted, Maitland most of all. He obviously hated having to work with Una Burt, who kept cutting across him to ask random questions. Shane was having trouble working out what she wanted and how he should answer. I presumed that was her intention, but I couldn't be sure, and certainly Derwent was annoyed enough to heckle whenever she spoke.

The door to our room opened and a uniformed PC leaned in. 'Do either of you know where DC Kerrigan is?'

'That's me,' I said, leaping up.

'There's someone in reception for you.'

I barely let him finish; I was halfway down the hall already. To get out of the stuffy room had been my dearest wish. Literally anything would do if it gave me a reason to leave.

I went through the heavy door into reception wondering

who knew I was even there. One of my colleagues, probably. I had an outside bet on Peake.

He was standing with his back to me, reading a road
safety notice pinned to a board. He was enormous in his
puffa jacket, and the baseball cap that was pulled down
over his eyes made him anonymous. I tacked sideways as I
approached, trying to work out how I knew him, and I was
feet away when he turned. I stopped dead.

'I heard you were looking for me,' he said.

Derwent came out through the reinforced door at that
moment, heading for the exit, still fighting his crutches
every step of the way. He glanced at me, then beyond me,
and his expression changed in a way that was almost comic,
going from bored to incredulous as his eyes opened wide.

'I don't believe it.'

Vinny Naylor grinned. 'Hello, Josh. Long time no see.'

Chapter 33

Here's what should have happened next: I should have arrested, cautioned, searched and processed Vinny Naylor, then handed him over to the custody sergeant who should have tucked him up in a cell to await the arrival of a legal representative and some new interviewers since Maitland and Burt would be worn out. Godley should have returned to claim his scalp and do a quick press conference on the steps of the police station, while inside Vinny confessed to all four murders and anything else we could think to throw at him. And then we should all have patted ourselves on the back for a job well done.

What actually happened was that Derwent limped past me at incredible speed, grabbed Vinny by the arm and hissed, 'What do you think you're doing? Do you want to go to prison?'

'No, of course not,' Vinny snapped. 'But I don't want to leave Shane here answering questions that you really need to ask me.'

'Shane's all right.'

'No, he's not. He'll be getting himself in trouble if I know him. And he doesn't deserve to be.' Vinny was the same height as Derwent and the two of them were nose to nose.

'Come with me.' He let go of Vinny and limped back to the door that led to the police station itself. 'Kerrigan, you need to come too.'

I was standing flat-footed in the middle of the reception area, my mouth hanging open. With his bulky coat I couldn't tell if Vinny was carrying a weapon, and neither could Derwent. And Vinny Naylor was a killer, of that I was absolutely sure. I hung back until Vinny went through the door ahead of Derwent, then caught up with him.

'What are you doing? We've got to do this properly. Godley—'

'Will go fucking mental when he finds out. I know.'

'You don't have any credit to use any more. You're already on your way off the team if you don't start acting like a copper again, and I'm not having you take me with you.'

He rounded on me. 'Look, I need to talk to Vinny. I haven't spoken to him for a long time, but I think I can get him to trust me. You don't know what he's like. He's the definition of hard as nails and none of the interviewers we've got will be able to get him to confess to getting dressed this morning, let alone murder.'

'But you think he might talk to you for old times' sake.'

'It's worth a try.'

'No, it's not. He's killed four women. Four.'

'If he killed them, why is he here?'

'Because he's arrogant enough to think he can get away with it, maybe. Because he knows we're after him and he's trying to do this on his own terms.'

'When the others find out he's here, he'll be charged with murder and I won't get near him, do you understand? This is the only chance I'm going to get.'

'Sir—'

But he was gone, pulling the door to slam behind him, leaving me on the wrong side. I waited for the receptionist to unlock it, fuming. I didn't know what to do. Call Godley and tell him what Derwent was doing? Try to persuade Derwent to stop committing career suicide? Go and sit in the same room so I could at least go and get help when Vinny kicked off, as he probably would?

Derwent had been reckless before. He fancied himself as a bit of a maverick and bull-headed wasn't the word for him: he truly believed he knew the right thing to do at all times. He wasn't going to listen to me, or anyone else. And if Vinny had come to finish off the job Shane started, he was offering him a golden opportunity. Pushing through the door I ran down the corridor, almost colliding with a couple of PCs who pressed themselves against the walls to get out of my way.

Derwent had taken Vinny to the little meeting room where we had been waiting. I opened the door quietly, wary of what I might find. The television was still on, though muted, and Vinny was standing there, staring at it with his hands in his pockets and a frown on his face.

'Have you searched him?' I asked Derwent, who shook his head and moved towards him.

'Come on, Vinny. Coat off.'

He obliged without making a fuss, pulling off his cap too and submitting to Derwent's quick but thorough pat down.

'Nothing,' he said to me.

I wasn't actually all that reassured. It was all very well, Vinny not carrying a weapon, but he'd been an infantry soldier and was trained in unarmed combat. I watched his hands, wished Derwent would stay out of range, and took up a position by the door so I could make a quick escape.

'Right,' Derwent said. 'Sit down.'

Vinny sat. Without the coat and hat I could see him properly. He was rugged rather than handsome and heavy-jawed under stubble that was getting towards being a beard. His expression was open and honest and I thought of the four women who had died, and how they had trusted their killer, and I cautioned myself not to fall for it.

'Here's what we're going to do. We're going to talk, the three of us, and you're going to tell us what's been going on since you got yourself in trouble in Afghanistan.'

He nodded.

'As soon as someone realises you're here, you're going to be arrested. So let's make it quick.'

'All right,' Vinny said. 'I'll do what I'm told if it gets Shane off the hook. I've got nothing to fear anyway. I didn't do anything.'

'You and Shane are doing a fine job of looking guilty,' Derwent said. 'There's nothing much I can do to help. I won't be involved in the interviews – they'll keep us apart.' He glanced at the screen. 'I wasn't allowed to talk to Shane at all.'

'Probably just as well,' Vinny said. 'He's got a bit of a bee in his bonnet about you.'

'He broke into my flat and tried to kill me.'

'Yeah, I thought that was the sort of stupid thing he'd do. I tried to stop him.'

'Thanks. Next time, try harder.'

'Fuck you,' Vinny said pleasantly. 'You haven't changed at all, have you?'

'I'm just saying, you didn't do a very good job.' Derwent sat on the edge of a table, propping his injured leg on a chair. 'Right. No bullshit now. Why did you come here?'

'To see her.' He nodded at me. 'Because she rang the priest who runs the place where I live and he told me she'd been asking for me.'

Damn. And he'd had time to get rid of any evidence he liked since Shane went missing. I could see this one going west, and fast.

'What happened in Afghanistan? Why did you decide to play dead?'

Vinny grimaced. 'I fucked up. There was this man I'd got to know, a local, but he was all right. Same age as us but he had three daughters and four sons. The oldest girl was fifteen. The boys were all under ten. Nice family. No money, but no one has any money there. They had some goats, I think. And some land.'

'And the oldest girl was raped.'

'No.' Vinny sighed. 'It was the youngest girl. The eleven-year-old.'

'Shit.'

'She was just a little kid. The guy who did it was a twat – I'd come across him a few times on patrol and he was always trying to annoy us so we'd beat him up and he could claim compensation. He had pretty good English – I don't know how because the only thing he ever heard from us was "piss off". His family were having a boundary dispute with the girl's dad, and he boasted about raping the girl to teach him a lesson. He said he'd made her worthless and he'd do the same for the others. The local police didn't want to know – they had enough to do just trying to keep the place relatively civilised. It's a crazy country, mate, you can't imagine.'

'So you decided to intervene,' I said. I was watching Maitland and Burt who were still plugging away. It was getting late. They'd be finishing soon. All I needed was for them to find us talking to the chief suspect behind closed doors.

'I was only going to talk to him.' Vinny shook his head. 'I can't explain it. I went mental. He just didn't care. He was talking about how much he'd enjoyed it. He said she was *tight*.' His hands spasmed into fists and I could feel the heat of anger radiate off him.

'I heard you ripped him apart.' Derwent's voice was neutral. I actually didn't know if he approved or not.

'I lost it. I just wanted to make him suffer. And I wanted to stop him from ever doing anything like that again.' Vinny put a hand up to his forehead, a tremor visible in his fingers. 'I can't really believe I did that. I was covered in blood, and I was kicking him, and suddenly I heard what he was saying and I stopped.'

'What was he saying?'

'He wanted me to kill him. He was begging me.'

'But you didn't.'

'I carried him to our camp and found a medic. He was airlifted to Kabul. Got the best medical treatment the British Army can offer, not that it did him much good.'

'Why didn't you kill him?' Derwent asked.

'Couldn't. Not like that. It would have been murder, not a fair fight.'

Oh, very virtuous, I thought. 'Why weren't you arrested?'

'It got hushed up. My CO didn't want a trial in case it turned the locals against us. They wanted to handle it their way, anyway – they didn't care if we had a court martial or not. I had a price on my head. It was too dangerous for me to stay in Helmand.' Vinny looked up at Derwent. 'I wasn't scared, Josh. But if I'd been on patrol and we'd come under attack and someone else had got injured or killed, because of what I did, I'd have been responsible.'

'So you quit.'

'I quit.'

'Why didn't you tell anyone? Why did you play dead?'

Vinny shook his head and looked away. 'It was my folks. I didn't want them to know.'

'Why not?'

'Because I didn't want them to know I had fucked up. The only thing I've ever done right was the army. They were so proud of me. They thought I'd turned my life around, found my feet, all that. I couldn't tell them that I was back to nothing.' He pushed up his sleeve and showed off a tattoo across one massive forearm: *Death Before Dishonour*.

'But they must have mourned for you,' I said. 'How could you do that to them?'

'It's a big family. Eight of us, and most of the others are married. Loads of grandkids. They wouldn't miss me.'

'I don't think that's true,' Derwent said quietly. 'I remember your mum. She wouldn't forget about you.'

'Do you see your family?'

Derwent flinched. 'No. Not since.'

'So you know sometimes it's better to walk away.'

'I didn't get a choice.'

'I didn't think I had one either.'

I moved to interrupt the pity party. 'How did you convince them that you were dead?'

'I'd changed my next of kin to my girlfriend before I went back the last time. We split up while I was there but I got her to tell them she'd been notified that I was dead.'

'No body, though. No funeral.'

'The story was I'd been doing something covert and top secret when I died, so for reasons of national security they couldn't admit publicly that I was dead, or the circumstances.'

'And your parents believed it?' Derwent's eyebrows were up around his hairline.

'Yeah. Apparently. I think they liked the idea I was someone important, doing something brave and risky. And they were used to keeping their mouths shut about what I was doing in the army.'

'Why did you come back to London?'

'I didn't have any money. I didn't know what else to do.'

'Is that why you got in touch with Shane?'

'Yeah. We had an agreement, the two of us, that if either of us ever got in trouble, the other one would do whatever it took to help out. Shane was so glad I was alive, he was well on for giving me a job and a bit of extra cash here and there.'

'What was the plan?' I asked. 'You came back and Shane put the bar on the market. Where was he going to go?'

'Thailand. We were going to open a bar or a restaurant there. I got to know it pretty well when I was younger and Shane was up for a change. Or he said he was. But he's turned down a few offers for the business, so I don't know.'

'What do you think he's waiting for?' Derwent asked.

'For his dad to die.'

'Or because he's found out he likes killing?' The two of

them turned to look at me. 'What? He's still a suspect. And so are you, Vinny.'

'I haven't killed anyone.'

'You didn't get a taste for it when you were beating that boy up? Get a reminder of how good it feels to be in control? To make someone scared? To hear them beg you for mercy?'

'It made me sick,' Vinny said, emphasising every word.

'I've been looking into the Angela Poole murder. Someone I consider to be a reliable witness told me you disliked her.'

Derwent looked at me, obviously surprised. 'Don't be stupid.'

Vinny turned to Derwent. 'It's not a big deal, Josh. I just thought she was a bit of a pain.'

'Angela?' Derwent was baffled. 'Why?'

Vinny glanced at me, then back at Derwent. 'If you must know, she was always trying to get me to kiss her. She was a massive flirt. Pinched my arse when you weren't looking. Rubbed up against me when she got the chance.'

'Bollocks. Why didn't you tell me?'

'You'd have gone tonto.'

'That's like lying to me.' Derwent was outraged. 'How could you keep that to yourself?'

Shamefaced, Vinny said, 'I thought you'd blame me.'

'Did you touch her? Did you kiss her?' Derwent demanded.

'No! Not at all.'

'You fucking *liar.*' The last word cracked through the room.

'It's the truth. Nothing ever happened – ever – but she was a prick tease.'

Forgetting his leg, Derwent jumped to his feet and suffered the indignity of pitching forward, almost falling, and having to be supported by the man he was intending to punch. I bit my lip to stop myself from laughing and looked away, towards the screen, just in time to see the solicitor shuffling her pages together. Maitland was yawning, one hand covering his mouth. Burt was talking.

'Looks as if they're winding up.' I snapped my fingers. 'Hey. Break it up. We don't have long.'

Derwent shook his head, bewildered. 'I can't even think what to ask him.'

'Well, I can. You didn't have an alibi for Angela's murder. Why not? Where were you?'

'Wandering round.' Vinny saw the expression on my face. 'It's the truth. I had a row with my girlfriend. I went and found Shane but he was with some guys who were really into pot and I wasn't in the mood. And Josh was with Angela. So I walked.'

'Did you see anyone or anything strange?'

'Nope.'

'Were you anywhere near Angela's house?'

'I went past late that night to see if you'd brought her home, but the light was off in her room so I thought you were still together.'

'She died around midnight.'

'I know. It was later than that. Half twelve or something. I didn't see her. I didn't see anyone.' He started to laugh. 'Oh, except that weird little fat kid from next door. He was looking out the window in the front room.'

'Why are you laughing?' Derwent asked.

'Because of you. You'd have loved it. He was wearing pyjama bottoms and a T-shirt with HOW SOON IS NOW on it, and you know you used to take the piss out of him for listening to the Smiths all the time. I was pissing myself laughing when I saw him. I couldn't wait to tell you about it the next day but I never got the chance.'

'How did he look?' I asked.

'Fat Stu? Fat.' Vinny started to laugh again. 'Stupid. He was just staring at me, like he always did. That was his life. Looking out of windows, watching people.'

'In his statement, he said he saw someone in clothes similar to the ones DI Derwent was wearing that night. Could it have been you?'

'I suppose.'

'He said he saw them leaving the garden. Did you go through the gate?'

'No. Just glanced up at the window.' Vinny's smile faded. 'I didn't even think she might be there.'

'And you didn't see anyone else running away.'

'No.'

I remembered what Derwent had said about the bruising on Angela's neck, and how the killer had had big hands. Vinny's were like shovels.

'Angela flirted with you, trying to provoke you. It worked on him,' I said, pointing at Derwent. 'Don't tell me you didn't find it a turn-on. You were a teenager. It doesn't take much, I seem to recall.'

Vinny looked uncomfortable. 'She was off-limits. And I didn't like her.'

'You don't have to like someone to want to have sex with them. Especially if you want to rape them.'

'I didn't want to rape her.'

'Did you see her that night? Follow her? Did you want to teach her a lesson?'

'No.' Vinny looked at Derwent. 'Really, no.'

'I don't believe you,' I said. 'And I don't believe that you're innocent. You killed Kirsty, and Maxine, and Anna, and Deena.'

'No.'

'You strangled them, just as you strangled Angela.'

'No.'

'You ran away afterwards. You left everything behind, and everyone.'

'We were all affected by it. It wasn't easy.' Vinny looked at Derwent. 'Tell her, Josh.'

'No, you tell us why you didn't mention being on

Angela's road that night when Orpen interviewed you. It's not in the file,' Derwent said.

'I don't know. It was better to lie. He was terrifying. If he'd put me in the right place around the time she died, I'd have been in the dock before I had time to say, "Please, sir, I didn't do anything wrong." He was desperate for someone to prosecute and I wasn't going to offer myself up on a plate.'

'The interview's over,' I observed. They were standing up and Shane was preparing to go back to his cell.

'*Fuck*.' Derwent pointed at Vinny. 'Don't think you're off the hook. I might not get to interview you but I'm going to be watching, and I'll know when you're lying.'

'I'm not lying about anything.' He smiled blandly and I felt a wave of anger. I knew they weren't going to get anywhere with interviewing him, and I knew he'd probably made sure there was no evidence to find at his address. But I was going to prove he was a killer, somehow.

'They'll have to let Shane go once they've got me in custody. Won't they?'

'They don't have to do anything. Is that why you're here? To save Shane?' Derwent asked.

'He's always looked after me,' Vinny said simply. 'This is the least I can do.'

'How moving,' I said, and the door behind me opened. Una Burt strode in and stopped.

'What's going on? Is that—'

'Vincent Naylor.' He stood up and held out his hand. 'Pleased to meet you.'

She didn't answer him, turning instead to Derwent and hissing, 'What have you done now?'

'Nothing at all. He's all yours.' Derwent swung towards the door at speed, so Burt had to jump back to get out of his way. I fell in behind him, leaving Vinny without a backwards glance. Maitland was just outside the door.

'You're going to need some cuffs.'

He looked surprised. 'What? Why?'

I didn't answer, hurrying to catch up with Derwent. He headed out of the main doors, his jaw set, and I knew better than to try to slow him down. We were halfway down the street before he stopped.

'What do you think?'

'Of him?' I shook my head. 'Guilty as sin.'

'Then why would he hand himself in?'

'He's playing games. I don't know why, and I don't know what the rules are, but there's definitely something he's hoping to achieve. He wants to rescue Shane, doesn't he?'

'So he said.' Derwent rubbed a hand over his face. 'Shit. And you really think he's our killer?'

'I have no reason to think anything else.'

'Do you think he killed Angela?'

'Very likely.'

Derwent winced, as if the very idea hurt. 'So how are we going to prove it?'

'I'm going to go back and talk to the witness.'

'Fat Stu?'

'One and the same. He was so sure it was you he saw. What if it was Vinny? You were very alike. You still are.'

'I'm better-looking,' Derwent said automatically. 'I'll come with you to speak to Stu.'

'Absolutely not.'

'I'd like to see him again.'

I shook my head. 'He'll never talk if you're there. Besides, it's too late to go and see him tonight.'

'Come on, Kerrigan. We work well together. We're a team. Let me come with you.'

'Give it a rest. I've got in enough trouble, thanks, because you want to be involved in my interviews.'

'You're not going to get anywhere without me. You need me.'

'I really don't,' I said, and started to walk away. Derwent hobbled after me.

'Kerrigan, wait.'

I picked up speed instead, leaving him behind.

'This isn't fair,' he yelled after me. 'Taking advantage of my disability. I'm not going to forget this.'

I didn't stop. I did slow down, though, but just so I could walk backwards for a couple of paces. I wanted to enjoy the look on his face as I waved goodbye.

FRIDAY

Chapter 34

The following morning I headed off to see Stuart Sinclair. I had gone back to the office to check my desk the night before and got waylaid by a request from the officer investigating my bunch of flowers, asking for a full statement about previous incidences of harassment. When it came to Chris Swain I could have written a book about all that he'd done and threatened to do to me, and the harm he'd promised to those I loved, but I just gave her the edited highlights. Kev Cox had agreed to take charge of the evidence I'd collected. I met him at the flat so he could pick it up. He was, as ever, unfailingly cheerful, even when handed a bag full of suppurating meat. It would have been a low priority for the forensics lab but he promised me he'd get it looked at sooner rather than later.

'I can't go home until I know if it's Swain,' I'd said to Kev, then wondered why I was in such a hurry to get back to the flat. It was cold, lonely and smelled a lot like work now that I'd had my very own bit of decomposing flesh in my home.

I had decided against going back to Derwent's flat to collect the stuff I'd left there; I'd had more than enough of him for one day. I packed a new bag and took a train out to Guildford, where Liv and Joanne were waiting to look after me and no one talked about work. Joanne found some arnica for my bruised neck, which made Liv snort, especially since she'd already slipped me some codeine. They were easy company. I laughed a lot. While the two of them were in the kitchen, squabbling over the recipe for the pasta sauce Joanne was making, I let myself think about Vinny Naylor, wondering if he was still being interviewed or if they would have stopped for the night.

'Whatever you're thinking about, stop.' Liv dropped down on the sofa beside me. 'You look grim.'

'That's just my face.'

'I think not.' She took my wine glass off the coffee table and handed it to me. 'Have a drink and forget about it, whatever it was.'

I clinked glasses with her and sipped the heavyweight Shiraz Joanne had opened, and I almost succeeded in forgetting, as instructed. Almost. At least, once the wine kicked in, I didn't care so much any more.

So it was the next day, in the company of a vile hangover that I retraced my journey to West Norwood and found Stuart Sinclair's house. I rang the doorbell and listened, resigned, to the ear-splitting screech from inside that told me Oliver was up and about, and in fine voice.

It wasn't Stuart who opened the door but his wife. She frowned at me, not quite recognising me, and she looked different too – jeans and a sweatshirt rather than the formal suit she'd worn the last time I'd seen her. Oliver was perched on her hip, wiping his nose on her shoulder. Her day for childcare, I thought, and smiled.

'Sorry to bother you. I came to talk to Stuart a couple of days ago. I don't know if you remember . . .'

As she placed me, it was as if a steel shutter had slid down behind her eyes. The smile disappeared and she started to close the door. 'Not interested, thank you. I said so at the time.'

'Wait.' I held up my ID. 'I'm a police officer.'

She stopped, looking from my warrant card to me. 'Seriously?'

'Detective Constable Maeve Kerrigan. I'm investigating a series of murders and I wanted to talk to Mr Sinclair again. Is he in?'

'*Stuart*?'

'I just need some information from him,' I said quickly. 'I'm not here to arrest him or anything like that. Do you know where he is?'

Her expression was blank. 'No idea. At his flat, probably.'

'His . . .'

'His flat,' she repeated. 'Where he lives.' *You moron*, I heard in her tone.

I was too confused to be suspicious. 'This is going to sound like a really stupid question, but doesn't Stuart live here?'

'Here? No. What gave you that idea?'

Well, actually, he *did*. Or I thought he had. Maybe I'd got it wrong. Maybe they were separated. 'Do you mind me asking what your relationship is with Mr Sinclair?'

'He's a friend.' She blushed. 'A friend of a friend, really.'

'He's not your husband. Or your ex. He's not Oliver's dad.'

'*No*. God, you don't have a clue, do you?'

'I must have misunderstood.' *I must have been meant to misunderstand.* In my mind, the pieces of the puzzle started to rearrange themselves to form a new picture, and I wondered how I could possibly have missed the way he had held the boy who was supposed to be his son. I wondered how I could possibly have thought he cared for him at all. And I wondered why anyone would lie to that extent, unless they had something to hide.

'Do you know him well?'

'Fairly. I don't know. Quite well. He's a friend.' She hefted Oliver, who had started to slip. 'Look, what's this about?'

'If you don't mind, I think it might be better if I came in so we can have a proper talk.'

'I don't really have time. I'm going out in five minutes.'

'Not unless it's urgent.' I put my foot across the threshold to stop her from closing the door. 'I'm sorry, but this is important.'

She had gone pale. 'Is he in trouble? Has he *done* something?'

'I'd just like to ask you a few questions about him.'

'I left him with my baby. Are you saying he's *dangerous*? Could he have *harmed* him?' Her voice was rising as she spoke, raw-edged with hysteria.

'I really doubt it,' I said. I stepped inside the door and closed it. 'Please, try to calm down.' Good advice for me too. My heart was thumping.

She was holding Oliver so tightly her fingernails were digging into him and he started to sob. 'It's all right, shh baby, shh baby,' she crooned, rocking him from side to side, but her eyes were wide and dark with terror.

'There's no suggestion he's ever harmed a child in any way. Please, don't worry.'

She closed her eyes tightly, trying to calm herself. 'Okay. Okay, I want to hear what you have to say. Of course I don't have to go out. Let me just send my friend a message.'

'Not Stuart,' I said sharply.

'No.'

'Don't mention it's about him. Make some other excuse.'

She nodded, still struggling for composure. Oliver wriggled and shouted, trying to break free.

I went into the kitchen and started to make mugs of tea. She sat down at the table and wrote a quick text, staring at me once she'd finished. Oliver wriggled off her knee and pounced on a toy snake that was on the floor.

'I don't know your name, I'm afraid.' *Not Mrs Sinclair, anyway.*

'Jenny Coppard.'

'Jenny, how long have you known Stuart?'

380

'Um.' She pulled her jumper down over her hands, thinking. 'A few months. Maybe six months.'

'How did you get to know him?'

'Through a friend. She got talking to him one day in a café and they had a lot in common. Too much, she said, because she really fancied him but she's married. She introduced us. I think she thought we might get together.' Jenny rolled her eyes. 'I get a lot of that.'

'Are you a single mum?'

'Yeah. By choice. I split up with my husband just before Oliver was born.'

'That's tough.'

'He was cheating on me. It's tougher to be lied to all the time and taken for granted. What's Stuart done?'

'Maybe nothing.' I poured boiling water over the tea bags and went looking for milk. 'But he definitely gave me the impression he lived here and Oliver was his child. He called you his wife.'

'I don't believe it.' She was red now, blushing. Flattered, in spite of her worries.

'Do you know where he lives? The address, I mean?'

She nodded, grabbed a flier for a pizza delivery place that was on the table and scrawled the address on it from memory. 'Larchfield Mews. It's about five minutes' walk from here. I don't know the postcode.'

'Don't worry.' I took it from her and put it away carefully, as if it was the Holy Grail and not junk mail. 'So you're just friends.'

'Yes.' The blush was back.

'Has he ever said anything to you that made you think he was romantically interested in you?'

'All the time. But he's like that. Flirty.'

'Has it ever gone beyond flirting?'

'He kissed me a week ago. We were playing around – I was trying to eat an ice cream and he said he wanted a bit and I wouldn't let him have any and – well, he kissed me.

And then he apologised. And I said it was all right, and he said that was good because he wasn't really sorry. You know.'

I did know. It was the sort of thing that a lonely woman with a small, demanding child would find charming. 'But nothing else happened.'

'No. I mean, there hasn't been an opportunity. And I didn't know if I should make the next move.' She shrugged.

'When you left Oliver with him, was that Stuart's idea?'

'Yes. Well, I had a job interview. That wasn't anything to do with him. But my mum couldn't look after Oliver because she had a hospital appointment, and there isn't really anyone else.'

'So that was the first time.'

'The only time.' She was back to looking anguished. 'I put him down for a nap and then I went out. I left him.'

'Jenny, I was here for most of the time he was alone with Oliver. Oliver was in bed when I arrived and he got up just before you came back. There's nothing to worry about.'

She put a hand to her head. 'Oh, thank God.'

I wasn't going to tell her what I suspected. If he really was the Gentleman Killer, she'd find out soon enough. 'What else can you tell me about him? Has he been living in West Norwood for long?'

'No. He came back from Japan about a year ago. He was an English teacher there for a long time but he got tired of it. It was somewhere rural and he said the fun of it wore off after the first five years but he stayed because he couldn't think of anything else to do. I think he was there for seven years in all.'

'What does he do now?'

'He teaches English as a foreign language in a college in Croydon.'

And he had the income from renting out the family home, I happened to know. He'd be doing all right for money.

'Does he live alone?'

'Yes.'

'And he doesn't have a girlfriend.'

'No. Not as far as I know,' she added, sounding disillu-sioned. She didn't have much luck with finding trustworthy men, all things considered.

I pressed her for any more information that she could give me, but there was nothing else useful. As we sipped tea and Oliver played, Jenny unwound enough to give me a fairly good idea of how hard she had fallen for Stuart, and how good he was at making himself indispensable. He'd never been violent to anyone as far as she knew. The idea shocked her. He'd helped people who needed it, buy-ing groceries for frail neighbours, mowing Jenny's lawn when it was overgrown. He was an all-round good guy, or pretended to be one. The more we talked, the more she forgot why I was there, and the more she spoke warmly of him. He was funny, and charming, and good at DIY.

'The perfect man,' she said wistfully. 'I thought, anyway.'

'He's clearly very good at getting people to trust him.' People, or maybe women. He presented himself as some-one you could trust. Someone to like. Someone to let in when he knocked on your door.

I had liked him, I remembered, and felt slightly sick.

When I'd finished my tea and when Jenny was start-ing to repeat the same stories about Stuart I thanked her for her time and help, asked her not to mention that I'd been around, and left. I took a stroll down to Larchfield Mews, a charmless apartment building behind a small parade of shops, not far from the A road that cut through the area. You probably couldn't see it from his flat, but you could definitely hear it. His flat was on the top floor, on the left, and I glanced up at the windows casually. No sign of life. The building had a small car park underneath it. A gate prevented me from getting into the premises to have a closer look, but I was sure one of the cars would belong to Stuart, and I was equally sure it would be worth a once-over.

But I had no idea how I was going to persuade anyone to believe me. *I* was convinced that Stuart Sinclair was the Gentleman Killer, but that was based on the most tenuous of details. He had lied to me about where he lived and pretended to be a married father of one when he was nothing of the sort. That was strange, but not evidence of a murderous mind. He looked pleasant; he sounded plausible. His connection with Angela Poole was obvious, but his movements on the night of her death were a mystery. All I knew was that he had lied to me about what he'd seen and heard, and even then I wasn't sure if it was a lie or a genuine mistake. He couldn't have seen Derwent but he might have seen Vinny. By all accounts he had been a strange, withdrawn, unattractive teenager who'd become a handsome and outgoing adult. Nothing about that was screaming 'killer' and yet everything was. And I knew that everyone thought Vinny was a cold-blooded killer – I had thought that myself – and Shane's behaviour was outwardly a lot more suspicious than Stuart's, but I still knew. I *knew*.

And I'd prove it if it killed me, I thought, not having the least idea that it might actually do just that.

Chapter 35

Back in the office, I got on the phone to the Japanese embassy and pestered them until they put me through to someone who could look up Stuart Sinclair's visa applications. The records showed he had settled in a place called Takayama in Gifu Prefecture and had a steady job teaching in a local high school. Based on what Jenny had said about when he returned to the UK, it looked as if he had left in the middle of the school year, a long time before his visa was due to expire. It was getting on for midday in London and Japan was nine hours ahead, so I didn't even bother trying to get in touch with the school. I put in a request for a Japanese-speaking translator and spent some time hunting around on the Internet for background information on Takayama and, more importantly, the telephone number for the local police. There was a chance that they would speak English, but since my Japanese was non-existent and this was important, I wanted to understand everything they said. I didn't know how long it would take – hours, probably – but I told myself to be patient and it sort of worked.

He had found a beautiful spot, a tourist destination in the mountains with old buildings and pretty countryside nearby. It was snowy in winter and hot in summer and it looked like a picture-perfect place to live. I couldn't imagine spending seven years there, but I was a city girl and I'd never done a lot of travelling. Freezing summer holidays in Donegal were no preparation for the exotic, even if they did make you hardy as a mountain sheep.

Maitland stopped on his way past. 'Booking a trip?'

'Following something up,' I said. 'Any luck with Vinny?'

'Nope.'

'Shane?'

'Nope.'

'Have either of them been charged yet?'

'Nope.'

'Keep me informed, won't you?'

'Yep,' he said, grinning, then relented. 'They've moved them to Charing Cross nick so they're not such a long way off. Godley's determined to persuade one or other of them to talk. He thinks one did it and the other knows about it, so it's just a matter of waiting until the innocent one cracks. And they haven't reached the custody time limit on either of them yet, luckily enough.'

'What do you think?'

'I don't know. I'd have thought we'd have got somewhere by now. And we've still got nothing on the forensics, from either of them.' He shrugged. 'We're a long way from taking anything to the CPS, put it that way.'

I was encouraged by the news that they were failing to make a case. It meant that Godley might be more receptive to a new suspect. Especially if I could find some reason to get a search warrant for Stuart's flat. In the past, I would have assumed I'd get a fair hearing from Godley and Burt, but I knew they would be a hard pair to convince now. I'd blown through a lot of credit in the past week – probably more than I had to spare.

I had been waiting for about two hours and was making my seventh or eighth cup of tea when Ben Dornton put his head into the kitchen. 'There's a nice Japanese lady asking for you.'

'Brilliant. At last.'

'You get all the interesting cases,' he said wistfully. 'I'm going to interview a guy who stabbed someone for his drugs out the back of Euston. He'll probably plead guilty in the end. That's my career.'

I tilted my head back to show him the aurora borealis of bruising around my neck. 'Interesting is overrated.'

'I wouldn't mind some of that. I could be the hero for a change.'

'Trying to impress someone?' I asked slyly, and laughed as he actually blushed. He was utterly smitten with the lovely Christine and I wished him the best of luck.

When I got back to my desk, the translator was standing near it and I could see immediately why Dornton had described her as a lady. She was in her mid-forties and impeccably dressed in a cashmere twinset, tweed skirt and pearls. More English than the Queen, I thought, and introduced myself.

'I am Akiko Larkin. How can I help?' Her voice was soft, her English practically unaccented. I dragged a chair over so she could sit beside me.

'I want to call a police station in Japan to find out about a suspect.' I filled her in as quickly as I could and she listened, taking in everything I said, making an occasional note.

'It might take a little while to speak to the right person. There will be someone there at this time, but maybe not the person we need.'

'Worth a try,' I said firmly, and handed her the phone. I was relying on her to do my job for me and I hoped she was as efficient as she seemed to be.

It took two or three phone calls to track down the right bit of the prefectural police for Takayama, and then a half-hour wait for the relevant inspector, Nakamura Shoichi, to phone us back once Akiko had explained why we were calling.

'Nakamura is his surname,' Akiko explained, having established that I knew more or less nothing about Japan and Japanese customs. 'In Japanese the surname comes first.'

'So you should be Larkin Akiko?'

She laughed politely. 'Before I was married I was Sakamoto Akiko. But I have been married to an Englishman for more than twenty years and I am used to being Mrs Larkin.'

The phone rang and I answered it, passing it to Akiko when the person on the other end tried to talk to me in Japanese. She spoke rapidly and softly into the phone, as I tried to pick out any phrases I recognised. Stuart's name sounded very odd rendered in its Japanese pronunciation. Aside from *'hai'* and *'arigatou'*, I didn't manage to understand much, but Akiko made copious notes. She ended on a flurry of thanks, hung up before I could stop her and turned to me.

'I can call him back if you have any more questions, but I thought you would want to hear what he had to say.'

'Go on.' I hated getting everything second-hand, but there was nothing else I could do.

'Inspector Nakamura knew who I meant immediately. Your suspect was a resident in Takayama for a long time and the local community knew him quite well. He had a Japanese girlfriend who lived with him. He was very settled there and happy, but then a tourist was murdered and he came under suspicion.'

'For what reason?'

'He had met her a couple of days before she died and made friends with her. His girlfriend had just left him and the victim's friends thought they had started a sexual relationship.'

'How did she die?'

'She was strangled,' Akiko said calmly.

'But they didn't arrest him.'

'There was no other evidence against him and he left before they could find anything.'

'Left as in left the country?'

'Yes. He abandoned his car and many belongings. The inspector was quite concerned that he was guilty but he wasn't able to pursue it because there was no evidence beyond his suspicion. Mr Sinclair called Inspector Nakamura from London and said that he was depressed because of his relationship breaking up and he wouldn't return to Japan. He said he left in a hurry because he was suicidal, and he made arrangements to have everything sold or given to charity.'

'Did the inspector tell you anything else?'

'He suggested that you speak to Mr Sinclair's girlfriend. Her name is Takahashi Yumi. She was reluctant to speak to Inspector Nakamura but now some time has passed she might have changed her mind.'

Another phone call to Japan. Super. 'Did he give you any way of contacting her?'

'He had anticipated we might want to speak to her and contacted her family before he phoned us. I have her name and address, and her telephone number. She lives in Bayswater.'

'In London?'

'She's a student at St Martins College.' Akiko put her notebook in her bag. 'She will speak English. You don't need me.'

I stopped thinking about the wonderful, glorious news that the girlfriend was in London, which was practically the first bit of luck I'd had so far. 'I might need you to translate something. I might need you to call someone else in Japan.'

She nodded, not smiling but obviously pleased. I rang the number she gave me and managed to get through to Yumi straight away.

'It's regarding Stuart Sinclair.'

There was a gasp at the other end of the line, and then she spoke again, very quietly. 'Is he in trouble?'

'I need to ask you some background information about him, but it's very important that you keep this confidential.'

She considered that in silence and I asked another, very important question.

'Are you in touch with him at the moment?'

'No. I never want to see Stuart again!' I thought she was going to hang up but after a second she sighed. 'When do you want to meet?'

'Now, if possible.' I gave her the address of the office and she promised to come straight away, even though she had a lecture. I hung up and Akiko picked up her bag.

'You have spoken with her. You know she speaks English well enough.'

'Please, stay.' Something made me feel she might be useful, still. 'Just until after the interview.'

'All right.'

'She does speak English well, but not as well as you do.' It was true. Yumi's speech was halting and she hesitated before each new clause, groping for bits of vocabulary. She seemed to understand everything I said but I couldn't be sure. 'Your English is amazing.'

'I've had a lot of time to practise.'

'Have you lived here long?'

'Twenty-four years.'

It was pleasant to have a conversation that wasn't going to end up with someone being arrested; it didn't happen often enough in my life. While we waited for the girl I found out how Akiko had met Mr Larkin (Paris, 1988, studying at the Sorbonne) and whether she missed Japan (yes, but her life was here with her children) and whether she liked her job (some days yes, some days no). I hoped she didn't mind the questions. I couldn't help myself. Curiosity was more than a habit now and I could no longer switch it off than I could stop blinking.

To prepare for the interview with Takahashi Yumi, I told Akiko what we needed: evidence that the man who had been her boyfriend would make a good suspect in the Gentleman Killer case. 'Did the inspector give you the name of the girl who was killed in Japan?'

'Grace Brumberger. She was American.'

'We'll need him to send us the file on the investigation.'

Akiko called him back while I did an Internet search on Grace Brumberger and turned up a treasure trove of information – her Facebook page, updated since she died with messages from grieving friends and acquaintances, a memorial page, a Grace Brumberger scholarship her parents were offering at the school she had attended, and most useful of all, a sixteen-page article from her local newspaper investigating what had happened to her in Japan. She was from Connecticut. She had been a cheerleader. Her parents were well off and she was an only child. She was bright, and diligent, and a good friend to those in need.

And she looked more or less exactly like Angela Poole.

I felt like bouncing up and down in my chair, but the presence of Akiko inhibited me. And anyway, the fact was that I was no closer to proving anything. Stuart had walked away from the investigation into Grace's death – he wasn't even alluded to in the article I'd read, which mainly focused on Grace's high hopes for her trip, the way the Brumbergers had found out the news and their journey from grief to acceptance.

But now I was absolutely sure I was right.

Akiko hung up the phone and immediately it rang again: reception, downstairs, to tell me that there was a Miss Tacky-something waiting to see me. I gathered up Akiko and my notebook and went to find her.

Takahashi Yumi conformed to the absolute template of a St Martins College fashion student, in that she was so determined *not* to conform. She was wearing lace-up red shoes with exaggerated, curved heels and a platform sole: they looked like an illustration from a fairy tale. Her tights were black but they had been embroidered with white thistles and ivy that snaked up from her anklebone to her thigh. She wore tiny black leather shorts and a big white fluffy jumper that was unravelling at the neck and cuffs. No coat, on a day when the temperature wasn't likely to rise above seven degrees, but she did have an umbrella with a duck's head handle. Small and slender, she wasn't quite pretty but she had dramatic eye make-up and had painted her mouth to match her shoes, creating a 1920s-style Cupid's bow. I stared at her for a good couple of seconds, taking it all in, before I remembered what I was supposed to be doing.

'Thank you for coming.'

She nodded. 'How can I help you?'

Time to be direct. 'I think Stuart might have harmed some women, but I can't prove it yet. I need to know if he ever did anything that made you uneasy, or if he hurt you, or if he acted in any way that made you suspicious of him.'

Three or four rapid blinks. Her false eyelashes had tiny hearts glued to the ends, I noticed. I couldn't begin to imagine how long it took her to get dressed in the morning.

'There were some things . . .' She trailed off.

'Can we start at the beginning? How did you meet him?'

'He was my teacher in school.'

'*Really?*'

'Yes, but we did not have a relationship then. We were friends.'

'I see.'

'I taught him Japanese and he helped me learn English. I wanted to come to London to study but I was very bad student.'

'So you helped each other.'

'For a year. And then I finished school and we became more than friends.'

'You moved in with him.'

392

She nodded, biting her lip gently. 'My parents were sad. I was in love with him.'

'How long did you live together?'

'Two years, almost. I would not go abroad to study or leave Takayama. I wanted to be with him. I stopped doing everything that made me happy. No fashion, no dressing up. No Internet. No friends. He was everything.' Her voice broke and she twisted her hands together, striving to keep the tears back.

'Was he controlling?'

She looked blank. Akiko leaned forward and offered a phrase in Japanese that made her nod. 'Yes.'

'He made you follow his rules.'

'And would not let me speak with my parents.'

'Was he nice to you?'

'Yes.' She looked away. 'No.'

'Was he violent?'

Two tears slid down Yumi's cheeks. 'Yes. No.'

'What do you mean?'

'He was but it was what I liked. I thought I liked it. I didn't know any different.'

Again, Akiko leaned in and said something softly, and Yumi replied to her, the words rapid. When the two of them were in full flow the sound of their voices reminded me of running water or gloved hands clapping. There was no harshness to it at all, no edge despite the subject matter.

Akiko turned to me. 'There was an element of sado-masochism in their relationship. She says that Stuart was unable to have sexual relations with her properly and only became aroused if he was choking her. He liked her to play dead and then he would masturbate on her.' There was something very odd about hearing those words come out of Akiko's mouth but she wasn't embarrassed. She went on: 'She says she had come to enjoy it and look forward to surrendering to him, but then on one occasion he choked her until she passed out. When she came round, he was elated, not sorry. She was terrified that the next time he would kill her. She refused to do it any more.'

'What was his reaction?'

'He started to go to the nearest city and visit prostitutes. He refused to speak to her. She apologised and told him she would do whatever he wanted.'

'And?'

Akiko turned to Yumi, who faltered through a few sentences before dissolving into tears.

'He choked her again and again she fell unconscious, but when she came round her eyes were bruised and swollen. She couldn't see anything for two days. The doctors were concerned that she could lose her sight but she recovered. After that, she knew he was too dangerous to stay with, and she left him.'

Yumi was crying properly now, a handkerchief pressed to her face. She peeled her eyelashes off and laid them on her knee, where they lay like two dead centipedes. 'I did not know anything else. I thought he did those things because he loved me. And I loved him.'

'Are you scared of him?'

She nodded. 'But he hasn't tried to contact me. Not since last October.'

Around the time Grace Brumberger died. I thought of Stuart killing her and realising he could make his fantasies a reality. It made me feel sick, but it also made sense.

'Are you willing to make a statement about Stuart?'

She looked horrified. 'I don't want to tell everyone what he did.'

'You don't have to be embarrassed,' I said gently. 'He was the one who decided to behave that way.'

Yumi muttered something and shook her head.

'May I?' Akiko murmured to me.

'Please.'

I couldn't guess what the older woman was saying to Yumi, but as she spoke the tears welled up in the fashion student's eyes again. Akiko kept talking, persuading, cajoling, and at last Yumi nodded.

'She'll give you a statement. I will help her,' Akiko said.

Yumi stood up, wobbly as a newborn fawn. 'I must go to the bathroom, I think.'

I showed her where to go. Once the door was closed behind her, I turned to Akiko.

'What did you say to her?'

'I told her I have a daughter. I told her my daughter is twenty, and very beautiful. I told her I worry about her. I told her the girls Stuart Sinclair killed had parents who loved them very much.' Akiko smiled, but her eyes were sad. 'I told her she was lucky.'

Chapter 36

I was pretty good at being a copper, which was lucky because I could never have been a burglar. The flat was empty, and I knew it was empty, but my heart rate was towards the upper limit of survivable. Perspiration was making my gloves slip a little on my hands. I pulled them further up my wrists and blew hair out of my face.

'Good to go?'

'Yeah.' Maitland stood behind me, in a heavy overcoat, with a police radio in one hand and a camera in the other. He looked as tense as if he was going on a picnic, and he grinned at me. 'Don't worry. We'll get plenty of warning if he shows up.'

'Are you sure that works in here?' Reception could be patchy. I really didn't want any surprises because the radio was only getting static.

'I've checked.' He folded his arms in front of him and looked at me expectantly. 'But the longer you take, the riskier it gets.'

'Okay, okay. Don't hurry me.'

We were standing by the front door in the narrow hallway that ran down the middle of Stuart Sinclair's flat. It was dark but smelled chemically clean. On my right was a bedroom, with a small bathroom beyond it. On my left, there was a living room and an equally small kitchen.

'At least you don't have many rooms to search.'

'That can be harder.' I could see telltale signs that he was both neat and a pack rat: an overfull bookcase stood at the end of the hall, with boxes stacked on top of it and piles of magazines underneath, all squared off and organised. Chaos would have been easier to rummage through. 'If everything is jammed in together, I'll have to take it all out to see if there's anything useful.'

'Go on, Chuckles. What are you waiting for?'

The truth was, I didn't know. I was waiting for the blinding flash of inspiration that would show me where Sinclair had stashed everything that related to his little hobby. I was also on edge in case he was expecting a visit from the police and had booby-trapped the place accordingly. Under the terms of our search warrant we could go through the place without getting his permission to be there. I had a feeling he wouldn't grant it, if he was offered the option. I didn't want to tip him off that we'd been there if we didn't find anything – we'd need to set up surveillance on him and try to catch him doing something incriminating, which would only work if he was confident our attention was elsewhere. So I was keeping my eyes peeled for stray hairs, black threads or artlessly arranged piles of paper that would give the game away. It was a lot easier to set a trap than to avoid springing it. That was why I'd been sent in on my own, with Maitland for muscle, just in case. The fewer people there were in Stuart Sinclair's flat, the less chance there was we'd leave a trace.

'Where are you going to start?'

'Bedroom.'

'Not the living room?'

'It doesn't look as if he has many visitors, but if he did, that's where they would go. I'm betting anything dodgy is in here.'

'On you go.'

I pushed open the bedroom door slowly and slipped inside, straining to see in the dim light. He had dark blue curtains that were still drawn even though it was daylight. I made sure there wasn't a gap in the middle, then took out my torch and started looking.

The bed was made, the duvet smooth. His shoes were lined up underneath it: many pairs of trainers, two pairs of smart shoes, one pair of desert boots. I checked the soles, quickly, and shook every shoe to check there was nothing inside it. The floor was carpeted and looked clean. I recalled that the killer had been scrupulous about leaving the crime scenes neat and tidy. It really would have been a lot more helpful if he'd been a slob.

I nudged the wardrobe doors open and bit back a gasp.

'You okay?' Maitland suddenly loomed in the doorway.

'Got a shock.' I swung the doors back so he could see the full-length mirror on one side and the full-length poster Stuart Sinclair had stuck on the other.

'Is that him?'

'It certainly is.' In the picture he was wearing a small pair of shorts and had a deep tan. His muscles were sharply defined, gleaming with oil, and he was posing with his hands on his waist in the best bodybuilder style, biceps bulging. 'Mr Fitness. I think this is his motivational material.'

'Twat,' Maitland said, and snapped a couple of pictures before he retreated. We needed to record anything remotely suspicious where we found it because Sinclair could remove it before we got a chance to come back.

I carried on searching, finding three smart suits with ties and shirts among the more casual clothes. To myself, I murmured, 'What do you need suits for? You're a teacher. Go to a lot of funerals?'

Nothing in the bottom of the wardrobe. Nothing on top. The bedside tables were empty. The chest of drawers contained neat piles of folded clothes. The drawers didn't pull out all the way but I checked the undersides anyway, lying on the floor, and even ran a hand along the back panel of the drawer to make sure there was nothing dangling down behind. I checked under the mattress and found nothing except slats. I checked under the pillow. Inside the pillow-cases. Inside the duvet cover.

'Anything?'

I took the torch out of my mouth, where I'd held it while I was replacing the bedclothes. 'You'll be the first to know.'

'Five minutes.'

'Got it.'

I did the bathroom in two minutes: whitening tooth-paste, hair dye and moisturiser. Expensive shampoo and conditioner. Eye cream. The guy used more products than I did.

The kitchen was tiny and so clean I wondered if he ever used it. The cupboards were full of protein powder and energy bars. The fridge contained egg whites, rice milk, turkey, chicken and cod, and a couple of bags of spinach.

'Fun,' I said.

Maitland was pacing up and down the hall like a bear in a zoo. 'Wish he'd invite me round for dinner.'

I kept searching. No wine or beer. A box of green tea, loose, with a Japanese tea set and little cups without han-dles. Some rice cakes and noodles.

There was a small freezer in the corner, with three draw-ers, and I ripped through it. Top drawer: more fish and lean meat. No ice cream. Middle drawer: frozen vegetables. No chips. Bottom drawer: plastic storage boxes opaque with frost. The top two seemed to be mince. A larger, flat one underneath them was far too light when I picked it up. I peeled the lid back and jumped.

'Whoa.'

'What've you got?'

'It's okay.' I lifted it up very carefully and draped it over my fingertips so it could hang properly. 'It's just a wig.'

'In the *freezer*?'

'Yep.' I couldn't stop smiling. 'Nice hiding place. The

colour matches Angela Poole's hair. The length and style is the same as hers was. And I bet we'll be able to match the hair we found on Anna Melville's body.'

Maitland took some pictures while I detached a couple of hairs and folded them into an evidence envelope. Then I replaced the wig in the box and the box in the freezer.

'Can I tell them?' He lifted the radio.

'Be my guest. I'm going to keep looking, though.'

In the living room I found weights and exercise DVDs, along with four stainless steel knives in a flat holder taped to the underside of the dining table. They were a Japanese make and exceedingly sharp. There was a gap in the middle.

'He could be carrying a knife.'

'I'll let them know.'

More bookcases, more books. I liked a room full of books, but not when I was in a hurry and trying to search with a light touch, because Godley had said to stay wary in case the wig wasn't a match. There was no way I could go through every book and check there was nothing hidden inside and I chewed my lip, knowing I was missing something.

Nothing hidden under a sofa cushion. Nothing inside the loose covers. Nothing under the rug.

A big rubber plant in the corner caught my attention. It was in a pot with wheels so you could move it around easily. I pulled it away from where it had been standing and saw that the fitted carpet wasn't quite level. It rose up in the corner, where the carpet tacks had been removed.

'Gotcha.'

It was easy to peel back the carpet, though I panicked a little when I saw nothing but floorboards. I stuck my hand in under the carpet as far as it would go and swept it back and forth in an arc, swearing as my muscles complained about the awkward angle. I forgot all discomfort when my fingertips brushed against something. I stretched even further and managed to get a grip on the corner of what proved to be an A4 envelope. I checked there wasn't any-thing else to find, and came up with two more.

'Harry? I've got something.'

He came and stood in the doorway, watching as I shook out the contents of the first envelope on the table. Pictures and medical notes. It was a history of remaking Stuart Sinclair from the tubby buck-toothed boy Derwent had tormented into, well—

'Is that Josh Derwent?' Maitland asked.

It was a picture I hadn't seen before, a close-up of Derwent smirking at the camera, wearing school uniform. Two smaller pictures were clipped to the back. The first proved to be a candid shot of him talking, in profile, while the second was him smiling at someone. He must have just been in the shower. His hair was wet and slicked back instead of hanging around his face, so you could see the details – the planes of his face, the line his hair followed, the shape of his ears.

'I think Derwent was his ideal. Like the world needed two of them.'

Maitland snorted. I skimmed through the paperwork.

He'd had dental work on the NHS but the major stuff – a jaw realignment and a set of crowns – had been done in Hungary. He'd gone to Los Angeles for a nose job and chin implant, at a cost that made my eyes wide. Over four visits to South Africa he'd had extensive liposuction and an eyelift, and had his ears pinned back. The pictures told the full story: a transformation from an unhappy, sagging young man to the toned, even-featured man I had met. He had removed body hair, tanned, reshaped his hairline, lightened his hair, exercised obsessively and it all *worked*. I tried to remember if I'd noticed anything strange about his face and how it moved, which was the usual giveaway with plastic surgery. The only thing I'd noticed was a resemblance to Derwent, which I'd put down to coincidence. And I'd noticed he was surprisingly hot.

'Creepy,' Maitland said. 'What else?'

The next envelope was a gut punch: a full set of crime-scene and autopsy pictures from the Angela Poole case.

'How did he get those?'

'Stole them. They went missing during the investigation. The SIO left them lying around. Stuart was the main witness – I bet he was in and out of the police station all the time.' I tapped one. 'He must have uploaded them to the website he showed me. These pictures were his reference material for the murders he committed and he had to make sure anyone could have seen them and done the same.'

'Clever.'

'No one is saying he's not clever.' I was really starting to hate Stuart Sinclair. I could taste it like bile at the back of my throat. He'd come so close to being discounted as a suspect. I'd come so close to overlooking him.

I'd met him and interviewed him before Deena died, and I hadn't suspected him for one second.

The third envelope was in some ways the most interesting. It contained maybe fifty file cards with names, addresses, personal details and physical descriptions of women, and a card wallet. I flipped it open. 'Bingo.'

'What've you got?'

'Fake police ID in the name of DI Josh Derwent, but that's Sinclair in the picture.'

Maitland leaned in to see. 'It looks rubbish. Nothing like the real thing.'

'Good enough to pass on the street, in the dark, especially if he just waves it at them.' I sat back on my heels. 'Got him.'

'I'd have thought so. What else is in there? What are all the cards?'

'Research.' I flipped through them, finding Jenny Coppard. Her card had a red asterisk on it, and the information that she was a mother was circled in the same pen.

He liked virginal women, I thought, not mothers. But Jenny had been useful all the same.

'I haven't found cards for any of our victims,' I said, shuffling through.

'Maybe he hides them somewhere else.'

'Maybe he doesn't keep them once they're dead.' They were no longer targets then. No longer a challenge. Not interesting.

I sped through the last cards and froze. 'You're fucking kidding me.'

'What?' Maitland leaned in. 'Oh, lucky you.'

Stuart had filled out a card for me, with my phone number and a physical description and – in capitals – KNOWS JD!!! There was a red asterisk on the top, though.

'I wonder why I failed.'

'Too tall,' Maitland suggested, and grinned when I glared. 'Too risky.'

'He doesn't like taking risks,' I agreed. 'He likes to feel safe.'

'Well, let's hope he's yearning for the comfort of home.' Maitland pointed with the radio. 'Collect all the paperwork. We'll take it with us. Let's put the plant back where it was, just in case he gets back here without us spotting him. But I'd say we've got more than enough to arrest him. And once we've done that, we can tear this place apart to make sure we've found everything.'

I rearranged the carpet and plant, then had a last walk through the flat, checking that everything was as I had found it.

'Happy?' Maitland asked.

'Ecstatic,' I said, and meant it. All we had to do now was catch him.

Chapter 37

Catching Stuart Sinclair, of course, was easier said than done, because all we could do was wait. Godley had a team of about twenty officers deployed in cars and vans around the area, all watching, all ready to go at any moment. The tension was a killer. The atmosphere was so highly charged I couldn't see how Sinclair would miss it when he came home. Or maybe he'd seen us already and was on the run. Maybe he'd had a silent alarm in his flat and he was never coming back.

For two hours and through four suspects who turned out not to be him I tortured myself with worrying about whether I'd done something wrong and scared him off. Eventually I put my head down on the steering wheel of the car and moaned.

'He's never coming back. We're never going to catch him. He's going to go abroad again and get more plastic surgery and a fake passport.'

'He's not a criminal mastermind,' Liv said. 'He's not any kind of mastermind. He spent hundreds of thousands of pounds to look like Derwent. What does that tell you?'

'Obsessive personality. Bad judgement. Serial killer. You're right. I'm not taking him home to meet my parents.' I stayed where I was, though, my hands gripping the wheel so hard my knuckles bleached.

'I don't think I've ever seen you so edgy. Are you okay?'

'This has been the week from hell. Of course I'm not okay.'

'Are you missing Rob?'

'Yes.'

Her eyes went round. 'Wow. No prevarication. No excuses. It must be love.'

'So what?' I was grinning, though.

'So I didn't think you'd ever admit it.'

'Yeah. I should really tell him.'

'Maeve Kerrigan, are you actually telling me you haven't said "I love you" yet to the perfect man? Your soulmate? The guy who makes you smile every time I even mention his name?'

'He knows,' I protested.

'That doesn't mean he shouldn't hear it occasionally.' The radio in the footwell by Liv's feet crackled and she picked it up.

'We've got an IC-1 male on foot towards the address. Just turned off Argyle Road onto Larchfield Avenue.' It was James Peake's voice, and he sounded calm and matter-of-fact. Good radio voice, I thought irrelevantly, trying to stop my heart from racing.

'He's coming from over there,' Liv said, having checked the map. She was pointing to the other side of the area we were watching. I sat back in my seat, the tension still knotting my stomach even though we were on the wrong side and too far away to be involved.

'Blue jeans, black jacket with a Superdry logo on the shoulder, grey trainers,' Peake added.

'Stand by,' Godley said. 'Let's confirm the ID before we move.'

I felt the tension in my arms as I put one hand on the door handle. Our car was parked near the main road, a short distance from the flat. I calculated there were ten or twelve officers closer than us or in a better position to bring him down, but I was still going to be in the game, and from Liv's face she felt the same way.

And I could see him now, in the distance. He was maybe thirty metres away from the gate to the flats. He was walking easily, looking relaxed, a gym bag slung over his shoulder. 'It's him.'

'Definitely our man,' Maitland said over the radio at more or less the same time.

It was all that Godley had been waiting for. 'Strike, strike, strike.'

The street came alive with people as everyone bundled out of their cars, converging on Sinclair. The strategy was to move fast, confuse and disorientate the target and control them by getting them down on the ground before they could think about fighting back. He had the reactions of a cat, though. He'd had no warning but in less time than it took to blink he was running, sprinting up the pavement towards our position.

'Coming this way,' I said to Liv in a rush.

Before Sinclair got close to us DI Bradbury got in front of him. Without hesitating, Sinclair threw the gym bag at his head, scoring a direct hit. Bradbury went down like a felled tree and the next officer, who happened to be Harry Maitland, tripped over him. Together they made quite a formidable obstacle for the pursuers behind, who crashed into each other and slowed themselves down. Sinclair didn't look back as he raced away, taking advantage of the mayhem. The smooth, organised arrest had disintegrated into chaos in seconds and I couldn't quite understand how, except that we'd had all the time in the world to prepare but Sinclair had had all the luck. James Peake kicked himself clear and put on an extra turn of speed but Sinclair had gained five or six metres on him.

Which left me and Liv to block Sinclair before he got to the open road. Seeing us in front of him he swerved, diving across the street to the opposite pavement. I bolted to do the same and cut him off, careless of traffic, my Asp racked and ready to use. Liv was right beside me, shouting to him to stop.

He didn't stop. He put his head down and ran straight at us. He hit Liv, hard, and I heard her stumble and go down with a cry as he straight-armed me out of his path, grabbing the Asp and using it to pull me off balance. I let go, twisted and stayed on my feet by a miracle, and the one thought in my mind was that I was not going to be the scapegoat for this going wrong, just because he had been more powerful than two female officers. I pelted after him, angry as hell, matching him stride for stride but with a height advantage that got me further than him with every step. He risked a glance back as we got near the end of the street: I was gaining on him, and he knew it.

My only focus was Sinclair. I was flying, close enough to touch him with the very tips of my fingers, almost close enough to grab him and bring him down . . .

I honestly don't know what he meant to do when he reached the metal barrier at the end of the street. It was designed to stop pedestrians from crossing the very busy A road that was four lanes of constantly thundering traffic, and it was roughly hip-height. I thought at the time, and I still think, he intended to jump over it and dodge through the cars, taking his chances. He was arrogant. He might have thought he'd be quick enough to avoid getting knocked down.

Whatever he'd intended, he clipped the top of the barrier as he jumped, and fell. He sprawled on the tarmac, arms and legs outstretched, and his head turned to see what was coming. That was all he had time to do before a fully loaded articulated lorry went straight over him, at speed. I felt the rush of wind as it passed me. I had been a split second behind Sinclair, and a lifetime. The wind dragged at my hair, my clothes, as I crashed into the barrier, going too fast to stop, and pitched forward over the top of it. I grabbed hold of it but I could do nothing about the momentum that had my feet off the ground as I pivoted, unable to prevent myself from following Sinclair into traffic that was nowhere near stopping, that hadn't even started to notice a man had just died there.

I was well past the point of no return when someone behind me grabbed a handful of my jacket and hauled me back, out of danger, to stand on solid ground. I stared into the road, at the red smear that was what remained of Stuart Sinclair. The cars and vans and trucks slammed on their brakes, just that little bit too late for me if I'd gone all the way over. I looked up into James Peake's face, then collapsed against his chest, too weak to stand. I was too shocked to think about what could have happened, or what had happened to Sinclair. I could barely form a coherent thought, let alone words.

It felt like for ever, but I finally managed to speak. 'You saved my life.'

'More than likely. It was no trouble.' He put his head down on top of mine for a second. 'Bloody hell, though.'

'I lost him. Another second, and I'd have had him.'

'Never mind about that. The important thing is that you're okay.'

I peeled myself off him and stood on my own two feet as the rest of the chasing police officers finally caught up with us. Godley's face was grim.

'Are you all right?'

'Fine.' I glanced into the road again. Dave Kemp and Ben Dornton were standing guard over the body, moving the traffic out of the lane where the various parts of Stuart were all too vividly displayed. It involved a lot of irritable shouting and furious gesturing as the drivers slowed to a crawl the better to get a good look, and it was as dangerous as anything I'd done that day even though they'd get little enough credit for it. Standing around on a fast-moving road without a high-vis jacket, without so much as a traffic cone, was one way to look death in the face. Neither of them appeared to be enjoying it much.

Further down the road, the truck had stopped, hazard lights flashing, and the driver climbed down from his cab. A couple of officers had gone down to speak him. He looked agitated, one hand to his head, one to his mouth.

'Better tell the driver not to worry about it,' I said. 'No one's going to miss this one.'

'I'd have liked the chance to arrest him,' Godley said softly. 'I'd have liked to hear what he had to say.'

'He'd just have lied.' I was starting to shiver as the shock kicked in. 'They all lie. You never really get near the truth.'

'That's truer than you know,' he said, so quietly only I could hear it, and I looked up at him, wondering what he meant. He didn't add anything else, striding off to speak to the lorry driver as a couple of response cars arrived, lights and siren on, to take over the traffic duties. An ambulance was right behind them, also on blues, and I wondered why they were bothering to hurry. Sinclair was far beyond anyone's help now.

Maitland finally made it to my side. He was looking anguished. 'Are you all right?'

'Never better.' I tried to stop my teeth from chattering. 'I'm fine.'

'Good.' He still looked upset.

'Really, I'm okay.'

'I believe you. But you need to come with me.'

'What's wrong?'

'You were right. He did have a knife.'

I stared at him, waiting, and I could see him decide there was no good way to break the news, given what it was. Two words were enough.

'It's Liv.'

MONDAY

Chapter 38

'Knock knock.'

I looked up from my work and gasped. 'No way.'

'Oh, there was a way. It just involved buying a new ticket.' Rob slung his bag on the floor and came across the deserted waiting room as I jumped up and ran into his arms. 'How are you doing?'

'I'm okay,' I said, my mouth muffled against his chest. 'I can't believe you came.'

'As soon as I could. I was away for a week and you almost got shot. And strangled.'

'Don't forget I almost got run over too.'

'I was getting to that.' He held me even closer. 'Then there was Swain. He's enough to get me on a plane on his own. Who knows what would have happened if I'd stayed the full two weeks?'

'Nothing good,' I said, shivering. 'But I'm not hurt. And I'm not scared of Chris Swain.'

'This again.' He shook me gently. 'You should be.'

'But then he wins.'

'So he wins. Be a good loser and live a long life. For me.'

'For you,' I said. I hadn't let go of him. It was still sinking in that he was really there. 'How come you were able to leave early? Did Debbie agree?'

'Not really.'

'Rob!'

'Look, I told her it was important. She'll get over it.'

'She doesn't even like me,' I said. 'She'll be furious.'

'Don't worry about it.'

'You can't destroy your career for me.' I was really worried now.

'I didn't destroy anything. I promise, she'll be fine.' He ran his thumb down my cheek, then bent his head and kissed me. I shivered in sheer pleasure this time and pressed against him, my arms around his neck. When we came up for air, he looked into my eyes. 'Let's be clear. If I have a choice to make between work and you, I'll always pick you. You come first for me.'

'I love you.'

His face went blank. Shock. 'What did you say?'

'You heard.'

'I don't know that I did.'

'I love you,' I said slowly and clearly.

He grinned, delighted. 'A hospital waiting room. Not the most romantic setting you could have chosen but I'll take it. I love you too.'

'I know.' I leaned my head on his shoulder, my cheek against his neck. I'd missed him more than I could have thought possible.

'Are you really okay? How's Liv?'

Tears caught at the back of my throat. 'Not great.'

For three agonising days we had been waiting to hear if Liv was going to pull through after emergency surgery to repair the damage Stuart Sinclair had done to her with the knife he had been carrying, the knife no one had seen, the knife I'd warned them about. He'd stabbed her in the stomach, almost casually, as he passed, leaving the knife in her as he ran on. She'd been wearing her protective stab vest but it had ridden up, as they tended to, and Sinclair had got lucky. Although the surgeons had been able to stitch her back together, she'd developed a post-operative infection that was causing a lot of headshaking and concern.

I felt paralysed, desperate to help but with no way of doing anything useful.

'Have you been here since it happened?'

'Most of the time,' I admitted. 'How did you guess?'

'You look as if you've just come off a long-haul flight.'

'Whereas you look just fine. How do you do it?'

'I make these things look good,' he said. 'But I am starving. I slept through the meal on the plane and I didn't stop for anything on my way here.'

'The café on the third floor is all right.'

'Not a rave review, but okay. I'll go and find it in a bit.' He pulled me a little bit closer. 'All this excitement. Your mum must be a wreck.'

'I think she's quite proud of me, for once. But she made me promise not to do it again.'

'Sensible woman. That was my next move.'

I leaned my head against him. 'Oh, Rob.'

'Very touching.' Derwent let the door slam behind him and limped towards us. 'Welcome home, lover.'

'Thanks,' Rob said drily, letting go of me. 'Good to see you too.'

Derwent was looking around. 'This place is like a morgue.'

'That remark is in poor taste,' I snapped.

'Sorry.' He didn't look it.

'I know you don't like Liv much but she's in intensive care. She's fighting for her life. The least you could do is show some respect.'

'I'm showing plenty of respect,' he protested. 'I'm here, for one thing. And I've just been along to see how she's doing.'

My heart jumped. 'Any news?'

Godley had come in behind him and answered for him. 'She's the same.' He nodded to Rob. 'Good to see you. How's the Flying Squad?'

'Fun and games.'

Godley grinned. 'Do you mind if we borrow Maeve for a minute? Just to catch up?'

'No problem. I was going to find something to eat anyway. I'll stay out of your way. Does anyone want anything from the café?'

'I need a coffee,' Derwent announced. 'I'll come with you.'

Rob looked at me. 'Coffee?'

I shook my head, and the two of them headed off together. I missed one of them before the door had even closed behind them. The other was welcome to stay away as long as he liked.

'You need to go home. Get some rest,' Godley said, sitting down.

'I'm fine.' I could work well enough in the hospital with my phone, which had at long last been returned, and my paperwork, and I wasn't going anywhere until I knew what was happening with Liv.

'You look tired.'

'I am. But I'll be okay.'

'I know the two of you are close.' He reached out and put his hand on my shoulder. I was surprised that he did it, but comforted by it too. 'You know, you've put us through this in the past.'

'It's easier to be the one who's out cold.'

'Very true.' He sat back.

'Do I have to talk to Derwent? Does he have to be here?'

Godley looked surprised. 'What's the problem?'

'I can't deal with him at the moment. Not with Liv the way she is. He doesn't even care.'

'He's been here every day, even if you haven't seen him. He's got the nurses eating out of his hand.'

'Am I supposed to be impressed just because he's flirting with the nurses?'

'They've been extra-nice to Joanne and Liv's family. It all helps.'

'He's totally motivated by self-interest.'

'He got here an hour ago. He's been sitting with Joanne, letting her talk about Liv. When I got there, he was making her laugh.'

'Seriously?'

'Absolutely.'

I swallowed. 'How did I not know this?'

'He keeps his good side well hidden, but it's there.'

'If you say so.'

Godley shifted in his seat. 'While Josh isn't here, I want to apologise.'

'For what?'

'For giving you a hard time. I don't want you to leave the team, Maeve. You're an asset I don't want to lose.' Godley looked at me. 'I don't know why you still want to work for me, given what you know about me, but for as long as you do, you have a job on my team.'

I could have wept. 'Sir—'

'It's not money. I want you to know that.'

I stared at him. 'I don't—'

'He didn't give me a choice. I try not to tell him anything he'll find useful. I take the view that if I wasn't doing it, someone else would be. At least this way I know what he knows.'

'You don't have to explain.'

'I want to.' He looked down at his hands, his expression rueful. 'You know, you're the last person I would have wanted to find out about it.'

'Why? I haven't told anyone.'

He looked back at me. 'Because you'd have said no and taken the consequences.'

Before I could put together a cogent reply, the door swung open as Derwent returned alone, except for a hospital orderly carrying two coffees on a tray, since the crutches meant he couldn't manage one. He had a genius for getting people to do things for him for nothing more than a smile.

'Thanks, darling,' he said, and winked at her as he lowered himself into a seat. The smile turned into a wince.

'How's your leg?' I asked.

'Agony. How's your neck?'

'Better.'

'For the record,' Derwent said, stirring his coffee, 'I'm glad you didn't fall under a truck the other day. But I wish you'd run a bit faster.'

'I did my best.'

'And it wasn't good enough.'

'I'm aware of that,' I snapped.

Godley cleared his throat. 'No one blames you, Maeve. You did a good job.'

'It pisses me off, though,' Derwent said. 'Twenty years I've been waiting to find out what really happened to Ange. Twenty years. And you're just a couple of seconds too slow, so now I'll never know.'

I took a deep breath before I replied. I needed some sort of mantra to cope with Derwent, something soothing and centring so that he didn't get to me any more, but the only things I could think of were swear words. 'Well, actually, I've been doing some digging while I've been sitting around here and I think I've worked out what happened. And almost all of this information was openly available, so you could have found it out for yourself at any point in the last twenty years. It's not my fault that you couldn't see the wood for the trees.'

'Hey,' Derwent said, hurt, and Godley shut him up with a look.

'Go on, Maeve.'

'Okay. Well, during the original investigation, the only people who told the truth were you and Angela's dad, and the two of you cancelled each other out as suspects. Orpen was a disaster. He kept really bad records of the interviews he did, and he had everyone running scared so they didn't tell him what he actually needed to know.' The next bit was mildly tricky. I hoped Derwent was concentrating on what I'd found out rather than how I'd done it. 'One of the witnesses I traced mentioned a guy named Craig – first name or last name, she didn't know – who'd been hanging around a couple of weeks before Angela died. He was a drifter, passing through on his way from somewhere in the north of England to France. He was a good source of quality dope and he liked to hang around with teenage girls although he was probably in his late twenties or thirties.'

'I don't remember him,' Derwent said, frowning.

'He might have only spoken to Angela once before she died, according to the witness. He seemed to disappear. He never came up in the original inquiry because no one ever told Orpen about him.'

'What makes you think he's relevant?' Godley asked.

'Because the night Angela died, Shane was smoking dope with people he described as friends, but they were really people he barely knew. I got in touch with him yesterday to see if he remembered anyone matching the description of Craig and he said he did, that the guy had given them the drugs and chatted to them for a bit. He'd never seen him before and he never saw him again. The guy wandered off halfway through the evening and I pressed Shane for the details but he really doesn't remember.'

'Drugs will do that to you.' Derwent sounded like his usual sanctimonious self but his eyes were fixed on me and he was very still, paying close attention.

'I think Craig was on the lookout for a girl to kill that night. I think he was hoping to get someone stoned and then take her somewhere private to kill her, but it didn't work out. He gave up on the teenagers in the park when no one suitable showed up, and went for a wander. He must have seen Angela walking home alone and followed her.' I laid a couple of sheets of paper out on the table in front of me so Godley and Derwent could see. 'He said he'd been up north before so I had a look through the records. Here's an unsolved murder in Bradford two months before Angela died – Laurie Morrows, aged sixteen. She was a drug addict and worked as a prostitute from time to time. She was raped and strangled and her face was mutilated. That case has just been sitting in West Yorkshire Police's files and no one ever thought it could be relevant until I went looking for cases that might be connected. Laurie's job confused the issue – they were looking for a client. Angela wasn't a prostitute, obviously, so that didn't ring any bells for West Yorkshire, and no one down here knew about Laurie's death in the first place. And this case: Coventry, the month before Angela's death. A teenage girl walking her dog was choked but managed to get away from her attacker. The description is patchy but it could be Craig.'

'Bit different from Angela.'

'Yes, it is. But after Angela, there are three murders in France.' I'd marked them on a map, in a curve that ran from the Pas de Calais to the Pyrenees. 'One, two, three. All teenage girls. All strangled. All sexually assaulted. All mutilated facially in various horrible ways – teeth knocked out, eyes removed. One had her nose and ears cut off. No one was ever caught for them though the French did make the connection between the three killings. They got DNA but they've never matched it to anyone.'

'And then what? He disappeared?'

'I'm still waiting to hear from the Spanish authorities but I bet there'll be more. They don't have any record of anyone with the name Craig being arrested for murder or anything else around that time, but that's where he was heading. From there—' I shrugged. 'Portugal? North Africa? Plenty of places he could disappear. I can't go any further at the moment. The trail is not what you'd call hot. I'm not giving up, though. Twenty years is a long time but people remember strangers, and Craig sounds pretty distinctive.'

'Why didn't he rape Angela?' Derwent touched one of the pieces of paper for no real reason, moving it around, rearranging the layout. The old OCD kicking in again, I thought.

'That's where Stuart comes in. He was in his bedroom, where he couldn't have seen what was going on in the garden next door but by his own account he *heard* it. That was why he woke up. That was what attracted his attention.'

'And?'

'And he thought it was you and Angela. I've spoken to Stuart's Japanese girlfriend a few times on the phone and she's been very helpful in filling in the background details for me. Stuart liked to get drunk about once every six weeks – his way of letting off steam because he was so disciplined about his diet and exercise usually. I told her about Angela and what we knew, as opposed to what Stuart had told us. She said he had talked about it a couple of times. That night, Stuart heard Angela moaning, thought he was listening to the two of you and his first thought was to disturb you and Angela if you were having sex. Then he decided it would be better to watch you. He was obsessed with you, wasn't he? And Angela was a flirt. Vinny said she was a tease. She loved the attention and you have to wonder if she'd been leading him on as well. He was a sexually frustrated teenage boy with absolutely no chance of finding a girlfriend, and he was never going to get closer to actual sex.'

'So he saw them?' Godley asked.

'He couldn't see anything out of the window. He had to go downstairs and out the front door. He found Angela lying in the grass, dead. It's just conjecture but if it was Craig who attacked the girl in Coventry, he might have been angry and frustrated. He seems to have started the attack by gouging Angela's eyes, to control her and subdue her. He was in a high-risk area, surrounded by people in their houses, so he would have wanted to keep her quiet too, and he strangled her. Maybe it didn't matter to him if she was alive or dead before he raped her. As it turned out, he didn't get the chance. Stuart's arrival on the scene disturbed Craig in the act, which meant that he had to run away before he could sexually assault her.'

'But all of this had a lasting effect on Stuart,' Godley said.

I nodded. 'I think he stole Angela's autopsy photographs because he found the sight of her arousing. He was troubled, unhappy and traumatised by his parents' divorce, and this was his first real sexual experience, according to his Japanese girlfriend. It was a shattering, exciting event and he never got over it. Afterwards he was, briefly, very important. He was able to get his revenge on the bully who'd tormented him.' I looked at Derwent. 'That's you, by the way.'

'Noted.'

'It was a turning point. He grew in confidence. He decided to remake himself in a different image. He became his ideal and then he was able to live out his fantasies. It just took him a long time to get up the nerve. And as it turned out, he had a gift for it. Killing came easy. Kirsty, Maxine and Anna didn't matter to him as people – that's why we had so much trouble making a connection between them. They looked right and that was all he wanted.'

'How did he get them to trust him?' Godley asked.

'He pretended to be me.' Derwent sounded weirdly detached, but he had to be upset about it.

I nodded. 'I've been going through the file cards we found in his flat, talking to the women who interested him. He was working on two or three at a time, I think, and sometimes he didn't pursue them – maybe if they asked too many questions or if they were too risky. From what I can work out, his technique was to stalk women who reminded him of Angela. He'd find out if they lived alone, then get talking to them. He told them he was a police officer named Josh and gave DI Derwent's surname and rank if they asked for more details. He gave them advice on their home security, probably culled from the Met website if you go by Kirsty Campbell's wish list. He promised to come round and check their locks, and he sent them flowers. White ones. So the flowers were there waiting for him, and the women trusted him when he went round to kill them.'

Derwent winced. 'Calculating bastard. What a creep.'

I narrowed my eyes. 'Let's not forget that you do actually follow women around for their own safety.'

'Leaving that aside.'

'Josh . . .' Godley looked appalled.

'Irrelevant,' Derwent said. 'It just sounds bad.'

'Angela's death had a big impact on both of you. Sinclair wanted to kill women because of it. You want to save them. You weren't all that different, really.'

Derwent glowered at me and Godley asked hastily, 'Why was it that he didn't have sex with them?'

'I don't think he could, from what his girlfriend says. Dr Chen would probably be able to explain it in technical terms, but my take on it is that he was squeamish. His flat was sterile. He didn't like mess. He didn't like getting dirty and that included having sex. The way he took out the eyes – it wasn't something he enjoyed, particularly, but it was part of the ritual. Killing Angela over and over again. Staring at her dead body for as long as he liked this time. Revelling in the moment. Being aroused but in control. I imagine that killing Deena was a very different experience for him because he was angry, not enjoying himself. He wouldn't have counted her murder because it was just practical, not for pleasure.'

'And now he's dead.' Derwent leaned back, his hands clasped behind his head. 'It seems like justice, somehow. Better than him getting fat and living a long life behind bars at the taxpayer's expense.'

'Happy to help,' I said, grinning.

Godley's phone rang and he glanced at the screen, then pulled a face. 'My wife. I'd better take this.'

He left the room and Derwent looked at me. 'You know, no matter what I say, you're a good copper.'

Before I could respond, the door opened again and Kev Cox poked his head in. 'All right? No news on the patient, I hear.'

'She's hanging on,' I said, coming down to earth with a thud. Oh, *Liv.*

'I just wanted to see you in person.' Kev advanced across the room, looking from Derwent to me. 'Is it all right to speak about that other matter?' he asked me.

'The flowers? DI Derwent knows all about it.'

Kev looked relieved. 'Well. This is unofficial, you understand, but we've got the results back on tests we did on the evidence you collected.'

'And?'

'We found a partial fingerprint on the tape that held the cellophane wrapper around the bunch originally, and we matched it to someone we have on file.'

'Chris Swain,' I said.

'Try DI Deborah Ormond.'

I stared at him, stupefied, as Derwent roared with laughter. 'Naughty Debbie.'

'Why would she do that?'

'Dunno. But she wanted you to know she'd done it,' Derwent said. 'Debbie knows enough to keep her fingerprints to herself. You can't tell me she'd make a mistake like that.'

'It was more than a smudge, if that helps. Pin-sharp. No mistaking it. Anyway, here's the report. I'll leave it with you. It's confidential at the moment but let me know what you want to do. I can always lose it.' Kev laid two pages down on the table and hurried out before I could so much as thank him.

Derwent picked them up, glanced at them and ripped them into pieces.

'What are you doing?'

THE STRANGER YOU KNOW

'This never happened.'

'Yes, it fucking well did.' I was livid. 'That *bitch*.'

'Forget it.'

'No way.'

'Listen, Kerrigan. I'm going to help you out.' He jabbed a finger at me. 'You don't want to do this. You don't want the publicity. You're already front-page news and the tabloids will be all over this. Your boyfriend works for Debbie. He likes the Flying Squad and he's not going to want to leave it. If you try to bring her down, you will suffer, and what's more you'll fuck up your boyfriend's career. Let it go. Be glad it wasn't Swain after all and move on.'

'I have to tell him. How can he work with her if she's done something so unprofessional? So *horrible*?'

'In blissful ignorance,' Derwent said. 'He doesn't need to know the truth.'

'I would.'

'You don't know what's good for you. You can't tell him because it's not fair. He can't work with her if he knows, and you've already done him out of one decent job by shagging him.'

I couldn't argue with that. Saying nothing made sense even though I was beyond outraged – too angry to see straight, let alone think straight. But I had the horrible and unfamiliar feeling that Derwent was right.

He picked up his crutches. 'Come on. You need to get out of here. Find your bloke. I'll even buy you lunch.'

'Wow.' I gathered up my pages of research and stuffed them into my bag. 'This is a red-letter day.'

'Don't get used to it.'

We had just come out into the corridor when someone called my name and I turned to see James Peake jogging towards me. 'Maeve. How are you?'

'I'm fine.'

'No ill effects? I'm glad. I still can't believe what happened the other day.'

'I was lucky.' To Derwent, I said, 'James saved my life.'

'I heard.' Derwent was glowering.

'I'm sorry about Liv. How's she doing?'

'Holding on.'

'Tough on you,' Peake said, full of sympathy, and I felt the tears start into my eyes. He reached out and folded me into his arms. 'Come here.'

I had enough time to register the situation as awkward before Derwent intervened.

'Hey, hey, hey. That's enough.'

Peake let go of me because he had to. The rubber ferrule on the end of Derwent's right crutch was pressing against his windpipe. He grabbed it but by now Derwent had him pinned against the wall.

'What are you doing?' I hissed.

'Letting him know to keep his hands to himself.' To Peake, who was turning purple, Derwent said, 'Back off, mate. She's taken.'

Peake knocked the crutch away and coughed. When he could speak, he said, 'Sorry. I didn't know. Are the two of you—'

'No,' we said in unison.

'She's got a boyfriend, though. And he's a big lad. Big muscles. Short temper. Two floors down as we speak.' Derwent made a shooing motion. 'Go on. Jog on, Ginger. She's not for you.'

I think if Derwent hadn't been on crutches, Peake might have punched him. As it was he glared, then nodded to me, all ice and wounded pride. I watched him go down the corridor and when he was out of sight I turned on Derwent.

'"She's taken." Thank you very much.'

'Sorry. I didn't think you'd be interested. Go on, go after him.'

'No, of course not. I'm not interested. At all. I'm glad he knows.'

'Why didn't you tell him?'

I tried to think how I'd explain to Derwent that you couldn't assume someone was interested in you in that way, and it was presumptuous to warn them off before there was even an issue, and anyway I was my own person and not Rob's chattel, but I gave up. 'It was never the right moment.'

'Not difficult, is it? "I have a boyfriend." There you go.'

'Whatever,' I said irritably.

'Poor guy.' I thought he was talking about Peake until he went on. 'He's never going to get a ring on it, is he? Never going to pin you down. You like your freedom too much.'

'That's not it, actually.'

He raised his eyebrows and waited.

'He's too good for me. He's better than I deserve.'

'Horseshit.' Derwent leaned one crutch against the wall and dropped an arm around my shoulders. 'Your trouble is low self-esteem. You need to start thinking more of yourself. Build up your confidence.'

'And you're going to help?'

'Probably not. I like you meek.'

'*Meek*?'

'Biddable.' He snapped his fingers. 'Oh, I've been meaning to tell you. You couldn't have seen the Philip Pace briefings. They were from anti-terrorism and you don't get them.'

It took me a second but when I worked out what he was telling me, I was outraged all over again. 'Did you know that when you were giving me a hard time about them?'

'Of course.' He retrieved his crutches and set off down the corridor. 'I felt a bit bad about it afterwards. Especially since you helped me.'

'I went above and beyond the call of duty, or even friendship. And we're not friends.'

'No, we are not. But hey, now we're even.'

'Because you told me you were just being an arsehole, deliberately, and I'm not actually incompetent, and that

427

cancels out me solving a twenty-year-old crime and clearing you as a murder suspect.'

'Exactly.'

We had reached the lift. I pressed the button and turned to look at him. He was the same as ever, despite everything that had happened. His confidence was undented.

'Has it occurred to you that all of this happened the way it did because Stuart Sinclair wanted to be like you?'

'Yep.'

The lift arrived and I stood aside while a motley collection of patients, visitors and medical staff trooped out. I waited until the lift was empty, then held the door for Derwent. When he was in and the doors had closed, I tried again. 'All of this was because of you. Don't you think that's strange?'

'Not really.'

'But you were his ideal. You were what he aspired to be.'

'So? Makes perfect sense, if you ask me.'

And Derwent gave me his widest smile.

ONE WEEK LATER

Chapter 39

I almost didn't go. I almost convinced myself that it was none of my business.

It just wasn't in my character not to interfere.

This time, I didn't call ahead. I rang the doorbell and waited. When she answered the door, Claire looked a lot better – younger, prettier, with more colour in her cheeks. She was just as hostile, though. 'What do you want?'

'Can I come in?'

She hesitated. 'It's not a good time.'

'I won't be long.'

'Can I tidy up first?'

'There's no need,' I said. 'I know.'

She got it straight away and her face crumpled. 'How did you find out?'

'I just worked it out. Can I come in?'

She went ahead of me into the sitting room and sat down on the edge of an armchair, shivering. I wandered up and down looking at the photographs of Luke that she had hidden before, seeing exactly why she had wanted to keep them out of sight. The pictures, on walls and shelves and every available surface, recorded his progress from adorable baby to toddler to small boy to teenager to university student, formal in an academic gown, and in each and every image he looked exactly, precisely like his father.

I sat down opposite her. 'You know what I'm going to say, don't you? You should tell him.'

'No.'

'He deserves to know.'

'We didn't need him. We did fine without him.'

'Yeah, you don't need him. But maybe he needs Luke.'

'Don't be stupid. He wouldn't be interested.'

'I don't think that's true, but even if it is, what do you have to lose? You don't have to tell Luke until you know either way. You don't have to tell Luke at all, if it comes to that. But you should tell his father.'

'I don't want to have to share him,' she said through gritted teeth. 'Luke is mine. Just mine. Nothing to do with Josh.'

I hadn't wanted to say his name until she did, even though I'd been absolutely sure Luke was Derwent's son. 'He's so like him, Claire. At least in looks.'

She stared away from me, her eyes streaming, and nodded. 'Personality too.'

'Really?'

'Josh all over again.'

I hoped for Luke's sake that wasn't completely true. 'What does Luke think? Doesn't he want to see his father?'

'He doesn't know who he is. I've never told him what happened. He thinks it was a random guy in Birmingham, just like everybody else did.'

'Didn't anyone else notice?' I asked, incredulous. 'They are identical.'

'People see what they want to see. My mother thought he looked just like Vinny did when he was a baby.' She rolled her eyes. 'I didn't argue, but really, no.'

'I didn't know that you and Josh had a relationship.'

She blew her nose. 'We didn't. It was just an accident. One of those things. You know Josh came and lived with us for a while after his parents kicked him out. He was so sad, and so hurt by his parents, and just heart-breaking, really.'

She shook her head. 'Such bad luck. It was pure chance that one Saturday evening, everyone was out. My parents and the younger kids were at Mass. I had homework. Vinny was with his girlfriend. Josh had been out for a walk but he came back, and I went in to see if he was all right. He was lying on the bed and I lay down beside him and just put my arms around him, just to let him know I cared. And one thing led to another.'

I could imagine it, very easily: the young Derwent, handsome and aching with sadness, in need of comfort. Claire trying to make him feel better. Being kind. Trying to take his pain away. The memory of the awkward, embarrassing, tragic sex with Angela was overwritten with a new experience – something tender and surprising that gave Derwent his confidence back and changed Claire's life for ever.

'Why didn't you tell anyone?'

'Vinny would have killed Josh. *Killed* him. And Josh wasn't exactly popular. I was scared to tell anyone about the baby. He was gone before I finally admitted it to my mother, and she just arranged for me to go and stay in Birmingham with my aunt and uncle. She believed me when I told her the father was a boy I'd been seeing. She never dreamed Josh was the one.'

'Did you get in trouble?'

'Oh my God, yes. And it got worse. I wasn't supposed to keep Luke, you know. He was supposed to be adopted, but I couldn't do it. So all the secrecy and running away was pointless.'

'Did your parents support you?'

'In the end.' Her face softened. 'Once they saw Luke, they loved him too.'

'Don't you think Josh would have felt the same way?' I asked carefully.

'Yes, I do. But he was just a kid. We were both kids.' She sighed. 'If I'd known I was going to bring Luke up I might have told the truth, but by the time I knew what I wanted to do it was too late. And then I'd lost touch with Josh anyway.'

I put a business card on the table, face down. 'It's up to you, but if you want to get in touch with him, here are his details.'

She looked at the card as if it was seeping poison. 'I don't want to. And you can't tell him. Or Luke. You mustn't go near him.'

'I won't,' I promised. 'But think about it. You're so proud of Luke. You've done such a good job of bringing him up. You should give Derwent the chance to get to know him too.'

She didn't reply, but she didn't say she wouldn't, at least. I had no idea what she would do, but I meant what I said – I wasn't going to tell him. Although I would have dearly loved to see his face when he realised he had something in common with Philip Pace after all. I left the card where it was and said goodbye. Claire was lost in her own thoughts and didn't answer. I let myself out, hoping I'd done the right thing.

I couldn't help feeling sad as I walked down the path back to the car. I wondered what the specific weight of secrets was – if that was why I felt I was shouldering an extra burden. But I could do it, and I would do it.

It was just one more secret to keep.

Acknowledgements

In some ways, this is the best bit: getting to say thank you to the many people who made this book become a reality. Firstly, the fiction team at Ebury – Gillian Green, Emily Yau, Hannah Robinson, Louise Jones, Helen Arnold, Jake Lingwood, Fiona MacIntyre, Martin Higgins and everyone in the sales department, as well as Beccy Jones in production and Jeanette Slinger. The world is divided into those who like Derwent and those who don't. My lovely editor, Gillian, thinks he can do no wrong. (Otherwise, however, she shows impeccable judgement.)

Secondly, I'm immensely grateful to all at United Agents for their support and guidance. My agent, Ariella Feiner, is as wise as she is lovely, and as glamorous as she is encouraging, which is saying a lot. They are all a pleasure to work with.

Thirdly, my thanks to all of the people who gave me the benefit of their knowledge. Without Gemma Golder and her wonderful friend Jon Morrell, who advised on Japanese geography, customs and names, I would have had a breakdown somewhere around Chapter 35. I learned a lot about Afghanistan from Rory Stewart's amazing book *The Places in Between*, and about soldiering there from *Dead Men Risen* by Toby Harnden.

Fourthly, my friends and family deserve at least a

round of applause for putting up with me while I fail to respond to phone calls, texts, emails and more. If I was inventing a husband for a crime writer, I would come up with something very like my own. In addition to being an encyclopedia of all things criminal, James has a great gift for remaining calm in the face of my impossible deadlines. Edward, Patrick and Fred are infinitely forgiving about my work and how little they see of me sometimes.

Fifthly, I must thank Frank Burns, Jonty Johnson and Caitriona Bennett for lending me their names for characters. The fictional Caitriona first appeared in *The Last Girl* and I liked her too much to leave her out of this book.

Finally, a note on places. London is a great backdrop for a crime novelist, with plenty of suitable locations for killings. This book ranges widely across London, but it's far from a guide to the city. I am reluctant to litter people's neighbourhoods with fictional corpses, so like the murderer, his victims and all the other characters, these specific locations exist only in my imagination.

THE YORKSHIRE
WOOLLEN AND WORSTED
INDUSTRIES

FROM THE EARLIEST TIMES
UP TO THE
INDUSTRIAL REVOLUTION

BY

HERBERT HEATON

SECOND EDITION

OXFORD
AT THE CLARENDON PRESS
1965

Oxford University Press, Amen House, London E.C.4

GLASGOW NEW YORK TORONTO MELBOURNE WELLINGTON
BOMBAY CALCUTTA MADRAS KARACHI LAHORE DACCA
CAPE TOWN SALISBURY NAIROBI IBADAN
KUALA LUMPUR HONG KONG

This book was originally published as Volume
10 of Oxford Historical and Literary Studies
issued under the direction of C. H. Firth and
Walter Raleigh.

REPRINTED LITHOGRAPHICALLY IN GREAT BRITAIN
AT THE UNIVERSITY PRESS, OXFORD
FROM SHEETS OF THE FIRST EDITION

TABLE OF CONTENTS

CONTENTS

MAPS AND DIAGRAMS

PREFACE TO SECOND IMPRESSION

A NEW preface to a very old book can scarcely avoid auto-
biography, acknowledgements, and an apology. This volume
originated in a thesis written in 1911 for the Honours School of
History at the University of Leeds. In that prentice work
I dealt with the Yorkshire textile industry of the eighteenth
century; but the award of a research scholarship, then of a
university fellowship, enabled me to spend most of the next
two years exploring the industry's earlier and later history.
The substance of the first three chapters earned me the M.A.
degree (Leeds) in 1912, and that of the whole book was submitted for the degree of M.Com. in the University of Birmingham, where I served under Professor W. J. Ashley as a junior
member of the Faculty of Commerce staff from 1912 till I
emigrated to Australia in 1914. At the last European port of
call I received a letter from Professor Ashley, reporting that
the degree had been granted and that he would endeavour to
find me a publisher. He quickly found one, whereupon I spent
two years thoroughly revising the script and making sure that
the two—or was it eventually three?—copies of each chapter
left Australia on different mail steamships travelling on different routes, in the hope that at least one copy would evade the
submarines. The book appeared in the autumn of 1920.

In it I traced the history of the Yorkshire industry from the
earliest times for which there was documentary evidence down
to what was then popularly called 'the eve' of the Industrial
Revolution. My original plan to carry the story through the
nineteenth century had to be abandoned when it became evident
that this would make far too long a volume; also that many
other scholars were hard at work on various facets of the modern
period. Mantoux's *La révolution industrielle au dix-huitième
siècle* (1906) and Cunningham's third volume of his *Growth of
English Industry and Commerce* (1903) had richly amplified
Toynbee's pioneer sketch, while six years' teaching of economics
(1902–8) at Leeds had switched J. H. Clapham's interests from

general history to economic, and by 1910 he had published a book on *The Woollen and Worsted Industries* (1907) as well as five articles on their modern development.

The later period was thus being well cared for ; but there were gaps to be filled in the earlier story. Medievalists had let their tale end with the Middle Ages or soon afterwards, while modernists had begun theirs with a brief survey of industrial society about 1760, but made little effort to penetrate further back. Moreover, their references to the country's major manufacture gave the impression that Yorkshire was, and for centuries had been, insignificant as a producer of woollen fabrics. My aim therefore was to link the twelfth or thirteenth century with the eighteenth, throw light on the Tudor and Stuart periods, give the Yorkshire industry its proper place in relation to those of East Anglia and the West of England, paint a detailed picture of conditions in the eighteenth century, but to stop at the factory gates. I hoped that circumstances would permit me later on to get inside those gates and write a second volume about what had happened there.

The Bibliography (pp. 438–45) lists the original manuscript or printed materials on which I drew, as well as the secondary works. This last category was the least rewarding, for economic historiography was only just passing out of the hands of the few founding fathers into those of a second generation which, though increasing in numbers, was not yet very productive in print. The interest in economic history was growing rapidly, not only in some universities but also in the 'tutorial classes' organized by the Workers' Educational Association in co-operation with the universities, and even in some schools. The number of tutorial classes mounted from two in 1908 to about 120 in 1912 ; a third of them were studying 'Industrial History', while at least another third tackled Economics ; and the list of full-time or part-time tutors included such names as Clay, Daniels, Gill, Gonner, Macgregor, Rees, Richards, and Tawney.[1] But it

---

[1] An interesting index of this booming popularity is supplied me by Blackie and Son, publishers of the most popular textbook of that period, Townsend Warner's *Landmarks in English Industrial History* (1899). They printed 7,000 copies in six impressions during the nine years 1899–1907, then 19,500 copies in eleven printings during the next six years 1908–13.

took time for the new flock of economic historians to finish and publish their own first books.

The manuscripts in the British Museum and the Public Record Office proved to be a gold mine. For a regional study, however, much depended on access to local records. Fortunately for the student of Yorkshire history, many important medieval and early modern documents had been edited and published by the Yorkshire Archaeological, Surtees, Thoresby, and other antiquarian societies. Beyond the frontier of these societies' interests and slender financial resources one had to search, often fruitlessly but on rare occasions with happy results, in the basements of local government bodies, the cellars of solicitors' offices, or the cupboards of local museums. The 'happy results' are catalogued on pp. 438–9. Only one item in that list comes under the heading of 'business records'; yet the two fragments, comprising less than sixty sheets of early eighteenth-century letter-books covered with copies of less than three hundred letters, gave invaluable information on the marketing of woollen cloths in London and the Low Countries and on the struggle of one clothier to develop the manufacture of worsted cloths in the Halifax region in competition with the well-established East Anglian industry. Of other such records I found no trace.

All that happened at least fifty years ago. The book was given a very kind reception by the reviewers and is still mentioned in footnotes and bibliographies. It went out of print in the 'thirties and only rarely appears in second-hand catalogues —at a fabulous price. Hence my publishers feel there might be a warm welcome for a reprint—they do not, I am thankful to note, insist on a revision—and offer me space for this new preface. I have therefore been obliged to re-read the book after a lapse of at least three decades. The immediate reaction has been a recurring exclamation: 'Did I really write that?', with the emphasis sometimes on 'I', but often on 'that'. My main concern has been to discover how far the contents of the volume have been chipped away, undermined, or converted into what Professor J. D. Chambers once called 'the economic history of yester-year' by the steady solid advance in research during the inter-war years—that 'age of monographs', as Sir Frederick

Rees once labelled it—and still more by the veritable 'academic explosion' of the last two decades.

That explosion has seen the number of workers in economic history grow many-fold. Old kinds of sources have become more accessible, and new ones, such as the records of business firms and of landed estates, have been thrown open for inspection. The collection and care of archives by county record offices, urban public libraries, and universities have supplemented the activities of the regional historical societies. Local studies have added depth, colour, and variety to the national panorama. Funds and facilities have become available to aid research and publication.[1] While some old labels and landmarks, concepts and questions, institutions and -isms have ceased to seem important, new ones have clamoured for consideration. Clapham's plea that 'every economic historian should acquire what might be called the statistical sense' and make an attempt 'to offer dimensions in place of blurred masses of unspecified size' has been heeded, and the quest of the quantitative proceeds apace on every possible front.

The story of the European woollen industry and of England's role in it has gained greatly from all this research. By mid-century Professor Carus-Wilson could re-tell it[2] from Roman imperial days 'through a thousand years of medieval history' in the three regions—Belgica,[3] Italy, and England—which became prominent above all others in developing a *grande industrie* 'operating under the direction of capitalist entrepreneurs and

---

[1] Younger members of the economic historians' guild might be reminded of the debt owed to Professor Postan and his band of volunteers who kept the *Economic History Review* going—with classic articles by Tawney, Habakkuk, Fisher, Postan, Clapham, Miss Carus-Wilson, and others—during the war years. Fear that the *Review*'s light might be extinguished, as all the continental journals had been, led us in the United States to start the *Journal of Economic History* in 1941. So now there are two.

[2] E. M. Carus-Wilson, 'The Woollen Industry' in M. Postan and E. E. Rich (editors), *The Cambridge Economic History of Europe*, ii (1952), 355–428. This chapter contains much of the author's own research on the English industry and trade. See also her *Medieval Merchant Venturers: Collected Studies* (1954). Her Ford Lectures, to be delivered at Oxford in 1965, will be published in due course of time.

[3] This was the Roman name of the province between the Somme and the Moselle.

organized for export to distant markets'. In this wide sweep over time and space the features and problems of the industry are analysed: the dependence on imported materials—wool into Belgica and Italy, dyestuffs into England; the task of organizing the passage of the wool through a long series of processes, sometimes at least two dozen, with the finished product of one group, such as yarn or undyed undressed cloth, serving as the raw material of the next; and the ever-present possibility that the flow of wool to the industrial centres or of cloth to market might be impeded by civil strife, hot or cold war, and the fiscal policies of rulers. In this setting are traced the rise of Belgica to its zenith in the urban capitalism of the thirteenth century and its troubles thereafter; the rapid growth of the Italian cloth trade and industry and the difficulties that checked it about the mid-fourteenth; and the advance of the English industry to pre-eminence by the end of the fifteenth.

That advance can now be followed quantitatively in the very thorough study by Professor Carus-Wilson and Miss Coleman of English exports of wool from 1279 and of cloth from 1347 to the mid-sixteenth century.[1] The tables and graphs have many blank spaces, and move precipitously up and down, thereby indicating the rocky road along which England's foreign trade was transformed from the export of one staple commodity, wool, to that of a manufactured article. In the mid-fourteenth century about 90 per cent. of that trade was in wool, but by 1500 the same percentage was in woollen fabrics. The number of cloths exported in 1500 was almost double the figure for 1400, while that of wool sacks was down to about one-third of its peak in the mid-fourteenth century.

For the expanding production of cloth that made this transformation possible little of the credit goes to the towns which had produced fine quality cloths for royalty, aristocracy, and the export market during the twelfth and thirteenth centuries. Most of it seems to have been due to the growth of the rural industry, whose infancy and adolescence in the West Riding, at the expense of York, Beverley, and Hull are dealt with in

---

[1] E. M. Carus-Wilson and Olive Coleman, *England's Export Trade, 1274–1547* (1963), especially the graphs on pp. 122–3 and 138–9.

Chapters I and II below. To the various reasons given there
for this development, it now seems necessary to add, or to stress
more heavily, the influence of the spread of fulling mills after
about 1200.[1] In these mills the cloth was immersed in a mixture of water and fuller's earth, where large wooden hammers,
operated by a water-wheel, pounded it. Under this treatment
the fabric shrank and grew thicker, and the fibres of wool were
felted together in a firm warm wear-resisting cloth. Formerly
this pounding had been done by the feet of teams of men or
women standing and 'walking'[2] in tubs or troughs. Hence the
mill was a great labour-saving, time-saving, power-using innovation; but it could operate only where—and when—there was
falling or rapidly-flowing water. Its location must be, not on the
eastern and central plains where the cloth-making towns were
situated, but in hilly country on the banks of streams in the
valleys of the Pennines, Lake District, Cotswolds, and West of
England. The mill involved some capital investment for its
construction, maintenance, and perennial repairs when floods
played havoc. In return it offered a new source of monopoly
income to the manorial landlord and to the fuller who rented it.
Hence it stimulated industrial growth in such regions as the
Stroud Valley and the West Riding.

For the Valley there is rich evidence, showing that almost
every bit of water-course was leased by 1450 to serve a thriving
industry.[3] For the Riding the manorial documents are scanty,
but Professor Le Patourel's volume of *Documents relating to the
Manor and Borough of Leeds, 1066–1400*[4] is full of references to
the renting and repair of one fulling mill after 1322 and of a
second mill built in 1356. We also know now that when monastic
lands in the Huddersfield region passed into the hands of local
yeomen and gentry in the mid-Tudor period, many of the new
owners hastened to erect more fulling-mills[5] to encourage and

[1] See E. M. Carus-Wilson, 'An Industrial Revolution of the Thirteenth
Century' in *Medieval Merchant Adventurers*, pp. 193–210.

[2] 'Marking time' would be a better description.

[3] E. M. Carus-Wilson, 'Evidences of Industrial Growth in Some Fifteenth-
Century Manors' in *Econ. Hist. Rev.*, Second Series, xii (1959), 190–205.

[4] Thoresby Society Publications, xlv (1957).

[5] W. B. Crump and Gertrude Ghorbal, *History of the Huddersfield Woollen
Industry* (1935), chap. v.

to profit from the expansion of the woollen industry in that area. On the other side of the picture Mr. J. N. Bartlett's detailed study of the expansion and decline of York in the later Middle Ages[1] shows that the city's textile industry and trade, after enjoying mounting prosperity during at least the last two-thirds of the fourteenth century, began to decline soon after the beginning of the fifteenth, and that this was intensified by growing competition from West Riding fabrics, the invasion of the York cloth market itself by them, and their diversion from Hull or York merchants to those of London.[2]

In my treatment of the West Riding's expansion I was delighted to be able to cite 'statistical evidence of an accurate character' from ulnage accounts.[3] In these accounts the ulnager reported, usually annually, the number of saleable cloths in his territory on which he had collected a subsidy of fourpence and an ulnage fee of a half-penny for measuring and sealing the cloth. He also gave particulars, sometimes including the names of the subsidy-payers in each town or locality and the number of cloths on which each person had paid the levy; at other times he was content to give only the number of persons and of saleable cloths in each district. The surviving Yorkshire accounts cover the years around 1395, then jump to those around 1470. Through them I traced the changes in the output of York and the various West Riding localities, and noted the scale of enterprise of men and women where individual figures were given. Then, after collecting the totals for other counties around 1470, I prepared a table and map to afford 'a rough general comparison of the production for sale' throughout the country.

The 'accurate character' of these figures was shattered by Miss Carus-Wilson's brilliant detailed analysis of the accounts, especially those for the West of England counties for the years

[1] His article on this subject in the *Econ. Hist. Rev.*, Second Series, xii (1959), 17–33, is based on his unpublished London Ph.D. thesis (1958).
[2] The story of York has been richly illuminated by the Yorkshire Archaeological Society's publication since 1938 of eight volumes of *York Civic Records* (1474–1588). Also by E. Miller's survey of the city's economy (1300–1500) in *Victoria County History, Yorkshire*, iv (1961), 84–113.
[3] See below, pp. 60, 68–75, 84–88.

1465–78.[1] She found (a) that the county totals were fictitious, often repetitions of figures copied from previous returns, at best no higher than the actual number but almost certainly not the whole truth;[2] (b) that the number of cloths attributed to each producer or merchant was fictitious, a juggling with figures to account for the total or a crediting of many men's outputs to one name in order to save time and ink; and (c) that even the names may be fictitious. True, the particulars arranged under the names of towns probably indicate the place where payments were made and hence the localities where cloths were being produced; but those of names and individual payments defy comprehension or credence.[3] True, also, Miss Carus-Wilson reports[4] that she found nothing so horrifying in Yorkshire as in other counties and that the northern ulnagers 'seem to have been free of the worst vices of the West Country ones'. Hence she does not see why almost everything in Chapter II cannot stand as it is, with an additional word of caution about the actual figures, general and particular. Nevertheless, this intimation of degrees of vice justifies her plea for 'the utmost caution', and in a wider context stresses the need for a similar attitude towards all kinds of statistical reports in all countries and all centuries. In the 1930's a Moscow statistician assured a visiting Minnesota agricultural economist that the figures of Russian grain production were absolutely trustworthy, since each annual return from a local official was corrected by applying to it the sender's known 'coefficient of mendacity'. There is, unhappily, no way of learning how mendacious the ulnager was, or how

---

[1] 'The Aulnage Accounts—A Criticism' in *Econ. Hist. Rev.*, ii (1929), 114–23; reprinted in *Medieval Merchant Venturers*, chap. viii.

[2] My grand total for the whole country (*c*. 1470) was about 39,000 saleable cloths; yet the customs records show an average of well over 37,000 cloths exported during the eight years 1466/7–1473/4, and for three of those years the average was 42,800. Hence either virtually the whole commercial output was exported, which seems absurd, or the ulnager's figures were far too low.

[3] For example, Emma Earle does not appear on the Wakefield list for 1394–5. Next year she is credited with 48 whole cloths, or over a quarter of the city's total score. Next year her figure is only 8 cloths, out of a total of 52. How does one classify her? As the city's leading but regular small producer, or as a spare-time dabbler at the job? (See below, pp. 23, 93.)

[4] In a recent letter.

lazy, or how many unreported fourpence-halfpennies went into his private purse.

Once the Middle Ages are left behind, the woollen industry and the sale of its products get a goodly share of the flood of new light thrown on the subsequent economic history of Tudor–Stuart England. The size of the domestic market remains a dark secret, since 'the industry did not suffer from the attention of the exciseman, its raw materials did not, for the most part, pass through the Customs House, and much of its output was sold on home markets and untaxed by bureaucracy'.[1] But of the overseas markets, on which the welfare of the three chief cloth-making regions became increasingly dependent, much more is now known about their character and size, their competitive features, their long-term trends and shorter-run vicissitudes in centuries that had more years of war than of peace, and their influence on public policy, especially when foreign skies grew dark.

Much has thus been added to, or has altered somewhat, the story told in Chapters IV–VIII below. Three instances must suffice. In the first place, virtually nothing is said in Chapter V about the remarkable growth of cloth exports, possibly by 150 per cent. during the first half of the sixteenth century, or about the collapse of the boom in the early 'fifties and the difficult, almost stagnant, decades that filled the second half.[2] The expansion was characterized by the increasing concentration of white unfinished fabrics—semi-manufactured products—in the hands of London merchants and their shipment for sale in Europe's great commercial and financial entrepôt, Antwerp. The collapse, followed soon by the decline and ruin of Antwerp, forced merchants to seek other market outlets across the English Channel and the North Sea, through the Sound, and even further afield. They had moderate success, and London's export score in the last years of the century, though far below the boom peak in the middle years, was double that of the first years,

---

[1] C. Wilson, 'Cloth Production and International Competition in the Seventeenth Century' in *Econ. Hist. Rev.*, Second Series, xiii (1960), 209.

[2] See F. J. Fisher, 'Commercial Trends and Policy in Sixteenth-Century England' in *Econ. Hist. Rev.*, x (1940), 95–117; also L. Stone, 'Elizabethan Overseas Trade', in ibid., Second Series, ii (1950), 30–56.

while merchants in York, Hull, and Newcastle made considerable headway with the sale of their kerseys and northern dozens to Dutch and Baltic customers. Thus England gained a foothold in the regions where the climate called for warm clothes, and it may not be idle fancy to estimate that the 100,000 'shortcloths'[1] shipped from London alone in 1600 provided 800,000 persons with durable outer garments.

In the second place, some of the 'Milestones in the Seventeenth Century' (Chapter VI) have been made easier to read and the road itself is much better marked on the map. The Great Depression of the early 'twenties and the string of smaller ones reflect the hard struggle to strengthen, or even to retain, the hold on the temperate zone market.[2] Competition grew keener as other countries developed their woollen manufactures and, in the case of the Dutch, shipping, commercial, and financial strength as well. Any comparative advantage England had once enjoyed in the supply of raw materials, in skill, or in production costs had shrunk to vanishing point, and no such technological innovations as those which revolutionized the whole situation in the late eighteenth century were forthcoming. Wages could not be cut much; deteriorations in workmanship or quality of product were self-defeating; and wars, whether short or thirty years long, whether civil or international, played havoc with the trade and the trade routes. 'From 1615 at the latest the old broadcloth industry which had been a bright jewel in the earlier Tudor expansion ceased to glitter and during the next quarter of a century its gleam became ever duller.'[3]

It was little consolation to the producers of these 'old draperies' to know that the production of 'new draperies', chiefly in East Anglia, had expanded so much since mid-Tudor times that on the eve of the Civil War the export of the new fabrics from London alone almost equalled in value the traffic

[1] The 'shortcloth' was a customs house official unit into which all kinds and sizes of cloth were converted.

[2] See B. E. Supple, *Commercial Crisis and Change in England, 1600–1642* (1959) for a detailed blow-by-blow survey and diagnosis of this period. Also F. J. Fisher, 'London's Export Trade in the Early Seventeenth Century' in *Econ. Hist. Rev.*, Second Series, iii (1950), 151–61. For the Baltic story see R. W. K. Hinton, *The Eastland Trade and the Commonweal* (1959).

[3] Wilson, *op. cit.*, 209.

in the old.[1] This expansion owed much to the energy and expertise of Flemish textile workers who had sought refuge in England from religious strife at home. It may also have been helped by an increase in the supply of its raw material, coarse long-fibred wool, which Mr. Bowden suggests was in part due to the enclosures and improvements in pasturage for sheep.[2] The products, a vast variety of fabrics made wholly or in part from this wool and known today as worsteds, were much lighter in weight than the old draperies and hence were suitable for wear on warm days or in such warm climates as that of the Mediterranean lands. A pattern or stripes could be woven into them to meet (or make) changes in fashion in almost any kind of climate. Since they needed little or no fulling or elaborate finishing processes their production costs could be lower and water-power was not needed.

Western and northern manufacturers were slow to take up the production of these fabrics. Instead Yorkshiremen met the declining sales of their kerseys by making pieces of greater length, finer workmanship, and higher quality. Wiltshiremen developed a new high-quality cloth, made originally of dyed Spanish wool and hence called 'Spanish cloth', which won favour at home and in northern Europe. Only after mid-century did the worsted industry make much headway outside East Anglia, when Exeter forged ahead as centre for making and exporting serges, a mixed cloth with worsted warp and woollen weft, which was middle-weight, cheap, and hard-wearing.[3] Somewhere in the same half-century Halifax men began to produce similar mixed cloths called bays, a fabric long known to East Anglian manufacturers.

In the third place, Dr. Davis's study of English foreign trade from 1660 to 1774[4] finds that English woollen cloths continued,

[1] Fisher, op. cit., 154.

[2] P. J. Bowden, The Wool Trade in Tudor and Stuart England (1959).

[3] W. G. Hoskins, Industry, Trade, and People in Exeter, 1688–1800 (1935), p. 40. Exeter's exports of serges in 1700 accounted for one-sixth of the country's total wool-textile exports (p. 68).

[4] R. Davis, 'English Foreign Trade, 1660–1700' in Econ. Hist. Rev., Second Series, vii (1954) ; and 'English Foreign Trade, 1700–1774', in ibid., Second Series, xv (1962), especially 291, 302–3.

even in the brief and rare intervals of peace, to face keen competition and protective tariffs in the European market; that the
official value of all types of wool fabric exports was stagnant
during the first quarter of the eighteenth century; and that its
increase by 40 per cent. during the next two quarters was due
overwhelmingly to the mounting demands of the West Indies
and the mainland American colonies. This transatlantic trade
doubled in the first half-century, then trebled in the next two
decades. By that time it absorbed nearly 30 per cent. of England's total woollen exports, with the thirteen mainland colonies
responsible for over half that figure. After the Revolution the
United States' share rose to 30 per cent., and remained at or
above it till the mid-nineteenth century. Yorkshire cloth and
traders were in the thick of this development; so thick that
when the Stamp Act (1765) provoked the Americans' boycott
of British goods, Leeds merchants joined in the demand for its
repeal and welcomed that retreat so enthusiastically that the
bells 'were immediately set aringing, and continued to do so
all day, and the evening concluded with bonfires, etc., etc.'.
On the eve of the Revolution the American coastal cities were
well sprinkled with Yorkshire cloth merchants; by 1800 they
swarmed with them.[1]

Once we enter the eighteenth century and stray beyond,
several recent studies of the Yorkshire story are available. They
reflect the growing interest of the local museums,[2] the historical
societies, and the University of Leeds in the region's economic
history and in the collection of its records. Mr. Crump's *The
Leeds Woollen Industry, 1780–1820* (1931)[3] was based on a fulling
and scribbling miller's diary (1808–14) given to the Thoresby
Society in 1928 and a fragmentary collection of the papers of
Benjamin Gott given in the same year to the University. The

---

[1] See my *Yorkshire Cloth Traders in the United States, 1770–1840* in Thoresby
Society Publications, xxxvii (1941), 226–87.

[2] The Tolson Memorial Museum, Huddersfield, published by W. B. Crump
and Gertrude Ghorbal, *History of the Huddersfield Woollen Industry* (1935). The
Halifax Museum published a re-edited and much enlarged edition of my *Letter
Books of Joseph Holroyd and Sam Hill* (1914), edited by Frank Atkinson and
entitled *Some Aspects of the 18th Century Woollen and Worsted Industry in
Halifax* (1956).

[3] Thoresby Society Publications, xxxii (1931)

diary paints a unique picture of a service station performing two power-driven processes for clothiers whose spinning and weaving operations were still manual. The Gott papers reveal how a young Leeds cloth merchant determined in 1792 to build a vast mill in which all the processes from sorting the wool to packing the finished pieces would be carried on. By 1800 this mill housed a thousand operatives; by 1830 Gott had 1,300 of them in three mills; yet all his weavers worked on hand-looms and he supplemented their output by purchasing heavily from small domestic clothiers. He thus was only an Industrial Half-Revolutionary.

In 1948 a generous donation by W. H. Dean to stimulate academic research on the woollen industry made it possible for Leeds University to finance historical studies in that field. The first task was a thorough search for surviving mill or mercantile records. While the results were often saddening, several collections, usually far from complete, were gathered into the Brotherton Library at the University. Most of them belong to the nineteenth century, but while they are useful for the light shed on the great changes of that period their introductory chapters cast some rays on the twilight of the *ancien régime*.[1] Some mercantile firms' papers run back to at least 1750, and have provided rich material for a very comprehensive study of 'Leeds Woollen Merchants, 1700–1830'.[2]

My own hope of writing a second volume was revived when I returned to the Northern Hemisphere in 1925. During two summer vacations and one sabbatical year I interviewed any octogenarians, or still older survivors I could find, and tracked down four substantial manuscript collections. The first covered four generations (1770–1880) of a village family which began as clothiers, turned merchants, then added a mill. A member of the first generation wooed the American market from Boston to North Carolina, but was stopped in his tracks by the Revolution. The representative of the second lived in New York City,

---

[1] For instance, E. M. Sigsworth, *Black Dyke Mills* (1958); F. J. Glover, 'Dewsbury Mills, 1811–1893' (unpublished Leeds Ph.D. thesis, 1959); R. M. Hartwell, 'The Yorkshire Woollen and Worsted Industries, 1800–1850' (unpublished Oxford D.Phil. thesis, 1956).

[2] By R. G. Wilson (unpublished Leeds Ph.D. thesis, 1964).

except when the War of 1812 turned him into an interned alien
enemy, from 1810 to 1825 as a member of a West Riding colony
of expatriate cloth merchants. The third and fourth did their
American business from their home base. The second 'find'
was the Lupton papers from 1750 onwards. The Luptons were
a famous Leeds merchant family which took to manufacturing,
did much business with the United States, and had a branch
office in Lisbon until the Portuguese royal family escaped
Napoleon's clutches by fleeing to Rio de Janiero; whereupon
the Luptons sent their son-in-law, John Luccock, author of a
classic work on *The Nature and Properties of Wool*, out to spend
ten years' exile in Brazil.[1] The third was a grimy mass of
miscellanea stacked under a stone staircase in a famous mill
near Huddersfield, and a volume, found in the office, which contained annual financial statements ranging unbroken from 1825
to 1893.[2] The fourth was a huge tin trunk filled with letters,
diaries, and memoranda of a Yorkshire mechanic who spent
sixteen years (1846–62) installing spinning machines in French
and Italian mills and teaching the natives how to work them.[3]
Meanwhile the Gott papers were a joy to examine and fit into
a growing jigsaw picture.[4]

On rare occasions I found a very old man or woman whose
hearing, memory, speech, and relevance were adequate. One
of them, a nonagenarian, was a perfect illustration of Clapham's
remark that the hand-loom, 'marked by the revolution for
death . . . was to be an unconscionable time in dying'. He told
how for thirty years he plied his loom in an upper chamber of
his home, making his weekly piece of high-grade cloth until his
fortieth birthday in 1880. But by that year the long battle
between power-looms and hand-looms for making high quality
woollen cloths had ended. Technically the power-loom could

[1] See 'A Merchant Adventurer in Brazil, 1808–18' in *J. of Econ. Hist.*, vi
(1946), 1–23.
[2] From these accounts and similar ones in the Gott MSS. it was possible to
produce a paper on 'Financing the Industrial Revolution' in *Bulletin of the
Business History Society*, xi (1937), 1–10.
[3] 'A Yorkshire Mechanic Abroad' in L. S. Pressnell (editor), *Studies in the
Industrial Revolution* (1960).
[4] 'Benjamin Gott and the Industrial Revolution' in *Econ. Hist. Rev.*, iii
(1931), 45–66.

now produce as good a fabric as did the older loom ; and, equally important, the cost advantages enjoyed by the domestic hand-loom—no wear and tear costs to be met by the employer, no bill for power or floor-space rent, no foreman's or loom-tuner's wages and 'other little et ceteras to pay'—had been wiped out. Consequently the weaver's employer, having erected a power-loom shed, told him that no more yarn would be put out to him and offered him a job in the new shed. 'And who else'll be working there? Lasses! Work wi' t'lasses? Not me. So I came home, chopped t'loom up for kindlin' wood, rented a bit o' land, and spent t'next forty years growing red cabbages for t'Leeds and Bradford markets.'

All this, and much more, was written up as a collection of draft progress reports. A sabbatical year's leave in 1939–40 was to be spent filling in the gaps and tying up the loose ends of research. But Hitler did not let it work out that way.

HERBERT HEATON

University of Minnesota
October 1964

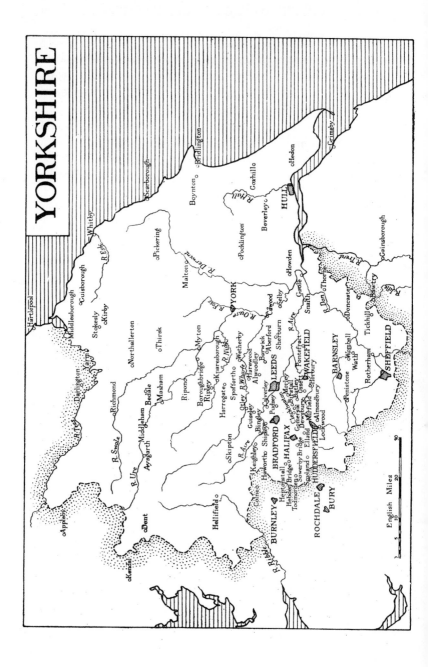

YORKSHIRE

English Miles

CHAPTER I

THE INFANCY OF THE WOOLLEN INDUSTRY IN YORKSHIRE

THE manufacture of woollen cloth has for centuries been an important occupation of Yorkshire men and women. From the twelfth century onwards there is abundant proof of the existence of the industry, and since that time generation after generation has worked at the spinning-wheel, loom, and dye-vat. The industry has been the architect of the social structure in each epoch, and has been the motive power of the county's progress. Finally, it has left its mark in the list of family names ; Lister, Walker, Webster, and other names common in the county, have survived from the days when a man took his surname from his trade.[1]

Until about 1300, however, the outstanding feature of economic life in the county (apart from agriculture) was the trade in wool. The production of wool, especially for the foreign market, provides a topic which lies outside the scope of this volume, and we can only notice it in passing. But it is necessary to remember that a great part of the wool produced on the manors and abbey lands [2] was exported to feed the looms of Germany, Italy, and the Low Countries. Native [3] and foreign merchants flocked to the wool fairs, or went direct to the producer, in their search for supplies. Long-period contracts were made frequently between these buyers and the Yorkshire abbots, and on one

---

[1] Lister was the trade name for dyer, Walker for fuller, and Webster for weaver.

[2] The abbeys were large wool-producers. In 1270, the Abbot of Meaux sold 120 sacks to merchants of Lucca (*Chronicles of Meaux Abbey*, Rolls Series, ii. 156). The list of about 200 monasteries supplying wool to Flanders, *circa* 1284, contains the names of thirty-nine Yorkshire abbeys (Cunningham, *Growth of English Industry and Commerce*, 1910 edition, vol. i, app. D, pp. 628 et seq.).

[3] Patent Rolls, 1 Ed. I, mm. 7, 8, and 14, give lists of licences to export wool. The licences were chiefly to alien merchants, but Hull, Pontefract, York, Lincoln, Newcastle, &c., are also represented. In 1230 merchants of Beverley were sending ships laden with wool, &c., to Flanders, and another ship was laden with the goods 'mercatorum de Eboraco' (Close Rolls, 14 Hen. III, m. 3) ; and in 1334, merchants of York, Beverley, Pontefract, and 'the parts of Craven' were residing in Flanders (Close Rolls, 8 Ed. III, m. 9 d).

occasion an Italian company agreed to purchase the whole of the Kirkstall clip for ten years.[1] The wool was exported from York and Hull, and between the merchants of these towns a keen rivalry existed for the monopoly of the trade.[2]

Meanwhile a certain amount of the raw material was being made into cloth at home, and this amount increased as time went by. We do not know what proportion was retained for the Yorkshire industry, but it is improbable that the local demand was a serious rival of the foreign until the fourteenth century. To the rise of that local demand, and the early growth of the Yorkshire textile industry, we must now turn our attention.

(a) The Rise of Cloth-making

Of the origins of the textile industry in Yorkshire, or indeed in England, very little is known. The discovery of rude textile implements in the lake-village of Glastonbury and elsewhere proves that the weaving of cloth is of prehistoric antiquity.[3] In Anglo-Saxon times cloth was widely used for garments by all classes, and the rough coarse fabrics worn by the poor were doubtless woven in the huts of the period, just as hearth-rugs are ' pricked ' and stockings knitted in the homes of the working-classes of Yorkshire to-day. At the same time a higher grade of cloth was being produced in some districts, and dyeing was practised, the dye being obtained from cockles, or from madder imported from France. By the end of the eighth century Mercia was exporting woollen cloaks, presumably made from English cloth, to the realms of Charlemagne, and owing to some apparently fraudulent reduction in the length of the garments Charles found it necessary in 796 to ask King Offa that the cloaks might be ' made of the same pattern as used to come to us in olden time '.[4]

---

[1] *Coucher Book of Kirkstall Abbey* (Thoresby Soc. Publications, vol. viii), pp. xxiii-xxiv, and 226–7, document cccxxiv, under date 1292.

[2] For details of this rivalry, see Poulson, *Beverlac* (1829), p. 89 n. ; also Wheater, ' Early Textile Industry in Yorkshire ', in *Old Yorkshire* (1885), p. 264 ; also Close Rolls, 6 Ed. III, m. 1, and Patent Rolls, 14 Ed. III, m. 14. The two towns were occasionally made Staples for the control of the wool export.

[3] For much interesting information concerning the early industry see H. Salzmann, *English Industries of the Middle Ages* (1913), chap. viii.

[4] Letter from Charles the Great to Offa, A.D. 796 (*English History Source Books*, no. 1, ed. Wallis, pp. 59–61). See also A. F. Dodds, *Early English Social History* (Bell, 1913), pp. 138 and 140.

Of evidence relating to the industry in Yorkshire in particular there is none. We know that York [1] was an important port and market long before A.D. 1000, trading in wool, and possibly in cloth to a small extent. Of the great mass of the Yorkshire rural population it is safe to surmise that they were dressed in cloth produced by the distaff and primitive hand-loom in the cottages scattered throughout the county.

With the twelfth and thirteenth centuries comes more documentary evidence relating to York, from which we can gather that the textile industry was firmly rooted in town and country alike long before 1300. The first traces are to be found in the two great ecclesiastical centres, York and Beverley, where the industry appeared early under gild organization. The weavers of York are first mentioned in the Pipe Roll of 1164,[2] and in the following year the payment is definitely stated to be ' pro gilda sua '.[3] The York gild was by no means the first in the field. Lincoln [4] had its weavers' gild in 1131, and the Pipe Rolls of the early years of Henry II record the subscriptions of weavers' organizations at London, Winchester, Lincoln, Nottingham, Oxford, and Huntingdon.[5] But when York appeared, the amount of its contribution leads one to believe that its weavers' gild must have been of some magnitude. Thus in 1164 the payments to the Exchequer were as follows :

		£
Weavers of London	. . . . . .	12
,, ,, York	. . . . . .	10
,, ,, Lincoln, Winchester, and Oxford	. .	6
Fullers of Winchester	. . . . . .	6
Weavers of Huntingdon and Nottingham	. . .	2 [6]

York jumped at once into the second place on the list, acknowledging only London as superior in the amount of its contribution. We may therefore assume that by the middle of the twelfth century there was a comparatively large body of men in York

---

[1] Alcuin remarked on the commercial importance of York in his day. See Drake, *Eboracum* (1737 folio edition), pp. 227–8.

[2] Pipe Roll Soc. publications, Pipe Roll, 11 Hen. II, p. 46.

[3] Ibid., 12 Hen. II, p. 36.

[4] Pipe Roll, 31 Hen. I (Record Com.), p. 109.

[5] See earlier volumes of Pipe Roll Soc. publications.

[6] Pipe Roll, 11 Hen. II. See under names of towns. Oxford does not appear in the Roll for 1164, but see Pipe Roll, 12 Hen. II, p. 117.

engaged in the trade of weaving, and able to pay a substantial sum (at least £150 in modern money) for the monopolistic privileges [1] conferred upon the gild by the Royal Charter.

Beverley did not lag far behind York. In the reign of Henry II there was buying and selling of cloth there,[2] and Spanish merchants were exporting pieces ' de scarlato et . . . de Staunford, de Beverlaco, de Ebor ' to the Continent.[3] In 1209 the ' Law of the Weavers and Fullers of Beverley ' was quoted alongside laws of Winchester, Marlborough, and Oxford,[4] and during the thirteenth century the wares of Beverley achieved widespread fame, the ' Beverley Bleu ' [5] and the ' Pann de Scarleta ' being especially famous, both at home and abroad. In fact, the prices paid for the Beverley fabrics indicate that these cloths were of the highest quality. Witness the following data :

(A. D. 1319) 1 robe and 2 whole pieces of Pers [6] cloth of Beverley were valued at £18 ; 4 whole cloths of Beverley were valued at £28. As a whole cloth was about 24 yards in length, this price was equivalent to about 6s. per yard, or quite £4 10s. in modern money. Compared with the current prices of other cloths the above statements indicate a high standard of workmanship,[7] and the Beverley pieces seem to have stood alongside those of Lincoln and Stamford, which were the best produced in England at that time.

The activity of York and Beverley was reflected in a less degree in the smaller towns of the county. In 1274 Whitby, Hedon, and Selby were mentioned as places in which cloth was made, and the inhabitants were accused of manufacturing it of dimensions contrary to the assize laid down in Magna Carta.[8] Whitby has been the home of many pursuits, and in the reign of Edward I it was a cloth-making stronghold, with John the Fuller, Roger the Dyer, Nicholas the Weaver,[9] and others of the same occupations amongst its inhabitants.

Meanwhile, what of the still smaller communities scattered

---

[1] See section on the textile gilds for the nature of these privileges.
[2] Madox, *The History and Antiquities of the Exchequer* (1711), p. 468.
[3] Poulson, *Beverlac* (1829), p. 58.
[4] Selden Soc. publications, vol. xiv (*Beverley Town Documents*), p. 135, quoting Add. MSS. 14252.   [5] Close Rolls, 20 Hen. III, m. 6.
[6] Probably a ' blue ' cloth.   [7] Close Rolls, 13 Ed. II, m. 14.
[8] Hundred Rolls (Records Comm.), Ed. I, Com. Ebor., i. 131–2.
[9] Lay Subsidy, 30 Ed. I (Yorks. Arch. Soc., Record Series, vol. xxi, p. 108).

throughout the rural area of the county? The evidence of a widespread industry here is no less conclusive, and in every Riding we find men whose attention had become concentrated on some branch of cloth-making.

At Leeds[1] in 1201 a certain Simon the Dyer was fined 100s. for selling wine contrary to the legal assize;[2] the nature of the entry and the amount of the payment indicate that Simon engaged in other trades besides that of dyeing, and was a wealthy man. Robertus Tynctor (dyer) de Ledes[3] was a witness to a Kirkstall Abbey charter not later than 1237, and an inquisition of 1258 records the names of William Webster (textor), Richard and Andrew Taillur (tailors?), and John Lister (tinctor), in the list of Leeds cottars.[4] A little later, in 1275, Alexander Fuller of Leeds was fined for making cloth which was not of the proper breadth,[5] and thus in Leeds of the thirteenth century we meet the weaver, the fuller, and the dyer.

The Calverley charters, which cover the thirteenth century, show that Calverley was a centre for the fulling of cloth. Standing on the river Aire, it was especially suited for this kind of work, and no less than five fullers are mentioned about 1257.[6] Turning to the south and west, the Court Rolls of the Manor of Wakefield provide abundant evidence of the existence of cloth-makers in the surrounding villages. These Rolls refer to the area between Wakefield and Halifax, and throughout this expanse the distribution of textile workers is almost uniform. In 1284 Thomas the Weaver of Hipperholme complained that his two cows had disappeared from the common,[7] and in the same year weavers of Sowerby[8] and Sandal[9] came before the Court. Ossett[10] was the home of Robert the Lister (i.e. dyer), 1274, and other dyers carried on their business at Alverthorpe[11]

[1] Wm. Paganel's charter to Drax (c. 1110) indicates the presence of mills in Leeds; possibly one was a fulling-mill (J. S. Fletcher, *Picturesque History of Yorkshire* (n.d.), i. 354).

[2] Jackson, *Guide to Leeds* (1889), p. 21. This 'Guide' is a scholarly piece of work, but no authority is quoted for the above fact.

[3] *Coucher Book of Kirkstall Abbey*, charter cvii. Thoresby Soc. publications, vol. viii, p. 81.

[4] Inquisition, 1258 (Yorks. Arch. Soc., Record Series, xii. 56-7).

[5] Jackson, *Guide to Leeds*, p. 21.

[6] *Calverley Charters*, Thoresby Soc. publications, vol. vi, pp. 8-55. No weavers are mentioned till 1357, pp. 170-1.

[7] *Wakefield Court Rolls* (Yorks. Arch. Soc., Record Series, 2 vols.), i. 182.
[8] Ibid., ii. 18.   [9] Ibid., ii. 203.   [10] Ibid., i. 81.   [11] Ibid., i. 269.

and Halifax.[1] Of fullers there were many. These men washed
the grease and other foreign matter out of the rough pieces
which had been woven in the cottages for home use; but the
existence of so many fullers leads one to believe that a great
part of the cloths which came to them had been made for the
home or foreign market. Certainly, all down the Calder Valley
we find the fulling-mill—at Sowerby, Halifax, Rastrick, Mirfield,
Dewsbury, Ossett, and Alverthorpe.[2] These mills were the
property of the lord of the manor, and the tenants were compelled to use the manorial mill and no other.[3] But though the
lord retained the monopoly for his mill, he did not manage the
work himself; instead, he leased the mill to one or two of his
tenants for an annual rent. Thus, in 1277, William the Fuller of
Wakefield and Ralph de Wortley paid forty shillings as one
year's rental for the mill at Wakefield.[4] It was no small mill
which could command a rental of £2, but William and his
partner would have plenty of business, washing the pieces before
they were cut up into garments by the cottagers or placed for
display and sale on the cloth-booths which stood in the market-
place. For Wakefield had its dealers also; there was Philip
the Mercer [5] (1274), William the Chapman,[6] Philip the Tailor,
and one or two merchants, all in or near Wakefield.[7]

Sufficient has been said to show that the industry was already
present in the parts which were eventually to become its stronghold. But these districts had not the monopoly of the rural
manufacture, for entries such as have been detailed above
can be found concerning all parts of Yorkshire. Away in
the dales we meet Thomas Webster and Isabel Webster, both
weavers, at Skipton.[8] In the Vale of York there were fullers
at Pocklington,[9] tailors and fullers at Thorp Arch,[10] walkers
(fullers) and 'litesters' (dyers) at Aberford and Alwoodley.[11]

[1] *Wakefield Court Rolls* (Yorks. Arch. Soc., Record Series, 2 vols.), i. 272.

[2] Ibid., both vols., *passim*.

[3] See Wheater, *op. cit.*, p. 262, for charter from Archbishop of York to
inhabitants of Sherburn (A.D. 1282), illustrating monopoly over fulling-mill.

[4] *Wakefield Court Rolls*, i. 176.

[5] Ibid., i. 81. In 1308, cloth booths mentioned, ii. 179.

[6] Ibid., i. 163.   [7] Ibid., i. 131.

[8] Inquisition, 31 Ed. I (Yorks. Arch. Soc., Record Series, xxxvii. 101).

[9] Yorks. Arch. Soc., Record Series, xii. 76 (A.D. 1260).

[10] Inquisition, 1301 (Yorks. Arch. Soc., Record Series, xxxi. 168).

[11] This is a little later, 1327. Thoresby Soc. publications, ii. 88 et seq.

Aysgarth,[1] Stokesley, and Pickering[2] carried on the various branches of the industry, and there was a dye-house at Richmond worth £4 per annum.[3] Northallerton, Yarm, and Ripon were flourishing communities, containing a full and strong contingent of cloth-makers, as well as tailors, glovers, mercers, &c.[4] In the southern areas of the county, Pontefract, Rotherham, and Sheffield were similarly provided with all the necessary men for making and selling woollen goods.[5]

The above is a mere catalogue of names and places, but it will serve to prove that by 1300 there was in town and country alike a big element of textile labour, which was supplying domestic needs and also a wider market. The cloths of Beverley and York were of no mean quality, and took their places alongside the high-class pieces produced at Lincoln, Stamford, and elsewhere, goods for which there was a big demand abroad. On the other hand, the rural fabrics were of inferior quality and coarse texture,[6] and did not take a prominent place even in the home market. Native manufacture could now meet some of the demands of the wealthy, and all the needs of the poor, and a few types of cloth were exported to the Continent. Still, one must not over-emphasize these facts, or convey the impression that by 1300 England had cut herself free from dependence upon foreign supplies. King and nobility, though they frequently purchased English wares, often had recourse to the produce of Flanders, and in the fostering ordinances [7] of the early fourteenth century, when the use of foreign cloths was forbidden, a saving clause was always inserted in favour of the finery of royalty and nobility.[8] Hence there was a steady importation of Continental cloths, and many merchants from Yorkshire loaded ships at Sluys and other foreign ports 'with cloth and other goods . . . for the purpose of bringing the same to Kyngeston-uppon-Hulle to trade therewith', taking back lead or wool in

---

[1] Lay Subsidy, 30 Ed. I (Yorks. Arch. Soc., Record Series, xxi. 100, 103, &c.).
[2] Ibid., *passim*.   [3] Yorks. Arch. Soc., Record Series, xii. 230.
[4] Ibid., xxi. 16, 27, 69.   [5] Ibid., xv. 76, 81, 145, &c.
[6] Kendal cloth in the fifteenth century was worth only 4½d. per yard (*Lord Howard's Household Book*, ii. 219).
[7] e.g. Ordinance of 1327, Patent Rolls, 1 Ed. III, pt. ii, m. 24.
[8] In 1242, for instance, Henry III ordered 'Rogerus le Taylur retineat duas navatas panni Flandrensis . . . ad robas regis contra instantem hyemem'. Close Rolls, 26 Hen. III, pt. iii, m. 4.

return.[1] The next three centuries were to witness a great change, as the export trade in wool declined, and British and foreign merchants carried more and more English pieces to every part of the Continent, making the produce of Yorkshire looms a commodity of international fame—or notoriety.[2]

(b) The Flemish Immigration

The definite emergence of the textile trade during the twelfth and thirteenth centuries has given rise to much speculation, and the question has been asked, Was this progress due to the natural development of the domestic industry, or to the influx of Flemish cloth-makers ? The question is of some importance, but unfortunately there is not sufficient evidence to enable one to give a definite answer. Hence on the one hand it can be urged that manufacture for the market evolved naturally from manufacture for home use ; whilst on the other hand many have maintained that the greater part, if not the whole, of the credit must be placed at the door of the Flemish immigrants. The latter theory has for long held sway, and the old historians made the alien weaver the hero of a story full of charm and heroics. Fuller[3] gave to him one of his most poetic paragraphs, and although later writers have almost destroyed the halo, the debt to the mediaeval immigrant is still admitted by many to be very great. Approaching the subject as it concerns the Yorkshire industry in particular, some popular writers have asserted that cloth-making was unknown until about 1331. Mr. A. C. Price, in his excellent little book on *Leeds and its Neighbourhood*, refers to the Flemish weavers who settled at York during the reign of Edward III, ' to whom probably the great clothing trade of the West Riding owes its origin ' ;[4] and when the statue of the Black Prince was erected in Leeds some few years ago, many speakers and writers justified the choice of subject on the grounds that the Black Prince's father was responsible for the introduction of the woollen industry into Leeds and district. Serious writers have, of course, long since repudiated any such extreme view, but Dr. Maud Sellers, in her

---

[1] Close Rolls, 13 Ed. II, m. 14.
[2] For the complaints concerning bad workmanship see Chapter IV.
[3] Fuller, *Church History of Britain* (1845 edition), iii, § 9.
[4] Price, *op. cit.*, p. 66.

account of the woollen industry in the *Victoria County History*, attributes great importance to migrations of Flemings, especially during the eleventh, twelfth, and fourteenth centuries.[1] The present writer must confess his inability to accept her conclusions, and feels that the part played by the Flemings in establishing and developing the Yorkshire industry has been over-rated by even such an eminent authority as Miss Sellers.

As to the influence of Flemings in Yorkshire during the Norman régime, one cannot safely pass any judgement, as there is so little evidence on either side. Miss Sellers bases her cases largely on the Domesday Survey, with its reiterated ' waste ', and urges that people must have come from somewhere to repopulate these stricken valleys. No part of England was sufficiently populous to be able to spare detachments for the West Riding. The Low Countries were overcrowded ; access to Yorkshire from Belgium was easy ; therefore Flemings came, settled in the vacant places, and built up the textile industry in these parts.

But was the West Riding really so entirely depopulated, desolate, and in need of a thorough resettlement ? In the pages of Domesday Book many Yorkshire villages are described by the melancholy word ' Waste '. William I, in his march of vengeance in 1069, had spread the destroying army over a large section of the county, and his ravages embraced the eastern parts of the West and North Ridings, almost the whole of the East Riding, the city of York, and the upper valleys of the Aire and Calder.[2] Scarcely had William departed southwards when Malcolm Canmore raided the northern counties, penetrating as far as the North Riding. He also plundered right and left, and those who fell into his hands were either killed or taken away as slaves to Scotland. Hence those who made the great survey in 1086 were impelled to write ' waste ' over almost the whole area north and west of Leeds and Wakefield.[3] But this term did not necessarily imply an absence of all human life, for some manors which were so described contained villeins or cottars in

---

[1] For Miss Sellers' discussion of this topic, see *Victoria County History, Yorkshire*, ii. 436–40.

[2] Matthew Paris, *Chronica Maiora* (Rolls Series), ii. 3–4.

[3] See map and article by Dr. Beddoe, ' The Ethnology of the West Riding ' (*Yorkshire Archaeological Journal*, vol. xix, pp. 57 et seq.).

1086. Further, as William's army approached, many Yorkshire-men doubtless fled into hiding in the forests or on the moors, where it would be easy to find solitude and safety. With them they might take cattle and sheep, and either settle there per-manently as moorland shepherds, or return to their old homes when the destroyer had departed. One need only know the West Riding countryside to realize the impossibility of a total destruction of population by William's troops.

Again, some of the important clothing centres of a later date were flourishing communities at the time of Domesday. York [1] had a population of over 5,000, and Beverley had been left untouched by William. Ripon and Pontefract were important settlements; Leeds, spared by the Conqueror, had a population of over 200 persons,[2] and was worth more than before 1066, and Wakefield, Batley, Dewsbury, and some other places were little, if any, smaller than before the Conquest. Thus the West Riding was far from being completely depopulated; in fact, it contained almost as many people as the other two Ridings put together.[3] If the Flemings had required a new home, easy of access, near a wool supply, and sparsely populated, they could have found such an area farther east than the West Riding.

It is possible that population was brought to the uninhabited manors of Yorkshire by the new Norman landlords, and this population might be brought from other parts of England or from abroad. The De Laci family, which had received almost the whole expanse from the borders of Lincolnshire to Lancashire, owned other parts of England as well,[4] and might thus move tenants from the south, or from the populous Pontefract area westward. At the same time Flemish landlords obtained many parts of the North Country, to which they may have brought Flemish artisans. For instance, William I gave large estates in Holder-ness to the valiant and restless Fleming, Drogo de la Boucerer,[5]

---

[1] H. B. de Gibbins, *Industrial History of England*, 16th edition, 1910, map, p. 38.

[2] Price, *op. cit.*, p. 33.

[3] Dr. Beddoe calculates the Domesday population as follows : West Riding, 3,143 ; East, 2,300 ; North, 1,311 : *Yorks. Arch. Journal*, pp. 56 et seq.

[4] Price, *op. cit.*, pp. 33 and 118.

[5] *Chronicles of the Abbey of Meaux* (Rolls Series), i. 89–90. Drogo built the castle at Skypse, but soon left the region, because of its infertility.

and Gilbert of Ghent received lands on the other side of the Humber.[1] A certain Reiner the Fleming[2] founded Kirklees Nunnery, and even so far west as Hellifield we find in 1202 a family which hailed from the Low Countries.[3] Further, during the strife of the twelfth century the Flemish mercenary was very much in evidence. William of Ypres, a leader of mercenary troops, was one of Stephen's right-hand men,[4] and Walter of Ghent led a body of his fellow-countrymen at the Battle of the Standard.[5] But there is nothing to show that these men were in any way connected with the textile trade. They were fighters rather than artisans. Still, the land from which they came was one in which the cloth industry had flourished for more than a century, and so some of the rank and file might be acquainted with the art, and a few might settle down to industrial pursuits. Further, the wealthy Fleming would bring his ' entourage ', which would almost certainly include a weaver and kindred workmen, and hence it is probable that amongst the Flemish immigrants were a number of men whose concern was the manufacture of cloth. But all this is conjectural, and the assertion that the Flemings were responsible for the establishment of the industry or the formation of the early gilds hangs on a very slender thread of possibilities.

When we reach the thirteenth and fourteenth centuries, documentary evidence is more abundant, and one can form more definite opinions about the presence and influence of the aliens. Perhaps the best plan would be to present all the available data, and then draw our conclusions.

During the thirteenth century Flemings were to be found scattered throughout the county. The affairs of a family of Flemings are frequently referred to in the Wakefield Court Rolls,[6] and the entries indicate that the family owned much property. In 1284 a certain William the Fleming held the vill of Wath-on-Dearne, near Barnsley, ' in capite ' from the King,

---

[1] Cunningham, *Growth of English Industry and Commerce*, i. 647.
[2] Halifax Antiquarian Society Reports, 1902–3.
[3] *Pedes Finium, Com. Ebor.* (1202–3), Surtees Soc. publications, vol. xciv, p. 78.
[4] Roger de Hoveden, *Chronica* (Rolls Series), i. 203–4.
[5] *Yorks. Arch. Journal*, x. 379.
[6] *Wakefield Manor Court Rolls* (Yorks. Arch. Soc., Record Series, 2 vols.), *passim*. See Index, under ' Fleming '.

and this district was occupied by a number of his fellow country-men.[1] Similar families dwelt in other parts of the county;[2] they were apparently landowners, but as to their interest in industry we know nothing that might help to prove that they were fostering the woollen manufacture in Yorkshire.

Turning to York, where trade was developing quickly during the early part of the fourteenth century, we find many Flemings in the ranks of the freemen of that city. All who desired to take up any trade or business there were obliged to qualify themselves, and be enrolled on the list of freemen; hence the names given in that register are those of men engaged chiefly in industrial and commercial pursuits. In 1291, Walter the Fleming and Giles the Fleming were admitted to the freedom.[3] In 1296 Giles of Brabant made his entry,[4] and others followed during the subsequent years. Some of these men occupied important positions. Giles of Brabant rose to the dignity of bailiff in 1308-9;[5] in 1298 Jacobus le Fleming was mayor,[6] whilst the doughty Nicholas the Fleming occupied the mayoral chair from 1310 to 1315,[7] and met his death when leading a York contingent against the Scots at the disastrous Battle of Myton (1319).[8] These men were evidently much esteemed by their fellow citizens; but the Roll tells us nothing about their occupations. They may have been ordinary merchants engaged in the exportation of wool and perhaps concerned with its manufacture into cloth. But whilst silent concerning the business practised by these aliens, the Roll shows the presence of a number of native workers in wool, drawn from many parts of Yorkshire and other counties. There are thirteen names of textile workers entered during the reigns of the first two Edwards,[9] and not one of them gives any suggestion of

---

[1] *Kirkby's Inquest* (Surtees Soc. publications, vol. xlviii, p. 1). See also Lay Subsidy, 25 Ed. I (Yorks. Arch. Soc., Record Series, vol. xv, p. 46).

[2] At West Lilling (*Kirkby's Inquest*, pp. 378-9) Nicholaus Flemyng, who became Mayor of York. Others at Fryton and Whitby (Lay Subsidy, 30 Ed. I, Yorks. Arch. Soc., Record Series, vol. xxi, pp. 53, 72, 108). Matthew de Luveyne living at Norton, mentioned in Assize Rolls, 36 Hen. III (Yorks. Arch. Soc., Record Series, xliv. 58).

[3] *Register of the Freemen of York* (Surtees Soc., vol. xcvi), 20 Ed. I, p. 5.
[4] Ibid., 25 Ed. I.   [5] *Kirkby's Inquest*, p. 380 n.
[6] Freemen's Roll, 26-7 Ed. I.   [7] Ibid., 4-9 Ed. II.
[8] Ibid., p. 18 n.
[9] *Victoria County History, Yorkshire*, iii. 438.

Flemish origin. There were William of Malton [1] and John of Wales,[2] fullers; John of Newcastle [3] and Robert of Marsk,[4] weavers; Williams of Easingwold [5] and Richard of Leicester,[6] chaloners (i.e. coverlet weavers); Wilfred of Leicester, dyer; [7] John of Craven [8] and John of Manchester,[9] tailors; to say nothing of chapmen from Bristol, Lincoln, Wakefield, and Craven, ' Mercatores de Beverle ', and mercers from Skipton, Ripon, Coventry, and Upsala.[10] Thus, to sum up, two things are clear from a study of the early list of freemen :—(1) That in 1327 the making of cloth and wool was in the hands of Englishmen ; (2) that increased numbers of enrolments were being made, showing a general expansion of trade in the city, and in this progress the cloth-makers stepped forward with the rest. All this was before the traditional migration began.

The granting of favours to foreign merchants had been a general feature of the economic policy of the thirteenth century. Now in the fourteenth the fostering of cloth-making took the place of importance, and in the Ordinance of May 1, 1326,[11] we have the declaration of a policy which was, in spite of many vicissitudes, to guide the development of the industry for some time to come. The most important points were :—(1) No person should wear foreign cloth, except royalty, nobility, and those paying an annual rental of £30 or over. (2) ' That in order to encourage people to work upon cloths, the King would have all men know that he will grant suitable franchises to the fullers, weavers, dyers, and other cloth workers who live mainly by this mistery, whenever such franchises are asked for.' (3) All alien merchants were taken under the King's protection. Edward III confirmed this declaration in the first year of his reign, and quickly added to it his offers of protection to foreign weavers. In July 1331 he issued letters of protection to John Kemp, ' Textor pannorum laneorum ', and his employees, and the proclamation concluded with a general offer of similar favours to all foreign weavers, fullers, and dyers.[12] Six months later [13]

[1] Freemen's Roll, 25 Ed. I. [2] Ibid., 13 Ed. II. [3] Ibid., 12 Ed. II.
[4] Ibid., 20 Ed. II. [5] Ibid., 17 Ed. II. [6] Ibid., 1 Ed. II.
[7] Ibid., 17 Ed. II. [8] Ibid., 11 Ed. II. [9] Ibid., 18 Ed. II.
[10] Ibid., 26 Ed. I.
[11] Patent Rolls, 19 Ed. II, pt. ii, m. 8. Also 1 Ed. III, pt. ii, m. 24.
[12] Rymer, Foedera, iv. 496.
[13] January 1333 : Records edition of Rymer, vol. ii, pt. ii, p. 849.

the King again dispatched a general mandate to the sheriffs :
' Be it known unto you that we have taken into our protection
all and singular weavers and other cloth-workers, from whatsoever part they come, along with their goods and implements.'
The sheriffs were commanded to see that the ordinance was
strictly obeyed.

Some years elapsed before the next declaration was made,
and on this occasion it concerned two aliens who wished to
settle in York.

' 12th December 1336. The king to his sheriffs . . . greeting.
Know ye that since William of Brabant and Hanekin of Brabant,
weavers of the parts of Brabant, have come into our realm of
England, and dwell in our city of York, there carrying on their
occupation ; we, being aware that if they engage in their industry
within our realm manifold advantage and benefits will accrue
to us and ours ; . . . and for this reason, wishing that William
and Hanekin should be free to attend to their business in peace
and quietness ; . . . we therefore take them . . . under our protection and defence, whilst they engage in the aforesaid occupation within our realm, along with their goods and all possessions
whatsoever ; . . . in which they shall be for the space of one
year.' [1]

This policy was firmly established in 1337, when an act was
passed, providing a wide statutory basis of protection, promising
security, and offering all necessary ' franchises ' to alien cloth-
makers.[2] Such offers came at an opportune time for the Low
Country men. All was not well in Brabant and Flanders. The
towns were full of faction strife, the gilds were drifting towards
oligarchy, and the poorer artisans found themselves virtually
disfranchised by the wealthier citizens. The gild monopoly was
so strictly enforced that rural industry was almost impossible.[3]
Hence, to the members of the defeated factions, and to the
poorer citizens, Edward's offers of protection would be very
welcome, and some packed up their effects and came to partake
of Edward's bounty.

Now arises the question, What was the extent of the migra-

---

[1] Rymer, *op. cit.*, iv. 723 ; also Patent Rolls, 10 Ed. III, pt. ii, m. 11.
[2] 11 Ed. III, c. 5 (*Statutes of the Realm*, vol. i, pp. 280–1). See also Rymer,
op. cit., iv. 751, and Patent Rolls, 11 Ed. III, pt. i, m. 6.
[3] Ashley, *Economic History*, I. ii. 197–8. Also Cunningham, *op. cit.*, i.
305–6.

tion to Yorkshire, and what was its influence upon the cloth industry there ? In York itself the influx was considerable, and we meet several Flemings and men of Brabant amongst the freemen.[1] For instance, note the following entries in the Freemen's Roll :

> 1344. Nicholas de Admare, de Braban, webster.[2]
> 1352. Thomas Braban de Malyns, tixtor (weaver).[3]
>   ,,   Laurentius Conyng de Flandre, webster.
>   ,,   Georgius Fote de Flandre, walker (fuller).
> 1357. Gerwinus Giffard de Gaunt, tixtor.[4]
>   ,,   Levekyn Giffard, frater ejus, tixtor.
> 1359. Petrus de durdraght (Dordrecht), walker.[5]
> 1360. Arnaldus de Lovayne, teinturer (dyer).[6]

This list of names, which is by no means exhaustive, shows that by 1360 there was a complete set of textile workers from Belgium settled in York ; weavers, dyers, fullers, in addition to tailors and merchants, had come from Ypres, Brabant, Malines, Ghent, Louvain, Bruges, &c. Some of these men were doubtless wealthy, had brought with them their households and workpeople, and had made homes in York.

The Fleming was in York. Further, there was a great expansion in the cloth trade, marked, as Miss Sellers has pointed out, by the enrolment of some 170 weavers, 100 dyers, 50 fullers, 30 chaloners, and a swarm of shearmen, wool-packers, &c., during the reign of Edward III.[7] But we cannot lay the honour for this expansion at the feet of the immigrant. From the early years of the century there had been a steady development in the trade of the city. The cloth-makers shared in it, and their progress was accelerated by the government's policy of favouring the English manufactures. Judging from the Freemen's Roll, the Flemings did not appear in any numbers until about 1346–50, and before this time the expansion had become very marked. Textile workers from all parts of the county, and of

---

[1] We do not find the names of the two men who received the special letters from Edward III. This was probably because they were under the King's direct protection and favour, but as the protection was only for one year, one would have expected to find them taking up the freedom eventually.

[2] Freemen's Roll, 18 Ed. III.   [3] Ibid., 26 Ed. III.

[4] Ibid., 31 Ed. III.   [5] Ibid., 33 Ed. III.   [6] Ibid., 34 Ed. III.

[7] *Victoria County History, Yorkshire*, iii. 439. The importance of these figures is discounted somewhat by the fact that many came in to fill the places of the victims of the Black Death.

the country, had taken the freedom of York before the Flemish invasion, as the following list will show :

1332. Willelmus de Hedon, tixtor.[1]
1333. Willelmus de Selby, walker.[2]
1334. Johannes de Bristow (Bristol), webster.[3]
1336. Willelmus de Ripelay (Ripley), taynturer (dyer).[4]
1342. Thomas de Huntingdon, litester (dyer).[5]
 ,, Walterus de Beverle, tixtor.
 ,, Willelmus de Cravene, litester.
1344. Johannes de Hertilpole, webster.[6]
 ,, Johannes de Novo Castro, litester.
1345. Johannes de Appleby, litester.[7]
1346. Willelmus de Lyncoln, sheregrynder.[8]

There were more cloth-makers from Lincoln than from the whole of the Low Countries, and Lincoln had a reputation for superior cloths even in the twelfth century.[9] It was therefore no decadent or infantile industrial community to which the men of Flanders and Brabant found their way. There was a boom already gathering force, and they simply helped to swell it. Their chief influence would be in the innovation of new varieties of cloth, and possibly of new methods of manufacture. The dyer of Louvain would introduce new hues, just as would his fellow-craftsmen from Lincoln, Stamford, and Grantham. The weaver of Ghent would have his favourite kinds of cloth, and his own ways of making them, just the same as the weaver of Huntingdon, Gloucester, Yarmouth, or Chester. Thus the aliens joined in the life of the city, but were by no means its dominating force. They shared in, and influenced to some extent, the progress of the fourteenth century, but they did not initiate it. Amid the developments of the following years, they occupied no positions of municipal importance, but took their places along with men from other parts of England in obedience to the decrees of city and gild.

Turning to the country districts, as seen in the Manor Court Rolls of Bradford [10] and the Poll Tax Returns, we find evidence

---

[1] Freemen's Roll, 6 Ed. III. [2] Ibid., 7 Ed. III.
[3] Ibid., 8 Ed. III. [4] Ibid., 10 Ed. III. [5] Ibid., 16 Ed. III.
[6] Ibid., 18 Ed. III. [7] Ibid., 19 Ed. III. [8] Ibid., 20 Ed. III.
[9] Salzmann, *op. cit.*, p. 136.
[10] A manuscript translation of these Rolls is in the Bradford Public Reference Library. It is in four volumes, and covers the period Edward III–Henry V.

of a flourishing cloth industry in almost every part of the West
Riding, but very few immigrants from the Low Countries.
The Bradford Court Rolls cover the first forty-five years of the
reign of Edward III, the period when the immigration was at
its height.   There are many entries concerning the textile
industry, but never once is there mention of a Fleming or
' Brabaner '.   From a most careful examination of the Rolls
one does not obtain the faintest trace of evidence indicating
any Flemish settlement in Bradford.   Mr. John Lister, who has
examined the Wakefield Court Rolls, has informed the present
writer that the name ' Fleming ' occasionally occurs in these
documents, but that there is no evidence to show that the
people mentioned had any connexion with cloth-making.   From
the Poll Tax Returns of 1379 one gets a similar impression.   Of
course some of the aliens might have forsworn their foreign
names, thus escaping our identification, and this possibility
must be borne in mind.   In the whole of the returns for the
West Riding only seven textile workers from the Low Countries
are recorded :

[1] Bawtry.   Iohannes de Braban et Agnes uxor eius,
    webster   .   .   .   .   vj$^{d.}$ (i.e. 6$d.$)
[2] Spofforth.   Iohannes Brabaner, Textor, et uxor eius   .   vj$^{d.}$
[3] Skipton.   Petrus Brabaner, Webster, et uxor eius   .   xij^{d}
    ,,   Petrus Brabayner, Webstre, et uxor eius   .   vj$^{d.}$
[4] Wetherby.   Iohannes Brabayner, Textor   .   .   ,   vj$^{d.}$
[5] Ripon.   Lamkynus de Braban, Textor   .   .   .   vj$^{d.}$
[6] Ripley   Iohannes Brabaner, Webster, et uxor eius   .   vj$^{d.}$

In addition to these names, there are about twenty-four other
entries of a similar character, but with no occupation attached ;
as for instance :

[7] Ledes.   Henricus Brabaner et uxor eius,
[8] Laughton.   Walterus Lovayne, et Alicia uxor eius,
[9] Acton.   Iohannes de Flaundres et uxor eius.

In these instances the poll tax payment was usually fourpence
or sixpence ; this denotes comparative poverty, and hence these

---

[1] *Poll Tax Returns,* 2 Richard II (published by Yorks. Arch. Soc., ed. by
Lister), p. 14.
  [2] Ibid., p. 223.   [3] Ibid., p. 267.   [4] Ibid., p. 222.
  [5] Ibid., p. 250.   [6] Ibid., p. 235.   [7] Ibid., p. 215.
  [8] Ibid., p. 57.   [9] Ibid., p. 165.

people would be compelled to engage in some work, which might be weaving.[1]

The number of aliens who entered the rural districts was small, and the new-comers were generally poor.[2]   Could such an element exert any powerful industrial influence ?   There are at least two tests we can apply, though neither can be regarded as final.   In the first place, does the distribution of the aliens mentioned above coincide with the active industrial areas, and was industry booming in the places wherein the ' Brabaners ' had taken up their abode ?   Secondly, admitting that their influence might be slow in bearing fruit, do we find that the industry developed during the fifteenth century in those places favoured by the Flemings in the fourteenth ?   Do we meet any aliens in the area which witnessed such a great expansion in cloth-making during the fifteenth century, namely the Halifax parish ?

Let us take one or two places conspicuous in the Poll Tax Returns for the number of persons engaged in the textile in-dustry.   Rotherham,[3] for instance, was a populous centre, in which the tax was paid for some 350 persons.   Here were five weavers, a coverlet weaver, three fullers, two shearmen, three dyers, in addition to tailors, drapers, and merchants.   In all, fourteen men were engaged in the manufacture of cloth ; but the most careful scrutiny fails to reveal the presence of any Flemings in the busy community.   At Wakefield,[4] payment was made by a ' wulchapman ' (i. e. a dealer in wool), eight weavers, five fullers, two coverlet weavers, one dyer, four drapers, and several mercers and tailors.   Here again there is no trace of exiles from the Low Countries.   Ripon [5] had its solitary ' Brabaner ', who had gone to live in a town which had long been a small textile centre.   He was only one out of the sixteen ' websters ' who paid poll tax in that town.   Pontefract, which paid the largest amount of taxation, had an abundance of cloth-makers, but no Flemings.   Where the alien weaver is found, he is often almost

---

[1] In the returns for the East Riding, I can find only three Belgian names, and these not specifically clothiers (*Yorks. Arch. Journal*, xx. 329 et seq.).

[2] It will be noticed that most of the rural immigrants came from Brabant, while those in York came from various parts. Further, all the former are poor, only one person paying more than sixpence. Again, all are weavers.

[3] *Poll Tax Returns*, p. 25.   [4] Ibid., pp. 160–2.

[5] Ibid., p. 249.

alone in his craft : Skipton,[1] with its two Flemings, had only
two other weavers, whilst the Wetherby alien [2] had the company
of only two native weavers. And so one might continue, showing
that in other places, large and small, where the industry flourished,
the alien was absent, and that when he did appear, it was
generally in some centre where cloth had been made for some
considerable period, or in an isolated quarter where he was
almost the only one of his craft, and he himself far too poor to
employ others in the trade. His influence in the latter places
does not seem to have been great, for Bawtry, Spofforth,
Wetherby, Ripley, Acton, and Laughton never appear at
a subsequent date as important clothing centres.

Further, if we turn to the valleys of the Colne and Calder, to
Halifax and the whole district west and south of Leeds, where
the ulnagers' accounts of the fifteenth century indicate a great
growth, we do not find the Fleming sowing the seed. In 1379
Halifax [3] had its ' lyster ', Liversedge its fullers,[4] Elland its
three weavers, coverlet weaver, three dyers and a fuller.[5] But
in the whole of the Halifax area the only name with a Flemish
appearance is that of Roger Flemmyng of Sowerby Bridge,
whose occupation is not stated. Indeed, with the exception of
the two solitary ' Brabaners ', father and son, at Skipton, one
does not find any weavers from the Low Countries in any parts
west of Leeds and Wakefield. And yet this region was the
stronghold of the textile industry from the fifteenth century
onwards.

One other matter is worthy of a moment's consideration.
The influence of the Flemings would probably have been towards
improving the standard of workmanship, and raising the quality
of the wares produced. Now York and Beverley made cloths
of considerable value, but the West Riding fabrics were always
of an inferior grade until the nineteenth century. Even in the
seventeenth century [6] it was pointed out that Yorkshire clothiers
used the same quality of wool as many West of England manufacturers, but the finished cloths from Yorkshire were much
inferior to the pieces made from the same kind of wool in Wessex.

[1] Ibid., p. 267.   [2] Ibid., p. 222.
[3] Ibid., p. 188.   [4] Ibid., p. 186.   [5] Ibid., p. 183.
[6] See evidence given during the big law-suit between the Yorkshire clothiers
and the ulnager, 1638 (Chapter VI).

The difference was said to be due to less skilful sorting of the wools, and lower efficiency in carrying out the various processes. The West Yorkshire clothier, like his fellows in Lancashire, Wales, and the corners of Devon and Cornwall, was deficient in industrial skill.. This may be due to the fact that few, if any, skilled workers, either alien or native, came to these parts, but concentrated in the towns and eastern districts.

Thus we come to the conclusion that the Flemish element in this county was small, and exerted little influence. In York the aliens came to swell a rising tide, but in the wide rural area over which cloth was being made their influence was negligible.[1]

From all this discussion we return to the question with which we set out: Was the establishment of the industry due to the growth of the native domestic industry, or to the immigration of alien craftsmen ? There is no proof of any large immigration of Flemish cloth-workers at any time before the middle of the fourteenth century, and then the influx was mainly confined to York. We are therefore driven to the other possibility, and to suggest that the establishment of manufacture for sale grew from manufacture for home use. Before the Conquest the domestic industry was in existence, the family demands for clothing being met by the family's work at the distaff and loom. This industry was not destroyed by the ravages of William I, and continued to be part and parcel of Yorkshire domestic life for centuries. Meanwhile, with the growth of population and the development of society generally during the twelfth and thirteenth centuries, it became possible for some men to earn a livelihood by devoting the whole, or the greater part, of their time to the manufacture of cloth. They then sold, or bartered, the produce of their labour to meet the local demand, and eventually supplied a wider market. This advance was first made in the towns of Beverley and York, but gradually specialized workers in wool appeared in the country districts. Such developments brought in their train the division of labour, one man becoming a weaver, the second a dyer, the third a fuller, and so forth. All this was a natural consequence of the growth

[1] Mr. J. Lister, who has spent twenty years on antiquarian research on the West Riding, agrees entirely with the conclusions arrived at above ; though my own opinion was definitely formed before I had met Mr. Lister.

of population, the increase in home and foreign trade, the presence in the county of plentiful supplies of wool and water, and the difficulty of making a livelihood out of agriculture alone. In its growth the industry possibly received some assistance and practical guidance from alien workmen, but there is nothing to show that these men were responsible either for the introduction of the industry, or for its subsequent development.

(c) The Character of the Rural Industry during the Fourteenth Century

From the Poll Tax Returns and other MSS. one gathers some impressions of the general character of the industry as practised in the country districts and small towns during the reigns of Edward III and Richard II. The largest centres of population[1] lay east of Leeds, at Pontefract, Doncaster, and in the Vale of York. In these parts cloth-makers were plentiful, and tailors, drapers, and merchants equally so.[2] West of Leeds the industry claimed a smaller number of professional adherents, and was in a more primitive stage as yet. Leeds, standing midway between the two areas, was well supplied, having two ' lysters ', two ' chalunhers ', one walker or fuller, two ' talours ', and one merchant.[3] Where population was gathered round a castle or abbey, the industry was well established ; Skipton, for instance, had four weavers, a fuller, draper, glover, merchant, and four ' cissores ' or tailors.[4]

Wool was to be obtained almost everywhere, and weaving might be either a person's staple occupation, or merely an auxiliary industry, carried on by the man in his spare time, or by the members of his household. Even the parish clergy occasionally devoted their leisure to cloth-making, and the Bradford Manor Court Rolls for 1354 speak of the ' chaplain ' of Bradford taking his cloths to the tenter-ground to be stretched and dried.[5]

---

[1] The Poll Tax Returns show that Pontefract had the largest population in the West Riding. Next came Doncaster ; then in order of size followed Sheffield, Selby, Tickhill, Rotherham, Wakefield, Snaith, Ripon, Leeds, Tadcaster, Knaresborough, Bawtry, Bradford, Huddersfield, Halifax. See Price, *op. cit.*, p. 52 n.

[2] *Poll Tax Returns* ; see for Doncaster, Selby, Pontefract, &c.

[3] Ibid., p. 215.   [4] Ibid., p. 267.

[5] *Bradford Manor Rolls*, 28 Ed. III, pp. 234–43.

The fulling industry was also widely scattered, and fulling-mills were to be found on the banks of every stream, even in the most remote places. Fulling had received an impetus from the act of 1376–7, which forbade the export of cloth until it had been properly fulled ;[1] this, coupled with the growing demand for English cloth, made the fulling-mill a good source of revenue. Every manor which stood on a water-course possessed its mill, which was leased to one or two of the tenants for an annual rental. The Bradford mill, for instance, was let in the early 'forties to William and James Walker, at a rental of ten shillings per annum.[2] In 1346 James resigned his share of the mill to William, being ' unable to hold the said mill on account of poverty '.[3] William retained his tenancy, aided by his son Thomas, and in 1353 managed to secure the monopoly of the fulling on the manor.[4] In that year father and son [5] went to the manor court, and gave to the landlord forty pence by the year of ' new rent ' for the term of the father's life, being promised in return ' that there shall no strange fuller enter within the town and liberty of the Court of the Lord of Bradford, . . . neither shall anything be taken or carried out of the said town to be worked upon, nor shall any one use that craft in the said town, except (the Walkers) and their servants '.[6]

The dyer was in a similar position to the fuller, in that he could not carry on his occupation without the licence of the lord of the manor. The landlord might allow many dyers to practise in the same locality, or he might hand over the monopoly of the trade to one man. Instances of both practices are found in the Bradford Rolls. In the 'forties there was no monopoly, but a licence was essential before practising in the industry. In 1342 William Nutbrown was fined threepence for using the office of dyer without licence,[7] and ten years later Walter Lister of Leeds was caught practising the same trade in Bradford

---

[1] *Statutes of the Realm*, 50 Ed. III, c. 7.

[2] Survey of the Manor of Bradford, 15 Ed. III. Transcript in the Bradford Reference Library.

[3] *Manor Rolls*, 20 Ed. III, p. 80.   [4] Ibid., 27 Ed. III.

[5] Thomas prospered greatly in his day. In 1360 he took a plot of the landlord's waste, 40 ft. by 30 ft., for a house to be situated there, and for the enlargement of his tenter-ground (*Rolls*, 34 Ed. III, p. 408). The Leeds fulling-mill let at 20s. per annum in 1342 (Survey, 15 Ed. III, printed in *Bradford Antiquarian*, ii. 137–8).

[6] *Manor Rolls*, 27 Ed. III.   [7] Ibid., 16 Ed. III, p. 18.

without having paid the four shillings which was charged for the privilege of dyeing within the manor of Bradford. Lister was brought before the court, and ordered to pay the necessary sum.[1] Two years later Lister assumed the offensive, and ' took the office of dyer in Bradeforddale, so that no other shall be received to perform that office there this year, rendering therefore to the lord by the year four shillings '.[2] This grant apparently amounted to a monopoly.

The cloth industry was in the hands of men and women alike. Women were the brewers of the day ; they might also be the weavers and dyers. Witness the following Poll Tax entries :

[3] Thorpe iuxta Rypon.   Alicia Gare, Webster .   .   .   vj[d.]
[4] Rypon.   Alicia de Bowland, Webester .   .   .   .   xij[d.]
    ,,   Christiana Lyttester, Lyster .   .   .   .   xij[d.]
[5] Eland.   Alicia and Isabella de Crosse, Websters .   .   xij[d.]

The ulnager's accounts for 1395–6–7 record payments for cloths made for sale by ' filia vicarii de Crayk ',[6] and Emma Earle of Wakefield ;[7] the latter was responsible for the manufacture of 48 cloths in 54 weeks, out of a total of $173\frac{1}{2}$ cloths produced for sale in the Wakefield area. These industrious women remind one of the Wife of Bath.

> ' Of cloth making sche hadde such an haunt,
> Sche passeth hem of Ypres and of Gaunt.'

In York women were admitted to the freedom.[8] No woman could carry on a trade unless her name had been entered on the Freemen's Roll, and consequently many such names appear in that list. But the women's special field was that of spinning the wool. The distaff, the primitive apparatus for this process, was part of the equipment of every household, and spinning belonged to the common round of the day's toil. Wife and daughters were responsible for this work, and it seems that even

---

[1] Ibid., 34 Ed. III, p. 385.
[2] Ibid., 36 Ed. III, p. 445. Similarly, Robert Lyster of Halifax in 1382 was granted the monopoly of dyeing in the manor of Halifax (Lister and Ogden, *Poll Tax Returns for the Parish of Halifax*).
[3] *Poll Tax Returns*, p. 254.   [4] Ibid., p. 250.   [5] Ibid., p. 183.
[6] ' Particulars of Account of Wm. Skipwith, collector of ulnage and subsidy of saleable cloths . . . in the County of York ', 1394–5 (Exch. K.R. Accounts, bundle 345, no. 15).
[7] Similar account 1395–6 (Exch. K.R. Accounts, bundle 348, no. 17).
[8] See preface to *Freemen's Register*.

at this date spinsters were employed, working for wages under a master. Thus, at the Halifax Tourn, April 6, 1372, Ibbot de Holgate and Matilda Winlove of Warley, spinsters, were accused of having taken wages contrary to the Statute of Labourers.[1]

The status of the cloth-makers varied. In the smaller settlements they usually contributed only fourpence or sixpence to the Poll Tax, but in many places a shilling was paid. The coverlet weaver, the dyers, the drapers, and some of the ordinary weavers of Rotherham were in the shilling class; [2] one of the weavers of Wakefield kept two servants, who probably gave assistance in the workshop, and his fellow wool-chapman paid 3s. 4d.[3] From earlier sources we learn that many of these men had their toft of land, like the two cottar weavers at Skipton (1307).[4] They generally had a little farm stock, with cows, horses, swine, and poultry, in addition to a little acreage under crops, thus being farmer and manufacturer in a small way.[5] As such they bear a marked resemblance to the small clothiers who were so numerous in subsequent centuries.

Mention of the Skipton cottars draws our attention to the fact that many of the weavers mentioned during the thirteenth and fourteenth century were cottars. These men would have a small tenancy of land, probably six to twelve acres of arable, the cultivation of which would take up part of their time. They would look after their live stock, and perform the requisite number of days' service on the demesne lands, unless those services had been commuted. When all this had been done, they would still have at their disposal each week a number of days which would be occupied with cloth-making. As to the origin of these cottar weavers, one hesitates to generalize. Were

---

[1] 'Ibbot de Holgate et Matilda Winlove de Warlonley sunt filiatrices ad rotam et capiunt stipendium contra Statutem de Artificiis.' Halifax Tourn, 6th April, 46 Ed. III (Lister and Ogden, *op. cit.*, p. 43).

[2] *Poll Tax Returns*, pp. 25 et seq.   [3] Ibid., pp. 160–1.

[4] Inquisition Post Mortem, 31 Ed. I (Yorks. Arch. Soc., Record Series, xxxvii. 101).

[5] Types drawn from Lay Subsidy, 25 Ed. I (Yorks. Arch. Soc., Record Series, xxv. 114): *Wakefield*, 'Thomas Tinctor, j vaccam, precium iiijs; ij quart. siliginis (wheat) vs; jv quart. avene (oats).' p. 2. *Burton-in-Lonsdale*, 'Ricardus Tinctor', 2 oxen 5s. each; 2 cows 3s. 5d. each, also various crops. p. 91. *Almanbir* (Almondbury), 'Iohannes Tinctor', 1 ox, 1 cow, 1 horse, also crops.

they small tenants because they were primarily weavers, or were they weavers because, being only small tenants, they had time to spare for weaving? The latter is the more likely, and probably explains the origin of the weaver class, one or two members of which appeared as cottars in so many villages during the thirteenth century. The cottar in his spare time might hire himself out as an agricultural labourer; or he might take up some industry, and in Yorkshire, as in the West of England, he turned to the manufacture of cloth.

There was some mobility of population throughout the county. In the ranks of the York freemen we find William the Cordwaner, Richard the Webster, William the Mercer, and John the Carpenter, all of Leeds; John of Holbeck, weaver, and John and Ralph of Pudsey, tailors. There were men of Leeds trading and brewing in Ripon, and merchants from Wakefield and Kendal were familiar figures throughout the West Riding.

The progress of the industry was frequently checked during the fourteenth century by great calamities. The Scottish Wars and the frequent raids [1] had disastrous effects on various parts of Yorkshire during the early decades, the most severe suffering being inflicted after the disastrous Battle of Myton-on-Swale in 1319. After a time the Scottish terror passed away, but the unseen scourge of plague now had to be faced. The loss of life caused by the Black Death was terrible, and Mr. Seebohm [2] estimated that quite one-half of the population of Yorkshire was carried away by pestilence during the reign of Edward III. The great outbreak of 1349 denuded abbeys,[3] towns, and villages of their population, and subsequent outbreaks of pestilence claimed heavy toll from the cloth-makers. The population of York, for instance, in 1340 was between 30,000 and 40,000. From the Poll Tax returns for the city, one gathers that by 1379 the population had been reduced to between 11,000 and 13,000.[4] There were many gaps in the ranks of the freemen, and each

---

[1] After Bannockburn the Scots raided as far as Skipton and the suburbs of York. After Myton they swept down the western parts of the county as far as Airedale (Price, *Leeds and its Neighbourhood*, p. 41; also *Chronicles of Meaux Abbey*, Rolls Series, ii. 337).

[2] 'The Black Death', in *Fortnightly Review*, 1865, p. 150.

[3] At Meaux only ten men survived out of fifty, and it was necessary to appoint the sub-cellarer as abbot (*Chronicles of Meaux Abbey*, iii. 37 and 77).

[4] *Victoria County History, Yorkshire*, iii. 441.

outbreak of plague was followed by a rush of new craftsmen to occupy the vacant places.[1]

The country districts suffered almost as severely during these years of war, pestilence, and famine, and in small communities the recovery was much more slow. There was more than one serious famine, which, coupled with the Scots' raids, reduced the manors to a miserable plight. At Bradford, for instance, in 1342 the Hall was in ruins ; the corn mill, which had been valued at £10 a year in 1311, now stood at £6 6s. 8d., and the fulling-mill, ' the building whereof is entirely unroofed ', had decreased in its annual value from £1 to 8s. in the space of thirty years.[2] Then came the Black Death, especially acute in 1349, but rapacious enough in 1362. The Bradford Court Rolls give vivid pictures of the effects of these visitations. In 1349 twenty-two tenants ' closed their extreme days ', to quote the euphemism employed in the Rolls, and under the stress of such events the whole social order collapsed for a time. Similar stories could be told of other villages, the sum total of which is that Yorkshire was depleted for many years of its population and wealth, and its progress seriously retarded. Hence the early career of the textile industry was very chequered. But the manufacture was never abandoned by the dwellers in the West Riding villages. Soil and climate prevented that, for these factors would not allow any population in the western parts of the country to subsist on a purely agricultural basis. Fourteenth-century farm-ing was so primitive that tillage could only be successful under very favourable conditions of soil and weather. The Yorkshire valleys would produce indifferent crops only, and the growth of grain at this time occupied a small part of the tenants' atten-tion. The land was most profitably employed in pastoral work. But even this, allied to a small production of crops, did not guarantee a livelihood to the population, and some supple-mentary occupation must therefore be followed. The district was naturally fitted for the manufacture of cloth, thanks to the supplies of wool and water, and the woollen industry therefore

[1] The number of new freemen admitted just prior to 1349 was about sixty per annum, but in 1349 no less than 208 enrolments were made. See *Victoria County History, Yorkshire*, iii. 441, for detailed figures.

[2] Survey of Manor of Bradford, 1342. See also M. C. D. Law, *The Story of Bradford* (Pitman, 1913), p. 52.

maintained itself amidst all the vicissitudes of plague and warfare, of high birth-rates and often higher death-rates.

(d) Gild Organization in the Urban Textile Industry

The manufacture of cloth in the chief towns of Yorkshire passed at an early stage under gild control, and remained so until the decline of the urban industry in the sixteenth century. The gilds of York, Beverley, and Hull were very similar in character to those which existed in the big industrial and commercial centres throughout England ; for this reason, therefore, a brief description of their economic functions will suffice. But whilst dwelling solely on the industrial work of the textile gilds, one must remember that their scope was much wider. The gilds embraced many of the most prominent features of social life. They concerned themselves with the tending of the sick, the burial of the dead, the support of religious observances, and the institution of regular feastings ; lastly, they developed the rudiments of popular dramatic art by their pageants and amateur theatrical displays.

As to the origin, as well as much of the early history of the textile craft gilds, we are left in a wilderness of doubt. They may have come into existence as a normal consequence of industrial evolution, being formed when the industry had become sufficiently specialized and differentiated from other occupations. On the other hand, they may have been formed as associations of aliens settling in certain towns under royal protection.[1] But there is no evidence which will enable us to come to any conclusion of a satisfactory character, and the whole matter must remain problematic until some evidence comes in from a source as yet unknown.

The first notices of textile gilds are found in the early twelfth century, but it is not until 1164[2] that we find any mention of the weavers' gild in York.[3] The city had evidently received its

---

[1] This is the general theory adopted by Dr. Cunningham. See Cunningham, op. cit., i. 337.

[2] Pipe Roll, 11 Hen. II, and subsequent years.

[3] The weavers' gild was soon followed by similar organizations amongst the glovers and curriers, saddlers, and hosiers, all of whom had gilds under royal warrant by 1179 (Pipe Roll, 26 Hen. II, printed in Bland, Brown, and Tawney, English Economic History, Select Documents, 1914, p. 114).

weavers' charter in that year or the previous one, and in return now began to make an annual contribution to the Exchequer. The charter was quite short, and its chief provision was the granting of a monopoly : ' No one except them (i. e. the York weavers) shall make any cloths, dyed or striped, in the whole of Yorkshire, except the men of York, unless it be others of the same occupation in Beverley, Kirkby, Thirsk, Malton, Scarborough, and other my royal boroughs (*aliis dominicis meis burgis*). And in return for this licence they shall give £10 annually to my Exchequer.'[1] The weavers of York were thus granted a monopoly for certain kinds of cloth, but for those kinds only Further, the exemptions were numerous and important, for in addition to the five towns mentioned there were other royal boroughs, to all of which the saving clause would apply. The charter did, however, give York the control over the rural areas, though the value of that power would depend on the success with which it was enforced upon those outside the walls of the city.[2] Hence the charter in actual practice probably only meant that the weavers of dyed and striped cloth who dwelt in the neighbourhood of York had to contribute something towards the annual payment. Even when we have made this necessary modification, the privilege granted by the charter must have been important, and the gild of considerable size, for the ' firma ' of £10 was a larger sum than that of any other weavers' gild in the country, London alone excepted. Moreover, £10 in the twelfth century would be equivalent to £150 to-day. Thus the privilege granted must have been of some value, or the gildsmen would not have agreed to pay so heavily for it.

The weavers' tribute was paid with great regularity throughout the reign of Henry II, and should one year have been missed, as in 1173, £20 was forwarded in the subsequent year.[3] During the turbulent times of the following century the payment fell into arrears, even though Henry III renewed the charter in

---

[1] Quoted in Patent Rolls, 20 Ed. III, pt. iii, m. 19.

[2] Similarly the weavers of Lincoln were given a monopoly over the country within a radius of twelve miles around that city (Patent Rolls, 22 Ed. III, pt. ii, m. 22).

[3] Pipe Rolls, 20 Hen. II, weavers' contribution omitted ; 21 Hen. II, payment made for two years.

1220.[1] In 1238 the debt amounted to £165, in 1246 it was £210, and at last, in 1268, matters reached a crisis, when the Sheriff received orders to enter the city and distrain the weavers for the whole of the arrears.[2] Whatever the result of the Sheriff's visit, matters were soon back in their former plight, and in 1275 the weavers once more appealed for exemption from payment, on the ground of their poverty.[3] This poverty was probably due in part to the Sheriff's distraint, which, even if only partially carried out, would exhaust the weavers financially. Under these circumstances, there would be a keen desire on the part of many to escape from this over-taxed city to some place where manufacture could proceed under less costly conditions. Also, as we have seen in the preceding sections, a considerable amount of cloth-making was being carried on throughout the county, and this rivalry between town and country was possibly diminishing the demand for York cloths. At such a pass had the competition arrived that in 1304 the city weavers petitioned the King, showing ' that divers men in divers places in the county, elsewhere than in the city or in the other towns and demesne boroughs . . . make dyed and rayed (striped) cloths, so that the weavers in the said city are unable to render their £10 yearly to the Exchequer '.[4] Edward replied by instructing the Exchequer to cause inquiries to be made, and to compel all such as were found plying the craft in illegal places to refrain from such work henceforth. Unfortunately we do not know the result of this order, but the evidence of the fourteenth century proves that the city weavers never succeeded in perfecting their monopoly, and that the rural manufacture continued to flourish.

Turning to Beverley, we find the weavers of the twelfth and thirteenth centuries in a strange position. A manuscript dated about 1209 [5] contains the ' Law of the Fullers and Weavers of

---

[1] *Close Rolls Calendar*, 1220, i. 421, quoted by Gross, *Gild Merchant* (1890), i. 108 n.

[2] *Victoria County History, Yorkshire*, ii. 437.

[3] Close Rolls, 3 Ed. I, m. 17.

[4] Close Rolls, 32 Ed. I, m. 12. At Lincoln in 1348 we find the same complaints of a declining industry. The weavers declared that there ' were no weavers working in the city and the suburbs and circuit thereof before the fifth year of the reign of the present king '. Apparently there had been an exodus from Lincoln also. Patent Rolls, 22 Ed. III, pt. ii, m. 22.

[5] Add. MSS. (Brit. Mus.) 14252, quoted by Leach, Selden Soc. publications,

Beverley '. This law declares that the weavers and fullers of
the town ' can dry no cloth nor go out of the town to do any
trade ; nor can any free man be attainted by them, nor can
they bear any witness. And if (a weaver or fuller) wishes to
forswear his craft, he must do to him who is called Mayor and
the Bailiffs of the town that which will make him to be received
into the freedom of the town, and turn the tools out of his
house.' No ostracism could be more complete. Here, evidently,
the weaver was outside the pale of the burgess roll and merchant
gild. So long as he remained a cloth-maker he had no caste in
the town ; he could not trade outside its walls, but must sell
his pieces to the merchants, who had probably made this rule
for his imprisonment. The municipal courts of justice were
closed to him, and he could neither bring accusations nor bear
witness against a free citizen of the town. If we try to explain
these harsh restrictions by suggesting that the outcasts were
foreigners, we are met at once by the fact that the prohibitions
were imposed not on the nationality but on the craft, and would
apply equally to native and alien. Leach suggests that the
cause of the disqualifications lay in the fact that the weavers
were the first important class of landless industrial workers,
who were therefore tyrannized over by the more powerful
sections of the community.[1] Salzmann holds that the cloth
trade was in the hands of big capitalistic merchants, who
utilized their power in the municipality to keep the cloth-
makers in subservience.[2] This may have been possible, for the
export trade in Beverley cloths would give the merchants
a grip on the makers. But the most satisfactory theory
is that which was put forward by Miss Bateson, who maintained
that the weavers and fullers already had their powerful gild
organizations before the town received its charter, and therefore
did not take up the new franchises, deeming themselves strong
enough behind the walls of their own society. Then, as the
town government grew stronger, it began to impose disabilities

xiv. 135. Another copy of the ' Law ' is found in the *Liber Custumarum* of
London (Rolls Series), i. 130–1.

[1] *Beverley Town Documents*, ed. Leach, Selden Soc. publications, vol. xiv,
p. xlix. Miss Bateson rejected this theory, and replaced it by the one outlined
above. See *English Historical Review*, xvi. 566.

[2] Salzmann, *op. cit.*, p. 135.

on the weavers and fullers, because of their obstinate maintenance of their own separate organizations. Such a state of
affairs would be similar to that existing in the fishmongers' and
weavers' fraternities of London.[1] These two trades had obtained
special immunities before the city had any really strong self-
government. When the London municipal authority became
more powerful, it resented the existence of these separate jurisdictions, and a long struggle ensued before the mayor and his
colleagues were able to bring the gildsmen under the common
rule. Meanwhile the weavers were denied the rights of freemen.
If the same struggle took place in Beverley, the Law quoted
above was the municipality's answer to the weavers' claim to
independence. The conflict ended with the defeat of the weavers
and fullers, for their next documentary appearance shows them
to be entirely subservient to the town and its rulers.

During the fourteenth century, and probably during the
thirteenth, there was a general movement towards organization
amongst the urban crafts, and by 1400 the number of gilds in
every large town almost equalled the number of occupations.
At Beverley in 1390, thirty-eight crafts took part in the plays
on Corpus Christi Day, amongst them being the weavers, dyers,
coverlet weavers, fullers, and shearmen.[2] The number of crafts
in York was naturally larger. A list of York plays, dated 1415,[3]
contains the names of 57 crafts, and a later list brings the
number up to about 80.[4] Of these the weavers, tapiters (or
coverlet weavers), fullers, dyers, shearmen, wool-packers, and
card-makers were connected with the cloth industry. The
strength of these textile gilds in York can be estimated roughly
from the ordinances edited by Miss M. Sellers in the *York
Memorandum Book*.[5] These ordinances, which are nearly all
dated about 1400, are prefaced occasionally by a list of the
masters of the fraternity. Probably the list of names is incomplete in some cases, and the actual membership was greater
than the list of names suggests. Taking the four cloth-making

---

[1] Unwin, *The Gilds and Companies of London* (1908), chap. iii.
[2] Selden Soc. publications, xiv. 33.
[3] Davies, *Municipal Records of York in the Fifteenth Century* (1843).
pp. 233–6 ; also Drake, *Eboracum* (1737), app. xxix.
[4] *Victoria County History, Yorkshire*, iii. 446.
[5] Surtees Soc., vol. cxx (1911).

crafts [1] of which a list of members is given, the numbers are as follows :

Fullers	. . .	30 names given	
Tapiters	. . .	57 ,, ,,	
Dyers .	. . .	59 ,, ,,	
Weavers	. . .	50 ,, ,,	and others referred to.
Total	. . .	196	

In addition to these crafts, there were the card-makers, shearmen,[2] wool-packers, and other small occupations, the total membership of which might amount to about 50. Thus there were some 250 masters in the city of York engaged in the manufacture of cloth and allied industries. York at that time contained a population of between 11,000 and 13,000 souls,[3] which is equivalent to about 2,500 families. Therefore out of 2,500 heads of families, 250, or about one-tenth, were masters of some gild which regulated the making of cloth. Such an estimate does not take into account the merchants who traded in cloth, the retailers of cloth within the city, or the journeymen employed by the 250 masters : were it possible to ascertain the number of these men, it would be found that the manufacture and sale of woollen goods employed a very large part of the population of York.

In Hull the number of gilds was not so large, and the weavers of that town favoured linen rather than woollen fabrics.[4] Pontefract had its craft gilds in the later years of the fifteenth century, if not before, for it is very probable that the largest town in the West Riding would have its gilds even before 1400.[5] Concerning such towns as Doncaster, Ripon, and Selby, there is no evidence to show the existence of any textile gilds, although the industry flourished in these centres. Of Wakefield we know little more, but the fact that Mystery Plays were performed there would

[1] See Ordinances of these crafts, *Memorandum Book*, vol. i.

[2] The Ordinances of this craft are prefaced by seven names, and others are referred to (*Memorandum Book*, vol. i, pp. 78–81).

[3] Estimate based on Poll Tax Returns ; see *Mem. Book*, vol. i, p. xxxiv. Also *Archaeologia*, xx. 525, where ThomasElyot, on the basis of a subsidy roll of 51 Ed. III, estimates the population of York at 10,800.

[4] Lambert, *Two Thousand Years of Gild Life* (1891), prints ordinances of Hull craft gilds.

[5] *The Booke of Entries of the Pontefract Corporation* (1653–1726) refers to gilds of the fifteenth century, p. 367.

suggest that there were gilds to perform these plays.[1] Thus our actual knowledge of Yorkshire textile gilds is confined to those of York, Hull, and Beverley; concerning the smaller towns in which the industry was carried on, we can only surmise that where industrial life flourished in any populous community some form of gild organization would be found.

The nature of the functions discharged by the textile gilds can be gathered to some extent from the ordinances which have been discovered. In no case do these ordinances go back beyond 1386, and are generally dated about 1400;[2] hence the picture presented is that of gild activity at the beginning of the fifteenth century. We know nothing of the work of the gilds during the twelfth and thirteenth centuries. Further, the picture is incomplete, for one cannot gain a comprehensive view of the gild through its ordinances any more than one can completely understand a nation by studying its statute book alone. Still we see enough to enable us to appreciate the extent to which the industry was subjected to regulation and restraint.

The purpose of the craft gild was to promote the welfare of its own particular industry. The policy always turned to that end, and in all decrees the gild sought to destroy evil practices, foster good work, and thus extend the demand for the wares of its members. Such results could only be achieved if it had complete control over all the workers at that craft within its area, and hence the first essential was that the gild should possess a monopoly of the local trade. In York the weavers obtained a limited monopoly over the county, but we have already seen the actual value of that privilege. Still York clung tenaciously to the letter of its rights, and at almost regular intervals petitioned the King, informing him ' that contrary to the charter of Henry II, many foreign weavers of the County of York have made and woven cloths dyed and rayed, and daily continue so to do, to the grave loss of the weavers of the city, and delay of the payment of the yearly ferm '.[3] The petition

---

[1] The Towneley Mystery Plays. See *Victoria County History, Yorkshire*, iii. 445.

[2] Dates of ordinances : *York*. Fullers, 1390 ? ; weavers, 1400 ; dyers, 1390 ; shearmen, 1405. *Beverley*. Weavers, 1406. *Hull*. Weavers, 1490.

[3] Patent Rolls, 22 Rich. II, pt. ii, m. 20 d, and 1 Hen. IV, pt. vii, m. 5. See Ancient Petitions, no. 10673, asking for commission, 1399.

usually resulted in a commission of inquiry, followed by a renewal of the old charter. Such renewals were effected in 1220,[1] 1346,[2] 1377,[3] 1400,[4] 1414,[5] 1468,[6] and at other times, nearly always, it will be noticed, at the beginning of a new reign. Similar monopolies were enjoyed by the weavers' gilds of Beverley and Hull, no person being permitted to establish himself as a weaver in these towns unless he was a member of the local gild. By this monopoly the gild hoped to control industry, check competition, encourage trade, and increase the membership of the gild, the new members helping to bear the burden of the craft's social expenditure and its contributions to the municipal or national exchequer.

The term ' foreign ' in the York petition quoted above might refer to Flemings or to Englishmen, for both were foreigners or strangers unless they belonged to the weavers' fraternity. All crafts made special provision for the stranger within the gate, and almost every set of ordinances contained some clause indicating the reception which was to be given to the man who came to the town, seeking permission to set up in a trade, or to serve as a journeyman. The weavers of York declared, in 1400, that no stranger should be received henceforth to work in that city, unless he first produced authentic and satisfactory certificates from the place of his former habitation as to his faithfulness and right conversation.[7] The dyers demanded evidence that the stranger had been fully apprenticed and was properly skilled,[8] and the shearmen and coverlet weavers [9] ordered that the new-comer should be examined by the searchers of the craft touching his moral and industrial character.[10] The stranger from beyond the seas received less kindly consideration, and the tendency was towards excluding the alien proper from participation in the industrial life of the city. Thus the coverlet weavers of York in 1419 issued very stringent anti-alien regulations. No

[1] *Close Rolls Calendar*, i. 421, quoted by Gross, *Gild Merchant* (1890), i. 108 n.
[2] Patent Rolls, 20 Ed. III, pt. iii, m. 19.
[3] Ibid., 1 Rich. II, pt. ii, m. 35. [4] Ibid., 1 Hen. IV, pt. vii, m. 5.
[5] Ibid., 2 Hen. V, pt. ii, m. 39. [6] Ibid., 8 Ed. IV, pt. ii, m. 13.
[7] Weavers' Ordinances, *Mem. Book*, i. 242.
[8] Dyers' Ordinances, ibid., i. 113. [9] Ibid., i. 85, 100, 107.
[10] The card-makers demanded that the stranger should produce ' sufficeant recorde . . . be (by) letters under sele auctentyke of hys conversacion and of hys gude fame ', or be able to find satisfactory pledges for himself and his deeds (*Mem. Book*, i. 80).

master was allowed to take an apprentice unless that apprentice was English-born and a freeman (' nisi ille apprenticius sit natus Anglicus et liber homo '), under pain of a £2 fine.[1] Further, it was decreed that if any alien wished to set up as a coverlet-master within York, he should pay to the city council £2 13s. 4d., and to the craft £1 6s. 8d., a total sum equivalent to £48 in modern money.[2]

Though membership of the gild was insisted upon, the conditions of entry were far from easy. One aim of the gild was to guarantee good workmanship, and this could only be effected by properly trained and experienced craftsmen : therefore apprenticeship was one of the corner-stones of the gild system. The would-be master must begin at the very bottom of the ladder, and become formally apprenticed to some fully recognized master of the trade which he wished to learn. The whole system of apprenticeship was hedged round with detailed regulations. The number of apprentices which a master might have at the same time was often fixed, and the Hull weaver was not permitted to take more than two youths into his charge at the same time.[3] On indenturing the apprentice, the master was to report his transaction to the executive of the craft, enter the name of his protégé in the register, and pay for him an entrance fee which varied from sixpence to half-a-crown, or even more.[4] The apprentice then entered upon a period of training which was fixed in almost every gild at not less than seven years. The card-makers [5] of York declared that ' Na maistre . . . take any apprentice or any servant in maner or fourme of apprentice . . . for lesse terme than . . . seven yerys togyder, and that be (by) indenture, (under) payne of xiij^s· . . . iiij^d· ' ; and the Hull weavers insisted that ' No mann sett up a loome wythyn hys howsse bot if he have bene 'prentyse vij yere at that occupacion, under payne of x$^{li.}$ (£10) ', a heavy fine if inflicted in full.[6]

During the seven years for which he was bound to his master, the apprentice learned the theory and practice of his trade. Having then reached years of discretion, and attained a fair degree of proficiency, he could now step at once to the rank of

[1] *Mem. Book*, i. 109.   [2] *Ibid.*, i. 109.   [3] Lambert, *op. cit.*, p. 206.
[4] See York Ordinances, *Mem. Book*, i. 100, 113, &c. The apprenticeship fee in the dyers' gild was £1.
[5] *Mem. Book*, i. 80.   [6] Lambert, *op. cit.*, p. 205.

a master, or enter an intermediary stage as a journeyman. In either case he was obliged to make his entry into the gild, and pay the required fee. Should he wish to become a fully fledged master, setting up a stock of weaving apparatus, the craft authorities came to his premises, to ascertain if ' his werkhowse be goode and able '.[1] At York the searchers were generally accompanied by a number of masters, who came down to the candidate's workroom and examined him to see that he was proficient, and sufficiently skilled to carry on the work of a master craftsman. The coverlet weavers were to be satisfied, through the investigations of their searchers, that any applicant for admission was ' habilis et sciens . . . ad operandum et occupandum ut magister in artificio '.[2] The fullers of York made a strange stipulation, based on the nature of the fullers' work. The master fuller, in his operations, would receive large numbers of pieces from weavers, to be fulled in his mill. He might tear or spoil a piece in the fulling stocks, or he might even lose it. It was necessary therefore that some security should be provided to those who placed their wares in the fuller's hands. The craft ordinances made provision to meet this possibility, and declared that the would-be master should not merely be proficient in his art, but should also prove that he possessed property to the value of four marks, so that if he lost a cloth entrusted to him he would have the wherewithal to make good his loss to the owner of the piece.[3]

Having passed his examination, the candidate now paid his entrance fee, two shillings at Beverley,[4] but much more at York. At the latter place the weaver, on setting up his loom, or the dyer, on acquiring his vat, was obliged to pay £1 for his ' upsett ';[5] the shearman paid only 6s. 8d.,[6] and the fuller half that sum (in addition to guaranteeing the reserve of four marks).[7] When we multiply these sums by twelve, so as to convert them into terms of modern money, it becomes evident that at the beginning of the fifteenth century entry into the York textile gilds was hedged about with many conditions, and barred by heavy entrance fees, which must have presented great obstacles

[1] Lambert, op. cit., p. 205.   [2] Mem. Book, i. 109.
[3] Ibid., i. 71.
[4] Beverley Weavers' Ordinances (Hist. MSS. Comm.), p. 94.
[5] Mem. Book, i. 243.   [6] Ibid., i. 108.   [7] Ibid., i. 72.

to the poorer members of the community who sought admission.

There were in the field of industry three classes of workers, the master, the journeyman, and the apprentice. Of these only the master enjoyed the full privileges of complete membership, and the craft gilds were thus associations of masters rather than associations of men. The master alone was eligible for the offices of the gild, and he alone voted in the elections.[1] But the gild did not confine its attention to the master alone; and affairs of the journeymen and apprentices were also regulated in every detail. The journeyman was an inferior grade of member, who did not pay so large an annual contribution to the gild coffers as his employer. The master could not employ him without the consent of the gild, and, should the journeyman have any cause for complaint against his master, he could complain to the searchers of the craft, who would take up his case and give a decision. Thus, if a master refused to pay the proper rate of wages, or fell into arrears with his wage payments, the journeyman could appeal to the alderman of the gild, who would insist upon due and complete recompense, and should the master fail in his obligation the municipal authorities could be called upon to make a distraint on the master's goods.[2] On the other hand, any misdemeanours on the part of the employee were punished with marked severity, and the regulations for journeymen were numerous. No man was to be employed simultaneously by two masters,[3] and any workman guilty of fraudulent or faulty work was heavily punished. The dyers of York declared that a man who did faulty work to the extent of twelve pence was to be fined forty pence for the first offence and half a mark for the second; if convicted a third time, he was to be expelled from the occupation, and forbidden to engage in the dyeing industry henceforth.[4] The journeyman's tongue was also placed under control; a heavy fine was inflicted upon the Hull workmen who ' of malice make any talys contrarey to treuth to th'entent to make discorde and debate among any of the sayd occupacon ',[5] and the Beverley weavers announced

---

[1] Lambert, *op. cit.*, p. 205.
[2] *Beverley Weavers' Ordinances (Hist. MSS. Comm.)*, p. 94.
[3] *Mem. Book*, i. 97.   [4] Ibid., i. 114 ; half a mark equals 6s. 8d.
[5] Lambert, *op. cit.*, p. 206.

' that if any of the servants of the craft called a journeyman is accused of fraud before the Keepers of Beverley or officers of the craft, he shall serve no master of the craft unless he be able to prove a lawful excuse '.[1]

The craft gilds also regulated the employment of women. We have already noted the presence of women workers in both urban and rural textile industries. They were in the ranks of the freemen of York, and they appear to have formed a large element in the weaving craft of that city, ranking both as masters and as employees. So strong were they that in the Ulnager's Account for the city in 1395 about one-quarter of the cloths entered for that year as subject to the payment of ulnage and subsidy were entered in the names of women,[2] which meant that these cloths were made either by women or by men who were in the employment of female masters of the craft. Their work about this time was evidently failing to give satisfaction, or it may be that their strength in the industry was beginning to arouse the envy of their male colleagues. Which of these alternatives was the correct one it is impossible to state, but we know that in 1400, when the gild underwent a thorough spring cleaning, it was decreed that in future only those women who had been well taught and approved by the craft officials should be allowed to weave, lest by their poor work the women should prejudice the craft and make it difficult to raise the annual £10 for the Exchequer.[3] In the dyeing trade[4] a woman was permitted to carry on the work for one year after the death of her husband, after which she must either pay 20s., the entrance fee for herself, or allow her chief servant to take up the business in his name as master of the craft. Hence in the list of members we find the names of two women, one the widow, the other the daughter, of former members. The women weavers of Beverley were under similar control,[5] and the earliest by-laws we possess of the Hull weavers (1490) declared that ' ther shall no woman

---

[1] *Hist. MSS. Comm.*, p. 94.

[2] Exch. Accounts, bundle 345, no. 16. For the calculation see *Mem. Book*, intro., p. xxvii.

[3] *Mem. Book*, p. 243. This clause may have aimed at the prevention of cheap female labour. The same trouble arose in Bristol during the fifteenth century. See *Little Red Book of Bristol*, ii. 127.

[4] *Mem. Book*, i. 114.

[5] *Hist. MSS. Comm.*, p. 94.

worke in any warke concernyng this occupacon within the towne of Hull, upon payn of xl[s.]'[1]

In the actual workaday life of the members, the power of the gild was constantly asserted. Work on Sundays and feast days was forbidden.[2] Many crafts regulated the hours of labour, and forbade night work, as in the case of the York coverlet weavers, who were permitted to weave only so long as the light of day was reasonably strong enough to allow them to ply the shuttle with ease.[3] The gild stated the fees which masters were to demand for fulling cloths, and other similar charges.[4] At the same time wage-rates were often fixed. In 1405 the shearmen of York established a maximum daily wage for their employees,[5] with fines to be levied on such as paid more than this sum ; and in 1400 the weavers drew up a piece-rate list for journeymen weavers.[6]

The gild aimed at inducing honest relations between the various members of the craft, and for this purpose made numerous decrees to prevent any member from enriching himself unfairly at the expense of his fellows. Masters were forbidden to attempt to entice any apprentice or journeyman to leave his master before his full term of service had been accomplished, and offences of this character met with strong condemnation.[7] Similarly, any attempt to entice customers, or to forestall a rival in obtaining orders, was forbidden, as being contrary to the principles of fair trade.[8] The same idea lay at the bottom of the prohibition of ' hawking ' or ' peddling '. Gildsmen were forbidden to go from house to house seeking customers ; they were to confine themselves to the proper market accommodation provided for them, and were not to attempt to push the sale of their wares by

---

[1] Lambert, *op. cit.*, p. 207.
[2] *Mem. Book*, Shearmen, i. 107 ; Fullers, i. 71.
[3] Ibid., i. 85.
[4] Ibid., i. 71. One penny per cloth for fulling, twopence for fulling and burling.   [5] Ibid., i. 107.
[6] Ibid., i. 244. The list was as follows : For weaving 8 ells or less, 14*d.* ; 9–10 ells, 16*d.* ; 11 ells, 18*d.* ; 12 ells, 20*d.* ; 13 ells, 2*s.* 4*d.* ; 14 ells, 2*s.* 8*d.*
[7] See Ordinances, *passim.*
[8] Ibid., i. 113–14. The dyers forbade any master to send his servants out of the city to bring in wool or cloth, or to meet strangers coming to York with wool or cloth to be dyed. Further, no master was by gifts or presents to entice the customer of another dyer to transfer his custom to himself. Such practices were regarded as violations of equality of opportunity and fair trade.

going ' thurgh the citee ' or in streets and lanes ' fra house to house in maner of hauking '.[1]

From fair trade to honest workmanship was but a short step, and the gild laid a heavy hand upon those whose work did not fulfil the required standard of quality. The weaver who put bad or insufficient material into his piece, or who wove it faultily, the fuller who lost or damaged the cloth in fulling, the shearman who was careless in finishing the fabric, the dyer who used improper materials for dyeing, all were liable to a heavy fine, and occasionally to the confiscation of the offending material. With the coverlet weavers of York the punishment for bad workmanship was especially severe. For the first offence the coverlets were confiscated, and if a master repeatedly transgressed he came under the special supervision of the searchers as an inefficient weaver. By them he was warned and admonished to improve the quality of his work, but if it was eventually found that he was quite incapable of improvement, his loom was confiscated, and he was forbidden to continue in that occupation.[2]

For the effectual administration of these and other branches of gild activity, certain officials, forming an executive, were necessary. The government of the weavers' gild at York and Beverley was in the hands of an alderman, who presided over the craft, stewards or bailiffs, who assisted him, and a beadle or summoner.[3] These men were elected annually by the whole body of master craftsmen, gathered together in the Prime Gild or annual general meeting. The alderman acted as judge on all matters relating to gild ordinances and their infringement, and was far more than a figurehead. He had the power to summon special meetings when any matter of importance called for immediate decision, and those who disregarded his summons to attend were fined the customary amount in wax or money. All masters were eligible for election to the office, and any one refusing to take office when elected incurred the displeasure of the craft, and was subject to a heavy fine. At the same time it was necessary that any person elected to office should know all the details of the trade, and be a fully qualified craftsman, and the weavers of York in 1400 declared therefore that no man

[1] Card-makers' Ordinances, *Mem. Book*, i. 81.
[2] Ibid., i. 86.   [3] *Hist. MSS. Comm.*, p. 94.

should be elected, unless he was known to be just and faithful, and also expert and perfect in his craft.[1] The weavers' gild of York was unique amongst the textile craft organizations of that city, in that it was founded by royal charter. The other gilds were based only on municipal sanction, and were much more directly subservient than the weavers to the municipality. In these gilds, therefore, there was no alderman at the head of affairs. The mayor of the city seems to have taken his place, and to have discharged most of the functions which fell to the lot of the alderman of the weavers. In the ordinances and lists of members of the shearmen, coverlet weavers, dyers, &c., of York there is no mention of the alderman and no provision for his election. In his place stands the mayor, the head of the city and also of the craft gild.

The most energetic members of the gild executive were the searchers, two or four in number, who were appointed to make periodical inspection of all workrooms, and by their vigilance enforce the ordinances of the fraternity. The searchers, when elected, took an oath of faithful service before the city magistrates, and their names were entered in the municipal records.[2] They then went forth on their task as industrial policemen, supervising the ' upsett ' of new masters, the employment and payment of journeymen, the taking of strangers and apprentices, the quality of the work done, and the method of disposing of the finished article. They were also financial agents of the society, and collected all levies and fines ; one of the chief functions of the searchers in the weavers' craft of York was the gathering of the annual farm of £10, and this was probably the most difficult part of their work.[3] In nearly all the York gilds the searchers were accompanied in their visitation by an equal number of masters, who were elected to assist and supervise them in the discharge of their duties. Once a week these men made a systematic tour of all the workrooms and shops under their control. When any fault or bad work was discovered,

---

[1] *Mem. Book*, i. 242.

[2] *Minute Book of Beverley Corporation* (*Hist. MSS. Comm.*), p. 113 : ' Supervisores : Iohannes Bayledon et Willelmus Belasys electi sunt scrutatores et supervisores artis textorum pro anno futuro et iurati sunt ' (1432).

[3] *Mem. Book*, i. 242–3. In the collection of this money the searchers could bring pressure to bear on the weaver, and as a last resort could distrain on his loom and weaving utensils.

the goods were at once confiscated (provided they belonged to the culprit) and the offender taken before the mayor, to receive correction and to be mulcted of the fine fixed in the craft ordinances. Part of the fine was taken by the city and part passed into the hands of the searcher, either to pay his wages or to meet the various expenses incurred by the gild.[1]

In his visitations the searcher was protected from insult and assault at the hands of the craftsman, and every gild imposed severe penalties upon those who refused admission to the searcher or behaved obstinately towards any members of the gild executive. On the other hand, the officials of the gild were by no means immune from control, or absolute in their power over the brotherhood. Any laxity or oppression in the discharge of their duties was severely punished, and those in charge of the gild's finances were held responsible at the end of their term of office for any arrears of payments or financial mismanagement.

In the preceding paragraphs we have observed that the municipal authority played a large part in the affairs of the gild. This was natural, for the gilds required sanction and recognition for their organization, such as would enable them to enforce their decrees. It would be useless for the weavers to draw up elaborate orders for the regulation of their trade, unless they had behind them the power to enforce their wishes upon every weaver in the community. From two sources could this power be drawn. The first was the King, who had granted the charters to some gilds during the twelfth century, and was frequently approached to grant new charters or renew the existing ones. Secondly, the craft might solicit the aid of the governing body of the town in which it was situated, and seek municipal assistance in discharging the duties for which it had been established. This course was necessary, even in the case of gilds which had been established under royal charter, and the York weavers, armed though they were with the sanction of kings, were also

---

[1] See Ordinances, *passim* (*Mem. Book*). Cases of searchers' work are to be found in the *Beverley Corporation Books* (*Hist. MSS. Comm.*). *Bad Work*, 16 Hen. VI. ' Ioh. Briggehous, webster, pro defectu artificii sui invento in medietate alterius panni lanei Aliciae Marshall. . . . Et fullones noluerunt operare dictum pannum quia non erat habilis : ideo ipse Ioh. Burgeys posuit dictum pannum ad unum fullonem patriae in deceptionem et defraudationem communis populi ' (p. 119). *Insolence*, 10 Hen. VI. Same man, Brighouse, ' pro rebellione et iniusta gubernatione sua versus aldermannum ', fined 3s. 4d. to city, and 3s. 4d. to craft (p. 113).

dependent upon the authorities of their city. Further, a study of the ordinances of many of the York gilds leads one to the strong conviction that many gilds were the actual creation of the town authorities.[1] Under these circumstances, the municipality exercised powerful control, legislative, judicial, and financial, over the gild. No gild decrees possessed any force until they had received the sanction of the mayor and his colleagues.[2] Should a revision of the craft ordinances be required it might be effected by the gild, but the new rules must then be submitted for the approval and endorsement of the municipal authorities. At the same time the town council, if it felt the need for such revision, might take the initiative and draw up amendments, which were then submitted to the gild for its assent and consent. Nor was this all, for the civic authority had power of itself to issue regulations for the general control of the whole industrial population or for the guidance of any one section. This was part of its economic function, and stood alongside the issue of by-laws concerning sanitation, the fixing of prices in the assize of bread, &c. Hence the city frequently made ordinances which applied to craftsmen as a whole, or to some particular craft, and which might supersede the gild by-laws, thus removing friction between divergent interests and shaping a unified municipal economic policy.

In the enforcement of its decrees and the infliction of punishment upon offenders the gild was dependent upon the municipal courts. The alderman of the weavers' gild had a certain judicial power, but it was frequently necessary to appeal to the judicial

---

[1] The town council was responsible for the general, social, and economic welfare of the community. In the city were many industries, some of which had voluntarily formed themselves into gilds, presumably with beneficial results. For those occupations which still remained unorganized the city must act as guide. The city authorities therefore took the initiative, called the craftsmen together, and led them to the drafting of ordinances, the appointment of searchers, and other steps necessary for the establishment of a gild. There is little direct evidence to support this view, but the whole tone of many gild ordinances convinces one that these gilds were brought into existence in this manner.

[2] The weavers' ordinances at Beverley were issued 'with the assent of the community of the town' (*Hist. MSS. Comm.*, p. 93). Weavers' ordinances at Hull (1490) were 'made amongst themselves, ratified and confirmed by the mayor, with the consent and agreement of all his brother aldermen' (Lambert, *op. cit.*, p. 204). Weavers' ordinances at York were put into operation 'with the approval and consent of all the weavers, by the licence, strength, and virtue of the royal charters, and by the licence and assistance of the mayor and sheriff' (*Mem. Book*, i. 242).

head of the city for moral support. In return for this and other favours, the municipality claimed a large measure of financial control over the craft gild. From industry, individual and organized, the city coffers received a considerable income. In Beverley the weaver paid a farthing for every four cloths he wove, and the fuller paid a similar amount for every two cloths fulled ; twopence was charged on the sale of each sack of wool, and a penny on each whole cloth sold.[1] Further, the city claimed a portion of all fees and fines paid by the gildsmen. In Beverley one-half of almost every fine inflicted by the gild went into the municipal purse, and the weaver of deceitful cloth, to quote one instance only, forfeited 3s. 4d. to the gild and the same sum to the town.[2] At York the proportion varied. The weavers' fines were allocated to the fund for paying the annual farm to the Exchequer, but in all the other gilds the municipal treasury claimed its share of the spoils. In some instances one-half the fine went to the ' communitas civitatis Ebor.', or, as it was expressed in some of the ordinances, to the ' chaumbre de counseil sur le pount de Use en Everwyk '.[3] In the coverlet weavers' and a few other crafts the city's claim was stronger, and in these cases no less than two-thirds of the various fines and payments passed into the hands of the municipality.[4]

Such was the gild life under which the manufacture of cloth was carried on in the urban centres about 1400. In each large town were these craft organizations, more or less highly developed, concerning themselves with the manifold activities of town life, social and religious as well as economic, and yet in all things subject to the general supervision of the municipal authorities. Whether the above is a fair picture of the gilds in their prime one cannot say, because of the lack of evidence of an earlier date. Before many decades had passed, the industry had begun to decline in the towns. Overtaxed and over-regulated, the weavers of York and Beverley were unable to withstand the competition which came from the rural areas, and the centre of gravity in the industry passed westward. In that day the fate of the gilds was sealed, and by 1600 their importance was a thing of the past. But the story of that decline from power must be left to the next chapter.

[1] *Beverley Town Documents* (Selden Soc.), xiv. 2.   [2] Ibid., p. 33.
[3] *Mem. Book*, i. 97.   [4] Ibid., i. 85.

CHAPTER II

DECAY AND EXPANSION DURING THE FIFTEENTH AND SIXTEENTH CENTURIES

The fifteenth and sixteenth centuries constitute an epoch of fundamental changes in the history of mankind. The discovery of new continents and the readjustments in social life, politics, religion, &c., were accompanied by the decay of much which had been all-important in the life of preceding centuries. Men were finding new worlds for themselves, and abandoning many of their old forms and systems.

In the sphere of English industry and commerce the same movements can be traced, and economic society underwent radical transformations. It is generally agreed that the fifteenth century was one of great expansion in the cloth industry.[1] The developments of the previous century were no whit abated, and as the manufacture spread over wider areas the ' makeng of cloth ' became, in the words of the House of Commons, ' the grettest occupacon and lyving of the poore people of the land '.[2] The policy of the government, from 1450 onward, was strongly protectionist, and efforts were made to foster native industries. In 1463 the importation of woollen caps, woollen cloth, and other manufactures was forbidden,[3] and scales of export duties were so framed as to encourage the shipping of cloth rather than of wool.[4] These efforts to keep the raw material in the country were partly successful, for in spite of the increasing output of wool an actually smaller quantity passed over to the looms of the Continent. The subsidy on wool exported to Calais amounted in 1348 to £68,000 ; in 1448 it had sunk to £12,000,[5] and the average for the years 1428–61 was only about £31,000.[6] The

---

[1] See Abram, *Social England in the Fifteenth Century* (1909), chap. i. Cunningham says that the cloth industry and the rise of the native merchant class were the only two bright spots in an otherwise gloomy century (*op. cit.*, i. 373).

[2] *Rot. Parl.*, v. 274, quoted by Abram, *op. cit.*, p. 2.

[3] 3 Ed. IV, c. 4. Renewed and made permanent by 4 Ed. IV, c. 1.

[4] Ashley, *op. cit.*, ii. 226.   [5] Cunningham, *op. cit.*, i. 434 n.

[6] J. H. Ramsay, *Lancaster and York*, ii. 267.

day of the great wool exporters was nearly at an end, and the
30,000 sacks exported annually in the fourteenth century
dwindled to less than 9,000 before 1500, and to under 5,000 by
the death of Henry VIII.[1]

Meanwhile the export of English cloth grew rapidly. In the
fourteenth century English pieces had gone to Germany,
Gascony, Spain, Portugal, and the Low Countries,[2] but the
total export, about 1350, was not more than 5,000 pieces per
annum.[3] This number had risen by 1509 to more than 84,000,[4]
and during the sixteenth century the amount increased still
more, as Hansards, Merchant Adventurers, and Eastland Merchants carried English cloths into the very heart of Europe, to
places which had formerly been the home of the industry. For
this expansion of the English manufacture had helped to bring
distress and decay on the foreign cloth-makers. Bruges, which
in the thirteenth century had boasted its 40,000 looms, stood,
at the end of the fifteenth, desolate and deserted. The 4,000
textile workers of Ypres (1408) had shrunk by 1486 to a mere
handful, and the whole industry of the Low Countries had
suffered the 'misery of a century of slow death—a misery on
which the English weaver throve and fattened '.[5]

With the growth of manufacture and the coming of 'high
commerce ', the mediaeval economic system was strained till it
eventually broke. The expansion in the cloth trade called for
a great increase in production, but the gild-ridden urban industry
was incapable of meeting the growing demand. Foreign trade
required an elasticity and enterprise such as were not to be
found under the gilds. The gildsman who wished to increase
his output found his path bestrewn with all manner of gild
regulations, restrictions, and financial burdens, which increased
the cost of production as well as the cost of living. Hence the
urban industry was ill-equipped to face the competition of the
manufactures already well established in the rural areas and

---

[1] Mrs. J. R. Green, *Town Life in the Fifteenth Century*, i. 51.
[2] Close Rolls, 22 Ed. III, pt. i, m. 8.   [3] Ashley, *op. cit.*, I. ii. 225.
[4] Mrs. Green, *op. cit.*, i. 51. The Hansards exported 4,464 pieces in 1422, and
21,389 in 1500 (Schanz, *Englische Handelspolitik*, ii. 28, quoted by Ashley,
op. cit., I. ii. 225–6).
[5] Mrs. Green, *op. cit.*, i. 65–6. The English competition was only a small
cause of the Belgian decline ; but England reaped a great amount of benefit
therefrom.

smaller towns. In these places there were few industrial laws to fetter the weaver's activities ; the 'rates were low ', and the cost of living below that of the town. Here also was a supply of unemployed labour, turned adrift by the economic upheavals of the sixteenth century. All these conditions were favourable for the production of cloth in increasing quantities at a comparatively cheap rate.

Such were the forces at work during the two centuries under consideration. We see the results, firstly in the decline of York and Beverley as industrial centres, and secondly in the outburst of industrial life in the West Riding.

(a) Decline of the Textile Industry in Beverley and York

One of the most tragic features in the history of these centuries is the decay in the economic life of the two towns within whose walls the industry of the Middle Ages had been fostered. It is impossible to fix a date at which the decadence began. The Black Death shook their prosperity for a time, but the rest of the county suffered equally. The Wars of the Roses brought misfortune on the towns, and by 1470 the competition from the West Riding had become severe. Hence, before the accession of Henry VII the decline was far advanced, and the complaints of the townsmen were frequent and serious. A similar development was taking place in many other towns which had built up a gild-controlled textile industry, and the history of York and Beverley excellently illustrates the interplay of economic, religious, and municipal influences on the textile trade.

York suffered heavily during the Wars of the Roses, when ' for their treuth unto ther Souverain Lord (Henry VI), such as abode in York was robbid, spolid, . . . and soo extremely empouverishered that few of them was ever after of power to diffend themselves '.[1] The weavers of York at this time were in a sorry plight, for the drift away from the city seems to have been great. The yearly fee of £10 weighed heavily on those who remained, and in 1478 they were ' granted pardon ', on account of their poverty, of half the annual contribution.[2]   When

---

[1] Petition from the York City Council to Henry VII, 1485 (Davies, *Records of the City of York in the Fifteenth Century*, p. 291).
[2] Patent Rolls, 18 Ed. IV, pt. ii, m. 12.

Henry VII came to the throne the poverty of the gild was again taken into consideration ; the greater part of the fee-farm was remitted, and the mayor made chief Serjeant-at-Arms to the King, with a salary to enable him to bear the expenses of his office.[1] At the same time the weavers were released for the time being from their annual payment, and allowed to have their 'gild, customs, and liberties without accompt in the same way as citizens in other cities do '. Their charter was renewed once more, with the proviso that all weavers without the city should be exempted from contributing anything to the gild coffers.[2] The reason for this extensive grant was specifically stated to be 'on account of the poverty and distress of the said weavers, which is so great that if they were compelled to pay the . . . farm, they would be obliged to remove from the city, and dwell elsewhere '.

These concessions appear to have had little effect in checking the decline which had already set in. Wolsey strove hard to bring back the vigour and energy of former days by obtaining Letters Patent which granted the city certain privileges in the exportation of northern wool and wool-fells. This favour allowed the cheaper wools of the northern parts of Yorkshire to be exported from York instead of Newcastle, as formerly.[3] ' By reason therof the seid cityzens dyd dayly encresse in gettyng of goods, as long as they contynued suche Shyppynge, the whych graunte so opteyned . . . was the hyghest and most especyall comodytye and Jewell that ever came to the foreseid Citye for the p'farrement and enrychyng of the Cytizens therof, and also great refresshyng to all the Cuntrey abowte the same.'[4] The great ' Jewell ' did not, however, spread its radiance upon the clothiers of the county, who soon complained that they could get no wool, because of the vigour with which the city merchants were exporting the raw material. The protests of York were disregarded, and an Act, passed in the same year as

[1] *Materials for a History of Henry VII* (Rolls Series), i. 462.
[2] Ibid.
[3] By the Act 3 Ed. IV, c. 1, the export of wool was forbidden except to Calais. But the fleeces of Northumberland, Cumberland, Westmoreland, Richmond-shire, and Northallertonshire might be exported from Newcastle to any part. By the Letters Patent given to York that city was given equal freedom to export.
[4] Cottonian MSS. (Brit. Mus.), Titus B. i, f. 279, June 24, 1526.

Wolsey's downfall (1529), annulled the privilege, and deprived the river port of its licence to export.[1]   Indeed, if we may believe the letter to Wolsey, the last state was infinitely worse than the first, for prior to the grant a considerable trade in lead had been carried on by the men of York.   When the wool licence was issued, declared the mayor, 'We were so gladde thereof that we did lytell regarde our old commodytye, in bying of leade. And at that tyme, the rich marchaunts of London gatt the treat of lead as we hadde before . . . and hath inhaunced yt to so hygh a pryce That we canne gett but lytell of yt ' ;[2] and indeed the trade in lead was partly lost to the city.

York had fallen upon evil days, but it was not the only sufferer.   The greatness of Beverley had already vanished, and much of its economic glory departed.   The cloths for which it had been famed in the thirteenth century were now unknown, and Leland, writing in the reign of Henry VIII, remarked that ' there was much goode clothe makyng at Beverle, but that is now much decayed'.   An Act of 1535[3] declared that there were many houses in ' greate ruine and decaye, and specially in the pryncipalle and chief stretes there, in which . . . stretes, in tymes passid, have bene beautifull dwellyng howses . . . well inhabyted, whyche at thys daye moche parte therof ys desolate and void groundys, with pittys, sellers, and vaultes lying open and uncoveryd, very perilous for people who go by in the night '. A later document[4] (1599) spoke of the town as being ' very poore and greatlie depopulated, insomuche as there are in the same fower hundred tenements and dwelling houses utterly decay'd and uninhabited, besides so great a nomber of poore and needie people altogether unhable so to be ymployed anie waie to gett their own lyvinge (that) the towne is constrayned for the reliefe of them yearly to disburse one hundreth and fyve pound, besides the chardge of bryngyng upp and keepinge of fower-score orphans at knytting, spynning, and other workes '. Similar complaints were made during the sixteenth century con- cerning Malton, Scarborough, Pontefract, Hull, and most of the older towns throughout the county.[5]

[1] 21 Hen. VIII, c. 17.   [2] Cottonian MSS., Titus B. i, f. 279.
[3] 26 Hen. VIII, c. 1 ; Act concerning many towns, including Beverley.
[4] Exemption from payment of all tenths and fifteenths ; quoted in Poulson, *op. cit.*, p. 338.   [5] See statutes 27 Hen. VIII, c. 1 ; 32 Hen. VIII, c. 18,

It would be futile to attempt to explain this decay of town life in the textile centres as being due to any one cause. Many forces were at work, and we must confine ourselves to the most powerful of these varied and far-reaching influences.[1]

First came the burden of gild demands. Industry had arrived at that stage where greater freedom was essential to further growth, but the gilds, instead of realizing this necessity, clung more closely to their old privileges, and attempted to make themselves even more exclusive than before. Their ordinances were marked by greater insistence on conditions of membership and citizenship. The privileges of the craft must not be watered down by being distributed amongst too great a number, and at the same time the growth of a class of interlopers must be prevented. . Hence town or gild restated with growing emphasis the conditions of labour and the gild monopoly over industrial life. The necessity for being a burgess was especially reiterated. In the past the craftsman who did not wish to become a burgess had paid various penalties, and these fines were now raised all round. The non-burgess weaver of Beverley had his payments increased in 1445, and again ten years later,[2] whilst in 1460 the municipal authorities declared, ' Every person of every craft of the town (Beverley) being a brother of the same crafts must be a burgess from this day forth '.[3] The position of aliens was becoming more difficult and unpleasant. In some gilds only English-born youths could be taken into apprenticeship, and the charges for the admission of adult aliens into the fraternities were forced higher and higher.

Details of internal organization were also receiving the closest attention.[4] The large number of closely allied occupations made demarcation disputes frequent and bitter. As the merchandizing organizations grew more powerful, the functions of the crafts-men were rigorously confined to manufacture. Between the making of cloth, clothes, and other articles composed of cloth, and the selling of these goods, there were at least six classes of

---

[1] For documents illustrating this matter, see Bland, Brown, and Tawney, *op. cit.*, pp. 279 et seq.   [2] Selden Soc., xiv, intro., p. li.

[3] *Beverley Town Documents* (*Hist. MSS. Comm.*), p. 46.

[4] In 1493 the Beverley authorities declared that no man should take up any occupation, except that of which ' he is brother withall, and in clothing ', i.e. in livery (Selden Soc., xiv. 60).

men—textile workers, tailors, glovers, drapers, mercers, and merchants—and the growing jealousy with which each class guarded its sphere of control can be seen throughout the fifteenth and sixteenth centuries. In 1561, for instance, it was decreed that ' No tailor, walker, or dyer within this towne of Beverley . . . shall bye no maner of wullen clothe or clothes to th'intent to selle againe by holesaile or retaile, by yards or otherwyse, under payne for every peace . . . to forfett xx^s to the drapers of the town '.[1] Specialization was pushed to extreme lengths, a development which was sure to fetter the growth of the industry as a whole.

The textile gilds began to suffer from over-legislation, either from the multiplication of their ordinances or from decrees and statutes issued by the municipality or the State. Both the manufacture and sale of cloth were subjected to increasingly minute regulation, and the liberty of the producer was more than ever curtailed. The weights and dimensions of cloths were fixed, and all pieces had to be sealed before exposure for sale.[2] In 1561 the coverlet weavers of York were forbidden to use more than one loom,[3] and were warned against using certain kinds of yarn. The number of prohibitions grew apace, and so numerous did the by-laws of the weavers' fraternity become that an early seventeenth-century set of ordinances contained over 70 clauses.[4] In the marketing of wares all manner of stipulations were laid down, special attention being given to the stranger and the alien. Here, as elsewhere, the gildsmen were unable to abandon their parochial outlook for one which would be national in its scope. The men of Kendal and other parts of England were still regarded as being little better than the alien.

The urban industry was over-regulated ; it was also over-burdened with financial demands. The gild levies [5] and exactions alone were heavy ; at York the fee-farm was a perpetual nightmare to the weavers, who, as the York municipal records declare (1561), ' beyng overchardged with the said yearly pay-

[1] Ibid., p. 99.   [2] York Minute Books, ix, f. 31 a (21 Hen. VII).
[3] Ibid., xx, f. 53 b.
[4] Ordinances of Weavers' Company (1607 and 1629) in Gildhall, York.
[5] In 1418 the entrance fee for the weavers' gild of Beverley was increased from 2s. to 3s. 4d. (Selden Soc., vol. xiv, p. li).

ment, have fled the most part forth of the said citie, inhabytyng in the country to the same nighe adjoynynge '.[1] Added to this was the load of municipal and national taxation. The former tended to increase, and the frequent calls for tenths and fifteenths were a severe strain on the resources of the towns-men.

The chief burdens of the gilds were therefore extreme exclusive-ness, excessive regulation, and heavy taxation. These might have been borne with equanimity had town life guaranteed in return peace and security. But from 1381 onwards, for at least two centuries, the Yorkshire towns were torn with civic faction and strife. There were quarrels in the council, there was enmity between those within the government and those without. Disaffection often gave birth to disturbances, in which the gilds-men played a prominent part, and occasionally the control of the city passed for a time into the hands of the craftsmen. In 1493 the Governors of Beverley, formerly the Keepers, were compelled to be liverymen of the crafts, just as their predecessors had been elected from men nominated by the crafts.[2] In York the gilds enjoyed a short spell of power in municipal affairs, before they finally sank into insignificance in the sixteenth century. Here, after the Wars of the Roses, the members of the various trades were ordered by Edward IV to name two alder-men from whom the council would elect a mayor ; and later they were commanded to gather together to choose a mayor from among the aldermen.[3] These elections gave rise to great tumults, in which economics and local politics were inter-mingled, and the voteless journeymen expressed their opinion of their own conditions and of the general management of the city. Constant disturbances led to the charter of 1517, in which the control of York was placed in the hands of a mayor, sheriffs, aldermen, and a Common Council. This last body was composed of two members chosen from each of the thirteen principal crafts, and one from each of the fifteen smaller frater-nities. These men, along with one searcher from each gild,

---

[1] York Minute Books, xxiii, f. 14 b, April 19, 1561.

[2] Selden Soc., vol. xiv, p. xxxv. See also *Beverley Corp. MSS.* (*Hist. MSS. Comm.*), p. 54.

[3] M. Sellers, ' York in the Sixteenth Century ', *English Historical Review,* xvi. 270.

formed a council of nomination which chose annually three aldermen, one of whom was then elected mayor by the sheriffs and other aldermen. This constitution, with some later re-adjustments, continued throughout the century, but failed to remove the causes of decay and discontent. Mayor and council fulfilled the ceremonial part of their functions with great éclat. Receptions, lavish displays of hospitality, the festivities of the Council of the North, venison feasts, and fish dinners made York proverbial for its good cheer. And all the time the com-monalty watched its industry taking wings westward beyond Micklegate Bar. Anger smouldered long, burst into flames, and died away, having achieved very little.[1] Remonstrances were of no avail, and it was useless to appeal to the heads of the town, who were, as one vexed soul complained, ' more mete to drive pigges to the feylde than to be Justices of the Peace '.[2] There was evidently no hope of regeneration from the local authorities, who were themselves interested in the feast, the pageant, and the *ancien régime*.

Other causes contributed to the decay of town life in York-shire. Owing to some negligence the condition of the Ouse had become unsatisfactory and the stream was practically un-navigable. Steps were taken, however, in the early 'thirties of the sixteenth century for the removal of the weirs, shallows, &c., and the water-course was greatly improved.[3] Beverley seems to have been injured by the migration of its merchants to Hull, this port being a much more convenient mercantile centre.[4] The Reformation was not without its economic consequences. It affected town and country alike, and York and Beverley suffered considerably, since they were ecclesiastical as well as industrial centres. The dissolution of the ' Mynster of Beverley, whyche before the dissolution thereof was invested with great lands and possessions, whereby many religious persons, in-habitants and poore people of the saide towne have bene mayn-tayned and relieved ' was given by contemporaries as one of the chief causes of the decay of that town.[5] At York the dissolution

---

[1] *English Historical Review*, xvi. 296.   [2] Ibid., p. 283.
[3] *State Papers, Henry VIII*, vol. x, p. 243 ; and statute, 23 Hen. VIII, c. 18.
[4] See Poulson, *Beverlac*, p. 338, in which Beverley mourns loss of staple.
[5] Ibid., pp. 338–9.

of the monasteries and religious gilds, and the confiscation of
such craft gild property as was held for religious purposes,
meant a great overthrow of charitable and religious life. The
monasteries had a firm hold upon the rural life of Yorkshire,
and the gilds played an equally important part in urban life ;
hence the actions of Henry VIII and Protector Somerset tore
up by the roots two very important growths. Part of the gild
money was to be spent in keeping up three hospitals,[1] as places
' where the poore could be set on worke ', but in spite of this
provision there were large gaps in the charitable institutions
of the city, as well as in its round of religious observance.

Faced with these handicaps, York and Beverley attempted
to retain their places as cloth-making centres. Had there been
no rival, free from such defects, ready to snatch away the
industrial prosperity from the cities, the faults indicated above
might not have had any serious effect on the welfare of the
craftsmen. But the rival was there in the field at the beginning
of the fifteenth century, and in the struggle which ensued during
the next 150 years the circumstances were favourable in almost
every respect to the West Riding clothiers. On the one hand
was an industry burdened with financial levies, with all skilled
enterprise and progress checked by the craft ordinances, industrial legislation, and the detailed system of inspection, with
prices and costs of production comparatively high, and with
local government in a state of almost constant chaos. On the
other hand was an industry free as yet from strict regulation or
heavy financial burdens, and with the cost of living and working expenses low. In such circumstances it was inevitable that
the rural districts and small towns of the West Riding should
triumph, and when the struggle really set in the old urban
industries could offer no successful resistance. The whole
situation is admirably described by a York writer, who was
reporting on the state of trade in that city in 1561 :

' The cause of the decay of the . . . weavers and loomes for
woollen (cloth) within the sayd cite as I doe understand and

---

[1] Sellers, *English Historical Review*, xvi. 287. The Chantry Commissioners
in their report on York stated that they found only twenty in place of thirty-six
in the College of Vicars Choral, ' th' occasion whereof is by reason of decaye
of landes and revenues of the Cytie of York, beyng sore in ruyne and decaye '.
Surtees Soc., vol. xci, pp. 25–6.

learne is the lak of cloth makyng in the sayd cite as was in old tyme accustomed, whiche is nowe encreased and used in the townes of Halyfax, Leedes, and Wakefield, for that not only the comodytie of the water-mylnes is ther nigh at hande, but also the poore folke as speynners, carders, and other necessary work-folkes for the sayd webbyng, may ther besyde ther hand labor, have rye, fyre, and other releif good cheape, which is in this citie very deare and wantyng.'[1]

This vast economic change was not carried out without much strenuous opposition from those who were being injured thereby. The most famous instance of such resistance was the apparently successful attempt of the coverlet weavers of York to retain for themselves the monopoly of that branch of the textile manu-facture. The weaving of coverlets for beds had long been an important branch of the York industry, but, although the weavers of the city claimed a monopoly of the trade, coverlet weavers were to be found in many places throughout the West Riding at the time of the Poll Tax Returns.[2] By the middle of the sixteenth century the competition of the outsider had grown so strong that it became necessary for the men of York to take steps in self-preservation. The most effective plan was to get the protection of Parliament, which would establish the citizens in the sole enjoyment of the manufacture. After con-siderable agitation the desired statute was obtained in the session of 1542–3.[3] The Act so fully describes the whole situation that it is worthy of quotation at some length :

' WHEREAS the City of York, being one of the most ancient and greatest cities within the Realm of England, afore this time hath been maintained and upholden by divers and sundry handicrafts . . . and most principally by making and weaving of coverlets and coverings for beds, and thereby a great number of the inhabitants and poor people of the said city, suburbs thereof, and other places within the County of York have been daily set on work in spinning, carding, dyeing, weaving, and otherwise, to the great comodity of the inhabitants and poor people, . . . having thereby honest livings, and not made else-where in any part of the county. For the true, substantial and

---

[1] York Corporation Minute Books, xxiii, f. 20 a, June 8, 1561.

[2] Coverlet weavers are also referred to as chaloners and tapiters. From the figures given below it will be seen that they made small pieces about the size of the present-day quilt or sheet.

[3] Statute 34–5 Hen. VIII, c. 10.

perfect making thereof, many good and beneficial ordinances and orders were devised and made, as well for the good quality . . . as concerning the length and breadth of them.[1] . . . And forasmuch as the same coverlets and coverings were well and substantially made and wrought, the King's subjects of divers parts of the realm and also strangers from foreign realms, knowing the goodness of them, were very desirous to have and buy them. . . . But now of late, divers and sundry evil-disposed persons, apprentices not expert in the same occupation, withdrawing themselves out of the said city of York into the county . . . and other places thereabouts, and also divers other persons inhabiting in villages and towns within the said county and nigh to the same, intermeddling with the craft and occupation, having little experience therein, not being bound to the said rules and ordinances, do daily make coverlets and coverings, neither of good stuffs nor of good assize, length or breadth, and for the utterance of the same use daily the craft and subtilty of hawking abroad in the country to villages and to men's houses, putting the same naughty ware to sale secretly, not only to the great impoverishing of the inhabitants of the said city and to the great deceit of the King's true and faithful subjects buying the . . . coverlets, to the great defaming and slandering of the said handicraft, but also to the utter decay of the same, if remedy the sooner herein be not provided.'

This statement of the grievance constituted the preamble of the Act. Stripped of its legal verbiage, it meant that the trade of the city weavers was being sapped by men who had always lived, or had recently gone to live, outside the walls and immediate neighbourhood of York. The mention of the ex-apprentice renegades indicates the occurrence of what is mentioned in other similar statutes, namely that ' weavers and workmen of clothiers, when they have been trained up in the trade of cloth-making and weaving three or four years, do forsake their masters, and do become clothiers and occupiers for themselves, without skill, stock, or knowledge, to the great slander of true cloth-making '.[2] In the hands of these upstarts, whose dignity did not scorn an occasional hawking of their produce, the fame of the Yorkshire coverlets was being dragged in the mire—at least, so said the men of York.

---

[1] Best coverlets were 3 yds. by 2½ yds. ; second grade, 3 yds. by 2 yds. third quality, 2½ yds. by 1¾ yds.

[2] Statute 4-5 Philip and Mary, c. 11.

For remedy against this outrage on law, order, and industrial honesty it was decreed by the statute that

' No manner of persons dwelling . . . within the said county of York or nigh unto the same, shall . . . make any coverlets or coverings, *to be put to sale*, unless such persons be inhabiting . . . within the city of York or within the suburbs of the same, upon pain of forfeiture of every coverlet wrought and put to sale. And it is further enacted that no manner of persons of the occupation of handicraftsmen of coverlets shall use the said craft of hawking or go as hawkers out of the city . . . but only in markets and open fairs.'[1]

The enforcement of these clauses was placed in the hands of the officials of the craft of coverlet weavers, just as if it was an ordinary by-law issued by the fraternity.

The wardens and searchers were given full power to search all fairs and markets from the Trent northwards, and to confiscate all coverlets which contravened the conditions laid down in the Act. When they went into any ' liberties and franchises ' other than their own, they might call upon the officials of those parts to assist in the search. A proviso declared that ' It shall be lawful for anyone to make coverlets as he shall please, for the use of his own household or for the lord to whom he is tenant, so always that the same coverlets shall not be put to sale '.

The coverlet weavers expected great results from this statute. The total cost of obtaining it amounted to about £1,000 in modern money, and of this sum the municipality paid one-half, as it considered that ' the same Acte is as muche for the comon wele of the city as of the coverlet weavers of the same '.[2] It seems probable that the weavers' expectations were partly fulfilled, for a survey of the Yorkshire industry made in 1595 reported that no coverlets were made in any part of the county except York, and that this city produced ' two packs of cov'letts and carpetts each moneth, and ev'y packe contaynes 14 or 15 stone weight '.[3] Evidently by this time York had become free from competition in the industry, a result probably due to the enforcement of the Act. But even if that were so the output was small and the industry quite insignificant.

[1] 34-5 Hen. VIII, c. 10.
[2] *York Memorandum Book*, vol. i, intro., p. xxxi.
[3] Peck's ' Certificate of New Draperies in the County of York ' (1595), *D. S. P., Eliz.*, cclii. 2.

As we are dealing with the woes of the coverlet makers, it is amusing to note that the black sheep complained of in the statute were to be found within the fold 'as well as without. Six years after the passing of the above law one of the searchers of the fraternity was found selling coverlets unsealed ; other weavers were summoned for keeping apprentices contrary to the ordinances, and about the same time one of the wardens, a man chosen to govern the craft and administer its decrees with honour and efficiency, was detected mixing ' hare and wolle together, and werkyng the same into coverlettes ', for which offence he was fined forty shillings and deposed from his office.[1] Again, in 1555, the mayor was petitioned to add two new ordinances to the regulations of the trade, one making it un-lawful to use certain devices in the making of coverlets, the other giving greater powers to the searchers.[2] The good name of York coverlets was evidently in jeopardy from the practices of those who fulfilled the conditions laid down in the Coverlet Act rather than from the outsiders against whom the statute was enacted.

Whilst men and industry sought the country districts and the smaller towns, Beverley and York continued their steady decline from former glories. Houses stood empty, streets were dirty and unkempt, and churches which once ' were good and honest livings for learned incumbents, by reason of the privy tithes of the rich merchants, and offerings of a great multitude ', became so impoverished as to be ' not a competent and honest living for a good curate ; yea, and no person will take the cure, but that of necessity there is some chantry priest, or some which for the most part are unlearned and very ignorant persons, not able to do any part of their duties, whereby the city is replenished with blind guides and pastors '.[3] Statutory permission was granted to unite two or more churches into one parish, and a number of disused edifices were sold into private hands.[4]

The gilds continued on their downward track, halting at intervals to issue new ordinances which were as vigorous in

---

[1] York Corp. Minute Books, xviii. 75, 130 et seq.

[2] Ibid., xxi. 112 b–113.

[3] Act 1 Ed. VI, c. 9, for closing various churches in York, and joining the endowments together.

[4] York Corp. Minute Books, xix, ff. 16 and 46 (1550).

language as they were ineffective in action.   In the distribution of 'voices' amongst the gild representatives for the York Common Council in 1517, the finishing and distributing fraternities took the most important places, the dyers being the only textile occupation in the list of greater crafts.   Weavers and fullers came amongst the fifteen less important industries, and shearmen and the remaining textile branches were not represented at all.   Some of these crafts were almost defunct by the middle of the sixteenth century, for in 1552 the people of York, petitioning for a reform in the craft representation on the Common Council, declared[1] that certain of the crafts which in 1517 were so important as to be able to claim one or two members on the Council were now 'decayd so that there is none of them to have voyces'.

For a number of the York crafts, however, death came more slowly.   They lost that industrial supremacy which they had formerly possessed, but they contrived to maintain some kind of existence for two centuries longer.   In some instances they gained strength by the union of two or three kindred crafts, as in the case of the haberdashers, feltmakers, and cappers, who were amalgamated in 1591 into 'one Companye and ffellowship', or of the tailors and drapers, who joined forces about 1560, with one set of ordinances and one team of searchers.[2]   Then, being transformed, and sometimes supported by a royal charter, a number of these 'companies' survived beyond the seventeenth century.

The decline of the weavers from the commanding position which they held at the end of the fourteenth century can be clearly traced, and we possess some reliable information relating to the days of their decadence.   The progress of the industry in the West Riding began to be specially marked in the first three-quarters of the fifteenth century, and that period synchronized with a serious decline in the output from the York looms.   This we know from the Ulnage Accounts,[3] which supply

---

[1] Sellers, *English Historical Review*, vol. xvi, p. 280 ; also *Victoria County History, Yorkshire*, vol. ii, p. 440.

[2] York Corp. Minute Books, ix, f. 25 a.   In 1505 it was stated that there were only three persons in the whole drapers' craft.   See also ibid., xx, ff. 56 and 60.   Also 14 Charles II, Add. MSS. (Brit. Mus.), vol. 8935 ; and Entry Book, Charles II, vol. v, p. 98.

[3] For more detailed explanation of the nature of these ulnage documents, see the next section of this chapter.

us with figures of the number of saleable cloths made in York during the reigns of Richard II and Edward IV. Each account states the number of cloths made for sale, and the amount paid for subsidy and ulnage, fourpence being the subsidy paid on a whole cloth of assize. The first record is for 1394–5, and from September 23, 1394 to September 22, 1395 subsidy was paid in York on 3,200 cloths of assize and one scarlet cloth, the latter being charged sixpence, the former fourpence each. This meant a total subsidy of £53 7s. 2d.[1] Seventy years elapse before we again have the necessary figures, and in the meantime misfortune had overtaken the weavers of the county town. The account is for 1468–9,[2] and the period covered is only ten and a half months; but if we calculate it out to a twelve-months' basis, we find that the number of cloths for the whole year amounted to 1,809, and that the subsidy realized £30 3s. Thus, during those seventy years, the amount of cloth made in York had *decreased by nearly one-half.* The records of subsequent years make the decline even greater, as will be seen from the following statement:

Year.		Cloths.					Subsidy.		
							£	s.	d.
1394–5	.	.	3,200 cloths of assize and 1 scarlet cloth		.	.	53	7	2
1468–9	.	.	1,809 cloths of assize	.	.	.	30	3	0
1473–5 [3] { annual average }		1,173¼ ,,	,,	.	.	.	19	11	1
1475–8 [4] ,,		922¼ ,,	,,	.	.	.	15	7	5

If one takes the annual average for the years 1473–8, it then appears that the output of cloth from the city of York had decreased by two-thirds during the preceding 80 years.

This diminution of output reacted on the fortunes of the weavers' gild, the membership of which declined throughout the fifteenth and sixteenth centuries. At the commencement of each new reign the weavers petitioned the Crown for relief from the burden of their £10 fee-farm, and were either excused

[1] Account, 18–19 Rich. II ; Exch. Accounts, bundle 345, no. 16.
[2] Account, 8–9 Ed. IV, Exch. Accounts, bundle 346, no. 22.
[3] Account, 13–15 Ed. IV (two whole years), Exch. Accounts, bundle 345, no. 24. This roll is for two whole years, so I have calculated the annual average.
[4] Account, 15–18 Ed. IV, Exch. Accounts, bundle 345, no. 24. This account is for two and a half years and eighty-three days ; the annual average has therefore been calculated for above.

from one-half, or exonerated entirely from payment by each of the Tudor monarchs.[1] So far gone was the craft that in 1517 it did not appear in the list of the thirteen most important trades, and the decline continued during the next half-century. In 1561 the City Council appealed on behalf of the weavers for relief from the fee-farm, and in the petition surveyed the rise and fall of the trade.

' Whereas in olde tymes past, the said citie hathe moche prospered in clothe makyng, and thereby th'occupacion of weavers of the same citie, beyng then bothe many and of goode substance, obteyned by charter of Your Highnes most noble pregenytours to be incorporat, yeldyng for a fee fyrme or gylde a certayne yerely somme . . . which yerely fee fyrme was payed accordyngly so long as webbyng in the said citie was used. But like as in processe of tyme the said occupieng decreased and at last utterly decayed in the citie, even so the weavers of the same, both wantyng their accustomed occupieing and also beyng overchardged with the same yerely payment, have fled the most part forth of the said citie, inhabtyng in the contry to the same nighe adjoynyng, sauf onely a few very poore men now remayn-yng, whoe no doubte if they shalbe compelled to paye still the said yerely fee fyrme, shall in short tyme be fayne alsoe clerely to forsake your Grace's citie.'

Elizabeth declined to cancel the payment, except for a sum of money to be paid at once, and the weavers, thanks to the loan made them by the municipality, were able to relieve them-selves of the yearly burden.[2]

Thirteen years before this happened the weavers of woollen cloth had taken a step such as most crafts were taking about this time. Their fraternity now numbered probably about fifteen members, and for purposes of economy had long been working in co-operation with the linen weavers, who were a craft of about the same size.[3] This co-operation rapidly grew stronger. In 1548 the two crafts were jointly bearing financial burdens, and almost immediately afterwards it was decreed that ' from hensforth for dyvers concyderacons th'occupacon of wollen wevers and lynon wevers shall be all one occupacon and to bere equal charges in all thynges, and to have serche togydder as all

[1] See, for instance, *Calendar of State Papers, Hen. VIII* (1511), vol. i, no. 1920.
[2] York Corp. Minute Books, xxiii, ff. 29 and 49.
[3] As, for instance, in 9 Hen. VII, York Corp. Minute Books, vii, f. 107 a.

one, and the said lyn wevers to be yerely at the eleccon of the master of the wevers, and to be ordered like unto them in every condicon '.[1]

This alliance resulted in the Weavers' Company of York, a company in which the linen weavers generally predominated throughout the next two centuries ; for this body existed until at least 1796, and possibly for a year or two longer. In the Muniments Room at York can be seen some seventeenth-century ordinances of the company, as well as the Account Books for the years 1564 to 1796. The ordinances of 1607 and 1629 are most elaborate, and show to what lengths of detailed super-vision the craft regulations had gone. There are over 70 clauses dealing, *inter alia*, with the elections of the executive, foreigners, hawking, apprenticeship, the behaviour of journeymen, the employment of women, the frequenting of taverns during divine service, and the practice of smoking tobacco in the meetings of the company.

The Account Books indicate the number of members in the society, and provide us with the data for a rough comparison of the numbers in the industry at different periods. The weavers' ordinances of 1400 are prefaced by the names of 50 members of the crafts, and others are referred to ; therefore the member-ship of the fraternity of woollen weavers in 1400 was *at least fifty*. In 1590 the company of linen and woollen weavers con-tained only about 20 members ; of these nearly half were linen weavers, and so the number of master woollen weavers could not have been more than a dozen—a strange contrast to the 50 masters of two centuries before.

Up to the time of the Civil War the company made some small progress, and increased its membership. This increase, however, was almost entirely due to the linen-weaving section, which did succeed in making a little headway. The member-ship of 20 in 1590 had risen to 27 by 1626, and to 36 in 1632.[2] In 1628 the weavers petitioned for a renewal of their charter, with certain additions of a strongly monopolistic character. The renewal was granted, but without the desired additions,[3]

---

[1] York Corp. Minute Books, xix, ff. 50 and 53.

[2] These figures are obtained by adding together the names of those who paid their annual subscription with those who are recorded as being in arrears.

[3] D. S. P., *Chas. I*, cix. 58 (July 9, 1628).

and the company prospered until the outbreak of the Civil
War.   Then, in the chaos of the next 20 years, it fell to pieces.
In 1663 there were only 7 brethren ; at times during the following years the number rose to about 10, and this small handful
of men kept the company alive in name until the end of the
eighteenth century.   The annual meetings, however, were very
formal.   There were no accounts to audit, for the annual subscriptions had disappeared, and the only business consisted of
the approval of a new apprentice or journeyman.   The meetings
were monotonous in their similarity and formality, and it seemed
possible that the company might continue indefinitely.   Suddenly
the Account Book presents a blank page after the entries of
1796.   The last meeting had been held, the last officers appointed,
the last apprentice approved.   Then came the end ; how, when,
or why we do not know.

This story of the York weavers is typical of the manner in
which the survivals clung to their shadowy privileges and
organization.   The economic forms of the Middle Ages were
slow in passing away, and the seventeenth and eighteenth
centuries are littered with the remains of mediaeval institutions.
In York the insistence upon the freedom of the city as a *sine
qua non* for trading was retained up to the end of the eighteenth
century, and a certain Rev. W. MacRitchie, passing through
York in 1795, remarked that the city ' has but little trade,
because no man can set up in business here without purchasing
the Freedom of the City, which is an expensive matter, and to
beginners almost, if not altogether, unattainable '.[1]   At Hull
most elaborate weavers' ordinances were issued in 1673, and, as
Lambert says, the members of the gild ' met yearly, elected
their Warden and their Searchers, ordered their dinner, and
displayed their plate, until at length the dinner was deserted,
the silver tobacco pipe unlit, and the punch bowl cold '.[2]   Then,
either in silent discontinuance, or in a last act of formal suicide,
the few remaining adherents dissolved the brotherhood which
had run through so many centuries.

For some years this industrial decline brought York into
a condition of depression.   Eventually the city regained part of

---

[1] *Antiquary*, November 1896, p. 332, quoted by editor of *York Freemen's
Roll* (Surtees Soc., vol. xcvi), p. xv.
[2] Lambert, *Two Thousand Years of Gild Life*, pp. 208 et seq.

its former activity, when the export trade of the Merchant Adventurers had developed to considerable proportions, and the cloths of the West Riding passed through York on their way to Europe. In this day the loss of industry was counteracted by the increased commercial activity. But in the meantime there was a period of dire poverty and distress. Unemployment was rife, and the poorer classes of the city were in great straits. The destruction of the monasteries and religious gilds had wiped out the chief philanthropic agencies, and the various private charities were inadequate for supplying relief to the poor. The problem of poverty became very pressing about the middle of the sixteenth century, and at last, following the example of other towns, the authorities of York began to grapple with the question of unemployment. They apparently admitted the principle of the 'right to work', and attempted to remove the poverty in their midst by providing work for those who were able to do it. Hence, from 1569 onwards for over a century, York was engaged spasmodically in municipal manufacture.

The first scheme was inaugurated in 1569, with Roger Lighe, a clothier by trade, in charge of the venture. The city purchased stocks of wool and textile apparatus, which were established in St. George's House. The constables of the various wards were ordered to gather together the poor in their constituencies, and bring them to the House, where they might be given work. Those who were acquainted with the methods of cloth manufacture were to pursue that occupation, being paid wages according to a piece-rate, and as to the inexperienced, Lighe was ' to do his digligens to instruct such of the sayd poore as he shall perceyve not perfect, to th'intent that lyttle by lyttle there may be of the sayd poore sufficient to serve the turne '.[1] The scheme was floated with a fair measure of success. Shears and other implements were purchased, men were sent into Lincolnshire to procure supplies of wool, and the weavers were soon so busy that the spinners could not keep pace with the demand for yarn. The municipal fabrics were exposed for sale in the City Hall on Ouse Bridge, and were generally purchased by the merchants of the city.[2]

[1] York Corp. Minute Books, xxiv, f. 138 b (May 18, 1569).
[2] Ibid., ff. 138-92 (1569-70).

The establishment of this textile scheme did not, however, solve the problem of poverty in York. The cloths were often of inferior quality and of higher price than those which the merchants could obtain from private makers, and thus the new venture finally collapsed, leaving the morass of unemployment undrained. Other new or similar schemes were therefore being constantly hatched to provide for the poor by the introduction of *new* industries. In 1590 a knitting school was instituted,[1] and so many children attended it that the services of three teachers were required. Seven years later the corporation made a contract with Thomas Lewkener, a Hartlepool gentleman, who undertook to begin the ' practice of the art, misterye, or occupation of making of fustians ',[2] and thus provide regular employment for at least 50 persons of the poorer sort. Lewkener was given the freedom of the city, granted the monopoly of fustian-making within the city for the space of ten years, provided with a house free of rent, and a loan of money. Armed with such powers and privileges he made onslaught upon the destitution in York, but only succeeded in denting the surface of that problem.

Throughout the seventeenth century the city authorities persisted in their efforts. Still more new industries were introduced, the chief being the manufacture of worsted cloth. As yet Yorkshire made scarcely any worsted goods, confining its attention to the old-fashioned woollens. But Norwich and various other places in East Anglia had built up a great trade in worsteds, or ' Norwich stuffs '. The success of these towns suggested to the aldermen of York the possibility of restoring the industrial prosperity of York by introducing the trade which had made Norwich so prosperous ; in this manufacture at least they would be free from the competition of the West Riding. In 1619, therefore, they induced Edward Whalley, a citizen of Norwich, to take up his abode in York, and there make worsteds, employing as many poor people as he possibly could. He was granted all the customary privileges, a house in which to work, a loan of money, and his freedom gratis. The

---

[1] *Victoria County History, Yorkshire*, iii. 468 et seq.

[2] York Corp. Minute Books, xxxi, f. 301 (1597). For much of this information I am indebted to Miss Sellers, either directly or through her article in the *Victoria County History*.

scheme was a failure, and in 1620, £280 having been expended
with little apparent result, the council decided that ' to erect
a new manual occupation in the city of makinge Norwiche
stuffes would be too burdensome to this citty '.[1] The worsted
project was therefore abandoned for the time being, but was
revived in the 'thirties, with a certain amount of temporary
success. A building known as the ' House of Workes ' was fitted
up with worsted-making utensils,[2] and many poor householders
were set to work under the charge of a master, who was paid
£20 per annum for his supervision and tuition. Alongside this
work the council had introduced the making of Kendal cloths,
and had provided cards and spinning-wheels for all the hospitals,
in order that the supply of yarn might be sufficient.[3]

After the Civil War similar efforts were made to coax industries to York. In 1655 the corporation signed an agreement with
two brothers, Chapman by name, who lived at Thornover, some
distance from York. By the contract[4] it was agreed that the
two men, clothiers by trade,

' shall . . . leave their habitations where they now dwell and
become Inhabitants and dwellers within the said City or Suburbs
thereof, to witt the House called comonly the Jersey House, and
accept their freedoms, and shall bring with them their familyes
and workefolkes and all their Loomes and materialls belonging
to their trade, to the house or place . . . which is intended for
their entertainment. They shall imploy their owne stocks and
such other moneys as are by these presents intended to be
given or lent to them . . . wholely for setting the poore people
of the Citty on worke, in spinning, carding and other Labours
concerning the said trade, and shall duely pay unto them for
carding and spinning of fine wool for every six pounds averdupois
weight sixteen pence, and of course wool twelve pence for every
six pounds, . . . and they are to sett up and continue four Loomes
betweene them at the least, and to make two clothes weekely at
the least, if there be vent and carding and spinning to be gott
in the Citty.'

The clothiers were to continue in the trade for at least seven
years, and during that time they were ' to bring or procure

[1] York Corp. Minute Books, xxxiv, ff. 177–8.
[2] *Victoria County History, Yorkshire*, iii. 471.
[3] York Corp. Minute Books, xxxv, f. 248.
[4] See Articles of Agreement between Mayor and Comonalty and Thomas and
Michael Chapman, both of Thornover, in the County of York, Clothiers,
April 30, 1655 ; in Muniments Room, York Guildhall.

Instructors to teach the poore to spin and card and doe other Labours belonging to the said Trade . . . at their own Charge, and the Citty not to be att any charge ' for instruction.

In return for these services the corporation undertook to give the men their freedom, presented them with a sum of £50, and lent them £100 each, free of interest, for seven years. Further, they were provided with Jersey House and some adjoining land at a nominal rent, and the corporation promised to ' find soe many spinning wheels and wool-cards as shall be thought necessary for the first yeare '.

The Chapman brothers took up their abode in York, and set to work, in accordance with the terms of the contract. But they also failed to effect a revival in the industrial fortunes of the city. Failure attended the efforts of their successors, of whom there were many. Again and again, throughout the rest of the century, clothiers, either of woollen or worsted fabrics, were engaged by the city authorities to take up the task of employing the poor.[1] Their work was small, and entirely insignificant in comparison with that which was being done in the Leeds, Wakefield, and Halifax districts and in comparison with the amount of cloth produced on the looms of York three centuries before. These municipal efforts were little more than expedients for the employment of the numerous poor who were

---

[1] The last effort of the York Corporation which has come to my notice is dated 1698. Richard Snowe of Masham, sergemaker, was invited on the usual conditions to come and supervise the textile work of the poor. The preamble to the indenture is very interesting, and worthy of a little quotation : ' WHEREAS it is very observable that the number of the poore within this Cittye dothe increase daily more and more, for want of employment and of some publick manufacture whereupon to sett them to worke, and therefore the Poore are not onely become very burdensome and chargeable to the . . . parishes where they live, but many of them for want of Employment under the motion of their Poverty do turn Vagabonds and idle wandring Beggars, and take and pursue evil courses of Life and Conv'sacon, to the utter Ruin and destruction of themselves, the great Scandall of the Citty and the evill Example of others, AND WHEREAS for the prevention of such mischiefes and Inconveniences as may in all probability happen . . . by such Encrease of the poore, it hath been considered that some publick Manufacture should be sett upp and carried on within the . . . Citty of Yorke, whereby the said poore or such of them as are able to worke may be kept in a constant employment and thereby rendered in a great measure capable to maintain themselves.' Snowe was to employ no more than four non-pauper persons, and was to pay wages ' according to the best and greatest Rates that are or may be for the time being given, allowed, or paid, in any other places within this Kingdom '. This indenture is in the Muniments Room at York ; it is impossible to give the reference number for it until the detailed catalogue of York MSS. is accessible.

on the hands of the authorities, and no industry could achieve a great success when it was practically limited to a pauper labour force.   Hence these efforts to reinvigorate an almost extinct manufacture were puny, fitful, and entirely ineffective. The merchants of York did not look to Lighe, Whalley, and the Chapman brothers for their supplies of cloth for the export trade ;   instead they went westward to the new home of the industry, to the area which is still to-day devoted to the same occupation.   How and when the manufacture of cloth assumed large proportions in this district we must now consider.

(b) The Expansion of the Woollen Industry in the West Riding

The Poll Tax Returns revealed the existence of the textile industry in almost every part of Yorkshire, though more vigorous in some areas than others.   In the central plain of the county there were more names attached to the industry than were to be found further westward, and in the Halifax and Bradford areas cloth-making did not appear as an important means of livelihood. The cloths produced in these parts were made largely for home consumption, and it is doubtful whether any considerable number of fabrics found their way into the English or foreign markets.   It now remains for us to trace the progress of the industry in that district which we regard to-day as its home, i. e. the part of Yorkshire which lies south and west of Leeds. Over this area there was in the fifteenth and sixteenth centuries a very rapid expansion, which brought the industry into a position of rivalry with East Anglia and the West of England long before the eighteenth century.

For this part of our story we have statistical evidence of an accurate character.   The Ulnager's Accounts,[1] though distributed irregularly over the period 1394 to 1478, give valuable figures of comparison as to the progress in various places.   It

---

[1] These Accounts are in the Public Record Office amongst the Exchequer MSS.   They were first examined by Mr. J. Lister, of Shibden Hall, Halifax, who very kindly lent the present writer the transcripts which he had made of some of the Accounts.   Mr. Lister's examination was not, however, exhaustive ;   further, he confined his attention almost entirely to Yorkshire. Miss M. Sellers went over the same ground in preparing her article on ' The Textile Industries ' for the *Victoria County History*, but owing to inaccurate cataloguing omitted to notice at least one important document.   The present writer has collected the figures from the Accounts for the whole country.

must be remembered, however, that only cloths made for sale passed through the hands of the ulnager. The pieces woven for home use would not be subjected to his scrutiny, and hence the ulnage figures apply solely to the cloths which were intended for the market.

The earliest returns for Yorkshire are for the years 1394-5 Mr. Lister points out the reason for this. By the Ulnage Statute of 1353 only those cloths which were equal to at least half a cloth of assize were liable to be called upon to pay subsidy. The cloth of assize measured 26 yards by 6½ quarters (i. e. 1 yard, 1 foot, 10½ inches).[1] The great majority of cloths made in the country districts of Yorkshire were narrow cloths, 'streit' cloths, kerseys, &c., which rarely exceeded 12 yards, and therefore escaped the payment of subsidy and the supervision of the ulnager. In 1393-4, however, a change in the policy of cloth regulation broke down this evasion. A law passed during that session[2] declared that any weaver might 'make and put to sale cloths, *as well kerseys as others*, of such length and breadth as him shall please, paying the subsidy, ulnage, and other duties, of every piece of cloth after the rate of the assize of cloth mentioned in the statute of Edward III', i. e. in proportion to the size of the piece. This Act made the smaller pieces liable to payment of subsidy, and the Yorkshireman now had to contribute his quota for the kerseys and 'panni stricti'. As the subsidy on a cloth of assize was fourpence, and as a kersey equalled about one quarter of a standard cloth, the levy on these shorter and narrower pieces was settled at one penny, and remained at that figure as long as the ulnage system existed.

The first *computus* or account for the whole county covers the 15½ months from July 20, 1394 to November 4, 1395[3] The return excludes the city of York, which had its own account, and paid the amounts already stated in the preceding section of this chapter. The names of the county cloth-makers, numbering

---

[1] Statute 27 Ed. III, i, c. 4. See J. Lister, 'Notes on early History of the Woollen Trade in Bradford and Halifax', *Bradford Antiquary*, ii. 33-50.

[2] 17 Rich. II, c. 2.

[3] Particulars of the Account of Wm. Skipwith, collector of ulnage and subsidy of saleable cloths, and of the forfeitures of the same, in the County of York, the City of York excepted, to wit, from the 20th day of July in the 18th year to the 4th day of November in the 19th year of Richard II (Exch. K.R. Accounts, bundle 345, no. 15).

357, are drawn from all parts of the shire. The local grouping
of the contributors is vague, and the only possible classification
is under marginal headings, which give the following approximate distribution :

Amount of subsidy.

	£	s.	d.
Ripon and Boroughbridge (grouped together) . .	7	5	0
Richmond, Bedale, and Allerton (grouped together) .	5	10	0
Wakefield, Leeds, and Doncaster (grouped together).	4	5	0
Pontefract, Howden, and Selby (grouped together) .	3	9	0
Malton (standing alone)	0	10	0

The figures placed against these groups give approximately
the amount of subsidy paid in each area, but as the districts are
so vaguely defined the returns only serve to show that the most
active areas were around Ripon or in the centre of the county.
The cloths were divided into two classes :

(*a*) 'Panni stricti', or narrow cloths, of which there were
221 pieces. Each of these was reckoned as being equal to one
quarter of a cloth of assize, and therefore paid one penny,
producing in all 18*s*. 5*d*.

(*b*) Cloths of assize, which amounted to 1,202 whole pieces
and 9 yards. On these the subsidy, at fourpence per cloth,
amounted to £20 0*s*. 10*d*. Thus the total subsidy for the Riding
equalled £20 19*s*. 3*d*. for 1,257¾ cloths. These figures are for
15½ months, but, reducing them to a twelve months' basis, the
returns for one year are as follows :

Number of cloths	974
Subsidy	£16 4*s*. 8*d*.

The account ends with a list of the offences committed against
the ulnage regulations. No cloth was to be exposed for sale
until it had been examined and sealed and the dues paid ; the
penalty for infringement of this rule was forfeiture of the cloth,
and one or two men were punished in this year for a violation
of the law.

The next account, from November 4, 1395 to November 20,
1396 (i. e. 54 weeks), is much more illuminating, for now the
West Riding had been placed under the supervision of William
Barker of Tadcaster,[1] whose duty it was to gather in the revenue

[1] Account of Wm. Barker for year November 1395 to November 1396
(Exch. K.R. Accounts, bundle 345, no. 17).

from this Riding alone. Hence the details are much more copious, and local classification is more accurate. The rivalry for first place in the quantity of cloth produced lies between Wakefield and Ripon. Seven names appear under the heading of Wakefield as paying subsidy for $173\frac{1}{2}$ cloths of assize. At Ripon nine men are named as being responsible for the production of $168\frac{3}{4}$ cloths ; thus Wakefield has more cloths to its credit, and pays a greater contribution to the Exchequer, than Ripon.

But this triumph is heavily discounted when we consider the extent of country covered by the term ' Wakefield '.[1] The only other town named in this area is Leeds, which had four men accounting for 120 cloths. This meant therefore that the two headings of Leeds and Wakefield included the whole district containing Bradford, Halifax, and Huddersfield ; in fact, the whole of the county to-day engaged in the manufacture of woollen cloth. Under such circumstances it was only natural that Wakefield and Leeds should make a brave show against their more northerly rival.

The other centres mentioned are responsible for much smaller quantities of cloth, and the whole list reads as follows :

	Names.	Cloths.	Subsidy.
Wakfeld . . .	7	$173\frac{1}{2}$	57/10
Rypon . . .	10	$168\frac{1}{2}$ & 8 yds.	$56/3\frac{1}{2}$
Ledys . . .	4	120	40/-
Pountfrett . . .	14	$105\frac{3}{4}$	35/3
Wethyrby . . .	6	$35\frac{1}{2}$	11/10
Doncastre . . .	9	27	9/-
Barnsley . . .	6	26 & 6 yds.	8/9
Selby . . .	4	$22\frac{1}{2}$	7/6
Skipton . . .	6	21 & 7 yds.	$7/1\frac{1}{4}$
Rodirham . . .	5	18	6/-

The total number of whole cloths on which payments were made was thus $718\frac{1}{2}$ plus 3 yards made by 71 master weavers, and the total subsidy £11 19s. $6\frac{3}{4}d$.

In the following year we have an account for November 20, 1396 to November 21, 1397 [2] which shows a great decline in the quantity of cloth produced and the amount of subsidy paid.

[1] Wakefield and Leeds eventually split up into Halifax, Bradford, Almondbury, and Leeds. See later accounts.
[2] Exch. K.R. Accounts, bundle 345, no. 18.

Only 474 whole cloths were accounted for, paying a subsidy of £7 18s. In these last two accounts we have returns stretching from November 4, 1395 to November 21, 1397, a period of just over two years. During that time subsidy was paid on 1,192½ cloths, or an average annual output for the West Riding of approximately 590 whole cloths of assize. Not by any means a large quantity, but yet one must remember that there was much manufacture for home consumption, and also that a whole cloth of assize might, and did often, mean two or four smaller pieces. Further, this average is admittedly unsatisfactory, since it is based on a calculation from two years, in which the output differed very considerably. But we have no other figures from which it is possible to obtain a more accurate estimate, and so we must be content with the facts as we have them, surmising in the light of the 1395-6 figures that 590 cloths is probably somewhat below the usual annual output.

In these early accounts we find mention of a surprising variety of cloths and colours. There were ' panni stricti ', ' panni de blankett ', ' panni de Cagsall ' (Coggeshall), russets, ' Panni blodii ' (blue), greens, ' blewe melde ', &c. Scarlet cloths were scarcely produced at all in the county, this manufacture being left to other parts of England. Thus, although the cloths were coarse and the processes were probably primitive, there was a certain amount of variety in the products of the West Riding looms.

From 1398 onwards until 1468 there is an unbroken absence of ulnage accounts for the county. This is probably due to the fact that the ulnage was ' farmed out ' to some person, who paid a fixed annual sum to the Exchequer and then appropriated to himself the whole of the contributions, realizing profit or loss according to the progress or stagnation of the industry. What was happening during that period of transition we would give much to know, and the next list of ulnage returns raises so many questions that the lack of accounts is doubly disappointing. Still, in spite of the absence of financial records, one can easily see from local documents that the textile industry of the West Riding was becoming more and more important, and that weavers, dyers, fullers, and other cloth-workers, or dealers, were developing the industry all through the period of Yorkist and Lancastrian strife.[1] The absence of the names of Bradford and Halifax from the early ulnage lists may possibly indicate that the industry in those places was not of great dimensions in the reign of Richard II ; or it may be due to the fact that the deputies appointed by the ulnager to collect the money throughout the Riding had their head-quarters at Wakefield and Leeds, and therefore grouped all the contributions under the names of these two towns instead of giving Bradford and Halifax credit for the cloths which were produced there. Whatever the reason, there must have been great progress during the first half of the fifteenth century in order to explain the situation as revealed in the returns for 1468. In 1439 Halifax had its dyer, fuller, glover, and drapers, and in 1467 eight men of Halifax were engaged in the work of fulling cloth. From lack of data it is dangerous to attempt any explanation of this progress. It may have been due to a migration from the city, or merely an acceleration in the rate of progress amongst the natives of the western parts of the Riding, who were favoured by the lower cost of production and the general facilities which these districts enjoyed.

It is indeed a great transformation which meets the eye in the next ulnager's statement. The account is for the period November 12, 1468, to Michaelmas, 1469, i. e. 46 weeks, and for the whole county, including York, Hull, Doncaster,[2] &c. The form and contents are so interesting that it may be well to quote a little of it in translation .

County of York. Particulars of the Account of Thomas Trygot, Approver of the Subsidy and Ulnage of Saleable Cloths in the County of York . . . from the xij[th] day of November in the viij[th] year of the reign of our Lord King Edward IV. to the Feast of Saint Michael next following, that is to say, for three quarters of a year and xlviij days.

City of York. Of John Clasyn, Christopher Marshall and other men of the City of York, for 1,596 cloths sealed in the aforesaid City during the aforesaid period . . . . . .   Subsidy, xxvj[li.] xij[s.] Ulnage, lxvj[s.] vij[d.]

[1] See H. Ling Roth, *Yorkshire Coiners*, article by Mr. Lister on ' The Making of Halifax '.

[2] Exch. Accounts, bundle 346, no. 22. This account has been incorrectly catalogued, and was therefore overlooked by both Mr. Lister and Miss Sellers.

Of Thomas Pykburn, Christopher ffrickley, and other men of the town of Doncaster, for 35 saleable cloths, and a half, sealed there   .   .   .   . } Subsidy, xj$^{s.}$ x$^{d.}$
Ulnage, xviij$^{d.}$

Of Richard Symmes, John Brokhole, and other men of Barnsley, for 88 saleable cloths and three quarters sealed there   .   .   .   .   .   . } Subsidy, xxix$^{s.}$ vij$^{d.}$
Ulnage, iij$^{s.}$ viij$^{d.}$ ob.

Of Miles Parker, Richard Mason, and other men of Wakefield, for 231 saleable cloths sealed there   .   .   .   . } Subsidy, lxxvij$^{s.}$
Ulnage, ix$^{s.}$ vij$^{d.}$ ob.

And so on ; the entries, arranged in order of magnitude, are as follows :

	Cloths.
York	1,596
Ripon	888
Halifax	853
Wakefield	231
Leeds	176$\frac{3}{4}$
Almondbury . . .	160
Hull	148
Pontefract	106
Barnsley	88$\frac{3}{4}$
Bradford	88$\frac{1}{2}$
Doncaster	35$\frac{1}{2}$
Selby	26$\frac{1}{2}$
Total	4,398
Subsidy and Ulnage .	£82 10s. 0$\frac{1}{4}$d.

Thus the output for the whole county for 46 weeks equalled 4,398 cloths ; this for a whole year would amount to 4,972 cloths. Of these, 1,972 pieces were accounted for by York and Hull; the figures for Beverley are presumably included in those for Hull, and cannot have been at all important. The West Riding can therefore claim 3,000 cloths. The year for which these figures are quoted seems to have been a ' boom ' year, and there was a diminution in the output during the subsequent period. According to the accounts, subsidy was paid for the West Riding as follows :

Year.	No. of cloths for West Riding.
1469–70	2,586
1471–3	1,894 (average over 2$\frac{1}{2}$ years)
1473–5	2,188 (average over 2 years)
1475–8	1,780 (average over 2$\frac{1}{2}$ years) [1]

[1] Exch. K.R., bundle 345, no. 24.

Therefore, taking the annual average production over the whole of this period, 1468–78, we get an output of 2,128 cloths. Compare this with the average output for 1396–8, viz. 590 cloths, and we see an increase of nearly 300 per cent., made largely at the expense of the county capital.

These later ulnage returns are valuable for the evidence which they afford about the comparative importance of the various districts engaged in the production of cloth. Let us first present the figures, and then point out the significant developments which they indicate.

1468–9 (46 *weeks*).		1471–3 (2½ *years*).		1473–5 (2 *years*).	
	Cloths.		*Cloths.*		*Cloths.*
York	1,596	York		York	2,346½
Ripon	888	Ripon	1,897	Halifax	1,493½
Halifax	853	Halifax	1,518½	Ripon	1,386½
Wakefield	231	Leeds	355½	Almondbury	427
Leeds	176¾	Almondbury	320	Hull	426½
Almondbury	160	Hull	295	Leeds	320
Hull	148	Barnsley	177½	Pomfret	214½
Pontefract	106	Wakefield	161	Bradford	178½
Barnsley	88¾	Bradford	125½	Wakefield	160
Bradford	88¼	Pomfret	108½	Barnsley	142½
Doncaster	35½	Doncaster	44½	Doncaster	35½
Selby	26½	Selby	26½	Selby	19

From these data we see that York still retained the leading position, although her supremacy had been much impaired, and the next hundred years were to witness a further decline in her output. In 1468 Ripon came second, but her position also was threatened by the growth of a rival. That rival was Halifax, a town not mentioned in the accounts of Richard II's reign, but now taking third place on the list. Beside these three centres, the rest were insignificant. Almondbury, representing the Huddersfield area, appeared next to Leeds, but Bradford made its entry in very humble fashion. The number of recorded places lying south-west of Leeds is large, and the output from this area equalled that of York itself.

In the list for 1471–3 Halifax still had to be content with the third place; Leeds and Almondbury passed Wakefield, and Bradford crept up one place. Finally in the third list, for 1473–5, Halifax outstripped its more northerly rival, and assumed second place; Almondbury and Hull overtopped Leeds, whilst Bradford advanced to the eighth place. These positions remained the same in the returns for the following years, 1475–8, when the accounts come to an end.

The outstanding feature of these statistics is the triumph of the Halifax clothiers.   From a position so humble as not to merit the inclusion of its name in the early accounts, Halifax had risen to a position of supremacy in the western industry, and outdistanced all but York itself.   Whilst noting this success, we must remember that the size of the parish of Halifax, for which these returns really are, was very great, embracing a wide area of hilly country.   Much of it had been entered in the fourteenth-century accounts under the names of Leeds and Wakefield, and so had helped to swell the total from these places, whilst leaving the real home of the pieces without recognition. Still, even admitting that the figures are not so wonderful as they would appear at first sight, it remains beyond dispute that over the area lying round Halifax there was a marked quickening of industrial life during the fifteenth century.   Nor was the progress stayed during subsequent years.   Halifax wares became known throughout the country.   They were sold at the cloth fairs at St. Bartholomew[1] and the market in Blackwell Hall, London ;   the stock-in-trade of a York tailor in 1485 contained lengths ' de pannis laneis Halyfax et Crawyn ', and many other cloths from the West of Yorkshire, including ' Halyfax tawny ', ' Halyfax grene ', ' Halyfax russet ', ' niger carsey Halyfax ',[2] &c. In 1560 there were 520 houses in the town of Halifax alone, and the whole parish was declared to be so populous that it sent 12,000 men against the Duke of Westmoreland's rising in 1569.[3]

This progress was the subject of comment by many writers during the sixteenth century, and was probably the cause of the legend, accepted by all historians until quite recently, that the population of Halifax township in 1450 was so small as to be accommodated in 13 houses.[4]   Such a statement was entirely untrue, but it was part of the glamour of romance which hovered round the head of Halifax.   Tudor writers waxed eloquent in

---

[1] Cloth booths in Bartholomew Fair are frequently mentioned in Halifax wills. See Chapter V, on markets and merchants.

[2] *York Wills and Inventories* (Surtees Soc., vol. xlv), p. 301.

[3] Camden, *Britannia*, ff. 709–10. Also most old Halifax historians.

[4] For a criticism of the statement see ' The Making of Halifax ', by J. Lister, pp. 142–4, in Ling Roth, *Yorkshire Coiners*.

their praise of the parish, and unsolicited testimonials were frequently bestowed. Camden declared, 'There is nothing so admirable in this town as the industry of the inhabitants, who, notwithstanding an unprofitable soil, not fit to live in, have so flourished by the cloath trade (which within these last seventy years they fell to), that they are both very rich, and have gained a great reputation for it above their neighbours '.[1] Edmund, Archbishop of York, wrote in 1584 of the populace of Halifax, ' It is a good people, and they well deserve to be considered of ' ;[2] and Ryder (1588), having eulogized the Yorkshire clothiers generally, singled out for special praise the ' inhaby-tants of Hallyfax '. Their virtues were extolled as follows :

' They excel the rest in policy and industrie, for the use of their trade and groundes, and after the rude and arrogant manner of their wilde country they surpas the rest in wisdom and wealth. They despise theire olde fashions if they can heer of a new, more comodyus, rather affectinge novelties than allied to old ceremonyes. . . . Yt sholde seem that desier of praise and sweetnes of their dew commendacion hath begoon and mayn-tayned ammonge the people a natural ardency of newe inven-tions annexid to an unyealdinge industry, and by enforcinge grounds beyond all hope of fertyllyty, so that yff the rest of the county wolde in this followe them but afar off, the force and welth of Yorkshier wolde be soon dubled.'[3]

In short, the Halifax area had witnessed a period of surprising prosperity during the fifteenth and sixteenth centuries, insomuch that its development was to contemporaries a matter for awe and wonder, and to the Halifax man himself a perennial theme for jubilant self-satisfaction.

The progress of Leeds, Wakefield, and Bradford, though not so rapid, was little less important. Here the woollen industry provided employment for the greater part of the inhabitants, and the output of cloth steadily advanced. The fulling mill at Leeds, which in 1381 was let for 30s. per annum,[4] was leased in 1488 for 46s.,[5] so the profits accruing from that mill must have

---

[1] Camden, op. cit., ff. 709–10.

[2] D. S. P., Eliz., Addenda, xxviii. 85 (1584).

[3] ' James Ryder's Commendations of Yorkshire, addressed to Lord Bur-leigh ' (1588), Lansd. MSS. (Brit. Mus.), quoted in Ling Roth, op. cit., pp. 192–3.

[4] Minister's Accounts, bundle 507, no. 8228, 7 & 8 Rich. II. For this reference see Victoria County History, Yorkshire, ii. 409.

[5] Materials for a History of Henry VII (Rolls Series), ii. 329.

increased somewhat in the intervening period.   Leeds and
Wakefield were becoming famous as markets and as the homes
of merchants.   By the seventeenth century Wakefield was the
principal wool market of the district, whilst Leeds had become
the emporium for cloth.   Wakefield ' chapmen ' [1] are frequently
mentioned during the fifteenth and sixteenth centuries, and
a complaint made in the reign of James I bore witness to the
rise of a native trading class in the Riding.   The complaint
occurs in a pamphlet analysing the causes of the decay of the
trade of Hull, and the grievance is stated thus :

' And that which is a further great and considerable damage
to the merchants of this towne (Hull) is a set of young adventurers that are lately sprung up at Leeds and at other places,
amongst the clothiers, who at little or no charges buy and
engross as they please, to the great hurt of the inhabitants and
merchants of this towne.' [2]

These upstarts we shall meet again when we consider the
methods of marketing and foreign trade, but it is desirable at
this juncture to note their existence.

When Leland came through Yorkshire in the reign of
Henry VIII, he made observations on the economic activities
of the towns through which he passed.   His remarks give us
an interesting, though fleeting, glimpse of the centres of the
industry : [3]

' *Wakefeld* apon Calder, ys a quik market toune, and meately
large ;   well served of flesch and fische from the Se and by
ryvers, whereof dyvers be thereabouts at hande.   So that al
vitaile is very good chepe there.   A right honest man shal fare
well for 2 pens a meale.   It standith now al by clothyng.

' *Bradeforde*, a praty quik toune, dimideo aut eo amplius
minus Wachfelda.   It standith much by clothyng.

' *Ledis*, 2 miles lower than Christal Abbay, on Aire Ryver, is
a praty market, . . . as large as Bradeforde but not so quik.
The toune standith most by clothing.'

Other writers make similar remarks, and supply abundant
evidence to show that the whole district of which Leeds, Wakefield, Bradford, and Halifax were the head-quarters, was hard

---

[1] Thos. Peyntour of Wakefield, chapman, in debt for £4 (1486) (Patent Rolls,
4 Hen. VI, pt. i, m. 23).

[2] Pamphlet by John Ramsden, of Hull, quoted in Hadley's *History of Hull*,
p. 115.   [3] Leland, *Itinerary*, vii. 41-2.

at work developing the textile industry. Further, there was already some degree of local specialization, and certain districts were becoming famous for the manufacture of distinct types of cloth. Leeds had already settled down to making ' broad cloth ', and kept almost entirely to trade in that variety during the next two centuries. But the Halifax men, intent on paying the minimum of taxation on their wares, ' were, for their own private lucre and gain, and in diminucion of the King's subsidy and ulnage, encouraged rather to make kerseys than . . . cloths of assize ',[1] and so, as a writer declared in 1588,. ' at Halyfax there is no clothe made but yearde brode carsies '.[2]

With the ulnage returns of 1478 we come to the end of our statistics, and have no further evidence which gives anything approaching a complete estimate of the number of cloths produced in the county. Fortunately, however, there is a document, dated 1595, containing a survey of the Yorkshire industry,[3] from which it is possible to glean a few figures, and to make one or two rough comparisons. The author of this report had been sent to carry out an inquiry into the extent of the manufacture of ' new draperies ' in the county. He found scarcely any such manufacture, but placed on record an account of the extent of the older industry. Thus he found ' At Wackefeilde, Leedes, and some other smale villages, nere there aboutes, there is made about 30 packes of brode cloths every weecke, and ev'y packe is 4 whole clothes ; the sortes made in Wackefeild are pukes, tawnyes, browns, blues, and some reddes ; in Leedes of all colours '. If 120 cloths per week was the average output of these places, we may assume that the annual production was about 5,000. Compare this with the figures given in the ulnage returns ; in 1468-9 these two towns were jointly credited with 408 cloths for 46 weeks, or about 460 for the year. Even supposing the estimate for the Elizabethan period to be excessive, the expansion must have been very great.

The same writer reported that ' At Penyston, Yellow, and Blackwood, and some villages there aboutes, are made about

[1] See Chapter V for account of trials of 1613 and 1638.
[2] Document concerning project for setting up woollen concern at Skipton, in *Hist. MSS. Comm.*, app. xiv, pt. iv, Kenyon MSS., p. 573 (1588).
[3] Brother Peck's Certificate of New Draperies (1595), *D. S. P., Eliz.*, cclii, 2.

1,000 peces of white Penystone '. A ' Penistone ' counted as
half a cloth of assize, so the output from the Penistone area
would be equivalent to about 500 whole cloths. In the ulnage
accounts the Penistone area would come under the heading
of Barnsley, the annual output of which in 1468-9 amounted to
about 100 cloths. Here again the development during the
Tudor period must have been considerable.

The comparison cannot be carried farther, since the Elizabethan survey makes no estimate of the number of cloths
made in the Halifax or Bradford districts. But the witnesses
in a lawsuit of 1613 declared most confidently that the output
of kerseys alone from the parishes of Halifax, Bradford, Bingley,
and Keighley amounted to over 90,000 a year. This was almost
certainly an exaggeration, but there can be no doubt that the
industry in this area made very great strides during the Tudor
period.

The result of all this progress was to give greater strength
to the West Riding, and to draw its industrial life and wealth
more into national regard. For centuries the district had
enjoyed comparative immunity from governmental interference,
since its cloths had been such as seldom found their way to the
wider markets, or attracted national attention. Now all this
was changing, as Northern Dozens and Yorkshire kerseys,
improved perhaps in quality, were purchased by such people
as the monks of Durham,[1] or for the choristers at Cambridge,[2]
or passed to Blackwell Hall and the markets of Europe. The
entry of West Riding goods more prominently into the field of
national and international commerce turned many eyes to this
hitherto despised portion of the county, and the ' cloathing
townes ' began to receive attention from many quarters.

The first of these newly interested parties was the State itself,
which, in the sixteenth century, cast aside the air of tolerance
with which it had formerly regarded the North Country in its
regulation of the cloth industry. Now that the cheap Yorkshire
pieces were being carried in large quantities to Germany, Poland,
and Russia, they must be subjected to the same scrutiny as the

---

[1] Thorold Rogers, *Hist. of Agriculture and Prices,* iv. 106.
[2] Several entries of northern russets and other northern cloths for choristers
at Cambridge about the middle of the sixteenth century. Rogers, *op. cit.,*
iii. 508 ; prices vary from 1s. to 5s. per yard.

wares of other parts, lest by their inferior quality the fair fame
of English fabrics should be dragged in the mire, and the ' vent ',
or sale, of cloths be lost to this country.   Hence there began
a long series of legislative attempts to bring the Yorkshiremen
on to the strait path of industrial honesty, and we must give
a whole chapter to a consideration of this State intervention.[1]

Secondly, the clothing area had gained some political strength
In 1597 there was a parliamentary election, and on this occasion
one of the candidates for Yorkshire was Sir Thomas Hoby.
The following letter from the Archbishop of York to Robert
Cecil explains itself.   Speaking of Hoby, the Archbishop says
he is ' a gentleman of very great hope, but is not yet so well
known, and was hindered specially by a rumour, true or false
I know not, spread abroad in the clothing towns of the West
Riding, which yield the greatest number of freeholders.   The
speech was that in the last Parliament his brother, Sir Edward
Hoby, did prefer a bill against Northern cloths, which they
thought did much concern them '.[2]

Thirdly, the pocket of the West Riding began to receive more
attention from the State, and from others.   This was especially
the case when the need for ships, in the last decades of the
sixteenth century, caused levies of vessels to be made on the
ports of the kingdom.   The demands generally took the form
of ordering each port to supply one or more ships, fully manned,
victualled, and equipped, for a period of service at home or
abroad.[3]   The Yorkshire orders came to Hull, and in 1588 and
subsequent years York and Hull, after violent altercations as
to their respective shares, joined in defraying the cost of the
Yorkshire ships.   In the early months of 1596 Hull was requested
to furnish one ship for the expedition of that summer.   But the
port had at last awakened to the fact that an El Dorado existed
inland, and therefore made suit that the ' three great clothing
townes and places belonging thereto, viz.   Halifax and the

---

[1] Chapter IV.

[2] The clothing area was not backward in its loyalty to Elizabeth.   When
the Bond of Association was drawn up, it was received with great favour by
' the meaner sort of gentlemen and of the principall freeholders and clothiers
. . . so that, especially about Halifax, Wakefield, and Bradford, 5,300 of that
sort have sealed, subscribed, and sworn thereto' (D. S. P., Eliz., Addenda,
xxviii. 102).   Letter quoted above is in Salisbury MSS., vii. 436.

[3] The story of this Ship Money encounter is drawn from the Salisbury
MSS. (Hist. MSS. Comm.), and the Ordinances of the Privy Council.

Vicarage, Leeds, Wakefield, and their several parishes ' should be compelled to share in the cost of the vessel. In a letter to Robert Cecil Hull explained the reason for making this request. ' They (the clothing towns) are many ways relieved by this port, by the uttering their cloth to a great proportion, and so have their oils, wood, alum, &c., and like helps for their trade brought in by the shipping of this place, . . . and consequently divers of them are not only clothiers, but merchants also, to the great hindrance of the merchants here and at York.' [1] An order was at once granted in accordance with Hull's request, and the ' cloathing townes ' were told of their liabilities. But with an astuteness typical of the Riding the clothiers refused entirely to stir a finger towards collecting the £400 demanded of them. They declared that they belonged to inland towns bordering on no river nor haven, ' nor having any vent of any comodity by the Porte of Hulle '.[2] The Privy Council, with obliging credulity, believed this statement, and the petitioners were graciously ' excused from any payment whatsoever '.[3]

This was in the spring of the year. Autumn came round, and with it the expedition returned, presenting to Hull a bill for £1,400. Again the port sent its lamentation to the Privy Council, and again the levy was imposed upon the West Riding.[4] Letters, petitions, commands, all were showered on the heads of the clothiers, who, led by Sir John Savill and other justices of the peace, took up a firm attitude of refusal to pay. The Privy Council hurled its thunderbolts, the Council of the North joined in with some forcible utterances, and the Archbishop of York made attempts at peaceful persuasion. For over a year these commands and entreaties were sent to the obstinate towns, but Savill and his followers calmly ignored the efforts of Archbishop and Council. On October 30, 1597, the Privy Council fulminated once more. ' We have many times heretofore written our letters for the contribution to be made by the clothynge townes in the West Rydynge of Yorkshire ', and the constant neglect on the part of the local justices 'shows an evident note of slack-nesse '.[5] Still the money was not forthcoming, and at last, in

---

[1] Salisbury MSS., vi. 58–9.
[2] Privy Council Ordinances, March 28, 1596, petition from Yorkshire.
[3] Ibid., April 1, 1596.   [4] Salisbury MSS., vi. 356, August 30, 1596.
[5] Ordinances of Privy Council, October 30, 1597.

February 1598, patience being exhausted, the Privy Council summoned four of the local magistrates to London to explain their passive resistance.[1]   Savill was especially reprimanded. ' You have not only refused to shewe your duties in contrybut-ynge to so necessarie and honorable a service, but have eluded our earnest direction by dillatory, frivolus and framed excuses.' Full of contrition, the quartet faced the Council, and were informed that now ' the money must be gathered of the clothiers and other chapmen, as of the welthier sort of the inhabitants of that Rydinge. . . . If there be any slacknesse, you must come along hether, and make up for your defaultes '.   At last the clothiers were driven to surrender, and in the next Quarter Sessions at Pontefract an assessment was made ' for the con-tribucon of fower hundreth poundes to be made by the clothiers and inhabitauntes of the Westridynge '.[2]

Though defeated at this encounter, the clothiers met every subsequent demand with similar silent obstinacy.   Thus, in 1626, when Hull was ordered to provide two ships, it had to go through a repetition of the former struggle, and eventually wrote to the Privy Council, ' Wee have sent sondrie tymes to them of Hallyfaxe, Leedes, and Wakefield, for their proportion-able assistance . . . and yet we have received no monies, neither from them nor from the countie '.[3]   In all this affair, it is im-portant to note the attitude of the justices of the peace.   They were evidently on the best of terms with the people around them, knew their needs and possibilities, and were prepared to stand up, even against the decrees of the central authority, in defence of their fellows.   This spirit would mean much when the regulation of industry was placed by law in the hands of the local magistracy.   The success of any Act would depend on whether or not the magistrates of the locality thought its enforce-ment would conduce to the welfare of the surrounding population. This must be kept in mind when examining the attempts made by the State to supervise the textile industry in the county.   The justices of the peace were the champions of local freedom in the matter of the Ship Money ; they would be equally the friend of the clothier against the demands of a new and oppressive cloth law.

[1] Ibid., April 14, 1598.
[2] West Riding Sessions Rolls, 1598 : Pontefract.   Yorks. Arch. Soc., Record Series, vol. iii.   [3] D. S. P., Chas. I, dxxv. 13, October 30, 1626.

Thus, to draw this chapter to a close, the West Riding cloth field of Elizabeth's reign had attained a position of importance, and was being recognized as one of the centres of general supply. Essex might boast its bays and serges, Norwich its fustians and worsteds, Devonshire its kerseys,[1] but the cloths of Kendal, the ' cottons ' of Manchester, and the Northern Dozens, kerseys, and broad cloths of Yorkshire were becoming famed at home and abroad, and the West Riding had already laid the foundations of its reputation as the provider of cheap cloths to the poorer classes of the whole world.

APPENDIX

THE DISTRIBUTION OF THE ENGLISH WOOLLEN INDUSTRY IN THE FIFTEENTH CENTURY

Ulnage Returns [2] are available for almost every county in England, and supply a mass of data showing the relative production of woollen cloth in various parts of the country. Unfortunately, we cannot be certain that the figures submitted by the ulnager's representatives are exhaustive. The subsidy may have been collected less thoroughly in some counties than others : judicious bribes may have secured exemption for some clothiers : the collector may have forwarded under-statements, and kept for himself a part of the revenue : and finally there may have been official exemptions from payment in some cases. On the other hand, these conditions might exist in all counties, or different conditions in different counties might to some extent produce a similar margin of error. On the whole, the returns are useful in affording a rough general comparison of the production for sale in the various areas, and it will be seen that some interesting conclusions can be reached.

Figures are obtainable for most counties for some part of the period 1468–78. For Northumberland and Hertford the latest returns are of a much earlier date, but with these two exceptions the following list is drawn from accounts dated between 1468 and 1473. An average annual output would have been preferable to a figure for some particular year, but the returns are not sufficiently full to allow the calculation of an average over the ten years following 1468. Further, in one or two instances the return actually made was for a period shorter or longer than one year. In such cases, the amount has been increased or reduced

---

[1] Fuller, *The Church History of Britain*, 1655 ed., p. 141.
[2] The Accounts are under the Record Office reference, Exch. K.R. Accounts, bundles 339–46.

to a twelve-months' basis. Such a step is open to the objection that the production was not uniform all the year round, winter being a bad period for drying and finishing cloths. Hence an account of nine months' production might include the busy season, and a fifteen-months' figure might include two busy seasons; calculations based on these figures might, therefore, over-estimate the annual production. Happily, this calculation was only necessary in the case of one or two of the smaller counties, and does not therefore produce any great error. In the case of Oxfordshire and Cornwall there is no separate figure, as the returns are attached to those of adjacent counties; but from almost contemporaneous returns it is possible to estimate the approximate output in these two counties. Subject to these limitations, the production of woollen cloths for sale about 1470 can be stated as follows :

County.	Year.	Number of Cloths.	
Bedford	1468–9	69	
Berkshire	,,	1,293½	
Bucks.	,,	68	
Cambridge	1469–70	41	
Cornwall	1472–3 (approx.)	30	
Derby	1469–70	40	
Devon	1472–3	1,036½	
Dorset	1467–8	707½	
Essex	1468–9	2,627½	
Gloucester, Co. of	,,	1,288	} Total = 4,874½
Bristol	,,	3,586½	
Hants	1471–2	1,450½	
Hereford	1469–70	339½	
Hertford	1447–8	249½	
Hunts.	1471–2	30	
Kent	1469–70	1,027	
Leicestershire	,,	66	
Lincolnshire	1472–3	286	
London and Middlesex	1469–70	983	
Norfolk (County)	,,	273	} Total = 830
Norwich, City of	1468–9	557	
Northants.	1472–3	780½	
Notts.	1469–70	69	
Northumberland	1441–2	120	
Oxfordshire	1468–9 (approx.)	200	
Rutland	1472–3	10	
Shropshire	1468–9	110	
Somerset	,,	4,981½	
Suffolk	,,	5,188	
Staffs.	,,	108½	
Surrey and Sussex	1469–70	769	
Warwickshire	,,	1,200	
Wilts.	,,	4,310	
Worcestershire	1468–9	477½	
York, Co. and City	,,	4,972	
	Total	39,345	

The counties for which no returns were made are Cumberland, Durham, Westmoreland, Lancashire, and Cheshire, i. e. those parts which manufactured only for domestic consumption, or which were still exempt from subsidy on account of the low value and coarse quality of their wares. All the counties of the southern, western, and midland areas produced saleable cloths, but in nine counties (Bedford, Bucks., Cambridge, Derby, Hunts., Leics., Notts., Cornwall, and Rutland) the annual output was less than 100 cloths. In three others (Northumberland, Shropshire, and Staffordshire) it was between 100 and 200, and in five others (Hereford, Lincolnshire, Herts., Worcestershire, and Oxford) it was between 200 and 500. A glance at the accompanying map reveals the significance of these facts, and points to the following conclusions :

1. The northern counties, excluding Yorkshire and Northumberland (which really meant Newcastle), were of no importance in the cloth market or in the eyes of the Exchequer.

2. Two midland blocks of counties, (a) Derby, Notts., Leics., and Rutland, (b) Cambridge, Hunts., Beds., and Bucks., separated by Northants., produced less than two cloths per week per county; in four counties (Cambridge, Derby, Hunts., and Rutland), less than one cloth was produced each week, and the whole eight counties together made less than eight cloths weekly.

3. With the exception of Warwickshire (where Coventry was responsible for seven-eighths of the production), Northamptonshire (where the county town produced $765\frac{1}{2}$ cloths out of a total of $780\frac{1}{2}$), and Yorkshire, the annual output was less than 500 cloths per annum in all the counties north and west of a line drawn from the southern part of Hereford to the south-eastern corner of Hertford, and thence up to the Wash.

Producing 500 to 1,000 cloths we find Dorset, Middlesex (including London), Norfolk (including Norwich), Northamptonshire, Surrey, and Sussex. The production in Middlesex had been higher earlier in the reign of Edward IV,[1] but experienced a heavy fall during subsequent years, and the average output in the reign of Henry VIII was only 856 cloths. Norfolk and the city of Norwich were evidently not great producers of woollen cloths. Possibly the worsted industry was by this time engaging the greater attention, and worsted cloths did not pay subsidy. But all the figures for Norfolk show that this county was quite a secondary field of woollen production. More pieces were made in Northampton than in Norwich. Surrey and Sussex together produced less than 1,000 cloths, but there is no evidence to show the output from each county.

[1] Production for Middlesex, 1463–4, 1,377 ; 1466–7, 1,711 (Exch. K.R., bundle 346, no. 20).

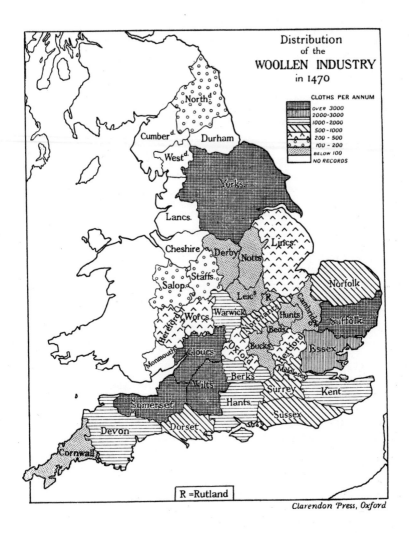

Distribution
of the
WOOLLEN INDUSTRY
in 1470

CLOTHS PER ANNUM

OVER 3000
2000-3000
1000-2000
500-1000
200 - 500
100 - 200
BELOW 100
NO RECORDS

R =Rutland

Clarendon Press, Oxford

Of the larger producers, eleven counties were responsible for over 1,000 cloths each. Of these, five made between 1,000 and 2,000 (Berks., Devon, Hants., Kent, and Warwick), Essex made over 2,000, four counties (Somerset, Yorks., Gloucester, and Wilts.) over 4,000, and Suffolk alone over 5,000. These five chief counties stood in order of production as follows :

Suffolk	.	.	.	5,188
Somerset	.	.	.	4,981½
Yorks.	.	.	.	4,972
Gloucs.	.	.	.	4,874½
Wilts.	.	.	.	4,310
	Total	.		24,326

Thus 62 per cent. of the total production of the country came from five counties : 12½ per cent. from Yorkshire alone.

The above figures and the accompanying map show that the West of England counties comprised the chief textile area. Gloucestershire, Wiltshire, and Somerset made 14,166 cloths (i. e. 36 per cent. of the total output), and if to this we add the yield of the adjacent counties, Oxford, Berkshire, Hants, Dorset, Devon, and Cornwall, the total for the nine counties is 18,884 cloths, i. e. 48 per cent. of the country's production.

The East Anglian area came second, though Suffolk was the largest producer in England. Norfolk, Suffolk, Essex, Hertford, and Middlesex together made 9,878 cloths, i. e. about 25 per cent. of the total production.

To sum up, two main conclusions are apparent from the above data :

1. That by 1470 the textile industry was largely concentrated in three chief areas (the West of England, East Anglia, and Yorkshire) and one smaller area (Warwick and Northamptonshire). The West of England counties were the largest producers, whilst in the northern counties (Yorkshire excepted) and Midlands (Warwick and Northamptonshire excepted) production was negligible.

2. That Yorkshire ranked third amongst the textile counties. The adjoining counties were of little or no importance, and hence as a clothing area the North of England was less important than its southern and western rivals. As generations went by, the Yorkshire production increased, until by the eighteenth century Yorkshire alone produced as much as either of the other two areas.

CHAPTER III

ORGANIZATION OF THE WEST RIDING INDUSTRY IN THE FIFTEENTH TO SEVENTEENTH CENTURIES

(a) *The Clothier and the Domestic System*

HAVING traced the growing importance of the extra-urban manufacture and the decline of the textile gilds, we can now turn to an examination of the economic structure of the woollen industry under the changed conditions. This leads us to a study of what has become known as the domestic system, with the clothier as the economic unit. The term ' domestic system ' is admittedly unsatisfactory, for it emphasizes only one fact, namely that manufacture was carried on in the home, in contrast to the factory system which came afterwards. As such, the term might be applied equally to that stage in industrial evolution which we label the gild system. The suggested alternative, ' commission system ', is open to criticism, and it seems impossible to invent a really adequate title to describe, in a couple of words, the distinctive characteristics of the industrial society which came between the gild and the factory. Confining our attention to the textile industry, we might use the phrase ' clothier system ', but usage has established the claims of the older term. Let us therefore retain the name ' domestic system ', understanding thereby that state of industrial life in which the clothiers controlled the trade, with industry established in the cottages scattered throughout the length and breadth of the county.

The domestic system did not hold all the field, for a small amount of manufacturing was carried on under factory conditions. The expansion of the industry in the fifteenth and sixteenth centuries had brought into existence a number of big producers, who in some cases gathered their many employees under one roof, and established a factory. Of the existence of the mill-owner (to use a modern term) there is conclusive evidence, but very little descriptive data. Jack of Newbury in the South had his counterparts in the North in the persons of

Hodgkins of Halifax, Byram (or Brian) of Manchester, and Cuthbert of Kendal.[1] These men are said to have been factory owners, though we know little of them except their names. But their existence shows that the economies of the division of labour and of direct supervision were becoming recognized, and the passage of the anti-factory Act of 1555[2] indicates that the trend towards factory organization was becoming sufficiently marked to merit national attention. But that Act did not apply to the North Country, the inhabitants of which area were left free to congregate looms as much as they pleased; and yet we do not find there any flood of factory organization. The reasons for the comparative rarity of the factory, especially in the North, are probably to be found in the following three factors. (1) The anti-capitalistic spirit of the age, so far as industry was concerned, expressed in the Act of 1555. (2) The absence of large sums of capital available for industry. This would be the case especially in Yorkshire, where the clothiers were comparatively poor, and where such capital as was available went into commerce. (3) The primitive nature of the cloth-making apparatus and processes. The utmost that a factory could do was to gather together a number of spinning-wheels, hand-looms, dye-vats, shearing-boards, &c. A factory so equipped would allow supervision more effectively to regulate the hours of labour, prevent idleness among the employees, and maintain uniform standards of production; above all, the concentration of employees on one spot prevented that waste of time which occurred when wool had to be carried a distance between each process. These advantages might have been sufficient to cause an adoption of factory production; but against them must be placed the initial cost of erecting a big building, providing homes for workpeople, and other preliminary charges, too heavy for a person not possessed of large sums of capital. The production of a ' Northern Dozen ' occupied fifteen persons for one week, so a factory would have to be large enough to hold a great number of workers to produce say half a score of such cloths weekly. In a few cases wealthy clothiers acquired deserted monasteries at a low price, and were thus provided

---

[1] Cooke Taylor, *Factory System*, early chapters, and De Gibbins, *Industrial History of England*, p. 66. [2] Statute 2 & 3 Philip and Mary, c. 11.

with a big building ready-made;[1] but, with the exception of such instances, the initial costs made the factory impracticable. Further, the Tudor factory could offer no advantages in the way of power or accelerated technical processes. In these circumstances, the balance between advantage and disadvantage was very slight, and the line of least resistance was to allow employees to remain scattered. Until the eighteenth century, therefore, the cottage was the centre of industry and the factory a rarity, treated by travelling authors as a curio so strange as to merit description along with the Strid at Bolton, the Dropping Well at Knaresborough, or the cloth market on Leeds Bridge.

We turn therefore to the predominant figure in English economic life, the clothier. Let us first define the word. According to the Statute of Artificers and Apprentices, 1563, the clothier was the person who 'put cloth to making and sale';[2] and the documents of a lawsuit in 1613 described four Yorkshiremen as ' clothiers, or persons that do trade and sell Yorkshire kersies '.[3] The ' clothyear ' (to give the spelling as it appears in some Yorkshire Tudor wills) was the person responsible for the production of cloths. He provided the necessary capital, purchased the raw material, saw it through the various processes, and then marketed the piece. He was the master, the employer, the ' head of the firm '. But the ' firm ' might be of any size, from the family unit upwards, and the exact character of the clothier's functions varied according to the size of his concern. If he employed only his own family and one or two outsiders, his own share of the work would of necessity be industrial as well as commercial: he was wool-buyer, weaver, and cloth-seller. If the scale of operations was large, with numbers of spinners, weavers, &c., employed, the clothier would not engage in any industrial processes himself, but confine his attention to buying the raw material, employing people to work it up, and selling the cloth. His employees might work entirely under his roof, in which case he would exercise a general supervision over their work. Sometimes a part would work in the clothier's establishment, the remainder in their own homes, but in very

---

[1] e.g. Malmesbury Abbey was so used after the Dissolution. See Ashley, *Economic Organization of England*, p. 150. It seems very probable that many factories had their origin in this way.   [2] 5 Eliz., c. 4.
[3] See Chapter VI for details of this lawsuit.

many instances all the work was done in the employees' cottages, in which case the clothier, stationed in his warehouse, would control the distribution of raw material and the payment of wages when the work was returned. Thus the way in which the clothier spent his time depended largely on the extent of his output, and that difference between the character of the Yorkshire and West of England clothiers so frequently commented upon by economic historians was entirely due to this difference in the scale of operations. It was a matter of degree rather than of kind.[1] The almost purely commercial activity of the Wiltshire clothiers was part of the division of labour which becomes possible with large-scale production. Wherever Yorkshire clothiers in the Tudor and Stuart periods attained any great heights of prosperity and large output, they became very much akin to their fellows in the West, commercial rather than industrial. But whilst the big man apparently predominated in Somerset and Wiltshire, ' meaner clothiers ' formed the greater part of the Yorkshire industrial army. This latter fact was responsible for those features which characterized the Yorkshire manufacture until the coming of steam-power and the factory, the chief of which were as follows :

(1) Industrial labour on the part of the clothier and his family was the general lot, and was accompanied in many cases by comparative poverty. The typical clothier of the south-western counties, working on a large scale, had become wealthy, and according to a pamphlet by May [2] (1613) increased in fame and riches, his house like a king's court, his table replenished with feasts, his hospitality bountiful, and with such plenty and content on every side that crowned heads were highly pleased with the entertainment received at his hands. The family of such a clothier would scarcely condescend to engage in textile work, or have industrial implements in the house. Hence there must have been a marked contrast between the condition of the clothiers' houses and families in the two areas.

(2) The small extent to which capitalism had developed in

---

[1] The report of the Parliamentary Committee of 1806 has created the impression that the differences between the industrial organization in Yorkshire and the West of England were fundamental. This was not so.

[2] May, ' A Declaration of the Estate of Clothing now used within this Realm ', Brit. Mus., 712. g. 16 (1).

the Yorkshire industry had as its counterpart a very slight cleavage between capital and labour, and a freedom from such serious labour disputes as marked the other textile areas.

(3) The inability of the small clothier to buy large quantities of wool made necessary the rise of middlemen whose business it was to provide the West Riding masters with wool according to their needs, both as to quantity and quality. (See last section of this chapter.)

(4) As the smaller men must sell their wares without delay, and were unable to take them to London or the Continent, numerous local weekly markets were necessary, with an army of factors and merchants acting as a medium between the small independent producers and the wider English and European market.

Throughout Yorkshire wills, from the fifteenth century onwards,[1] we encounter the last testaments of clothiers in all parts of the West Riding. The nature of these clothiers varied with the man and the district and there was an unbroken gradation from the ' meaner ' up to the wealthy. One feature was common to all, namely the alliance between farming and industry. Even the busiest clothier had his plot of land, and some part of his sustenance was drawn from that source. The word ' yeoman ' was often only an *alias* for ' clothier ', and it was by the joint produce of the land and the loom that the Yorkshireman found his livelihood secured.

The most numerous section of the Yorkshire textile community was that of the smallest clothiers, who were to be found all over the Riding, but especially concentrated in the Halifax area, where they seem to have constituted the greater part of the population. We first make the acquaintance of these men in the Ulnage Returns for the reign of Richard II, when the West Riding contained none but small producers. In the Account for 1396–7, Emma Earle was the largest contributor of -ulnage, being responsible for 48 whole cloths of assize in 54 weeks. If, as was probably the case, each cloth really meant two ' Dozens ', the leading clothier of Wakefield produced $1\frac{3}{4}$ ' Dozens ' in a week. The average for the whole of Wakefield

---

[1] See volumes of wills published by Surtees, Yorkshire Archaeological, Thoresby, Bradford Antiquarian, and other similar societies. For detailed references, see Bibliography.

was less than one ' Dozen ' per clothier per week. In Leeds the average weekly output of each of the four clothiers mentioned in the Account was just over one ' Dozen '; in Ripon it was one-third of a whole cloth of assize, and for the whole Riding the production amounted to about ten whole cloths per clothier per annum. By the sixteenth century many bigger producers had appeared, and the weekly output of the smallest men was now, as a rule, one kersey.

The best description of the small clothier class is found in the preamble to the ' Halifax Act ' of 1555.[1] Doubtless, as in most preambles, there is hyperbole in the praises, both moral and material, but apart from this glossing the description is accurate.

' Forasmuche as the Paryshe of Halyfaxe and other places theronto adjoyning, beyng planted in the grete waste and moores, where the Fertilite of Grounde ys not apte to bryng forthe any Corne nor good Grasse, but in rare Places, and by exceedinge and greate industrye of the inhabitantes, and the same inhabitantes altogether doo lyve by clothe making, for the greate parte of them neyther gettethe Corne nor ys hable to keepe a Horse to carry Woolles, nor yet to bye much woolle att once, but hathe ever used onelie to repayre to the Towne of Halyfaxe, and some other nigh theronto, and ther to bye upon the Woolldryver, some a stone, some twoo, and some three or foure accordinge to theyre habilitee, and to carrye the same to theire houses, some iij, iiij, v, and vj myles of, upon their Headdes and Backes, and so to make and converte the same eyther into Yarne or Clothe, and to sell the same, and so to bye more Woolle of the Wooll-dryver, by meanes of whiche Industrye the barreyn Gronde in those partes be nowe muche inhabyted, and above fyve hundrethe householdes there newly increased within theis fourtye yeares past.'

In view of these local conditions the district was granted special permission to purchase its wool through middlemen (wooldrivers), whilst the rest of the country was forbidden to do so.[2] Similar pictures were painted by witnesses in the clothiers' lawsuits of the following century ; many spoke of the parish of Halifax, with its ' very mounteynous and barreyn soyle ', and its poor people, ' who, making every week a coarse kersey, and being compelled to sell the same at the week end,

---

[1] 2 & 3 Philip and Mary, c. 13.
[2] See last section of present chapter.

and with the money received for the same to provide bothe stuffe wherewith to make another the week following, and also victualls to susteyne themselves and their families till another be made and sold ', supported themselves only by dint of frugal living and ceaseless toil.[1]   Such clothiers were not peculiar to Halifax, but formed the lower grade of independent workers throughout the Riding.   It must have been a hand-to-mouth existence for such men.   Unable to make long journeys into the wool-producing areas, they bought their wool from dealers or wool-staplers, made it up into yarn or cloth, and then sold the yarn to weavers or the rough unfinished piece to merchants or agents.   Thus they trod the weekly round of production and sale ; profits were small, but the men were independent, and that was probably worth a great deal.   They leased or owned a cottage, with a toft of ground adjoining, on which they fed a little live stock.   They had their loom, spinning-wheels, a set of ' walker sheres ', and often a dye-vat or ' lead '.   Employing their own family, and occasionally one or two outsiders, they produced one piece weekly, and so were able to jog along more or less contentedly, provided no new burden was imposed on them in the way of a levy for Ship Money or an increase in the subsidy on their kerseys.   One gets an interesting glimpse of the family life of such men from such wills as the following, wherein Robert Sydall, clothier, of Holbeck, makes the following bequest : ' To Elizabeth, my wife, such vessels and furniture as belongeth to her brewinge, and all that stock of money which she haith gotten by her bakinge and brewinge.'   Sydall also shares out certain lands which he holds on lease, and to his wife and children leaves ' one fatt cowe, and the fletches of a little swyne that is already kill'd '.[2]   Evidently the live stock kept on the plots of land did much to provide meat and milk, whilst the earnings of the wife's spare hours had been laid aside for a rainy day.

One reason for the existence of this large class of meaner clothiers is probably to be found in the fact that the kersey was the staple cloth manufactured, especially around Halifax. According to a document of 1588, *six* persons would be occupied

[1] Depositions of witnesses in Metcalfe case of 14 Chas. I.   See account in Chapter VI.   [2] Thoresby Soc. publications, vol. i, p. 384.

for a week at sorting, carding, spinning, weaving, and shearing, in order to produce one finished but undyed kersey.[1] The wool-driver, by selling sorted wool, freed the small clothier from the first of the above-enumerated processes : most kerseys were sold without being sheared : fulling and possibly tentering would be done by the fuller. Hence the small clothier, assisted by *four* workers, would be able to carry through the carding, spinning, and weaving of a kersey in a week. The four assistants might all be members of the clothier's family, especially as children were inured to work at a very tender age : but should the family supply of labour be inadequate, an apprentice was taken, or one or two women were hired to assist in spinning. Thus there was a distinct connexion between the labour supply required to make one kersey a week and the normal size of the clothier's establishment. Further, it seems certain that there existed a small class of independent men who were weavers only.[2] The preamble of the Halifax Act states that some of the small clothiers only went so far as to work the wool up into yarn, and then sold it. At the same time the Yorkshire wills reveal the existence of independent weavers, who probably purchased the yarn from the yarn-makers, and simply carried out the weaving processes.

From the poorer clothiers there was a gradual rise to their more wealthy neighbours, who engaged in a little farming as a by-occupation, but whose chief interest lay in the production of cloth in larger quantities. These men, who were to be found especially in the villages near Leeds, lived in a state of simple plenty.[3] Their houses were surrounded by a garden or orchard, and several closes of land were owned or rented, which, combined together, allowed for the keeping of numerous domestic animals. Cows, a horse or ass, swine, and poultry were always kept, and as winter came along a cow or pig was killed and salted to provide meat during the months of frost and snow. Of cloth-making utensils there was a full set. The 'brode lome' on

---

[1] *Kenyon MSS., Hist. MSS. Comm.,* app. xiv, pt. iv, p. 573. Draft of scheme for establishing some cloth-making venture at Skipton.

[2] *D. S. P., Jas. I,* lxxx. 13, describes such a class of weavers. For a typical weaver's will, see that of George Goodall, of Tong, 1552, in Thoresby Soc. publications, vol. xix, pt. ii, no. 4, 1913.

[3] See Surveys of Manor of Leeds, Wills, miscellaneous MSS., and Leeds Parish Church Registers, all in Thoresby Soc. volumes.

which the ' Northern Dozens ' were woven, the ' leade ' or ' lyttinge leade ', in which the wool was dyed, the ' shere borde ' and ' walker sheres ', with which the surface of the cloth was cropped fine and smooth after fulling, all were to be seen in the loom-shop or work-chamber.[1] Outside, in the garth or close, stood the ' wool hedge ', on which the wool was spread to dry after dyeing, and the long wooden tenter frame, on which the piece, after shrinking in the fulling process, was finally stretched to the desired dimensions and left to dry.

In most cases these larger clothiers were at the same time employers and workmen. They took apprentices, who learned the various branches of the trade during long years of service under the master. They employed journeymen and women, who either in the workshop of the clothier or in their own cottages prepared the yarn and wove the piece. The clothier then took the piece to the fulling-mill, or ' walk-miln ' as it was still commonly called, and, after it had received a thorough washing and milling, brought it home, sheared, dressed, and tentered it, and finally carried or sent it to the market.

The character of these more wealthy clothiers can be well realized by examining an inventory of the stock-in-trade of one of their number. Let us take that of ' John Pawsone, late of Kyrkgaite in Leeds . . . Clothier ', dated 1576.[2] Pawson belonged to what one might call the upper middle class of his fraternity. His house was small, containing three chief rooms —the ' Offyse house ' or kitchen, which was the only room to possess a fire-place ; the parlour, which also served as a bed-room, and store-room for the ' xij beiff flickes ', or stock of salted meat for the winter ; and the chamber, which contained the following stock of cloth-making materials :

' xiiij stone of collered wool (i. e. wool dyed before weaving), . . . fyve stone of Butter (for greasing the wool before working it), a quartren and a half of allum (for use in dyeing). . . . Item, xxvij stone of Collered Woll, more certeyne thrums (waste ends of yarn and wool), xv stone of whyte woll, vij paire of woll combes.'[3]

[1] At death it was customary to bequeath ' my best beast for my mortuary ' to the parish priest. In one or two cases the ' best loom ' took the place of the beast. [2] Printed in Thoresby Soc. publications, iv. 163–6.

[3] In view of the fact that worsted cloths were not made in the West Riding until a century later, it is difficult to decide the use to which these combs were put.

Attached to the house were a workshop and loom-house, a dye-house, and ' laith ' or barn.   The contents of these rooms were :

' *In the Shopp and Lomehouse*, Inprimis, xxj dossans in Clothe (i. e. 21 pieces of cloth 13 yds. by 1¾ yds.), price xxxiiij$^{li.}$, one shere borde coverynge, xxij$^{s.}$, . . . Item, x stone of yarne att spynners, and v stone of woll, viij$^{li.}$ v$^{s.}$ One lome, Damyselles, Bartrees, Horne, Wheile (spinning-wheel), and other thynges theronto belongyng.'

' *In the Leadhouse* (*dye-house*), *Laithe and Back Yearde*, One Leade, . . . iiij tubbes, certeyne . . . yarne, baskettes, ij tenter heades, tenter rope, a cock and two hens, two kye, three styrkes, one horse, one pack saddle, two swyne, xxij$^{s.}$'

In addition to these goods, there were some ' good debtes ', a few ' Desperat debtes ', and notices of several leases and holdings of land.   Pawson had under his care three apprentices, who slept at their own homes, and this, along with the quantities of material in stock or out at the spinners' houses, shows that his business was comparatively large.

Taking another instance, the will of John Hollyred of Halifax, clothier (1574–5), makes special bequests alone to the extent of £130.[1]   One might multiply instances of similar men, clothiers in comfortable or affluent circumstances,[2] with all the requisites for cloth-making, and also their many garths, orchards, ' hearbe gardens ',[3] tenter closes, and ' woll hedges '.   At their death they bequeathed considerable sums to their relatives and servants, to the poor, or to ' mendinge of the hie wayes '.   They made minute provision for the distribution of jackets, doublets, hose, shoes, houses, corn, cattle, horses, sheep, bedding, candlesticks, and silver spoons.   In some wills we get a glimpse of another side of the clothier's life, as for example, in that of John Walker of Armley, clothier (1588) :

' To my son, my sword and my yewe bowe, and sixe of my best arrowes.   To (another son) another bowe and six arrowes.'[4]

Amongst such men the idea of large-scale production was not unknown.   In 1588 a detailed scheme, apparently for some

---

[1] *North Country Wills*, Surtees Soc., vol. cxxi, pp. 70–1.
[2] See *Testamenta Leodiensia*, Thoresby volumes, *passim*.
[3] Will of Wm. Sydall, Holbeck, clothier, January 1583–4 : Thoresby Soc. publications, i. 383.
[4] Will of John Walker of Armley, clothier : Thoresby Soc., i. 385.

charitable institution, was drawn up, by which sixty persons were to be employed under one roof at Skipton. What came of the suggestion is not known.[1] In practice some of the largest men in Leeds employed over a score of workpeople, and a petition from that town, dated 1629, says that many of them were ' dayly setting on worke about forty poor people in theire Trade '.[2] In such cases the clothier would not engage in industrial work himself, but resembled textile leaders of the West of England.

It is amongst these men that we find the beginnings of the great families which directed social and municipal life in their locality during the next two centuries. Of them probably the most important name was that of John Harrison, the famous Leeds philanthropist, who was himself a clothier by trade. Harrison's work for his native place puts him in the first rank as a public benefactor.

' He builte one parish church, a very faire one of free stone (St. John's, Briggate), . . . he founded an hospitall of twentie almes howses, he built likewise a chapell to itt, and a howse for a vicar to live in, . . . he built a free schoole, . . . he builte a wholle streete with faire howses on booth sides . . . and att his owne proper cost and charge did he all this, and left large revenews to maintaine these thinges.'[3]

Harrison's property extended north of Upperhead and Lowerhead Rows, and his income was very large. But it was practically all devoted to public service, and the Grammar School, St. John's Church, and the provision for aged and poor were amongst the chief of his benefactions. He was also a man of great intellectual power, energy, and inspiration, and in his capacity of deputy alderman (the equivalent of deputy mayor) he did much to guide Leeds through critical times.[4]

Another figure of Elizabethan times is less famous in the general social life of Leeds, and so, although he seems to have been one of the most prominent industrial figures of his day, very little is known of him. This was Randall Tenche. Tenche was a clothier of no small importance, and an enterprising man,

---

[1] *Kenyon MSS., Hist. MSS. Comm. Reports*, app. xiv, pt. iv, p. 573.
[2] *D. S. P., Chas. I*, cxxxix. 24. See Chapter VII.
[3] *Life of Marmaduke Rawdon* (Camden Soc. publications), p. 121.
[4] Price, *Leeds and its Neighbourhood*, p. 198.

ever ready to explore new fields.   In 1589 he was in negotiation
with Sir Francis Willoughby of Wollaton Hall, near Nottingham,
at a time when the latter was engaged in certain fancy-cloth-
making ventures.   In a letter Tenche undertook

' the dyeing of Sir Francis Willoughby's wool, and the spinning,
dyeing, and working of Arres work of all sorts, which he is
emboldened to do, more especially as he has found out a workman or two who will join with him or be under him, who will
work any work that shall be set unto them by a painter in
colours, and to work the same in woollen yarn . . ., or in silk or
in silver or gold or altogether.'

For proof thereof Tenche was willing to visit Wollaton Hall,
' and Sir Francis shall draw a little carpet or cushion in what
colour shall be thought fittest for the same ; and Tenche will work '
it to the satisfaction of the worthy gentleman before the contract
be finally made.   Tenche's work seems to have satisfied Sir
Francis, who was quite willing to pay him £50 per annum as
well as the desired wages to his workmen, 6s. 8d. per week.
The two began to draw up various plans for dyeing and weaving
these fancy wares, but nothing is known of the subsequent
history of the scheme.[1]

In his own county Tenche was chiefly famous as an orthodox
upholder of the law.   In 1590 he wrote to the President of the
Council of the North of York, ' with the full consent of all other
clothiers in the North partes ', complaining that ' by reason of a
corupt practise of a great number of broggers, engrocers, wool-
gatherars, regratours and such like ', all the wool of the county
had been snatched up, and could only be obtained by clothiers
at ' prisses . . . exceedingly enhaunsed and increased '.[2]   In view
of this lamentable state of affairs, he pleaded for a vigorous
enforcement of the law against middlemen in the wool trade.
In the same year he was appointed, on the nomination of the
Privy Council, to check evil practices in the making of West
Riding cloths.[3]   The letter from the Privy Council to the President of the Council of the North was most flattering to Tenche.
After stating the evil practice to be dealt with, it declared that
' forasmuch as this fraude . . . will best be suppressed by

[1] Letter in Middleton MSS. (*Hist. MSS. Comm.*), pp. 498–9, April 4, 1589.
[2] Acts and Ordinances of the Privy Council, May 28, 1590, xix. 169.
[3] Ibid., December 24, 1590, xx. 163.

th'aucthorising of some honnest and discreete personnes for the overseing of the said abuses ', the President ' is praied to license Randoll Tenche, a man of honnest conversacion and good skill and experience in such cases, together with one or two more to joyne him ', to take all possible steps to root out the fraud. At a later date he was entrusted with the task of enforcing another law[1] concerning the true making of cloth, and had power to seize all pieces which did not conform to legal demands. Again Randall discharged his duties with customary thorough ness : in fact, so energetic was he that he brought upon his head the angry complaints of many of his victims, who appealed against him to the Quarter Sessions at Wakefield, 1598. Hence the order of the Court :

' Whereas this Court is informed that Randall Tenche and others the Searchers of Leedes have seized many clothes of dyvers personnes, who desire of this Court that the Searchers may be called in, and showe cause why they dyd the same : yt is therefore ordered that a warrant shalbe made against them to appeare att the next Sessions and answeare for the premisses.'[2]

Apart from these facts, little seems to be known of this interesting figure. He was evidently of some importance in the religious life of the town, and acted as churchwarden at the parish church in 1591.[3] His home was situated in the Tenters,[4] or lands by the river side near the church, and here he had his garth and tenter close.[5] One of his sons was buried in the parish church,[6] and Randall himself died in the last days of the year 1628.[7] His name has sunk into oblivion, for, though he was a stalwart pillar of Church and State, he did not endow any churches or almshouses.

(b) *Apprenticeship*

As we have seen, apprenticeship was an important part of the gild system, and aimed at maintaining the standard of

---

[1] 39 Eliz., c. 20.

[2] *Quarter Sessions Records*, 1598, Yorks. Arch. Soc., Record Series, iii. 141.

[3] *Leeds Parish Church Registers*, Thoresby Soc. publications, i. 269.

[4] Entries in register always read ' Randall Tenche of the Tenters ', e.g. Thoresby Soc., iii. 316.

[5] *Survey of the Manor of Leeds*, 1610, Thoresby Soc., xi. 411.

[6] Thoresby Soc., ii. 41.

[7] Burial Register, Leeds Parish Church, 1628–9 : ' Jan. 1st, Randall Tenche of the Tenters ', Thoresby Soc., iii. 316.

workmanship by demanding that every man, before becoming an independent master, should have received a thorough train-ing during a long period of service under the guidance of some competent master. Apprenticeship had become systematized under the old local control, and entry into it hedged about with many formalities and restrictions. As the effectiveness of local industrial regulation declined, national supervision became more necessary. An Apprenticeship Law had been passed in the reign of Henry IV, but its effect was rather to injure the towns than to regulate the country industry.[1] The expansion of the textile industry in the new centres during the next hundred years was accompanied by a comparative neglect of formal industrial training. The State had not yet evolved its elaborate code of economic law, and so cloth-makers were virtually free to act according to their individual desires. In Yorkshire, as else-where, men took up the manufacture of cloth without having undergone any lengthy period of apprenticeship. Hence, in the sixteenth century, many complaints were made concerning the ' multitude of clothiers lately encreased in the realme ', since ' every man that wolde had libertie to be a clothier ' : and it was urged that laws should be made to ensure that ' none shoulde meddle with clothemaking, but such as had been prentises to th'occupacion '.[2] Various enactments [3] eventually brought apprenticeship under legal control, but the North Country was exempted from their scope until the great Act of 1563,[4] which surveyed the whole field of relationships between master and man.

This Act spread its tentacles over town and country alike. The enforcement of apprenticeship, and the maintenance of high freehold qualifications for apprentices, marked all the clauses concerning training for work. Merchants, mercers, drapers, and ' clothiers that put cloth to making or sale ' were forbidden to take any apprentice unless the youth was their own son or the child of a ' forty shilling freeholder '. The forty-shilling qualifica-

---

[1] See Cunningham, *op. cit.*, i. 449. Also Statute, 7 Hen. IV, c. 17.
[2] Ordinances of the Privy Council, 1550, vol. iii, p. 19.
[3] e.g. 2 & 3 Philip and Mary, c. 11.
[4] 5 Eliz., c. 4. This Act exempted the makers of the coarsest wares of Cumberland, Westmoreland, Lancashire, and Wales, i.e. friezes, cottons, and ' huswives' cloth '.

tion applied only to those living in corporate towns or cities, such as York and Beverley : in market towns and rural districts the freehold was to be of the annual value of £3. The local magistrates were to see that this clause was enforced, and all indentures of apprenticeship had to be duly registered and endorsed by them. The Act also reiterated the demand for a training period of at least seven years, and in order to guarantee that all workers, whether employer or employee, should be properly skilled, laid down the following rule :

' It shall not be lawfull for any person to sett up, occupy, use, or exercise any craft, mistery, or occupation . . . except he shall have been brought up therein seven yeares at the least as an apprentice, nor to set any person on work in such occupation . . . except he shall have been appriced as is aforesaid.'

The penalty for infringement of this clause was 40s. for every month the offender had worked at the trade.

The Act applied to all existing industries, and the Quarter Sessions records, both of the North and West Riding,[1] show that some of the clauses of the statute were enforced, especially that demanding a seven years' apprenticeship. Instances similar to the following are numerous :

Malton, Jan. 12th, 1607. ' Thomas Cooke, . . . webster, for trading, having never served vij years' apprentice.'[2]

Pontefract, April 1647. ' George Copley of Skelmanthorpe, did for the space of eleven whole months occupy . . . the art, mistery, and manual occupation of a weaver making woollen cloth, in which said art, mistery or occupation he had not been educated or apprenticed for the space of seven years.' He was therefore fined in accordance with the provisions of the statute, £2 per month, or £22 for his eleven months of illicit industry.[3]

Wakefield, Jan. 1648. Elizabeth Wayte of Thorne, mercer, for carrying on the trade of a mercer for ten months without having previously served the necessary apprenticeship. Elizabeth had incurred the enmity of a neighbouring mercer, who, being legally qualified, had informed the authorities of Elizabeth's misdemeanour, and in return received half of the £20 fine imposed upon the offender.[4]

[1] *West Riding Quarter Sessions Rolls*, 1597–1602, ed. by J. Lister.
[2] *North Riding Q. S. Records* (ed. Atkinson), i. 121.
[3] *West Riding Quarter Sessions Rolls*, Indictment Book B, April 27, 23 Chas. I.
[4] Indictment Book B, Wakefield Quarter Sessions, Jan., 23 Chas. I.

Thirsk, 1681. A Hewby yeoman indicted for using the trade of a weaver without having been properly apprenticed.[1]

The master took his own son as apprentice, or accepted the lad of some neighbour or friend. In addition to this, he was liable to receive forced gifts of apprentices from the poor law authorities. The poor relief system of the seventeenth century made provision for the employment of pauper children in some school or workhouse, or for them to be placed out in the hands of a clothier or other ratepayer. Thus the clothier was destined, sooner or later, to have an apprentice thrust upon him by the churchwardens and overseers of the poor. It was wellnigh impossible for him to refuse the child, and the following entries indicate some of the attempts made to wriggle out of the obligation :

Skipton Quarter Sessions, July 1638. ' Upon Informacon given unto this Corte by the Churchwardens and Overseers of the Poore in the parishe of Kighley that one Robert Cloughe of that parishe refusethe to take his apprentice, beinge legally tendred unto him, Itt is ordered that the saide Robert Cloughe shall take the said poore child apprentice, if he have not a scald head, or els be taken bounde to answeare his contempt before His Majestie's Judges of Assize at the next Assizes.'[2]

At the same Court, ' Thomas Backhouse doth wilfully refuse to take . . . a poore child putt apprentice to him. Ordered that the apprentice shallbe confirmed to him, and that he shalbe taken bounde to answeare his contempte at the next Sessions, . . . and that he shall pay and satisfie the chardges that the parishe hath beene putt for providing and maintaining the saide poore child since he was tendred unto him.'[3]

During the seven years of apprenticeship, the lad was entirely under the control of his master, especially if provided with board and lodging. Any attempt to abscond could be severely punished,[4] and should the master be seriously dissatisfied with the pupil he might lay his case before the magistrates, who were empowered to ' cause such due correction and punishment to be ministered to him as by their wisdom and discretion shalbe thought meet '.[5] This might mean a flogging, expulsion from

[1] *North Riding Q. S. Records*, vol. vii, p. 53.
[2] West Riding Quarter Sessions, Order Book A, July 1638.   [3] Ibid.
[4] April 5, 1608, North Riding Records. Man indicted for enticing John Smith, apprentice, to leave his master.
[5] 5 Eliz., c. 4.

the service of the master, or a period of incarceration in the
' Soletary Cells ' which were provided in the Wakefield House
of Correction for ' the purpose of confining unruly apprentices,
vagrants, etc.' [1] The parish apprentice was occasionally a burden
to his master, who missed no opportunity of ridding himself of
useless pupils. Thus, in 1639, a clothier of the Halifax parish
complained to Quarter Sessions that a parish apprentice, given
him three years before, was ' a Lunatique and a Caytiff, and not
fitt to doe him any service ',[2] and in the following year a Bradford clothier declared that the apprentice placed with him was
' blynde, and utterly disabled and unfitt for service '.[3] In such
cases the applicant was released from this useless charge, and
another parish child given him. On the other hand, the apprentice was not without a measure of protection. His master was
not supposed to ill-treat or neglect him, under pain of the lad's
removal ; and if the master became bankrupt, or was manifestly
not discharging his obligations to the youth, the apprentice was
liberated by the justices, and could seek for a new master elsewhere. Witness the following quaint order of the Pontefract
Quarter Sessions, April 1638 :

' Whereas Thomas Farrey hath beene bounde apprentise to
one Matthew Usher of Wakefield, . . . to the trade of a mercer ;
now forasmuche as the said Usher is decayed in his Estate, and
given over his Trade, and lyen two years in the King's bench,
and his wife lives by brewing or Tipling of Ale, and hath not
ymployed or assigned the said Farrey to any person of that
trade, but forceth him to live idlely and fill Ale, and loose his
tyme and trade ',[4]

therefore the lad was freed from bondage, and allowed to seek
a master of better repute.

As we examine the system of apprenticeship in the light of

---

[1] Order Book of Quarter Sessions, quoted by J. Horsfall Turner, *Wakefield
House of Correction*, p. 122.

[2] Quarter Sessions, Order Book A, 3rd October, 14 Chas. I (Halifax Sessions).

[3] Ibid., p. 15, 1st October, 15 Chas. I.

[4] Ibid., April 1638. Similar one in North Riding Records : ' Whereas Thos.
Pant, apprentice to Christopher Simpson, of Egton, shoemaker, complains that
he has not been employed in his occupation, . . . but hath been trayned up
these three yeres in wandering the country and playing Interludes, and for the
said Simpson is an obstinate convicted Popish recusant, . . . and warrants are
issued for his apprehension, . . . the said Pant shalbe free of his apprenticeship ' (North Riding Sessions, 1610, vol. i, p. 204).

the Act of 1563, the questions inevitably arise—Did it work? Did it achieve its aims? Was it a permanent part and parcel of the industrial organization? To these queries it is difficult to give a comprehensive answer. In the mind of the clothier there were two interpretations of the term 'Apprenticeship'. The first was that it was essential for future masters to be thoroughly trained, and this could be best effected by a course of tuition, the duration of which had been settled by custom at seven years. Secondly, there was the legally ordained apprenticeship, hedged in with freehold qualifications, attestations of local magistrates, &c., as demanded by the Elizabethan Act. The first of these views was generally admitted, and to some extent enforced by the local courts. But even here it is difficult to believe that all fulfilled the term of seven years. Such a period was far more than sufficient for acquiring proficiency in the various processes, especially since the average Yorkshire cloth was not a 'super-fine', and would not require very great skill or delicate work-manship. Hence it is very probable that apprenticeship was regarded by many as a matter rather of industrial convenience than of legal necessity, and that the West Riding justices of the peace were speaking of a practice common in the textile industry when, in 1604, they complained of the 'unskillfull persons that daileye sett upp trades and misteries in those thinges wherein they were never lawfull apprentises '.[1]

As to the observance of the 'freehold' and other clauses of the Act, we have the answer to our query in a confession made in 1640 by the Yorkshire weavers themselves. It appears that some men had been perusing the Act, and had seen the possi-bility of making money by informing the authorities of the manner in which various clauses were being disregarded by the clothiers.[2] The latter were up in arms at once, and dispatched to the King ' The humble petition of the poore Clothiers of Leedes, Hallifax, and other the Clothing Townes in the Countie of Yorke '. In the petition they cited the clauses which were the cause of the trouble, namely, ' that no Clothier shall take any apprentice but hee whose father hath 40s. of ffreehold

[1] Complaint of justices of Agbrigg and Morley wapentakes to constables of those parts. Printed in *Old Yorkshire*, vol. ii, pp. 41–2.

[2] The informer was the bane of life in some parts, but the fear of his activities did not deter the clothiers from straining the law.

estate of Inheritance, to be certified under the hands of three
Justices of the Peace, . . . and also for everie three apprentices
to keep one Journeyman, and these upon pain of severall great
penalties '.   These clauses, the petitioners candidly confessed,
were ' never observed nor put in execution in ye said Countie of
Yorke, nor can be observed, for many wise reasons '.   The
clothiers therefore asked that the clauses be repealed, and also
sought grace and pardon for those clothiers who were to be
brought before the next Assizes for offences against them.
A sentence imposed upon these men would ' tende to their utter
undoeing, if some remedie be not speedily had, *there being not
one Clothier in ye Countie but is guiltie of ye Penalties of ye said
Statute* '.[1]

(c) The Journeyman

The extent to which journeymen were employed depended
largely upon the scale of the clothier's business.   It is very
doubtful if any of the smaller men employed any male adult
labour, but in the case of the larger clothiers and the cloth-
finishing trades considerable numbers of journeymen were
engaged.   The journeyman's position was carefully regulated
by the Act of 1563.   Any clothier who had three apprentices
must employ one journeyman, with an additional one for every
further apprentice ;   but in practice this rule was disregarded,
and the Yorkshire clothier made the matter one of personal
option, utilizing the services of apprentices or journeymen as
best suited his purpose.   The employee was required by law to
have first completed a seven years' term of apprenticeship, and
in many cases looked forward to the day when, having saved
sufficient money, he would be able to become a clothier himself.
He was to be employed for not less than one year, and could
neither leave nor be dismissed before the end of that period.
His hours of labour were fixed by the Act of 1563 ;   from March
to September he was expected to work from 5 a.m. to 7 or 8 p.m.,
with not more than $2\frac{1}{2}$ hours interval for meals and after-dinner
sleep ;   from September to March he must work ' from the spring
of the day in the morning until the night of the same day ',
upon pain of losing a penny for each hour's absence.   These
hours were not strictly observed, except possibly by those who

[1] *D. S. P., Chas. I,* cccclx. 64.

worked under the employer's roof. Dyers, fullers, shearers, and apprentices carried on their occupation under the direct supervision of their employer, and to them the legal hours of labour might apply. But a great proportion of journeymen weavers worked in their own homes, and were in consequence free to work or idle when they pleased. These men often owned their own tools, but occasionally the employer provided the necessary implements.

The supply of male adult labour was strongly supplemented by the employment of women and children. In 1588, one loom consumed the yarn carded and spun by five or six persons, and most of the work of preparing yarn for the weaver was performed by women and young persons. Every cottage had its spinning-wheel or distaff, as an almost essential part of the domestic equipment. The clothier sent his wool out to the spinners, who, in their homes, spun the mass of raw material into fibre ready for the loom.

The technique in the various textile processes was primitive, and the number of cloths produced appears very small in relation to the number of persons engaged, and the time and energy expended. From a document dated 1588 [1] we gather some idea of the distribution of labour in the industry, and the speed at which cloths were produced. The document gives details for the manufacture of broad cloths (as in Leeds), and for that of kerseys (as in the Halifax area).

In the making of short broad cloths or dozens (12 yds. by $1\frac{3}{4}$ yds.), sixty workers were distributed as follows :

Persons.

Sorting, dressing, and dyeing the wool	12	
Spinning and carding . . .	30	
Weaving and shearing . . .	12	of whom four were probably shearmen.
Odd jobs, taking wool to spinners, and cloth to fulling mill . .	6	

This labour force in the course of a week worked 12 stones of wool up into four ' dozens ' : in other words, fifteen persons were employed for a week in producing a cloth 12 yds. by $1\frac{3}{4}$ yds. Such a piece was too wide to be woven by a single weaver, and

[1] *Kenyon MSS., Hist. MSS. Comm. Report,* app. xiv, pt. iv, p. 573.

the broad loom therefore occupied the attention of two work-men, who utilized the yarn prepared by three sorters, dressers, and dyers, and seven or eight carders and spinners.

In the kersey trade the distribution was a little different, and the sixty workers would be employed as follows :

Persons.

Sorting and dressing	.	.	.	6
Spinning and carding	.	.	.	40
Weaving	.	.	.	.	8
Shearmen	.	.	.	.	6

of whom two were to help the rest of the workers.

Kerseys were usually sold ' in the white ', and so the list made no provision for dyers. The forty spinners could prepare 20 stones of yarn in a week, and this made 10 kerseys (18 yds. by 1 yd.). Thus one kersey occupied six workers for a week. The kersey, being a narrow cloth, could be woven by one weaver, who apparently made $1\frac{1}{4}$ cloths per week, utilizing the yarn carded and spun by five persons.

The apparent slowness of production was due to many causes. The actual process of weaving occupied many days, by reason of the crude method of passing the shuttle across the warp. But before and after making the cloth many things had to be done which took up much time. First came the journey from the weaver's home to the clothier's head-quarters, to get the supply of yarn. Then, when the yarn had been brought home, that part of it which was intended for the warp had to be spread out, wound to the back ' beam ' or roller, placed in the loom, threaded through the healds or heddles which were to raise and lower the warp threads in alternate series, and finally, after being fully adjusted in the loom mechanism, fastened to the front beam, on which the cloth itself was to be rolled. These processes all required time, care, and patience, as any error in the arrangement of the warp would cause trouble in the course of the weaving. The weaving was liable to be interrupted by a scarcity of yarn for the shuttle. Finally, the fulling, tentering, and drying were slow processes, as the Yorkshire climate was not suitable for the rapid drying of cloths. Thus, when one takes into account the primitive methods of manufacture, the passing of materials from hand to hand,[1] and the climatic diffi-culties, it is not surprising that a single cloth should represent so great an outlay of time and energy.

The wages of the textile workers were regulated by the justices of the peace, in accordance with the Acts of 1563 and 1603. The Elizabethan statute had been confined in its practical application almost entirely to agricultural labour and the build-ing trades, and there was some doubt whether it was really intended to deal with the textile trades. In 1603, however, it was declared that the Act of 1563 had ' been found beneficiall for the commonwealth ', and its bounds were therefore more carefully defined. The justices were now given instructions ' to rate the wages of any labourers, weavers, spinsters, and work-men or workwomen whatsoever, either working by the day, week, month, year, or taking any work at any person's hands . . . to be done in great or otherwise '.[2] These assessments were intended to state minimum wage figures for textile workers, and any clothiers who refused to obey the commands of the magistrates, or pay as great wages to their weavers and spinsters as should be ordained in the assessment, were to be fined ten shillings for each offence. The weaver was not to be underpaid, if the State could prevent it. Further, in order to exclude the employers' influence when assessments were being made, it was ordered that no justice who was a clothier by trade should be allowed to assist in the fixing of wages for textile workers.

The new Act was not at first administered with any enthusiasm in the West Riding. The chief and petty constables were apathetic in declaring the assessment which had been drawn up, and in searching for offenders. This negligence roused the ire of some of the more conscientious magistrates, and in Novem-ber 1604 three of them expressed their severe condemnation of ' the many complaints arisseinge betwixt masters and servants . . . through the negligence of the Chief and Petty Constables, and the masters and the men who do not obey the law as they ought to do '. The constables were therefore ordered to rouse themselves, and bring to justice all masters and men who should continue to disregard the law.[3]

---

[1] See Pawson's inventory quoted above ; amount of wool ' yarne att spyn-ners '.   [2] Statute, 1 Jas. I, c. 6, amending and extending 5 Eliz., c. 4.
[3] Document quoted in *Old Yorkshire*, vol. ii, pp. 41–2.

To what extent this order was obeyed, and subsequent assessments drawn up during the next forty years, it is impossible to
state,[1] but it is certain that wages lists were actually framed
during the reigns of James I and Charles I.   In 1641, for instance, an assessment was issued, and the constables were ordered
to make its provisions known to all concerned.   Six months
later it became apparent that the rates fixed by the justices
were being disregarded, and at the Doncaster Sessions there was
a general complaint ' that servants refuse to worke for reasonable wages, and cannot be hired for competent allowance as
formerlye, makeing advantage of the much busines of the times '.
The magistrates therefore, ' takeing into consideracon the many
inconveniences that now doe and are like to arise therby if
some speedy course be not taken herein ', ordered the constables
to make a full and thorough proclamation of the rates fixed,
and of the penalties for disobedience, after which they were to
bring for punishment all such persons as they found ' refrac-
torye in not observing thereof, either master or servant '.

During the years which followed, the West Riding was too
much distracted by plague and civil war to give any attention
to the matter of wages.   But when some measure of peace had
been restored the justices returned to the question, and at the
Pontefract Sessions, April 1647, they drew up a comprehensive
assessment.   This document is the first of such assessments
accessible, but is doubtless very similar in form and figures to
its predecessors of the earlier years of the century.   The assessment touched all the West Riding industries—agriculture,
building trades, tailoring, mining, and textile work.   The clause
relating to textile work ran as follows :

' Cloathworkers and Dyers.
Noe Weaver, Cloathworker, Shereman or Dyer Shall not take
for his wages above iiij$^{d.}$ with meat and Drinke, and without
meate and Drinke viij$^{d.}$ And if hee be hyred by the yeare, and
if hee bee a very Skilfull workman in these Sciences, hee shall
have iij$^{li.}$ per annum.   And other comon weavers, Cloath-

---

[1] This is due to the fact that the Quarter Sessions Records, prior to 1639,
are not accessible.   After that date the records are continuous, being in the
custody of the Clerk of the Peace at Wakefield.   Some of the Elizabethan
Sessions Records have been edited by Mr. John Lister, and published by the
Yorks. Arch. and Topogr. Soc. (vol. iii), and another volume is now in course
of preparation.

workers, Shearemen, ffullers and Dyers shall not have for their wages above ij[l.] x[s.] yeareley.'[1]

There are many points to be noted in this short clause. The first is that the assessment laid down a maximum figure for the wages of the employee, and consequently any master paying more than this amount was liable to a severe fine, as was also the man who accepted an excessive wage. This feature runs throughout the whole of this and other wages assessments. ' Shall not take above ' is the ever-recurring phrase, the key-note of the proclamation. In no case was a minimum wage stated, and apparently the master might pay as little as he pleased ; the justices were only concerned to see that he did not pay too much. This was contrary to the spirit of the Act of 1603, which presupposed the fixing of a minimum rate for textile workers, and, as quoted above, stated the penalty to be inflicted on those clothiers who did not pay to their work-people ' so much or so great wages' as were ordered by the local magistrates.[2] But in practice the assessments were confined solely to establishing maximum rates, and all cases of punish-ment under the Act were those of masters who had paid, and servants who had accepted, higher wages than were allowed by the assessment.[3] The orders given to the constables in 1641 show clearly the attitude of the justices, and there can be no doubt that the real motive in their minds when issuing any assessment was to prevent workpeople from taking advantage of any temporary or permanent scarcity of labour to extract increased wages.

Secondly, it is somewhat surprising to find all classes of cloth-makers placed in the same group, with one rate for all, and that rate a time rate, eightpence a day. For those engaged in dyeing, cloth-dressing, fulling, and shearing, a time rate would be natural, for their work was of such a kind that it

---

[1] Doncaster Quarter Sessions, October 1641. Sessions Order Book A, f. 186. ' A proclamation of the Rates and appointment of the Severall wages for Artificers, handycraftsmen, husbandmen, Laborers, Servants, Workemen and Apprentices of husbandry within the Westridding of the Co. of Yorke, &c.' (Pontefract Quarter Sessions, April 27, 1647, Order Book C, p. 10). See article by present writer in *Economic Journal*, June 1914.

[2] 1 Jas. I, c. 6.

[3] See, for instance, the numerous offences brought before the North Riding J.P.'s, *North Riding Q. S. Records*, vol. vii, pp. 34, 45-7, &c.

would be difficult to pay a man according to the amount of work done. Similarly, for those weavers who lived and worked with their master, and devoted their whole time to weaving in his loomshop, a time rate might be satisfactory. But a large part of the weaving was performed by men who, though employed by a clothier, carried on their occupation in their own homes. These men were also in possession of a piece of ground, and combined the cultivation of their patch of land with their work at the loom. At times they had to wait for further supplies of yarn, and these intervals were doubtless filled up with agricultural work on a small scale. In these circumstances, one would have supposed that the justices would have stated a piece rate, and limited the amount which could be paid for the weaving of each piece. In actual practice the piece rate was general, and it is probable therefore that the assessment figures bore some relation to the amount which a weaver could earn when paid by the piece.

A third point of interest lies in the comparison of the rates paid to industry and agriculture. The most important maxima fixed in the 1647 assessment were :

Agriculture.	*Maximum Wages.*
Bailiffs or foremen hired by gentlemen or wealthy persons per annum	£3 10s. 0d.[1]
Chief servants in the employ of ordinary yeomen or husbandmen	£3 0s. 0d.
Female servants	25s. to 30s.
Mowers of grass and corn, per day, with or without food	5d. or 10d.
Ordinary farm labourers, per day, with or without food	Summer, 3d. or 6d. / Winter, 2d. or 5d.
Building Trades.	
Master masons and carpenters . . .	6d. or 12d.
Their men	Summer, 4d. or 8d. / Winter, 3d. or 6d.
Plumbers, glaziers, bricklayers, slaters, tylers, and others engaged in branches of building . .	Summer, 4d. or 9d. / Winter, 3d. or 8d.
Miners.	
Colliers, per day, without meat or drink . .	10d.
Banksmen or drawers-up of coal, without sustenance	8d.
Clothworkers.	
All classes, per day	4d. or 8d.
If engaged for year, presumably with meat and drink	Skilful, £3 / Common, £2 10s. 0d.
Tailors, with meat and drink	2d. to 4d.

[1] In addition the bailiff received a livery or 10s. per annum in lieu thereof. The large sums denote the maximum annual rates, and include food and probably lodging.

From these figures it will be seen that textile workers were not the most highly paid in the county. The ' very skilfull ' weaver or fuller was to receive less than the skilful collier, less than the higher grades of farm servants, less than the heads of the building trade, less even than the mower of grass or corn. The superiority of mining wages over textile rates, which has lasted up to the present day, was probably due to the presence of a strong female element in the textile trade. The weaver was not the sole bread-winner of the family ; his wife, and children over four or five years of age, were all potential wage-earners, a fact which would help to keep the male adult's earnings lower than might otherwise have been the case. The weaver was paid less than the harvest workers, and this had the effect of drawing large numbers of the industrial population to the agricultural areas in harvest time. The weaver laid aside his shuttle, and, often accompanied by his family, went eastward to the Vale of York and the East Riding to assist in mowing and reaping. This annual excursion served as a summer holiday, a holiday for which the weaver was paid more than he could earn by working at the loom.

A comparison of the West Riding rates with those established in other counties shows that the Yorkshire textile workers were allowed quite as good wages as their fellows in East Anglia, and better wages than those assessed in the West of England.

County.	Best Weaver.	Common Weavers.	Fullers, Dyers, Shearmen. Best.	Others.
Yorks. W.R.	£3	£2 10s.	£3	£2 10s.
Essex (1651) [1]	£3 and livery	£1 10s. and livery	£2 10s. and livery.	
Suffolk (1630) [2]	£3 and livery	£2 and livery	£3	£2 10s. and livery
Norfolk (1610) [3]	£2 and livery	£1 13s. 4d. and livery	£2 and livery	
Wilts. (1604) [4]	£2 and livery	£1 6s. 8d.	Dyers £2 10s.	£2
Devon (1654) [5]	2½d. or 8d. per day.		Shearmen ⎫ Fuller ⎬ £2	£1 6s. 8d.

Turning from these assessments to the actual wages which were being paid to workers in wool, we are faced with a scarcity

[1] Thorold Rogers, *Hist. of Agriculture and Prices*, vi. 694–7.
[2] *English Historical Review*, xii. 307–11.   [3] Ibid., xiii. 523–7.
[4] Bland, Brown, and Tawney, *op. cit.*, p. 349.
[5] Hamilton, *Quarter Sessions from Queen Elizabeth to Queen Anne* (1878), pp. 163–4.

of data.   Thorold Rogers gives no figures for the West Riding
industry, but a few facts are available from the evidence given
in the clothiers' lawsuits of 1638 and 1676, and from one or
two other sources.   In 1638 the weaver would be under an assessment similar to the one already quoted, and his maximum wage
would not be greater than that stated in 1647, namely, fourpence
with, and eightpence without, food and drink.   In practice the
weaver was paid by the piece, receiving a certain amount for
each cloth worked.   This payment in 1588 amounted to 1s. 8d.
for each kersey,[1] and in the Leeds area 3s. 4d. was paid for the
weaving of a ' dozen '.   These rates had scarcely changed by
1638.[2]   As seen above, a weaver was able to produce about
$1\frac{1}{4}$ kerseys in a week, and statements were made in the lawsuit
of 1638 to the effect that one kersey was the weekly output of
the average weaver.   At the most, therefore, his weekly earnings
would be 2s. 1d., or less than 5d. a day.   The weaving of a
' dozen ' occupied the attention of two workers for a week, who
for their joint labour received 3s. 4d.   If this had to be shared
equally between the two, the weekly wage of each was a beggarly
1s. 8d., the same amount as was received by the kersey weavers
who only produced one cloth in a week.   It was, however,
a common practice to set an apprentice to assist a journeyman
in weaving broad cloths, in which case the journeyman's share
of the 3s. 4d. might amount to about 2s. 6d., an average of 5d.
per day.   This was the rate in 1588, and in 1676[3] the earnings
seem to have been about the same.   According to one of the
witnesses giving evidence in the trial of that year, ' weavers of
Cloath can hardly earne fivepence a day . . . and find themselves
meate, though they be stronge and able to worke '.   Another
man stated that the daily earnings were 6d., and a third
declared that ' the wages of a Clothier [4] for weaveing of cloth
is but three pence a day besides meate ', which may be taken
as equivalent to at most 6d. per day.   Thus the average daily
earnings of the weaver in the seventeenth century were less
than 6d., and therefore well below the maximum fixed by the

---

[1] *Kenyon MSS., Hist. Comm. Report*, app. xiv, pt. iv, p. 573.
[2] Exchequer Depositions by Commission, 14 Chas. I, Mich. 21, York.
[3] Ibid., 28 Chas. II, Mich. 29, York and Lancaster.
[4] The word ' clothier ' is used here in a vague sense, and really means
the employee weaver.

assessment of 1647. It was not until the eighteenth century
that the weaver's remuneration crept up to the 7s. or 9s. per
week which was paid in the days of Arthur Young.

The spinners, whose wages were untouched by the assessment,
were very badly paid, and here again the wages of 1588 were
almost the same as those of a century later. Payment was by
piece, and the spinner received from 1s. 8d. to 2s. 8d. per stone,
according to the quality of the wool and the standard of the
spinning. It took a skilful worker about a fortnight to spin
a stone of wool, and so the earnings of spinners varied from
2d. to 4d. per day,[1] the lower rates generally going to children
and young women, or to adult women in the badly paid areas.
As one witness declared in 1638, ' A spinner may earn, some
twopence, some threepence, and the strongest a groat (fourpence), and none usually earne more by spinninge for and
towards meat and drink and wages '. A fellow-witness confirmed this statement by declaring that ' the ordinary rate of
a stone of wool spinninge is eight groat (2s. 8d.), and a good
spinner cannot ordinarily earne above threepence a day towards
meat, drink, and wages, and the most spinners adle (i. e. earn)
but twopence a day in the parish of Kighley '. In 1676 these
rates had diminished rather than increased. Witnesses declared
that ' spinners can scarce earne threepence a day, findinge
themselves with meat ', ' a very good spinner can scarcely earne
twopence a day, they finding themselves with meate, a pound
of wool a day beinge as much as an ordinary person can carde
and spinne '. Others estimated the general wages at fourpence
for the best workers, whilst one man declared that in his district
(Lockwood) ' the wadges for spinninge is not above one penny
a day besides meate '.

In taking stock of these figures we must remember the relatively larger purchasing power of money, and make allowance
accordingly. But it is also necessary to emphasize the fact that
between 1588 and 1676, the period when weavers' and spinners'
wages were stationary, there was a very great increase in general
prices. This was due in part to the debasement of the coinage
in the early decades of the sixteenth century, and also to the
influx of silver from the mines of South America, which began

[1] The same scale of wages for spinners prevailed in Wiltshire, 1605. See
Bland, Brown, and Tawney, op. cit., p. 351.

to affect English prices about 1570. It is impossible to state
with any measure of accuracy the extent of the movement, but
one is safely within bounds in stating that prices doubled in the
century which followed 1570.[1] The effect of this increase on
the wage-earner must have been very serious. True, he would
be independent of market supplies of foodstuffs in so far as he
added agriculture and the rearing of stock to his industrial
pursuits. There would be the eggs from the poultry, the milk
from the cow (if the weaver were fortunate enough to possess
one), and the slices of ham or bacon from last year's pig. But
the supply of cereals would have to be purchased from elsewhere, especially by those who lived in the barren districts of
the Pennine slopes, and the rise in the price of wheat, oats, and
rye would have a very serious effect upon the purchasing power
of the weekly wage. Hence, whilst recognizing the big expansion
of the industry and admitting that many clothiers were finding
their way to riches, we are forced to the conclusion that the
poorer classes of the county lived on the poverty line, and
that the vision of a Merrie England is dimmed when we see at
closer quarters the economic vicissitudes and general industrial
conditions of Tudor England. Profound shocks had been
experienced in every branch of national life, and in such upheavals
it is usually the poor who feel the blow first and are the last to
recover. In addition to the rise in prices, there was the dissolution of the monasteries, the enclosure movement, and the
constant drain of men and money for wars in Scotland and
elsewhere. In 1558 the Earl of Shrewsbury wrote of Yorkshire
that ' the state of the shyre was poore . . . by reason of the
greate chardge they have bene at since the begynnynge of these
last warres about the furnyture of bothe horsemen and foot-
men to the Borders '.[2] Half a century later matters had not
improved, and Thomas, Lord Burghley, writing from York,
exclaimed to a correspondent, ' You will not think to what
pouertye this country (Yorkshire) is growne into at this present.
. . . I pray God sends us peace, or els I dare assure you it wyll
brede grete discontent in these Northe partes, where they say
there is nothyng dayly but payinge and punishynge '.[3]

[1] On the question of prices, see Cunningham, *Growth*, ii. 162–70 ; L. L. Price,
Money, and its Relation to Prices, chap. iii.
[2] *D. S. P., Mary*, Addenda, viii. 87.   [3] *D. S. P., Eliz.*, cclxxxi. 28.

(d) The Wool Supply and the Middleman

Had we asked the Elizabethan clothier which aspect of his work gave him the most cause for anxiety, he would probably have replied, ' The obtaining of my raw material '.

There was a great diversity of wools throughout the kingdom, in quality, nature, and price. Some wools were naturally suited for particular classes of cloths, and the wool grown in one county was frequently worthless to clothiers of that district, but met the demands of some county which lay at the other end of the land. This caused the rise of a considerable trade in the transit of wools. The sheep of Yorkshire could not supply all the needs of the Yorkshire clothiers. The quantity was inadequate, and for many purposes the quality was not sufficiently good. For this reason, the native wool of the West Riding was largely handed over to the makers of the very coarsest cloths, whilst the clothiers drew their supplies from other counties. A paper dated 1615[1] states that the wool of Lincolnshire, Rutland, Leicestershire, Warwickshire, Oxfordshire, and Buckingham-shire was carried to Leeds, Wakefield, Halifax, and Rochdale ; and from an earlier source (1588) we learn that ' the Hallyfaxe men occupie fyne wolle most out of Lincolnshire, and there corse wolle they sell to men of Ratchedall '.[2] Thus there was a well-developed system of internal trade in wool, and Yorkshire drew its supplies from many of the most famous wool-producing counties of that period.

This transference of wool was carried on in many ways. The wealthy clothier went himself, or sent his assistants, into the wool counties, and made his purchases either at the wool fair or in the parlour of the wool-grower. The witnesses in the lawsuits of the seventeenth century[3] declared that they often journeyed into the wool areas of Lincolnshire and Leicestershire to purchase their supplies. We have an excellent instance of such direct purchase during the early part of the same century in the case of John Priestley, who lived in London, and made a practice of riding out into Kent and the surrounding country to buy wool from the growers. He then packed up the fleeces

[1] D. S. P., Jas. I, lxxx. 13.
[2] Kenyon MSS., Hist. MSS. Comm. Report, xiv, pt. iv, p. 573.
[3] Depositions in lawsuit re subsidy and ulnage, 1638 (see Chapter VI).

and brought or sent them north to his brothers, who lived and worked as clothiers at Soyland, near Halifax.[1] Similarly, the Leeds clothier [2] saddled his horse and rode out to the country fairs at Ripon, Doncaster, and Pontefract, or to the moorland farms, and there made his purchases.

But many could not afford to make these excursions, and few of the clothiers had kind-hearted brothers in the capital. The lower grades were therefore unable to buy in this direct manner. They could not afford to make big purchases, pay down large sums, or get long credit, and so lead home a team of laden pack-horses. Also, the farmer required some surer means of sale than the chance visits of prospective buyers ; the wool-fair was often far distant from his own home ; and lastly he preferred ready money to the notes of credit which the big clothiers might offer. Thus between wool-grower and clothier there was a distinct gap, which made exchange difficult and laborious to all but the most wealthy. The situation called for the intervention of a middleman, whose business would be to buy up the wool from the farmer, sort and classify it according to its quality, and then retail it to the clothiers in amounts to meet their needs, and in quality and fibre to answer the demands of the particular types of cloth. Such a man would bring the wools of the East and Midlands to the North, and try to meet the most varied wants of the clothiers for whom he catered.

The middleman, the woolchapman, the brogger, is a very common figure in the sixteenth and seventeenth centuries. But the reputation of such men during this period was black, and the treatment they received at the hands of the State was very severe. They were popularly associated with all that was bad in the trading life of the day, and seem to have alienated every class by the dangerous monopoly for which they strove. Countless complaints were made against them, and they were accused of engrossing every fleece of wool in the kingdom, so that none could be obtained even in the open fairs and markets, except through their hands. The clothier found himself at their mercy, and the farmer declared that he could not sell his wool as he pleased. The sixteenth century saw a large increase in

[1] Surtees Soc. (*Priestley Memoirs*), vol. lxxvii, p. 26 et seq.
[2] Blome's *Britannia* states that Leeds clothiers frequented Ripon very much.

the price of wool, and the cost of a stone in 1570 was about three times the sum paid for the same amount at the beginning of the century.[1] This was really part of the general revolution in prices which marked the period, but it may be that the wool dealers had some small share in enhancing prices. Whether justly or not, they were blamed abundantly, and served as scapegoats for the various economic grievances of the times. The attitude of the public and the State towards the middleman is seen in the Act of 1552. In that year legislation took the bull by the horns :

' Whereas by the gredye and covetous myndes as well of suche as have the grete plentye and habundance of sheepe and woolles as also by the corrupt practyses of dyv'se Broggars, Ingrocers, Woolgatherars . . . and sondrie other persons, . . . it manifestlye appeareth that the prices thereof be wonderfullye and excedynglie enhaunsed and raysed, to the grete hurte, detrimente, and decaye of the Realme ' ;

therefore it was decreed that none should buy wools, except (1) the Merchants of the Staple of Calais, who exported it to the Continent, and the Merchant Adventurers of Newcastle, who were allowed by charter to export the cheap qualities of Northern wools ; (2) the manufacturer, who intended to make it into cloth.[2]

This meant the annihilation of the wool-middleman, since by the above decree only direct purchases between grower and clothier were to be allowed, and the intervention of a wool-dealer was declared illegal. Such an order was also a fatal blow to the system by which the small clothier of Yorkshire was fed, and immediately the Halifax men rose in protest against the Act, seeking exemption from its scope. With powerful plea they stated their case, and the success of their agitation was seen in the Halifax Act of 1555. The preamble has already been quoted, with its picture of the clothiers' stern struggle against a barren soil, and of their trudging to market, ' ther to bye upon the Woolldryver, some a stone, some twoo, and some three or foure, accordinge to theyre habilitee, and to carrye the same ', on head or back, several miles to their homes. By persistence

---

[1] *Price per tod* : 1500, 6s. 0½d. ; 1570, 16s. 0d. (Thorold Rogers, *Hist. of Agriculture and Prices*, iv. 305–6).

[2] 5 & 6 Ed. VI, c. 7.

in this rough mode of life and work they had achieved considerable success, but were ' nowe like to bee undone and dryven to beggery, by reason of the late statute made, that takethe awaye the Woolldryver, so that they cannot nowe have theyr wooll by such small porcions as they were wont to have, and that thei are not hable to kepe anye horses wherupon to ryde or sett theyr wolles further from them in other places '.   In consideration of this insuperable difficulty, it was enacted

' That from hensfurth, yt shalbe lawfull to any persons in-habyting within the parishe of Halyfax to buye any wooll or woolles at suche tymes as the clothiers may buy the same, otherwyse than by engrossing and forestalling, so that the persons so bying the same doo carye . . . the woolles so bought by them to the Towne of Halyfaxe, and there to sell the same to suche poore folkes of that and other parishes adjoyning as shall work the same in clothe or yarne . . . and not to the riche and welthye clothyers, nor to any one to selle agayne.'

The wooldriver who sold his wares in any other part besides Halifax, and the purchaser who sold the same again unwrought, was condemned ' to lose and forfeite the dooble value of the wooll so sold or uttered '.   Thus, in the special case of Halifax, middle-men were allowed to buy wool, and bring it to the Halifax parish, for sale to the meaner clothiers only.   Those who could afford the journey to the wool areas were still to make it, but the services of the wooldriver were permitted, to meet the needs of the poorer classes, whose weekly demand did not exceed one or two stones per family.[1]

The Halifax Act is of further interest in that it served as a beacon light and a precedent to the rest of the North Country.[2] In 1577 a petition was presented from the clothiers of Lanca-shire, Richmondshire, Westmorland, Cumberland, and Durham, protesting against the restraint of middlemen in the wool trade. These counties put forward a very strong case, pointing out : (1) ' The clothyers (are) cotegers, whose habylytye wyll not stretch neyther to buy anye substance of wolles to mayntayne any worke or labor, not yet to fetch the wooll, the markets beyng four or five score myles away att the least.' (2) The wool

---

[1] 2–3 Philip and Mary, c. 13.

[2] Bill introduced March 5, 1562, ' to allow to buy wools in Lancaster and Yorke, to sell againe in fairs and markets ' (*House of Commons Journals*, vol. i, March 5, 1562).

was needed in small quantities only, and for coarse goods, rough ' cottons ', ' frizes ', &c.

The petitioners also quoted the Halifax Act, and declared that the folk of Halifax were evading it, and utilizing it to get the whole trade of wool-dealing into their hands.[1] The request of these Northern clothiers was eventually granted in 1585.[2]

Similarly, in 1588, Rochdale, which was really a part of the Yorkshire cloth field, complained of the proceedings which were being instituted against certain Rochdale wool-dealers, and declared ' that yf the same statute (of 1552) were executed in this countrie, where the poore clothyer is not able to go to the grower of the wooles, neyther the grower able to come hither, ther were thowsandes of poore people utterlie undone '. The Rochdale clothiers therefore asked for the same liberty ' which the men of Halyfax have '.[3] Their case was espoused by the Earl of Derby, and eventually they obtained the desired freedom.[4]

Under cover of such licences, or in the face of the full rigour of the Act of 1552, the middleman continued to rule the sale of wool. In 1590 the clothiers of Leeds were feeling the inconvenience of the monopoly, and Randall Tenche headed a petition [5] to the Council of the North, complaining ' of a corupt practise of great nomber of broggers, engrocers, wool-gatherars, . . . and such like inhabiting therabouts, that have too much liberty of buieng, keeping and occupieng of wooll ', and had made ' the prisses of wooles exceedingly enhaunced and increased, notwithstanding the sheepmasters and wollbreders are nothing benefitted therby '. For remedy of this evil, Randall asked the Privy Council to grant that the statute of 1552 might ' be proclaymed and read in open markets and like places and assemblies . . . and that diligent inquiry bee made after all such broggers, etc.', getting the names of all men engaged in such work, and then ' take bondes of them . . . in good somes of money, with condicion that they shall not buy or bargaine any manner of wools contrary to the tenour and forme of the said Statute '.[6]

[1] *D. S. P., Eliz.*, cxvii. 38, October 1577.
[2] Brit. Mus., Add. MSS. 34324, ff. 8–10 (May 23, 1585). Also f. 14.
[3] *Kenyon MSS., Hist. MSS. Comm.*, p. 595 (June 26, 1588).
[4] *Acts of Privy Council*, August 9, 1590, vol. xix, pp. 370–1.
[5] Ibid., May 28, 1590 (vol. xix, p. 169).
[6] Add. MSS. 34324, f. 14.

It seemed impossible either to end or mend the wool-chapman ; firstly, because he was an economic necessity ; secondly, because he was linked up in close alliance with the Merchants of the Staple, who still possessed some strength ; and thirdly, because the justices of the peace, in whose hands rested the administration of all these social and economic statutes, might enforce the Act or leave it a dead letter, according to their temper and the need of the locality for the wool-man. James I tried to solve the problem by making certain places staple towns, at which alone wool could be exchanged. Kendal[1] and Leeds[2] were amongst the towns chosen, and all dealers were ordered to become members of the Company of Staplers. This attempt only helped to make still more difficult the work of exchange in wool, and before long the middleman was as powerful as ever. A general ordinance was made some time in the early seventeenth century, allowing the terms of the Halifax Act to be extended over the whole clothing area, and the wool-dealers were not slow to take an ell when allowed an inch. We may conclude this chapter with a recognition of their triumph by quoting a little more of the clothiers' petition of 1640. Here the petitioners, after pleading for a stoppage of the apprenticeship prosecutions, mentioned the extension of the Halifax Act alluded to above.

' But soe it is . . . that under Colour and pretence of doeing good . . . to ye Clothier (by bringing wools for him from a distance), they, on the contrarie, if any Countryman or any woolman that dwells farre remote, doe bring in his wolle to ye Townes of Leedes, Wakefield, Rippon, Doncaster and Pomfrett, which are Markett Townes within ye Compasse of 20 miles of ye clothing townes, and are such marketts where the Clothiers can and doe usualie frequent, even there the said woollmen doe come, purposelie to forstall ye woolle, soe that ye poore Clothiers cannot be served but at theire handes againe, which is a very greate grievance to them.'

It was requested, therefore, that ' the woollmen may be restreyned from buying and ingrossing the woolle comeing to ye Markett townes of Leedes, Wakefield, Rippon, Doncaster, and Pomfret '. The dealer had seized upon every stronghold of wool-dealing, and secured his position as a permanent factor in the economy of the domestic system.

[1] D. S. P., Jas. I, xcii. 28.   [2] D. S. P., Chas. I, cccclx. 64 (1640).

CHAPTER IV

THE STATE REGULATION OF THE YORKSHIRE CLOTH INDUSTRY UP TO THE SEVENTEENTH CENTURY

' TRICKS of the trade ' are not peculiar to the modern industrial world, and in view of the many popular attacks which are made to-day on the dishonesty of business it is refreshing to find that questionable practices in industry are as old as industry itself, and that ' business secrets ' of fraud and deceit formed part and parcel of production long before the days of the power-loom, the big firm, and the world-market. The record of our own county is as disreputable as that of any other industrial area, and the perverted ingenuity of the Yorkshire clothier presented a constant puzzle to the forces of government, so long as the State attempted to maintain a code of industrial ethics.

The regulation of the cloth industry by the State was guided by two primary considerations. Firstly, there was a real and genuine desire to keep the English pieces at a high and uniform standard of quality, and to maintain the good name of English fabrics both at home and abroad. As the export trade in cloth grew, this motive became very important, and countless statutes were prompted thereby, all of which aimed at keeping up the reputation of our textile goods in the European markets. Secondly, there were financial considerations, which regarded the cloths from the point of view of revenue. As English wool began to be worked up more at home, the revenue which had formerly been drawn from the export of the raw material must now be obtained from levies imposed upon the manufactured article. Hence, just as the staple was intended to supervise the finances of the wool revenue, so some machinery must be devised for controlling the sale of cloths in the interests of the Exchequer.

These two motives, interwoven almost inextricably at times, but with the former eventually predominant, guided the State regulation of the industry almost from the beginnings of cloth-making down to the nineteenth century, when the State abandoned all attempts at controlling the quality of the goods, and contented itself with supervising the conditions of labour. The attitude of the State was somewhat as follows : For the purposes of revenue, the same quantity of cloth of the same quality must always pay the same contribution to the national chest. Therefore the most simple method was to order uniformity of dimensions for all pieces of the same kind ; let the length, breadth, or weight of each variety of cloth be laid down by law, with severe penalties upon such as disregarded these specifications. Then, with all cloths reduced to standards, let subsidy be paid according to the nature and value of the piece. Again, in the interests of honest workmanship, it would be better to have uniformity of dimensions, for only by the rigid enforcement of legal standards of length and breadth did it seem possible to check the ' fraude and deceipt ' which for so long were the bane of legislators. Laws were therefore enacted which fixed standards of length, weight, and breadth, forbade the use of certain materials or processes, and laid down in a more or less comprehensive manner the conditions of manufacture.

To pass an elaborate measure is one thing ; to have its clauses enforced and obeyed is a very different matter. It is not necessary to enlarge on the incentives to law-breaking in such cases as this. The clothier made pieces with a view to selling them, rather than for the purpose of demonstrating his law-abidingness. The statutory specifications might not present any difficulty ; but often they did, for it was seldom possible to satisfy all the law's demands. Obedience sometimes meant all the difference between profit and loss, especially if the needs of the foreign markets and the regulations of the home government did not happen to coincide. Hence the decrees of the rulers ' up yonder ' in London were looked upon by many Yorkshiremen as orders made only to be disregarded whenever business enterprise and private gain disagreed with the laws made for the common weal. Those who framed the laws saw all this, and realized that industrial legislation would be nothing but a mass of empty phrases unless means were provided for the enforcement of such decrees. For this reason they made arrangements for the appointment of men whose business it was to see that the cloth laws were obeyed, men with power of search amongst the scattered clothiers of the rural areas, men with authority to confiscate all products of illegal workmanship, and, at the same time, men in whose hands lay the task of collecting the subsidies on cloth for the replenishing of the Exchequer. Thus we have the ulnager, and later the searchers, appointed for the difficult work of collecting revenue and enforcing legal restrictions upon an industry which was becoming increasingly flexible in character and more scattered in the area of its activity.

These are the broad lines of the subject ; we can now approach it in more detail. The Assize of Measures (1197) regulated measurements of almost every description.[1] Concerning cloth it was ordained that ' woollen cloths, wherever they are made, shall be made of the same width, to wit two ells within the lists, and of the same goodness in the middle and sides '. Here was regulation of width and also of quality. The ' width clause ' was repeated in Magna Carta,[2] and further declarations of a similar character were issued during the reign of Henry III. English merchants, however, found these restrictions most inconvenient, and many obtained liberty to deal in cloth of any breadth, whilst foreign cloths imported into this country could not be expected to conform to the English official measurements.[3]

Edward I [4] made a return to the Assize (1278), but admitted a certain variety of standards and qualities :

' Henceforth every cloth of England worth four shillings an ell and upwards shall be of the breadth of two ells within the lists, and other cloths of lower price shall be seven quarters (of an ell) . . . and that all foreign cloths shall be 26 ells and 6 quarters wide. And that all cloth which is not of assize, except the serges of the parts beyond the sea and of Scotland and Ireland, for which there is no certain measure in this realm, shall be confiscated.'

Here the length of a whole cloth was fixed for the first time ; foreign cloth was ordered to conform to English standards for

---

[1] Roger de Hoveden, *Chronica*, iv. 33. The ' list ' was, of course, the narrow strip of waste on both edges of the cloth, useful in tentering, &c.

[2] Magna Carta, c. 35 ' Una latitudo pannorum tinctorum et russettorum et habergettorum, scilicet duae ulnae infra listas.'

[3] e.g. Statutes 9 Hen. III and 56 Hen. III ; see Close Rolls, 6 Ed. I, m. 7 d : Madox, *Exchequer*, chap. xiii, p. 324.

[4] Close Rolls, 6 Ed. I, m. 7 d (1278).

easier assessment of import dues, but the cheaper wares of the North and West were allowed to be of any dimensions.

In order to enforce this declaration two men were appointed to view all cloths exposed for sale, whether home-made or of foreign manufacture, and to confiscate all wares not in accordance with proper dimensions.[1]   Shortly afterwards the work passed into the hands of one man, who was generally appointed for life to the ' office of ulnage of canvas, linen, kerseys, serges, and all kinds of cloth of London, York, Winchester, Bristol, Lincoln, Essex, Norfolk, Suffolk, Kent, Stamford, Beverley, St. Osyth, Devon and Cornwall '.[2]

This man was the ulnager, a person destined to play an important part in the textile world for the next four centuries. His work was to enforce the assize of cloth as fixed by the government of the day, and to collect the subsidy levied on cloth manufactured for sale.   His province was the whole of England and Wales, and consequently he was obliged to enlist the services of a large number of deputy-ulnagers.   There was one for Yorkshire, Cumberland, Westmorland, and Northumberland, one for Lincolnshire, and one in each of the remaining cloth-making areas of the kingdom.   The deputies lived in the locality to which they were appointed, and were responsible for the enforcement of the assize in their respective districts.[3] They were to examine and seal all taxable cloths before the fabrics could be exposed for sale.   Pieces which were not of assize, or were exposed for sale without having first received the ulnager's seal and sanction, were to be confiscated, and in some cases were conveyed to the Tower of London, there to be disposed of as the King should deem best.[4]   From this inspection the cheapest saleable cloths were exempt.   ' Cogware ' and ' Kendal cloths ', made from ' the worst wool within the realm ' and sold chiefly to ' poor and mean people ', were of such small

[1] Patent Rolls, 7 Ed. I, m. 3 (1279).

[2] Patent Rolls, 9 Ed. II, pt. i, m. 25 (1315).   See also Patent Rolls, 22 Ed. III. pt. i, m. 27.

[3] Patent Rolls, 23 Ed. III, pt. i, m. 12, and 25 Ed. III, pt. i, m. 6.   Also 22 Ed. III, pt. i, m. 27.   E.g. John Pathorn of York, draper, and Wm. Belle, appointed by Wm. Hervy, ulnager of cloth for England, to be his deputies in the County of York (Patent Rolls, 3 Rich. II, pt. ii, m. 26 (1380)).

[4] Order to bailiffs, sheriffs, mayors, &c., to provide carriage for John Marreys, King's Ulnager, for conveying to the Tower of London all cloths arrested as forfeit for not being of assize (Patent Rolls, 1350, m. 1).

value that the State did not think it worth while to enforce its decrees, or levy taxation, upon such cheap wares.[1]

A fixed assize of length and breadth was apparently of doubtful value, and at times during the fourteenth century was abolished. For instance, an assize of cloth was issued in 1328,[2] fixing the dimensions of cloths in the raw state. In 1353 freedom was given to make cloths of any dimensions, provided, however, ' that the King's Ulnager shall measure the cloth and mark the same, by which mark a man may know how much the cloth containeth '.[3] Thirty-six years later, in 1389, the assize was revived,[4] except for the coarsest qualities of cloth.[5] This remained in operation until 1393, when all persons were once more allowed to make and sell cloth of such lengths and breadths as they pleased, provided each piece was searched and sealed by the ulnager before being sold.[6] This Act was important, in that it affected all kinds of cloth intended for sale, whatever the size or quality.

The examination of saleable cloths, whilst important in itself, was only the preliminary to the real work of the ulnager, i. e. the collection of the subsidy on cloth.[7] The ulnager was primarily a financial agent of the Crown, and as such had to collect the sums levied on cloths made for sale. When the cloth had been sealed, the ulnager demanded an ulnage fee of one halfpenny, and a subsidy of fourpence for each whole cloth of assize, or sixpence in the case of scarlet cloths. The whole cloth of assize was 26–28 yards in length, and 6–6½ quarters in breadth.[8] Half cloths paid twopence, but by the statute of 1353 no subsidy was to be paid for cloths containing less than half a cloth of assize. The kerseys and many other cloths made in the West Riding were less than half a cloth : hence they escaped not merely the payment of subsidy but also the preliminary inspec-

<hr />

[1] Statute, 13 Rich. II, c. 10.   [2] Statute, 2 Ed. III, c. 14.

[3] *Statutes of the Realm*, i. 330.   [4] Statute, 13 Rich. II, c. 10.

[5] The Act of 13 Rich. II, i, c. 10, has an interesting paragraph on cheap cloth : ' Forasmuch as it hath been a common custom to make certain cloths in divers counties called Cogware and Kendal cloth . . . sold to cogmen out of the realm, and also to poor and mean people within the realm, of the which cloths a great part is made of the worst wool within this realm, that cannot well serve for any other cloths ' ; these cloths were therefore allowed to remain free of any regulation or taxation.

[6] Statute, 17 Rich. II, c. 2 (1393).

[7] Patent Rolls, 27 Ed. III, pt. iii, m. 5 (1354).

[8] Statute, 27 Ed. III, stat. i, c. 4. ' Quarter ' here means a quarter of a yard.

tion by the ulnager. This was all altered by the Act of 1393, which imposed the payment of revenue on all cloths ' as well kerseys as others '.[1] From that time onward, the kersey makers of the West Riding had to place their wares under the ulnager's rod and pay their tribute. Since the average kersey made in Yorkshire was equal to about a quarter of a whole cloth of assize, it contributed one penny as subsidy. In practice, the Kendal cloths, ' cottons ', and ' Cogware ' of the far north-western counties remained exempt from control all through the fifteenth century, and no ulnager's documents exist for the area west of the Pennine Chain.

With the expansion of the woollen industry during the fifteenth century the yield from the subsidy and ulnage became a more important part of the royal revenue. Monarchs regarded it as a constant and regular stream of income, which could be utilized in paying off debts or in providing annuities for old and faithful servants. For instance, in 1410 Henry IV granted to one of his serjeants-at-arms ' twelve pence daily for life from the issues of the ulnage and subsidy of cloths in the County of York ',[2] and three years later he made a similar grant to another serjeant ' of £34 11s. 3d. yearly from the subsidy and ulnage of cloths in the City and County of York '.[3] When Henry died, his widow received a large annuity, including £33 6s. from the revenue on Yorkshire cloths, £100 from that of Somersetshire, and other sums from the money paid by the clothiers of Dorset, Southampton, Surrey, Sussex, and East Anglia.[4] To give a last instance, Edward IV, immediately upon his accession to the throne, sought to reward the Nevilles, and also to bind them more closely to his side, by handing over to John Nevill, Lord Montagu, the whole of the ulnage of Yorkshire, with all its revenues from subsidy, ulnage, and the sale of forfeited cloths.[5]

---

[1] Statute 17 Rich. II, c. 2.   [2] Patent Rolls, 11 Hen. IV, pt. i, m. 1.
[3] Patent Rolls, 14 Hen. IV, m. 18.
[4] Patent Rolls, 1 Hen. V, pt. v, mm. 10 and 11 (1414). More ambitious still was the grant in 1442, to Leo, Lord of Welles, and late Lieutenant of Ireland, ' of the sum of 113 marks yearly . . . out of subsidy and ulnage of cloth for sale in the County and City of York . . . and in Kyngeston-upon-Hull . . . until he be satisfied of the sum of £2,000 and more, due to him by the King ' (Patent Rolls, 20 Hen. VI, pt. iii, m. 15 (1442)).
[5] Patent Rolls, 1 Ed. IV, pt. iv, m. 2.

The work of the ulnager was supplemented by the activities of the searchers appointed by the crafts, who strove to enforce the legal assize, and at the same time attempted to maintain the quality of the fabrics made in the towns. That this dual system of inspection fully achieved its aim is very improbable. The frequent revisions of the law and the declarations of municipal authorities and gilds seem to indicate that the mediaeval cloth-maker was not invariably law-abiding. Numerous instances of fraud and deceit are recorded, and commissions were occasionally sent out to study the working of the Cloth Acts and to suggest improvements in legislation and administration.[1] In short, it seems to have been impossible effectively to regulate the industry even when it was largely confined to the towns. Hence when the expansion of the following centuries began to make itself felt, when the drift from the towns weakened the control of the craft searchers and the rural areas became the strongholds of the industry, it was even less possible for the old local and national machinery to be effective. The industry was becoming much more important as a source of national wealth, but its development was on such lines that the old police systems were more and more inadequate for keeping it under supervision. One arm of control, that of the gilds, was losing its strength, and it was therefore necessary that the State should provide stronger regulations to uphold a fair standard of quality in the English pieces. So we enter a bewildering maze of legislation throughout the fifteenth and sixteenth centuries, regulating every detail of dimension for every variety of cloth, forbidding certain processes, and prescribing the general and detailed character of the manufacture. One Act succeeded another with great rapidity, and the Yorkist and Tudor Parliaments evolved some measures which in complexity and intricacy rivalled a modern Insurance Act.

What were the tricks of trade against which these statutes were directed ? Particular complaints occur from time to time,

---

[1] There were constant attempts to evade the ulnage, and nearly every ulnage account contained records of forfeiture made by some one who had attempted to sell cloth unsealed. In 1358 there was a Commission for the whole kingdom, with seven commissioners for Yorkshire, because the ' King learned he is greatly defrauded by the subtle machinations of merchants and others, who are selling cloths before they are sealed ' (Patent Rolls, 32 Ed. III, pt. ii, m. 6 d).

but the general faults which run throughout the whole story, and which were concerned with all the processes, from weaving onwards, can be briefly summed up as follows :

(1) The use of flocks, thrums (i.e. waste ends of wool and yarn), and other inferior materials and rubbish in the weaving of the cloth. This working of waste odds and ends into the body of the cloth when weaving seems to have been a common practice, which called forth general condemnation from pamphleteers and legislators.

(2) The mixing of wool of various kinds and standards of spinning in the same piece, and also the use of better qualities of weft at the ends of the piece than in the middle. These practices caused the fabric to be composed of material of very uneven quality and standard. The inequalities were accentuated after the fulling, when certain parts had shrunk more than others, and thus the piece would be uneven, of varying width, thickness, and quality, exhibiting that strange effect known to contemporaries as ' cockling ' or ' banding '.

These practices, however, were mere trifles compared with (3) the frauds practised in tentering the cloth. The piece had shrunk considerably during the washing and fulling ; the extent of the shrinkage varied according to the fineness of the yarn which had been used in making the cloth, and other considerations, so that the size of the piece after fulling might be doubtful. In the tentering process, the cloth was stretched upon a long wooden frame, and was then pulled out to its final dimensions. These measurements were those fixed by the particular statute which was at that time in operation, and so the cloth, no matter what its length after fulling, must be stretched to the stipulated legal length and breadth. This often meant that the piece was excessively stretched, and the cloth which could have undergone a little tentering without any harm was, by this over-tentering, rendered thin and threadbare in places. In such circumstances ' medicine ' was applied to restore the cloth to its pristine thickness and firmness. This was done by covering the cloth with a coating or pigment of some concoction, in which flocks, waste wool, thrums, chalk, oatmeal, and similar substances were to be found. Thanks to this reinforcement, the cloth now appeared firm to the touch

and pleasing to the eye ; it was not until the fabric was worn
and the rain came down that the deception became apparent,
as the ' medicine ' was washed out and the cloth shrank towards
its minimum dimensions.[1]

It was against such practices as these that legislation hurled
its prohibitions. The frauds debased the name of English cloths
in the foreign market, and would lose for this country the
foreign cloth trade unless they were speedily checked. The
Government therefore did its utmost to stamp out all such
nefarious practices. It did not attempt at first to meddle with
the coarser wares, and Kendal cloths, ' frizes ', ' cottons ', and
similar qualities of North-Country textiles were generally
exempted from the force of these reformatory statutes. The
better class of goods, the kerseys and broad cloths, were not
excused, and many of the cloths on which the West Riding was
building up a thriving industry would therefore come within
the scope of these enactments. Certainly, as the sixteenth-
century Statute Book shows, Yorkshire needed to be watched,
for its reputation was in many respects very bad.

From the accession of Edward IV to the reign of James I
there is an almost unbroken succession of enactments, all of
which attempted to encourage the cloth industry by making
orders for its moral welfare, and by forbidding dishonest
practices in the manufacture of textile fabrics. It would be
unprofitable to enter into the details of those statutes, but it is
possible to study their general character, and to note how the
framers of such legislation learned wisdom and gained experience
in the course of time. The Act of 1464 gives an excellent
illustration of the nature of these enactments.[2] Its preamble is
typical :

' Whereas for many years past and now at this day the
workmanship of cloths and things requisite to the same is and
hath been of such fraud, deceit, and falsity that the said cloths
in other lands and countries be had in small reputation, to the
great shame of this land.'

---

[1] These details of the nature of the frauds are drawn from pamphlets,
complaints such as Leake's *Discourse* (see below), and other State papers, in
addition to the statutes themselves.

[2] Statute 4 Ed. IV, c. 1. These Acts were generally worked out with
minuteness of detail, and attempted to provide as adequately as possible
for the control of the industry.

Therefore, for the reformation of the industry, it was ordered that various kinds of cloth, ' after the full watering, racking, straining and tentering of the same, ready for sale ' should conform to certain stipulated lengths and breadths. Clothiers were forbidden to work lamb's wool, thrums, or chalk into the pieces, and officers were appointed to see that the Act was obeyed in all its details.

This Act of 1464 failed to bring about the reformation expected from it, and the statute of 1483 was intended as a supplement and extension.[1] The note of the new Act was its attack on excessive tentering ; some cloths had been stretched to far more than the legal limits, and pieces which should have been only 24 yards in length had been ' drawn out to xxx yerdys, and in brede from seven quarters unto ye brede of ij yerdys '. The root of the evil seemed to lie in the fact that tentering was done privately, within doors, out of the public gaze. The Act therefore forbade the use of any cloth-stretching devices within houses or workrooms. Tenters were to be set up in open places only, and the mayors, bailiffs, and governors of boroughs, towns, and villages were to survey these open places diligently, in order to prevent excessive tentering. The assistance of the local authorities was thus enlisted, a policy which was materially developed during the next century. From the force of this Act there were numerous exceptions, especially of the cheaper northern cloths.[2]

Henry VIII, in the midst of his manifold activities, found time to attend to economic legislation, and the cloth laws of his reign were numerous ; but they always exempted Kendals, Northern whites, ' frizes ', and Devon cloths, the cheap wares of the period.[3] Yorkshire, however, was not to escape, for in 1533 a commission was appointed to inquire into some aspects of the West Riding industry. The details of the story are scanty, but it is clear that the Yorkshiremen had been using flocks in the manufacture of their cloths, in a manner contrary to law. The commissioners had great difficulty in obtaining

---

[1] Statute 1 Rich. III, c. 8.

[2] Kendals, ' frize ware ', &c., were exempted.

[3] e.g. 14–15 Hen. VIII, c. 1 and c. 11. Also Statute 6 Hen. VIII, c. 9, for avoiding deceits in making woollen cloths, excluding Cornwall, and friezes made in Wales, Lancashire, and Cheshire.

any information; witness the following letter, sent by Sir Marmaduke Constable to Thomas Cromwell, and dated October 3, 1533 :

'Please it you bee aduised that accordyng to the Kyng's comyssion to me and others directed for reformacon of fflokkyng of clothes in the West Parties of the Shyre of Yorke, by force whereof Sir John Nevyll, John Pullayn, and myselff have setten at Leydes, emong diuers of the clothmakers, wherby all the polycye we could devyse came not any to the knawllege of prove to be made agaynst the grett nombre of the offenders. Whereupon we appoynted another settynge att Pountfrett . . . trustyng by the same that the offenders shalbe brought to better knawllege, and the Kynges grace to profyt.'[1]

After considerable trouble, the commissioners succeeded in drawing up a list of such as were weaving cloth with weft made of flocks.[2] This catalogue of offenders includes names from all the cloth-making centres of the West Riding, and mentions no less than 542 clothiers. Alongside each name stands the number of illegal cloths which were found in the possession of the offender. The general entry is one half-cloth, and the largest culprit is entered for three cloths only. Evidently this manufacture of cloths by using flocks as weft was a very small and insignificant matter. The explanation seems to be that the clothiers, in the course of their occupation, gradually accumulated a stock of flocks, thrums, waste yarn, &c. These scraps they kept on one side until they had a considerable pile at their disposal, when they worked up the whole into yarn of an inferior quality, and wove it into a cheap cloth. This was scarcely

[1] *State Papers, Henry VIII*, § 79, p. 139.
[2] Exch. Accounts, bundle 345, no. 25 : 'Nomina eorum qui operaverunt pannos licia vocat. fflocke.' This list contains 542 names, distributed as follows :

Halifax	.	.	182 names	Heaton	. .	18 names
Heptonstall	.	.	60 ,,	Birstall	. .	18 ,,
Almondbury	.	.	55 ,,	Wakefield	. .	13 ,,
Leeds	.	.	49 ,,	Dewsbury	. .	13 ,,
Elland	.	.	49 ,,	Batley	. .	13 ,,
Huddersfield	.	.	40 ,,	Mirfield	. .	8 ,,
Bradford	.	.	24 ,,			
				Total	.	542 ,,

The names cover the whole of the cloth area, and a good percentage come from what is now the heavy woollen and shoddy district. Amongst the culprits appear most of the well-known industrial families of Yorkshire—Baynes, Walker, Musgrave, Kitson, Harrison, and Wilson, in Leeds ; Crowther, Hirst, Wormald, Lee, Walker, Holdsworth, &c., in other parts.

a forerunner of the modern shoddy industry, for shoddy is made out of wool which has already been woven or knitted, and worn, whereas these sixteenth-century clothiers were utilizing the waste material which they accumulated in weaving kerseys, Northern Dozens, &c. To the clothier this practice was obviously a splendid piece of economy, and a utilization of waste products. In the eyes of the law it was a deceitful and lawless device which must be stopped. The commission reported to Thomas Cromwell, who entered in his ' Remembrancer ', at least three times, ' To remember such as have caused cloths to be flocked in the North, and to know the Kynges pleasure '.[1] Little was done, for in 1534 a writer declared to Cromwell that in spite of the commission ' they doe nowe the same (flokkyng and false cloth making) moche more and worse than ever they dyd '.[2]

Commissions and legislation appear to have produced little effect upon the morality of the industry, and complaints began to come from the foreign countries which purchased English cloths.[3] During the sixteenth century the number of varieties of native fabrics increased rapidly, and it was therefore possible for new types of cloth to escape the letter of the law, since they belonged to a class not mentioned in the statutes then in operation. In 1552 a great and comprehensive attempt was made to bring all existing varieties of cloth under the power of the law, and to establish a thorough scheme of regulation. A commission of ' certain wise discreet and sage knights and burgesses of Parliament ' was given the task of inquiring amongst ' honest clothiers . . . drapers, merchant taylors, cloth-workers, shearmen and other artificers, . . . of such matters as touch as well the false as the true making of clothes, by whose declaration, consent and advice, after divers and sundry meetings ' the new Act was to be framed.

The first point of importance about this statute[4] was the variety of cloths for which regulation was ordered. No less than

---

[1] *Calendar of State Papers, Henry VIII*, vol. vi, nos. 1370, 1371, and 1382, October 1533.

[2] *State Papers, Henry VIII*, § 88, pp. 119–20.

[3] Prohibition by Spain on foreign cloths. English cloths were admitted for a time, but the writer said that this favour would be quickly removed unless the English cloth-makers amended the faults in their cloth. Written at Valladolid, September 18, 1538 (*Calendar of State Papers*, vol. xiii, pt. ii, no. 383).

[4] Statute 5–6 Ed. VI, c. 6.

22 different types of woollen cloth were catered for, and in each case full specifications were laid down. There were ordinary kerseys, sorting kerseys, Northern cloths, Northern dozens, Pennistones, Manchester, Lancashire and Cheshire ' cottons ', Manchester rugs and ' frizes ', &c.[1] The Act really did attempt to embrace every variety of English woollen cloth which came into the market, and in order to do so it had to make provision for this great number of different fabrics.

The second feature of importance in the statute was the stress laid on the weight of cloths. It had become obvious at last that the provision of legal dimensions alone was insufficient, and was even provocative of fraud, since it tempted the clothier to stretch his pieces abnormally in order to bring them up to the legal length and breadth. In order to remedy this defect the new Act declared the weight of wool which must be put into each piece, or rather the weight of the piece when washed and dried, as well as the length and breadth of the fabric.

The dimensions stated in the Act were those of the cloth when fully wetted and shrunk, and the weight was to be that of the piece when thoroughly cleaned and dry. It was hoped now that by measuring the piece before tentering its real size could be ascertained. Makers of short-weight pieces were to be fined, and really faulty cloths confiscated. No cloth was to be stretched in tentering more than one yard in length or a quarter of a yard in breadth.

For the administration of this Act searchers were to be appointed. The mayors, bailiffs, and other chief officers of cities, boroughs, and corporate towns· were given authority to appoint two or more ' discreet, honest and expert persons ', who were endowed with full power of searching, measuring, and sealing, and with the right to confiscate cloths which infringed

---

[1] ' Pennistones ' or ' forest whites ' were cloths which seem to have been made especially at Penistone, near Barnsley. Or they may have taken their name from a coarse type of Yorkshire wool, known as Pennistone. For instance, the Northern wares were ordered to be as follows :

Ordinary kerseys .   .   Length, 17–19 yds. Weight, 20 lb.
Sorting kerseys   .   .   ,,   17–18 ,,   ,,   23 ,,

Northern whole broad cloths, of the kind made around Leeds, were to contain 23–25 yds. by 1¾ yds., ' and being well scowered, thicked, milled, and fully dried, shall weigh lxvj lb. (66 lb.) at the least '. Northern dozens : Length, 12–13 yds. ; breadth, 1¼ yds. ; weight, 33 lb. Pennistones : length, 12–13 yds. ; breadth, 6½ qrs. ; weight, 28 lb.

the clauses of the statute. But all these provisions applied only
to towns, and to cloths which were finished or made within the
towns. There was no provision of machinery for the regulation of the rural industry, and so, apart from the ulnager, whose
work was now little more than financial, the country cloths
might pass uninspected, provided they did not come into the
towns to receive their finishing touches. Hence the Act, full
of good intentions, achieved very little. It was amended and
strengthened in 1557,[1] when attention was given to the broad
cloths of the West Riding, and, in a small degree, to rural cloths
generally. But still no reformation was effected, and the
famous complaint of Leake, written twenty years afterwards,
revealed a lamentable lack of orthodox industrial morality
amongst the clothiers of the North Country.[2] Leake's chief
accusations against the Yorkshiremen and their neighbours
were :

(1) 'fflockes, chalke, and other false oyntementes cast uppon
clothe is specially used in the Northe partes, *wher no true clothes
are made*, and this is the pryncipall poynte in the which the
clothyer doth offend ' :

(2) For faulty dyeing, ' all the coulored clothes made in ye
Northe is worst of all ' :

(3) ' And especially for streatchinge and strayninge, Suffolke,
Redding, and ye Northe partes . . . are greatly abused, . . . and
generally where the clothyer doth dresse clothe at home before
he sell itt, ther doe they moste stretche and strayne abomnably,
6, 7, 8, 9, and 10 yardes.'

(4) ' All other sortes of lowe prised clothes, and Northern
clothes of all sortes and Kerseys, and cottons, freyse, etc., will
not hold their contentes, beinge wette.'

And so Leake's indictment continues, against every fraud,
conceivable or otherwise. He condemns all manner of deceits
as practices which ' can nayther bee answered before God nor
the World '. As to the cloth laws, ' better laws cannot bee
made, onely there wants execuc'on, for wante therof bothe
clothyer, alnager, searchers, merchantes and retaylers of clothe
be growen into suche securitye yt ye lawe is forgotten, and they
do what they liste '. The magistrates, noting the prevalence
of such evil-doing, have let the laws fall into abeyance, ' and

---

[1] Statute 4–5 Philip and Mary, c. 5.

[2] D. S. P., *Eliz.*, cxi. 38. Also a copy in cclxxxvii. 96.

therbye all the falsehood hitherto hath bene couered, as it were under a bushell '. ' I am fullie of opinion ', concludes Leake, ' that . . . generallie for all clothes the lawes were never yett observed in any place within the realme.'

These processes, so obnoxious to the legislator, were practised as commonly in the West Riding as elsewhere, especially that of stretching the piece to an excessive length, and then thickening it with a pigment of flocks. In 1590 [1] complaint was made to the Privy Council of the ' great deceiptes used and permitted in the chopping of flockes and rubbing the same into cloth by the greatest parte of clothiers in the County of Yorke '. The Council took the matter into consideration, and eventually appointed Randall Tenche to ' deface and cutt in peeces or burne all such blockes or bordes as have been or are now used for the chopping of flockes '.

Whilst complaints were coming from within the country, the murmur of discontent from abroad grew louder concerning the inferior quality of some of the cloths which were bought from England. In 1589 [2] the Estates of Holland dispatched to Elizabeth a complaint ' of the great defectes and fraudes in the Englische clothes brought thether ', and in 1592 Monsieur Carron, the agent of the Low Countries, resident in England, presented a long list of grievances against English wares. He declared that the fabrics imported into the Low Countries by the Merchant Adventurers were ' not only full of holes and in certen faults muche worse than can bee seen outwards, but also [were] narrower and shorter than they ought to bee, wherby the merchants which cometh to buy them without openinge or measuring of them, . . . when they sell them by the ell or measure they find themselves shortened and deceaved of that which they thought to have ; which is the cause that manie merchant clothbuyers of the United Provinces can not of late profite anie waye by the said clothes, but become poore '. Carron asserted that the faults mentioned were especially prevalent amongst the kerseys and ' Dozens ', which were often two yards below

[1] Acts of Privy Council, December 24, 1590.

[2] Ibid., December 28, 1589. In 1593 the soldiers then in the Low Countries were complaining that ' the apparel is not equal to the patterns, and is of bad stuff which soon wears, the cloth shrinks, the stockings are short, and the shoes bad '. This was due partly to Elizabeth's economy, and partly to the antics of the English clothiers (D. S. P., Eliz., ccxliv. 821).

the proper length ; all of which, he declared, ' is wholie against the goodwill of her Matie and contrarie to your good and laudable Statutes of Parliament therupon made, which ought to be observed as well for the Lowe Countries as for Englande '.[1]

These protests at last bore fruit in a renewal of industrial legislation, and it is significant that the first sweeping enactment concerned itself solely with cloth made north of the Trent.[2] This Act of 1597 [3] was surprisingly harsh in tone, and aimed with deadly intent at ' checking the deceiptfull stretching and taintering of Northerne Cloths '. The preamble was as illuminating as it was prolix ; it spoke of the ' many goode and wholesome lawes heretofore made for the true makyng of good and true clothes and karseis, which lawes, either by some wants in the statutes already made, or for lacke of the due execucon of the saide lawes have not only not restrayned the great abuse in makyng of clothes and karseis, but rather have increased the same, insomuch that the Northerne clothes and karseis doe yerely and dayly grow worse and worse, and are made more light and moche more stretched and strayned than heretofore they have bene, to the greate deceipt of all nations . . . and to the shame and slaunder of the countrye where the same is made, and in short tyme like utterlie to overthrowe the trade of clothynge '. This great depravity the legislators imputed chiefly to the ' greate nomber of tentors and other engines daylie used and practised . . . for the stretchynge and strayninge of the . . . clothes and Karseis '. Therefore the Act, with righteous indignation and firm determination to destroy the evil, root and branch, declared that ' no person or persons within any of the counties on the Northside of the Ryver of Trent shall stretche or strayne . . . any clothes, dozens, kersies, pennistones, rugs, frizes, Kighley whites, . . . or any other clothes made within the counties aforesaid, upon pain to forfeit £5 for every default. And further that no person . . . shall use or occupie any tenter or any manner of wrinche rope or engines to stretche or strayne

[1] *Salisbury MSS., Hist. MSS. Comm.*, pt. iv, p. 216, July 1592. Also *D. S. P., Eliz.*, ccxlii. 75, July 1592 : ' The Copie of the first five Articles exhibited by M. Carron in the names of the State Generall of the United Provinces of the Low Countries.'
[2] As early as 1580 a Bill for the search of cloths made in the County of York had been before the House of Commons, but had been abandoned (*House of Commons Journals*, i. 124).   [3] Statute 39 Eliz., c. 20.

any clothes ' under a penalty of £20 fine. In other words, the use of tenters was entirely forbidden.

Secondly, all cloths were to be made of the weight and dimensions stated in previous Acts, and the manufacturer was to place on the end of each piece, before selling it, a seal, on which was his own name, as well as the specifications of the cloth.

It was not intended that this statute should fail in its objects through faulty administration ; further, it was not intended that the rural industry should escape any longer from thorough supervision. The Act therefore gave detailed and elaborate orders for the provision of administrative machinery, both for town and country alike. The Justices of the Peace were to appoint searchers for the rural areas, whilst the municipal authorities chose similar officers for the towns. The searchers were elected for one year,[1] during which time they had full power to go, once a month at least, into the houses or workrooms of all workers in wool, to search for faulty workmanship, and to measure and seal all cloths when ready for the market. At the same time they were to hunt for tenters, and when they found any they were to deface the frames so that they could not be used henceforth.

The main provision of the Act [2] was ' Death to the tenter '. This would be a staggering blow to every cloth-maker in the county. There was scarcely a clothier of any standing but had his tenter frame, on which he stretched the shrunk fabric, after its visit to the fulling mill, into uniformity and legality of length and breadth. Without tentering, the piece would be contracted to small and uneven proportions, it would present a dishevelled and unkempt appearance, and would not sell at any profitable price. Industry without the tenter was impossible. And yet the ' big folk ' up in London, ignorant of the needs and the means of the clothiers, had ordered that all stretch-

[1] The searchers on election were to take oath, and be bound with a guarantee of £40, to do their duty faithfully and thoroughly. The exhortation administered them by the J.P. read as follows : ' You shall swear that you shall use your best endeavours by all lawfull means dureing your continuance in the office of searchers, . . . to see all lawes and statutes concerninge clothinge bee well and truely observed and kept, and that you shall make a true presentment with accompte in wrytinge at every generall sessions for your division within the said Rydinge of all your whole proceedinges in your office, soe helpe you God.'

[2] The Act was extended to the whole country four years later ; 43 Eliz., c. 10.

ing of cloth should cease, and threatened a St. Bartholomew's Day on all tenters.

The Act was received with very mixed feelings by the various parties concerned. The French Ambassador in London caused it,[1] along with other cloth laws, to be translated into French, and disseminated in his own country, and the French Government began to confiscate any English pieces which went into that country bearing signs of stretching. In England the Privy Council, which was chiefly responsible for supervising the administration of such Acts by local authorities, dispatched frequent letters to the justices of the Northern counties, exhorting them to enforce the Act of 1597, and destroy the accursed tenters. But the justices, who had fought so strenuously in the battle over the Ship-money levies, did not intend to surrender without a hard struggle on a matter which was much more important in its permanent effects. They, who lived in the very heart of the clothing area, knew that the tenter was a necessary piece of apparatus to the clothier's art, and that the industry could not be carried on without using the tenter frames. They were also fully aware that any attempt to demolish these tenters would mean an attack on the property of nearly every clothier, and would bring about their own ears such a storm of protest and opposition that their lives would be unbearable. Hence, little wonder if they allowed their loyalty to their county to outweigh considerations of obedience to Her Majesty's Government. They ranged themselves on the side of the clothiers, and refused to put the Act into operation. The Privy Council sent long letters to the West Riding magistrates, informing them of the confiscations which were taking place in France, bewailing the fact that cloth came to the markets as bad as ever it had been,[2] and finally urging the need for a rigorous administration of the Act. To those letters the justices presented a front of masterly indifference and inactivity, which irritated the Privy Council in no small measure. At last the Council threw persuasion to the winds, and spoke in terms of anger to the disobedient Yorkshiremen. This was in 1600, after two years had been wasted in peaceful persuasion; and the

[1] D. S. P., Eliz., cclxix. 45.
[2] D. S. P., Eliz., cclxix. 45, declared that ' cloth cometh to the market woorse than better '.

wrath of the Privy Council was now turned against the justices
for Yorkshire, Lancashire, and Westmorland jointly :

' It ys not, or ought not to be unknowne unto you that there
ys a statute made in the xxxixth yere of her Majesty's raigne,
against the deceiptfull makinge . . . of certaine clothes. . . .
Nevertheless, notwithstandinge the Statute so latelie made with
soche care and provicion to redresse and remedie thes sclanderous
abuses, by which the credit and estymacion of our cloths ys so
moche demynished and sclaundered as of late there ys an edict
sett forth by the French Kinge by which all Englishe clothes
which shalbe brought into that realme are declared confiscable
that have bene tentered or stretched, or made of two wolles,
rowed, cockled, and stuffed with flockes.'

Still, in spite of the good intentions of the legislators, the
laws are left inoperative by those who should enforce them,
and cloth is as bad as ever it was. Concerning this ' contempt
of the lawe and prejudice of the Common Wealth ', the Council
continues, ' wee have cause to note a greate wante of care in
you (i. e. the Northern magistrates) in that you neglect the due
execucion of that lawe, and therefore wee doe will and com-
maunde you in Her Majesty's name that you will have due
regard hereafter to see the said statute observed and put in
execucion accordinge to the tenor, purport and true meanynge
of the same in all places within the countie '. The justices are
to enforce the Act at once, and order that all tenters shall be
completely defaced. The letter concludes with a stern note of
warning : ' Otherwyse . . . you will be called to a strict accompt
for the neglect of your duties, . . . and further notice maie be
taken of soch of you as shalbe fownde negligent and remisse
herein, as other more carefull persons maie supplie their
places.' [1] Even such a minatory epistle failed to make the
justices stir in the matter, and six months later, in 1601, the
Council declared in most injured tones, ' nothinge hathe bene
as yet don for redres of the said deceipt, . . . and wee cannott
but fynde it strange that you should use such slackness in
a reformation . . . of so greate waight and ymportance '.[2]

Hard words indeed, but not sufficiently strong to move the
justices to attempt the impossible. What matter if the French
monarch had ordered all English cloths taken into France to be

[1] *Acts of the Privy Council*, August 24, 1600, vol. xxx, pp. 602-3.
[2] Ibid., January 22, 1601, vol. xxxi, p. 111.

soaked in water, and was confiscating those which shrank under that test ? The tenter was a necessity for trimming up the piece, and one might almost say that no tentering meant no profit. Hence protests were sent to the central authorities from the justices of the peace, clothiers, and merchants.[1] The traders who were engaged in selling the English wares declared that the practice was carried on by their foreign competitors, and that it would be impossible for English cloth to gain a market abroad unless tentering was allowed. They stated, with how much truth one cannot say, that Muscovites, Russians, and ' they of Barbarie ' desired cloth which would shrink, and did not in the least object to stretched cloth. Finally, they urged that unless the cloth could be stretched it would be too costly for the inhabitants of those regions to which it was formerly exported.[2] The result of these agitations was to obtain a number of exemptions from the full force of the Act, and these privileges were eventually crystallized in a statute in 1623.[3] In this new Act, tenter-frames were permitted to exist and to be used, but they were to be so constructed that no more than a certain specified amount of straining could be effected by them. The distance which the bottom beam of the framework might be lowered was not to exceed a certain amount, and all tenters which violated these conditions by allowing more than the legal ' chase ' were to be defaced instantly, and their owners fined 40s. for the benefit of the poor.

This was a great triumph for the clothiers, for the permissive Act amounted in practice to an admission of the injustice of the anti-tenter laws, and a surrender to the clothiers. Probably the passing of the new statute made no actual difference in the procedure of the industry, and certainly it failed just as much as its predecessors to achieve anything substantial. True, the various enactments were not quite dead letters.[4] Searchers

---

[1] The J.P.'s of Lancashire gained the concession in 1600 that tenters should be permitted to remain in existence, but were to be so made as not to allow excessive tentering (*Acts of Privy Council*, January 4, 1600–1, vol. xxxi, p. 78).   [2] Cotton MSS. (Brit. Mus.), Galba E, vol. i, 320–2, April 1605.
[3] Statute 21 Jas. I, c. 18.
[4] In West Riding Quarter Sessions Indictment Books one occasionally encounters cases of excessive tentering being punished, but such cases are comparatively rare. One man in 1648 was fined £20 for the offence (Indictment Book B, Wakefield Quarter Sessions, January 1649). In the Sowerby Constable's Accounts, mention is made of warrants for bringing such as had

were appointed, and clothiers were hauled before the magistrates for deceitful making of cloth and for excessive tentering.
But in spite of the activity, more or less spasmodic, of these
local inspectors, there was little improvement in the ' tone ' of
the industry, and the cries of fraud and deceit continued almost
without abatement during the seventeenth century. New types
of cunning workmanship came into prominence, new complaints
were voiced, and new attempts made to check these practices,
either by reinforcing existing laws and reviving old forms of
regulation, or by inventing new methods of control. These
attempts will form the subject of a subsequent chapter, but we
can conclude this section by quoting the lamentation of May
in 1613, to show how completely the Tudor legislation had
failed to fulfil its purpose. May cites a long list of nefarious
practices, and piles a terrible indictment upon the heads of the
clothiers. He then concludes as follows :

' Whiles the true making of cloth endured in reasonable
manner, it was most vendible in all parts. But what maketh
those now to refuse it, being brought to their owne doors, which
before time earnestly sought it at ours ? Falsehood ! . . . What
maketh the gentleman complain of the wool that lyeth on his
hands ? The clothier complain of his dead sales ? The merchant complain of his losse ? All but falsehood ! How thick
are certificates of falsehood returned upon our merchants from
beyond the seas ! In provinces beyonde the boundes of Christen-
dome, when· a Turk or Infidel brusheth his garment bare that
he may number the threads, and findeth here and there holes
and faults, then our Christian profession is called into question
by these prophane people. In Kingdoms nere us, these abuses
have bene founde so odious, and their people so much wronged,
that they have made laws and edicts to banish our cloth out of
their countries, rather desiring our wool wherewith to make true
commodities. In our own countrie, where muche of our wool
may be vented, the falsehood of clothing is so common that
every one striveth to wear anything rather than cloth. If
a gentleman make a liverie for his man, in the first showre of
raine it may fit his Page for Bignesse ! ' [1]

made deceitful cloth ; there is a warrant for one man who had flocked some cloth,
and another for refusing to take up the office of searcher (Halifax Antiq. Soc.,
1902). In 1648 it was stated at the Leeds Quarter Sessions that there was
great complaint of the abuse of clothiers in making tenters of greater chase
than was allowed by the statute, and searchers were consequently ordered to
give careful attention to the matter, and deface all offending frames (Quarter
Sessions Order Book C, 101 a and 148 a).

[1] *The True Estate of Clothing in the Realm,* by J. May (1613).

CHAPTER V

MARKETS AND MERCHANTS: THE ORGANIZATION OF HOME AND FOREIGN TRADE IN YORKSHIRE CLOTH, UP TO THE RESTORATION

LONG before 1600, Yorkshire pieces had become a commodity of commercial importance. As we have seen already, the wares of York and Beverley had been noted in their day, and during the sixteenth century the produce of the Northern counties generally was meeting a certain kind of demand, both at home and abroad. The broad Northern Dozen and the narrow kersey, which were the best of the Yorkshire fabrics, commanded only low prices when compared with the high-class fabrics of the West of England. Pennistones, 'Keighley whites', and other varieties made in Yorkshire and the North belonged to even lower grades of quality. The merchants of the Northern ports were partly within the bounds of truth when they declared in 1591 that ' the clothes shipped in those cuntryes (counties) bee course clothes, and most of them made of course wooll of the growthe of those cuntryes and ffloxe and thrummes '.[1]

Such fabrics met the needs of the poorer classes in Yorkshire and elsewhere. Many of the pieces were therefore sold in the local cloth fairs and markets, where, as in the eighteenth century, clothier and merchant met on certain fixed days. Scarcely anything is known of these markets until the days of Defoe, beyond the fact that they existed.[2] The merchants or factors who purchased the pieces then sold some of them locally, but the great bulk of the cloth either passed to London, and thence

---

[1] *D. S. P., Eliz.,* ccxxxix. 54 (1591). The broad cloth, either in its full length of 24 yds., or as a ' Dozen' of 12–13 yds., represented the highest grade of Northern fabrics. It was made of the best wool, chiefly drawn from Lincolnshire or other southern counties. Next in order of merit came the kersey, which was very little inferior in quality to the broad, but longer and not so wide. It was made of the same brands of wool as the Dozen, and sold at 1s. 6d. to 2s. 6d. per yard in the early seventeenth century, when broads sold at 4s. to 5s. These two cloths were the staples of the Yorkshire industry and export trade. See next chapter for details as to further varieties and standards of manufacture.

[2] For account of Yorkshire cloth fairs see Chapter XI. Also Chapter VI for position of merchants.

to other parts of England, or went, via London, York, Hull, Newcastle, or Chester, to serve the poor of Europe.

At the same time many of the wealthy clothiers took or sent their own cloths to London, instead of relying on the Yorkshire markets for sale. This trade between Yorkshire and London was of great importance, and thousands of pieces travelled south each year, to be sold at the annual fair of St. Bartholomew or in the more frequent sales at Blackwell Hall. The yearly fair in London was opened on the day before the Feast of St. Bartholomew,[1] and continued over the two subsequent days. The venue was the churchyard of the Priory Church in West Smithfield, and the fair had become famous as a cloth exchange.[2] Here the booths of the clothiers were erected and the pieces exposed for sale ; at night the gates were locked to prevent the theft of the goods. The cloth booths seem to have been the freehold property of the clothiers, who used them annually for the display of their wares and at their death bequeathed them to their heirs. Yorkshiremen journeyed regularly with their goods to this great textile concourse, and owned cloth booths there. Thus in 1518 William Hardy of Heptonstall in his will made the bequest of his booth at ' Sainct Bartholomews juxta London '[3] to his wife and children ; in 1542 Henry Farrer of Halifax assigned to his son Brian his ' boith within Sancte Bartilmews in London, to be hade and holden to the saide Brian and to his heres and assignes for euer '.[4] Others held stalls on lease, as for instance John Crossley of Huddersfield, who in 1562 made the following bequest :

' To my eldest sone, William . . . all my interest and tearme of yeares which I have, or ought to have, of and in one standinge or bowthe in the clothe faire called great Sainct Bartilmewes, nere west Smythefield of London.'[5]

This annual journey to the fair must have been a great event to the clothiers, who approached the capital with mixed feelings of wonder and fear, much akin to the emotions of the modern countryman when he makes his first visit to the metropolis.

---

[1] ' Halifax in the Days of Henry VIII ', by J. Lister, in *Halifax Almanack*, 1913.

[2] Ashley, *Economic History*, I. ii. 214. See also *Encycl. Brit.*, 11th edition, iii. 450.   [3] *Halifax Wills*, ed. by Clay and Crossley, p. 53.

[4] Ibid., i. 156.   [5] Ibid., i. 53 n.

Fears for the safety of their precious cloths might well be entertained in an age when the length, breadth, and weight of a cloth were fixed by law, and when these legal data were constantly being revised and amended. The clothier living away up in Yorkshire would have some difficulty in keeping abreast of the latest statutory demands, and so when he reached London he might with good cause entertain doubts about the legality of his pieces. Hence we find that in 1558 'dyvers clothiars of sundry partes of the realme, havinge repayred to this Barthylmews Fayre with a greate nomber of course clothes and karseys to be uttred and solde there do forbeare to open their said clothes and put the same to sale, fearing they be not made according to the Statute ordeyned in this behalf'. In order to clear away such doubts, and to dispel the fears of the clothiers, the Privy Council called before it a number of those concerned, including, amongst others, ' John Sutclif of Hallyfax, John Hardy of the same, John Lyster of Manningham, William Lunsdale of Selby, Ollyver Brigges of Bewdeley (Co. Salop), who occupyeth in the Northe partes '. With these men the Privy Council conferred, the state of the Cloth Acts was considered, and every possible step taken to allay the fears of the clothiers.[1]

The fair was an annual occurrence, and hence did not provide facilities for continuous intercourse between the provincial clothiers and the London traders. As the cloth trade grew, the capital became more and more important as a market for cloths made in the country. Clothiers wished to sell their wares to the people of London, or to London merchants for export. They needed, therefore, some more convenient channel through which their cloths could flow week by week into the hands of London buyers. The need was met by the institution of Blackwell Hall.[2] This Hall was a building in Basinghall Street, purchased by the Mayor and Commonalty of London in 1396. to serve as a market for country clothiers and drapers. Here, and here alone, countrymen were to expose and sell their cloths, and sales could take place only between Thursday noon and Saturday noon in each week. Strict rules were drawn up for the control of the market, and offenders punished by the con-

---

[1] Acts of the Privy Council, Aug. 23, 1558.
[2] Ashley, I. ii. 215, and Cunningham, *Growth*, i. 382.

fiscation of their goods.[1] As the commerce in cloth expanded, the importance of Blackwell Hall grew proportionately, since there was no relaxation of the monopoly of sale which the Hall possessed. Hence pieces were forwarded from every part of the country, on pack-horses or by sea, to this central sales-room, and in the seventeenth century special rooms were set apart for the produce of the various districts. There was a ' Northern Hall ', which in 1622 contained over 5,000 pieces waiting to be sold ; there was a ' Manchester Hall ', full of ' frizes ' and ' cottons ', whilst Wiltshire, Suffolk, and other parts of the country claimed their local ' Halls ' (as the rooms were euphemistically called), each with its keeper or clerk.[2] Later in the century two other buildings were utilized as cloth markets, the ' Welch Hall ' for coarse goods from the western areas, and Leaden Hall for the wares of East Anglia and the new draperies of Yorkshire. The country cloths, when ready for sale, were packed up in bundles suitable for carriage by pack-horses or for transmission by sea, and then the clothier either took them himself to the capital or, as was more frequently the case, dispatched them by a professional carrier.[3] The goods were forwarded to some agent [4] or factor in London, who took them to the Hall and there disposed of them, charging his client with a certain proportion of the receipts as commission. Those clothiers who accompanied their goods might have a stall of their own in the market, but during the seventeenth century the factor succeeded in encroaching upon the trade to such an extent as practically to forbid any sales by the producer. Bitter complaints were constantly being made of this monopoly and tyranny on the part of the middleman,[5] and legislation attempted to keep him in check.[6] But the factor was a necessary part of the industrial organization

---

[1] Early in the fifteenth century, drapers' and merchant taylors' companies obtained the right to search all cloth exposed for sale, and to mark it according to its size (Ashley, *op. cit.*, I. ii. 214).

[2] *D. S. P., Jas. I*, cxxviii. 73–7.

[3] In the seventeenth century there was a constant stream of carriers plying between Kendal, Wakefield, and London (*Kendal Corp. MSS., Hist. MSS. Comm.*, Report x, pt. iv, p. 317).

[4] See Surtees Soc., vol. lxxvii, p. 19. The Priestley family had a factor in Blackwell Hall. See also will of John Hollyred of Hallyfax, clothier, 1574 (copy in hands of Mr. J. Lister) : ' I have in Blackwell Hall Foure score and one peces of Kerseyes, in the Hall that Mr. Gray kepes.'

[5] See pamphlet extracts in Smith, *Memoirs of Wool*, vol. i, pp. 315–30.

[6] Statute 8–9 Will. III, c. 9.

of the century, and so he throve out of the needs of the many clothiers who used the London market for the disposal of their wares.

Blackwell Hall was taken advantage of by the State to facilitate the inspection of cloth in accordance with the various cloth laws, and several Acts declared that all goods going to London should be searched there.[1] Further, the cloth-dealing companies of the capital attempted to take advantage of the market to engross all trade into their own hands, and forbade any direct dealing between the country manufacturer and the consumer. Though never quite successful in this policy, the· companies and the city authorities in unison could make matters exceedingly unpleasant and inconvenient for the outsider, especially by the levy of excessive hall dues and fees. This was particularly the case after the Restoration, and in 1664 the clothiers and merchants of Leeds petitioned the Commons, complaining that the city of London had increased ' ye auncient Hallage for ye entrance and pitcheinge ' of the cloths, which obliged ' a pitchinge lodgeing and long continuance of our clothes in Blackwell Hall and Leaden Hall ', with consequently heavier charges, so that the petitioners did ' every day meet with new discouragement and inconveniences in their trade '.[2] The House of Commons tried to remedy these grievances, but the city quickly reimposed its heavy dues, and continued its attempt to ' make the foreigner pay '.[3]

The cloth sold in London might be for distribution in London or in other parts of England, amongst the poorer classes of the population. But English cloth, and with it Yorkshire cloth, had now become the most valuable article of foreign trade, just as English wool had been in the thirteenth and fourteenth centuries. The export trade was now a very important factor in the textile industry, so important that any diminution of the foreign demand brought depression, unemployment, and distress upon large numbers of the English cloth-makers. During the Tudor period our fabrics found their way into almost every part of Europe. ' Bristow frizes, Welsh cottons, Manchester

[1] Rymer, *Foedera*, xx. 221–2.
[2] *D. S. P., Chas. II*, xcv. 82–6 ; also vol. 449, m. 14.
[3] See pamphlets on wool (1678), Brit. Mus. 712. g. 16. (22).   Yorkshire cloths were obliged to pay 8*d.* per pack (10 cloths) for hallage.

cottons and Northerens ' equally with the best qualities of white and coloured cloths, were exported to the Low Countries, to the various parts of High and Low Germany, to Muscovy, Russia and the Baltic area, to France, Spain, Italy, Barbary, Hungary, ' and contries beyond the same '.[1]   In the seventeenth century the troops of Russia were dressed in English fabrics, and the gentlemen of Poland used to clothe their attendants with English cloth until, after the various wars of the early seventeenth century, they were too impoverished to be able to afford the rough but durable wares of England, and had to be content with the still cheaper fabrics of their own country and of Silesia.[2]

In this export trade the three great cloth areas shared. East Anglia was now essentially the home of the new draperies ; in the West of England goods both of high and low quality were produced, and Yorkshire comprised the third important source of supply for the export trade.   In 1623, a time of depression, the merchants of York claimed to have shipped more than 50,000 kerseys during the previous thirteen months,[3] whilst in the famous lawsuit of 1638 a witness who was keeper of the ulnage seals declared that 80,000 kerseys were manufactured annually in the county, of which 60,000 were exported by way of York, Hull, Newcastle, Chester, London, and other ports.[4]

The Yorkshire ports naturally played the most important part in the exportation of the Yorkshire cloth.   York had to a very large extent lost its industrial activity, but had developed its commerce instead, so that it was now, in the seventeenth century, the home of many merchants, a city renowned for its pleasant society, its venison pasties, its ' good fires, good chere, and good company '.[5]   Hull had developed considerably during the Tudor period,[6] and was now the port and fort of the Humber.   Its harbour had been renovated so as to give better

---

[1] *D. S. P., Eliz.*, xv. 67 (1560).

[2] Sellers, *Ordinances of the Eastland Merchants* (Camden Soc.), Intro., p. lix.

[3] *D. S. P., Jas. I*, cxxxviii. 120.

[4] Evidence of J. Crabtree of Halifax, innkeeper, who ' keepeth the booke of the seales for the whole viccarage of Halifax '.

[5] *Life of Marmaduke Rawdon of York* (Camden Soc., 1863), p. 84.

[6] At the time of the Reformation, Hull sold all its church plate and jewels, and paved the town with the proceeds (*Calendar of State Papers*, vol. xii, pt. i, p. 481).

accommodation for the loading and unloading of ships. At the same time increased provision had been made to protect the town and shipping from the ravages of pirates and hostile fleets. Henry VIII had ordered the building of blockhouses and other fortifications,[1] and in the following century the scheme of defence had been extended, so that the port was now surrounded by strong walls, only to be entered by drawbridge and portcullis, and all bristling with arms.[2] Hull was now the ' Key of the North ', and, as Fuller quaintly remarked, the key had been well mended and the wards of the lock much altered, for they succeeded in shutting out Charles I when the Civil War began.[3] The trade of Hull was both coastal and foreign. The traffic with London and Newcastle was important, and ships left the Humber for most of the ports of Europe, especially those facing Hull across the North Sea. Cloth was one of the chief, if not the chief, articles of export. Grain [4] from the basins of the Ouse and Trent, and lead [5] from the mines of Derbyshire, also figured prominently at times in the bills of lading, and Hull was for many years the centre of the Greenland whale-fishing industry,[6] the northern market for fish, and the chief port to which wool was brought from the southern counties.

Now let us turn our attention to the men who were carrying on this foreign trade in Yorkshire cloth. The first fact to be noted is that they were Englishmen, and very often Yorkshire-men. Even as early as the thirteenth century English traders were engaged in foreign commerce, and it is probable that the importance of these men has been vastly underestimated by economic historians. But at that time the Englishman undoubtedly had to take second place to the alien. It was the

[1] *D. S. P., Eliz.*, cxi. 10.

[2] Baskerville's Tour, temp. Chas. II, *Portland MSS. (Hist. MSS. Comm.),* ii. 313. Celia Fiennes entered the town over a drawbridge.

[3] Charles himself had spent over £1,600 on fortifying the town (*D. S. P., Chas. I*, xvii. 130 and 140 ; also xviii. 433).

[4] Harley MSS., vol. 306, ff. 26–8. Also *D. S. P., Eliz.*, cxix. 50 (1577), licence to mayor and burgesses of Hull to transport 20,000 qrs. of grain in twenty years.

[5] *D. S. P., Chas. II*, vol. 265, f. 17 (1669). Just departed from Hull, three ships for Bordeaux, with coals, cloth, butter, &c. One ship for Holland, with lead, cloth, and rape seed. One for Hamburg, ' richly laden with cloth ', and three other vessels preparing for Virginia.

[6] Bigland, *Topographical and Historical Description of the County of York* (1812), pp. 508–9.

Italian and the Hansard who bought up the supplies of wool
from the monasteries and at the big fairs, and exported it to
the textile centres of Italy, Flanders, and Germany.   High
finance was in the hands of the Florentines, and the import
trade in spices, silks, and general luxuries was carried on chiefly
by foreigners.

With the reign of Edward III [1] the high tide of alien commercial
supremacy began slowly to ebb before the rise of a strong native
mercantile class.   This movement continued with much irregularity and frequent halts during the two subsequent centuries,
until by the end of the Tudor period the alien influence had
almost entirely disappeared, and English foreign trade was
really ' active ' and carried on by natives.   In its early stages
the battle was waged by the wool merchants, organized eventually in the Company of the Staple.   In its later stages native
cloth merchants played a prominent part and reaped the
greater share of the benefits which accrued.   Of the trading
companies which then took up the control of English commerce,
two in particular drew their export commodities from Yorkshire
and traded largely in Yorkshire cloth.   These were the Societies,
Fellowships, or Companies of the Merchant Adventurers and the
Eastland Merchants ;   in them the merchants of the county
were enrolled ;   by them Yorkshire pieces were carried to the
Continent.

The two companies were alike in that their chief export trade
was in cloth, though the Merchant Adventurers exported only
white cloths, whilst the Eastlanders could only traffic in coloured
pieces.   They were akin in that they were associations of men
rather than of capital.   They were not based on joint-stock
principles.   The company ordered the rules of life and the laws
of trade, but had ' no banke nor common stocke, nor common
factour to buy and sell for the whole companie, but every man
tradeth apart and particularlie with his own stocke, and with his
own factour or servaunt '.   The companies differed in the market

---

[1] For details of the rise of the native merchant class, see Law, *The English
Nouveaux-Riches in the Fourteenth Century* (Trans. Royal Hist. Soc., New
Series, ix) ;   Guiseppi, *Alien Merchants in England* (Trans. Royal Hist. Soc.,
New Series, ix) ;   Cunningham, *Growth*, i. 290 ;   Ashley, *Economic Organiza-
tion of England*, chap. iv.   See also Patent Rolls, 14 Ed. III, pt. iii, m. 55 d ;
also Close Rolls, 13 Ed. III, pt. iii, m. 8.

which they supplied, having the bounds of their respective activities clearly mapped out in their charters, with one small area open equally to the members of both companies.

Of the two organizations, that of the Merchant Adventurers was the older and more important.[1] As internal trade developed in England, special trading classes grew up, such as the mercers, drapers, and grocers, with men earning their livelihood solely by the exchange of commodities. Some specialized in retail trade, whilst others devoted their attention to wholesale transactions. These wholesale traders formed the raw material out of which foreign merchants were evolved, and gradually there arose an important class of English merchants dealing with foreign ports. These men received favours from the English kings and from foreign rulers, such as the Count of Flanders. They built up trade centres abroad, especially in the Low Countries, and here they began to organize some common life and scheme of government. In 1407 a charter was granted to all English merchants trading abroad to erect and maintain proper means of government to watch over their interests and regulate their actions in foreign parts. This grant did not establish the Merchant Adventurers: it only gave powers of self-government to all English merchants when abroad, and in accordance with this grant local groups of merchants organized themselves and drew up common rules in various foreign towns during the fifteenth century.

Throughout that century, the adventurers, as these cloth merchants were now generally called, grew in strength, after many a hard fight against the Staplers, who exported wool, and the Hansards, whose trade in cloth was now seriously challenged by the Englishmen.[2] During this period there was also a movement towards concentration and centralization, and the various local organizations were being brought within the fold of one adventurers' society. In this unification of the forces of English traders abroad the London element predominated, and London merchants and mercers, organized in a fellowship,

---

[1] The following pages give only those details concerning the Adventurers which are necessary in order to understand the work of the Yorkshire merchants. See Wheeler, *A Treatise of Commerce* (1601), and Lingelbach, *The Merchant Adventurers of England* (1902), for a full treatment of the topic.

[2] For this early history see Lingelbach, *op. cit.*, preface.

succeeded in gaining the mastery over the whole body of traffic
with the Low Countries.   This control amounted to something
approaching a monopoly, and by the end of the fifteenth century
traders from the provincial ports were loud in their complaint
of the manner in which the London organization of ' mercers and
other merchants and adventurers ' was imposing financial levies
and trading disabilities on the foreign commerce of those who did
not belong to the capital.   The most famous of these protests
was contained in the petition of 1496, in which the merchants
from the outports railed against the men of London, who ' by
confederacie made amonge theym self of their uncharitable
and inordinate covetise for their singuler profite and lucre,
contrarie to every Englissheman's libertie and to the libertie
of the (foreign) Marte there . . . have contrarie to all lawe reason
charite right and conscience, . . . made an Ordinaunce . . . that noe
Englishman resortyng to the seyd Martes shall neither bye nor
sell any godes . . . except he first componde and make fyne with
the seid feliship merchauntes of London . . . upon payn of forfeiture to the seid feliship . . . of suche Merchandises godes or
wares so by him bought or sold there '.   This fine or entrance
fee, amounting to £20, had been instrumental in crippling the
trade of many provincial merchants, and the Yorkshire cloth
exporters had suffered as much as any others engaged in the
Netherlands traffic.   In response to this petition, an Act was
passed in which the London fellowship was confirmed in the power
to levy a fine or entrance fee, but that fee was reduced to ten
marks (£6 13s. 4d.).[1]

This enactment was of great importance to the men of the
outports, and York benefited considerably by the terms of the
statute.   Here the mercers had become a large and flourishing
body, and had received a royal charter of incorporation in 1430.
The merchant class grew up as a specialized branch of the
Mercers' Company, and the merchants turned their attention
to foreign trade.   They traded with the Netherlands throughout
the fifteenth century, and acted to some extent in harmony

---

[1] The London mercers and merchants had first levied this fine in the name
of the fraternity of St. Thomas of Canterbury, and originally the levy was
a quite small one.   It had been subsequently increased, until it stood at
£20 in the time of Henry VII.   See Statute 12 Hen. VII, c. 6.   Also Lingelbach,
op. cit., preface.

with merchants from other Northern ports.[1] In fact it seems to have been the custom at one time for the London merchants and mercers abroad to be organized under the control of one governor, and for the merchants and mercers of York, Hull, Beverley, Scarborough, and all other ports north of the Trent to be grouped together under another independent governor. During the fifteenth century this sytem fell into abeyance before the encroachments of the London organization, and the southern merchants rode roughshod over the interests of their northern rivals, to the great inconvenience of the latter. Eventually the men of York complained to Edward IV, who issued a proclamation in 1478 ordering the governor of the London merchants to mend his ways : ' From hensfurth ye (shall) demeane and intrete ye said mercers (of the Northern ports) in the parties beyonde the see with all favour and honestee accordeyng to ye said auncient custumes . . . as ye lust to do us singler pleasor and would answer to us at your peryll.' [2] How much regard was paid to this command we do not know, but it is certain that the heavy financial levy continued to be imposed upon the Northern merchants and mercers until its reduction to ten marks by the statute of 1497.

With the granting of this cheaper privilege, the merchant class in York sprang forward into increased activity and larger operations. Numbers of mercers enrolled themselves in the ranks of the central organization, known by this time as the Fellowship of the Merchant Adventurers of England, and a local Court of Merchant Adventurers was added on to the York Company of Mercers. Eventually this wholesale traders' branch eclipsed the retail section, but there was never any separation into two bodies, and the retail trader and the wholesale merchant remained side by side in the same organization. Other ports soon had their Merchant Adventurers, organized in local courts, but also enrolled in the larger body.[3]

During the sixteenth century the growth of the society was continuous. Its membership increased, as did also the number of cloths which passed through the hands of its members. It

[1] Sellers, ' The Merchant Adventurers of York ', *Brit. Assoc. Handbook*, 1906, p. 213.
[2] Quoted by Miss M. Sellers, *The Merchant Adventurers of York* : pamphlet published 1913 (York). [3] Sellers, *Brit. Assoc. Handbook*.

gained privileges abroad, and strengthened its position both in England and in foreign ports. The pieces exported were almost entirely white cloths, which were dyed and finished in the Low Countries, where they were said to provide employment to 20,000 persons in Antwerp and 30,000 in other parts of the land.[1] In the latter part of the century wars in the Low Countries caused complications, and necessitated frequent removals of the Company's head-quarters ; but operations were extended nevertheless, and the trade with the Baltic and Germany shared with the Eastland Company. Hence in 1601 Wheeler was able to declare that ' the Merchant Adventurers do annually export at least 60,000 white cloths, worth at least £600,000, and of coloured cloths of all sorts—kersies, bayes, cottons, northern dozens, and other coarse cloths—more than 40,000, worth £400,000, in all £1,000,000 sterling '. Probably these figures are too large, for Wheeler was here defending the organization of which he was secretary.[2] But admitting this, the statement serves to show the greatness of this Tudor trading company.

In 1564 and 1586 new charters were granted by Elizabeth defining very clearly and comprehensively the scope and powers of the society, and arranging for its government and administration.[3] As we see it at this time the company consisted ' of a great number of wealthy and well-experimented merchants dwelling in diverse great cities, maritime ports, and other parts of the realm, to wit—London, York, Norwich, Exeter, Ipswich, Newcastle, Hull, &c.', men who had ' linked and bound themselves together in company for the exercise of merchandise and seafare, trading in cloth, kersie and all other as well English as foreign commodities vendible abroad '.[4] There were men from all parts of the country united in this fellowship, but not as shareholders of a joint-stock company. All obeyed the rules and ordinances of the central authority or of the local court. The members sent their cloths to Europe in the same ships, and might make partnerships among themselves. But the company

---

[1] *Newcastle Merchant Adventurers*, Preface, p. xxxvi. A letter (1564) states, ' The subjects of King Phillip doe gaine yerly by woll and wollen cloth that cometh out of England almost £600,000 ' (Brit. Mus., Sloane MSS., vol. 817, f. 21, quoted by Cunningham, ii. 224).

[2] Wheeler, *A Treatise of Commerce* (1601), p. 24.

[3] Lingelbach, *op. cit.*, pp. 19–69.   [4] Wheeler, *op. cit.*, pp. 10 and 19.

itself was not an association of capital. It left each man to carry
on his own business and conduct his own affairs, provided he kept
to the stipulations laid down by those in authority. What then
was the value of membership? In the first place, membership
admitted a man to a share in a monopoly. The society had
succeeded in breaking down the monopoly of the Steelyard,
only to erect another one in its place. None but members of
the company could export cloth to the special area of control
allotted to the company, and any member guilty of selling the
goods of a non-member was severely punished. This monopoly
was often defied, especially in the seventeenth century, by
' interlopers ' who competed with the real Adventurers, to the
constant annoyance of the latter. Still, in spite of these men,
the monopoly was on the whole well maintained. Secondly,
the company had its head-quarters abroad and attempted to
make commercial bargains with foreign Powers. This was
a great part of the work of the Merchant Adventurers, who were
sufficiently wealthy and strong to be able to extract favours,
temporary or permanent, from the home Government, or from
Continental rulers. Along with this the company tried to
ensure to its members protection from violence and loss of goods
when travelling by land or by sea. This was exceedingly important in those centuries of active commercial jealousy and
international strife, and if the authorities could only provide
safe escort by sea, and protect the merchants on land, they had
met a very pressing need. Thirdly, the company did its best
to regulate the markets with a view to preventing a general
glut at any time or in any area. This was perhaps the most
difficult task of all, since markets were opened and closed to
English goods according to the diplomatic situation of the
moment, and the company was forbidden by its very nature to
turn to other parts of the world in order to get rid of wares which
had been denied entry to the old markets. Also there was
an absence of that intimate inter-relation between the producer
and the merchant which is necessary to check over-production.
The clothier went on making cloth with little regard to the state
of the market, expecting the merchant to take his pieces as
a matter of course. Hence the Adventurers failed to avert
many serious trade depressions, due either to inflated supply

or to some sudden prohibition on the part of a European government.

The Fellowship traded by special licence to a certain part of
Europe. Its territorial limits were the mouth of the Somme
on the one extreme and the Skaw on the other. Between these
points the society was given an absolute monopoly of English
trade, whilst it shared on equal terms with the Eastland Merchants
the trade of Denmark (Copenhagen and Elsinore excepted),
Jutland, Silesia, Moravia, Lubeck, Wismar, Rostock, Stettin,
Stralsund, and the Oder mouth.[1] The company was a fellowship
of English merchants and of Englishmen alone. No alien could
qualify for membership, and no Englishman married to a foreign
wife or holding real property abroad could claim admission.
Further, entry could be obtained only on terms akin to those
which regulated admission to the craft gilds. A person might
be made an honorary member; he might purchase admission
by paying a high redemption fee ; he might gain access on the
grounds of patrimony when he attained the age of twenty-one
years ; or, lastly, he might enter through the ordinary gateway
of apprenticeship.[2] A youth who desired to be an Adventurer
became apprenticed to some free brother of the company at
the age of sixteen, and served for a period of eight years, during
which time he attended his master's business both at home
and abroad. Then, armed with his certificate of fitness and ' dew
servyce ', he presented himself at the next Court, held at some
trading centre abroad.[3] Here he took the oath, paid his entrance
fee, purchased his livery, and became a recognized freeman of
the Fellowship. He was not yet full-grown, however, for a
maximum limit was fixed to the quantity of his trade for fifteen
years. In each of the first three years he could not export more
than 400 cloths ; in the fourth year not more than 450, and
then the maximum increased 50 cloths per annum, until at his
fifteenth year he was permitted to export 1,000 pieces.[4] Also
for the first seven years he might keep one apprentice, from
the seventh to the twentieth year he might take two, and
after that the number was limited to three.[5] Aided by appren-

[1] M. Sellers, *Ordinances of the Eastland Merchants*, pp. xvi–xvii.
[2] *Brit. Assoc. Handbook*, York, 1906, p. 221.
[3] Lingelbach, *op. cit.*, pp. 23–8.
[4] Ibid., p. 32.   [5] Ibid., pp. 31–2.

tices and journeymen, he was to devote his energies to trade in cloth, and this trade was almost entirely wholesale. The mercer element in the organization still survived in the provincial branches, but the division between the wholesale trader and the retailer was now quite distinctly marked. At York, for instance, it was ordained that there must be no cutting up of cloth for purposes of sale by merchants, no keeping of an open shop or ' shew house '. Members were also forbidden to stand at the corners of the street or in other men's shops, or frequent any ' comon Inn ' where chapmen were wont to resort, but at .the same time they were prohibited from hawking their wares, or from keeping any shops in the country districts.[1] In place of these practices, the Merchant Adventurers of York had a hall and here the merchant was ordered to make his purchase from the clothiers who came to this market with their wares : ' No brother of this fellowshipp shall hereafter go to se or buye anie clothe broughte to this Cittye to be sold in no place but in our Hall therefore appoynted, in paine of a fine.'[2] The punishment for infringement of these regulations was generally confiscation of the goods concerned, and the records of the Newcastle Merchant Adventurers show that such confiscations were of frequent occurrence. The company also fixed the dates of sailings, and arranged them so that the consignments should reach the Continent in time for the four large cloth fairs which took place each year. The ships sailed in as large numbers as possible, accompanied by a convoy, provided the Government could spare a frigate or two.

The affairs of the Company as a whole were administered by a central executive, which had its head-quarters, not in London, but abroad. The centre of the association migrated from place to place during the sixteenth and seventeenth centuries, impelled chiefly by political dangers and commercial rivalries. Bruges, Antwerp, and Emden were in turn the centres of the trade, and in 1564 the Burgomaster of Hamburg invited the Adventurers to make that town their head-quarters.[3] Hamburg seemed a doubtful centre, but those in authority decided to test its value as a market, so in 1567 they ordered each port to

---

[1] M. Sellers, *Brit. Assoc. Handbook,* p. 223.   [2] Ibid., p. 224.
[3] Cunningham, *Growth,* ii. 224–7.

dispatch cargoes to that city. The letter to York stated that
' of late the Citie of Hamborowe have at our speciall instance
and sewte graunted to us divers goodly privileges upon hope
yt we shulde occupie and use somme trade thither, and for that
purpose have according to their grant prepared a howse for us '.
Therefore the Court requested the merchants of York to engage
in some trade with the Elbe port, and ordered ' that ye first
four shippes which shalbe laden aftar the last daye of Marche,
. . . shalbe laden and departe for and to the said Citie of Hamborowe '.[1] The venture was successful and the trade soon
settled on Hamburg. Here, with minor temporary migrations
to Stade and Middelburg, the Adventurers stayed throughout
the seventeenth century, and became known generally as the
Hamburg Merchants.[2] At these head-quarters the real government of the company was to be found. There was a Governor
and a Court of twenty-four Assistants, chosen by the General
Court of the Fellowship. In the hands of this elected Court
the real legislative and executive power rested. ' It not only
made the Statutes and Ordinances but it was also entrusted
with the duty of enforcing them. It administered the general
affairs of the society, represented its interests with the Government and with strangers, and maintained order and discipline
among the members of the Fellowship.'[3] The decrees of the
Central Court were obligatory upon merchants of all the local
districts ; even London received its orders from this source,
and the Court had almost complete power in the selection
of the officials of the local branches.[4]

Local branches of Merchant Adventurers were to be found in
all the large ports. In the case of Newcastle, the Adventurers
claimed entire independence of the central body, and declared
that they were in no manner subservient to the Merchant
Adventurers of England, an assertion of autonomy which was
the cause of long and acrimonious quarrels between Newcastle
and the larger organization. York, Hull, Bristol, Ipswich, &c.,
all had branches which were admittedly under the control of the
central authority, and were ruled by the Court of Assistants
which sat abroad. This subordination was the outcome of the

[1] M. Sellers, *Brit. Assoc. Handbook*, p. 218.
[2] Cunningham, *op. cit.*, pp. 228–9.
[3] Lingelbach, *op. cit.*, pp. 66–7.   [4] Ibid., p. 63.

encroachments which were made by the central body during the fifteenth century, and was none the less complete even when the local branches had obtained considerable powers by means of royal charters. The branch at York is an excellent illustration of this. Here the Merchant Adventurers' organization, evolving from the Company of Mercers, had been deprived of its independence abroad by the growth of the national Fellowship. In 1581 a charter of incorporation was obtained from Elizabeth. After lamenting the alleged decayed state of commerce in York, the charter gave very considerable powers to the ' Society of the Merchant Adventurers of the City of York ' (*societas mercatorum adventurarum civitatis Ebor*') for controlling all men exercising the art or mystery of merchant or mercer within the city and its suburbs. Thus the Merchant Adventurers of York were to control both the internal and external trade of their city.[1]

This control was to be in the hands of a Court, consisting of a Governor and twelve Assistants, who were to be elected annually, and who would make laws and regulations binding upon all under their sway, with power to fine or imprison those who were guilty of disobedience.[2] The Court enforced the eight years' apprenticeship, forbade illicit trading amongst the merchants and mercers, repelled the invasion of interlopers, insisted on the wearing of livery, and generally ordered and controlled the occupation, morals, and manners of its members. But although giving these important local powers, the charter was very careful to keep the provincial body in a position of subservience to the Central Court of the Merchant Adventurers of England. The local Governor and his Deputy were to be members of the larger company, and the Central Court had a voice in the election of these men. Apprentices at the end of their period of service were compelled to go to the foreign Court to receive their freedom, and decrees from head-quarters had precedence over all local by-laws.[3] Thus the society at York, whilst possessing considerable powers of self-government, had to bow to the commands of the larger body.

The Eastland Merchants were very similar in their aim and organization to the Merchant Adventurers, though their company

---

[1] Gross, *Gild Merchant*, vol. ii, p. 282.
[2] M. Sellers, *op. cit.*, pp. 221–2.   [3] Ibid., p. 222 ; Lingelbach, pp. 67–8.

was not of such ancient standing, and was certainly much smaller in the scale of its operations. Trade with the Baltic ports had grown up during the fifteenth century in spite of the opposition of the Hansards, and English merchants carried cloth there, bringing back corn, flax, hemp, timber, and the other commodities which the Baltic area could supply. The story of this trade is obscure until the granting of a charter by Elizabeth in 1579. This charter was bestowed upon the ' Governour, Assistants and Fellowshipp of the Marchaunts of Eastland ', in order to help these ' expert and exercysed marchaunts in their lawfull and honest trade ' and to restrain those unskilled and interloping traders who, as ever, were said to be degrading the fair fame of English commerce abroad. The company resembled that of the Merchant Adventurers in its general structure and in most of its details. It had its well-defined geographical limits ; Norway, Sweden, Poland, Letto, the Gulf of Pomerania, and the islands within the Sound were closed to all Englishmen who were not free of the company. Thus Eastlanders held control over such ports as Danzig, Elbing, Braunsberg, Königsberg, and Revel on the east coast of the Baltic, and Elsinore and Copenhagen in Denmark. They were forbidden, on the other hand, to trade in Holstein, Hamburg, or the Elbe mouth, these being the preserves of the Adventurers, but were given free passage through these parts ; finally, one expanse comprising much of the south and the west coast of the Baltic was open to members of both companies on equal terms.[1]

Like the Merchant Adventurers, the Eastland Company had its Central Court, consisting of a Governor, his Deputy, and twenty-four Assistants, but this Court was held in London, and not abroad, with the result that the power and the government of the organization fell largely into the hands of London merchants, much to the dissatisfaction of those from the outports. This Central Court had power to issue ' Statutes, Lawes, Constitucyons, and Ordinances ' binding on the whole Fellowship, and was able therefore to assert a large measure of authority over the rank and file. In practice it succeeded in establishing an autocracy, placed the ordinary member, and especially the provincial member, in a position of insignificance, and virtually

---

[1] *Ordinances of Eastland Merchants,* pp. xi and 147 ; also p. xiv.

destroyed the value of his vote.[1] The officials were surrounded with pomp, circumstance, and ceremony; no criticism was allowed from members, and any merchant who was found scoffing at the Court or its members was fined £5. This Central Court issued ordinances of every conceivable kind; elaborate codes of etiquette and ethics were drawn up, and all fighting, ' reviling, indecent speeches, tanglinge, lewd communications ', and other lapses from grace were punished by severe fines. The Court had large financial powers; it could levy dues of various kinds, and therefore placed taxes on the person who imported, the merchandise he brought with him, and the vessel in which the goods were carried. A stint was established, which limited the amount of goods each member could export, and the Central Court fixed the dates at which shipments could take place from the English ports.[2] At times this restriction weighed heavily on the outports, as, for instance, in April 1625, when the merchants of Hull and York addressed the following petition to the Privy Council : ' At a generall Court of the Eastland Company held at London in ffebruarie last, it was agreed by the Merchants of London and the coast Townes that the first time or season for shipping of cloath into the Eastland this yeare from Hull and Newcastle should be the 21st of March past and the last of April instant, And that no goods should be put aboarde theire shippes for the Eastlande after these tymes upon a great penaltie. The Petitioners had not dared shipp at that time ' because of the Dunkirkers who were hanging off the coast, and therefore they did not dispatch their cloths in the time allowed, for want of a convoy. Now the time for shipping was past, but the wares of the Yorkshiremen still lay at the port, and could not be dispatched for fear of the ' great penaltie ' which would be inflicted by the Central Court of the Company. The petitioners, therefore, asked the Privy Council for permission to ship their cloth and make the journey, in spite of the Company's regulation to the contrary.[3] All these points serve to illustrate the autocratic nature of the Eastland Company's government; in fact,

---

[1] In 1616 it was declared that ' the power of ruling the whole company, of making Bylaws and appointing officers, is by the Charter vested in ye Court of Assistants only, and if all ye generallity of ye Company were present, they could have no voices in any question ' (ibid., p. 136).

[2] Ibid., p. xxiii.   [3] *D. S. P., Chas. I*, vol. 521, p. 33 (April 1625).

the ordinary unofficial member was ' hampered by many restrictions, his speech curtailed, his manners regulated, his morals supervised ', by an oligarchic Court which imposed taxation without allowing any measure of representation.[1]

The Eastland Merchants, like the fellow Company, had their local courts and branch organizations, but here again the power of the central authority was strongly in evidence. The charter of 1579 allowed courts to be established ' as well within some convenyente place within our cyttie of London, or els where within our domynyons as also within the said Realmes and domynyons of the Easte partes afforesaid ', i.e. at the outports in this country or in the foreign centres of trade.[2] York, Hull, and Newcastle, which were strongholds of the Eastland traffic, soon had their local bodies, but these provincial communities were kept under the thumb of the London assembly. The local courts were administered by a deputy, aided by a secretary and beadle, and their work was purely administrative, devoid of any legislative power. The Central Court made laws and ordinances without the knowledge or consent of the districts, and then ordered the branches to see that they were properly administered. The London governors placed their nominees in the local offices, levied impositions, regulated the times of shipping and the quantity of goods to be exported by the provincial merchants. Apprentices were compelled to journey to London in order to take up their freedom, and almost the whole of the money paid in entrance fees in the districts had to be forwarded to headquarters. Occasionally, however, the northern Courts obtained concessions, as for instance when the London executive consented not to admit any northerner to the freedom unless he held a certificate or testimonial from a northern Court,[3] and in 1681 the Londoners declared, in a letter to York, ' we have lately denied some from Leeds their admission for want of your certificates '.[4] But such concessions were small, and in both the companies the central authority possessed large powers of jurisdiction over the districts, powers which, as we shall see, the outports strongly resented.

[1] M. Sellers, *Eastland Merchants*, pp. xxii and lxxii.
[2] Ibid., p. 144.   [3] *D. S. P., Chas. I*, cccvii. 73–4 (1635).
[4] Quoted by M. Sellers, *Eastland Merchants*, p. lxxxiii.

In these big trading companies the exporters of Yorkshire
cloth were enrolled.[1] Hull and York had their local branches
of each company, between which harmonious relations existed,
especially during the second half of the seventeenth century.
This was natural, for their interests were allied whilst their
spheres of action were different, and hence they were not to
any great extent in competition with each other. The Eastland
Merchants had special entrance fees for Merchant Adventurers,
who were admitted on paying a fine of 40 marks (£13 6s. 8d.),
whereas other men were charged £20 for admission. Many
merchants were members of both companies. In 1661 the
Eastland Merchants of York numbered eighty members, of
whom fifty-four were Merchant Adventurers also. By being
a member of both companies the merchant possessed the right
to exploit the whole field of the North Sea and the Baltic.
Occasionally the companies held joint meetings, generally of
an extraordinary nature, and at times they had joint officials,
both having the same beadle, and with the Deputy of the Eastlanders also acting as Governor of the Adventurers in York
from 1646 to 1698.[2]

The chief consideration which these Yorkshire cloth merchants had at heart was the development of their northern trade.
In pursuing this object they found themselves faced with two
great difficulties, namely, (1) dangers on sea, and the opposition
of foreign powers, (2) the competition of London rivals, and the
despotism of their central organization. The first of these
obstacles received a great deal of attention from the central
executive, both societies doing their utmost to gain concessions
from foreign powers with whom they came in contact, and to
protect shipping from attacks at sea. The second was the cause
of long and bitter quarrels between the northern merchants and
their southern rivals. The Central Court of the Merchant
Adventurers was largely under the control of London merchants, although its meeting-place was abroad, and thus both

---

[1] The two companies embraced practically the whole of the Yorkshire
merchant class. Sons of the best-known wealthy families were constantly
being enrolled as apprentices, and entering into commercial life. Ralph
Thoresby in 1684 went to London, and became a freeman of both companies.

[2] *Eastland Merchants*, pp. xxxv–xxxvi. In December 1651 the Adventurers and Eastlanders of York held a joint meeting to protest against the
seizure of some ships at Rotterdam (*Eastland Merchants*, p. xxxiii).

companies were ruled by a limited number of rich metropolitan traders. As one writer complained (1585), in lamenting the temporary stagnation of Hull, ' The merchants are tyed to companies, the heads whereof are citizens of London, which make ordinances beneficiall to themselves, but hurtfull and chargeable to others in ye country '.[1] The northerners often objected to the rulings of the central power, and either at their individual local courts or in joint meetings of the various branches gave utterance to their grievances against the autocrats at head-quarters. York was the leader in the fight against the London Eastland Merchants, and succeeded in obtaining some small concessions, though it failed in its greatest struggle (1663–80), when it attempted to procure a local legislature.[2] The Merchant Adventurers of Newcastle, who claimed independence of the national body in domestic affairs, led a similar revolt against the government of the Merchant Adventurers of England. All this antagonism sprang from a sense of bitter rivalry and opposition against the London merchants, who were accused of damaging northern trade alike in England and abroad. We have already noted the existence of this struggle in the fifteenth century, and subsequent years brought no greater degree of harmony or goodwill. In 1548 the Newcastle Merchant Adventurers decreed that no man ' should latt no loftes, scellers nore housses to no Londyners nor straungers ', or ' from hensfurth bye no maner of marchaundice of any Londyner nor of none other straunger '.[3] Some years later a writer from Hull lamented that ' by means of ye said companies, all the trade of merchants is drawn to London '.[4] During the seventeenth century this feeling rose to great heights of bitterness, and was the cause of constant demonstrations of antagonism between the northern ports and the capital. In 1651 the merchants of York convened a general meeting of their fellows from Newcastle, Hull, and Leeds. At this conference it was decided to ' ioyne in peticioning the councell for trade agaynst the ffayres and marts held by the Londoner, that noe Londoner

[1] D. S. P., Eliz., clxxvii. 56.
[2] Eastland Merchants, pp. lxxvii and lxxx : also Cunningham, op. cit., ii. 242 and 242 n.
[3] Newcastle Merchant Adventurers, pp. 51 and 64.
[4] D. S. P., Eliz., clxxvii. 56 (1585).

... directly or indirectly shall come or send to keepe any fayres or mart on the north side of Trent . . . chiefly because the northern Traders are exceedingly prejudiced by their coming downe, they haveing layd their moneys and creditt to furnish the countrie. Soe that by these ffayres the Londoner ingroseth allmost all the trade of the northern partes, and in equity and reason the benefitt of trade should be equally disposed into all the vaines of the commonwealth '.[1] Similar sentiments were expressed in a letter written in March 1655 by the merchants of York and Hull, requesting Adam Baynes, M.P. for Leeds, to procure a convoy for a cargo of cloth. The letter concluded by urging Baynes to prompt action, and declared ' If at the day prefixed wee demurr to saile for want of Convoy! its 100 to one but the Londoners will be at the Markett before us . . . and if they be, . . . it will tend very much to the prejudice not onely of us that are Adventurers, but alsoe of the Northern Clothiers. Wee, Like little fishes, are swallowed up by a great whale! London hath almost ingrossed all the traid of this Nation into their owne hands, specially for goods importable, more's the pitty ! ' [2]

Antagonism towards the Southron was a sentiment which most northern merchants could share. But this unanimity did not prevent the existence of feuds, at times almost as bitter, between the two Yorkshire mercantile centres, York and Hull. Hull possessed a good strategic position on the Humber, and so could control the trade which passed inland, either for the Ouse or Trent. The port had been exceptionally favoured by Henry VIII,[3] and Elizabeth's minister Cecil frequently granted further privileges. In 1592 Hull attacked the fairs which had been granted to Gainsborough,[4] and then set to work to check the growth of Grimsby and other ports at which southern merchants entered the north country. So successful was this campaign that in December 1592 the Privy Council ordered ' that from henseforthe no marchant either of the Cittie of Lundon or of any other Cittie, towne, or place within the realme

[1] *Newcastle Merchant Adventurers,* i. 166–7, March 25, 1651.
[2] *Baynes Correspondence* (Brit. Mus.), xi. 225, Leeds, March 1, 1654–5.
[3] *Henry VIII, Calendar of State Papers,* vol. v, p. 1139 (22), 1532. Grant to Mayor and Burgesses that no stranger shall sell or buy merchandise to any stranger within the borough, except at fair time, on pain of forfeiture of the goods.
[4] Acts of Privy Council, June 14, 1592.

shall carry convey or transport . . . any kindes or sortes of marchandise (coles and milnstones only excepted) to any porte, creeke, or haven within the Northerne partes of this realme of England between Boston and Hartlepoole, . . . unless he be first admitted into the incorporation of the towne of Hulle '.[1] Then came the encroachment upon the liberties of York and its merchants. So heavy were the levies imposed upon the traders from the county town and their goods[2] that in 1623 the men of York petitioned the Privy Council for relief against ' the grievance and wrong done unto them by the maior and burgesses of the Towne of Kingston-upon-Hulle '. It appears that Hull was attempting to monopolize the import trade in corn, and to exclude York from any share in that trade, by engrossing and forestalling all corn which entered the Humber. Further, when York traders, who had exported over 50,000 kerseys in thirteen months, brought back corn in return, the Mayor of Hull refused to allow the grain to pass up the river, but insisted upon its being sold to men of Hull ; for which reason, declared the petitioners, the corn market of York was empty, and the cloth trade discouraged.[3] This was only one of many occasions on which Hull attempted to cripple some part of the trade of York, and to control the commerce of the county. During the latter part of the century the Eastland Merchants of the two ports were generally on unfriendly terms. Hull was loyal and obedient to the decrees of the Central Court, whilst York was in a ' chronic state of dissatisfaction ' and revolt.[4] York desired local self-government, and disliked having to pay its dues and impositions to head-quarters through Hull. These and other factors combined to keep aflame the animosity between the two commercial centres.

Lastly, the merchants of the two historic ports looked with unfriendly eyes upon the traders who came from other parts of their own county. As quoted in a previous chapter, Hull complained in the reign of James I that ' a set of young adventurers had lately set up at Leeds and other places amongst the clothiers, who at little or no charges buy and engross as they

---

[1] Acts of Privy Council, December 22, 1592.
[2] *Lansdowne MSS., Burghley Papers*, vol. cx, f. 65.
[3] *D. S. P., Jas. I*, cxxxviii. 120.
[4] *Eastland Merchants*, ed. M. Sellers, Preface, pp. lxvi–lxviii.

please, to the great hurt of the merchants and inhabitants of
this town '.[1]   These West Riding merchants generally sprang
from local families of clothiers.   The father would be a clothier,
probably on a rather large scale of business, selling his cloths
in the market at Leeds, or at Blackwell Hall and Bartholomew
Fair.   Thanks to the father's energies and thrift, the son was
able to become apprenticed to some merchant, and in time set up
as a fully qualified merchant and member of the trading companies, taking the wares of the West Riding to foreign parts.
One instance of this is seen in the rise of the Denisons, a family
prominent in the history of Leeds.   George Denison, born in
1626, lived at Woodhouse, and engaged in the occupation of
a clothier.   His son, Thomas, became a merchant and member of
the Merchant Adventurers; Thomas's son in time followed the
same career, and was elected Mayor of Leeds in 1727 and 1731.[2]
Other branches of the family had a similar history.   The Denison
family had its origins in clothiers' cottages.   Its members
afterwards numbered three knights, a baron, a viscount, a
Speaker of the House of Commons, a judge, a colonial governor,
and a bishop, not to mention Mayors of Leeds and lesser digni-
taries.   The history of other families is largely a repetition of
the above story ; and this line of development accounts in part
at least for the rise of the Armitages, the Jacksons, the Metcalfes,
the Walkers, the Wades, and other families which have played
a large part in the economic and political life of Leeds.

These West Riding merchants were naturally in closer touch
with the cloth-producing area than the traders from the port
towns, and a large proportion of the traffic in broad cloths and
kerseys fell into their hands.   They were, however, compelled
to join the trading companies, and enrol themselves as Adventurers or Eastlanders, or both, ranking themselves along with
their ' bretheren at Yorke '.[3]   But the aristocratic merchants
of York did not welcome this upstart breed of traders.   The
Leeds merchants were not willingly recognized, and as no new
member could be admitted to the local residencies without the
consent of the members of that branch, the York merchants

[1] Pamphlet, by John Ramsden, quoted in Hadley's *History of Hull*, p. 115.
[2] Thoresby Soc. publications, xv. 252.
[3] *Baynes Correspondence*, xi. 225.

were able to bar the entrance of this new blood. In 1681, for instance, the London Court of Eastland Merchants informed the York branch that it had lately refused admission to a number of men of Leeds, because these candidates had not been able to produce a certificate of approval from the York officials.[1] Similarly, the merchants residing in York did not approve of these West Riding merchants living in the cloth area, instead of sharing in the social life and civic expenses of York. In 1654, therefore, when the traders of Leeds were seeking to make some arrangements with their brethren of York, probably about the next cargo of cloth, the Eastland Merchants of the county town haughtily replied ' that if ye Merchants of Leeds and other y^t live in Clothing Townes will come and inhabitt in port Townes, we will joyne with them in anything y^t may conduce to ye good of this country '.[2]

Such were the two institutions which controlled the export trade in Yorkshire cloth at the end of the sixteenth and throughout the first half of the seventeenth century. They gained many victories abroad, and opened up new markets for English commercial enterprise. The cloths which they exported from Yorkshire and the northern counties were not of the best quality, and this was recognized by the state when levying customs. Thus, in the later years of the reign of Elizabeth, the customs were fixed at 6s. 8d. for a whole cloth of assize. This was a heavy burden on cloths of small value, even when three, four, five, or six pieces were counted as equivalent to one whole cloth. In 1591, therefore, the merchants of Newcastle, York city and county, and other northern centres, along with those of the western counties, complained of the excessive rate which was levied on the cloths of these parts.[3] They asserted that a customs levy of 6s. 8d. was a very heavy impost on fabrics made of coarse wools and low in price. The case was referred to the Lord Treasurer, who admitted the justice of the complaint, and recommended that the customs dues should be reduced by two shillings per whole cloth for all these coarse northern cloths, whilst one piece in every five should be free of

---

[1] *Eastland Merchants*, Preface, p. lxxxiii.
[2] Ibid., p. 76, October 30, 1654.
[3] *D. S. P., Eliz.*, ccxxxix. 54, June 1591.

any impost, being counted as a wrapper for the other four. These recommendations were carried out, and the northern merchants paid reduced customs, with the ' gyfft of the ffifthe cloth for a wrappar ' free of duty. The concession was of great value to the trade, and the merchants stoutly resisted any attempt to abolish this preferential treatment when subsequent revisions of customs were being made.[1]

Foreign trade was beset by many dangers, not least of which was that of capture by pirates, or by the ships of some hostile country. Security at sea was a luxury seldom enjoyed by Tudor and Stuart merchants, who really were 'adventurers' in a double sense of the term. Piracy was rampant, and powerful associations of pirates patrolled the North Sea and the Channel.[2] Throughout earlier centuries, cargoes of wool, cloth, lead, and coal had been seized on the high seas, and the coast towns and villages were always liable to be raided by a horde of these wild men of the sea. Or if the pirates were subdued, the ships of a hostile country were scarcely less dangerous. England was generally on unfriendly terms with some Continental power, and this enmity expressed itself in regular seizures of goods and vessels. Even if no state of actual hostilities existed, political and commercial rivalries were sufficiently strong to justify an attack on a foreign ship and the confiscation of its cargo. Instances of such occurrences are abundant. Thus, in 1319, fifteen merchants of Beverley, along with other traders, loaded three ships of Flanders, then lying at Hull, with cloths of Beverley, sacks of wool, woolfells, and other merchandise to the value of £4,000. This rich cargo was on its way to Flanders, when ' certain armed malefactors ', subjects of Count Robert of Flanders, attacked the ships, captured them, and escorted ships and cargo to Flanders, where they shared out the booty. The English government repeatedly made representations to the Count on behalf of the Beverley merchants, but without avail. Edward II, therefore, following the regular custom, retaliated by ordering the seizure of the goods of Flemish merchants who were then in England. Action was stayed for

---

[1] See revival of question, *D. S. P., Jas. I*, cxi. 69–72.
[2] Cunningham, *Growth*, i. 301. Also Clive Day, *History of Commerce* (1907), ch. ix.

a time, as the Count promised to send envoys to England to settle the affair. But the envoys never came, and so Edward ordered the seizure of a large quantity of Flemish merchandise, and imprisoned several Flemings until the Count adequately recompensed the English merchants.[1] Similar occurrences were frequent throughout the fifteenth, sixteenth, and seventeenth centuries, and bore witness to the dangers to commerce, whether coastal or foreign. In 1577 a writer complained of the great prevalence of pirates up and down the coast, which was preventing fishermen and merchants from venturing out of harbour.[2] In the last years of the sixteenth century Dunkirkers haunted the Yorkshire coast, chasing the coal, cloth, and fishing fleets and racking the nerves of the whole sea-going population ;[3] later, in 1625, the Eastland Merchants dare not put out to sea with their cloth ships, for fear of the Dunkirkers who were hanging outside the mouth of the Humber.[4] England still had no adequate navy, and during the various wars of the seventeenth century the Dutch and other enemies were able to inflict severe blows upon the country by harassing its mercantile ventures.

Merchants tried to fortify themselves against these dangers in many ways. The ports occasionally acted on their own initiative, and in 1577 Hull armed certain ships for the purpose of stamping out piracy. The attempt was attended with success, and the ships captured Lancelot Greenwell, a notorious pirate who had given Hull merchants a vast amount of trouble.[5] But generally the merchants looked to the government to provide protection. They paid Ship Money, customs, and other dues, and therefore they expected in return some measure of security in their trade. The northern merchants voiced the general opinion when, in 1651, they asked ' that in regard wee pay so greate custome and excise, wee may bee constantly supplied with convoy and secured from the great danger of the enemyes, and that the merchants

---

[1] Close Rolls, 13 Ed. II, m. 14, October 24, 1319.
[2] D. S. P., Eliz., Addenda, xxv. 11 (1577).
[3] Ibid., cclxx. 109.   [4] D. S. P., Chas. I, dxxi. 33.
[5] Ordinances of Privy Council, October 29, 1577. Piracy was almost one of the learned professions, and a sound business investment. Thus in 1527, the Abbot of Whitby, two gentlemen, and a number of other men prominent in the affairs of the East Riding were the financiers of a famous piratical band (Yorks. Arch. and Topogr. Journal, ii. 247).

may have some reasonable reparacions for their losses at sea by robbers from tyme to tyme, in respect of the greate tax they pay for the maintenance of the navie'.[1] Hence, when the periodical shipments were ready to be dispatched, the merchants of the ports from which the consignments were to go wrote to the government, asking for a convoy, or for some other guarantee of safety. Prior to the existence of a national navy, the government allowed the merchant ships to take soldiers with them to provide the necessary defence. For instance, in 1483, the merchants of Hull were granted permission ' to take up as many souldeours and mariners as shalbe requisite for the defense and Waughting (wafting) of certain shippes, now being at poort of Hull, laden and chardged with Wolles and Wollfelles to the Staple of Calais '.[2] With the improvement and extension of the navy, it occasionally became possible to spare men-of-war, and throughout the seventeenth century ships were detailed to act as convoys to the mercantile fleets. The northern merchants, who in 1625 had missed the market for want of a convoy, were compensated in the following year, when three ships were sent ' to wafte the cloathe ffleets of the Northeren partes bound unto places of securities ', and also ' to wafte the said shipps home againe in their retourne '.[3] This grant of a convoy was repeated on several occasions, the most famous of which was that of 1630. In that year, at the earnest petition of the cloth merchants of Hull, York, and Newcastle, a vessel called the *Reformation* was sent, under the command of Sir Henry Mervyn, to convoy sixteen ships, laden with cloth, to the Low Countries, Hamburg, and the Eastlands.[4] This was a large cargo, comprising the wares of Adventurers and Eastlanders, and the ports were jubilant at the prospect of a safe and profitable journey. The Mayor and Corporation of Hull wrote to the Privy Council, thanking them for the favour granted,[5] and the authorities of York followed suit, expressing ' the comforte . . . received by his Most Excellent Ma[ties] gracyous and royall favour, in that it pleased his Ma[tie] in our greate extremity, after sundry losses by pyratts, and when wee had noe power of ourselves to help

---

[1] March 25, 1651 (*Newcastle Merchant Adventurers*, i. 166).
[2] September 16, 2 Rich. III, Harleian MSS., 433, ff. 159 b and 187 b.
[3] *D. S. P., Chas. I*, xxv. 22 and 47.
[4] Ibid., clxiii. 59.   [5] Ibid., clxvii. 3.

ourselves, that then his Matie out of his princely disposicion' should send Sir Henry Mervyn.[1]

The mercantile fleet set out from Hull on May 18, 1630, under the aegis of Mervyn. On the 21st the men of Hull sent their letter of thanks to the Privy Council, and were congratulating themselves on the assured success of the expedition. Imagine, therefore, their dismay and surprise when they saw some of the ships returning up the Humber the following day. The story was quickly told, how, soon after getting well out to sea, Sir Henry had sighted a Spanish warship, and had set off to the north-east in pursuit, instead of keeping to the straight course for Holland. The merchants and mariners had protested angrily against this diversion, whereupon Sir Henry calmly replied 'That if they would not go his way, they could go their own'.[2] The merchants had argued in vain, and Mervyn eventually left them, to follow up the Spaniard. Some ships put back into port, and two of them were lost on this sad return journey. The others evidently continued their voyage, though with what result we do not know.[3]

During the period of the Civil War, the Commonwealth, and the wars with the Dutch, the state of the high seas was more dangerous than ever. Hence, year after year the Yorkshire merchants inundated their Members of Parliament or the Government with requests for convoys. These letters are so full of energy and interest that one is worthy of quotation :[4]

' Leedes,
' 1st. March, 1654-5.

' (To Adam Baynes, M.P. for Leeds),
    Honoured Sir,
        ' Wee, whose names are hereunto subscribed, make it our humble request on the behalfe of our selves and other merch^{tts} of Yorke and Hull, that you would be pleased to procure us from the State a good Convoy, to be if possible at Hull the last day of this moneth, to take charge of Thomas Robinson's shipp and goods, (and his lugg alsoe if need bee for one), for the Porte

---

[1] *D. S. P., Chas. I*, clxviii. 27.   [2] *Ibid.*, clxvii. 7.

[3] In 1627 four York merchants had their vessels seized by the Dunkirkers, entailing a loss of £600. They therefore asked Buckingham for permission to take compensation from a ship of Rouen, which had been captured by some Englishmen (*D. S. P., Chas. I*, lxxxiv. 29).

[4] *Baynes Correspondence*, xi. 225.

of Hamburge in Germanie. And what charges you or any that
you employ shall be at, wee shall thankfully repay.

'S^r, if it please you to consult Sir Thomas Witherington
herein it will not bee amisse, for wee beleeve the Deputie and
rest of our bretheren at Yorke have desired his favour and
Assistance as being a matter of moment to this poore Country !
Though there be noe visible enemies to annoy us, yet pickaroones
and lurking knaves there may be in the way to come from farr !
for roavers at Sea are seldome or never out of their way ! they
will goe any way for a rich Bootie. S^r, wee know you soe much
to be our good friend, and a zealott for the welfair of your
Country, as that wee shall not trouble ourselves to lay downe
any motives before you to incite you to the worke, onely this
one ',

namely the fear of the London traders, who, as already quoted,
seemed like great whales to the northern minnows. For that
reason alone, if no other, Baynes was intreated to be sure
to secure a convoy, so as to enable the Yorkshiremen to
reach the foreign market promptly and in safety. Baynes had
also to extract another favour from the Commonwealth authorities. In these times of national danger the ordinary sailor was
at any moment liable to be pressed into the service of the navy.
Therefore, having gained his point in the request for a convoy,
Baynes at once asked for a licence for the sailors on the two
cloth-laden ships ' y^t [they] may be freed from being prest,
ffor if they loose the Markett at Hamburgh the 10th of the next
month, the Dutch will reape the benefitt of it, and the pore
people of the Northe loose halfe a yeares imployment, this cloth
being the fruits of halfe a yeares labour '.[1]

Twice a year at least the Yorkshire merchants carried their
cloths to Hamburg or to the Baltic, and on every such occasion
they sought the protection of the State. In the later years
of the Commonwealth and during the wars of the subsequent
reign they often failed to gain the desired provision. Occasionally the convoy was promised but did not come,[2] and often
when it came it was hopelessly inadequate, and could offer no
satisfactory guarantee of security to the merchant ships. Thus
in 1666 there was a fleet of fifty sail at Hull, ' very riche ladened

---

[1] Letter to Lambert, March 29, 1655 (*D. S. P., Interr.*, xcv. 84).
[2] *D. S. P., Interr.*, cxxx. 40 and 44, September 1656 ; convoy promised
but did not come.

with lead, corne, butter, and clothe, with other goods, vallewed at 100,000^{li.} and above '.   This great mercantile flotilla was provided with one man-of-war to guard it on the high seas. The solitary ship had been convoying a fleet of eighty coal ships along the coast, and had ' met with fower great [Dutch] men of warr about 40 guns apeese ', with very disastrous consequences to the colliers.   The four Dutch vessels now hung about the entrance to the Humber, waiting for more merchant fleets to plunder, and hence the fifty laden ships dare not stir out of the estuary, although it was now November, and the time for sailing to the Continental markets had almost passed by for that season.   No wonder that ' the people in those parts murmor crouelly that these coasts are noe better garded, and say they pay all there great sesments to small porpose, and thatt in Olliver's time there was better care taken to secure the coast trade than is now '.[1]

It was amidst such difficulties as these that the Yorkshire merchants sought to develop their foreign trade, and to expand the market for northern cloths.   Bound by the restrictions of the companies, open to the opposition of neighbouring or distant ports, and devoid of continuous security on the waters, foreign trade was far from being an easy road to opulence.   That these were not the only obstacles will become evident in the next chapter.   In this chapter we have attempted to describe the general organization of foreign commerce, the nature of the societies which did the pioneer work in the Continental markets, and the constant state of insecurity which prevailed on the North Sea during centuries of warfare, undeveloped international law, and rival commercial empires.

D. S. P., Chas. II clxxviii. 92.

CHAPTER VI

SOME MILESTONES IN THE SEVENTEENTH CENTURY

The textile history of Yorkshire during the seventeenth century is full of complications and vicissitudes. The first sixty years are marked by a series of events of a more or less catastrophic nature, under the influence of which economic progress became very difficult, if not altogether impossible. There were distractions at home, where plague and civil strife were demanding their heavy toll. State attempts to regulate the industry had disastrous effects upon its prosperity, and the efforts which were made to push the sale of English cloth abroad were met by the opposition of foreign governments, who were desirous of establishing economic independence and of fostering their own national industries. Forces, economic and political, were acting and interacting in blind and often purposeless conflict. National and local interests clashed in bitter rivalry ; economic thought was laboriously pushing through to the light ; the laws of economic action were dim and vague, and those who set them forth generally did so with interested motives. Under such circumstances the textile industry pursued a chequered career, and it was not until the later decades of the century that it really set out on that course of prosperity which preceded the Industrial Revolution. In this chapter we shall consider those events which were most potent in their influence on the welfare of the Yorkshire industry.

The first great event of the century, so far as Yorkshiremen were concerned, was the famous trial of 1612–14, one of at least three in which the interests of the Yorkshire clothiers were at stake. The trial was a test of strength between the clothiers and the ulnage officials, so it will be necessary to state in a few words the exact position of the ulnage at this period.

By the end of the sixteenth century the ulnager had been largely displaced by the local searchers, and his work was now entirely financial. All cloths had to bear the ulnager's seal before they could be sold. The clothier paid subsidy and ulnage, obtained his seals, and was then allowed to expose his cloths for sale. Should he attempt to evade his obligations to the ulnager he was liable to heavy penalties, including forfeiture of his cloth. But provided that the seals were obtained and the fee paid the ulnager or his representative did not trouble about the dimensions or quality of the cloth. These aspects of regulation he left to the searchers, who were appointed by the justices of the peace in accordance with the legislation outlined in a previous chapter.[1]

The ulnage of the county was farmed out by the Crown, and during the sixteenth century the farm of the ' ulnage of saleable woollen cloths in the city and county of York and the town of Kingston-on-Hull ' changed hands frequently. In the reigns of Edward VI and Mary it was held by the Wentworths [2] and the Waterhouses, who paid about £96 a year as rent to the Crown. Later it passed to Sir Walter Raleigh, and in the reign of James I it became the property of the Duke of Lennox,[3] who had by that time absorbed the ulnage of the whole kingdom. Occasionally the tenant-in-chief sublet a part of his holding to others, as in the case of Lennox, who re-farmed the Yorkshire ulnage to Sir Thomas Vavasour, Sir John Wattes, and Sir John Middleton. These men employed two deputy ulnagers, George Nixon and Thomas Snydall, who carried on the actual administration and collection of the ulnage fees, appointing assistants where necessary to help in the distribution of seals and the collection of the ulnage dues. It was the business of these officials to live in the heart of the clothing districts, and to go to the houses of the clothiers, when sent for, to seal the cloths and to receive the necessary fees.

What were the dues on each cloth ? What ought they to be ? These were questions around which centred several agitations

---

[1] The ulnager's men and the searchers were not always in perfect harmony. Thus in 1618 the deputy-ulnagers of Leeds declared that the ' Comon Searchers appointed . . . for searching of cloths do usually set their search seal to cloths that are not truly contented . . . and that the said searchers who are by their office and oath to search truly the cloths within their charge are clothiers themselves, and do usually make faulty cloths themselves as other clothiers do.' Copy of Memorandum transcript kindly lent by Mr. J. Lister.

[2] *Calendar of State Papers*, vol. xxi, pt. ii, 770, f. 77 (1547).

[3] *D. S. P., Chas. II*, xvi. 87.

and lawsuits during the Stuart period. In these controversies law and long-established custom were at variance, and usually custom gained the victory. To go fully into the details of the cases would lead us into a maze of legal and technical data of very little real interest ; but the broad features of the disputes are easy to understand. The amount of subsidy on a whole cloth of assize was 4d., and the ulnage ½d. When the smaller Yorkshire cloths first came within the scope of these charges in 1393 each kersey was reckoned as a quarter of a whole cloth, and so paid subsidy of 1d., whilst on every four kerseys ½d. was paid as ulnage. Eventually the ½d. fee seems to have been dropped, and in the sixteenth century 1d. per kersey was the only payment made by the clothiers. In the meantime, however, the variety of Yorkshire cloths was increasing rapidly. The ' Northern Dozen ' still remained about 12–13 yards in length, but kerseys had been increased considerably in size, and might be of any length up to 18 yards. Still, although they approximated now to a third, or possible one-half, the dimensions of a whole cloth of assize, they only paid 1d. as subsidy. Other varieties of cloth had also been increased in length, but were paying small fees, especially the long cloths (32 yards), which should have been contributing about 4d., but were still paying 2½d. These customary payments were evidently accepted by the collectors, who were content to confine themselves merely to giving out seals and receiving pence, without taking any measurements, for a witness in 1596 declared that he had ' never known any cloths measured which have been bought and sold within the county of York, by the ulnager or collector of the subsidy, nor by any others by their appointment '. It was custom alone which had kept the subsidy on kerseys down at 1d., and a great opportunity therefore presented itself to any staunch upholder of the law who might care to demand payment proportionate to the size of the cloth.

There was a slight preliminary skirmish in 1596,[1] when a collector of these dues attempted to compel two Birstall men to pay more than 2½d. per piece for certain long cloths which they had made. But the real struggle did not take place until the following reign, when ' a penny a kersey ' was the battle-cry.

---

[1] Exchequer depositions, 38–9 Eliz., Mich., no. 23, York and Hull.

At this time Sir Thomas Vavasour, Sir John Wattes, and Sir John Middleton had taken the Yorkshire ulnage in farm from the Duke of Lennox, and had as their deputies George Nixon of London, and Thomas Snydall of Halifax. The aim of these men was to increase the levy on kerseys from 1d. to 1½d. They declared that the statute of 1393–4 decreed that subsidy should be paid in proportion to the dimensions of the cloth, and that since three Yorkshire kerseys now equalled one whole cloth of assize, the payment should be 4½d. for the three (i. e. the amount of subsidy and ulnage for a whole cloth), or in other words 1½d. each. In further justification of this demand, the deputies pointed out that the Customs authorities now regarded three kerseys as equal to one whole cloth when levying Customs charges. Therefore let the kersey pay its just and proper tribute, instead of stealing into the market under false pretences. But the ulnage collectors recognized that it would be an unwise policy to attempt to levy the extra ½d. all at once, and therefore decided to proceed as gently as possible. In May 1611 the collectors began to demand 1¼d. per kersey, and by means of arguments and threats succeeded in obtaining the additional ¼d. from some clothiers. St. Bartholomew's Fair was drawing near, and large numbers of clothiers were preparing their consignments of cloth to send to that great meeting ground. But no cloth could go unsealed, and as the deputies refused to seal any cloths unless the clothiers paid the increased subsidy, many submitted and gave the sum demanded.[1] Whereupon, deeming the time to be ripe for a further advance, Nixon and Snydall began to demand 1½d. per cloth. This was in November 1611. The makers of kerseys were in arms at once, in opposition to the new demands. They applied as usual for their seals, and tendered 1d. for each cloth, only to be refused by the deputies. Many therefore dispatched their cloths unsealed, either to the Yorkshire ports or to London, and the deputies retorted by seizing all the unsealed cloths upon which they could lay hands. Some men had their pieces captured in their own districts, and had to pay a heavy ransom, in addition to the 1½d., in order to get them back. One man, Thomas Davye, of Midgeley in the parish of Halifax, had ' Tenn of his owne carseyes . . . sezed

[1] *D. S. P., Jas. I*, lxv. 78, August 18, 1611.

and taken att Hull by a pursuyvant, and by one Nixon '. He had asked for seals before dispatching his pieces, but Snydall the deputy had refused to give them out for less than $1\frac{1}{2}d.$ each, and so, fearful lest he should lose the continental market, Davye had dispatched the goods unsealed, only to have them confiscated at the port. The packs of cloth which were being forwarded to Blackwell Hall or St. Bartholomew's Fair shared a similar fate, and a number of clothiers were arrested for the resistance which they had offered to the ulnager's men. Finally, adding insult to injury, the deputies threatened ' that if the clothiers of the Vicarage of Halifax would not agree with the ulnager the payment would be enhanced to 2d.'

The demand for an increase of 50 per cent. in the amount of subsidy and ulnage was accompanied by other acts of aggression on the part of the ulnage officials. The clothiers were now subjected to new inconveniences, against which they had no power of redress, since the deputy could always punish them by refusing to issue seals and by seizing the pieces. The chief annoyance was the discontinuance of the practice which had formerly allowed the clothiers to procure their seals quickly and cheaply. This grievance was well expressed by one of the witnesses in the subsequent lawsuit. ' The farmers [of the ulnage] have used to keepe severall deputyes or sealers in severall towneshippes or hamblettes of the Parishe of Hallifaxe, to be readie to seale the carseyes there made with more speed and conveneance, and they have also used to come to men's houses for the same purpose.' This practice, however, had been discontinued about 1610 by the deputy Snydall, and now the clothiers were compelled to go ' fetch their seales, some a myle, some two myles, some three, some fowre, some seven. myles from their dwellinge houses, since the sealers gave over to come to the said clothiers' houses to seal their cloth '. Many clothiers had sent for Snydall to come to their loom-shops and seal their pieces, but he had refused, and the clothiers were therefore compelled not only to pay the extra subsidy, but also to go to Snydall's establishment. The deputies had further begun to insist upon the measuring of the cloths, even although the pieces had been previously ' searched ' by the local searchers. Since the cloths were generally dried and tentered after the 'search', and would have to be wetted again if the deputy wished to measure them, the clothier was now faced with the possibility of a double 'making up' of his pieces.

These attacks on long-established customs roused the opposition of the clothiers in the kersey-making districts, and although many eventually submitted to the new exactions, a few of the braver spirits put forward a sturdy resistance. Chief amongst these was Robert Lawe, one of the more wealthy clothiers, who had contrived to dispose of 290 unsealed cloths, and was in consequence overwhelmed with threats of imprisonment and other penalties. Along with him were others equally obstinate in their attitude towards the ulnage officials, and at last, in 1612, the Attorney-General, at the request of Nixon, the deputy ulnager, instituted proceedings against 'Robert Lawe, Richard Lawe, John Drake, and Michael Godley, clothiers that do trade and sell Northern Kersies'. In his Bill of Complaint, the Attorney-General quoted the complicated series of Acts relating to the dimensions of kerseys, and argued that as three kerseys equalled one broad cloth they ought to pay $1\frac{1}{2}d$. each, or $4\frac{1}{2}d$. for three.

'Yet so it is that Robert Lawe, Richard Lawe, John Drake, and Michael Godley, being clothiers or persons that do trade and sell Yorkshire kersies in great quantities, do refuse to answer and pay to his Majesty's ulnager . . . or his deputy 4d. for subsidy and $\frac{1}{2}d$. for ulnage for three of the saleable Yorkshire kersies . . . and by their examples divers of the clothiers and sheeremen of the County do also refuse to answer and pay such subsidy and ulnage for three of the Yorkshire saleable kersies, and do daily put their saleable kersies for sale without paying the said subsidy and ulnage, to the great loss and diminishing of the King's profit and revenue, which should and ought to grow to his Majesty by the wools and cloths of the said County of York, and to the manifest contempt and breach of his Majesty's laws and statutes in that behalf provided.' [1]

The defendants replied with the plea that they were only upholding a traditional and long-accepted custom. Their defence ran as follows :

That all have used, time out of mind, in the parishes of Bradford, Halifax, and Keighley, ever sithence subsidy and ulnage was payable on Northern Kersies, to pay for subsidy

[1] Bills and Answers, Exchequer, Jas. I, York, no. 1296, 10 Jas. I, Mich.

and ulnage 1*d.* and no more, until within two years last past or thereabouts. About two years ago the deputy ulnagers asked for five farthings, alledging that to be a proportionable rate, and by menaces and indirect means compelled some poor men to answer after that rate, and that sithence, they have lately demanded $1\frac{1}{2}d$.'

This the defendants had refused to pay, and they reiterated the fact that for two hundred years and more only 1*d.* had been paid, and was the proper proportionable rate ; they ' have paid or tendered to be paid to the ulnager's deputy the accustomed duties of 1*d.* per kersey, and nevertheless have been much vexed and troubled, whereby the trade of clothing is in danger of decay '. Finally, they declared that this extra $\frac{1}{2}d.$ would mean the exaction of an additional £200 per annum from the parishioners concerned.

Not content with acting on the defensive, the clothiers instituted a counter-action against their accusers,[1] and Robert Lawe, with four other clothiers, brought in a suit against Vavasour, Wattes, Middleton, and their deputies Nixon and Snydall. The burden of this complaint was that the deputies had exacted and extorted more than they ought to claim, had seized the wares of those who resisted their extortions, and had been negligent in their duties by not coming to the clothiers' houses when sent for to seal the cloths. The plaintiffs took this opportunity of blowing their own trumpet very lustily, and their Bill of Complaint therefore contains some admirable purple patches of self-praise. The clothiers declared that 20,000 men, women, and children were employed in ' the trade of clothing ' in the four parishes of Halifax, Bradford, Bingley, and Keighley ; they stated that in the Halifax parish alone poor relief amounting to £40 per month was administered to 600 impotent, aged, and poor people, and they pointed out that the inhabitants of the parish of Halifax ' out of zeal to God's holy religion, do freely and voluntarily, at their own Charges, maintain and give wages to ten preachers, over and above the payment of all tithes and oblations, . . . and by the special grace of God there is not one Popish recusant inhabiting in the said great and

---

[1] The plaintiffs in this counter-suit were Robert Lawe, John Dixon, John Jenkinson, John Oldfield, and Richard Smith ; they were not the same as the defendants in the first case.

populous parish of Halifax, . . . all of which benefits do arise and growe from the said trade of making . . . Northern Kersies '.

The cases having been instituted, long series of elaborate interrogatories were drawn up covering all the points at issue, and witnesses were called to give evidence on these questions.[1] The hearing of the trial was conducted by commissioners, who sat at Leeds in September 1613 to receive evidence. The plea of the clothiers was one of custom, and they therefore called the oldest men available, in order to have testimony which would go as far back as possible. Venerable clothiers, 75, 78, and 80 years of age, gave evidence based on a life-long experience of the industry, and although there were differences on minor points, there was perfect unanimity on the central question as to the amount of subsidy and ulnage on the kerseys. Witnesses declared that from time ' when the memory of man is not to the contrary ' the makers of Northern kerseys had only paid 1d. They refuted the statement that three kerseys were regarded by the Customs officials as equal to one whole broad cloth of assize by pointing out that the three kerseys paid only 5s. 4d. at Hull, whilst the broad cloths paid 6s. 8d. each ; and they reminded their opponents that considerations of quality must be taken into account, as well as mere dimensions and weight. The evidence was overwhelmingly in favour of the clothiers, and the decision of the Court showed this.

' Upon the hearing, it appeared to this Court that it hath been heretofore used and accustomed of very long and ancient time without any interruption, until now of late, . . . that the clothiers inhabiting within the parishes of Halifax, Bradford, Bingley, and Keighley have only paid the sum or rate of 1d. for the subsidy and ulnage of every Kersey, and no more. And that the same hath been during all the said time accepted as the proper and one sum payable for the subsidy and ulnage of a Kersey as this Court now conceiveth, and therefore, without great and just cause to be shown to the contrary, the Court thought it not fit to be altered. Therefore, it is thought fit and ordered by this Court that the said clothiers . . . shall from henceforth continue the payment of one penny only, . . . without demand or exaction of any further sum.'

The clothiers had gained an absolute victory, and for twenty-four years they remained in undisputed possession of the fruits

[1] Exchequer Depositions, 11 Jas. I, Mich., nos. 9 and 11, at Leeds.

of that victory. But almost immediately they were faced with a new situation, which brought far greater misfortune upon the industry than that which the ulnager's extortions could have inflicted. From 1614 onwards there are constantly recurring complaints of bad trade, and of the decay of industry and commerce, and although these dolorous jeremiads were often uttered by persons who had interests to advance, still there can be little doubt that the next half-century was marked by frequent and surprisingly periodical fluctuations, with serious depressions in industrial and commercial life. As to the causes of these fluctuations the seventeenth century writers could not agree, but one important reason seems to be that our foreign trade in cloth was now of great importance, and that it was being called upon to encounter many powerful influences and tendencies, which might bring temporary or more permanent depression. These deterrents might come from some government action or conditions at home, or from the economic and political movement of some foreign power with whose subjects England carried on trade. The textile trade was therefore subjected to many strong blasts of adversity during the next few decades, and those engaged in the manufacture of cloths were often plunged into depression and unemployment.

The first heavy blow came from the Cockayne experiment in dyeing English cloths at home. In the sixteenth century it had been thought desirable that fabrics should be dyed and finished at home, instead of providing employment for the people of other lands, as was the case when English cloth was exported undyed and unfinished. The Reformation Parliament of Henry VIII therefore found time, in the midst of its manifold labours, to declare that henceforth no piece above a certain value should be exported until it had been properly dressed and finished.[1] This Act, however, was rendered inoperative time and time again, by granting licences allowing merchants to export cloths contrary to the statute.[2] The Merchant Adventurers exported large quantities of cloths of good quality in an unfinished condition, and were said to provide employment for 50,000 persons in the Low Countries, finishing the raw cloths

---

[1] Statute 27 Hen. VIII, c. 13.
[2] *Calendar of State Papers*, vols. xv–xx, frequently.

exported from England. In fact, the whole area served by the Adventurers took scarcely any but white cloths from England, and the English merchants seem to have made few efforts to push the sale of coloured wares. Restrictions, and eventually prohibitions, were raised against such a trade; the governments of these parts attempted to ban any import of finished cloths, and in April 1612 the Archduke Albert of Austria declared that 'after the last contract made [with a certain merchant] shalbe expired, he will give out no more passports for English cloths to come into the Countie of fflaunders, but that there shall onelie come in white clothes to Antwerpe by that river, there to be dyed and drest as in tymes past'. The English representative in Flanders fumed against the decree, but without avail, and the volume of coloured cloth exported to Flanders shrank to nothing.[1]

This prohibition gave a stimulus to many ideas which were already in the air in England. Why not foster a national industry, by compelling all cloths to be dyed and finished at home? Why not retaliate on Flanders by forbidding the export of white cloths, which alone Flanders would admit? Why not tap another source of revenue, by granting to some person or company the monopoly of this finishing industry? And lastly, why not take this opportunity of breaking down the power of the Merchant Adventurers, who were already becoming the object of considerable hatred? In this manner the national industry, the national honour, and the royal purse could all be benefited at the same time, a tempting combination of advantages. In July 1614, therefore, James issued a proclamation forbidding the exportation of unfinished cloth, and by so doing practically deprived the Adventurers of their occupation.[2] In the following February a new company was set up, with Sir William Cockayne at its head, and this company was to deal with the cloth which before this time the Merchant Adventurers had exported. Cockayne had a new patent method of dyeing and finishing the pieces, and his company undertook to dye the cloths and to export an increasing quantity of finished

---

[1] Cotton MSS., Galba E, 1. 399. Letter dated Brussels, April 13, 1612.

[2] Cunningham, *op. cit.*, ii. 294. For a detailed study of the whole episode see Durham, ' Relations of the Crown to Trade under James I ', in *Trans. of the Royal Hist. Soc.*, New Series, xiii. 208–18.

goods each year, thus developing a branch of industry which the policy of the old company had certainly allowed to be neglected. In return for the favours granted, the new company was to pay a handsome fee to the Exchequer. It then entered into its fair domain, to buy the white cloths from the country clothiers, dye and finish them, and find a foreign market for them. From the first the venture was a dismal failure in every respect, and entirely dislocated the cloth trade. The provincial weavers, who had formerly prepared stocks of cloth for the Merchant Adventurers, made similar supplies for their successors, but as the new company had no market it could not take these cloths out of the hands of the country clothiers. Further, the old company, though not defunct, was barred from any export of unfinished cloths, and could therefore do nothing to relieve the situation. Hence clothiers were thrown into great distress, and Sir John Savill, in the House of Commons, declared that in Leeds, Halifax, and Wakefield the clothiers were being ruined, and at least 13,000 persons affected by this *impasse*.[1] The export of cloth declined considerably. From December 1613 to March 1614 (a period of three months), the export from the port of London amounted to 37,494 whole cloths. During the same three months of the following year, when the scheme was in full operation, the export fell to 20,283, a decrease of 17,211.[2] The new company failed entirely to secure a footing in foreign markets. Hence, in May 1615, three and a half months after the company had been established, a writer declared [3] that

' The great project of dieing and dressinge of cloth is at a stand, and they knowe not well how to go forward nor backward, for the clothiers do generally complain that theyre clothe lies on theyre hands, and the clotheworkers and diers wearie the Kinge and counsaile with petitions, wherein they complaine that they are in worse case than before, . . . and indeed yt is found that there hath not been a cloth died or dressed since Christmass more than usual, . . . whereby the Customes do fall, and many other inconveniences follow both at home and abroade, whiles the new companions differ amongst themselves and draw dyvers wayes, so that the old companie hath been dealt withall to resume the trade, and set al straight again, yf yt may be.'

---

[1] Quoted by Miss Hewart, in *Economic Journal* (1900), p. 28. No original reference is given. [2] *D. S. P., Jas. I*, lxxx. 58–9.
[3] Letter from Chamberlain to Carleton, May 25, 1615 (*D. S. P.*, lxxx. 108).

The industry was indeed almost at a standstill, especially amongst the white cloth manufacturers. Clothiers complained of the supplies of cloth which were left on their hands, and the Government ordered the old company to relieve the makers by taking the supplies which had been prepared. The new company pleaded for permission to export white as well as coloured pieces, thus admitting its failure to establish itself as a cloth-finishing concern. Eventually,[1] in 1617, the scheme was abandoned, and the old company of Merchant Adventurers reinstated with greater powers than before, in order to win back the trade which had been lost during those unfortunate years of experiment.[2]

The Cockayne venture was intended to foster one branch of the textile industry. It failed dismally, and was partially responsible for the plunging of the whole industry into many years of depression. For the period which followed was one of economic dejection, especially acute in 1621–3. This depression affected every part of the country, and complaints came from all clothing counties, from Devon to Yorkshire, from Kent to Anglesey.[3] Industry was at a standstill, and foreign trade was reduced by more than half. The Merchant Adventurers declared that their trade had fallen in value from £200,000 to £70,000, and a contemporary writer stated that the export of cloth had diminished by two-thirds.[4] There seemed to be no vent for cloth, and in March 1622 over 5,000 Yorkshire pieces lay unsold in the ' Northern Hall ' at Blackwell Hall ; the Manchester Hall had 850 ' frizes, Cottons, and Bayes ' unsold, ' besides that thear is far greater quanteties of clothe of these sortes lyinge in the Cuntrye, redie to bee sent upp if the market wear not soe loded '.[5] Clothiers did their utmost to keep their workpeople employed, but in vain, even though in some parts the justices of the peace ordered them not to dismiss any hands.[6] Through-

---

[1] D. S. P., Jas. I, xciii. 23, August 12, 1617. Also Smith's Memoirs of Wool, vol. i, p. 145.

[2] See D. S. P., Jas. I, lxxx. 110–12 ; also S. R. Gardiner's History of England, ii. 385–90.

[3] See D. S. P. for these years, passim ; especially Jas. I, cxxvii. 76.

[4] D. S. P., Jas. I, cxv. 100, and Stowe MSS., 354, ff. 63–5.

[5] Ibid., cxxvii. 73–7.

[6] As in Gloucester and Suffolk, D. S. P., Jas. I, cxxviii. 49. See E. M. Leonard, English Poor Relief, p. 148.

out the clothing counties money was scarce, bankruptcies were common, unemployment was rife. In Yorkshire the effect was keenly felt, for that county supplied large quantities of white cloths for exportation, and the shrinkage in the foreign demand brought great suffering on the clothing population. In addition to this, the scarcity of corn was ' greater than ever known in the memory of man ',[1] and one complaint from Yorkshire, Gloucestershire, Wiltshire, and the other clothing counties declared that ' the poore have assembled in troops of forty and fifty, and gone to the houses of the rich and demanded meat and money, which has been given them through fear '. In places the provision markets were raided.[2] The mercantile centres were equally dislocated by the depression. The corporation of Hull spoke of ' the sudden and great decay of this Towne, happenynge as well by the generall decay of Trade as also by the late losse of many of our shipps and men at sea, as by the present pynchinge dearth with us '.[3] Similarly the authorities of York lamented ' the decayinge estate of this Cittie for want of commerce and tradeinge, the Artificers therein haveinge much Ado to get bread to susteyne them and ther familyes, in this tyme of scarcety of corne and money, the like wherof hath not fallen out in the memory of man '.[4] The problem was indeed acute, and all classes were affected. As the clothiers of fourteen counties declared, ' these tymes do more than thretten to throw us and every one of us, yea, many thousands of poore and others yt depend uppon us, into ye bottomles pitt of remediles destruction '.[5] Similar depressions occurred in 1630–1, when the ravages of plague helped to bring the fortunes of Yorkshire to a very low ebb ; and again in 1638, 1649–50, and in the last years of the Commonwealth, when a letter from Lord Fairfax and other leading men in Yorkshire referred to ' the particular Decay and Ruine of the Cloathing Trade of this County '.

These periodical depressions of trade, coming at intervals of eight to ten years, attracted a great amount of attention from individual writers and from the Government. Explanations

[1] *D. S. P., Jas. I,* cxxxi. 78.   [2] Ibid., cxxvii. 102.
[3] Printed in Cartwright's *Chapters in the History of Yorkshire,* p. 275.
[4] Ibid., p. 277.   [5] Stowe MSS., 354, f. 65.

of their causes, and suggestions as to infallible remedies, were never lacking. In 1622 the Privy Council decided to appoint a commission,[1] consisting of a 'convenient Nomber of Persons of Qualitie, Understanding, Experience and Judgement', to whose 'Judgement, Industrie and Care [it] might commit the further searching out and better discerning of the true Causes of the Decaie of Trade, and the finding out of fit and convenient Remedies to be applied to the same'. The Commission was to receive evidence from all parts of the country, and for that purpose the justices of the peace in each county were to call the clothiers before them, in order to select two representatives who should be able to place before the Commissioners the grievances of the county from which they came.[2] Armed with a number of points of reference, the Commissioners set to work, and after 'many conferences had with the Marchaunts Adventurers and the marchaunts of other Societies and Companies, with the gentry of quality of severall Counties, with the Cloathiers of the severall cloathynge sheires, with the officers of his Ma[ties] Customes and the drapers and diers of London, and after manie dayes spent in this waightie service', presented a long report of the 'true Groundes and Motives of the great decaye of the sale and vente of our English Cloth in fforaigne partes'.[3]

The causes enumerated in this report apply to some extent to all the depressions of the seventeenth century, and illustrate the difficulties with which the progress of the cloth trade was confronted. They were :

1. 'The makeing of cloth . . . in fforeigne partes in more aboundance than in former times, being theareunto chiefly enabled by the woolles and other materialls transported from the Kingdomes of England, Scotland, and Ireland, wee conceive to be the cheifest cause that lesse quantitye of ours are vented there.'

2 'The false and decitfull makinge, dyinge, and dressinge of our clothe . . . and stuffes, which disgraceth it in foraigne partes.'

3. 'The hevy burthen uppon our cloth, wheareby it is made soe deare to the buyer that those that were wont to furnish

---

[1] Brit. Mus., 190 (g). 13 (317), quoted in Cunningham, *Growth*, Appendix E; Rymer, *Foedera*, xvii. 410.

[2] See D. S. P., *Jas. I*, cxxix. 81, for report from Bishop of Chester and justices of Lancashire concerning the election of representatives.

[3] Stowe MSS., 554, f. 45.

themselves therwith in fforraigne parts either by [buy] Cloth in other countries, or cloath themselves in a cheaper manner.'

Another document explains that the dues inflicted by the English Government, by the companies monopolizing the export trade, and by the foreign powers through or into whose countries the cloths went were so heavy that they made

'ye charg of our English clothe from ye hands of ye maker to ye back of ye wererer exceede ye charg of a duche [Dutch] clothe made and worne in Hollande by iiij^{li}. and xiij^s., and in ye Archduke coontry by v^{li}. xij^s.' [1]

4. 'The present state of the times by reason of the warres in Germany is conceived by many to be some present impediment to the vent of our cloth, partly by the interupcion of passages, partly for want of mony.'

5. 'The pollices of the Marchaunts Adventereours, which bringe uppon themselves suspicion of combinacion in tradinge, and the smallnes of their number which doe now usually buy and vent cloth, and the like pollicies of other marchaunts who are not able or willinge to extend themselves in this time of extremitie to take off the cloth from the handes of the clotheirs.'

6. 'The scarcety of coyne at home and the basenes of fforraigne coynes compared unto ours.' For the scarcity the East India Company was especially blamed.

7. 'The want of meanes of retorne for our marchauntes, especially out of the Eastland Countries, which discorage them to carry out cloth thether, because they can neither sell for redy money nor barter for vendable comodities.'

Another paper complains of the trade of the Dutch, who were said to bring French, Eastland, and Russian commodities, and who ' fill the Marketts here and carry no clothe or Englishe ware [back], but only reddy monnys '.[2]

8. 'The too little use of waringe cloth at home, and the too muche of silkes and fforraigne stuffes, which overbalance our trade.' [3]

The first reason offered by the Commission was very true. Throughout the sixteenth and seventeenth centuries many of the countries of Western Europe were building up industrial systems, and attempting to meet their own demands for cloth. First the Low Countries tried to regain some of their former

---

[1] Stowe MSS., 354, f. 65. Report and petition of clothiers of Yorkshire and thirteen other counties, presented to the Privy Council.

[2] Ibid., f. 65.   [3] Ibid., 554, f. 45 ; also *D. S. P., Jas. I,* cxxxi. 55.

fame as clothmakers,[1] and then at a later date the policy of Colbert succeeded in establishing in France a strong textile industry. The Dutch Government levied heavy import duties on English cloths passing into the country, severely punished any importation of false wares, and in 1612 forbade the entry of any but white cloths. The Cockayne bungle resulted in a tariff war, and enabled the Dutch to make progress as cloth-makers. The Dutch Government gave a bounty to all who set up looms,[2] and many Englishmen, weavers of broad cloths and serges as well as woolcombers, were soon to be found in Holland.[3] The Dutch contrived to get supplies of English wool and English fuller's earth, and therefore manufactured bays, serges, and other cloths, which were sold on the Continent cheaper than the English wares, thanks to the various imposts under which the English pieces laboured.[4] The exportation of wool to foreign parts was a perennial theme of complaint, and though the English Government had forbidden its exportation to Holland, the wool was smuggled there from Newcastle,[5] Scotland, and Ireland, to the great disgust of English clothiers.[6] Thus, assisted by English labour, receiving supplies of raw material from England, and aided by strong protective duties, the Dutch were able to produce large quantities of cloth, which replaced the English pieces and so reduced the amount of our cloth sold in Holland. The troubles before and during the Civil War in England further assisted the progress of the Dutch, and a writer in 1649 speaks very emphatically concerning 'the greate number of clothe workers, weavers, dyers, cottoners, and pressers repayring from England' to Holland, as well as to Hamburg, Altona, and other centres across the North Sea, where Englishmen were competing against their fellow workers in England.[7]

[1] As early as 1527 various towns in the Low Countries were refusing admission to English cloths (*Calendar of State Papers, Henry VIII*, vol. iv, p. 3433).

[2] Unwin, *Industrial Organization in the Sixteenth and Seventeenth Centuries*, p. 192.   [3] *D. S. P., Chas. I*, ccxxiv. 44 (1632).

[4] Ibid.   [5] *D. S. P., Jas. I*, lxxxviii. 76 (1616).

[6] Add. MSS., 34324, f. 203 (1622).

[7] *D. S. P., Interr.*, i. 34 (1649). Another writer (*D. S. P., Interr.*, ix. 5, (1650)) declares that 'great quantities of white and coloured cloths which are made here (i. e. in Hamburg) and being endraped of Spanish and other sorts of wool, are offered at cheaper rates than we English can do ours, and are

Similar industrial developments had taken place in France, though there was scarcely any immigration of English cloth-workers into that country. As early as 1622 it was declared that the French and Dutch now made so much cloth 'that they have noe needs of our English drapery '.[1] Large quantities of wool and fuller's earth were carried thither in spite of all pro-hibitions, and the French trade flourished, nourished partly by English raw material. Even Poland turned against English cloth, and the Eastland merchants were hit hard by the growth of manufactures

'not only in Holland but also in Germany . . . and Brandenburg, and Silesia, and divers places in Poland and . . . Prussia, and the cloth can be afforded cheaper than any such like that can be carried out of England. . . . And whereas the gentlemen in Poland formerly used to cloath their attendants with English cloth, they, being now impoverished by reason of the late wars, do now cloath them with Silesia and such as is made in their own Country, not being able as formerly to go to the price of English cloth.'[2]

In refusing admission to English fabrics, foreign Governments generally stated that they were only protecting themselves against the false and deceitful wares made in England. The legislation of Elizabeth and James I was no more effective than previous attempts had been in preventing fraudulent making of cloth, and the pieces exported were open to the usual complaints of uneven weaving, excessive stretching, and deceitful finishing. In about 1604 [3] the Dutch placed an embargo on faulty English cloths, and thirty years later a writer from Delft declared that 'the Dutch merchants avoid the buying of [English] cloths, finding them now worse made and yet as faulty as before, whereby our English cloth grows more and more in disgrace, and causeth the Dutch to go on with more courage in the making of cloth '. In 1635 the London merchants trading with France lamented that ' the ffrenche, (who are very prone uppon the

finer ; by long continuance of the clothing trade they make them very good and substantial, whereas ours are made thin and faulty . . . (therefore) they outsell us, thanks to this and the impositions which the States have put on our cloths, i.e. 12s. on all white cloths of £16 and under, 40s. on all £16–24, and £2 13s. 4d. on all above £24, . . . from which impositions their own cloths are free '.   [1] Add. MSS. 34324, f. 203.
    [2] Coke MSS., i. 465 (1632).   [3] Cotton MSS., Galba E, i. 284–6.

least occasion to interrupt the trade of the English and to villifie their manufactures) . . . doe daylie complayne of the badness of the English draperie ', especially of the Welsh and northern cottons and other coarse northern cloths which found their chief markets in France, but which were now being made so ' vicious ' that the French had begun to return them to the exporters, ' desiring a reformacion '.[1]   Two years later the Government of Poland issued an edict prohibiting the vent of strained cloths, and went a step further by permitting only those pieces to be imported which were of sizes different from those fixed by the English cloth statutes.[2]   In 1652 the Senate of Hamburg sent a representative to the English Government to complain of the ' abuses wch are in the makeing of the English cloaths '.[3]   The reputation of English pieces abroad was apparently bad, and may have helped considerably to bring about these serious trade depressions.

The remedies recommended by the Commission of 1622 and later inquiries followed the main principles of the mercantilist theories, which were in almost general acceptance at that time. Forbid the exportation of wool and fuller's earth, and establish a coastal police to prevent smuggling ; take precautions ' that no coyne be carryed out of the realme ' ; abolish some of the export dues, and curb the power of monopolistic organizations such as the Merchant Adventurers, so that these societies may not levy heavy tolls on non-members, or impede the expansion of trade.   These were the usual suggestions advanced for the improvement of economic affairs.   Then, having deprived our rivals of their supplies of raw material, reorganize and strengthen the machinery for ensuring a high quality of workmanship ; simplify the cloth laws and administer them more thoroughly ;[4] then, ' all theis being duelie reformed there is great hope that clothing will flourish again, which hath mayntained more when clothing was goode and comodities cheape than all the trades in this kingdom besides '.[5]

These varied suggestions occupied the attention of Stuart

[1] *D. S. P., Chas. I,* ccxciv. 93 (1635).
[2] Eastland Merchants' petition, *D. S. P., Chas. I,* ccclxvi. 71.
[3] Order Book, *Interr.,* i. 66, p. 511.   Order of Council of State, April 6, 1652.
[4] Report of Commission, 1622, Stowe MSS. 554, f. 45.
[5] Add. MSS. 34324, f. 213.

rulers from time to time, and we shall have cause in the next
chapter to observe how some of the recommendations were
carried out.   For the present, however, we must continue our
survey of some of the chief events which influenced the Yorkshire cloth industry up to the Restoration.   Gradually the
stagnation of 1622 gave place to greater briskness in our home
and foreign trade, and for some years the cloth industry enjoyed
a period of comparative prosperity.   But in 1630 the cries of
the decay of trade were renewed, and cloth-makers once more
plunged into depression, though happily not so keen as that of
eight years before.[1]   These years, 1630–1, were memorable,
however, because of the terrible plague which swept over Yorkshire, and which helped to bring the cloth industry to a standstill.   We are apt to underrate the frequency and the fierceness
of the epidemics which periodically ravaged some part of Europe.
We are well acquainted with the horrors of the Black Death,
the Great Plague of London, and the outbreak of cholera in the
early thirties of last century.   But really these were only the
most important in a long series of plagues which visited this
country.   There was a serious outbreak in Yorkshire in 1596–7.
The death-roll was heavy in Leeds, rising from an average of
162 for 1590–5 to 271 in 1596, and to 311 in the following
year.[2]   This pestilence passed northward and claimed heavy
toll at Richmond, Knaresborough, and other northern towns.
In 1610 there was another outbreak, the death-roll at Leeds
being increased by 50 per cent. ;   and so terrible was the
mortality at Beverley that the register of St. Mary's Church
speaks of two score victims ' yat was shuffled into graves without any reading over them '.[3]   Leeds suffered from further
visitations in 1617[4] and 1623, a famine in the latter year helping
to swell the death-rate.   The outbreak of 1631 was national in
its scope, and even embraced most parts of Western Europe.
London, Birmingham, Leicester, and Nottingham all suffered
from ' the sickness ', and so great was the distress in Cambridge
that the mayor and the heads of the various colleges petitioned

---

[1] See *D. S. P.* for those years, *passim*.
[2] Figures of births, marriages, and deaths in Leeds : Thoresby MSS.
(Thoresby Soc. Library, Leeds).
[3] Cook, *Hist. Notes on Beverley* (1880), p. 8.
[4] Death Roll : 1615, 195 ; 1617, 520.

the King for leave to employ part of their moneys for the relief of the poor. The progress of this pestilence in the clothing district of Yorkshire is vividly depicted in a long letter written by Wentworth, who was at that time President of the Council of the North.[1]

'True itt is (that leauing our neighboures of Lancishire and Lincolnshire miserably distressed with the pestilence), that now wthin thes sixe weekes the infection is cum'd to ourselues in diuers partts of this county, and last of all into this Citty [York]. Upon the Edge of Lancishire ther is the toune of Heptonstall, wch hath neare forty howses infected. Mirfeild, a little toune not farre of itt, hath lost ninescore persons, and both thes tounes wthin four miles of Halifax, wch yett, God be praysed, stands sownde, but much indangered, by reason of the great number of people and lardge trade of clothing thereaboutes. It is likwise in the tow tounes of Beeston and Holbecke wch are wthin one mile of Leedes, and if it should please God to visit either of thos greate townes Hallifax or Leedes, wch tow allone trade more then all the cuntry besides, in good faithe it would mightily distresse and impouerishe all that side of the cuntrye.'

In similar fashion other parts of the county had been attacked, and eventually York itself was stricken, in spite of the precautions taken by Wentworth.

Leeds escaped the pestilence of this year, but 1635 and 1637 were marked by abnormally high rates of mortality, whilst in 1640 and 1641[2] a similar outbreak seized upon the whole of the West Riding. Leeds, Bradford, and Halifax, all were swept by pestilence, and in January 1641 the justices of the peace in their Quarter Sessions at Wakefield declared 'that by occasion of the heavye visitation with wch itt hath pleased God to visitt the inhabitaunts of Dewesbury [several months before] the same contagion still continueinge in some particular places there, the trade and commerce of those inhabitaunts are soe muche decayed and the poor soe exceedinglie encreased . . . that about two hundreth seaventie and odd persons . . . are to receive weekly allowance and relief '.[3] The justices had already

---

[1] *D. S. P., Chas. I*, cc. 14.

[2] Thoresby MSS. Death-roll for parish of Leeds : 1634, 406 ; 1635, 615 ; 1636, 479 ; 1637, 516 ; 1638, 398 ; 1640, 561.

[3] Quarter Sessions Records, January 14, 1641, Wakefield ; Order Book A, 145 d.

charged the inhabitants within five miles of Dewsbury with one contribution for the relief of the sufferers, and they now ordered £100 to be raised throughout the Riding; but when the collectors attempted to obtain this money they met with sullen and stubborn refusals, for most other districts were in similar plight, and needed the money for their own suffering and poor.[1]

Meanwhile the clothiers of the kersey-making area had been compelled to make another stand in defence of their ancient customs. After the legal decision of 1613 peace had reigned between the ulnager and the clothier, and during the subsequent years, in spite of plagues and depressions, some industrial progress had been registered. The number of clothiers had increased, especially in the Aire valley, and one witness in the 1638 lawsuit declared that 'in the towne of Shipley, and places adjoyning [i. e. Keighley, Bingley, and Bradford] there are now about an hundred clothiers for one that was in these Townes' about thirty years before. Keighley had become famous for a certain kind of cloth known as Keighley kerseys or 'whites'; the parishes of Bradford, Bingley, and Shipley were said to contain 10,000 persons engaged in cloth-making, and the parish of Halifax alone claimed no less than 12,000 textile workers.

Further, a change had come over the nature of the wares which were being produced. In 1613 large numbers of 'broad-list kerseys' were being made. These were cloths 14 to 17 yards long, and less than a yard in width, with a very broad list, or waste edge, which sometimes amounted to one-fifth or one-sixth of the whole cloth. These pieces were of inferior quality; they were often excessively tentered and deceitfully finished, and were therefore very cheap, selling at 1s. to 1s. 6d. per yard. Such pieces had found a market in Holland, Germany, and Poland, being sold there by the Adventurers or the Eastland Merchants, but between 1613 and 1638 there was a heavy fall in the demand for 'broad lists'. This was due partly to a rise in the price of wool, and to the heavy customs and other imposts, which in proportion to value weighed most heavily on the cheaper cloths. At the same time the defective manufacture of the pieces brought them into bad repute abroad, and thus a witness declared in 1638 that 'very few have been vented

[1] Ibid., May 4, 1641, Pontefract; see also 184 d and 197.

[abroad] these late yeares, by reason of the basenes and ill-making thereof. This witness hath heard by the people in the Country of Silesia that by reason of the badness of the said kerseis which were then vented, they took upon them to make kerseis in those countries like in length and bredth ' to the ' broad lists ' formerly imported from the West Riding.[1] Further, the merchants were beginning to find that cloths of ' nientien and twentie yeards are more vendible and desired in forreigne partes than those of eightiene ', and that they found a more ready and a more profitable sale for long pieces than for short cloths. Hence the very cheap cloth of short length, the broad list kersey, quickly disappeared. It succumbed because of its evil repute, because of the competition of the cheapest cloths made abroad, and because of the enterprise of merchants in pushing the sale of longer pieces of better quality. Some young merchants, giving evidence in 1638, had never dealt in ' broad lists ', so quickly and completely had the demand for this cloth disappeared. In its place kerseys of all lengths up to 30 yards were being manufactured. The most popular pieces were from 18 to 23 yards, though merchants occasionally gave orders for cloths up to 30 yards. The cloths were of greater lengths ; they were also of better quality and finer workmanship. There seems to have been considerable improvement in this respect since the contest of 1613, and many witnesses in 1638 agreed that the kerseys, although now made of inferior wool, were ' both finer, better made, and of greater value and price than the said kersies were ' a quarter of a century before.[2] Thus, on the whole, Yorkshire kerseys had increased in variety, in length, in quality, and in value.

And yet they were only paying a penny each for subsidy and ulnage ! This was bound, sooner or later, to bring about another conflict between the clothiers and those interested in the collection of the cloth fees, and the legal battle took up the years 1637-8. At this time the control of the ulnage for the West Riding was in the hands of Thomas Metcalfe of Leeds,

[1] Evidence of Wm. Busfield of Leeds ; Exch. Dep. by Comm., 14 Chas. I, Mich., no. 20, York.

[2] In 1613, average price for Halifax kersey 1s. 3d. to 2s. per yard. In 1638 the cheapest valued at 1s. 10d. ; others sold at 2s. 6d. to 4s. 6d. per yard. Even Keighley kerseys, 18 yards in length, sold at 2s. to 2s. 6d. per yard.

described as a gentleman of great estate, but also a merchant who carried on foreign trade in the very wares over which the dispute arose. Metcalfe was assisted by a number of deputies, who lived in the various villages and towns, distributing the seals and collecting the pence. These deputies carried on some other occupation, and did the ulnage work as an additional means of livelihood. Some were yeomen, and might be actually engaged in making cloth ; others were inn-keepers or shop-keepers, or persons of other employments who possessed a little spare time to devote to these duties in return for the two, three, or four pounds which Metcalfe paid them. These ' deputyes did repayre to the clothiers' houses upon notice given, and there seal their karseis ', though, if the clothier wished, he might go down to the deputy's house and there purchase as many seals as he required, paying the customary penny for each.

The relations between Metcalfe and the kersey-makers were harmonious until October 1636, but in that year the former decided to raise the fee to $1\frac{1}{2}d.$, since the cloths were now much too large to be allowed to escape any longer on payment of $1d.$ He therefore instructed his three chief assistants, Thomas Walker, Christopher Scaife, and John Crabtree, to demand an extra $\frac{1}{2}d.$ per kersey from the clothiers, and these men were so successful in their threats and cajoleries that they were said to have wrung an additional £100 out of the clothiers of the four parishes in a short space of time.

Four men stood out in sturdy opposition, and refused to pay the extra toll. These men were Thomas Lister, Robert Hall, James Robinson, and Nathan Drake, clothiers who lived in or near Halifax, and who bore the brunt of the fighting. Lister, Hall, and Drake already had several cloths sealed on the penny basis of payment ; these were packed up ready for carriage to London when the ulnage officials came and demanded an additional halfpenny on each cloth. They were met by a refusal, and the clothiers proceeded to dispatch the pieces on the backs of pack-horses, escorted by two carriers, to the metropolis. The deputies decided to follow the carriers, and seize the goods *en route.* They therefore made their way southwards, and overtook the loaded train of pack-horses at Wombwell, where the carriers were resting for the night, at the end of the first day's journey. Here the horses were stabled, the packs stored away, and the carriers retired for the night. At three o'clock in the morning (October 20) they were awakened by noises outside, and on making investigations found the three deputies busily engaged in tearing open the packages of cloth. The two carriers rushed out and defended their charges with success, but the deputies had already opened some of the packs, and had scattered the cloths about in the yard of the inn, so that they were ' much spoiled and made unfitt for sale '. Scaife, perceiving that the carriers were making a strong resistance, fetched the constable of Wombwell, and, by reason of their official status, the deputies had the carriers arrested, taking the packs, containing thirty-three kerseys, into their own possession. On November 5, 1636, a similar raid was made on the wares of James Robinson, another Halifax clothier. Robinson had dispatched a pack of ten cloths to York. All these pieces bore ulnage seals, for which Robinson had paid a penny but had refused to pay the additional halfpenny. The deputies therefore determined to seize the offending cloths, and just as the carrier was bringing the load over Kirkstall Bridge, near Leeds, his horse was seized, led to a house near by, and Robinson's goods were confiscated.

In making these seizures, the deputies felt somewhat dubious about the rights of their case, and they therefore reinforced their position by pointing out that not only ought the kerseys to pay three-halfpence, but also that, being 20 to 21 yards in length, they were above the legal maximum of 18 yards allowed to kerseys by the Act of 1623.[1] This Act, still nominally in force, was in actual practice a dead letter, and few Yorkshire kerseys were less than 18 yards in length. Nevertheless, for want of some better justification, the deputies were ready to invoke the assistance of an obsolete law, and to declare that their seizures were made in the interests of the majesty of law and the purity of industrial life.

The four clothiers did not agree with these contentions. They stated that as their goods were all properly sealed the action of the deputies was entirely unwarranted, and they complained that by reason of the confiscation of the goods they had ' lost

---

[1] Statute 21 Jas. I, c. 18.

the benefitt of their market, and will be putt to great charges
and expences in getting ye same againe, and their said karseis,
with opening and throwing in ye dust, are much spoiled and
made unfitt for sale '. They therefore instituted proceedings
against Metcalfe and his subordinates, and the case was opened
in the Court of Exchequer in 1637.

In their bill of complaint,[1] the Halifax men indulge in the
customary eulogy concerning the industrial activity of their
district, ' by meanes of which trade and of godly and true
religion there professed and embraced, manie thousand of his
Ma$^{ties'}$ subjects are nourished and exercised in godly labour,
manie poore people and theire families honestly mainteyned
and vertuously brought up, a great number of impotent and
aged persons relieved, manie godly Preachers mainteyned, and
his Ma$^{ties'}$ Revenues much encreased '. There is boasting concerning the 22,000 persons engaged in the four parishes in
cloth-making, the £40 per month distributed to the Halifax
poor, the ten additional preachers maintained, and the claim
that ' by the speciall grace of God there is not one Popish
Recusant inhabiting in the great and populous parish ' of
Halifax. The clothiers also state that the cloths exported from
the four parishes furnish the Customs officials with over £6,000
per annum, and as eleven kerseys paid about £1 for customs
dues, the export of kerseys must have been between 60,000 and
70,000 each year. All this, declare the clothiers, is effected ' by
the travell and industry of the people dwelling there, the places
which they inhabitt being soe mountainous and rough, soe
barren and unfruitfull as it will not suffice to yield victualls
for the third part of the inhabitants, and the poor that spin the
wooll there, though they work very harde, cannot gaine for
theire laboure fowre pence a day towards their livinge '. The
plaintiffs then complain of the illegal impositions and infamous
practices of which the deputies have been guilty, namely the
extortion of the additional halfpenny, the seizure of the cloths,
and the refusal of the deputies to come to the clothiers' houses
when sent for ; ' by means whereof yor Orato^{rs} and other ye

---

[1] Exch. Bills and Answers, Mich., 14 Chas. I, York, no. 485. The whole
of the documents relating to this case have been transcribed by Mr. J. Lister,
who kindly placed them at the writer's disposal.

Clothiers aforesaid have been much impoverished and hindred, and the trade of clothing much decayed in theis parts and a great sort of people undone and forced to live unproffitably for wante of worke, to ye great hurt of ye weeale publique and his Ma^{ties'} subjects in those parts, and to ye great diminucion and impairing of his Ma^{ties'} customs and duties for exportacion of Northern kersies into forraigne countries '. Finally, as if the above pleadings are not sufficient, the plaintiffs conclude with a grim and almost pathetic picture, which might do credit to any modern book on poverty. They point out that the levy of the additional halfpenny would produce £200 per annum, and ' ye greatest waight of ye said exaccion will fall uppon very poor people y^t are sore oppressed with ye same, who making every week a coarse kersie, and being compelled to sell ye same at ye week-end, and with ye money receaved for ye same to provide both stuffe wherewith to make another ye weeke following, and also ye victualls to susteyne themselves and their familyes till another be made and sold, by which means ye said poor and distressed people, making hard shifts with continual labour to preserve themselves, their wives and children from begging, are nevertheless constrained out of their necessities to yeild and contribute every week one halfpenny a peece more than is due '.[1]

The procedure was similar to that of the suit of 1613. Commissioners sat at Halifax and Leeds, and here hosts of witnesses were called to answer the long series of questions put before them. Young men and old, clothiers from the parishes, drapers, chapmen, merchants of Leeds, aldermen of York and Customs House clerks from Hull, all gave their evidence. All bore testimony to the increase in the length of cloths, but all were equally emphatic on the recognition of the custom of paying only one penny for subsidy and ulnage.[2] Metcalfe eventually recognized the hopelessness of his case, and therefore, ' after he had spent a greate deale of money, did desist the suite and accept of a penny seale '.[3] For the second time the ' penny custom ' triumphed, the force of an old-standing usage out-

---

[1] Exch. Bills and Answers, Mich., 14 Chas. I, 485.

[2] Exch. Dep. by Comm., Mich., 14 Chas. I, York, 20 1.

[3] The actual verdict is missing, but this quotation comes from the suit of 1676 : Exch. Dep. by Comm., 28 Chas. II, Mich. 29 (York ; Lancaster).

weighing considerations of changed circumstances. But the matter was not finally settled even then, for in 1676 the whole dispute was raised once more. The actors were different, but the plot was the same. The verdict was also the same as in the two previous suits, but there was occasional trouble between the ulnage officials and the clothiers[1] until the ulnage expired, early in the eighteenth century.

The evidence presented by the witnesses in 1638 enables us to get many interesting side-glances at the character of industrial life during this period. There are many varieties of people engaged in the manufacture and sale of cloth, and though there is no rigid stratification it is possible to classify the Stuart textile workers into the divisions which were studied in Chapter III. There was the small clothier making one piece weekly, and living from hand to mouth ; the yeoman, who combined agriculture and industry, either making cloth, or finishing it, or both ; the large clothier, with his flock of spinners and weavers, and with apprentices learning their trade under his care. These large clothiers often bought pieces from the small men of the first class, and sold them along with the cloths of their own manufacture to London or Yorkshire merchants. The great merchants of York and Hull now drew their supplies of cloth for export, not from the looms of York or Beverley, but from the West Riding generally, whilst Leeds merchants, chiefly young men,[2] formed a large proportion of the witnesses in the lawsuit. The dealings in cloth were carried on in two ways : either in open markets and fairs, or according to orders given by the traders to the clothiers. To the cloth markets of Leeds, Halifax, and Wakefield the clothiers brought their goods once

---

[1] There was a case concerning the sale of ulnage seals in 2–3 Jas. II, Hil. (York ; Lancaster). The Yorkshire suit of 1638 was followed in 1640 by one almost identical to it in Lancashire (D. S. P., Chas. I, cccclxxv. 61). Here the complaint was that the ulnager ' hath by many indirect practices endeavoured to extract farr greater fees, and from some hath by threats obtayned his desyre, and to others hath denyed the seale to make them subject to seizure and forfeyture, and instituting Exchequer proceedings, by which grievance our trade of Clothynge is like to be overthrowne, and our poor people to perish for want of employment '.

[2] e.g. the following Leeds merchants : Wm. Busfield of Leeds, merchant, aged 60 ; Richard Lodge of Leeds, merchant, 28 years ; John Baines, of Leeds, merchant, 26 years ; Wm. Sykes, Leeds, chapman, 33 years ; Michael Lister, Leeds, woollen draper, 30 years ; Wm. Lodge, Leeds, chapman, 28 years.

or twice a week, or sent cargoes to Blackwell Hall and Bartholomew Fair.   Here the cloths were sold either directly to the
merchants, cloth dressers, and dyers, or, as was often the case,
to a middleman.   This middleman, factor, or chapman, occupied
an important position in the mercantile world of this period;
and his chief business was the purchase of cloth on commission
for absentee merchants.   To give one instance of the middleman's methods: a certain chapman, giving evidence, declared
that he bought Keighley kerseys, half-fixed, mingle-coloured,
and ordinary kerseys, from clothiers in Wakefield market;
then taking these wares to York, he sold them to merchants for
exportation.[1]   Or secondly, cloths might be made to the order
of the merchant.   If the merchant required only the standard
types of cloth he could satisfy his needs through the ordinary
open markets; but if he desired to obtain some special quality,
or some cloth of more than ordinary length (30 yards, for instance), he ordered it from some clothier.   Also, in many cases,
merchants developed permanent connexions with particular
clothiers, who therefore made their goods with the intention of
selling them privately to one or two merchants.

During the years between the suits of 1613 and 1638 there
had been considerable developments in the use of credit.   The
price of cloth was higher at the later date than in 1613, and
witnesses explained this partly by the improvement in the
quality, partly by the rise in the price of wool, and partly by
the expansion in the scope of credit dealings.   One witness
summed up the situation when he declared that ' what he sells
dearer now, he gives far longer time for payment for them than
he did for those he sold a little cheaper of like making and
substance thirty years ago ', and another dealer stated that
' the clothiers give to the Marchaunts and the Chapman longer
tyme with payment '.   In most cases a partial payment was
made, and a period of six months allowed for the payment of
the remainder ; one man who sold kerseys for about 43s. received
on delivery all above 30s., and gave ' six monthes tyme usually
for the payment of the rest '.   As such a system came into
general use, the need for the chapman became more pressing.
The small clothiers, making one kersey a week, could not afford

[1] John Dickson, of Shipley (Exch. Dep., 14 Chas. I. Mich., 20–1 York).

to wait six months for payment. They needed to be paid on the delivery of the piece, in order to be able to buy wool and victuals for the forthcoming week. Hence, they must sell their pieces to a man who was willing to trade on cash terms, a man with some spare capital, who could afford to wait for his returns. The chapman was the man who filled this position.

In the making of kerseys, the supply of wool was a pressing problem for the clothiers. They had been accustomed to using the higher qualities of northern wool, and also the fleeces of Lincolnshire and Leicestershire. In the thirties, however, there had been a heavy demand for the wool of these two counties, since southern clothiers were now using larger supplies of wool from these sources. This had been partially instrumental in causing an increase in the price of Lincolnshire wool. From 8s. or 9s. per stone in 1610 it had risen to 14s. in 1638,[1] but there had been no improvement in the quality of the material. Yorkshire makers of cheap cloths were compelled therefore to supplement their supplies of Lincolnshire wool by drawing upon the cheaper grades from Ireland, Scotland, and other parts. This would have caused the production of an inferior quality of cloth, had not the clothiers paid attention to the improvement of their methods. This raising of the standard of work in sorting, carding, spinning, &c., had been very considerable, and nearly all the witnesses agreed that the cloths of 1638 were better than the fabrics of 1613, because of the finer workmanship.

The discussion on the wool supply led many witnesses to a comparison of the relative merits of Yorkshire cloths and those manufactured in other clothing areas. All admitted that the Yorkshire fabrics were inferior in quality to those of East Anglia and the West of England, although ' the wolles of Lincolnshire and Leicestershire are as fyne wolles as the wolles of Kent, Essex, Suffolke, Norfolke, Cambridgeshire, and Huntingdonshire '. The wools of Wiltshire were no better than those of the northern parts, and yet Wiltshire pieces sold at much higher prices than the Yorkshire woollen goods. The greatest contrast, however, came in comparing the cloths made in different parts

---

[1] This increase was also partly due to the general rise in prices which was going on throughout the period.

from the same wool. The clothiers of Suffolk and the West of England were using large quantities of Lincoln and Leicester wool. The cloths which they made from this raw material sold at the rate of 12s., 20s., and in some cases 26s. a yard, whilst the Yorkshire fabrics made of wool from the same sources only commanded 3s. or 4s. This superiority of the south was explained as being due to 'the Industry and Skilfulnes of the Manufactor thereabouts. On this point some witnesses gave greater detail. One declared that ' he conceaveth the good sortinge of wolles in the Southern partes is the reason why the clothiers in the South partes doe make their cloathes fyner and of greater values by much than the Northern kerseys and cloathes are made of, though the wolles be alike in fynenes from the sheepe '. Another witness stated that the contrast was due ' to the good dying of the Southerne cloathes, the skill of the manufactors, and the carefull sorteinge of their wolles, but he holdeth the principall reason to be the well-sorteinge of their wolles ', and a third witness concluded with the optimistic assertion that ' if the clothiers in Yorkshire would as well severally and carefully sorte theire woolls as the cloathiers in Wiltshire doe, the same might be made as good cloathes as the cloathes in Wiltshire are ordinarily '. Evidently the West Country clothiers had developed their processes to a high level of perfection, and had built up the reputation for high-class work which they retain to this day. The reason may have been that the industry in those parts was more capitalized than its northern rival, and was therefore more highly organized and carried on with a greater degree of division of labour. It may have been that the Yorkshire clothiers were content to keep to their lower qualities of fabrics, and did not deem it worth while to raise their industrial methods to a high state of efficiency. But whatever the cause, it is evident that the Yorkshire manufacturing processes were still inferior to those of other counties, and that the produce in consequence could not bid for a place in the high-class textile markets of Europe.

In the conflict with the ulnagers, the clothiers had been completely successful, but they were soon to be faced with another danger, beside which all previous troubles sank into insignificance. The relations between Charles I and his Parliament were now growing very strained, and the Civil War was shortly to be a grim reality throughout the land. On January 1, 1642, Charles attempted to arrest the five members ; on April 23 he was refused admission to Hull, and finally, after a short sojourn at York, he set up his standard at Nottingham, on August 22.[1] The political tension had begun to exert an untoward influence on trade months before the actual outbreak of hostilities, and in April 1642 the clothiers of ' the Parish of Leeds, the Vicaridge of Halifax and other partes adjoyning ' presented an account of their grievances to the King. In their petition the clothiers complained of the various ' illegall pressures and impositions ', and then went on to state that they had been ' diversely vexed and grieved with Sealings, Searchings and the like devices most rigorously executed by promoters and other officers, . . . by which means not onely considerable sommes of money have been screwed out of your Petitioners' purses, but also divers of the meaner sort have beene utterly disabled to mannage theire trades, their stockes being exhausted by those crafty inventions '. With the assembling of Parliament in 1640, the clothiers had hoped for redress of these grievances, but with the quarrel between King and Parliament all their ' hopes of reliefe and justice have become over-clouded by hopeless despaire, . . . especially because merchants, fearing what evill event may ensue upon these distractions, do not take up . . . Cloth as they used to doe '. Hence stocks lay dead in the hands of the clothiers, ' and many thousands of poore people, who onely subsist by spinning and cardinge of . . . woolles, are like to be brought to suddaine want, for want of worke '. The clothiers therefore besought the King to take steps to restore freedom and security to the merchants, such as would allow them ' to goe on comfortably in their vocations '. Charles replied by protesting that the political troubles were not of his seeking, and promised to bestow upon the clothiers any favours which they could ' in Reason or Justice ask, or Hee graunt '.[2]

Such promises were as vague as they were plentiful, and the lot of the clothiers went from bad to worse. July came round,

[1] Ransome and Acland, *Handbook of English Political History*, p. 95.
[2] Brit. Mus., E. 144 (6). Printed copy of petition.

and with it the time for the midsummer shipment of cloth from Hull to the Continent. But Hull was in the hands of Sir John Hotham, who had defied Charles in April, and who now refused to allow a ship, laden with cloth, to sail, declaring that he could not spare any men from the town.[1] This prevented the Yorkshire pieces from reaching the market at Hamburg, and reacted disastrously upon merchants and makers alike.

At the outbreak of the war, Yorkshire was divided in its allegiance. The King's party predominated in the agricultural districts and amongst the gentry. York was a royalist stronghold, and the King's supporters also held the castles of Scarborough, Pontefract, Knaresborough, Tickhill, &c.[2] Only in Hull and the manufacturing areas of the West Riding was the Parliamentary cause in favour, and here, to quote Clarendon,[3] ' Leeds, Halifax and Bradford, three very populous and rich towns, depending wholly upon clothiers, naturally maligned the gentry,' ranging themselves under the command of Lord Fairfax and Sir Thomas, his son. When hostilities commenced, however, Leeds and Wakefield were actually in the hands of Royalist troops, whilst Bradford and Halifax were garrisoned in the Parliamentary interest. Such an arrangement was fatal to any continuance of trade, for these four towns were most intimately connected. Wakefield was a large market for kerseys and wool, Leeds was a finishing centre and the home of many merchants. Further, Wakefield blocked the road to the London markets, and could prevent cloth from going south and wool from coming north. . Leeds was on the highway between the cloth area and York, and controlled the road along which food supplies came into the West Riding. Some rearrangement of forces was very necessary before any trade could be revived, especially after the Royalist attempt to capture Bradford on December 18, 1642. The clothiers of Bradford and Halifax began to urge their leader, Sir Thomas Fairfax, to some decisive action, and on January 9, 1643, Fairfax wrote to his father, ' These parts grow very impatient of our delay in beating [the Royalists] out of Leeds and Bradford, for by them all trade

---

[1] *Hist. MSS. Comm., House of Lords Cal.*, v. 38. Petition of West Riding clothiers.   [2] See general histories of Yorkshire.

[3] Clarendon's *History of the Great Rebellion*, Clarendon Press edition, vol. ii, p. 464.

and provisions are stopped, so that the people in these clothing towns are not able to subsist, and indeed so pressing are these wants [that] some have told me if I would not stir with them, they must rise of necessity of themselves '.[1] A fortnight later, January 23, Fairfax took the offensive, and seized Leeds, an event which ' did strike such terror into the Earl of Newcastle's army that the severall garrisons of Wakefield, Sherburn, and Pontefract fled all the way presently, before any assaulted them '.[2] The clothing district was thus entirely in the hands of the Parliamentary forces ; but the victory was short-lived, for Fairfax had only a small army, and after the victory of Newcastle at Atherton Moor (June 30) Royalist troops captured the clothing towns, and held them until larger Parliamentary forces entered Yorkshire, smashed up the King's supporters at Marston Moor (July 1644), and drove the Royalists out of the county.

After Marston Moor the Civil War was practically at an end so far as Yorkshire was concerned, but those twenty months of hard fighting (December 1642 to July 1644) had brought the most terrible sufferings upon the clothing population. Leeds and Bradford, bombarded and captured time after time, were damaged the most severely. At Bradford the tower of the church was used as a centre of defence, and was fortified by being covered with sheets and packs of wool, the property of the clothiers. Joseph Lister describes it, in his account of the Royalist attack after Adwalton Moor, as follows : ' We took every precaution and again hung sheets of wool on that side [of the tower] facing the [Royalist] battery. They presently began to play their cannon upon us with the greatest fury and indignation possible, so that their shot cut the cords whereon the sheets of wool were hung, and down they fell, which the enemy, immediately perceiving, loudly huzzaed at their fall.'[3] When the Royalist troops entered the place they ransacked it, took everything of value which they could lay hands upon, burnt down houses, ruthlessly destroyed property, confiscated cattle and live stock, and generally wreaked their vengeance on

[1] Bell's *Memorials of Civil War*, i. 33, quoted in *Yorks. Arch. and Topogr. Journal*, i. 91.
[2] Extract from Fairfax's letter, quoted by Miss Law, *The Story of Bradford*, p. 104. [3] Ibid., p. 107.

the little town which had made such a sturdy resistance.[1] Bradford paid heavily for those years of strife, not only in property and industry, but also in lives. The entries in the parish register [2] indicate the extent of that misfortune :

Year.	Baptisms.	Marriages.	Deaths.
1639	209	61	183
1659	113	38	117
1739	182	94	134

The town had never been so important as Leeds, Halifax, or Wakefield in the output of cloth, and petitions from the West Riding cloth-makers of the early seventeenth century always mention these three towns, but never speak of Bradford. Now, after the sufferings of the Civil War, its trade in woollen cloths declined and became practically negligible. Later it arose from its ashes in the eighteenth century, not as a woollen, but as a worsted centre. Even in 1739 the above figures seem to indicate that the population of the town was smaller than that of a century before.

The plight of Leeds was scarcely less pitiable. Held by the

---

[1] When some semblance of peace had been restored, Bradford clothiers began to petition the Commons for relief from the burdens which they had borne for the Parliamentary cause. They speak of houses burnt down, of woolsacks employed as defences against the enemy's cannon, of goods plundered and spoilt, of wives and children starving, and of themselves bankrupt and in despair. If not actually engaged in fighting, the town was being called upon periodically to raise money for the maintenance of troops, and to supply men. Witness the following documents coming from the pens of Bradford men after the war : (1) To Fairfax : ' The humble petition of the Inhabitantes of the Towne of Bradford. Whereas there is charged and ymposed vpon our Towne, by one warrant lately from your hono[rs] for a daily Assesse to the value of 25s. and 000d. per diem, And wee have bene putt to 200 and 50 lbs. charges in Billitting of Souldiers man and horse for these 16 dayes last past. Wee humbly beseech yo[r] hono[rs] That you would bee pleased to take it into Consideracion, and to consider of our former Annoyance, and what wee have suffered. And that yo[r] Hono[rs] would be pleased to release us of this daily Assesse (for God knowes) wee cannot gather itt of our poore neighbors in regarde of their poore and weake estate (*in regarde Tradeing failes*) ' (Add. MSS. 36996, f. 58. See also *Hist. MSS. Comm., House of Lords*, Report vi. 193). (2) The Petition of Isaac Elleston of Bradford, clothier, states that he was a supporter of the Parliamentary cause, for which he lost the whole of his goods, value £130, when Bradford was captured by Newcastle. His only son was slain at Bristol, ' and yo[r] petitioner being an aged man of 75 yeares and in great debt and past his labour, having nothing left to preserve his life . . . Humbly beseeches your Highnes to take his sadd and distressed condicion into your pious and serious consideracion ' (*D. S. P., Interr.*, lxxiii. 57 (1654).

[2] James, *History and Topography of Bradford*, p. 144.

Royalists, captured by Fairfax, recaptured by Newcastle, and
again taken by the Roundhead army, its loss of life and property
was very great. At the orders of Fairfax and ' for the greater
safety of the town ' many clothiers burnt their houses to the
ground and destroyed at the same time most of the implements
of their trade ; and in 1647 these men had still received no
compensation which would enable them to return to their
calling or provide new stock-in-trade.[1] The mortality in the
parish rose from 523 in 1642 to 1,104 in 1643,[2] though whether
this increase was due solely to deaths by fighting or to an outbreak of pestilence one cannot say. In the Riding generally,
the poor were in dire straits, for ' all trade and business was
interrupted and laid aside '.[3] The supplies of foodstuffs from
the Vale of York were never sure of reaching their destination,
and the heavy assessments and billetings drained the last few
pence out of the pockets of many. Then when the Royalists
were victorious for a short space of time, they ransacked towns
and villages, confiscating all they could lay hands upon. Large
numbers of the poor inhabitants fled to the solitudes of the
Pennines or across into Lancashire, where they succeeded in
getting some slight relief so long as their homes were in the hands
of the enemy.[4]

As for trade, it was either impossible or was carried on under
the greatest difficulties. When Marston Moor destroyed the
Royalist power in Yorkshire the county subsided into a state
of comparative peace, and trade via York and Hull could be
carried on, though there were still the difficulties and dangers
of the high seas to be encountered. But internal commerce
between the north and the capital was fraught with much
greater insecurity, for here one had to carry goods through two
hundred miles of a country divided against itself. In a few
instances this traffic was actually continued with success, as
in the case of Thomas Priestley, a member of the famous family
which had its home at Soyland near Halifax. This family

[1] *Hist. MSS. Comm.*, vi. 188 (b), July 19, 1647.
[2] Thoresby's figures, in MSS. in Thoresby Soc. Library, Leeds.
[3] *Priestley Memoirs*, Surtees Soc., vol. lxxvii, p. 26.
[4] *Stewart MSS., Hist. MSS. Comm.*, vol. x, pt. iv, p. 67, October 12, 1643.
Deputy-Lieut. of Lancashire ordered that ' Yorkshire poor exiled from the
West Riding and now residing in this county shall have relief out of the
sequestrations of Royalist property'.

ranged itself on the Parliamentary side, and paid heavily for its devotion to that cause. Its house was plundered, and members of the family were forced to seek refuge in Lancashire ; the father died a prisoner in the hands of the enemy, and one son died of fever whilst serving in the ranks. Thomas, however, cared for none of these things. He escaped the war fever, and continued his business as a chapman throughout the whole period of the war. He bought cloths in the West Riding, and journeyed to London with eight or nine pack-horses, travelling in company with one or two other venturesome spirits. Sometimes the party hired a convoy of armed men to protect them on the journey ; at other times they travelled without any protection. And yet Priestley ' was never taken, he or his horses or goods, all that dangerous time '. He made regular journeys up to London, and realized about £20 clear profit on each trip.[1] Such a man was exceptionally fortunate, and many others who ventured to continue their commercial dealings during the period of the war met with a very different fate.

Scarcely was the sphere of military activity removed from the West Riding when the coping stone was added to the arch-way of misfortune which had been built over the lives of the cloth-making population. This took the form of a further outbreak of pestilence, which on this occasion eclipsed by its severity the memories of all previous visitations.[2] The cause of the plague of 1645 is doubtful. It may have been due to the usual lack of sanitary provisions, augmented by the after-effects of the war. Whatever the cause, the pestilence swept down upon the district with unparalleled severity. The outbreak began in 1644 and lasted until the last months of 1645. It was especially severe in Leeds, where from March 1645 to the follow-ing December 1,325 persons died. During the hottest parts of the summer as many as 130 persons a week succumbed to the disease, and in all it is calculated that about one-fifth of the

---

[1] *Priestley Memoirs*, Surtees Soc., vol. lxxvii, pp. 18, 23, and 27.
[2] The plague attacked most of the northern counties. *D. S. P., Chas. I*, vol. 506, p. 59 (1644–5), says : ' The sickness is much dispersed of late into severall parts of the country, as Auckland, Darlington, and Wakefield. . . . May God in his mercy turn away his judgement of the sword and pestilence and keep us from the other great judgement of famine.'

population of Leeds was destroyed by the pestilence. According
to one chronicler, ' the air was so thick and warm and so in-
fectious that dogs and cats, mice and rats died ; also several
birds in their flight over the town dropped dead '.[1] Life in the
town became unbearable, and there was a general exodus.
' There is scarce a man to be seen in the streets ', reported one
writer,[2] and all who could possibly get away from the town did
so, living in rough-and-ready cabins built on Woodhouse Moor,
or other open spaces around Leeds. The markets were transferred to Hunslet Moor and Chapeltown Green, where corn, wool,
cloth, &c., were to be brought, but only those who held certificates
of freedom from infection might use these markets. The justices
of the peace made stringent orders for preventing the spread
of the disease. All woollen cloths and wool-packs were to be
scalded in hot water, or put in a running stream for two
days and then dried in the open air. Appeals for relief and
financial assistance were made to other parts of the county, and
the Corporation of York appointed several persons to ' make
a colleccion through the cittie for everie one to give towards
their releife what they shall thinke fitt, and the ministers to be
moved to invite them theirunto '.[3] In similar vein, the justices
of the West Riding commanded the towns and villages around
Leeds to contribute to the relief of the sufferers in the borough,[4]
but these parts needed the money for their own sick, since the
plague was scattered throughout the whole clothing area, and
not merely confined to its chief market centre. Wakefield lost
245 inhabitants in one year, victims of the pestilence, and
Pontefract, Aberford, and other places were stricken with ' the
sickness '.[5] Only when the ·heat of summer gave place to
November's cold and fog was there any great decrease ' of ye
sicknesse which has . . . of late overspreade the whole West-
ridinge ',[6] and by that time the population of many a clothing

---

[1] See Whitaker, *Loidis and Elmete* (1816), i. 76. The task of recording
deaths was so heavy that it was eventually abandoned, and the figure 1,325
was the number of deaths reported to the Governor-General of the town.

[2] ' As for Leeds it is utterly spoilt ; there is scarce a man, &c.' (*Graham
MSS., Hist. MSS. Comm.*, vi. 329, July 16, 1645).

[3] York House Books, xxxvi, f. 138 a, July 1645. A similar step was taken
at the request of the inhabitants of Bradford (House Books, xxxvi. 154 a).

[4] *Yorks. Arch. and Topogr. Journal*, xv. 437 et seq.

[5] *Graham MSS., Hist. MSS. Comm.*, vi. 329.

[6] *Yorks. Arch. and Topogr. Journal*, xv. 454.

community had been terribly thinned. The years from 1640 to
1650 were a dark decade in the annals of Leeds, Bradford, and
Halifax, and the effect is briefly summarized in the following
vital statistics for the parish of Leeds :

Year.	Births.	Marriages.	Deaths.
1640	557	157	561
1650	345	69	345
Decrease	38 %	55·5 %	38·5 %

Or, if we take triennial averages, the fall between 1639–41 and
1649–51 amounted to

Births, 37 % ; Marriages, 62 % ; Deaths, 33 %.

Thus, taking the figures of births and deaths, we are justified
in supposing that quite *one-third* of the population of Leeds
had been swept away in those ten years of sword and pestilence.

During the years of the Commonwealth Yorkshire was busy
attempting to recover from the exhaustion of the previous
decade, but there was little if any progress. In 1654 the Corporation of Leeds declared that ' tradeinge at present is beginninge
a little to revive ',[1] but there were many obstacles to be overcome. The war with Holland and the prevalence of piracy
rendered the North Sea very dangerous to cloth ships, unless
well convoyed. But the Government was quite unable to
provide adequate, or even inadequate, protection, so that the
export trade suffered heavily, and, as the Leeds merchants
wrote to Adam Baynes, ' the countrie in generall did smart by
it, and eccho'd forth dolefull complaints '. Thus, at the end of
a period of constitutional chaos and economic blight, the
country poured out its complaint to Monk in 1659, when asking
for the restoration of a free Parliament in place of the parodies
of the Interregnum. Fairfax, the staunchest of Parliamentarians,
joined with ' the rest of the Lords, Knights, Esquires, Citizens,
Ministers and Freeholders of the County and City of York '
when they declared themselves to be ' deeply sensible of the
Confusions and Distractions of the Nation, the particular Decay
and Ruine of the Clothing Trade of this County, which necessarily bears an influence upon the Publick '.[2] Another letter

[1] *Baynes Correspondence*, xi. 224.
[2] See Cunningham, *Growth*, app. E, vol. ii, pp. 921–7.

from York about the same time stated that the 'Trade of
Cloathing being dead . . . makes those Parts rise in abundance
to do anything for the having of a Free Parliament, which (they
think) will procure the opening of Trade again '.[1]   There were
many who for political and religious reasons were bitterly
opposed to the Restoration, but the great majority of the
people were willing to submit to any change which might dispel
the clouds of depression in which industry and commerce had
been enveloped.   The Commonwealth had been only common
woe for many, and the nation welcomed the return of Charles II
in the hope of a better time coming.   Whether or not these hopes
were realized we shall see in a later chapter.

It has seemed desirable to dwell at some length upon these
more gloomy aspects of the industry's development.   Our conception of progress often needs to be modified.   We look at the
position of the woollen industry in the sixteenth century, and
then turn to the state of affairs of our own times.   The difference is very marked, and we are apt to explain it as being the
result of constant and steady development, such as might be
expressed in a curve that mounts higher and higher as the years
go by, without any break in the continuity of its ascent.   The
events narrated in this chapter will have proved the error of
such an idea, for they will have shown that industry fluctuated
as much and as frequently in the seventeenth century as in the
nineteenth.   The woollen industry in 1660 was probably some
distance ahead of its position at the accession of James I, and
progress had actually been made.   But that progress had been
checked and at times more than cancelled for a time.   War,
pestilence, famine, and international politics had played their
part, and if the clothier or merchant now looked forward to
a period of peace and progress, he was quite warranted in hoping
for such recompense after the years of stress and strain through
which he had just passed.

[1] Leeds, February 13, 1659.   Brit. Mus. 190. g. 13. (317), quoted by Cunningham, *op. cit.*, ii. 926.

CHAPTER VII

STUART EXPERIMENTS IN INDUSTRIAL REGULA-
TION—GILDS AND COMPANIES

In an earlier chapter we have considered the various attempts which were made to regulate the cloth industry with a view to maintaining a high standard of commodity. The gilds had their ordinances and searchers, and when the industry spread over the extra-urban areas the State drew up appropriate legislation, and ordered the appointment of searchers, whose duty it should be to detect fraudulent work and bring offenders to justice. The last of a long series of acts was passed in 1623,[1] and fixed the lengths, breadths, and weights of the chief kinds of cloth which were then made in England. The statute laid down rules concerning the extent to which cloth could be stretched in tentering, and gave detailed instructions as to the duties of the searchers, the amount of the fines, and the objects to which the fines were to be devoted. But in spite of laws and searchers the evil still remained, and complaints about faulty cloth are to be found throughout the early seventeenth century. The searcher was often a clothier, or the friend of clothiers, and we have at least one instance of a searcher who was also a clothier taking advantage of his official position to have a tenter frame of dimensions which were illegal according to the very laws he was employed to enforce.[2] Sometimes the searcher was an ale-house-keeper, who would naturally do nothing to offend his customers, and so, notwithstanding the presence of the searcher, there were still ' many false clothyers who make bad and slight cloth '.[3]

The difficulties of the searchers were enhanced by the flood of ' new draperies ' which had sprung up during the latter half of the sixteenth century. These cloths were new varieties intro-

---

[1] 21 Jas. I, c. 18.

[2] John Tottie of Wakefield, Clothier : ' being appoynted one of the searchers of Wakefield did alter the size of his Tenter and made the chase thereof bigger than was agreed and sett downe by hym and the residew of the Searchers of Wakefield aforesaid ' (*West Riding Sessions Rolls, Wakefield, 1598*, ed. by Lister, p. 133. See also Quarter Sessions Order Book, A, p. 132 (1640)).

[3] *D. S. P., Chas. I*, ccccviii. 15.

duced partly by the refugees who came to England during the period of religious upheaval on the Continent; they were also the result of English attempts to imitate foreign wares. There were Bays, ' Stamells of fflorence sorte, Searge of ffrench sorte, Sayes of the fflaunders sorte, Mockadowes of everie sorte, Carrell ffustayn of Naples, Blanketts called Spanysh ruggs, etc.' [1] Thus, as May declared in 1613, ' there are many sorts of cloths or stuffes lately invented, which have got newe godfathers to name them in ffantasticall fashion that they which weare them knowe not howe to name them '.[2] These cloths could evade the legal stipulations by passing under some name for which there was no provision in the current statute. True, they had been brought under the scope of the ulnager's impositions in 1594, and James I had given the ulnage of both new and old draperies into the hands of the Duke of Lennox; but the aim of the ulnager was the collection of revenue rather than the propagation of industrial ethics, and hence the searcher, unaided by the ulnager, found himself baffled by the bewildering complexity of the cloths to which he had to attend.

The failure of the searcher to meet the needs of the situation, and the interested vigilance of certain classes of men, brought about the demand for some better mode of regulating industrial life. From many sides men preached that the immorality in industry was due to the absence of organization, and to the individual freedom which was allowed by the State. Representatives of existing companies and corporations were always ready to declare that the decay in trade was due to the existence of interlopers and others outside their particular association. The drapers of London explained the depression of 1622 as being largely caused by the operations of inexperienced cloth-makers, who sold the cloth either directly to the consumer or to hawkers who carried it to the villages and towns throughout the country.[3] Therefore, to remedy such evil, let the cloth be sold by drapers alone, and let the arm of the Drapers' Company be strengthened accordingly. In a similar vein, May [4] declared that ' the dispersing of clothiers and makers is a principall cause to breede ... defects ' in cloth, and urged that industry should be carried

---

[1] Originalia Rolls, 36 Eliz., July 13, pt. iii.   [2] May, *op. cit.*, p. 21.
[3] *D. S. P., Jas. I*, cxxx. 140.   [4] May, *op. cit.*, p. 26.

on only in towns. This idea of the necessity for bringing industry more under the control of economic organizations became very popular during the reign of James I and Charles I, and suggestions for the institution of a number of corporations were frequent. Since the local government official had proved a failure, let a local trade association be formed to regulate and maintain the standard of craftsmanship in that particular trade. Such an association would represent the best industrial interests of the district, and so, backed by local opinion, its officials would be able to carry out their police work with greater hope of success. The idea found favour with the Commission which was chosen to report on the causes of the depression in 1622. This Commission, it will be remembered, condemned the false making of cloth as being one of the causes of that 'stand of trade'. In its recommendations it suggested

(1) The simplification of the laws concerning cloth, for ' the lawes now in force concerning the makinge and dressinge of cloth are so many and by the multitude of them are so intricate that it is very hard to resolve what the law is '. Also the issue of ' playne rules and easy to be observed . . . for new draperies '.

(2) 'That a Corporation in every Countie be made of the most able and sufficient men . . . to look fullie to the trewe makeing, dyeing, and dressing of cloth and stuffs . . . and not truste to meane men '. These corporations were to have their searchers, and the ulnager was not to place his seal on any cloth until it had been ' searched, tryed, and proved by such as shalbe appoynted '.[1]

Some writers were in favour of a corporation in which the clothiers and merchants should be entirely self-governing; but in most of the schemes the suggestion was that the organization should be dual, containing representatives of the industrial and commercial interests on the one hand, and representatives of the Crown, such as justices of the peace or the Lord Lieutenant of the county, on the other. Some urged that such societies should be established in each of the clothing counties ; others suggested the incorporation of the chief clothing towns, and the granting of charters which would create municipal authorities with considerable powers of control over the industry of the

[1] Stowe MSS. 554, f. 45.

community. But though varied in detail, all these numerous suggestions agreed upon one essential point, namely that the regulation of industry must now be placed in the hands of local organizations, in which the leaders of local economic life were to find a place.[1]

Such recommendations, which had been in the air prior to 1622 and now became insistent, were partly responsible for the marked revival of industrial association which took place about this time. Old companies took on larger powers,[2] and new associations were established in various parts of the country. In the cloth trade we have already seen some of the York companies striving to regain control over their particular branches of industry. The suggestions outlined above were receiving attention, and a scheme was drawn up for the establishment of corporations in thirty-two counties, for the regulation of the manufacture of the new draperies which were becoming important during the seventeenth century. Only one county (Hertfordshire) actually set up such a corporation, and the life of the institution was short.[3] The Government of Charles I was too busily engaged in foreign affairs during the early years of the reign, and hence the scheme for the erection of these county associations remained a scheme. We shall see, however, that the idea was not abandoned, but that an organization of this character was instituted at a later date to supervise the broad-cloth industry of the West Riding.

Though the proposal was put aside for the time being so far as the counties were concerned, less ambitious suggestions were acted upon. The establishment of corporations had been urged for cities and towns as well as for counties, and it is in this

[1] See, e. g. 'A redy course propounded for thestablishment and certaine Settlinge of the Manufacture of all maner of draperies, &c.' (Add. MSS. 34324, f. 201 (1622). Also Report of Commissioners of Trade (1640), in *Portland MSS., Hist. MSS. Comm.*, vol. viii, pp. 2–3.

[2] See Unwin, *Industrial Organization during the Sixteenth and Seventeenth Centuries*. Also Cunningham, *op. cit.*, ii. 303–6.

[3] Add. MSS. 34324, f. 201. See also *D. S. P., Chas. I*, i. 24 and 62. The whole topic of these provincial corporations still remains to be worked at in greater detail. The idea of an association controlling the industry of a wide rural area was very strong during the seventeenth century, and many attempts were made to put such an idea into practice. Mr. Unwin's work is largely confined to London. But much light still remains to be thrown upon the nature of these county organizations, as well as upon the actual work and nature of the companies which were still to be found in the provincial towns.

connexion that we turn to the story of the incorporation of Leeds. Leeds was one of a number of towns in which clothing corporations were set up, Bury St. Edmunds, Ipswich, and Colchester being other centres to which similar attention was given ; and it was out of this need for industrial regulation that the Corporation of Leeds came into being. The preamble to the first Leeds charter emphasizes the economic aspects of the town's life, and declares that the charter was granted for the improvement of the industrial ' tone ' and for the fostering of industrial honesty. Leeds historians have regarded this as a picturesque but irrelevant preamble, bearing no actual connexion with the real motives which prompted the incorporation of the town. When, however, we regard the charter of 1626 and its successors in the light of the Stuart policy of regulating industry by corporations, we see at once that the economic factor was probably the predominating influence in the granting of civic powers.

During the half century preceding its incorporation Leeds had grown in size and industrial importance. Its population had more than doubled between 1576 and 1626,[1] and it was now established as the centre of a district occupied in making broad cloths, superior in size and quality to the kerseys which were made in the Halifax area. The Leeds market was already famous, and here the merchants of Leeds, along with traders from York and London, purchased the pieces from the clothiers. When, in 1616, James I established staple towns for wool in England, Leeds immediately petitioned the Privy Council, asking to be placed on the list of staple towns in order that the sale of wool in the West Riding might be carried on with ease and official sanction.[2] The request was granted, and Leeds remained a staple so long as the new arrangements were adhered to.[3]

During the years of depression in the early 'twenties complaints came from Leeds concerning the deceitful practices of clothiers and dyers, especially in the use of logwood for dyeing.

---

[1] Annual average (for parish of Leeds) :

	Births.	Marriages.	Deaths.
1576–80 .	150	37	142
1621–5 .	349	79	352

[2] Cunningham, *op. cit.*, ii. 298–9 n. Also *D. S. P., Jas. I*, cv. 147.

[3] *D. S. P., Jas. I*, xcii. 28. Also Jackson's *Guide to Leeds* (1889), pp. 36–7.

Logwood had been the subject of legislation in the time of Elizabeth, and an Act of 1580 had declared that 'forasmuch as the colour made with the said stuff [was] false and deceitful ', therefore, all existing stocks of logwood were to be seized and openly burned by the authority of the justices of the peace, and henceforth no logwood was to be used under pain of forfeiture of the cloth, and imprisonment of the offender.   This Act was reinforced in 1596 by a statute which ordered that fines and the pillory should be additional punishments.   Such legislation was enforced occasionally, as for instance in 1598, when Thomas Cummy of Holbeck, clothier, was indicted for ' dying wooll and Wollen cloth ' with logwood or blockwood.[1] But in spite of prosecutions the practice continued.   The clothier who dyed his own wool or cloth in his own dye-vat required some inexpensive colouring material for his cheap cloths, and logwood met his needs in that respect.   Hence the grievance of those who sought the incorporation of the town was expressed in the charter,[2] namely, that the 'fame and estimation ' of Leeds was being ruined by ' divers clothiers [who] have begun to make deceptive cloths and to dye the same with wood called logwood, to the damage and prejudice of [the Crown], subversion of the clothiers of the town and the discredit of the inhabitants there if immediate remedy for that purpose be not applied '.

The petition asking for a charter was said to be presented by ' clothiers and inhabitants ' of Leeds, but really it was the work of the wealthier clothiers and merchants of the parish, and not the demand of the whole community.   Documents are very scarce concerning this first charter, but the few manuscripts which are extant seem to point to the fact that those who sought to obtain the charter did so with a view to gaining control over the industrial and political affairs of the community, and that in this effort they were opposed by a considerable body of the population of Leeds.   The opposition probably came from the smaller clothiers, who were scattered over the thirty-two square miles which comprised the ancient parish of Leeds.   The charter was partisan, and those who worked to obtain it did so

---

[1] *West Riding Sessions Records*, ed. by Lister, p. 174 : ' Logwood alias Blockwood callide ac deceptive usitavit '.

[2] 1626 Charter ; see Wardell, *Municipal History of Leeds* (1848), appendix.

with the intention of establishing an oligarchical control over the town and its multitude of small cloth-makers. This clash of rival parties is seen in the first document which exists relating to the incorporation of the borough. The request for a charter had been made in 1622 or 1623, and the charter was drawn up in accordance with the wishes of the petitioners. On December 21, 1624, came a protest from the opposing party :

'The inhabitants, being many hundreds of people, desier a stay of the Corporacion latly procured by some of the ablest men of Leedes for their owne ends, in the name of the whole Towne, without the Consent of the greater number, and to their prejudice, desiers a referrence to Sir Thomas Wentworth, Sir Henry Savill, Kts. and Barotts. . . . and to examine the conveniency or inconveniency of the said graunt, and to certefy his Majesty thereof.' [1]

Note the phrase 'the ablest men of Leedes for their owne ends'. It evidently refers to the industrial and commercial magnates who were seeking to obtain the charter, and expresses the hostility of the poorer inhabitants. This opposition succeeded in delaying the incorporation for a while, and the death of James I caused still further delay. Eventually, however, opposition was swept aside, and on July 18, 1626, Charles signed the charter which incorporated 'the Borough of Leedes in the County of York'.

The economic significance of the charter is seen throughout, from the preamble onwards. 'Whereas our town of Leedes . . . is an ancient and popular town, and the inhabitants . . . for many years past have had and skilfully exercised . . . the art or mystery of making and working woollen cloths, commonly called in English 'Northern Dozens', to their perpetual praise and great increase of the Revenue of the Crown of England for the custom of the said cloths ' ; and whereas complaints have been made of deceptive manufacture and dyeing of cloths, ' and divers other enormities and inconveniences for some time have sprung up and do still increase as well concerning the cloths aforesaid as the town and parish aforesaid, which in no way can be reformed without good rule by our royal authority and power established, and whereas the former methods of government have failed to

[1] Harleian MSS. 1327, p. 9 b, December 21, 1624. See also Atkinson, *Ralph Thoresby, his Town and Times*, vol. i, p. 20.

check these abuses' ; therefore Charles made the town and
parish into a borough with a proper corporation, consisting of
an alderman, nine principal burgesses, and twenty assistants,
all of whom were nominated in the charter. The powers of this
corporation were fully defined, and two paragraphs indicate the
manner in which the newly created body was to regulate industrial affairs.

' We will and do grant that the Council shall and may have
full power and authority to enact, constitute, make, and establish
. . . such reasonable laws, statutes, and ordinances which to
them shall seem wholesome, useful, honest, and necessary, . . .
as well for the fit, good, true, and perfect working, making, and
dyeing of cloths from time to time, . . . as for the good rule and
government ' of the whole body of citizens.

Secondly, and more important, ' we do grant to the aforesaid
Alderman and burgesses . . . that for the better government of
the inhabitants, . . . especially the workers and labourers for
making woollen cloths, . . . they shall have all reasonable gilds,
and that they shall and may be able to divide themselves into
separate fraternities, Societies, and mysteries, . . . and that no
fraternity or gild . . . shall have power, authority, or jurisdiction,
of constituting, ordaining, or making of any statutes, laws etc.,
. . . to bind any burgess or inhabitant, . . . unless they shall
have authority, power, and licence to make such laws . . . from
the Alderman, and Common Council . . . under their common
seal first had and obtained.' [1]

Such was the corporation of 1626, a body of men chosen to
enforce legislation, to issue by-laws for the regulation of industry,
and to grant permission for the formation of sectional economic
associations or gilds under the general supervision of the council.
The personnel of the corporation was drawn from the men who
had secured the charter. Sir John Savill, who had conducted
the campaign in London, was nominated first alderman, and the
chief burgesses and assistants were nearly all prominent clothiers
or merchants. John Harrison, the famous clothier and philanthropist, was chosen as deputy-alderman, and Richard Sykes,
Thomas Metcalfe, Benjamin Wade, William Busfield, Ralph
Hopton, and others, men in the front rank of local industry and
commerce, found places on the council. The corporation was
a close oligarchy. Its charter had been ' procured without

---

[1] See Wardell, *op. cit.*, appendices, for translations of charters.

a generall consent of ye Clothiers and inhabitants ',[1] and the first members were nominated by the King. When vacancies occurred, new members were elected by the council itself, without any appeal to the wishes of the great mass of clothiers outside. With such a divorce between the corporation and the industry which it was set to govern, friction was inevitable, and an important dispute soon arose.

This conflict between the town and its rulers centred round the provisions made in the charter for the establishment of gilds. The clause concerning gilds was vague in one respect. Did it mean that the formation of gilds and companies was optional, and that the various industries could organize themselves into associations only if they felt inclined to do so? Or did it give the corporation power to compel the clothiers and others to enrol in such trade societies? The point was disputable, and furnished the basis for what must have been a keen conflict. Many members of the council adopted the compulsory attitude, and did their utmost to secure the institution of gilds, so as to increase the power which the corporation possessed over the various industries. On the other hand, a majority of the clothiers was averse to such organization. The clothier enjoyed a certain measure of individual freedom and was at liberty to develop his industry along the lines which seemed most suitable to his needs and circumstances. True, there was legislation touching apprenticeship, dimensions and quality of cloth, &c., legislation administered by the local justices. But these enactments weighed lightly upon the clothier, and he did not conform to the strict letter of the law except when it pleased him to do so. Hence he was antagonistic in the first place to a corporation which might curb his freedom by a strict enforcement of rules which he had held in light esteem in the past. If the erection of a corporation signified the substitution of a keen and active urban administration for the easy-going methods of the justices of the peace, then his sympathies were decidedly against the innovation. Further, he was opposed to the institution of additional restraints in the form of gild regulations. As a clothier, he was a man of many parts, especially if his establishment was of any size. He went to buy his own wool, he employed people

---

[1] *D. S. P., Interr.,* cxxxi. 7.

to spin that wool, he dyed and wove it himself; probably he did part of the finishing himself, and then marketed the fabric. Thus his activities were varied, and were marked by a large measure of elasticity and freedom. Now, if the gilds were to be set up, he would be subjected to a host of regulations and ordinances such as would destroy that sense of freedom. There would be fines and fees to pay, and if the gild system became at all minutely sectionalized he would be compelled to enrol himself as a member of several gilds, or might have the variety of his occupation curtailed. These were the doubts which would arise in the mind of the Leeds clothier, objections based on the dislike of further and more thorough supervision of his work, and fears as to the restriction of his economic liberty. Hence, many clothiers had been opposed to the incorporation of the borough, and were now inimical to the formation of gilds and companies.

Soon after its institution, the municipal council began to insist on the establishment of fraternities, and at once there was opposition from the clothiers of the town. The details of this struggle are scanty, and are best narrated in the following petition, dispatched from Leeds in March 1629 : [1]

'The humble peticion of Robert Sympson, and Christopher Jackson, and many thousands of poore Clothiers of the parish of Leeds in the County of York,

'Showeth That whereas it pleased your most excellent Ma^{ty} by your l^{res} patents dated the 12 day of July in the 2nd yeare of your Ma$^{ty's}$ most happy Raigne to incorporate the said towne and parrish for the better increase of the Trade of Cloathing, And your highnes said l^{res} patents did give Liberty and power to all the said parrishioners and inhabitants to distinguish and devide themselves into guilds and fraternityes, not giving authority to the Aldermen and assistants there to inforce or compell any to bee Companyes unlesse they willingly submitted thereunto.

'Soe it is . . . that the present Alderman, (beeing an Attorney at the Comon Lawe) and a few of the Cheife Burgesses, for the increase of theire owne authority and for their owne gaine (as the peticioners conceave) and not for the good of Cloathing, contrary to the goodwill and liking of most and of the best of the parrish (there beeing not the fortieth part of the Clothiers that doe consent thereunto, as the peticioners hope to make it appeare)

---

[1] *D. S. P., Chas. I*, cxxxix. 24, March 21, 1629.

endeavour to inforce the peticioners to bee a Company and to submitt themselves to such Rules and constitutions as they shall please to make, to bee fined, imprisoned, and called from theire Labour at their wills.

' Your peticioners show that many of them dayly setting on worke about 40 poore people in theire Trade, and that compelling them to come hither [i. e. London] (dwelling 150 Miles hence) tendeth much to theire impouerishing and overthrowe of theire trade.'

Therefore the petitioners pray that the King will be pleased ' to referre the examinacion [of the matter] fully unto such Lords, Knights and Gentry of the County as shall seeme best to your Ma^{ty} and whoe best understand the nature of Cloathing.'

The King referred the whole matter to the Council of the North, along with Sir Henry Savill, Sir Richard Beaumont, Sir John Ramsden, and two other prominent Yorkshire personages. Of the result of the deliberations we know nothing, but evidently the companies continued, for the next document relevant to Leeds (1639) refers to the ' Companies that now are in that Borrough '.[1]

This document is a petition from the corporation itself, asking for parliamentary representation, and is of such interest from the economic point of view that I venture to quote it at some length. The petitioners strongly emphasize the industrial importance of the borough;

' w^{th}in ye . . . Corporacion and places adiacent, great Quantities of woollen clothes are yerelie made. . . . And in all theis Northe partes where clothe is now made, there is no place Incorporated but ye pet^{rs} wherby ye regulacion and true making of cloth might bee provided for. And that this corporacion of Ledes, nor any Clothing towne in this county, are not enabled to choose any burgesses in parliament to have voice upon any occasions arising touching abuses or other matters of Cloathing. Nor none can be soe apt or able to judge of as those who live amongst theis places of Cloathing, and have use and experience of their deceipts and of ye Conveniences and Inconveniences of ye lawes already made or wch may be propounded touching the same, and that ye most part of Cloathing townes in ye Kingdome have one or two Burgesses in parliament for the purposes aforesaid.'

The petitioners, therefore, asked for a number of important

[1] *D. S. P., Chas. I,* ccccxxxix. 5, 5i, and 6.

favours, the chief of which was that the town might have two members in parliament.

The corporation pleaded its case very powerfully, and appended to the petition a number of reasons why the town should be enfranchised. These statements are doubtless to some extent exaggerations, but they contain a great deal of truth. The chief assertions were :

' There is Cloth made in this Corporacion of the value of two hundred thowsand pounds, and most of it is yerelie sent beyond the seas. His Maties Customes for Cloth made in this parishe and exported amounteth to above 10,000^{ll}. per annum, besides the Customes of foreigne comodities for ye said Clothe into yor Maties kingdome imported. . . . Ye people that make this cloth are laborious and industrious, and this trade growne of late yeres and much increased since the towne was incorporated. Noe parte of the Kingdome can afford clothe soe reasonable, by reason of Cole, wood, Mills, and house rent as this part, And by well ordering and true making Noe doubt by God's blessing this trade will daylie encrease. . . . All places of the Kingdom where Clothe is made have Burgesses in parliament and by reason thereof in former tymes Sundry Lawes were made much to the prejudice of the clothing of theis parts, because they never had (till the late Lo: Savyle's time) any man in parliament experienced in the clothing of this Countrey. By this trade the Countrey subsists and many thousands of poore people, woomen and children set on work, and many able men maynteyned in labour fitt for yor Maties Service uppon any occasion. . . . The pet^{rs} upon all occasions of publique charges and taxes for his Maties service have beene willing and forward.'

In short, the men of Leeds declared their industrial greatness, their loyalty, and their sense of the injustice of being ruled without enjoying representation.

Leeds did not get its member of parliament, and the grant of a new charter with a mayor and aldermen was only made by Charles I at Nottingham on the eve of the Civil War,[1] when the outbreak of hostilities prevented this new constitution from materializing. At this time the town was divided in its allegiance. The wealthy merchants, who comprised the municipal government, were Royalists, but the great mass of the people were Parliamentarians. When the town was occupied by the Parliamentary forces the corporation fell into abeyance, and

[1] *D. S. P., Interr.*, cxxxi. 7, and *Chas. II*, xxviii. 71.

from 1643 to 1646 the government of the town was in the hands of Major-General Carter.[1]   In 1646 the corporation was restored on the lines of the charter granted twenty years before, but all Royalists were excluded, and their places taken by supporters of the Parliamentary cause.   The new-comers carried on the oligarchic tradition of their predecessors, and ruled the industrial population with a heavy hand.   Hence, in 1656, a monster petition signed by about 850 clothiers and inhabitants of the town and parish of Leeds expressed the grievances against the council :

'They doe rule and act illegally as may appeare by their unjust By-Lawes, and Ordinances (whereby they oppresse ye poore Clothiers and much preiudice that Trade), theire unlawfull Taxes put upon the people . . . theire imprisoning men's persons, etc., . . . to ye great damage and disquiet of ye Inhabitants and disturbance of ye publique Peace.'[2]

From this time onward the demand for a new charter grew in force, and with the accession of Charles II that document was obtained, placing the government once more in the hands of the ' wealthiest and best affected merchants and inhabitants of the Towne of Leedes '.[3]

The industrial activities of this new corporation can be studied in some detail, since the Minute Books of the council from 1662 onward are still available, and give a fair picture of the manner in which the city rulers attempted to supervise industry and commerce during the later seventeenth and early eighteenth centuries.   Before turning to the consideration of this work, it will be best to glance for a moment at an attempt which was made to establish an organization to regulate industry over the whole field of the West Riding.   This corporation had a short life, and we know practically nothing of its actual work ; but the project serves to illustrate the manner in which the idea of supervision by local organizations was put into practice in Yorkshire.

The powers of the Leeds corporation were circumscribed by the boundary of the borough.   Within that limit the municipal

---

[1] List of Aldermen (MSS. volume in Thoresby Soc. Library) : ' 1643–6 in ye Wars a Vacancy '.   [2] D. S. P., Interr., cxxxi. 7.
[3] For this, see proceedings of Council of State, Chas. II, i. 78, p. 63. Also D. S. P., Chas. II, xxviii. 71 ; xxx. 28 ; xl. 62.

authorities administered both the laws of the nation and their own by-laws touching the making and finishing of cloth. Outside the boundary such work was carried on by the justices of the peace, and the searchers whom they appointed. Thus it might happen that whilst the laws against excessive tentering and deceitful manufacture were administered with exemplary thoroughness within the borough, clothiers outside the pale were allowed a great amount of licence. This might be possible because of the leniency of the justices of the Riding, the slackness of the searchers, or by reason of the fact that the rural clothiers were scattered over a very wide area, stretching from Wharfedale to Derbyshire, and from Wakefield to the borders of Lancashire. The disparity actually did exist, and hence, whilst Leeds clothiers were subject to constant supervision in the manufacture of broad cloths, their fellows outside the boundary were producing similar fabrics, comparatively immune from police inspection. During the Civil War the system of search broke down for a while, but in 1647 the restored Corporation of Leeds determined to resume work. The alderman and burgesses therefore approached the justices of the Riding and complained ' of the great decay of the trade of Cloathing, and more especially of broad cloth, commonly called " Leedes Cloath ", occasioned by ye great deceipt therein used, in makeing Tenters of a farr greater chase [1] than by the statute is limitted, and other sleights and subtiltyes by diverse of ye clothyers practised, to the great deceipt of those countryes to wch ye same [is] transported, and to ye great shame and slaunder of all ye good clothyers in these Northerne parts '. In consequence of this complaint, the West Riding magistrates promised to co-operate with Leeds in a crusade against illegally constructed tenters ; they were to attack the offenders in the clothing areas of the Riding, whilst the Leeds Corporation set its own house in order. ' Whereupon ye said Alderman and Burgesses caused ye tenters within ye . . . Borrough to be reformed and proceeded in such other lawfull courses as to ye regulacion of ye said trade, expectyng ye like to be done in all parts of ye said Ryding.' The justices, however, failed to fulfil their promise, and took no steps to administer the

---

[1] Chase, the allowance made for the movement of the movable parts of the tenter frame, which did the actual stretching.

cloth laws. Thus the clothiers of Leeds were 'moche greived and molested, they beeing onely restreyned' whilst their rivals outside the borough were allowed to continue their malpractices free from interference. In January 1655 the corporation drew the attention of the magistrates of the Riding to the injustice under which the Leeds clothiers were labouring, and the bad workmanship which was being permitted to continue in the rural areas, which, 'if not reformed, when tradeinge at present is beginninge a little to revive, will inevytably tend to ye absolute disgrace, if not faile of trade in these parts, and soe consequently not onely impoverish ye clothyer, but many others thereupon depending.' Leeds asked that the statutes concerning tenters should be put into operation throughout the Riding, frames either reformed or defaced, and proper seals of lead placed upon cloths, stating their length and weight. Further, in order to ensure the equitable and effectual administration of these measures, the corporation suggested that 'some speciall persons may be joyntly commissionated to acte together, as well within as without the Borrough'.[1] The justices did not accept this last suggestion, but they ordered their searchers to be more careful and thorough in their duties, 'and to see that noe tenters for broad cloathes have chase or liberty for or to the under barr above halfe of a quarter of a yard, and for narrow cloathes above halfe of halfe of a quarter, but that they shall presently deface the same, according to the statute upon paynes and penaltyes mencioned.'[2]

The suggestion of the Leeds Corporation that joint officials should be appointed is a weak reflection of a strong policy which some of the broad clothiers were advocating about this time. Broad cloths were made in all the district round about Leeds, especially at Birstall and Wakefield, and the clothiers of Leeds were probably experiencing the keen competition of these outsiders. They therefore wished to bring the broad clothier who dwelt outside the city under the same control as themselves, either by having a broad clothiers' corporation for the whole Riding, or by extending the scope of the Leeds municipal regulations to all broad clothiers, whether within or without the borough. To bring about this result they enlisted the services

---

[1] *Baynes Correspondence*, xi. 224, January 1655.   [2] Ibid., xi. 148.

of Adam Baynes, the Leeds representative in the fitful parliaments of the Interregnum.[1] In August 1654 [2] a petition of the
more affluent broad clothiers of Leeds was dispatched to Baynes,
in which the cloth magnates declared that the best way to
foster the trade of Leeds would be to carry out the following
proposals :

    1. 'That the hole trade of brode cloth makinge . . . in the
Countie of Yorke maye be incorporated into one bodie politick.'
    2. 'That soe many officers maye be chosen by the holle
number of clothyers as may be thought requisit ffor the carry-
inge on the worke, with a certan number of asistants and a Comon
Councell.'
    3. 'That they [the executive] have power to chuse officers
and overseers to put the lawes in execucion provided ffor good
of trade, and to gain [extension] where they are short, if needs be.'

    Such an organization would almost inevitably place the control
of the industry throughout the whole Riding into the hands of
a few wealthy Leeds clothiers, and so establish the supremacy
of Leeds and of the more important and opulent men in that
borough. The proposal was, therefore, strongly opposed by
the ' adverse partie', which consisted of the clothiers living
outside Leeds, at Wakefield, Birstall, and in the open districts
generally.[3] These men made a hard fight against the Leeds
magnates. They attempted to get Baynes's election declared
null and void, and sent several deputations up to London to
state their case before Cromwell.[4] Baynes, however, pursued
his mission with eagerness, and succeeded in obtaining a commission of inquiry into the whole question. The purpose of this
inquiry was

    1. To study the existing statutes, see where they were defec-
tive, and suggest amendments if necessary.
    2. Granted that the laws were good, to consider how they
might be put into more effective operation.
    3. With regard to the second term of reference, to consider
if it would be more practicable that ' a select number of discreet
and able persons, consisting of Gentlemen, merchants, and

---

[1] Leeds, along with Manchester and Halifax, was granted parliamentary
representation in 1653, and Adam Baynes was elected to represent Leeds.
See Ingelwick, *The Interregnum*, p. 93.   Also Atkinson, *Ralph Thoresby, his
Town and Times*, vol. i.   [2] *Baynes Correspondence*, xi. 210.
    [3] Ibid., xi. 211.   [4] Ibid., xi. 213.

clothiers, be invested with all the power that the Justices of the Peace had by former statutes, with such additional power ' as the inquirers should think desirable.[1]

Meanwhile, the opposition from without was making itself felt. At a general meeting of the Leeds clothiers all present expressed their willingness to be incorporated, provided the whole of the West Riding clothiers were included. Whereupon the promoters of the scheme were compelled to admit that they ' feared itt could not bee done . . . they having alwayes received such stronge opposicion from the clothyers without '.[2] For the present, therefore, the scheme fell into abeyance, and the men of Leeds concentrated their energies upon an attempt to get the borough charter modified.

With the Restoration came a flood of charters, reinstating old organizations, such as the Merchant Adventurers, and erecting a number of new corporations. At such a time the scheme of the Leeds broad clothiers was more likely to receive favourable consideration, and the Leeds men returned to the attack. They were successful on this occasion, and in 1662 an Act was passed ' for the better regulating of the Manufacture of Broad Woollen Cloath in the West Riding of the County of Yorke '.[3]

This statute enacted that ' there shall be a Corporation to continue for ever . . . consisting of all the Justices of Peace of the West Riding, Two Masters, Ten Wardens, Twelve Assistants, and Commonalty. All which [officers] . . . are to be of the ablest and best experienced Clothiers within the Riding, and such as have served and been brought up in the Trade and Mistery of Clothing by the space of seven yeares . . . ; one of which Masters, Five of which Wardens, and Six of which Assistants to be chosen the first Monday after Pentecost annually at some public place by the Free Clothiers . . . inhabiting within the Parish of Leeds '. The other half of the executive was to be elected in like manner by the clothiers residing in the rest of the Riding. Such a society was to be ' one Body Politick and Corporate . . . and . . . a per-petuall Succession, and to be called by the name of the Super-visors, Masters, Wardens, Assistants, and Commonalty of the Trade or Mistery of Clothiers for the well making of Broad

---

[1] *Baynes Correspondence*, xi. 147.   [2] Ibid., xi. 218.
[3] Statute 14 Chas. II, c. 32.

Woollen Cloath within the West Riding'. The executive
was to meet on the first Saturday in each month at the Sessions
House in Leeds, and at any other time and place if the members
should think fit. Here by-laws, rules, and ordinances were to be
drawn up for the better spinning, working, making, fulling, and
milling of woollen cloth, and these regulations, after having been
endorsed by the justices of assize, were to be published at least
four times a year. Any clothier breaking such rules could be
fined up to twenty shillings, half the levy being retained by the
corporation, the remaining portion being handed over to the
relief of the poor of the parish in which the offender lived.

Searchers were to be appointed to enforce the observance of
all ordinances, and to bring offenders to justice. They were to
examine all broad cloths, and affix a seal on which was stated
the length and weight of the piece. The searcher was given right
of entry into houses, shops, and warehouses where cloths were
made or stored. These provisions were not intended to replace
the ulnager, who still collected his pence and supplied his seals.
The searcher of the new corporation replaced the searcher
formerly appointed by the justices, and enforced not only the
laws of the realm but also the decrees of the local trade association.

In order further to guarantee the best possible workmanship
the statute made a pronouncement concerning apprenticeship.
No person was to make broad cloths unless he had served an
apprenticeship of at least seven years to that trade, under
penalty of £5 for each month he engaged in the occupation ;
the penalty was a heavy one, especially as the Act of 1563
inflicted a fine of only £2 per month. A proviso, however, stated
that any one might make broad cloths ' for the use of themselves,
their Children and families, but not to sell them ', without
having served the requisite period.

One last clause was intended to safeguard the interests of the
employees. It ran as follows :

' Provided alwaies that neither the Supervisors, Masters,
Wardens, and Assistants, nor any of them, nor any other persons
free of the Corporation of Broad Woollen Clothiers shall by any
Authority derived from this act . . . set or impose any other or
lesser Rates or Wages upon any inferiour Workmen, Servants,

or Labourers to bee imployed by them . . . in the said Manufacture than such as shall bee from time to time allowed and
approved of by the Justices of the Peace in their Quarter
Sessions.'

This clause was based on the assumption that the minimum
wage clauses of the statute of 1603 were being enforced. As
we have seen (Chapter III) the justices were actually fixing
maximum rates for weavers as for other workers, and no minima
were ever laid down.

The men of Leeds had gained their point, and the Corporation
of Broad Clothiers was established in accordance with the terms
of the statute. Of its actual work we know nothing. It continued until 1680,[1] and was then given another five years of
life by a renewal of the Act. In 1685 a further renewal was
mooted, but not actually effected.[2] In 1692 [3] came a vigorous
attempt to reinstate the corporation, when a number of gentry,
clothiers, and cloth-workers petitioned the Commons for a
revival of the provisions of the Act of 1662. In the petition these
men spoke of the divers abuses which had arisen since the demise
of the corporation, and asked for its resuscitation. Their
request was not granted, and the Corporation of Broad
Clothiers passed permanently into the shades, along with
many other associations and institutions which were by that
time either defunct or in a state of advanced senility. The
corporation had been an interesting experiment, an attempt
to regulate an industry which was carried on by a widely
scattered population, working under domestic conditions.
Effective supervision under such circumstances was naturally
very difficult, and hence the corporation failed to establish itself
as an efficient instrument of industrial regulation. When next
the State stepped in to provide machinery for supervising the
trade, it had abandoned all idea of a trade association, and
reverted to the old sixteenth-century method, by which the justices
of the peace and their nominees were to carry on the work.

Meanwhile, the revised corporation of the borough of Leeds,
established by the charter of November 1661, had commenced
operations, and was making provisions for the control of industry

---

[1] *House of Lords Calendar, Hist. MSS. Comm.*, vol. xi, pt. ii, p. 163.
[2] *House of Commons' Journals*, lx. 729.   [3] Ibid., x. 741.

and commerce within the town.[1] Additional powers had been
given, and the newly organized body could do much more than
its predecessor. In the first place, the borough could hold its
own petty and quarter sessions, at which all necessary steps
were to be taken to enforce the observance of the cloth laws
of the realm. At such sessions the dignity of the national
decrees would be upheld, and offenders punished by the municipal
magistrates. Secondly, the corporation had power to issue
special by-laws for the regulation of the cloth trade in the
borough. On this the charter was very explicit, and outlined
the *modus operandi* in making such ordinances :

' When the mayor of the borough . . . shall judge it just or
necessary to make . . . any new laws, ordinances, or statutes,
for or touching the making, dyeing, or sale of woollen cloth,
or the art or mystery thereof, . . . then the mayor, aldermen
and assistants . . . shall cause to be summoned forty of the
more honest and sufficient clothworkers, craftsmen . . . inhabitants within the borough . . . to meet on a certain day and
place, which assembly shall be called the common assembly,
and then and there may be proposed . . . such laws, statutes
and ordinances as the mayor or common council shall think fit
and just to be established, and they shall ask advice thereupon
of the said common assembly. . . . Such laws, . . . which shall be
approved by the greater part of those present, shall become
laws and ordinances, and thence after shall be of good force
and effect, and be inviolably observed by all clothworkers,
artificers, and merchants, under pains and penalties in the said
laws contained.'

In addition to these specific powers, the corporation was granted
all such general rights as were necessary for the full and thorough
control of the industrial life of the town.

During the sixty or seventy years which followed the granting
of the Restoration charter the municipal authorities attempted,
with doubtful success, to carry out the policy which their powers
enabled them to formulate. They administered the various
statutes relating to cloth, and appointed searchers to see that
the laws were respected.[2] Eighteen searchers were elected

---

[1] See Wardell, *Municipal History of Leeds*, app. xiii.

[2] Leeds was divided into fourteen districts, for each of which searchers
were elected. Some districts only claimed one searcher, others (Farnley and
Wortley) claimed two, whilst Hunslet had three. See *Leeds Sessions Books*,
vol. ii, pp. 147, 164, 284, &c.

annually, and took solemn oaths to discharge their duties
faithfully ; those who neglected their office, or refused to serve
as searcher when appointed, were severely punished, and many
such cases actually occurred.[1] On the whole, these men did their
work thoroughly, and many offenders were brought to court.
Witness two typical instances :

July 17, 1717, a man indicted for attempting to sell a piece
of white Birstall cloth, declaring it to be well spun, good and
' merchantable ', when really it was badly spun, very deceptive,
and unmerchantable, as an evil and pernicious example for other
men to do in like manner.[2]

January 13, 1735. ' Sam Lumley of Stanningley, possessed of
one end or half cloth of broad woollen cloth, which had been
very greasy, full of holes, mill bracks, and not merchantable.'
These holes had been artfully cunningly, and with a fraudulent
design sewed up, and the cloth sold to John Berkenhout,
a prominent Leeds merchant.[3]

Many other instances might be given of the manner in which
clothiers and cloth-workers were fined for making cloths of
deficient length or weight, or for having infringed some clause
of one of the Acts passed during the two preceding centuries.[4]

The corporation also made an attempt to regulate and enforce
the laws concerning apprenticeship, and to compel all apprentices in the borough to become registered in the town's Apprentice Roll. In 1703 the court of the corporation therefore declared[5]
that ' It is ordered that every Artificer, Shopkeeper, and Trader
whatsoever, being a freeman or Burgess of this Burrough, that
shall take any Apprentice or Apprentices, shall enter the names
of every such Apprentice with the Town Clerk . . . in a book to
be kept for that purpose, and pay Sixpence for the entry thereof '.
The apprentice then served his allotted period, at the end of which
he was able to set up as a clothier, if he possessed the necessary capital, or become a journeyman.   In the former case, the

---

[1] e.g. August 1703, for instance of cloth searcher who ' executionem officii
contemptuose et totaliter refusavit et neglexit ' (*Sessions Books*, ii. 164).

[2] *Leeds Sessions Books*, iii. 28 : the above is one out of twenty-six indictments made at that court.

[3] Ibid., vol. iv, 13th January, 8 Geo. II.

[4] In one instance an Act of the reign of Philip and Mary was cited, and
a kersey maker indicted of having violated it.

[5] *Leeds Corporation Records*, i. 408 (1703).

corporation made a further claim upon him ; ' at the end and
expiracion of his Terme, [the master must] bring such Apprentice to a courte of Mayor, Aldermen and Assistants, to take
his Freedome, which apprentice shall pay for registring such
freedom the sum of three shillings and fourpence.' To what
extent these rules were enforced it is impossible to state, but
it seems that the corporation occasionally awoke to the fact that
large numbers of apprentices had completed their terms of
service, and were setting up as masters without having sought
enrolment as freemen of the borough.   On such occasions the
corporation issued a sweeping command ' that the severall
persons be respectively sumoned to appear at the next Court of
the Mayor, &c. . . . to be held for this Burrough (whereof they
shall have notice), to take their freedomes and be registred as
the case shall require '.[1]   In September 1706 and May 1707 [2]
numbers of apprentices were summoned to take up their
freedom ; the list included weavers, cloth-drawers, and card-
makers, as well as barbers, joiners, drapers, and other tradesmen.
It is very doubtful whether these men obeyed the summons,
for there is no mention of their appearance at the subsequent
assemblies of the corporation.   In its relations with strangers
who came to reside in Leeds the corporation seems to have been
more fortunate.   It would be easier to obtain obedience (and
money) from a stranger setting up his home and business in the
town than from those who had grown up there, and whose
familiarity with its governors might breed contempt for their
demands. The corporation kept a sharp look-out for strangers,
and occasionally ordered its constables to submit lists of all
men practising any trade within their divisions who had not
taken the freedom of the borough.[3] Men from all parts of the
county and from all quarters of England were thus constrained
to take up the burdens and privileges of citizenship : a stationer
from Manchester, a merchant from Hull, a saddler and joiner
from Wakefield, clothiers from the surrounding districts, a mercer
from Bradford, a haberdasher from York, a linen draper and
a brazier from London, a barber from Oxford, with goldsmiths,

[1] Ibid., ii. 20.
[2] Ibid., ii. 28–9. In 1706 nineteen persons were summoned ; in 1707 forty-
six.   [3] Ibid., ii. 235, and ii. 170.

apothecaries, and dyers from other parts. These men came before the Court of the Corporation, took the oath of allegiance to the King and that of a freeman of the borough, paid their entrance fees, and were then admitted to the citizenship.[1]

Finally, the corporation attempted to foster gild organization amongst the various industries of the town. Unlike its predecessor, the charter of 1661 made no provision concerning the establishment of gilds and fraternities. The early societies established during the reign of Charles I were probably now defunct, and the new charter gave no orders for their renewal. But this omission was either an oversight or was due to the supposition that a municipal charter carried with it such power and that any town authority had the right to set up as many gilds as it pleased. At any rate, the new corporation took that view of its powers, and one of its first ordinances dealt with this subject. On November 4, 1661, the court declared that

' fforasmuch as all or most of the traders within this Burrough are much decreased, and the poore thereof much increased, occasioned by the undue takeinge of apprentices, setting on worke fforeners and strangers, and by fraudes and abuses therein used, ffor Remedy whereof and in pursuance of the Powers and Authority given in His Maties Letters Patent, This Court thinks fitt and soe orders that all and any persons useing and exerciseing the trade of a Clothworker shalbe a Guild or ffraternity, and are by this Court constituted a Guild or ffraternity, . . . themselves, their servants, and apprentices, to be guided and governed by and under such Lawes, Ordinances, and Constitutions, as John Dawson, Esq., Major, [and ten

---

[1] The amount of the entrance fee varied according to the new freeman's occupation, and to the estimated benefit which he would be likely to receive by pursuing his vocation in Leeds. Thus in 1703 it was declared that ' if any stranger for the future shall be desirous to purchase his freedome of the Burrough, it shall be upon such termes as the Court of Mayor, Aldermen, and Assistants . . . shall agree upon, having respect to the trade that he shall exercise within the said Corporation, and the benefit and advantage that he may be presumed to reap thereby' (*Corp. Mins.*, i. 414 (1703)). This consideration made the fine vary to a great degree, and whilst a small trader or clothworker paid only about £2, a strange merchant, seeking his freedom, was charged as much as £50 (ibid., ii. 155, and ii. 165). If the newcomer happened to be one of the many foreign merchants who were settling in Leeds in the early eighteenth century, he was called upon to pay a much larger fine. The English merchant paid £50, but the alien was ordered ' to pay ffines which shall not exceed ffive hundred pounds, nor be less than one hundred pounds for any ffreedom to be taken by such fforeign merchant, who shall be naturalized before such ffreedom is taken ' (ibid., ii. 165).

Assistants or Aldermen], or the major part of them shall approve and allow.'

The Company of Cloth-workers, thus established, was not the only one to be instituted, for at the same time the other occupations of the town were brought under similar organized control. The size or nature of some occupations was such that they needed a 'guild or ffraternitie' of their own, but in other instances kindred trades were grouped into one company, so that in all there were six such companies established by the municipal authorities.[1]

These companies had proper constitutions, with executives and officials, ordinances and by-laws for the control of their members. The Cloth-workers' Company strove for a time to further the interests of its members by attempting to prevent any person from working at the art unless he was a member of the fraternity, by protesting against any obstacles which might hinder the sale of Leeds cloth at home or abroad, and by seeking favourable legislation. Thus in 1664 [2] the company joined the municipal corporation in a petition to the King, protesting against the increased charges which the Blackwell Hall authorities had placed upon Yorkshire cloths going to that market. Similarly, in 1690 the company was busy attempting to prevent cloth from leaving the West Riding before it had been dyed and dressed.[3] But in all such activities the companies were under the control of the corporation. Their ordinances carried no weight until they had been sanctioned and engrossed by the local authorities; if any dispute arose amongst the members, the word of the corporation overrode the decision of the company, and if any neglect occurred either in the control of finances or in the election of the executive, the mayor and his fellows had the power to settle the affair as seemed best to them.[4]

---

[1] *Leeds Corp. Mins.*, i. 27. Dawson was the first deputy-mayor, and the second to fill the mayoral chair. The remaining companies, in addition to that of the cloth-workers, were :
    1. 'Milnewrights, Carpenters, Joyners, Plaisterers, Coopers, and Bricklayers,' i. e. the building trades.
    2. 'Mercers, Grocers, Salters, and Drapers,' i. e. a company of shopkeepers.
    3. Cordwainers.
    4. Tailors.
    5. Ironmongers, smiths, glaziers, cutlers, pewterers, i. e. a hardware company.
[2] *D. S. P.*, March 23, 1664, vol. 449, f. 14.
[3] Stowe MSS. 746, ff. 110, 128, 136, 138.
[4] See sections on tailors' ordinances, i. 5c and 55.

In short the gilds were the creation of the corporation, and were entirely under the control of the parent body.[1]

The absence of any detailed records prevents us from approaching nearer to these Leeds fraternities, and it is therefore dangerous to be dogmatic as to their success or failure between the years 1660 and 1710.[2] During this time the Corporation Minute Books furnish occasional references which seem to indicate that gild activity was not very important. In 1691 it was suggested that statutory power should be obtained to fuse the six gilds into one company, but the idea did not materialize.[3] From 1700 onwards the corporation made frequent demands for the enfranchisement of traders and craftsmen, and during this time the Tailors' Company was very active. The Cloth-workers' fraternity, however, was gradually drifting into desuetude. This continued until 1720, when the corporation, suddenly awakening, made frantic efforts to whip the clauses of the charter and their own powers of industrial regulation into some semblance of life and reality. The demands for a general enrolment of freemen were peremptory, and the slumbers of the cloth-workers' organization rudely disturbed. Witness the minutes of the court held on May 7, 1720 :

'Whereas by a long disuse and failure in the Company of Clothworkers in this Corporacion to put in force their Orders, by-Laws and Ordinances which have been made for the good Government of the said Company and the Artificers belonging to the same, and for the well making, dying and manufacturing of woolen cloth made and sold within the Burrough aforesaid ; and touching the sale thereof great abuses and deceits have crept in, to the great Disparagement and debaseing of the said Manufacture and to the great loss and hindrance of the fair and honest Traders therein. And whereas the aforesaid Laws were not sufficient to prevent the inconveniences and abuses aforesaid, for remedy whereof It is thought fitt and Ordered that the aforesaid By-Laws and Ordinances be carefully inspected and revised, and that such alteracions and amendments be made therein, or additions thereto as by Councel Learned in the Law shall be advised, and that they be prepared and ready to be proposed at the next Court . . . or at a Comon Assembly for the Burrough aforesaid, which shall be called for that purpose, And that the persons following [forty names given], being forty

---

[1] The companies all met in a place known as the Gildhall (*Mins.*, i. 88).
[2] *Mins.*, i. 418 (1704) ; ibid., ii. 32–3 (1707).   [3] Ibid., i. 313.

of the more sufficient and honest Clothiers and Clothworkers Inhabiting within the Burrough . . . be Sumoned to appeare at the Same time and place, to the end their approbacion may be had to the said By-Laws, Orders and Ordinances as shall then be proposed by the Mayor and Comon Councell . . . for the purpose aforesaid.'[1]

How this conference ended we do not know. It was the last effort of the corporation to reinvigorate the gild organization, and it seems to have failed most completely. From this time onward there is an entire absence of any records throwing light on the subsequent history of the companies, and it seems that the fraternities died a slow death and perished from starvation and disuse. Even if they had served a useful purpose at the time of their institution (which is doubtful), they had by this time become much too small to be adequate for the proper control of the industries which were advancing so rapidly during the eighteenth century. The woollen industry in particular had entered upon its period of adolescence, and just as a suit of clothes rapidly becomes too small for a youth who is growing at a great rate, so the organization of the Restoration period was eminently unfitted for the nature and extent of the trade which was carried on within the Leeds boundary during the eighteenth century. Thus the corporation ceased to attempt to order and control the cloth-workers, as well as the other branches of economic activity. In 1725 the supervision of the broad cloth industry was handed over by legislation to the justices of the peace and their searchers,[2] and the Leeds Cloth-workers' Company, after existing a little longer as a convivial society, quietly disappeared from view.[3]

The final years of the seventeenth century and the early decades of the eighteenth witnessed the decline in economic importance of many other institutions which had played a prominent part in the activities of Tudor and Stuart times. This period, in fact, was an era of transition, in which the older forms of organization were breaking down, and the ground was being prepared to some extent for the flood of individualism

[1] *Leeds Corp. Min.*, ii. 159–60, May 5, 1720.
[2] Statute 11 Geo. I, c. 24.
[3] Webb, *History of Local Government* (The Manor and the Borough), ii. 418. The ten pages devoted to the history of the Leeds Corporation by the Webbs contain much valuable information on the work of the corporation.

and the great changes which were to create modern commercial society. The Leeds gilds disappeared, the West Riding Broad Cloth Corporation had already made its departure. These were comparatively mushroom growths, but they were accompanied in their demise by such old-established institutions as the ulnage, the companies which had developed out of the mediaeval fraternities, and the big trading companies of the Eastland Merchants and the Merchant Adventurers.

The ulnage had continued to be collected, though it was some-what neglected during the Interregnum.[1] In 1664 the grant of its farm had been renewed to the Duke of Lennox for a further period of sixty years, and, on the death of the Duke in 1672, the farm was transferred to his widow.[2] The ulnage was now purely a revenue machine, and its officials did nothing to administer the cloth laws relating to dimensions, weight, or quality. In the West Riding it had become customary for the clothiers to buy a large number of seals from the local representa-tive of the ulnager, and affix them to the cloths which they had woven. In one case, for instance, a witness in a lawsuit of 1676 declared that he was accustomed to fetching one hundred seals at a time from the ulnager, then fixing them to the cloth without any representative of the ulnage being present. This practice was forbidden in a similar suit during the reign of James II (1687),[3] and clothiers were expected to have their cloths examined and weighed before the ulnager's seal was affixed. The old practice continued, however, so long as the ulnage was levied.[4]

---

[1] *D. S. P., Chas. II*, xvi. 87 (1660) : ' Since the late war, divers clothiers and others, taking liberty to themselves by the dysorder of the late tymes, have and still doe putt sett and send to sell divers cloathes . . . without payment of the said subsidye '.

[2] Treasury Books, 1672–3, February 19 ; *Calendar*, p. 67. Lennox paid £900 for the old draperies, and £98 for the new.

[3] Exch. Deposition by Comm., 2–3 Jas. II, Hil., York and Lancs., 14.

[4] Witness the following letter written by Joseph Holroyd, a cloth-factor of Halifax, who acted as ulnager's representative for the West Riding during the early years of the next century :

ffarm[rs] of Aulnage

Srs   Hallifax y[e] 25th 9b[r] 1706.

. . . I desire y[v] to Send by first Carriers 4 a 5000 1½ Seales. If y[w] please may make itt up 1 horrse pa: wth 2 a 3,000 1[d] and 1,000 ½[d] the rest 3[d] Seales.

I am

Yo[rs], J. H(olroyd).

(*Letter Books of Joseph Holroyd and Sam Hill*, ed. Heaton (Bankfield Museum Notes). See nos. 81, 94, 100.)

By the end of the reign of James II there had grown up
a considerable amount of opposition to the ulnage fee; many
were demanding that the office should be abolished, and the loss
to the Crown compensated by increased customs dues on exported
cloth.   The Yorkshire clothiers were amongst the strongest
supporters of this suggestion, and in 1693 they petitioned the
House of Commons, declaring that the office 'is now useless and
no-ways answers the end of its first constitution, but is become
very burdensome to the subject, and a great hindrance to the
woollen trade'.[1]   The farmers of the ulnage naturally opposed
the destruction of their office and means of revenue; they
pointed out that the patent granted in 1664 had still thirty
years to run, and they did not intend to renounce such a profitable investment.   Hence, though many bills were introduced
to bring the institution to an end, all failed, and the ulnage did
not finally expire until the termination of the Lennox licence in
the reign of George I.[2]

The two great cloth-exporting companies were also rapidly
falling from their former high estate, and were losing the
monopoly they had enjoyed during the early years of the
seventeenth century.   The Civil War had affected adversely
the trade of both Eastlanders and Adventurers, and when
the Commonwealth was established the opponents of the companies prevailed.   The charters of the organizations were not
annulled, but suspended, the companies were deprived of their
monopolistic powers, and 'interlopers' were granted liberty in
foreign trade.   With the Restoration, this 'anti-company'
policy was reversed, and by confirmation of their charters in
1661 the two companies were restored to their old position.   But
the day of great things was now past, and from the Restoration
onwards both bodies declined from their former strength.
The entrance fees were being reduced very substantially, and
admission had thus become comparatively cheap and easy.[3]
Once begun, the process of pulling down the walls of privilege
could not long be stayed, and in the first year of the reign of

---

[1] *House of Commons Journals*, xi. 16.   Also *House of Lords MSS., Hist.
MSS. Comm.*, xiii, pp. 225–6.

[2] See also *House of Lords MSS., Hist. MSS. Comm.*, xiv, pt. vi, p. 42.

[3] For this later history of the Adventurers, see Lingelbach, Introduction;
also *Newcastle Merchant Adventurers*, Preface to volume ii.

William and Mary there was much agitation in favour of
' a general liberty to all persons to export [woollen goods] to
Hamburgh ', the very centre of the Adventurers' activity. This
campaign ended successfully, and in the same year an Act was
passed allowing freedom to all who wished to trade in what
had formerly been the preserves of the Merchant Adventurers.[1]
Such a statute would materially affect the merchants of Hull,
York, and Leeds, whose control over the export trade in Yorkshire cloths would thus be destroyed. They therefore made
many attempts to obtain a revision of the above Act, and pleaded
for the re-establishment of the power of the Hamburg Company
under ' such regulations or other provision . . . for carrying on
the trade in a regulated way ' as the Commons should think
best.[2] In 1693 the Merchant Adventurers declared that they
were willing to allow any Englishman who was not a handi-
craftsman to be ' admitted into the freedom of the . . . Company
for forty shillings, to trade within all their limits, except the
Rivers of Elbe, Weser, and Eyder '. In other words, would-be
merchants were allowed to enter the company at a very much
reduced fee, and then trade over a large part of the Merchant
Adventurers' territory. This arrangement pleased neither the
Yorkshire Adventurers nor the House of Commons, for the former
thought it opened a way to infinite debasement and fraud,
whilst the latter refused to make any alteration in the statute
of 1688.[3]

In similar fashion the power of the Eastland Merchants was
being undermined. The records of the Eastlanders of York
end in 1696. The last thirty years had been spent in an acrimonious correspondence with Hull, and in violent quarrels with the
Eastland Merchants at head-quarters ; and now at the last
meeting, with only six members present, there was no indication
(except in the smallness of the attendance) that the branch
had come to its ' extreme day '.[4] The quantity of cloth exported
by the whole company throughout the realm had fallen very
heavily during the middle years of the century. In 1640 the
export was said to be 120,000 cloths annually, whilst in 1670

[1] Statute 1 William and Mary, c. 32.
[2] *House of Commons Journals*, x. 759.   [3] Ibid., xi. 80–1.
[4] *Ordinances of the Eastland Merchants*, ed. by Miss M. Sellers, p. 139, and
Preface.

the number was stated to be only 11,000.[1] These figures are probably far from accurate, but they express an exaggeration of an actual fact, namely, that the old monopoly was breaking down, and that the outsider was engrossing more and more of the foreign trade. This decline continued during the rest of the century, and although the York branch probably did not actually expire after that last recorded meeting of January 27, 1696, it gradually ceased to control any appreciable proportion of the Baltic cloth trade.[2] The York Merchant Adventurers were more numerous ; their influence was stronger ; and so they continued throughout the eighteenth century as a trading society, though deprived of the monopoly which had formerly been theirs. They pursued a rather conservative policy, clinging to the old traditions and customs in an age which was needing more and more individualism and progressive thought. Hence they were left behind in the great developments of the eighteenth century, and the major portion of the foreign trade in cloth passed into the hands of others. Still the organization survived, and exists even to this day. A flood of new life has been infused into it by the historical labours of Dr. Maud Sellers, which have done much to remind the citizens of York of the former greatness of what was once the driving force in the foreign trade of that ancient city.[3]

This decline had two important consequences. In the first place, it gave Englishmen freedom to engage in foreign trade unhampered by the restrictions and regulations of the trading monopolies. Secondly, it allowed foreign merchants to trade with greater ease between this country and their own shores. This second possibility affected considerably the trade in Yorkshire cloths, and many foreign merchants settled in Leeds and other parts of the West Riding during the eighteenth century. In the discussions which followed the establishment of free trade to Hamburg, Leeds merchants continually expressed their opinion that the new conditions would certainly flood Yorkshire

---

[1] *England's Improvement*, by Roger Coke, p. 21, quoted in *Ordinances of Eastland Merchants*, Preface, p. li.

[2] Eastland Merchants were existing in Macpherson's day (*Annals of Commerce* (1805), iv. 166).

[3] The Adventurers meet in Trinity Hall arrayed in proper robes, have a sermon preached ; also go to service every 27th of January.

with foreign merchants, who would take the trade out of the
hands of the Englishman. This contention availed nothing, and
the risk of such a foreign invasion was braved. The influx of
foreign merchants actually did take place, in the person of such
aliens as John Berkenhout,[1] a native of Hamburg, who played
an important part in the economic life of Leeds as a trader in
cloth. These foreigners were looked upon with great disgust by
the native clothiers and merchants, and the whole attitude of
the Yorkshiremen is seen admirably in a petition sent by them
to the House of Commons upon the subject, drawn up some time
during the reign of Anne.[2]

The petition

'Sheweth that the Incouraging the Exportation of Manufactures by her Majesty's natural born Subjects directly to
Germany in a Regulated way of trade, exclusive of fforaigners
would, as your Petitioners humbly conceive, With due Sub-
mission to the great Judgement of this hon[ble] House, be for the
generall benefit of the Nation. That since Forreigners have
been suffered to export the said Manufactures they have occa-
tioned them to be debased, and not to be so truly made as
formerly, wherby the esteem thereof abroad hath been lessened
and Forreign Manufactures Incouraged, and a long Credit hath
been introduced and many losses hath happened to ye Clothiers
of their debts to a considerable value ; the Members of the
Company of Merchant Adventurers, who whilest they were
supported were generous traders, exported great Quantitys and
paid well, have been discouraged and doe not send out near
such Quantitys as formerly, and severall of them have wholly
left off ye said trade, which it is feared will in a little time come
wholly into the hands of Forreigners, and Occation an irre-
parable damadge to the Nation ; that the supporting of the
said Company in their . . . trade to Germany would as ye Petitioners conceive be a means to prevent and put a stop to those
evils provided ye said Company were obliged to admit all her
Majesty's subjects into ye freedom of there Society upon easy
terms.'

In spite of such protests, the old barriers to freedom of inter-
change were swept away, and we are in the throes of the
eighteenth century. That century is of the greatest interest,

---

[1] See Thoresby Soc. publications, vol. iv, p. 226. Berkenhout died in 1759.
[2] This is the petition of 'divers Clothbuyers, Clothiers and Clothworkers
and others concern'd in ye Woollen Manufacture in Hotherfield and places
adjacent' (Cookson MSS. in Thoresby Soc. Library).

because it is such a wonderful mixture of the old and the new. In it we have the decease of so many ideas and institutions which either had their origin in mercantilist theories, or which even pushed their roots down into the soil of the Middle Ages. And at the same time the new movements which are to dominate the modern economic world are already groping through to the light. The century which lay between 1750 and 1850 was one of stupendous development in industry, commerce, and in the relations between these branches of national life and the State. But this progress would not have been so easy or so rapid had it not been for the manner in which the systems and organizations of a former age were passing away during the first half of the eighteenth century. A new order was knocking at the door seeking admittance. When it did gain entrance it found the room more or less swept and garnished. There were still many survivals of the former system, but the great landmarks which had so strongly characterized the Tudor and Stuart régimes were gone, and their places were waiting to be filled by the ideas and institutions of a new world.

CHAPTER VIII

FROM THE RESTORATION TO THE INDUSTRIAL REVOLUTION—THE PERIOD OF PROGRESS

THE years which lie between the accession of Charles II and the coming of the Industrial Revolution constituted a well-defined epoch in the development of the Yorkshire textile industry, and on the whole comprised a period of progress. The progress, however, was far from unbroken or constant. The reign of Charles II was marked by depressions quite as acute as those of the Commonwealth, and similar spasms of bad trade occurred during the subsequent century. But in spite of the black outlook at the commencement, and the periodical blasts of misfortune, the epoch is one during which the cloth-makers of Yorkshire prospered, and built up a powerful industry, before steam and machinery came along to point the way to still greater progress.

When Charles II came to the throne economic society was smarting under the effects of twenty years of civil strife and political disorder. The complaints of bad trade which came from all parts of the country in 1659 were quite justified, for industry and commerce were alike under a cloud. Nor did these depressing circumstances vanish at the appearance of the restored monarchy. Throughout Charles's reign the complaints continued; in 1663 a committee was appointed to inquire into ' the reasons for the generall Decaye of Trade ',[1] and a similar commission was chosen in 1669 to consider the ' causes and grounds of the fall and decay of trade '.[2] At later stages stagnation was general, and there were many periods of temporary or more lasting languor.

The causes of these depressions are easily discovered. In the first place it took time to recover from the exhaustion of the previous thirty years. Secondly, the intense commercial enmity of the Dutch expressed itself in naval warfare, and during these wars (1665-7 and 1672-4) the Dutch harried the English

---

[1] *D. S. P., Chas. II*, xcv. 53.   [2] *Hist. MSS. Comm.*, viii. 133-4.

coast, hung about the river mouths, and pounced upon such coal and cloth fleets as dared to venture on the North Sea. Further, even if no actual war was in progress, the Dutch did their utmost to exclude finished English cloths from their country, and to take from England only raw materials or semi-manufactured cloths. They were still superior to the English as dyers and finishers, and thousands of Dutchmen still found employment by dressing the cloths which were imported, white and undressed, from England. This arrangement had been fostered by the Merchant Adventurers, who still exported annually large quantities of such pieces to the Low Countries. As the monopoly of the Adventurers broke down, private factors and middlemen carried on the trade. Joseph Holroyd, of Soy-land, near Halifax, of whom more will be said later, was such a man. His letter books show him, during the years 1706–7, to be engaged in making large purchases of white kerseys on behalf of Dutch finishers and merchants. Also, especially after the Restoration, Dutch agents settled in the manufacturing areas, where they bought and shipped new and old draperies, unfinished, to their native land. Such men were to be found in Leeds and the West Riding, and one man, Kyte by name, a Dutchman living in Halifax, was in 1665 dispatching via Hull and Newcastle thirty or forty packs of white kerseys each week.[1] Many of these cloths were then exported from Holland by Dutch merchants to Turkey and elsewhere in competition with the wares of English merchants.[2]

The third and greatest cause of this halting progress lay in the very keen competition to which English traders were subjected in foreign markets. The mercantilist policy which was being pursued by most European countries aimed at building up strong industries, and the attainment of self-sufficiency in the supply of cloth as in most other branches of economic life. France and Holland did not want English cloths ; they intended to make their own. But to do so they must have wool and fuller's earth. Of these raw materials they had only a scanty native supply, and were therefore compelled to seek for such commodities in other lands. England was especially fortunate in possessing

---

[1] D. S. P., Chas. II, cxi. 59 (1665).
[2] Report of Turkey Merchants, D. S. P., Chas. II, xcviii. 35 (1664).

large supplies of those necessaries of the textile trade, and English writers often boasted that, in their opinion, England held the world's supply of these precious substances. 'Wool is the flower and strength, the revenue and blood of England . . . and in the supply of wool and Fuller's Earth this nation is by God peculiarized in these blessings. . . . It is possible and probable that other parts of the World may produce Fuller's Earth, but neither in such fineness nor abundance as this in England '; [1] so declared the author of *The Golden Fleece*. France and Holland were fully aware of the high quality of the English raw materials, and made great efforts, openly or surreptitiously, to obtain supplies. Wool was a popular commodity for smuggling to these countries, and, having obtained the desired supplies and placed heavy impositions upon English cloths, the French and Dutch were able to 'suck the sweetness of the Sinews of our Trade ',[2] and develop their own textile industries. This growth of rivals, fed partly on English materials, caused constant controversy, much thought, and frequent legislation, and the Government spared no pains to prevent the growth of the industry in other countries at our expense. Further, when a continental country such as Prussia or Russia set out to initiate and build up a textile industry, it attempted to induce Englishmen to go over and instruct the natives in the art of cloth making. We hear repeatedly of ' divers Workmen transported . . . together with ye said comodities [i. e. wool, &c.], to the end and intent to sett up the Manufacture of Clothing in other countries '.[3] In 1738 a writer instances the case of a Mr. John Hudson of Yorkshire, who went out to Altona and began to make cloth there in 1732, ' and now [1738] there is at that place above 100 looms, and those that are gone over lately are to set up the making of stuffs and stockings and narrow goods, and have carried their engines and other utensils along with them, . . . and severall broad looms to make calimancoes, camblets and divers other stuffs.' [4]

The protectionist policy of Colbert dealt a hard blow at the North Country, for the cheap northern cloths had found one of

[1] *The Golden Fleece*, by W. S., Gentleman (1656), pp. 60–4.
[2] *England's Glory*, by a true lover of his Country (1669).
[3] *D. S. P., Chas. II*, xcv. 20 (1663).
[4] Pamphlet, *Observations on British Wooll and the Manufacture of it*, by a Northamptonshire manufacturer (1738), pp. 10–11.

their best markets in France. The French, however, had quickly acquired the art of making cheap wares, and in 1670 a writer from Lille declared that ' the French are now got into a way of making a Low-price-sort of Cloath called " Searge de Berry " which comes as cheap as Northern Cloaths and of much better wool . . . in which they have cloathed a great number of their souldiers '.[1] Four years later another writer gives the following lamentable picture of the decline in the demand for northern fabrics :

' There have, about 12 or 14 yeares agoe, come from Kendal to this towne [London], 6 or 8,000 peeces a yeare, and not now 300 peeces ; of Kearseys from the West of Yorkshire 10,000 peeces a yeare, not nowe 500 to be shipped for france ; from Lancashire severall thousand peeces of bayes formerly, and nowe scarce one ; and all, from the excessive customes, discouraged and disabled to send to France.'[2]

Thus, from the Restoration to about the end of the century, the woollen industry experienced a period of stagnation, due to the expansion of the textile industries in those countries where English cloths had formerly found a substantial market. ' In divers foreign countries, France, Holland, Flanders, Spain, Portugal, Sweden, Silesia, Luneberg, and other parts of Germany, new manufactures have been set up, which we take to be another reason why our trade in woollen has not been further enlarged.' In these words a commission reported to the House of Lords in 1702. Men of Yorkshire were of the same opinion ; in 1703 the merchants and clothiers around Leeds declared that ' the Woollen Manufacture doth sensibly decline in severall branches, particularly in the vending thereof into fforaigne countreys ', and the men of Halifax, with their usual personal frankness, asserted that ' upon the Woollen Manufactures and Trade depends in a great Measure the Wealth of your Maj[sty's] Kingdome, the Imployment of the poor, and the Incouragment of Navigation, which Trade is greatly Decayed of Late in these Northerne partes '.[3]

This unsatisfactory condition of the industry attracted much

---

[1] *England's Interest by Trade Asserted*, by W. Carter (1671), who quotes the above extract.

[2] *D. S. P., Chas. II*, vol. 361, p. 171 (July 27, 1674).

[3] Treasury Papers, lxxxiv, no. 15 (1703). A similar petition came from Wakefield.

attention from the Government, and persistent and varied attempts were made to infuse the cloth trade with vigour and new life. The first attempt was by means of a series of statutes which aimed at increasing the demand for woollen goods. The idea dated back to at least the reign of Henry III, when the Oxford Parliament decreed that every one 'should use woollen cloth made within the country'.[1] During the depressions of the reign of James I many people complained that the wearing of silks and foreign fabrics was displacing the good old English woollens, and clamoured for legislation to compel the wearing of English woollen cloths in preference to these fancy and foreign materials.[2] Others made a different suggestion which was now embodied in the statute of 1666. This act, 'for the encourage- ment of the Woollen Manufacture of the Kingdom', demanded that ' noe person . . . shall be buryed in any Shirt . . . or Sheete, made of or mingled with Flax, Hemp, Silk, Haire, Gold or Silver, or other than what shall be made of Wooll onely . . . or be putt into any Coffin lined or faced with anything made or mingled with Flax, Hemp, &c., upon paine of the forfeiture of the Summe of Five pounds, to be imployed to the use of the Poore of the Parish where such person shall be buryed'.[3] This order neither produced the desired boom in trade nor materially enriched the poor of the parishes, for it seems to have been generally disregarded. In 1678, therefore, it was replaced by a much more formidable decree, which directed that a register should be kept in every parish by the incumbent or his substitute, in which some one must certify that everything about the corpse was made of sheep's wool only.[4] This information was to be supplied in an affidavit made by the relations of the deceased, and lodged with the incumbent within eight days of the inter- ment, under penalty of five pounds. The Act, reinforced in 1680,[5] remained on the Statute Book until the nineteenth century. Entries in accordance with its clauses and instances of its infringement are occasionally encountered in the local parish registers, and generally run as follows :

1724. 'Mary Higgins, of Allerton, makes oath that May Mitchell, of the same place, was not wrapt . . . in any sheet . . .

[1] Ashley, *Economic History*, I. ii. 194.
[2] *D. S. P., Jas. I*, cxxxi. 55.
[3] Statute 18–19 Chas. II, c. 4.
[4] Statute 30 Chas. II, c. 3.
[5] Statute 32 Chas. II, c. 1.

or shroud but that was made of sheep's wool only as by Act of Parliament decreed.'[1]

Richmond Quarter Sessions, 1679. 'Fine of five pounds levied on the goods of Thomas Norton, late deceased and buried in the Bedale Parish Church, no certificate having been made to the Rector of Bedale within eight days of the buriall that the said Thomas was buried in wool according to the Statute.'[2]

These statutes were far from being dead letters, but it seems probable that here, as in all legislation which relied for its effectiveness on the vigilance of local administrators, there was every degree of laxity and rigour, according to the character and the temper of the local clergy. Again, the poorer classes, to whom woollens were the everyday cloths at hand, would have little inclination to brave the law by using linen and cotton fabrics ; the wealthier neighbour was willing to take the risk, as was Thoresby in the case of his father, who died in October 1679.[3] Hence Macpherson, writing at the end of the eighteenth century, complains that ' such is the vanity of the rich and great that they continue to pay the penalty rather than not adorn the deceased with fine linen, lace, &c., though this is so contrary to our true and national interest '.[4]

Legislation with a similar aim strove to forbid the growth of the manufacture of calico,[5] cotton, and similar upstart fabrics, under the belief that any development of such new industries could be made only at the expense of the older manufacture.

The second method adopted to foster the woollen industry comprised new determined efforts to improve the quality of the wares. But, as we have seen already, the corporations and companies which were instituted for this purpose by the Stuarts failed dismally, and in the eighteenth century therefore the State was compelled to fall back on direct legislation, administered through the justices of the peace and their officials. With these somewhat elaborate efforts we shall deal in a subsequent chapter.

[1] Thornton Register, June 1724.
[2] *North Riding Quarter Sessions Records*, vii. 18.
[3] Atkinson, *Ralph Thoresby, his Town and Times*, vol. i, p. 72. Also Leeds Parish Church Register, November 1, 1679.
[4] Macpherson, *op. cit.*, ii. 592. In the registers mention is made as follows : ' affidavit and certificate given '.
[5] Calico Acts, 7 Geo. I, c. 7 ; and 9 Geo. II, c. 4.

The third method was an attempt to prevent France and Holland from obtaining their supplies of raw materials from this country. The exportation of wool and fuller's earth was stringently forbidden, and repeated attempts were made to suppress the illicit traffic, which, however, continued in spite of legislative efforts. The story of these fruitless exertions is of considerable importance in its bearing on the Yorkshire wool supply, and so a fuller consideration of the topic must be postponed until we deal with the manner in which the eighteenth-century clothiers obtained their raw material. But we must note here, in passing, that the State also attempted to forbid the exportation of technical skill. In 1718 a statute was passed denouncing the compacts which were being made between foreigners and Englishmen, and laying down penalties against those who enticed workmen, and those workmen who consented, to go abroad to set up English industries in the land of the enemy.[1] This Act failed to check the emigration of artisans, though occasionally the law did seize upon some suspected person, as for instance in October 1727. At the Leeds General Sessions of that year John Windsor and William Simpson, cloth-dressers, were accused of having 'promised and contracted to leave the realm of Great Britain and go to Spain, there to exercise their art and to teach the mystery of cloth-dressing to the subjects of the King of Spain'. The prosecution, however, broke down, and the men were acquitted.

Thus over the broad field of English economic life the outlook was often gloomy, and it might even seem possible that in the struggle between the great commercial empires England would come out defeated. Why should not France or Holland secure the mastery of the industrial and commercial world, and become the workshop and the carrying agent for mankind? Nay more, would England ever emerge from the cloud under which she lay in those later decades of the Stuart period?

The answer to these questions is to be found largely in the general history of the next century, and also in the development of certain factors which had begun to exert their influence before

---

[1] Statute 5 Geo. I, c. 27 ; renewed and strengthened, 23 Geo. II, c. 13 (1750). The penalties inflicted by these Acts were very severe. For the first offence £500 and twelve months' imprisonment, for the second £1,000 and two years in prison.

the Revolution of 1688. First amongst these was the building up of our commercial and colonial empire, the foundations of which had been well and truly laid during the seventeenth century. India, North America, and other territorial acquisitions opened up new sources of raw material or provided new markets, and a brisk trade in cloth soon developed between Yorkshire and the North American colonies.[1] At the same time the European market was extended by the Methuen Treaty of 1703, which opened Portugal still further to English cloth dealers, and by the relations of William of Orange and the Hanoverian kings with the Continent. As the English navy gained greater mastery over the sea the complaints of piracy and of the dangers of the ocean highways became less frequent, and merchants could make their journeys in peace and security.

Secondly, the whole standard of economic activity was raised by the various steps which were taken during the last decade of the seventeenth century. The founding of the Bank of England, the institution of the National Debt, the restoration of the currency, and the developments in credit, paper money, and marine insurance, all helped British commerce to feel its way towards a state of greater efficiency and more complex organization. The commercial class was growing in wealth and importance, and although the old pioneer companies had lost their former influence, newer associations, such as the East India Company, had acquired great power, political and economic, over the regions in which they traded. The mercantile and financial magnates found their way into parliament,[2] took on an air of respectability, and even attained the greatest social heights by marriages with the nobility of the realm. Defoe marvels at that new product, the gentleman merchant, and declares that ' Trade is so far from being inconsistent with a gentleman that in England trade makes a gentleman, for after a generation or two, the tradesman's children come to be as good gentlemen, statesmen, parliament-men, judges, bishops and noblemen as those of the highest birth and most ancient families '.[3] The nobility as yet showed little general interest

[1] D. S. P., Chas. II, vol. 362, p. 47.
[2] Gee, *Trade and Navigation of England considered* (1739), p. 239.
[3] Defoe, *Complete Tradesman*, p. 246. See also Gibbins, *Industry in England*, pp. 322–3.

in commerce, probably because the ' youth of liberal education, never reading anything of manufacture, &c., in Homer or Virgil, or their college notes, . . . are either generally silent in this matter, or speak of it with contempt ; . . . thus they are accurate in Logic and Philosophy, which do not add twopence per year to the riches of the nation, . . . whilst the notions of trade are turned into ridicule, or much out of fashion '.[1] A more probable explanation was that the more spirited landed proprietors devoted their enthusiasm and energy to agricultural pursuits, and were in the van of agricultural improvement. Arthur Young is full of praise for the splendid work done by the landed gentry ; Townshend left politics for turnips ; Walpole was intended by his father to be the first grazier in the country, but preferred the political field.[2] In the north the nobility were giving much assistance, pecuniary and otherwise, to commercial enterprises and to the improvement of the means of communication. The Earl of Thanet, on April 16, 1692, ' spent in a journey to Yorke, to discourse with Mr. Thompson about the linen manufacture . . . o. 13. 10.', and Viscount Irwin provided the Cloth Hall at Halifax, and gave assistance in the erection of the first White Cloth Hall in Leeds in 1711. The turnpike and canal ventures were generally sure of the favour of the neighbouring gentry and nobility, and greater facilities for the purchase of land for roads and canals were extended by them than the smaller holders.

The mention of the means of communication brings us to the third important influence in the economic progress of the eighteenth century. Capital began to be called into greater use, though not to any great extent for purposes of production. Vast sums of money were, however, laid out in the very necessary task of improving the means of transit throughout the country. The few spare pounds of the clothier and yeoman farmer, or the larger sums of the landed gentry, were pooled together to make a turnpike road, to render a river navigable, or to construct a canal. For this work the geographical features of the country were very favourable. There were no outstanding difficulties to be overcome in the form of vast deserts, lofty mountain ranges, or great distances. The carrying of a canal over the

---

[1] *Britannia Linguens, or A Discourse of Trade* (1680), in Smith's *Memoirs of Wool*, vol. i.   [2] Morley, *Walpole*, p. 2.

Pennine Chain was about the only great obstacle to be faced, and thus the improvement in the means of communication was carried out with comparative ease. By the end of the eighteenth century the network of roads and waterways, though far from complete, enabled transport to be carried on with infinitely greater celerity than had been the case in the days when Thoresby recorded his travelling experiences during the early part of the century. When one remembers that the wool had to travel many miles in going through the various processes of manufacture, and considers the extremely unkempt state of the highroads prior to the revolution in the means of transit, it is surprising that an industry so widely scattered as the woollen manufacture should make any progress whatever. Certainly few improvements could be more welcome to the clothier than a reformation of the highways. From the time when he travelled into the wool-producing areas to the time when he deposited his cloth on the stall in the market he was constantly on the road, and hence the making of good highways was to him a veritable blessing.

Finally, the closing years of the seventeenth century and the whole of the eighteenth century were marked by the rapid growth of two new branches of the textile industry in the north. Lancashire had formerly resembled Yorkshire in its textile activity, and had been famous for the production of various types of cheap cloths, 'frizes', 'cottons', fustians, &c. Now in the eighteenth century this manufacture of woollens was partially replaced by the production of cotton goods. Cotton was imported from the American colonies, and, thanks to the suitable climate, Lancashire made rapid progress in the manufacture of cotton fabrics, especially when released from legal disabilities. Thus by the end of the eighteenth century cottons had displaced woollens in Lancashire, although the manufacture of certain kinds of woollen cloth lingered on in the Pennine districts and round about Rochdale. Whilst Lancashire was transforming its industry, the woollen area of Yorkshire received new vigour by the institution of the worsted industry, which quickly found a congenial home in the West Riding, and therefore allowed Yorkshire to develop along dual lines, as a woollen and also as a worsted manufacturing county.

These and other forces combined to make the eighteenth century one of progress and general prosperity. The peace of Walpole's régime, the internal order and security from invasion which this country enjoyed even in times of commercial warfare, were factors which allowed the new commercial and industrial developments to make headway. Old industries found fresh worlds to conquer, and new industries quickly assumed considerable dimensions. The home market expanded with the growth of population, whilst the figures of our foreign trade gradually mounted higher and higher. In 1662 the exports reached £2,022,812, a figure which was less than that of the year of depression 1622.[1] During the next ten years there was little improvement, but the following figures indicate the subsequent expansion :

	Total Exports.	Exports of Worsted and Woollen Cloth.[2]
	£	£
1688	4,310,000	2,600,000 (circa)
1700	7,621,053	3,128,366
1720	6,910,899	2,960,000 (average 1718–24)
1730	8,548,982	3,669,734 (1741)
1750	12,699,081	4,206,762 (1751)
1760	14,694,970	4,344,078 (1761)

The second column gives the values of woollen and worsted exports. In the reign of Charles II these exports constituted two-thirds of the total exports in value, but during the following century, although there was an actual increase in the value of such exports, the increase was not proportionate to that of general exports. Woollen goods lost some of that predominance which they had held for so long.

When we turn from a consideration of the national field to that of Yorkshire, we find that progress here was very marked. True, the *national* woollen and worsted industry was not expanding at a very great pace, and the increase in the value of its exports between 1700 and 1760 was only about 30 per cent. But such a figure fails to express the growth which was taking place in Yorkshire, for in reality the West Riding was appropriating to itself a greater and greater share of the national industry, and was attracting the trade from other parts of the country. The worsted

---

[1] *House of Lords MSS.*, New Series, vol. v, pp. 69–70.
[2] Figures for 1700 from *House of Lords MSS.*, New Series, v. 69–70. Others from Macpherson, *op. cit.*, vols. ii and iii.

industry which grew up around Bradford was not a new national asset; it was an expansion made largely by outrivalling the East Anglian worsted manufacturer. Similarly, the increase in the output of ordinary woollen goods in Yorkshire was made at the expense of the woollen areas of Lancashire, the Midlands, East Anglia, and the West of England. Thus, though there might be no extraordinary increase in the national production of cloth, Yorkshire was developing very rapidly by appropriating to herself a larger proportion of the cloth manufacture of the nation, and was preparing for the still greater progress which the Industrial Revolution was to bring. For this assumption of supremacy the West Riding was peculiarly equipped, both before and after the advent of steam. The facilities which existed for the use of water had been of great value from the earliest times in influencing the settlement and progress of the industry in the valleys of West Yorkshire. The legion of fulling mills could never have existed but for the abundant supply of water. Now, in the eighteenth century, when water power was being utilized for grinding logwood and working machines of various kinds, even the most insignificant little mountain brook was of service, and the ubiquity of water was a valuable natural asset to the industry. Then, when the Industrial Revolution came along, a giant of iron and coal, all the materials for the new machinery and for the power to drive that machinery were found near the existing seat of the industry. The West Riding had water power at hand so long as water power was needed; but when steam came to be the motive force, and iron the material of which machines were made, iron and coal were at the very door. Hence there was no necessity for an extensive migration, and the industry remained in its former place, though of course more concentrated in certain centres.

As already indicated, the outstanding feature of Yorkshire's textile development during the eighteenth century was the growth of the worsted manufacture. It is necessary, therefore, to turn our attention to this aspect of the story, and trace the rise of this new branch of the trade. First, however, let us make quite clear the general difference between worsteds and woollens, and note briefly the technical distinctions between the two types of cloth. The following description is quite inapplicable to modern conditions, for the developments in textile knowledge, machinery, and procedure have entirely transformed the technique of the two industries, and effected a revolution in the possible uses to which the various kinds of wool can be put. Whatever, therefore, is said here must be regarded as referring only to the old hand days.

The wool fibre differs from hair and some other fibres in two respects. Firstly, it is waved and curly, and tends to twist round anything with which it comes in contact. Secondly, under the microscope, wool shows its edges to be covered with scales or serrations, somewhat like the edge of a saw, or like a fir-cone, if one could imagine such a cone with parallel edges. These serrations all point the same way, and hence whilst the wool is on the sheep's back, and the fibres all lie the same way, they have no opportunity of interlocking. But if the various fibres are placed across each other, or in any way thrown out of a parallel arrangement, interlocking takes place. Not merely do the wavy fibres curl round each other, but under pressure the serrations of one fibre hook on to those of neighbouring strands. This process is known as *felting*; by it the various threads lose their identity, and become mixed and entangled in a homogeneous mass of wool, the strength of which depends not merely upon that of each separate fibre, but also on the grip which the threads have taken upon each other in the matted texture. The process of felting is always accompanied by a shrinkage in the volume of the wool, popularly known as ' running up '.[1]

Thanks to this felting property, wool can be made into cloth the strength of which comes not from the firmness of its warp and weft, but rather from the completeness with which the fibres comprising warp and weft become interlocked and entangled when submitted to the necessary treatment. As the felting is accompanied by shrinkage in dimensions, the resultant fabric is thicker, firmer, and stronger than when woven. It is no

[1] The details such as are here given can be obtained from any technological work on the textile industry. See especially McLaren, *Spinning Woollen and Worsted* (1884) ; E. Baines, paper on ' Woollen Manufactures of England ', read before the British Association at Leeds, 1858 ; Clapham, *Woollen and Worsted Industries* (1907) ; Bean, *On the Wool Track* (1913).

longer possible to distinguish the separate threads of warp and weft amidst the maze of interwoven fibres, and hence the cloth does not unravel at the edge or end.   This type of cloth is known as *woollen*; it is comparatively rough in texture; little ends of fine fibres protrude from the surface, and can be seized and pulled out with one's fingers or a pair of pincers.

On the other hand, cloth can be made which largely neglects the strength given by felting, but relies almost entirely on the strength of weft and warp.   For certain kinds of cloth a smooth surface is required, approaching that obtained on silk and cotton goods.   In order to achieve this effect, the cloth must be made of yarn which is firm, even, and smooth.   Such yarn would by reason of its smoothness have no protruding fibres, and be unsuited for felting.   It must therefore be strong enough to give the cloth firmness and durability without seeking the aid of felting.   In short, if the yarn must be smooth, the cloth loses a great part of that strength which comes from interlocked serrations, and this strength must be supplied by using a stronger yarn.   Such cloth is known as *worsted*, and the navy blue serge so extensively used for men's suitings to-day is an excellent type of the whole class.   Smooth, firm, and even in texture, it has almost a glossy appearance in a bright light, and the gloss becomes more pronounced with wear.   A piece of worsted unravels at the end, and the thread which comes out is seen to be quite firm and strong.

The essential difference between woollens and worsteds lies therefore in the character of the yarn used.   For the woollen, the wavy and serrated properties of the fibres must be utilized to the utmost in making the fibres into yarn and in fitting the yarn for interlacing with neighbouring threads.   For the worsted, the fibres must be made into a strong thread, whose felting proclivities are ignored or actually repressed.   Before the Industrial Revolution, differences in the character of the yarn depended partly upon the character of the wool used and partly upon the processes through which the wool passed prior to spinning.   Short-fibred wool was used for woollen yarn, long-fibred for worsted; the former was carded, the latter combed.   Short-fibred wools were more curly than long, and therefore were more easily entangled.   This cohesive faculty was accentuated by carding, in which the fibres were converted into a maze by being worked between two boards covered with wire spikes. The fibres were crossed and doubled over each other in every possible direction, and the handful of wool was thus held together by the interlocking of the serrations and the curling of one fibre round another. When the carded wool was spun, the twist given increased the cohesiveness of the tangled material, whilst the loose ends of fibres which protruded offered further facilities for the rough yarn to interlace itself with adjacent weft and warp.

Whilst the aim of carding was to arrange the fibres in as con-fused a manner as possible, combing was intended to lay all the threads in the same direction. The long-fibred wool could more easily be kept straight than the short, and combing increased this straightness. Combing achieved two things. It extracted from amongst the long fibres any short ones which might be present, the latter by reason of their greater curl twisting round the teeth of the comb : at the same time it gave all the long fibres a similar parallel direction. There were now no crossed fibres, no fibres running contrary ways, and therefore scarcely any interlocking. The combed wool when spun therefore depended for its strength upon the natural firmness of the fibres, plus that given by twisting them altogether.

Perhaps the accompanying diagrams (see p. 263) will help to make the foregoing explanation more clear.

The difference in treatment of the material continued after weaving. With one or two exceptions, all woollen cloths were fulled, in which process the fibres of warp and weft, under pressure and moisture, interlocked still more thoroughly, giving a compact piece of material. Worsteds needed no such treat-ment.

The establishment of a worsted industry in Yorkshire there-fore meant the introduction of one new process in the existing woollen industry, i. e. combing. From the account of the law-suit of 1638 it appears that the long wools of Lincolnshire and

---

[1] Modern conditions in the woollen and worsted industries are very different from those described above. To-day, short wool can be combed, long wool is sometimes carded, and much worsted wool is carded before it is combed. Further, some worsteds are now milled in order to obtain greater firmness, whilst some woollens are not milled. See McLaren, *op. cit.*, chap. iv.

Leicestershire were being used for the manufacture of kerseys, and were presumably carded. All that was required was to replace carders of that wool by combers—by no means an easy task. Combing required a considerable measure of skill, and the necessary body of skilled wool-combers could only be obtained gradually. Further, Yorkshire worsted cloths would have to bear the competition of similar fabrics from the traditional centres of the industry. How the West Riding confronted these two difficulties we must now see.

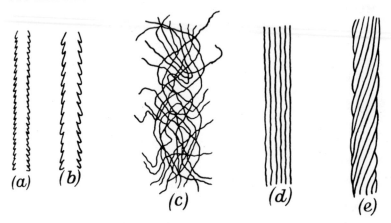

(a) Merino fibre, showing serrations.
(b) Lincoln fibre, showing serrations.
(c) Carded wool, showing entangled arrangement of fibres.
(d) Combed wool, showing fibres lying parallel.
(e) Worsted yarn, showing, in exaggerated form, the smoothness of surface.

The Rise of the Worsted Industry in the West Riding

The manufacture of worsteds in England dates back to at least the middle of the thirteenth century. Worsted cloths were exported from Boston in 1302,[1] and in 1315 formed a sufficiently important article of commerce to be placed on a list of commodities on which Hartlepool was allowed to claim port tolls.[2] By 1329 the manufacture of ' cloths of Worstede ' was large enough to need regulations for the prevention of fraudulent workmanship.[3] The industry developed most rapidly in East

[1] See Lipson, *op. cit.*, chapter on the woollen industry, for early evidences ; also Salzmann, *op. cit.*, p. 139.
[2] *Registrum Palatinum Dunelm.* (Rolls Series), iv. 124.
[3] Ashley, *Economic History*, I. ii. 206.

Anglia, and from the sixteenth to the eighteenth century Norfolk and the eastern counties were easily foremost in the worsted trade. Norwich was one of the largest, most wealthy, and handsome towns in the kingdom ; ' an ancient, rich and populous city ', said Defoe,[1] and Arthur Young described it as follows : ' In Norfolk we see a face of diligence spread over the whole country. The vast manufactures carried on chiefly by the Norwich weavers employ all the country around in spinning yarn for them, besides many thousand packs of yarn which they receive from other countries, even so far as Yorkshire and Westmorland.'[2] Norwich was, in the seventeenth and early eighteenth centuries, the ' Worstedopolis ' which Bradford has since become. Its prosperity continued until about the sixties of the eighteenth century, when the competition of the north and the general adoption of new and lighter fashions began to bring about its decline.

Other centres and localities had risen into prominence during the centuries, and in 1700 Exeter was famous for its serges,[3] Canterbury and Colchester made good ' says ', Coventry was doing a large trade in ' tammies ', and many smaller places were centres of some branch of the manufacture, thriving and populous.

When did the industry settle in the northern parts, and find a home in the West Riding ? Briefly, the answer is that the making of worsteds was taken up in Yorkshire almost as soon as in East Anglia, but was apparently forsaken during the sixteenth century in favour of the staple kerseys and dozens. During the Stuart régime fitful attempts were made to reestablish the manufacture, but it was not until nearly 1700 that West Riding manufacturers seriously turned their attention to shalloons, says, and tammies. From that time onwards the industry progressed, though at first only slowly, and by 1770 was large enough to be a most formidable rival of East Anglia.

The coverlets or ' chalons ' mentioned so frequently in the first chapter were worsted cloths. As we saw, their manufacture

---

[1] Defoe, *op. cit.*, 1763 edition, i. 59–64.
[2] Arthur Young, *Eastern Tour*, 1771, ii. 76.
[3] Smith's *Memoirs of Wool*, i. 204. Defoe, *Tour*, 1727 edition, i. 323, points out that the serge market at Exeter was, next to the Leeds market, the largest cloth market in England.

was carried on in many parts of the county during the fourteenth century, and York had its gild of coverlet weavers by about 1400. But this branch of cloth-making never attracted any great amount of attention : possibly the difficulty of getting supplies of long-fibred wool impeded its progress. Hence, whilst woollens flourished, worsteds languished. The coverlet weavers of York in 1543 made their famous protest against the competition of the country weavers, and had their monopoly over the industry confirmed. But their own production was very small, whilst that of the country chaloners was probably reduced considerably by the Act of 1543. Thus we find from a document dated 1595 that at the end of the century the manufacture of coverlets or any other kind of worsted goods in the county was very small indeed. During the sixteenth century the varieties of worsteds, which came under the heading of ' New Draperies ', had been increasing rapidly, especially after the influx of refugees into East Anglia during the Reformation period. These new draperies were not brought under the control of the ulnager until 1594, when the ulnage of new draperies was farmed out to Sir George Delves and William Fitzwilliam for twenty-one years.[1] The farmers at once set out to investigate the probable yield of their investment, and requested a certain Peck to draw up an account of the extent to which new draperies were being made in Yorkshire. Peck's report, or rather as it is endorsed, ' My Brother Peck's Certificate of New Draperies in the Countie of Yorke ', is a most interesting and illuminating document.[2] It shows that only a very small quantity of such draperies was being produced in the county, and the figures which it contains indicate that the farmers of the ulnage could not expect to reap a fortune from the manufacturers of the West Riding. The chief articles of manufacture which came under the scope of Peck's inquiry were ' cushions ', of which Bradford and Halifax together made less than 3,400 yearly, coverlets and carpets, of which York made a few, and knitted stockings, which were made in large quantities at Doncaster, Richmond, and throughout the North Riding. Of worsted cloths proper there is no mention, apart from the few coverlets,

[1] Originalia Rolls, 36 Eliz., part iii, July 13.
[2] D. S. P., Eliz., cclii. 2.

and thus by 1600 that industry had almost disappeared from the West Riding. According to the Yorkshire wills of the sixteenth century, worsted fabrics were occasionally used for garments, but whether the cloth was made in the county or not there is no indication. The inventory of John Pawson, the Leeds clothier, dated 1576 (quoted in Chapter III), notes the possession of 'vij paire of woll combes', but all the cloths on his premises were woollens, not worsteds. During the subsequent years visitors to Bradford are equally silent concerning the existence of any worsted trade in the town or neighbourhood. A traveller in 1639 declared that Bradford was 'a towne that makes great store of Turkey cushions and carpetts',[1] articles which were 'new draperies', but which can scarcely be regarded as forerunners of the great industry which was subsequently to develop there. Thus, up to the end of the Commonwealth, the clothiers of the West Riding were still engaged almost solely in making the old staple cloths, kerseys, pennistones, broad cloths, and northern dozens.

Meanwhile the worsted industry was receiving the attention of certain other inhabitants of the county. We have already noticed the attempts made by the municipal authorities of York to establish the manufacture of 'Norwich stuffes', in order to find employment for their poor people. This seems to have been a popular idea with many Yorkshire Poor Law authorities, who hoped by the introduction of a new industry to solve the problem of pauperism. In 1652 the North Riding justices of the peace drew up a similar scheme for the House of Correction at Pickering.[2] The details of this scheme are interesting in the light which they threw on the position of the worsted industry in Yorkshire at that time. The plan was drawn up 'for setting persons to work on spinning and knitting woolen drapery in the House of Correction . . . and instructing them in the art of weaving such searges as are the most usual manufacture of the weavers of the Eastern counties'. The pupils were to be drawn from those who had been incarcerated in the House for wandering or idle loitering, and also such other persons as were able

---

[1] *Journal of John Aston*, 1639, Surtees Soc., vol. cxviii, p. 30. See also *Life of Marmaduke Rawdon*, Camden Soc. publications, vol. lxxxv, p. 121.

[2] Order Book of the J.P.'s of the North Riding, April 1652, printed in *Hist. MSS. Comm.*, ix. 331–2.

and willing to work, provided they came between the ages of seven and sixty, and were 'not decrepitt'. The inmates were to be employed at the occupation for which the North Riding was noted, namely 'knittinge and spinninge both wollen and Jersey, and all woollen drapery, makin stockins of wollen and Jersey'. But at the same time, the House was to enlist the services of 'a sufficient able woolcomber, who shall likewise instruct others in the same faculty'. Further, whilst the comber initiated his disciples into one branch of the worsted manufacture, the master of the House was at the same time to 'setle and employe one lowme sufficiently and well wrought by a worsted weaver for Searges of the best sorts . . . such as are most usually manufactured in Norwig, Norfolke and Suffolke'. The home of punishment was to become also the training college for a new industry. The project achieved no lasting success, nor did the North Riding become the centre of a flourishing worsted manufacture. East Anglia still retained its virtual monopoly of the industry, and the most that Yorkshire could do was to prepare and spin yarn, which was then carried south to feed the looms of Norwich and the surrounding counties.

During the last four decades of the seventeenth century a gradual change came over the scene, as the industry once more began to find a home in the West Riding. How exactly this transformation took place one cannot say. James [1] suggests that the industry may have been imported direct from East Anglia by the settlement of southern merchants and manufacturers in a county where land and labour were cheaper, where there was freedom from regulations and restrictions such as existed in the Norwich area, as well as from the labour troubles which frequently harassed East Anglian masters. Or it may have been that some enterprising inhabitants of the West Riding, finding the trade in woollens at a standstill, turned their attention from kerseys and broad cloths to serges and shalloons, and either forsook woollens entirely, or ran both manufactures together in double harness. Probably both these courses were adopted. Norfolk merchants and manufacturers had been putting out wool to be spun in Yorkshire, and had then taken the yarn back to East Anglia for further treatment. Why not

[1] James, *op. cit.*, p. 200.

transplant the whole of their industry to Yorkshire and have all the processes of combing, spinning, and weaving carried out by north country labour?   At the same time, Yorkshire clothiers, yeomen farmers, and merchants began to turn their attention to the possibility of improving their outlook by a change in policy.   The districts around Bradford and Halifax had suffered severely during the Civil War, and their trade in cheap cloth had been seriously injured by the various depressive influences which we have already noted.   The foreign nations had begun to make their own cheap cloths, and were ceasing to purchase the wares of Yorkshire.   There seemed little prospect of much future development in the manufacture of kerseys and other such low-priced fabrics.   Very well; why not abandon the manufacture of such commodities, and turn to other branches of the trade in which other countries were still unoccupied; in short, why not manufacture worsted cloths, as did the men of Norwich?

This change occurred during the latter years of the seventeenth century and the first two or three decades of the eighteenth. All the earliest evidence concerning worsted workers clusters round this period.   The first step seems to have been to make bays, cloths which were half wool, half worsted—the warp being of combed wool, the weft of carded.   In 1688 the output of bays in Yorkshire was sufficiently great to justify the inclusion of this fabric in a short list of cloths on which subsidy and ulnage were paid.[1]   Eighteen years later we find Joseph Holroyd,[2] a cloth factor who lived near Halifax, engaged in a large trade in bays.   Holroyd made big purchases for London and foreign merchants, and his letters for the years 1706-7 show him to be buying heavily in all varieties of bays both for London and the Low Countries.   Consignments of 40 pieces are quite common, and one invoice mentions the purchase of 250 such cloths for a big customer in Rotterdam.   There is no evidence in the letters as to the manufacture of full worsteds, but from other sources we know that serges and shalloons were now being made in many parts.   Watson, in his *History of Halifax* (1775) states that ' The Shalloon trade was introduced here about the

---

[1] *House of Lords MSS., Hist. MSS. Comm.*, xiv, pt. vi, p. 42.
[2] *Letter Books of J. Holroyd and S. Hill* (Halifax, 1914), Intro., and letter 34.

beginning of the century'.[1]   From an indenture of apprenticeship dated March 1, 1715, we learn that a certain James Haggas
was bound apprentice with John Jackson of Halifax,[2] to learn
the art of weaving shalloons, the type of worsted for which the
Halifax district eventually became famous.   Obviously, therefore, by 1715 there were men in the Halifax area busy at work
as fully fledged masters of the craft.   Similar evidence from
other parts is abundant.   A 'Searge Weaver' who resided in
Marsh Lane, Leeds, was brought before the Leeds justices in
1705;[3] wool-combers were numerous in the same town about
1710, and in 1721 Mr. Thomas Jackman, worsted comber, paid
his five guineas and was admitted to the freedom of the Corporation of Leeds.[4]   In the Skipton parish register, wool-combers
are mentioned in 1717, and the Keighley register records the
death of a shalloon maker in 1724, and a woolcomb maker in
1725.[5]   Denholme and Haworth were now flourishing worsted
centres; Keighley was regularly sending pieces of shalloon to
London before 1725, and when Defoe came north, about the
same year, he found the manufacture established in many parts,
but especially around Halifax, where at every house he saw
a 'tenter and on almost every tenter a piece of cloth, kersie or
shalloon, which are the three articles of this countrie's labour'.[6]

From this time onwards the growth was rapid, though in some
cases fitful and subject to strong opposition and keen discouragement.   That at least was the experience of Sam Hill, a clothier
in the Halifax district, who in 1737–8 turned his attention from
kerseys to shalloons.   A fragment of Hill's letter-book, covering
only three weeks, is extant, and gives a vivid idea of the difficulties to be overcome.   Hill apparently decided to develop
a trade in shalloons, Bocking Bays and Exeter Long Ells, and
so began to solicit the buyers of his kerseys to take a few worsteds
as well.   The response was far from satisfactory, and at first those
who took Hill's shalloons and bays found it difficult to get rid
of them.   At times Hill grew weary at the non-success which

[1] *Op. cit.*, pp. 67–9.
[2] See Dawson, *Loose Leaves of Craven History*, p. 20.
[3] *Leeds Sessions Records*, ii. 293.
[4] *Leeds Corp. Records*, ii. 176. See also *Sessions Orders*, ii. 561 and 627.
[5] Keighley and Holmes, *Keighley Past and Present*, p. 105.
[6] Defoe's *Tour* (1727 edition), iii. 134–5.

attended his efforts. 'Am perfectly sick of the little or no hopes of the Shalloon Bussiness ',[1] he writes to one customer, and to another he declares, 'Am much concerned to hear you have not any Trade for Shalloons pray you as soon as possible revive me with the Contrary '.[2] Hill struggled hard to gain greater skill and experience ; he experimented with different varieties, wrote eager requests to his customers for information and advice, sent samples, and strove hard to imitate in quality and appearance the worsteds of Norwich and Exeter. Amid all his worries, Hill was buoyed up by his immense confidence— one almost wrote conceit. Witness the following extracts from his letters : 'I am studying to outdo all England with the sort Sam Hill [shalloons] if quality and price will do it ... but must earnestly beg of you to lett them go for a small profit however till they be known.'[3] 'I like to make [Shalloons and Long Ells] and fancy I shall in time doe It well.'[4] 'I will send you the 6 pieces Shaloon which shall be such as never was sent to Leeds at that price.'[5] 'The narrow Shaloons . . . are I think such goods as I may say are not to be out done in England by any Man, let Him be who He will (I don't value).'[6] So Hill plodded on : the competition from the older fields of industry was terribly keen, but he was not daunted. In the darkest hour, when reports from his customers were very bad, he boldly declared, 'I think it now evident these Manufactories [Bocking Bays and Exeter Serges] will come in spite of fate into these northern Countrys '.[7] A true prophecy, for within fifty years Yorkshire had usurped the position of supremacy and become the stronghold of the industry.

By 1750 the industry was widespread throughout the Riding, and shalloons, calimancoes, tammies, camlets, &c., were made so far east as Leeds and Wakefield. Of the industrial centres, Halifax[8] was the most important in the output of worsteds. The greatness of the town was twofold ; it was alike a worsted and woollen centre. The demands for cloth for the troops in the various wars of the eighteenth century were met by the

---

[1] *Letters Books, Holroyd and Hill,* no. 102.
[2] Ibid., no. 135   [3] Ibid., no. 112.   [4] Ibid., no. 116.
[5] Ibid., no. 130.   [6] Ibid., no. 133.   [7] Ibid.
[8] Halifax population, 1738, 5,500 ; 1775, 7,500.

supply of Halifax kerseys, i.e. woollens. The North Sea trade in these cloths grew to such an extent that Defoe noted a Halifax factor who traded by commission to the extent of £60,000 per annum in kerseys alone.[1] On the other hand the worsted trade was very considerable, and Defoe estimated that the parish of Halifax was producing 100,000 pieces of shalloons yearly.[2] Spain, Portugal, Italy, and the Levant were markets for Halifax wares, and a trade with Guinea was being developed in ' Says ' of a strong blue shade. ' These last were packed in pieces of $12\frac{1}{2}$ yards in length, wrapped in an oilcloth painted with negroes and elephants to captivate the natives.'[3] To the busy market, or to the Cloth Hall erected by Viscount Irwin, was brought the produce of the parish itself, Keighley, Haworth, and Colne, and merchants from Leeds, or their factors, came and bought great quantities of white undressed cloths, which they exported to Holland and Hamburg.[4] The position of Halifax was there-fore that of a powerful centre for a widely scattered district, and it seemed quite possible that Halifax would forge ahead as the metropolis of the worsted industry. That it lost that supre-macy to Bradford is a matter the causes of which we cannot stay to consider. It is one of the strange incidents in the history of the West Riding that a town which had been supreme in the woollen industry, and then in the worsted, should fall from that position as Halifax did with the coming of the Industrial Revolution.

Wakefield, which was the second most important worsted centre, enjoyed a period of great prosperity during the eighteenth century. It had long been engaged in the woollen industry, and now took to itself the manufacture of ' tammies ', a thin worsted fabric, a glazed variety of which was used for window-blinds and curtains, with a considerable sale both at home and abroad.[5] The opening of the Aire and Calder navigation in 1699[6] and the following years brought enormous wealth and trade to the town, for the long wool of Lincolnshire and Leicestershire, the very heart's desire of the worsted maker, was now brought by boat

---

[1] Defoe, *op. cit.*, 1762 edition, iii. 139. Also Dodsley's *Road Book*, 1756.
[2] Defoe, *op. cit.*, iii. 139.
[3] Pennant, *Tour in Scotland*, 1770 (1776 edition), iii. 362.
[4] *Halifax and its Gibbet Law*, by Wm. Bentley, 1708, p. 27.
[5] *Brit. Assoc. Handbook*, Leeds, 1890, p. 144 n. Also James, *op. cit.*, p. 265.
[6] See Chapter XI, section on communications.

up the Calder, to be sold in the busy market at Wakefield. Wool growers and dealers forwarded wool from all parts of England to the factors at Wakefield, who had then little difficulty in disposing of it over the vast industrial field situated to the west and north of that town. Wakefield therefore figured largely as an emporium for raw materials. In addition to this, it was also a growing market for cloths, and in the production of tammies it gradually stole from Coventry its monopoly of that fabric. In the Tammy Hall,[1] built in 1766, these worsted pieces changed hands, and the Hall became one of the most important centres of trade in the county. Further, Wakefield was becoming important as a ' dressing ' and ' finishing ' town [2]; undyed and unfinished goods were sent there for further treatment, before their final dispatch to London and the Continent. And, whilst an important textile centre, Wakefield had become a great corn market. Large supplies of corn were brought up the Calder, and many people declared that Wakefield was the ' greatest corn market in the North of England '. Such a town was naturally the abode of wool-factors, wool-staplers, merchants, dyers, corn-dealers, &c., in addition to the official class, which was already there in considerable numbers. Here were many warehouses for cloth, corn, and wool, and so far had the mammon of unrighteousness invaded the place that even the little chantry chapel on the bridge had succumbed, and ' had been converted into a warehouse which was let to an old cloath's man, who used it as a warehouse for goods '.[3] The general appearance of the town seems to have been very pleasing to the various travellers who have left on record their impressions. ' A town exceedingly populous, upon account of the great number of hands it employs in the woollen manufacture ' [4]; ' an opulent and handsome town ' [5]; ' one of the most wealthy and genteel of the clothing towns of Yorkshire ' [6]; ' the handsomest of the trading towns in the West Riding ' [7]—such were the verdicts of four tourists, and the fame of this town, with its clean but narrow streets, its

[1] James, *History of the Worsted Manufacture*, p. 265.
[2] Arthur Young, *Northern Tour*, i. 151.
[3] Defoe, *op. cit.*, iii. 112.
[4] Oxford's Journey, *Portland MSS.*, vi. 142.
[5] Housman, *Topographical Description . . . of the West Riding* (1800), p. 183.
[6] Edmund Dayes, *Works* (1805 edition), p. 35.
[7] *England Described*, by Aikin (1818), p. 61.

elegant houses, its pleasant buildings, cheap food, and abundance of social life, still kept for it the title of ' Merrie Wakefield '.[1]

Of Bradford it is difficult to gather much. We have already
noted its depopulation and the decay of the small woollen
trade which had flourished there, and there can be no doubt
that the fortunes of Bradford had sunk to a very low ebb.
Whenever petitions were forwarded to Parliament concerning
the woollen trade, Halifax, Wakefield, Leeds, and Huddersfield
made their voices heard, but never Bradford. Only very
slowly did the worsted manufacture establish itself there ;
hence Defoe, who knew Yorkshire very well, treated the town
in a most cursory manner, declaring that it had become a market,
but was ' of no other note than having been the birthplace of
Dr. Sharp, the good Archbishop of York '.[2] In 1752 it began
the construction of the canal which joined it to the Leeds and
Liverpool Canal ; in 1773 it obtained a Piece Hall, and in the
nineties one or two mills were erected there. Its expansion
had been considerable between 1740 and the end of the century,
but it was still only a small town, with a population in 1780 of
about 4,200.[3] Even in 1818 Dr. Aikin, in his *England Described*,
devoted only seven lines to Bradford as against thirty to Halifax.
Its reputation was bad, if we can gather anything from the
frequent legislation against frauds committed by workers in
worsted, or from the following somewhat damaging verse in an
eighteenth-century Methodist hymn : [4]

> On Bradford likewise look Thou down
>   Where Satan keeps his seat.

This insignificance of Bradford is partly to be accounted for
by the fact that the industry grew up scattered over the whole
of the district round about, and was not concentrated in the
town itself. Again, Leeds and Wakefield were of considerable
size, either because they were the abodes of merchants, middle-

---

[1] In a letter printed in *Old Yorkshire*, i. 13, and dated 1766, it is stated that
the Calder was so clear at Wakefield that salmon were to be seen leaping the
dam stakes at Kirkgate.

[2] Defoe, *op. cit.*, 1762 edition, iii. 145. Also 1748 edition, iii. 147.

[3] This figure is quoted and accepted by all Bradford local historians, e.g.
J. W. Turner, *Bradford Antiquary* (1884), i. 135.

[4] Verse 38 of a hymn with 104 verses, ' The progress of the Gospel in Yorkshire and other parts ', 1751, by Wm. Darney.

men, &c., or because they were finishing centres. Thus their
population was either largely concerned with marketing transactions, inns, and offices, or consisted of men engaged in the
dyeing, dressing, shearing, and other finishing processes. Now
Bradford was, until the latter part of the century, only a small
market, and not a finishing centre. The goods were bought
there ' in the white ' [1] by Leeds merchants, and then taken
down to Leeds to be finished before export.[2] It was not until
the last years of the eighteenth century, and the advent of
steam power and machinery, that Bradford really began to
make rapid progress. In the adoption and improvement of
machinery, and in the manufacture of new types of wares, men
of Bradford showed great enterprise, and enabled the town to
outstrip Halifax. Further, the linking up of Bradford with the
Leeds and Liverpool Canal gave to the town greatly improved
means of communication. This ease of access was further
developed to Bradford's advantage when the railway, especially
the Midland Railway, brought Bradford almost on to the main
line, whilst Halifax remained more or less isolated. Halifax
was then left wide of the main arteries of traffic, its importance
diminished, and Bradford rapidly assumed the position of
metropolis of the new industry.[3]

Even Leeds, stalwart heart of the woollen body, was partly
captured by worsteds. Arthur Young in 1770 [4] noted that in
addition to broad cloths there were ' some shalloons and many
other stuffs, particularly Scotch camblets, grograms, and calimancoes, etc.', manufactured in and around Leeds. The ' camblet ' was the chief of these, and consisted of a rough, thick,
worsted material, which was considered especially valuable for
resisting rain, and was therefore used to a great extent in the
making of cloaks and wraps for those who were travelling by
coach ; it also formed the customary dress material of the poorer
classes of women.[5] The substitution of lighter cloths, the adop-

---

[1] i.e. undyed and unfinished.

[2] This was the case until well into the nineteenth century. About 1840
Bradford goods began to be finished on the spot.

[3] Population of Bradford (town) : 1780, 4,200 ; 1801, 6,393 ; 1831, 23,233 ;
1851, 52,501.

[4] Arthur Young, *op. cit.*, i. 152.

[5] *Reminiscences of an Octogenarian*, by Henry Hall, of the firm of Clapham
and Hall ; printed in James, *op. cit.*, p. 311.

tion of the macintosh, and the growth of the railroad rendered the camlet unfashionable, and Leeds remained true to its first love, the woollen.

With these and other towns as its strongholds, the worsted industry grew steadily throughout the century. It had its years of bad trade and of good,[1] it lost old markets and gained new ones.[2] It gradually won from the more southerly manufacturers the monopoly or predominance which they had formerly enjoyed. The tammies of Wakefield replaced those of Coventry, the serges of Exeter fought in vain against the growing popularity of Halifax and Bradford wares, and East Anglia, far from claiming the yarn of Yorkshire spinners for its looms, was soon content to send north some of the yarn spun in its own homes.[3] From Arthur Young [4] and from the Report of a Parliamentary Committee in 1774 [5] we can gather the relative position of east and north about 1770. Eighteenth century statistics can seldom be taken as accurate ; they are often little more than estimates based on a few facts and a host of suppositions. Still if we do not treat them as being perfectly accurate, the general position can be ascertained.

Output of WORSTEDS for WEST RIDING in 1772=£1,404,000
    (committee's figures).
Output of WORSTEDS for NORWICH area in 1770=£1,200,000
    (Arthur Young).

Thus the West Riding produce at least equalled that of Norwich by 1770. Again, James and others estimated that about 80,000 persons were employed in the industry of the West Riding. Young gives the corresponding figure for Norwich as 72,000,[6] and thus in terms of employees, as well as in quantity of output, Yorkshire had won a high position even before the great changes came to accelerate its progress.

[1] 1764–80 had many years of bad trade. Agitations, disorders, charitable doles, &c., figure in the records of the times. See Newspapers, Mayhall's *Annals*, vol. i, and Arthur Young. 1783–93 comprised the hey-day of Yorkshire's industrial prosperity in the eighteenth century.

[2] The Napoleonic Wars made trade with Western Europe unsafe. Still in 1793 Halifax was exporting thousands of pieces of shalloons to the Levant and Turkey (*Brit. Dir.*, 1793, iii. 320).

[3] James, *op. cit.*, p. 307. Also Arthur Young, *Eastern Tour*, ii. 76. Young says that the great day of Norwich was 1749–60.

[4] Arthur Young, *Eastern Tour*, ii. 76 et seq.

[5] This report is printed in both James, pp. 280–4, and Bischoff, *Wool, Woollens, and Sheep*, i. 186–90.   [6] Arthur Young, *Eastern Tour*, ii. 76.

There was considerable intercourse between the northern worsted area and that of East Anglia during the century. Partnerships were occasionally formed between Yorkshiremen and inhabitants of Norfolk, as for instance, ' the co-partnership between Mr. John Hodgson of Leeds, woolstapler, and Messrs. Joseph Ames and John Roe of Norwich ', which was dissolved in 1757.[1] Also in matters of general interest to the trade the two districts worked in unison, joining in petitions to Parliament whenever their prospects were in danger, and after the formation of the Worsted Committees in Yorkshire and East Anglia these two committees kept in constant correspondence until the demise of the Norfolk industry.

Progress of the Woollen Industry during the Eighteenth Century

Meanwhile the woollen industry had been pursuing a similar career, though its progress was perhaps more slow and fitful. The home demand was proportionately reduced by the adoption of worsteds and cottons, and Sam Hill in 1737 declared that ' the encrease of the Bocking Bayse makeing I doe realy believe causes one third fewer kerseys to be made '.[2] The foreign market was subject to all the vicissitudes of eighteenth century wars and enmities. The series of commercial wars, chiefly with France, placed foreign trade in a position of unstable equilibrium. First one section and then another of the foreign market was closed to English wares, whilst the growth of textile industries abroad and the smuggling of wool helped to cause acute depressions at various stages in the century. In 1742, for instance, the Leeds Corporation was bewailing the fact that ' trade and manufactures are every day declining ', and attributed it to the illicit exportation of wool.[3] Nine years later, the merchants and clothiers of Leeds asked Parliament to approach the Austrian Government with a view to removing the recent heavy duties, which were said to have closed the Low Countries to Yorkshire cloths.[4] In 1756 the same petitioners complained of the recent decrees of the Regent of Hanover that all Hanoverian troops, who had formerly been clad in Yorkshire cloth, should hereafter

[1] *Leedes Intelligencer*, August 9, 1757.
[2] *Letter Books*, no. 124.
[3] Wardell, *Municipal History of Leeds*, p. 74.
[4] Add. MSS., 15873, f. 70, November 19, 1751.

wear Hanoverian fabrics only.[1] The growth of clothmaking in
the German States was a constant source of uneasiness to
English dealers, who were afraid that one of their best markets
would slip from their grasp.[2] The Yorkshire cloths were especially
suited for military garments, and had enjoyed the favour of
many European Governments until the rise of the native industries dispensed with the need for the imported article.   The
policy of Peter the Great had definitely aimed at the cultivation
of a textile industry in Russia,[3] in order to supply the requirements of his armies.   Hence the Yorkshire clothiers had to fight
hard to maintain a hold on the European markets, and their
trade with the Continent was subject to all manner of vicissitudes.

Yorkshire had also built up a considerable trade with North
America, and hence the war with the colonies brought about
a temporary slump in the sale of woollens.   The years 1771–3
had been gloomy, with bad harvests, dear food, and depression
in trade.   Then came the American War, which closed a valuable
market against the clothiers and merchants.   The extent of the
consequent depression is seen in an interesting letter written by
John Wesley, dated August 23, 1775 :

' I aver that in every part of England where I have been (and
I have been east, west, north, and south within these two years)
trade in general is exceedingly decayed, and thousands of people
are quite unemployed.   Some I know to have perished for want
of bread ; others I have seen walking up and down like shadows.
I have seen three or four manufacturing towns which have
suffered less than others.   Even where I was last, in the West
Riding of Yorkshire, a tenant of Lord Dartmouth was telling me
" Sir, our tradesmen are breaking all around me, so that I know
not what the end will be."   Even in Leeds I had appointed to
dine at a merchant's, but before I came the bailiffs were in
possession of the house.   Upon my saying " I thought Mr. . . . .
had been in good circumstances ", I was answered " He *was* so,
but the American War has ruined him." ' [4]

---

[1] Add. MSS. 32863, ff. 259–60, March 1756.
[2] Home Office Papers, November 16, 1764.
[3] Clive Day, *A History of Commerce*, chaps. 27 and 44.   Also 1806 **Report,**
iii. 373.
[4] *Dartmouth MSS., Hist. MSS. Comm.*, Report 15, app. i, vol. iii, p. 220.
Also *Parl. Rep.*, 1806, iii. 163, speaks of depression in latter years of American
War.   In 1774 a Parliamentary Committee made inquiry into the depression
in the county.   It found trade depressed, wages down, and the Poor Law

Foreign trade in the eighteenth century was no easy highway to success ; and yet in spite of all these obstacles the Yorkshire woollen trade made magnificent headway, progress which seems almost incredible in the light of the difficulties outlined above, but as to the reality of which there can be no possible doubt. The proof is of a reliable official character. In 1725[1] Parliament ordered the examination and registration of all the broad cloths manufactured in the West Riding. In 1738 [2] the same regulation was extended to narrow cloths, whilst after 1768 the length of each piece was also noted, as the cloths were being made of various lengths. The registers were added up annually, a report was presented to the Quarter Sessions at Pontefract, and then made public. The figures were common property, and were well known to all writers of the period. Arthur Young quotes them to 1770,[3] and the local directories of Leeds bring them up to 1800 and even beyond. The statistics present ' an Account of the Number of [Broad or Narrow] Cloths Milled at the several Fulling Mills in the West Riding of the County of York '.

Broad Cloths.			Narrow Cloths.	
No. of Pieces.	Yards.	Year.	No. of Pieces.	Yards.
28,990		1727		
31,579½		1730		
31,744½		1735		
41,441		1740	58,620	
50,453		1745	63,423	
60,477½		1750	78,115	
57,125		1755	76,295	
49,362½		1760	69,573	
54,660		1765	77,419	
93,075	2,717,105	1770	85,376	2,255,625
95,878	2,841,213	1775	96,794	2,441,007
110,942	3,427,150	1779	93,143	2,659,659
157,275	4,844,855	1785	116,036	3,409,278
172,588	5,151,677	1790	140,407	4,582,122
250,993	7,759,907	1795	155,087	5,172,511
285,851	9,263,966	1800	169,262	6,014,420

This table is for woollens only ; it takes no account whatever of worsteds, and it does not even include all kinds of woollens.

bill mounting rapidly. Extensive charity attempted to cope with the distress, but the general unrest and suffering expressed itself in numerous riots, outrages, and violent robberies. For this, see Report in James, *op. cit.*, 280–4, and Bischoff, *op. cit.*, i. 186–90. Also Mayhall, *Annals of Yorkshire*, i. 153 and 180.

[1] 11 Geo. I, c. 24.   [2] 11 Geo. II, c. 28.

[3] See Arthur Young, *Farmer's Tour*, i. 404. Also Bischoff, *op. cit.*, app. iv. A complete copy of the table from 1726 to 1819 is in the possession of the present writer.

Certain woollen cloths such as ' bearskins, toilonets, swans-downs, and kerseymeres ' are not included in the above figures.[1] Hence the statistics are not quite exhaustive even for the woollen industry, but they embrace the great staple kinds of cloth, and furnish a reliable indication as to the progress of the industry.   From them we trace a growth both in the number of pieces and in the length of cloth produced.   The output of broad cloths in 1770 is nearly three and a half times that of 1727. In 1785 it is almost six times the 1727 production.   Similarly, the number of narrow cloths milled in 1785 is more than double that of 1740, whilst in both broad and narrow cloths the output in 1800 is about three times that of 1770.   The importation of foreign wool had begun some time prior to 1770 ; wool-staplers scoured the southern countries to find supplies, and brought large quantities into Yorkshire.   The improvements in the breeding of sheep helped to swell the supply of raw material, and Adam Smith declared that ' the wool of the Southern Counties of Scotland [was], a great part of it, after a long land passage through very bad roads, manufactured in Yorkshire '.[2] The cloths of Leeds were supplanting the wares of the South and West of England, and various travellers and observers writing between 1790 and 1818 remark on the effects of northern competition on the southern textile areas.   Dr. Aikin, writing in 1809, states that the textile industry in Gloucestershire is ' somewhat on the decline.   Its cloth has been successfully rivalled in Yorkshire '[3] ; that of Somerset is ' somewhat declined on account of the rivalship of Yorkshire and other places '.[4]   The manufacture of superfine cloths in Wiltshire is ' less affected by the rivalry of Yorkshire than the other branches of the woollen manufactory '.[5]   In Dorsetshire ' on the whole, the clothing manufacturers have greatly declined from their former importance, and have for the most part, migrated into other counties '.[6]   Turning to East Anglia, the trade of Norwich has declined somewhat by reason of the competition of the cotton industry[7] ; that of Bocking[8] and other adjacent towns

---

[1] *Leeds Guide* (1806), p. 110, or *A Walk thro. Leeds* (1806), p. 17.
[2] Adam Smith, *Wealth of Nations*, ii, chap. v, pp. 281–2 (Routledge ed., 1913).   [3] Aikin, *England Delineated* (1809), p. 144.   [4] Ibid., p. 277.
[5] Ibid., p. 254.   [6] Ibid., p. 273.   [7] Ibid., p. 188.
[8] Ibid. (1818 edition), p. 252.   The 1818 edition is called *England Described*.

'has much decreased within these sixty or seventy years', and that of Suffolk has 'for many years been on the decline'.[1] Thus with one or two exceptions the whole of the eastern and south-western clothing centres were by 1809 feeling keenly the ' rivalship ' of Lancashire and Yorkshire, and as machinery and steam were more widely adopted the supremacy of the north became absolute.   Across the English Channel, the weavers of France were experiencing the same effects of keen competition from the West Riding.   Arthur Young in his *Travels in France* pointed out that the fabrics of Elbœuf and Vire were unable to hold their place against the cloths of Leeds called ' Bristols '.[2] Leeds was expanding rapidly ;   if we take vital statistics as a general guide, the population doubled between 1666 and 1731,[3] and again doubled between 1760 and 1801.[4]   As a finishing centre, and as a market for cloth, its prosperity advanced by leaps and bounds.   There was an abundance of money available for building cloth halls, chapels, a theatre, a library, &c.,[5] and the increase in population called for so many new houses that in 1786 400 dwellings were in course of erection.   The conclusion of the American War reopened the American market, and the merchants of Leeds poured their goods into the new republic.   When the struggle with France began, Yorkshire was flooded with orders from every part of Europe for fabrics for the clothing of troops ;   a Wakefield master in 1825 declared that he had been employing 400 hands for the last twenty years making broad cloths for the army,[6] and in 1797 Mr. Sheep-shanks of Leeds was supplying scarlet and white cloth for the militia to the extent of £1,400 a year.[7]

The latter half of the eighteenth century was indeed a period of phenomenal progress.   If we take our stand in 1770, we see the sister industries thriving to an extent which augured well

---

[1] Aikin, *op. cit.* (1818 edition), p. 237.

[2] Extracts from pamphlet, ' Observations sur le traite de commerce entre la France et l'Angleterre ' (1786), quoted in Arthur Young, *Travels in France*, 1794 edition, i. 525.   [3] Whitaker, *History of Leeds*, i. 25.

[4] *Leeds Guide*, 1806, p. 121.

[5] *Brit. Dir.*, 1790, iii. 533.   From 1765 to 1800 Leeds revelled in the erection of chapels, churches, &c.   The General Infirmary was opened, 1771.   A theatre in Hunslet Lane, 1771 ;   a Methodist Chapel in St. Peter's Square, 1771 ;   a Quakers' Meeting House, 1788 ;   Salem Chapel, 1791 ;   and many others about the same time.

[6] *Reports*, 1825, iv. 631.   [7] Add. MSS. 35670, f. 146 et seq.

for their future prosperity. The estimates of the committee of 1774 throw much light on the extent of the industries, their relative size, and their national importance. The following figures are given for the Yorkshire industry :

		£
Annual amount of manufacture of woollens .	.	1,869,700
,, ,, worsteds .	.	1,404,000
Total .	.	3,273,700
Of this, exports of woollens	.	1,248,740
,, ,, worsted	.	1,123,200
Total exports	.	2,371,940

Thus the worsteds almost equalled in value the output of woollens. Further, the total textile exports (including cottons, silks, &c.) for the whole country amounted to £4,436,783 in 1772 ; of this the above figures enable us to claim that at least £2,300,000 came from Yorkshire, or, in other words, more than half the entire export trade in fabrics.

In conclusion, therefore, the West Riding had reached a position of pre-eminence even before the great inventions came into operation. The supply of wool, the possibilities of water power, the possession of a population which could not produce by tillage of the bleak slopes all that was necessary for sustenance, and which, by the inherited skill of generations, was especially suited for industrial work, these were the chief forces which carried the county along the highway of progress, and prepared the road for the gigantic developments which lay before her when the wits of men revealed new sources of power, and discovered untold mineral wealth at her very door.

> No more the rugged North with tyrant might
> Shall shivering poverty evade to fight.

So wrote Maude in 1782.[1] He saw clearly the future of wealth before the ' rugged North ', but little did he perceive that ' shivering poverty ' would still retain its stronghold a century and a quarter after his words were penned.

[1] Maude, *Verbeia* or *Wharfedale*, p. 22 (York, 1782).

CHAPTER IX

THE DISTRIBUTION AND ORGANIZATION OF THE CLOTH INDUSTRY DURING THE EIGHTEENTH CENTURY

THE remaining chapters of this book will be devoted to a survey of industrial life in the textile area of Yorkshire just prior to the Industrial Revolution. They will endeavour to indicate the geographical distribution of the industry, the main features of its organization, and the general processes by which cloth was made. The methods of marketing will be discussed, and finally we shall study the efforts which were made during the eighteenth century to regulate industrial activity and to inculcate honesty and morality in the economic sphere. In these chapters we shall stop short at the Industrial Revolution, and make no attempt to follow the fortunes of the cloth trade through the great transformation which produced modern economic society.

Such a limitation of the subject demands some explanation as to what one means by the Industrial Revolution, and some statement of the approximate date at which the survey is to conclude. The term ' Industrial Revolution ' is here used in the narrowest sense of the words ; it is not meant to imply the great expansion of trade or the vast increase in population : it does not embrace the growth of capitalism, the freeing of industry and commerce from customary or legal restraints, or the attempt to formulate and apply exact economic science.[1] It is used to imply solely the invention of machinery, and the application of steam, for it was these two factors which constituted the real revolution, and were the cause of many of the other developments. The inventions of Arkwright, Hargreaves, Cartwright, and the rest comprised the first step ; the ' discovery ' (if so one might call it) of iron, coal, and steam-power was the second. As the possibilities of these two revelations were more clearly realized, and the inventions brought nearer

[1] See J. H. Clapham on ' Economic Change ', *Cambridge Modern History*, x. 727.

to perfection, machinery and steam-power were adopted, and
the inevitable outcome was the congregation of labour in the
factory system.   Thus in these chapters we are concerned with
the state of the cloth industry before the adoption of steam-
driven machinery.

Can one fix a date for the Industrial Revolution as here
defined ?   It is dangerous to attempt to assign definite dates to
any social or economic change, and the Industrial Revolution
is no exception in this respect.   Since the inventions, the application of steam, and the tremendous expansion in the use of coal
are the outstanding causes of the change, it might be argued
that the dates on which these discoveries were made should be
regarded as marking the inauguration of the new era, and the
invention of the power-loom by Cartwright in 1785 should be
reckoned as the commencement of the Industrial Revolution.
Such a course would be attended by many possible misconcep-
tions ; one must keep in mind the imperfections of the machines
themselves, and the need for improvements before they could
be generally adopted ; also, there was the difficulty of getting
the new methods known and adopted, as well as the violent
opposition of the workpeople.   Therefore the adoption of
factory organization and the introduction of machinery came
very slowly.   There were scarcely twenty factories in Yorkshire
in 1800 ; the power-loom was not introduced into Bradford till
1826, when it was the cause of fierce strife and riots [1] ; combing
was done by hand until well into the forties,[2] and many technical
difficulties rendered it undesirable to use the power-loom in the
woollen industry until about 1850.   Writers in the middle of
last century speak of the widespread existence of the cottage
system,[3] and the memories of people still alive reach back to
the days when the hand-loom was to be found in almost every
cottage.   Thus we come to the conclusion that the Industrial
Revolution had little more than its beginnings in the eighteenth
century.   The great change came first in the cotton industry,

[1] James, *History of the Worsted Manufacture*, p. 356 n.
[2] Burnley, *History of Wool and Wool-combing*, p. 195.
[3] Forbes, Lecture at 1851 Exhibition, ii. 316–17, estimated that 50 per cent.
of the textile workers were still outside the factory.   Jackson, in his *History
of Barnsley* (1858), p. 168, states of the linen industry that 4,000 hand-
looms were still in use as against 1,000 power-looms.

then in the manufacture of worsteds, and lastly in the making
of woollen cloths. In the Yorkshire branches of the textile
industry, the revolution did not actually take place until the
nineteenth century ; the face of Yorkshire had been little altered
by 1800, and half a century had still to elapse before it could
be claimed that the factory and the power-driven machinery
had displaced the old hand methods. Our survey, therefore,
will broadly consider the whole of the eighteenth century.

(a) The Distribution of the Industry

In the eighteenth century the manufacture of cloths was
carried on in the same regions as in 1470, though concentrated
even more than at that date in the three areas of East Anglia,
the West of England, and Yorkshire. A famous agitation in
1752, concerning the false winding of yarn, brought petitions
from such widely scattered districts as Leeds, Halifax, Norwich,
Frome, Colchester, London, Wiltshire, Devonshire, Saffron
Walden, Andover, Taunton, Nottingham, Grantham, Lancashire, Stourbridge, Kidderminster, Kendal, Coventry, &c.,[1] thus
indicating the widespread national character of the industry.
As in the country so in Yorkshire. The industry was carried on
in most parts of the county, but still there were certain tracts
which could definitely be labelled textile, or non-textile, and,
further, could be marked out according to the predominant type
of cloth produced, whether worsted or woollen, white or mixed.
Descending to a further subdivision, one could point to the
specialization of Wakefield on ' tammies ', Leeds on broad cloths
and camlets, Halifax on shalloons and kerseys, and so forth.

As a rough generalization, one might say that Leeds was the
north-eastern limit of the clothing area. A line drawn along
the watershed between Airedale and Wharfedale would mark
the northern boundary, whilst another line, passing from Leeds
south to Wakefield, and then turning south-west towards
Huddersfield, would denote the eastern limit. ' Not a single
manufacturer is to be found more than one mile east or two
miles north of Leeds ',[2] declare many writers and directories of
the century. Chapel Allerton, now part of Leeds, was entirely

---

[1] *House of Commons Journals*, xxvi. 320.

[2] This quotation is found in all the histories, guides, &c., of Leeds, 1797
onwards, e.g. *Leeds Guide* (1806), pp. 100–1.

outside the clothing district, and there was 'scarcely a single manufacturer of cloth to be found in the whole village '.[1] As for Barwick-in-Elmet and neighbouring villages, they were as entirely without the clothing area as was the quietest little village in the Vale of York, being solely agricultural.[2]

Before elaborating the above statements, one must make the necessary modifications. With an industry as yet free from absolute dependence upon coal and iron supplies, it was an easy matter to carry on some branch of the manufacture wherever wool could be obtained and labour was available. Thus throughout almost the whole of the North and East Ridings there were to be found persons occupied in one or other of the many processes involved in the manufacture of the finished cloth. Around Ripon and Middleham there was a considerable ' manufactory ' of woollen goods and preparation of yarn.[3] Even so late as 1810 the drawback on soap for Masham amounted to £89 9s., and the total for the North Riding reached £204 15s. 7d.[4] Some of the yarn prepared in these northern dales was sent to be woven in the West Riding area, but a considerable quantity was utilized at home, being made into woollens at Masham [5] and Middleham,[6] into carpets at Ripon,[7] or into knitted goods in the recesses of Wensleydale and Swaledale. This latter occupation was an extension of the old Westmorland knitting industry. The women of the East Riding were preparing linen yarn, and they of Cleveland were ' spinning of worsted ', or knitting.[8] Defoe found at Richmond ' a manufactory of knit-yarn stockings for servants and ordinary people. Every family is employed in this way, both great and small. Here you may buy the smallest

---

[1] The same applies to this extract. It is a stock sentence, in all the local publications of the period.   [2] *Leeds Guide*, p. 164.

[3] See advertisements in Leeds newspaper, e.g. *Leeds Mercury*, October 12, 1773 : ' Wanted, 4 or 6 hands to card and spin . . . Can be either a family or individuals.' This was for Middleham.

[4] See table in James, p. 369. This drawback was a rebate paid to clothiers and preparers of yarn out of the duty paid on soap. The rebate was allowed on all soap used for industrial purposes. See section on Worsted Committee. In 1810, the drawback for Leeds, £353 17s. 11d. ; Wakefield, £111 13s. 3d.

[5] *British Directory*, v. 131.   [6] Dodsley's *Road Book*, 1756.

[7] Numerous advertisements of Ripon Carpet Manufactory, in *Leeds Mercury*, e.g. 1769 and 1775.

[8] Young, *Northern Tour*, ii. 180. The ' worsted ' was not the thin fibre used for weaving, but the thicker thread such as is used in knitting, and is to-day referred to indifferently as ' wool ' or ' worsted '.

sized pairs for children at 1s. 6d. the dozen pairs, sometimes less.'[1] Another line was the making of 'knit wool caps for seamen '.[2] These goods, evidently of a common order, were either worn by the producers, sold at the small fairs and markets of Dent, Bedale, &c., or taken by the more hardy over the moors to Kirkby Stephen and Kendal, whence they went to supply the needs of 'servants and ordinary people' of other counties.[3] A similar industry was carried on at Doncaster, on a somewhat more ambitious scale. In the sixteenth century Doncaster was famous for the knitting of stockings, waistcoats, gloves, and other articles of attire,[4] the industry being almost entirely in the hands of women. The manufacture continued through the seventeenth century, and was flourishing at the time of Defoe's tour (1723-4), and even much later. This industry employed large numbers of spinners and combers, who also spent part of their time preparing yarn for the weavers of the West Riding. Thus over the whole of the North and West Riding, and in part of the eastern area, some form of working in wool was being carried on. But in scarcely any centre, except Ripon, was it considerable, and this diffused manufacture was insignificant when compared with the activity of the Leeds, Halifax, and Wakefield regions.

The cloth area, stretching from Leeds and Wakefield to beyond the border,[5] can be roughly divided as follows : (1) The *worsted* field, i. e. the country stretching from Bradford to 15 miles west and north-west of Halifax, comprising the upper valleys of the Aire and Calder, and including Halifax, Keighley, Haworth, and Colne. To this list must be added Wakefield and Leeds, which were of secondary importance as centres of the worsted industry. (2) The *woollen* district, lying within a pentagon of

---

[1] Defoe, *op. cit.* iii. 148.

[2] Dodsley's *Road Book*, 1756, under ' Richmond '. In 1595 Peck stated that there were above 1,000 knitters in and about Richmond, engaged in knitting stockings (*D. S. P., Eliz.*, cclii. 2).

[3] Defoe, *op. cit.*, iii. 149, and Bigland, *op. cit.*, p. 739.

[4] Peck stated in 1595 that there were 120 persons knitting stockings in Doncaster. See also *Life of Marmaduke Rawdon* (Camden Soc.), p. 116 (1664). Also Baskerville's Tour, in *Portland MSS., Hist. MSS. Comm.*, ii. 310-12. Also Defoe, *op. cit.*, iii. 107.

[5] Rochdale, Bury, and even Manchester, with a large slice of east Lancashire, were engaged to a considerable extent in the manufacture of woollens. Rochdale and Bury are noted by Defoe as being ' very considerable for a sort of coarse goods called half-thicks and kersies ' (*Tour*, iii. 133).

which the corners were, roughly, Wakefield, Huddersfield, Halifax, Bradford, and Leeds, with its great market at the latter town. In this district a further important subdivision is possible, according to the nature of the product : (*a*) the district containing the following places manufactured *mixed* cloths, in which the wool had been dyed before it was woven : Leeds parish, Morley, Gildersome, Adwalton, Drighlington, Pudsey, Farsley, Calverley, Eccleshill, Idle, Baildon, Yeadon, Guiseley,

Clarendon Press, Oxford

Rawdon, and Horsforth (i. e. chiefly in the Aire valley) ; also Batley, Dewsbury, Ossett, Horbury, and the Calder Vale generally, making smaller quantities ; (*b*) the *white* cloth came from the district occupied by the following places : Alverthorpe, Ossett, Kirkheaton, Dewsbury, Batley, Hopton, Mirfield, Cleckheaton, Littletown [1] (i. e. chiefly in the Calder valley), Bowling, Shipley, Morley, Idle, and a little from Bradford.

[1] i.e. what we now know as the heavy woollen and shoddy districts ; this division of the clothing area is drawn from the directories, &c., of Leeds, e.g. *Leeds Guide*, 1806, pp. 100–1, and the documents connected with the Leeds Cloth Halls.

Thus the white cloth area was a tract of country forming an oblique belt across the hills separating the Aire and the Calder, beginning about one mile west of Wakefield, leaving Halifax and Huddersfield a little to the left, terminating at Shipley, and nowhere coming within six miles of Leeds on the eastern edge. The two districts, as will be seen from the map, are generally distinct, but intermingle a little, especially at their south-eastern and north-western extremities.[1]

Throughout the whole of the county west of Leeds, scattered in isolated farm-houses in the western reaches, but gathered into villages in the valleys to the east,[2] the industry was carried on. The growth of villages as centres of industry during the seventeenth and eighteenth centuries was one of the great features of the period. Such villages as Woodhouse, Beeston, Armley, Hunslet,[3] Haworth, Holbeck, Churwell, and Morley had grown steadily as cloth-making centres, and this growth was probably in part at the expense of the larger towns. Thus Leeds, Wakefield, and Halifax were quite correct when they declared, in 1627, that 'there is not that quantitie of cloth made in these three towns and their precincts as is made in the severall and dispersed towns and villages about us . . . and the most of the inhabitants in these places that are of anie abilitie are not clothiers, but gentlemen, yeomen, ffarmers, and men of other trades and professions '.[4] This statement applied with greater force to the eighteenth century, when the commercial progress of the towns caused a large increase in rents, and drove many clothiers out to the suburbs or even farther afield. The demand for land in and around Leeds was very great during the last half of the century, because of 'the encrease of opulence and population in the town and neighbourhood of Leeds '.[5] One witness before the Parliamentary Committee of 1806 declared that 'since my remembrance there were many hundred clothiers in the township of Leeds, and I believe there are but five now ; . . . they have been driven out and found habitation where the rents were cheaper '. Another Yorkshire-

---

[1] *Leeds Guide*, 1806, p. 101.   [2] Defoe, *op. cit.*, p. 144.
[3] Hunslet was by 1650 a thriving place with 200 families, and demanding that its chapel should be made into a church (Thoresby, *Ducatus*, p. 177).
[4] *D. S. P., Chas. I*, lxi, 82 and 84. Petition concerning ship money.
[5] *Report on the Woollen Manufacture*, 1806, iii. 158.

man spoke of the 'decrease of master manufacturers in the immediate neighbourhood of large towns, especially in two or three populous hamlets adjoining to Leeds, whence they had migrated to a greater distance in the country, where they might enjoy a little land and other conveniences and comforts '.[1] The towns were not the centres of manufacture, but were chiefly engaged in the finishing processes, in the marketing of raw material, cloth, and food-stuffs, and in providing accommodation for merchants, clothiers, and travellers ; or they were the homes of merchants, clergy, officials, and professional men. Leeds, for instance, in 1797 was the home of over 1,400 merchants and traders,[2] whose genteel residences lined Hunslet Lane, Boar Lane, Meadow Lane, and Albion Street. For the accommodation of travellers and villagers coming to market there were no less than 103 inns. Thus on the eve of the Industrial Revolution the distribution of the manufacture might be summed up as follows : Spinning and weaving in the villages and farms scattered over the whole of the Riding ; fulling along the banks of the streams ; dyeing, dressing, finishing, and marketing in the towns. This resulted in a fairly uniform distribution of population throughout the Riding. Most of the towns had less than 10,000 inhabitants, and the total number of urban dwellers as late as 1811 [3] amounted to only about a quarter of the population of the whole Riding.

(b) The Homes of the Workers

When Leland passed through Yorkshire in the sixteenth century he noticed wooden houses in many parts of the county. By 1700, however, brick and stone were general throughout the whole clothing area, and the wooden structures had almost, if not entirely, disappeared. Stone was largely used wherever available, and the houses of the Pennine slopes and the western districts were entirely of stone,[4] giving the landscape that grey cold appearance which still survives, mellowed by a century's deposit of soot and smoke. Bradford was largely built of stone, but in Leeds [5] and Wakefield brick buildings preponderated.

---

[1] *Reports*, 1806, iii. 11. Also Eden, *The State of the Poor* (1797), iii. 847.

[2] *Leeds Directory*, 1797, List of Merchants, &c.

[3] See Aikin, *England Described* (1818), pp. 68–9 ; and Census Returns, 1841.

[4] Defoe, *op. cit.*, iii, *passim.*   [5] *Description of Leeds*, by Dodsley, 1764.

The houses were of all shapes and sizes; the larger possessed two storeys, but the greater number of dwellings enjoyed only one. In the smaller dwellings the work was carried on in the living-room or the sleeping-chamber, but to many houses a low shed was appended, with a long 'weaver's window', in front of which the loom was erected. As the type of house grew larger, other rooms and outhouses were added, and the dwelling of the average well-to-do yeoman or clothier could boast living-rooms, pantry, attic, loom-shop, stable, farm-buildings,[1] and a yard. The upper storey of many houses was approached by an external staircase, instances of which are still to be seen. Casement windows with pebble glasses let in the light, and there was often some simple attempt at decoration of the exterior by training ivy and creepers over the walls.

Few cottages were without a piece of land. The West Riding was one of the strongholds of the small freeholders, who possessed holdings ranging from half a dozen acres to 15 or 20. The sides of the hills around Halifax were 'spread with enclosures from two acres to six or seven each, seldom more, and every three or four pieces of land had a house belonging to them'.[2] All parts of the Riding exhibited the same feature. Where there was not a definite freehold, many Yorkshire proprietors had attempted with success to foster the joint occupation of farming and weaving. Sir Walter Calverley in the early part of the century induced many clothiers to come and reside on his estate by providing fulling mills, and by making it possible for the farmer to be a clothier, and the clothier to work as a farmer.[3] In the last decade of the same century many landlords took advantage of the exodus which was taking place

[1] Note the following typical advertisements of houses: 'To be lett. A house, stable, and croft, adjoining on the upper side of Woodhouse Moor, very convenient for a clothier' (*Leeds Mercury*, April 11, 1738). 'To be lett. One good fashionable new built house, six rooms on a floor, one large shop with a chamber over it, a handsome court planted with wall fruit, a garden and orchard, and all other convenient outhouses . . . fit for a gentleman or any substantial tradesman dealing in the woollen manufacture . . . also four closes of land adjoining the same, about sixteen days work' (*Leeds Mercury*, August 27, 1737). 'To be Lett. A very Commodious Dwelling House, with Stables, Dye-House, Tenters, and all other conveniences proper for a Cloth Maker; together with nearly seven Acres of land adjoyning. There is also a Cottage House contiguous thereto very convenient for a Journeyman Cloth Maker (*Leedes Intelligencer*, February 27, 1759).

[2] Defoe, *op. cit.*, iii. 135.   [3] Laurence's *Duty of a Steward* (1727), p. 36.

from Leeds to induce clothiers to come and live on what had formerly been farming centres. Mr. J. Graham, in his evidence before the Committee in 1806, dwelt upon this aspect, and indicated the nature of the movement. He himself had an estate which had been let out in agricultural leaseholds. The leases terminated in 1796, whereupon Graham divided the farms into small allotments for clothiers. He visited the clothiers' houses in the neighbourhood, in order to discover the most suitable type of building, and then erected about fourteen houses, to each of which he attached five to ten acres.[1] These holdings were immediately occupied by clothiers, and the venture was so successful that other landowners followed in Graham's footsteps. Farmers became clothiers, and small villages grew rapidly into flourishing, though scattered, communities. Thus Leeds was surrounded by a great body of clothiers, living dispersed over the countryside, in houses to which holdings of land were attached.

But these small holdings in land were not intended to make farming a serious rival to the textile industry. They were a subsidiary source of livelihood, and might provide facilities for farming as a by-occupation, or might be utilized largely for textile purposes. On these pieces of land the tenter frames and wool hedges were erected, and tenter frames were as familiar features of the landscape as advertisement hoardings are to-day. The clothier might erect these frames on his own parcel of ground, or on some piece of waste land on which the clothiers of the district obtained permission to set up wool hedges and tenter frames, paying a small sum annually for the privilege.[2] If not used in this manner, the land was devoted to the growth of hardy crops which required little attention, or was turned into a pasture, for the rearing of live stock. Defoe found the land round Halifax employed in sustaining horses and cows (which were owned by all except the very poorest), ' by which means the small pieces of land about each house are occupied. As for corn, they scarcely sow enough to feed their poultry.'[3]

---

[1] *Reports*, 1806, iii. 444.

[2] See maps of Leeds in Thoresby Soc. publications, e.g. ix, p. 204. Also extracts from Leeds Manor Court Rolls (vol. ix), for reference to wool hedges and tenter frames on Woodhouse Moor.

[3] Defoe, *op. cit.*, iii. 135.

Around Leeds a similar state of affairs existed ; the land was used generally ' not in corn, but in grass, in keeping cows and keeping a galloway (horse or pony), or something of that kind, and in tenters '.[1] Crops received little attention, even in the most fertile districts. Graham remarked that some of his new tenants had expressed a desire to have a little ploughed land, but he had found that whenever a manufacturer engaged in working arable land he was sure to waste all the money he was earning by making cloth.[2] In some parts oats were grown in order to supply meal, whilst potatoes were cultivated in all parts of the Riding. But these products were of secondary importance, and hence the husbandry was of a perfunctory character, and the tillage backward and unprogressive. Traditional methods held undisputed sway, and the clothiers were so busy advancing their textile businesses that they had little time to devote to improving their methods of agriculture. Custom therefore reigned supreme : ' Such is the force of prejudice ', declared a writer, about 1800, with reference to the weavers of Pudsey, ' that if any one does not follow the old course of husbandry, he is laughed at as a visionary and innovator. The chief reason which they advance in defence of this old and antiquated pro-cedure is that their forefathers have practised it.' [3] The majority of the clothiers' lands were therefore generally under-utilized, but, provided the horse did not die of starvation, the cow cease to yield milk, or the hens refuse to lay, there was no call for a revision of the accepted order, and no need for a reformation of the agricultural and pastoral economy which was the heritage of centuries.

Such were the homes in which the industry of the eighteenth century was carried on. The alliance of land and loom was a great benefit to the clothing population, especially to the weavers, who often were compelled to lay aside the shuttle because of scarcity of yarn, but who were able to fill up this time by working in their garden, or by performing some neces-sary piece of work on the land attached to their house. Life in these cottages and farms was far from luxurious ; the hours

[1] *Reports*, 1806, iii. 14.

[2] Ibid., p. 144. Some of Graham's tenants, with large families, kept two or three cows, and in such cases held land up to 15 acres, all pasture.

[3] *Annals of Agriculture*, xl. 135, quoted by Cunningham, ii. 564.

of labour were long, the tasks arduous, and the fruits of hard toil far from being rich or plentiful.   In fact, as all the early Leeds directories boasted, the domestic worker, whether master or man, was 'for the most part blessed with the comforts without the superfluities of life '[1]—a statement which was quite true, provided we place the standard of ' comforts ' sufficiently low.

(c) Industrial Organization

In considering the structure of the Yorkshire industry it is necessary to remember now the existence of two branches, namely, the worsted and the woollen.   The organization of the two manufactures was different in many respects, so we must distinguish therefore between the two, and study each separately.

The woollen industry was still largely in the hands of the small independent clothiers.   These were the men who occupied the small freeholds throughout the Riding, and were cloth-makers on a small scale with a little farming as a by-occupation. They possessed their own spinning and weaving machinery, and carried through most of the processes themselves.   The father went to the market and purchased his wool, his wife and children carded and spun it, and if they were unable to provide him with an adequate supply of yarn some of the wool would be put out to be spun in neighbouring cottages.   With the help of a son, apprentice, or journeyman, the clothier dyed his wool, wove the piece, took it to the fulling mill, and thence, in its rough and unfinished condition, to his stall in the market or his stand in the cloth hall.   Out of his receipts he had to pay for raw materials, a fee for fulling, and wages for any external assistance ;   then the remainder was entirely his own, the profit on his venture, and the price of the labour of himself and family. Such a man would never produce more than two pieces per week,[2] and many would get only one cloth to the weekly market. The profits,therefore, would not be large, and a livelihood could be obtained only by dint of hard work and frugal habits.[3]   The majority of these men had their three to fifteen acres of land,

[1] This extract will be found in every directory or guide published between 1790–1810.

[2] Defoe, op. cit., iii. 117.

[3] Committee on Woollen Manufacture, Reports, 1806, iii, passim. See also Aikin, op. cit., p. 52, for remarks concerning ' frugality and industry '

on which the family cow, pigs, and poultry were fed. They also had a horse or ass on which to carry their wares to and from the market; but many of the poorer clothiers could not afford this luxury, and the sight of a man carrying his piece of cloth on head or shoulders was very common. Mayhall instances a man, Richard Wilson, of Ossett, who had two pieces of broad cloth ready for sale.[1] Not possessing a beast of burden, he carried one cloth on his head to Leeds, a distance of about seven miles, and there sold it. His customer also offered to buy the other piece; Wilson thereupon walked back to Ossett to fetch it, delivered the cloth at the merchant's warehouse, completed the transaction, and then returned home. The day's business had included a 28 miles walk, for half of which the clothier had been carrying a somewhat heavy load.

The existence of this class was rendered possible by the fact that only a small amount of capital was required for setting up as a clothier on such a scale. According to the *London Tradesman* (1757), £100 to £500 was the sum required in order to set up as a master weaver in London,[2] and as rents, &c., were probably lower in a Yorkshire village than in the capital, £100– £150 would be more than ample for the purpose in the West Riding industry. The initial expenses were comparatively light, and it was generally easy for a man with a clean reputation to get credit to the extent of a week's supply of wool. Thus the apprentice, at the end of his period of training, could look forward with some degree of confidence to the day when he would have acquired a sufficient amount of capital and be able to set up as his own master. He might borrow the money at once, or work as a journeyman until he had saved the requisite sum; then he acquired his house, ground, and loom, and set to work as an independent manufacturer. Added to this consideration is the fact that the system of open marketing placed the small producer on almost equal terms with his larger rival. The street markets and cloth halls made it possible for the small clothier to dispose of his wares easily, and long after the big men had adopted other methods of sale the cottagers clung to their old form of market.

---

[1] Mayhall, *Annals of Yorkshire*, i. 122, under date 1734.
[2] *The London Tradesman*, by R. Campbell, 1757; see pp. 201 and 340.

But although entry was so easy, and although the class of small clothiers was very numerous in Yorkshire, the small man did not hold the whole of the woollen field. During the seventeenth and eighteenth centuries there had been a steady increase in the number of big clothiers,[1] and although this class probably never attained the status or the extent of the West of England clothiers, it did comprise the upper stratum of the Yorkshire cloth-makers, and was a powerful body during the later years of the eighteenth century.

The wealthy clothier was generally a development from the lower grade which we have just described, and only differed from the meaner master in the number of outside hands he employed, and in the amount of trade which he transacted. Thus there were clothiers of every gradation, from the smallest independent master, employing only his own family, to the wealthy clothier, employing a large number of people in his house and loom-shop, as well as others who worked for him in their own homes. The big man went to the wool markets, or into the wool-producing counties, to purchase his supplies of raw material. These he brought home, and then set his apprentices and journeymen, his own family, and the children of his employees to work converting the raw wool into yarn, and then into cloth. He often took a hand at the loom (especially if he was engaged in training an apprentice), he generally dyed the wool or the piece himself, and when the cloth was finished he took it to the merchant's warehouse or to the cloth-market. Let us take one or two instances to illustrate the nature of such businesses. These cases are drawn from the report of 1806, and they therefore represent the state of industrial organization just before the factory had begun to assert its influence. Elijah Brooke, of Morley, had served his period of apprenticeship, and then, after working for some time as a journeyman, in 1780 he set up as a clothier, making mixed broad cloths in Morley.[2] His own house accommodated only one loom, and this was worked by himself, his son, or an apprentice, his own daughter spending her whole time

---

[1] A witness in 1806, *Reports*, iii. 160, stated: 'Fifty years ago he was thought a great clothier that made two pieces in a week, and now if he makes six, or eight, or ten, he is not the largest by far. Some make two in a week and some make twenty.'

[2] *Reports*, 1806, iii. 129–38.

spinning wool for this loom. He employed twelve journeymen, who were all engaged either spinning or weaving in their own homes, and who were paid by piece rate. Similarly, J. Ellis, of Armley,[1] was a maker of superfine broad cloths ; he had a spinning jenny and three looms, all of which were in his own workrooms. His wife did not take part in the affairs of the business, but he, his apprentice, and a journeyman each worked a loom. Another man and his wife spun yarn for him in the master's shop, two or three children sorted his wool, and another woman was engaged in spinning in her own house. These two clothiers belonged to what one might call the middle class, and there were many such men, employing eight to twelve persons, either in the rooms of the master or the homes of the workpeople themselves.

Higher still in the industrial scale came the really big clothiers who were to be found in many parts, especially around Leeds, during the latter half of the eighteenth century. These men were large employers, and, in the congregation of workpeople in their shops, they established miniature factories many years before the perfection of the power loom or the application of steam. For instance, James Walker of Wortley employed twenty-one looms, of which eleven were in his own loom-shop, and the remainder erected in the houses of his weavers.[2] L. Atkinson, of Huddersfield, had seventeen looms in one room, and also employed weavers who worked in their own abodes.[3] These looms were all worked by hand, and in addition to the men engaged in weaving there were many women and children busy preparing yarn. Thus we see that there was no standard size of master clothier. He might be of any status, from the small man, employing his own family and one or two outsiders, to the wealthy clothier, with his two-score looms and his half a hundred workpeople.

Turning to the organization of the worsted industry, conditions were somewhat different. Here was an industry introduced comparatively late, and superimposed on the woollen manufacture. It had to fight its way to a place in the home and foreign markets, and this could only be done by men who possessed some amount of capital, who were capable of defraying

---

[1] *Reports*, 1806, iii. 5–30.   [2] Ibid., pp. 174–83.   [3] Ibid., pp. 219–23.

the initial costs, and willing to overcome many difficulties before they achieved success. Whether these men were Norfolk merchants or of local origin, they built up the industry on a much more capitalistic basis than was the case in the woollen trade. The small independent clothier never existed in the worsted industry, but in his place stood a man who closely resembled the clothiers of the West of England or those wealthier woollen clothiers of the West Riding whose status we have just been considering. The worsted master was usually a large employer, with a flock of workpeople at his command. This contrast is seen in the difference between the cloth halls at which woollens and worsteds were sold. The halls at Leeds were intended to accommodate the legion of small woollen clothiers who sought the Leeds market; hence, the White Cloth Hall provided 1,210 stands, and the Mixed Cloth Hall found room for 1,770 stallholders. The number of worsted masters was much smaller, but the amount which each man had for sale much greater, and thus the Worsted Cloth Hall at Bradford accommodated only 258 salesmen, but allowed each to have a separate room for himself and his pieces.

This then was the great difference between the two branches of the cloth industry; in the woollen trade a large number of small men, in the worsted a small number of big men. The worsted master was generally the head of a comparatively large establishment. He went to the chief fairs, or to the farmers, buying considerable quantities of wool, which he then brought home and gave into the hands of his sorters and dyers, who worked under his supervision. The wool was then given out to be combed and spun over a wide expanse of country. The yarn thus produced was again collected. Sometimes it was sold, especially to the southern weavers, but in most cases it was handed out to domestic weavers round about, by whom it was woven into cloth, the weavers being paid according to a piece rate. Professor Clapham cites the case of Mr. Greenwood of Oxenhope,[1] near Haworth, who bought wool, combed and dyed it at home with the assistance of a few journeymen, gave it out to be spun, and then sold the yarn. There were many such

[1] Article on ' Industrial Organization of Yorkshire Woollen and Worsted Industries, in *Economic Journal*, xvi, p. 517.

men, master woolcombers and spinners, who prepared yarn on
a large scale. On the other hand, many worsted masters carried
on all the processes of manufacture from sorting to weaving.
The early history of the Haggas family gives an admirable
instance of the kind. In 1715 James Haggas was bound apprentice to a Halifax worsted weaver. On the completion of his
training he went to live at Weethead, above Fell Lane, Keighley,
and here set up as a manufacturer of stuffs, employing hand-
combers and weavers, and selling his pieces at Halifax every
Saturday. His son James went to the Lincolnshire fairs to buy
long wool, which was brought home, sorted at Oakworth Hall,
where was the warehouse, and then given out to the various
workpeople. The pieces were woven in the houses scattered
over the hillsides, and every Friday, the day before market-
day, men might be seen going to Weethead, with heavy pieces
on head or shoulders, and returning with bags of warp and weft.[1]
Sam Hill of Soyland, near Halifax, is an excellent illustration
of the large woollen clothier who became a producer of worsted
goods. On February 3, 1737, he dispatched 200 shalloons to
a London merchant, and a week later announced that he would
forward a second 200 within seven days. How many of these
cloths were the products of his own employees we are not told,
but from one or two remarks concerning his workmen and the
amount of his wool purchases we gather that he was quite
a large employer.[2]

Thus, to recapitulate, the manufacture of woollen cloth was
still in the hands of small clothiers, though the larger employer
was by no means uncommon, whilst the worsted industry was
entirely in the hands of masters who carried on business upon
a considerable scale. These men made the cloth; but they
seldom finished it. The small woollen clothier in particular had
no equipment for the adequate dressing of the pieces which he
and his assistants wove. Hence when the cloth was taken from
the loom it was carried to some fulling mill, the property of
another man, and then, after being fulled, dried, and tentered,
was sold at the market 'in the white' or 'in the raw'. The
cloth had still to undergo the processes of shearing, dressing,

[1] Hodgson, *Textile Manufactures of Keighley*, pp. 47–8.
[2] *Letter Books*, nos. 116, 125, 133, and 134.

dyeing, &c., and these branches of the industry were carried on by another class of men, who possessed the necessary equipment. The master cloth-dresser, cloth-worker, dyer, and fuller lived in the market-towns, or along the banks of some stream as near the cloth-market as possible. They rented or owned the building in which they worked, laid down capital in providing the necessary machinery, and employed journeymen to assist them in the task of dressing and finishing pieces. They worked on a commission system, for they seldom owned the pieces upon which they were working. In a few cases the dyer or finisher went into the market, bought the rough pieces from the clothier, finished them, and then sold them to merchants, middlemen, shopkeepers, or tailors ; but generally the cloths at which the finisher was working were the property of some merchant, who had purchased them from the makers and then handed them over to receive the final treatment before taking them away to sell. In such cases the finisher received a fee for each cloth which he finished, out of which he had to pay the wages of his journeymen, the remainder being interest on his capital and profit to himself as *entrepreneur*.

There are still two figures in the eighteenth-century organization with which we have not dealt—namely, the merchant and the middleman. Their position and functions can most profitably be discussed when we turn to a consideration of the methods of marketing the Yorkshire cloths. But it may be well to state at this juncture that these men were very important elements in the domestic system. The merchant, either directly or through his agent, was rising to an altitude from which he could largely control the industrial field. Under the conditions of the seventeenth century, when the industry was not nearly so extensive or so highly developed, he had confined his attention almost entirely to the commercial aspect of the cloth trade ; he had met the clothier in the market, bought pieces, which he handed over to the cloth-worker, and finally sold to his customers at home and abroad. He had little direct influence over the clothier or the finisher. But during the eighteenth century, and especially with the rise of the worsted industry, the merchant began to get a firmer grip over the industrial units. He commenced to buy direct from the maker, without going into the market. He gave orders for large supplies of goods to be made according to a sample presented by the clothier, or in accordance with his own specifications. Some clothiers, especially worsted manufacturers, spent their whole time producing goods for one merchant or middleman, and their wares never saw the cloth-market. Thus these men became dependent upon the merchant, and worked directly under his control, executing his orders. The letters of Joseph Holroyd, a cloth-factor of Soyland, show him in 1706–7 acting as the agent of London and foreign merchants, and placing large orders for them with local clothiers. Merchants, when sending their orders, supplied detailed specifications and fixed maximum prices, and it was then Holroyd's business to obtain the required cloths in accordance with the wishes of his patrons. Many clothiers apparently spent their whole time supplying Holroyd, and their pieces never went into the public market.[1] The next step came when the merchant actually set up as a clothier himself, and figured in the double rôle of manufacturer and merchant. As manufacturer he owned looms and other utensils, and employed spinners and weavers making cloth out of his raw material according to his specifications. When the cloth was woven, it was finished in mills which were also his property, by men who were his employees, and when the cloth was actually completed it came into his hands and was sold by him in his capacity as merchant. Thus the maker and the merchant were combined in the same person, with the merchant as the pre-dominating partner. These two important developments, the working to the order of the merchant, and the engrossment of the whole industrial procedure by the merchant, were very evident in the eighteenth century. A cloth-dresser declared in 1765[2] that 'some merchants make cloth themselves', and twenty years later Charles Clapham of Leeds described himself as a 'Merchant and Manufacturer of Worsted Stuffs'.[3] The tendency developed rapidly during the next twenty years, and when the new possibilities of machinery and power were revealed,

---

[1] See *Letter Books*, Intro., pp. 6–8, and letters *passim*. For further treatment of the nature of merchants and factors, see chapter on markets and merchants, Chapter XI.

[2] *House of Commons' Journals*, xxx. 264.

[3] *General Collected Reports* (1788), vol. xxxviii, no. 87.

it was chiefly the merchants who, possessing the necessary capital, seized upon them, set up mills, allied industry and commerce, and provided the capitalist system of the nineteenth century.

(d) Apprenticeship in the Eighteenth Century

In a previous chapter we have observed the extent to which apprenticeship prevailed in the domestic system of industry, and have noted the attempts of Elizabethan legislation to enforce certain conditions upon those who sought an industrial education. Apprenticeship, and the law which regulated it, still survived in the eighteenth century, and found general theoretical acceptance in the North of England long after it had been placed in disregard elsewhere.

The clothier augmented his labour supply by taking one or more apprentices, who might be drawn from one of three sources. In the first place he might take his own son as a pupil, and teach the lad all that he himself knew concerning cloth-making. In such a case the apprenticeship was often an unwritten arrangement between father and son. There was no indenture, probably no promise to work for a stipulated number of years ; it was a family agreement, intimate, loose, and informal.

Secondly, the clothier might take the son of a neighbour or friend, or some other youth whose father wished him to receive a definite and practical training. In this case a proper indenture was drawn up and duly signed. The clothier was frequently paid a premium to take the apprentice, and the indenture stated in the most minute detail the terms of the contract, and the obligations which were accepted on either hand. The nature of the agreement and of the relations between master and pupil will be best seen by quoting the following indenture, the original of which is in the Halifax Reference Library : [1]

'This Indenture made the Eleventh Day of December, . . . one thousand seven hundred and sixteen, BETWEEN Stephen ffirth of Wyke in the County of York, Clothier, on the one part, and Thomas Gleadhill, Son of Jeremy Gleadhill of Halifax on the other part : WITNESSETH that the said Thomas Gleadhill hath of his own free Will and with the Consent of his ffriends,

---

[1] The indenture is made out on the customary printed form such as was used for the purpose. The special details were then filled in as required.

Put and Bound himself Apprentice to and with the said Stephen ffirth, and with him after the manner of an Apprentice to Dwell, Remain and Serve from the Day of the Date hereof, for, during and until the Term of 13 Years thence next following to be fully compleated and ended. During all which said Term the said Apprentice his said Master well and faithfully shall serve, his Secrets shall keep, his lawfull Commands shal do, Fornication or Adultery he shall not commit, Hurt or Damage to his . . . Master shall not do, nor Consent to be done, but he to his Power shall Lett it, and forthwith his . . . Master thereof Warn : Taverns or Alehouses he shall not haunt or frequent, unless it be about his Master's Business there to be done. At Dice, Cards, Tables, Bouls, or any other unlawfull Games he shall not play. The Goods of his Master he shall not Waste, nor them lend nor give to any Person without his Master's License. Matrimony with any woman within the Said Term he shall not Contract, nor from his . . . Master's Service at any time absent himself ; but as a true and faithful Apprentice he shall order and behave himself towards his Master and all his, as well in Words as in Deeds . . . And true and just Accounts of all his Master's Goods, Chattels, and Money committed to his Charge, or which shall come into his Hands, faithfully he shall give at all times when thereunto required by his Master.

' And the said Stephen ffirth, ffor and in Consideration of the Sume of thirty shilling of Lawfull Money to him paid at the Ensealing hereof, doth Covenant, Promise and Grant by these Presents to and with the said Thomas Gleadhill his Apprentice that he shall and will Teach, Learn, and Inform him . . . or cause Him to be Taught . . . in the Trade, Mystery or Occupation of a Clothier, which he the said Master now useth, after the best manner of Knowledge that he . . . may or can, with all the circumstances thereunto belonging. And also shall find, provide to and for his . . . Apprentice sufficient and enough of Meat, Drink, Washing, and Lodging, together with all his Wearing Apparell, Linen, as well as Woollen Clothes, Shoes and Aprons, dureing the said Terme, And at the end of the Terme shall and Will allow him one Suit of Cloths for the Workinge Days, and another for the Holidays, fit and sufficient for Such an Apprentice to have.'

(Signed by) STEPHEN FFIRTH,   (Seal.)
        his Mark

THOMAS T GLEADHILL,   (Seal.)

If the master was a worsted clothier, or a woollen clothier on an extensive scale, the indenture often stated that the apprentice should receive tuition in wool-buying, marketing, and all the other branches of the trade in which the large manufacturer engaged. The following extract throws light upon this subject, and is taken from a unique type of indenture. In this agreement, dated 1792,[1] the master, a worsted manufacturer of Bingley, received a premium of sixteen guineas, in return for which he promised to train the apprentice in the ' art and Mystery of a Worsted Stuffmaker, in all its Branches . . . and also shall and will take his apprentice, in the last year of his Apprenticeship, to the Market, or into the Country, and instruct him in the buying of Wool, the Apprentice finding his own horse, and paying his own Travelling Expenses. And also shall and will allow unto his said Apprentice one Fortnight in each and every year during the said Term [five years], to go to School to improve himself in learning '.

If the youth was apprenticed to a cloth merchant, the master was to instruct him in the ways of foreign trade, and was expected to fake his pupil with him when he went abroad.

Frequently the apprentice paid no premium, and on some occasions the master actually agreed to pay a small nominal wage to his pupil. Thus in 1704 John Burton of Bramley, clothier, undertook to teach James Wilkinson ' the misterie, craft and occupation of a cloathier, with meat, drink, washing and lodging and beding, and paying one shilling per year as sallerie or wages, and finding him all cloathes and nessessories '.[2]

Thirdly, the apprentice might be drawn from the ranks of the Poor Law children. When the churchwardens and Overseers of the Poor had a ' poor child ' of whom they wished to dispose, they could practically compel some eligible person to take the child as apprentice. In Leeds this power of binding a parish apprentice upon an unwilling ratepayer was very capriciously exercised, and caused many complaints during the eighteenth century. The Poor Law officials kept a book, in which they entered the names of those persons they thought were fit and able to bear the gift of an apprentice.[3] Then, when a child had to be got rid of, one of the townsmen was approached and

---

[1] Apprenticeship Indenture of Thomas Lister, apprenticed to William Smith of Harden, near Bingley. Copy in Bradford Reference Library.

[2] Indenture, printed by J. H. Turner, *Shipley, Idle, and District*, p. 67.

[3] *Poor Law.Commission Reports*, 1834, xxviii. 729.

informed that he must take the child.[1] Sometimes a clothier,
knowing that his turn to take a parish apprentice was coming
round, would anticipate the command of the Overseers by
asking for a child.   Generally, however, the clothier awaited
the order, and then made his objections.   He might point out
that he still had with him the parish apprentice last allotted to
him, and that it was not just to saddle him with another at that
moment.[2] He might protest, as did Samuel Durrans of Hunslet,
in 1711, that ' there are severall other persons that are more
fitt and propper than him to have apprentices putt to them,
in regard he is unmarried '.[3] He might explain that he was
maintaining by his exertions an orphan relative, an aged father
and mother, or some other person, who, but for his support,
would be thrown upon the Poor Law charges, and hence, as he
was doing his duty to the community, he should not be further
burdened with a pauper child.   Or he might refuse point-blank
to take the apprentice.   These objections, however, were seldom
regarded (unless the plaintiff carried his protest to the local
justices), and the citizen was ordered to welcome the child into
his house.   If he still refused, he was heavily fined.   In 1775,
for instance, Alice Halstead, a widow of Morley,[4] was fined five
and a half guineas because she refused to take a town apprentice.
In Leeds the fine was generally £10, and the Poor Law funds
of that town often profited to the extent of £1,000 a year by
reason of the fines imposed upon those who refused to take such
children.[5] The Overseers were only too pleased to get children
off their hands, and often placed out those who were obviously
physically or mentally unfit.   Fortunately, the person with
whom the child was placed could appeal to the justices of the
peace for relief from his burden, in case the apprentice proved
to be useless.   Thus in Leeds the justices from time to time
ordered the Overseers to take back such children ; one because
he had a lame leg, another because he was afflicted ' with sore
fface, and not fitt to be put out Apprentice ',[6] whilst a few were
returned to the Poor Law authorities because it appeared to

[1] *Reports*, 1806, iii. 134.   [2] *Leeds General Sessions*, ii. 581 (1711).
[3] Ibid., ii. 582 (1711).
[4] Morley Town Book (1775), quoted in Smith's *Rambles round Morley*, p. 47.
[5] Poor Law Commission, app., Yorkshire section, *Reports*, 1834, xxviii. 729.
[6] *Leeds General Sessions*, 28 Geo. II, vol. vi, pp. 378–9.

the court that they were 'afflicted with a distemper called the Evill, and not fitt to be an Apprentice'.[1]

The apprentice was placed out when he reached the age of twelve or thirteen years, though Poor Law children were often disposed of at an earlier age. In the indenture quoted above the child was apprenticed for thirteen years; it seems that he had been left an orphan, and was therefore indentured at an early age for such a long period. Such a case, however, is exceptional, and generally apprenticeship was formally taken up between the twelfth and the sixteenth year. During the years which preceded apprenticeship the boy would frequently have been learning some branch of the trade whilst in his father's house, where he would help in wool-sorting, spinning, and other occupations such as were carried on in most houses in the textile area. We must never lose sight of this consideration, namely, that the domestic atmosphere was charged with in-dustrial activity, and that the child grew up with the processes of manufacture going on all around him. Thus, before he was indentured, he would have a practical acquaintance with some phases of the industry. During his period of tuition he was a member of his master's family, an unpaid servant, and a pupil. He was tied carefully by the terms of his indenture, and his master had very considerable powers over him. His leisure-time and his morals were under supervision. 'Taverns and alehouses he shall not frequent; games, etc., he shall not play', so ran the indenture, and in 1757 the magistrates of Leeds made a declaration for the uplifting of the moral tone of both apprentices and journeymen.

'Publicans permitting Journeymen, Labourers, Servants, or Apprentices, to play at Cards, Dice, Draughts, Shuffleboards, Mississippi, or Billiard Tables, Skittles, Ninepins, or any other Implements of Gaming in their Houses, Outhouses, or Grounds, shall forfeit 40s. for the first offence, for every subsequent offence £10, to be levied by distress and sale; a quarter to the Informer, the rest to the Poor.'

If an apprentice or journeyman was known to be in a public house, his master could obtain a warrant from the justices for his apprehension.[2]

[1] Ibid., vi. 388, and vii. 126.   [2] *Leedes Intelligencer*, August 30, 1757.

At times the youth made a bold bid for freedom, and ran away. One constantly encounters advertisements in the eighteenth-century newspapers similar to the following : [1]

'Run away, on the fifteenth of November last, John Oldham, Apprentice to Jonathan Roebuck, Clothier, of Jacksonbridge, near Scholes. . . . The said John Oldham will be twenty years old the last Day of March next, is about five feet high, of a fair complexion, has light coloured flank Hair, and his little finger on each hand crooked. He had, when he absconded, a blue Waistcoat, and a light blue-grey Singlet, and a Shread Apron, red and blue, a pair of good Shoes with bright Metal Buckles, and slouch'd Hat. If the said Apprentice will return to his said Master, he will be kindly taken in, or if any Person harbours him after this Notice he will be prosecuted.'

Such occurrences were only to be expected, even in cases where the master was the very embodiment of kindliness and good nature. The apprentice was bound for a number of years, generally seven, in some cases less, in others for a longer period. Long before that time was expired, he would be able, or suppose himself able, to do a man's work and earn man's wages. He would chafe at the terms of his indenture, and eventually seek his freedom. In 1806 Mr. William Cookson, a Leeds magistrate, declared that disputes often arose between apprentices and masters, especially towards the end of the period of apprenticeship. This, he stated, was due to the fact that the young men, as soon as they had learned their trade and were able to do the work of a journeyman, became arrogant, and made themselves obnoxious to their masters, in the hope that the latter would release them before the expiration of their full time. If the master refused to grant the apprentice his liberty, then the pupil ran away, and so, stated Mr. Cookson, 'there is scarcely a week that we (i.e. the magistrates) are not obliged to grant warrants to apprehend runaway apprentices.' [2] If the master was highly dissatisfied with the work and conduct of his apprentice, he could release him from the contract,[3] and if the youth

---

[1] *Leedes Intelligencer*, February 26, 1782. Similar picture in *Intelligencer* for June 4, 1782.

[2] *Reports*, 1806, iii. 172. Unruly apprentices were often placed in the House of Correction, e.g. 1710, *Leeds. Gen. Sess.*, ii. 545, an apprentice put in the House of Correction ' as an Idle, dissolute and disorderly person '.

[3] *Leeds Gen. Sess.*, ii. 56, 9th October, 12 William III ; quarrel between master and apprentice. Court decided it was best they should part.

had been taken from the Poor Law officials, the justices of the peace could relieve him of a charge which was an unprofitable burden upon him.

The master was also protected by law against any attempts to entice away his pupil. From time to time the justices of the peace were called upon to order the restoration of an apprentice who had been seduced by another master from the care of his proper guardian. For instance, in 1698 Antony Dobson, of Armley, clothier, had taken a parish apprentice and formally indentured him, ' yet notwithstanding, one Peter Broadbent, of Armley, clothier, hath invegled and Seduced the said [apprentice] out of the Service of the said . . . Dobson, and doth detain and keep him in his own Service, contrary to Law and Justice '. Dobson appealed to the justices of Leeds, who ordered that Broadbent should return the apprentice, or ' answer the contrary at his perill '.[1]

On the other hand, the apprentice could appeal through his father or some relative to the justices of the peace for protection against the abuses of his master. The justices had to insist on both sides keeping to the terms of the indenture, and masters were constantly before the bench, charged with some breach of their trust. At almost every General Sessions held in Leeds during the first sixty years of the eighteenth century some apprentice was freed from his agreement to serve, because of offences on the part of his master. The grievance might be persistent cruelty, starvation, or neglect ; it might be that the master was bankrupt, had fled his home, or was in gaol. Whatever the circumstances, the apprentice could obtain his freedom, if he proved that his master was not properly discharging his duties. Witness the following instances. In 1708[2] William Killingbeck, of Horsforth, made petition to the magistrates on behalf of his son, John, whom he had placed apprentice with Richard Hodgson, of Holbeck, clothier. The complaint was ' that Richard Hodgson hath left his ffamily, and is run to Ireland, and that Sarah Hodgson, his wife, doth not follow the said Trade, nor take care that the Apprentice be instructed therein, whereby he is in danger to be Deprived of the means of

---

[1] *Leeds Gen. Sess. Records,* October 5, 1698, ii. 4.
[2] Ibid., October 6, 1708, ii. 425.

getting his Liveing ' ; therefore it was ordered that the indenture
should be cancelled and the youth allowed to serve the remainder
of his time with another master. In the same year another
apprentice obtained his freedom, because his master was incarcerated in Rothwell Gaol for debt,[1] and similar entries are
scattered up and down the North Riding Quarter Sessions
records. Charges of cruelty and neglect are no less common.
In 1709 complaint is made ' that John Atkinson doth not
allow his Apprentice Sufficient and necessary Meat, drink, and
Apparel, and ffurther, that he doth not take care that he be
kept att and instructed in his Trade '.[2] In 1714 another apprentice reports that he ' hath not had sufficient Meat and Drink
allowed him, and that his Master hath several Times immoderately
corrected him ' ;[3] and four years later Sarah Brown complains
that her master, a clothier, is teaching her nothing by way of
a trade, and ' that she hath been very much crushed and abused
by beating and otherwise in her master's service '.[4] In all these
instances the indenture was cancelled. If the apprentice was
nearing the expiration of his time he seems to have been excused
the remaining period, but if he had still some considerable time
to serve he was ordered to place himself at once under another
master.

One more topic remains to be discussed, namely, to what
extent legal conditions of apprenticeship were being maintained.
The Commission of 1806 declared that apprenticeship had maintained its ground more generally in the north than in the west,
but it also went on to state that this survival was ' rather from
custom than from a sense of the Law '.[5] The apprenticeship
system had woven itself into the fabric of the domestic industry,
and was now part and parcel of the economic structure. The
youth who some day hoped to become a master needed a training
in the various parts of the work, since he would have to be
a man of many parts, and this comprehensive training could
best be obtained by serving a period of apprenticeship under
a fully qualified master. The law demanded that the period
should be at least seven years, and the Leeds Cloth Halls at first

[1] *Leeds Gen. Sess. Records*, ii. 407.   [2] Ibid., ii. 466.
[3] Ibid., ii. 706.   [4] Ibid., iii. 77.
[5] *Reports*, 1806, iii, p. 13.

forbade entry to any clothier who had not served the full legal
period. We have seen, however, that in the early seventeenth
century the full letter of the Elizabethan statute was not being
observed in the West Riding, and during the eighteenth century
the Act fell into greater neglect. This was inevitable in the
widely scattered districts, and the justices of the peace never
seem to have attempted to enforce the full demands of the Act
of 1563.[1] In Leeds, where supervision was more easily effected,
and where the Corporation was alive to a sense of its authority,
some attempt was made, from the Revolution of 1688 to the
middle of the eighteenth century, to enforce the terms of the
Statute of Apprentices. The chief offenders in Leeds were the
cloth-workers, i. e. those engaged in dressing the cloth. This
industry seemed to be full of men who had not served an apprenticeship. They were constantly being brought before the justices
on the charge of having violated the laws concerning apprenticeship, and were fined in accordance with the length of time they
had been engaged in the occupation. Cloth-workers abounded
as defendants in such cases, but clothiers, drapers, mercers,
bricklayers, tallow-chandlers, and tailors also appeared amongst
the offenders.[2] Occasionally there was an indictment of a master
for having employed a journeyman who had not served the
legal minimum of seven years.[3] Thus the authorities of Leeds,
during the first fifty years of the eighteenth century, tried
to administer the statute, and to uphold the standard of

[1] The West Riding justices were not the only ones who looked with a lenient
eye upon offenders. In February 1702 the Kendal weavers petitioned Parliament, declaring that when persons were prosecuted for violating the apprenticeship Act they met with such favour from the local justices that the law
was of no avail.

[2] The indictments generally ran as follows : ' That XY . . . on the first day
of May, in the fifth year of the reign of our Sovereign Lord George the Second,
and continually after until the first day of May then next following, to wit
for the space of one whole month, at Leeds, unlawfully, voluntarily, unjustly,
and for his own gain hath sett up, occupyed, used, and excercised the Craft,
Mistery, or Occupation, of a Broad Woollen Clothworker, being an art, Mistery,
or Manuall occupacion, used or occupyed within the Kingdom of England
[at the time of the passing of the 1563 Act] in which said Craft . . . the said
XY never was brought up or served as an Apprentice therein by the space
of seven years, in Evill Example of all others in the like case offending and
against the peace of the King his Crown and Dignity, and against the form of
the Statute '. It would seem from this indictment that offenders were
seized after having practised the illegal occupation for the space of a month,
and hence the statutory fine of 40s. was inflicted (*Leeds Sess. Records*, April 2,
1733).   [3] Ibid., v. 222, 228–9.

apprenticeship in the town, whilst to some extent the rule of the Cloth Hall would maintain the same standard amongst the clothiers around Leeds.

After 1750, however, there is an absence of apprenticeship prosecutions in the Leeds General Sessions records, which seems to indicate that the justices had abandoned their attempts, and the latter part of the century was marked by a general break-down of any legal restraint upon apprenticeship. The witnesses in an inquiry in 1802 all agreed on this point. One man declared that he always thought the Act of 1563 was obsolete ; he himself had only served for four years, and of the general body of Yorkshire cloth-makers not one in ten of the workmen employed in the woollen manufacture had served a regular apprenticeship : many had not been apprenticed at all, and the others had done only three, four, or five years, according to the age at which they were indentured.[1] Another witness stated that, as cloth-dressing could be learned in a little over twelve months, there was not the least occasion for seven years' training, whilst a Mirfield representative in 1806 remarked that ' the apprentice-ship law has never been thought of : . . . I never heard it men-tioned before that I know of '.[2]

The system of apprenticeship received a hard blow from the growth of the worsted industry in the West Riding. The Act of 1563 was understood to apply only to certain industries which existed and were of importance at the time of the passing of that statute. The worsted industry, however, came to the West Riding subsequent to that date, and so the question arose, Did the regulations concerning apprenticeship apply to the new industry ? This was a difficult question, which no one could answer. Hence, although many young men were apprenticed to learn the worsted manufacture, many others entered into no such formal pledge of service. Further, in the manufacture of worsteds there was much greater division of labour amongst the employees. One was a wool-comber and nothing else, another spent all his time weaving, and so there was no need for that many-sided industrial proficiency which the woollen worker possessed. It would be quite unnecessary for a wool-

---

[1] *Reports*, 1802–3, v. 305.
[2] *Reports*, 1806, iii. 197. Evidence of Mr. Staincliffe.

comber to serve seven years when he could learn his trade in one or two, and it would be equally undesirable that a man whose whole task was to be weaving should bind himself as an apprentice for a long space of time. Thus, both in the worsted and woollen industries, apprenticeship was becoming obsolete. It was now entered upon only by those who intended to become masters; the rank and file of the workpeople never became formally indentured, and so a Bradford witness in 1806 asserted his belief that ' nineteen out of twenty have not served regular apprenticeships in the textile industry of the West Riding '.[1]

This decline of the system is seen in the gradual relaxation of all attempts to enforce the legal period. The prosecution of a man for not having served seven years was a thing unknown in 1806,[2] and it was only the fear of the onslaught of machinery which made the domestic clothiers at that time seek for the reinvigoration of an Act which most of them had transgressed. The Cloth Halls of Leeds had long ago reduced their seven years' stipulation to five years, whilst the later Halls, at Colne, Bradford, and Huddersfield made no demand whatever concerning apprenticeship qualifications. Moreover, during the century, legislation itself admitted the justice of the case against the Elizabethan Act, and provided a loophole of escape from the rigour of its demands. In 1725 Parliament renewed its attempt to regulate the industry and to stamp out deceptive practices in the manufacture of broad cloth. This Act contained certain clauses concerning apprenticeship, and declared that ' no person who shall not have served for the space of seven years as an apprentice . . . in the trade of a broad clothier shall make or cause to be made any broad cloths, under the penalty of forfeiting £10 for every month ' he has worked.[3] This meant that a fully qualified clothier could not make broad cloths unless he had served for seven years as an apprentice to the broad cloth trade. The broad clothiers lived around Leeds, the narrow clothiers around Huddersfield and Halifax, and thus a distinction was fixed against the latter. This clause was obviously intended to reinvigorate the statute of 1563, but it seems to have had little effect, and when the Act was renewed in 1733[4] the appren-

---

[1] Reports, 1806, iii. 184.   [2] Ibid., passim.
[3] Statute 11 Geo. I, c. 24.   [4] 7 Geo. II, c. 25.

ticeship clauses were removed entirely. In 1749[1] soldiers and sailors who might be unemployed in times of peace were allowed to take up a trade without having previously served an apprenticeship to that trade. A further enactment came in 1795, and attempted to deal with another special case, namely that of the wool-comber. Wool-combing formed a distinct part of the worsted industry, and combers held a virtual monopoly of their trade, because of the skill required. They spent the whole of their time at one particular process, and seem to have earned comparatively large wages by combing only. In 1795 it was felt that these skilled hand-workers might be left stranded in consequence of the coming of machinery, and some relaxation of the law must therefore be made in order to allow them to migrate to some other part of the textile field. The Act of 1795 therefore stated that all wool-combers who had served an apprenticeship to combing, but were willing to apply themselves to other branches of the trade, might transfer themselves to some other occupation without legal let or hindrance.[2] By this time legal apprenticeship was practically dead. It had fallen into neglect, and the clothiers who sought to revive the Elizabethan statute during the next few years did so not from love of the system, but because they wished to erect a bulwark against the onslaught of the factory and machinery. Their efforts ended in failure. Circumstances were changing, and economic conceptions were becoming modelled on the *laissez-faire* plan. The petitions of the domestic workers were of no avail ; Parliament temporarily suspended the law concerning apprenticeship, and finally repealed it entirely in 1813. Apprenticeship for the future was to be a voluntary agreement between master and pupil, and as the factory system advanced its frontiers, and machine production gained ground, the scope for individual tuition and intimate personal relations largely disappeared. In the modern textile world there is little room for the apprentice.

(e) *The Journeyman in his relation to the Clothier*

The position of the journeyman during the eighteenth century varied according to the nature of his employer. Amongst the

[1] 22 Geo. II, c. 44.   [2] 35 Geo. III, c. 124.

smaller clothiers engaged in the woollen manufacture the gulf between master and man scarcely existed ; the two often worked side by side, took their share of duty at the loom or the dye-vat, with very little apparent difference in status between them. The employer had probably been a journeyman in his day, and the journeyman looked forward to the time when he might possibly be able to set up as a small clothier for himself. With the larger masters such as the worsted chiefs, the big woollen clothiers, and the master cloth-finishers we rise to a more highly developed type of employer, and therefore the contrast between master and man is much more evident. The worsted master, for instance, carried on his trade with a real division of labour ; he employed his wool-combers, spinners, and weavers, each a well-defined class in itself. He utilized a considerable quantity of capital, and thus stood in a position high above that of the people he employed. The big woollen clothiers, with their ten or twelve looms in one room, and the master dyers or cloth-dressers belonged to the same class, and in these branches of the cloth industry there were quite distinct bodies of employers and of workpeople.

In accordance with the statute of 1563 employees were still engaged in some cases by yearly contracts, but it is doubtful whether this rule was general throughout the whole industry. In Leeds the justices occasionally punished master cloth-workers for hiring, taking into service, and retaining men for a period of less than one year, but spinners and weavers were probably engaged on the same terms as to-day, given work whenever the clothier had any for them, and paid according to piece rates.

In a previous chapter we studied the assessment of textile workers' wages by the justices of the peace, and noticed the maximum rates allowed in 1647.[1] During the next hundred years this practice of assessment was continued, but the regulation of woollen workers' wages was soon abandoned. The assessment of 1647 was renewed, without any alteration, up to 1672. In that year a new assessment was drawn up,[2] in which an all-round increase in wages was permitted, but from which

---

[1] For a fuller treatment of the assessment of wages in the West Riding, see an article by the present writer in the *Economic Journal*, June 1914.

[2] *Sessions Order Books*, H, pp. 35–7.

the textile clauses were entirely deleted. There is no mention whatever of the wages which were to be paid to ' Cloathworkers and Dyers ', and from this time onwards no assessment was made for this very important section of the community. The reasons for this abandonment are very obscure, and one can only guess what were the motives which induced the justices to remove from their sphere of control so important an industry. It may have been due to the difficulties encountered in revising the rates for textile workers   Time rates had been fixed in 1647, and it may have been that an attempt was now made to convert them into piece rates in accordance with the custom actually in practice in the industry.   Such a step would be exceedingly difficult, because of the variety of cloths made in the Riding.   A second possibility is that the heads of the cloth-ing trade were averse to any such increase in the textile wages list as was being granted in most of the other occupations. There is no evidence on this point, but one must remember that there was in existence at this time the Corporation of Broad Clothiers, established in the early years of the reign of Charles II. When this organization was brought into being, the statute which incorporated it forbade the Corporation to meddle with wages, or to attempt to ' set or impose any other or lesser Rates of Wages upon any inferiour Workmen, Servants or Labourers . . . than such as shall bee from time to time allowed and approved by the Justices of the Peace in their Quarter Sessions according to the Lawes and Statutes . . . in that case made and provided '.[1] This clause is quite in harmony with the provisions for a mini-mum rate laid down in the Act of 1603, but it is grotesquely unreal in the light of the maximum figures which were being assessed by the justices. The Corporation was set up in 1662, and in the same year the assessment had been renewed as in 1647, continuing without any alteration until 1672. But now, in the latter year, when the whole schedule was to be revised, there may well have been some searchings of heart amongst clothiers and justices at the manner in which the assessments of maxima for cloth-makers violated the law of 1603 and the clause in the statute of 1662. The justices may have felt some-what uneasy at their neglect of duty, whilst the Corporation of

[1] Statute 14 Chas. II, c. 32.

Broad Clothiers was probably opposed to any increase in wages, since times were bad and the textile labour market was so over-stocked that any number of workpeople could be obtained at the old rates. In the circumstances, it seemed best to leave out entirely the textile workers' wages list, and so from 1672 onwards the wages in the cloth trade were thrown open to individual bargaining. In the eighteenth century the State stepped in and made various enactments for the regulation of the wages to be paid in the industry, and an Act of 1756 [1] gave the justices power to fix piece rates for weavers. But all these statutes were practically useless, and did not actually affect the Yorkshire branch of the cloth industry. At the same time there were many enactments to protect the worker from payment in truck, and the various anti-combination laws of the century demanded the proper disbursement of ' full wages . . . agreed on, in good and lawful money of this Kingdom '.[2]

But the workman of the eighteenth century did not rely much upon the justices of the peace for an increase in his wages. Workmen were already beginning to be conscious of their class-strength, and were embarking upon experiments in the methods of industrial warfare. Mr. and Mrs. Sidney Webb have shown, in their early chapters on the history of trade unionism, the growth of organized labour during the eighteenth century, especially in the more capitalistic areas of London, Norfolk, and the West of England. Here the division between master and servant had become complete, with a class of wealthy industrial and commercial magnates on the one hand and a proletariat on the other. Here there were trade unions, strikes, and riots, to say nothing of countless petitions to the King and Commons. These expressions of labour unrest, which were most prevalent during the first third of the century, called forth a series of anti-combination laws which culminated in the Acts of 1799 and 1800, and laid the foundation of that opposition against which trade unionism had to fight throughout the nineteenth century.

The early Acts were aimed specifically at workers in wool,

---

[1] Statute 29 Geo. II, c. 33. This statute was repealed in the following year (30 Geo. II, c. 12).

[2] e.g. 12 Geo. I, c. 34 ; 13 Geo. I, c. 23 ; 22 Geo. II. c. 27.

and forbade the formation of clubs, societies, and all other forms of combination such as should attempt to regulate the trade, advance wages, and generally help to improve the conditions of employment. Any person entering into such combination was to be sent to prison for three months ; any wool-comber or weaver leaving his employment before the termination of the period for which he was engaged was similarly punished, and any workman who should ' damnify, spoil, or destroy . . . any of the goods, wares, or works committed to his charge ' was to pay double their value to the owner. Finally, any person or combination of persons who attempted to intimidate or victimize an employer, by endangering his life, or destroying his property, because he refused to comply with any demands made by his workpeople, was to be transported for a period of seven years.[1]

Legislation of this type was inspired by the outbursts in the south-western counties, but the north was not free from industrial disturbances during the century. Capitalism was established and developed in the worsted and finishing trades. The worsted trade of Yorkshire was in constant touch with the southern branches of the industry, where the wool-combers were very strongly organized, whilst the cloth-workers of Leeds, living in a town and working in groups, would enjoy that social and industrial intercourse from which springs combination and concerted action. Hence in the cloth finishing and the worsted branches of the industry symptoms of labour unrest presented themselves during the century which preceded the Industrial Revolution. Take, for instance, the two following examples of strikes in Leeds. The first was in 1706, and the heroes were six cloth-drawers employed in that borough. These men banded together and vowed that at a certain day and time they would 'down tools', and thenceforth refuse to work for any person who declined to pay them $1\frac{1}{2}d$. an hour, in place of the $1d$. an hour which was the general rate. Apparently the men fulfilled their promise, and consequently attracted the attention of the judicial authorities of the town. They were brought into court and heavily fined.[2]   In 1743 another body of strikers incurred

---

[1] Statute 12 Geo. I, c. 34, extended in 22 Geo. II, c. 27.
[2] *Leeds Gen. Sess. Books* (1706), ii. 300.

the wrath of the guardians of law and order.[1] On this occasion there were three men named, 'and divers other persons as yet unknown', all of them 'workmen and journeymen in the Art, Mystery, or Manual Occupation of a broad Woollen Clothier'. These men were 'not content to work and labour in that art and mystery at the usual rates and prices for which they and other journeymen and workmen were wont and accustomed to work', but were 'falsely and fraudulently conspiring and combining unjustly and oppressively to enerease and augment the wages of themselves and others'. In pursuit of this policy they 'did on the 24th January . . . at Holbeck, in the Burrough, with fforce and arms unlawfully, riotously, and tumultuously assemble and meet together, and so being assembled and met, did then and there, with like force and arms in a Warlike manner, unlawfully, riotously, and tumultuously incite, move, and stir up other workmen and journeymen in the said . . . occupation to conspire with them not to make or do their work . . . at any lower or less rate or price than twelve pence for each day's work . . . To the great Terror of his Majesty's Liege Subjects, and to the evil example of all others'. This was evidently a very spirited outbreak; the leaders were seized and brought before the Leeds magistrates, but with what result is unknown.

The cloth-workers were meek as lambs when compared with the worsted workers. The worsted industry had become strongly organized in its southern home, and that organization spread to the north with the establishment of the industry in the West Riding. Time and time again the stuff weavers around Leeds rose in riot and outrage, and attacked some fellow workman who was probably a non-unionist, or struck at the fountain-head and raided the employer's house. Two instances in particular stand out as showing the energy which was put into these concerted attacks on an unpopular employer. In 1770 thirty-two stuff weavers of Leeds, being 'assembled, unlawfully, riotously, and routously, did redeliver and return, unwoven and unmanufactured, unto Joshua Musgrave, 14 lbs. of Worsted Yarn, which by him had been delivered to one John Day, to be wove and manufactured into two pieces of Camblet; then, being gathered together, they did remain and continue together

---

[1] Ibid. (24th February, 16 Geo. II), v. 239.

in a tumultuous manner for a Space of half an Hour, Shouting and making a great noise and Disturbance, and otherwise greatly misbehaving themselves to the great Disturbance and Terror of diverse of his Majesty's Liege Subjects '; for which expression of their animosity towards the master worsted manufacturer they were fined five shillings each.[1] Two and a half years later 28 worsted workers of Leeds did 'with force and Arms . . . unlawfully . . . assemble and gather together . . . and being so assembled then and there in and upon one John Rider [a master manufacturer of worsteds] in the Peace of God and our said Lord the King . . . did make an assault, and him did beat, wound, and illtreat, so that his life was despaired of, and then did Rioutously, Routously, Wrongfully, and Unjustly break and enter the Dwelling-House of John Rider and did take and carry away 200 pieces of Woollen Stuffs, value £300 '.[2]

The wool-combers, who were the aristocracy of labour in the cloth trade, and who earned the highest wages, were organized in a union which had an almost national constituency. This union was instituted some years before 1741, when it was described in detail by a pamphleteer, who screened his identity behind the pseudonym ' A Lover of his country '.[3] The organization evidently began as a friendly society, paying benefits to those who were sick or unemployed, out of funds raised by weekly payments of 2d. or 3d. Gradually the union gained strength, and then commenced to dictate terms to the masters ; minimum piece rates were to be fixed for combing, and no master was to employ a non-unionist. If the employer defied the union in these respects, the members refused to work for him until the outsider was dismissed. When a member was out of employment, he was given a ticket and money to enable him to go and seek work elsewhere, and found a welcome amongst fellow-members in other parts of the kingdom. Thus in spite of legislation, this union of wool-combers existed as a highly developed association, resembling in many of its methods the big societies of the following century. How long the club lasted we do not know, but it is certain that throughout the century the wool-

---

[1] *Leeds Gen. Sess. Records* (28th May, 10 Geo. III), vii. 183–4.

[2] Ibid. (1st September, 12 Geo. III), vii. 290.

[3] *A Short Essay upon Trade in General*, by ' A Lover of his Country ', 1741, quoted by James, *op. cit.*, p. 232.

combers of Yorkshire were a strong and stalwart body of men, who stood together for purposes of offence or defence, and were the bane of their employers. Legislation existed which allowed the clothier to indict his workpeople for false spinning, bad workmanship, or embezzlement of materials; and yet the worsted master was so much afraid of the united opposition of the labouring classes that he did not dare to put the law in operation against offenders. It was not until the worsted chiefs were given power to establish what was practically an employers' union, namely the Worsted Committee, that the individual master dare attempt to get his grievances redressed. The wool-combers occasionally demanded increased wages, and, should a master refuse, the three or four combers employed by him declined to continue their work. Such incidents as the following were therefore quite common : In 1777 three journey-men wool-combers were convicted at the Bradford Quarter Sessions ' for keeping up, continuing . . . making, entering into, and being knowingly concerned together at Bowling in a Con-tract, Agreement, or Combination, contrary to the fform of the Statute in the case made and provided, to advance their wages as journeymen woolcombers, and for presuming to put such Contract, Agreement, and Combination into execution, and in consequence thereof refusing to work for reasonable and accus-tomed wages ; . . . [they were] therefore committed to the House of Correction . . . at Wakefield, there to be confined and kept to hard labour for a space of three months.'[1] Again in 1791 the Worsted Committee prosecuted three Halifax wool-combers upon ' a charge of Combination or Conspiracy in raising their Wages '.[2]

During the later years of the century organized labour became much more powerful in the West Riding. In January 1787 the carpet weavers of Leeds, after a ' turn out ' of several weeks, obtained an advance in wages ; during this strike there had been much rioting and robbery.[3] In 1793 the Corporation of the borough began to feel anxious at the growing industrial unrest, and appointed a committee to consult with the Recorder

---

[1] *Quarter Sess. Order Books, Bradford*, July 31, 1777, vol. FF, p. 2.
[2] *Minutes of Worsted Comm.*, January 3, 1791.
[3] Mayhall, *Annals of Yorkshire*, i. 166.

' as to the necessary and proper measures to be adopted for the amending and explaining the Acts of Parliament for punishing Servants and Workmen for breach of their contracts, and for preventing combination amongst workmen '.[1]   In the previous year the Worsted Committee had looked askance at any extension of liberties for friendly societies, because such societies might have a ' prejudiciall Tendency, by enabling the members thereof to form illegal Combinations '.[2]   The Acts of 1799 and 1800 forbade combinations of masters and men alike, but in spite of these Acts labour organizations continued. The evidence before the Commission of 1806 revealed the existence of various societies and unions, which were attempting to keep out non-unionist workmen (or ' snakes ' as they were labelled), striving to force up wages, by strikes if necessary, rebelling in sympathy with any of their fellows who might be wrongfully dismissed, and also acting as sick and provident societies. One society, that of the clothworkers, had evidently succeeded in gaining considerable control over that industry. It insisted that no person over fifteen years of age should be taken as apprentice, and a Leeds master finisher in 1806 admitted that he dare not attempt to defy his men in this particular, ' because the men would have left their work '. Another witness tells how he dismissed a man (William Child) because of his advocacy of a union called the ' Institution ', and because he spent too much of his time ' going round to persuade men to think as he thought in the villages, endeavouring to make converts, and exhorting the workmen to stand up for their rights '. Strikes were carried on with much bitterness, destruction of property, personal attacks, and vigorous picketing.[3]

The strange feature about most of these later unions is that they belonged essentially to the eighteenth century, by the way in which they attempted to stamp out the first flames of the Industrial Revolution.   With the appearance of machinery many people foresaw the inevitable. The employees and the small clothiers saw clearly that the advent of machinery and the entire abandonment of Tudor legislation would spell ruin for

[1] *Corporation Minutes*, January 28, 1793, iii. 96.
[2] *Worsted Comm. Minutes*, April 2, 1792.
[3] *Reports*, 1806, iii. 15, 36–8, 178, 187, 193, &c.

them.   Labour-saving machinery would remove the need for many workmen, and the cost of purchasing and erecting the new machines would mean that only the big clothiers and the merchants would be able to take advantage of the new possibilities.   Hence the workmen and small independent clothiers had to fight for their very existence, and many of the unions established between 1780 and 1810 spent their time and energy in trying to stop the flow to the factory.   They pleaded for the maintenance of apprenticeship, for the revival of the Act of 1555 which forbade the congregation of machinery into one place, for the prohibition of the use of gigmills, and for the maintenance of all the old and now obsolete safeguards which the flood-tide of *laissez-faire* was sweeping away.   When they found there was no help to be obtained from Parliament, they took the law into their own hands, and for the next twenty years fought against machinery wherever it made its appearance.   Then came the destruction of looms and spinning jennies, burnings and gunshots, imprisonments, transportation, and executions, but all without avail.   The day of little things was past, and the small clothier, the domestic unit, and the little trade union gradually passed out of sight.   The next few decades were full of circumstances which militated against unionism, and only since 1914, amid the difficulties created by the Great War, has labour organization become really strong amongst Yorkshire textile operatives.

CHAPTER X

THE PROCESSES OF MANUFACTURE—FROM THE SHEEP'S BACK TO THE CLOTH HALL

IN the preceding chapters no attempt has been made to describe in detail the various processes through which the wool passed before it became a piece of cloth, ready for the market and the consumer. It now becomes necessary, therefore, to take up this theme, and to make a brief survey of the stages of manufacture as they were carried on in the eighteenth century. In many respects this description applies to all the centuries during which the industry was being practised in Yorkshire, for there had been little development in the industrial arts between the fourteenth and eighteenth centuries. The implements were almost the same, the treatment of the wool had scarcely altered, and in industrial knowledge the clothier who paid his penny a kersey in the days of the Lancastrian kings was not very much behind his descendants who sold their pieces on Leeds Bridge in the days of Anne. In the intervening period the spinning-wheel had become universal in the North, and new varieties of cloth had been introduced. Many minor improved devices had made the hand-loom easier to work, and the clothiers in the lawsuit of 1638 spoke with pride of the increased efficiency of their methods. Further, during the eighteenth century there was some adoption of better machinery and methods. But the great fact remains that in the four centuries preceding 1760 there was not one tithe of that technical progress which was made in the next half-century. Inventive genius lay almost dormant during those centuries, and did not awaken until the reigns of the Georges.

The reasons for this are not hard to find. Inventive activity is stimulated chiefly by an increased demand from the market. So long as production, jogging along on old-fashioned lines, can meet the demand, there is no powerful stimulus to the discovery of better methods. This was the general situation up to about 1700. A slowly growing demand could be met by traditional methods of production, thanks to the increase in population. But with the eighteenth century came a largely increased demand for textile goods, in order to cope with which it was necessary to devise some means for accelerated production. Once this had begun in one branch of the industry it spread to others. Quicker weaving called for faster spinning : therefore the flying shuttle made necessary the discoveries of Hargreaves and Crompton, which in turn necessitated further acceleration in the rate of weaving, in order to consume the swollen supply of yarn.

Increased demand is, however, only part of the explanation. The fact that most of the inventions came in the cotton manufacture suggests that in a new industry, free from tradition, technical progress is likely to be more rapid than in older trades. The woollen industry was bound tight in the customs of centuries, and its devotees were therefore loth to venture on new lines. Inventions applying solely to the treatment of wool, e. g. combing machinery, were slow in making their appearance, and even when the big textile inventions had proved their worth in the cotton trade they were adopted very slowly in the West Riding industry. The cotton manufacture, rising in the eighteenth century, had no age-worn creed to fetter its development, and therefore supplied conditions far more favourable to the advancement of industrial methods.

Now let us turn to the processes of manufacture as practised in the eighteenth century, and first we must consider

The Wool Supply

The story of the English wool supply from 1660 to 1825 is one of reiterated but scarcely successful attempts to keep English wool for English looms, and thus deprive foreign workers of their supplies of English fleeces. An Act of Charles II had revived the absolute prohibition on the exportation of the commodity, and this Act, frequently reinforced by subsequent statutes, remained in operation until 1825. William III drew up elaborate plans for patrolling the coast, and appointed inspectors to keep watch for smugglers.[1] The Yorkshire coast was placed under the control of a surveyor, who, aided by eighteen ' riding

---

[1] Various Acts, e. g. 10 Will. III, c. 40. See also *Memoirs of Wool*, vol. ii, *passim*.

officers,' attempted to suppress illicit exportation from the big ports as well as the tiny creeks.[1] Ingenious schemes were suggested for the detailed registration of all wool immediately it was sheared, for the erection of big bonded warehouses to which all the wool should be brought, for the prohibition of coastwise trade in wool, except by special vessels ; and a commission which inquired into the matter in 1732 was advised by some witnesses to recommend that the whole English wool clip should be bought by the State at fixed prices, and then sold to those who needed it under stringent rules concerning its use.[2] The question was indeed a very pressing one, and the Government was willing to do anything to stop the flow of wool to foreign parts.

In spite of these efforts English fleeces found their way to the Continent. The coasts of Kent and Sussex formed a happy hunting ground for southern smugglers, and on the more deserted northern coasts ' owling ' proceeded merrily throughout the eighteenth century. At the same time much wool crossed the Cheviots and passed from Scottish ports across the sea.[3] France now took the chief share, especially of long wool needed for making worsteds, of which wools England had large supplies, whilst France had very little. English writers of the period spoke with indignation of the manner in which they had seen English wool landed at Dunkirk, and referred to the places where French and Dutch looms were kept at work by the supplies of raw materials smuggled from England. Dyer lamented the existence of the traitor who would so far sink his patriotism as to carry away supplies of long wool ' to the perfidious foe '.[4] The Northamptonshire manufacturer-pamphleteer in 1738 waxed angry at the fact that ' we have the misfortune to have among ourselves some who are so base as to contrive all manner of ways and means to owl . . . wool abroad . . . to those who are utter enemies to our interests and happiness ' [5]; and the Leeds Corporation in 1742 and 1767 appealed to the House

[1] *Memoirs of Wool*, ii. 67. This was in 1717.
[2] Add. MSS. 33344, ff. 63 et seq.
[3] See *Treasury Papers*, vol. lxxiv, and *passim* 1690–1730.
[4] *The Fleece*, by John Dyer, LL.D. (1757).
[5] *Observations on British Wool*, by a Manufacturer of Northamptonshire (1738), p. 2.

of Commons to give its earnest attention 'for the preventing
the pernicious practice of running our Wooll from Great Brittain
into fforeign Countrys '.[1]

During the 'seventies the wool market became somewhat
easier. The improved breeding and closer attention now devoted to sheep rearing had increased the production of English
wool, whilst the importation from Ireland and other sources
was becoming considerable. These factors, along with the
slump caused by the American War, brought down the price of
wool very quickly. In 1775 the price was $8\frac{1}{2}d.$ per lb. ; in 1779
it was only $6d.$[2] This severe decline brought the wool-growers
to their feet ; they were compelled to sell cheaply, and yet they
had considerable stocks remaining on their hands. If only they
could obtain permission to export the surplus, they would be
able to get a good price for the wool abroad. In 1780 and 1781,
therefore, an agitation began, especially among the Lincolnshire wool-farmers, to obtain permission to make a limited
exportation of English wool, and also to forbid the importation
of Irish yarn. In October 1781 a general meeting was held at
the castle of Lincoln, where a committee was chosen to prepare
petitions to Parliament asking for these favours. Outwardly,
the Lincolnshire men seem to have been very moderate in their
demands, and did not seek the repeal of the anti-exportation
laws. They asked only for licence to export a limited quantity
of the surplus wool which the period of depression had left on
their hands, and sought for protection against imported supplies
which might deprive them of part of their home market. But
in a moment the industrial and commercial interests of Yorkshire and East Anglia sprang to arms, as if their very existence
was at stake. This insidious proposal of the men of Lincolnshire must be met by the strongest opposition, and the clothing
districts set to work to defeat the wishes of the wool-growers.
The first big meeting of the woollen manufacturers and merchants was held in Leeds on December 19, 1781, when many
resolutions were carried. It was decided that ' the exportation
of any sort of wool is injurious, and must be strenuously opposed,
and that applications for stopping the importation of Irish yarn

[1] *Corporation Minutes*, ii. 323 and 466.
[2] Bischoff, *op. cit.*, app. vi.

be resisted '.   Two committees, one of merchants, the other of manufacturers, were elected to carry on the campaign.   They were to open up correspondence with merchants and manufacturers in other parts of the kingdom, and so rouse general opposition.   Lastly, it was decided that since the welfare of the landed interests was thought to be at stake, the assistance and support of the gentry should be sought.

Similar meetings were held at Halifax, Huddersfield, Rochdale, Newcastle, Carlisle, Exeter, Norwich, and in all the East Anglian counties.   At all these gatherings the resolutions passed at Leeds were endorsed, or similar ones carried.   The High Sheriff and Grand Jury at York in March 1782 declared against the men of Lincolnshire, and the justices of the peace in the West Riding expressed their practical sympathy by granting £100 to help in defraying the expenses of the campaign.   The whole clothing interest was in arms against the wool-growers. Some pointed out that although the price had fallen the quantity had increased, and so the growers were really more prosperous, and Arthur Young urged that over-production should be checked by turning some of the pastures into arable land, and by growing hemp or flax under a Government bounty.   The men of Lincolnshire stuck to their guns as the national attack concentrated upon them.   Delegates from various parts met in conference in London in January 1782 and drew up a monster petition, expressing the abhorrence of the whole industry at the proposals of the wool-growers.   Against such united action Lincolnshire could not hope to succeed in gaining what it desired, and when the wool-farmers' requests eventually came before the Commons they were summarily rejected.[1]

This failure only urged the wool-dealers to take the risks of illicit trading, and smuggling of wool continued apace.   In 1784 42,000 lb. of wool were seized at English ports, but large quantities evaded the vigilance of the customs inspectors. Sometimes the material was carried abroad in bags labelled ' Hops ' or the like ; at other times small boats, laden with wool, pushed out to sea, and met the ships some distance from port. Few ships in fact left the Yorkshire and Lincolnshire coast

---

[1] For all the details of this agitation see *Leedes Intelligencer*, 1781–2 ; also Bischoff, *op. cit.*, i, pp. 209–15.

towns without having one or two sacks surreptitiously stowed away in their holds.[1]   The merchants and clothiers therefore clamoured for stricter legislation and more rigorous enforcement.   The Worsted Committee set the ball rolling, and evidence was given before a Parliamentary Committee by Mr. Charles Clapham of Leeds and Mr. John Hustler, the grand old man of eighteenth-century Bradford, to show the extent to which the home industry was being baffled by the unlawful traffic. The trustees of the cloth halls prosecuted a vigorous campaign, and the West Riding justices gave financial support.   These exertions were rewarded by the stringent Act of 1787-8[2]; by this statute any person concerned directly or indirectly in the exportation of wool was liable to a fine of £3 for every pound weight he had exported, and also to three months' solitary imprisonment for the first offence, and six months for the second, along with the forfeiture of ships, boats, carriages, &c., concerned in the smuggling operations.   Regulations were imposed on the carriage of wool from one part of the kingdom to another, and other provisions made to ensure that the foreigner should no longer feed upon English raw materials.   When the news arrived that this measure had passed all its stages in both chambers there were great rejoicings and processions of workmen in all the Yorkshire clothing towns.   The bells of the churches and cloth halls were rung, speeches and self-congratulations indulged in, and bonfires illumined the skies at dusk.[3]

As to the exact value of such Acts one can make no accurate estimate.   They required an efficient and alert machinery for their enforcement.   Popular feeling and commercial interests would aid in the detection of offences, whilst the officials of the Worsted Committee did much to bring culprits into the dock. Still, a dark night, a lonely expanse of coast, and a handful of experienced sea-dogs were sufficient to evade the strictest watch, and smuggling of wool continued.   Some cases of detection are recorded, as for instance the following :

1788.   Edmund Barker of Thorne was committed for three months to York Castle for exporting wool from Goxhill

---

[1] *Report of Parl. Committee*, 1786, *Gen. Coll. Reports*, vol. xxxviii, nos. 82–5, 87.

[2] 28 Geo. III, c. 38.   See also West Riding Quarter Sessions Order Books, HH, *passim*.   [3] Mayhall, *op. cit.*, i. 170.

in the East Riding to Dunkirk, besides forfeiting all his goods and chattels, and paying £3 for every pound of wool exported.

In the same year three Swedish ships were seized at Hull for smuggling wool out of the kingdom.   For a number of years they had been surreptitiously exporting some 1,300 packs annually.[1]

1789. Messrs. Hainsworth & Son, Leeds merchants, were found guilty at Appleby Assizes, ' both of illegal package and . . . exportation ' of fleeces.[2]

The home supply of wool was therefore of vital importance to the Yorkshire manufacturer.   The wools of the Lincoln and Leicester breeds, with heavy fleeces and long fibres, were the special demand of the worsted weaver, whilst the Yorkshire and other strains supplied the shorter fibres for the woollen cloths.   The supply from the Yorkshire sheep was wholly inadequate, and its quality was not sufficiently good for many of the fabrics woven in the county.   Until about 1770 no one in Yorkshire had paid serious attention to sheep-breeding, and the average fleece of the sheep reared on the wastes and commons seldom weighed more than 3½ lb.   True, this was an improvement on the conditions of the seventeenth century, for Best in his *Rural Economy* (1641)[3] says that ' usually six of our ordinary fleeces make a just stone ' of 14 lb.   Luccock at the end of the eighteenth century allowed one sheep to eight acres, and remarked that the fleeces of Yorkshire sheep were small in weight, very dirty, and generally used in the district where they were produced, never going out of the county.[4]   In the eighteenth century, therefore, as in Stuart times, it was necessary to draw upon the wool supplies of other counties, and the southern parts of England supplied large quantities of raw material for

---

[1] Mayhall, *op. cit.*, i. 163.

[2] Ibid., i. 167. Also *Gentleman's Magazine*, September 1789, p. 855.

[3] *Rural Economy of Yorkshire*, by Best (1641) ; Surtees Soc., vol. xxxiii, p. 24. See A. Young, *Northern Tour, passim*.

[4] Luccock, *Observations on British Wool* (1800), p. 323. When attention began to be paid to the improvement of sheep the fleece increased in weight from 3½ lb. to 7 or 10 lb. (see Young's *Northern Tour*). A story is told of a moorland shepherd who, when asked by Sir John Sinclair how many sheep he allowed to the acre, replied, ' Why man, ye begin at t'wrang end first. Ye should ax how many acres to a sheep ' (' Essay on farming of West Riding ', by Charnock, *Journal of Royal Soc.*, lx. 300).

the Yorkshire looms.   Further, foreign supplies were being drawn upon to a much greater degree during the century.   In 1752 Yarmouth and Lancaster were opened as ports for Irish wool and yarn,[1] through which new supplies of raw and semi-manufactured materials flowed into East Anglia and the West Riding.   Additional stocks were obtained from the southern counties of Scotland,[2] and in 1766 nearly 2,000,000 lb. of wool were imported, chiefly from Ireland, Spain, Portugal, and Saxony.[3]

The wool, when shorn from the sheep's back, might be sold in a number of ways.   In the first place, clothiers and wool-staplers made annual excursions to the wool-farms, and purchased part or the whole of the year's clip.   Secondly, many wool-buyers, especially the large clothiers and wool-staplers, made contracts to purchase the whole yield of a farm for a number of years. Thirdly, the wool-grower, instead of waiting for buyers to come to the farm, might bring his wool to the fair or market, and there dispose of it.   All three courses had their adherents. The visit to the farm was a recognized method of purchase : long-period contracts were common, and the big wool markets and fairs of Guisborough, Beverley, and Wakefield, or the smaller meetings at Dent, Bedale, and similar market towns, were great events in the life of the district and the county. The greatness of the Beverley wool sales was now a thing of the past, whilst Wakefield had stepped forward rapidly in the seventeenth and eighteenth centuries, and was now the great wool market of the clothing area.   Growers and dealers in Lincolnshire and other counties forwarded their wool to Wake-field, where it was sold by agents and staplers to the clothiers of the surrounding districts.

The wool-stapler, described in the *London Tradesman* (1757) as the ' Sheet-Anchor of Great Britain ', is worthy of a moment's attention.   He was the descendant of the Merchants of the Staple and the broggers who were so abominated in the sixteenth century   The Merchants of the Staple had developed an internal trade in wool as their foreign trade declined, and now, although

[1] Statute 25 Geo. II, cc. 14 and 19.
[2] Adam Smith, *op. cit.*, II. v. 281–2.
[3] Hobson, *Evolution of Modern Capitalism*, p. 63.

the society was dead, the wool-stapler survived,[1] and was, according to Defoe, ' a very important and considerable sort ' of tradesman in the eighteenth century.[2] Success in the business required a large amount of capital, £1,000 to £10,000 being the sum regarded as necessary for setting up as a master in the trade in London.[3] The stapler was to be found in every part of the kingdom where wool was produced or required. His business was to buy and collect large quantities of wool from varied sources. Hustler, one of the most famous Bradford staplers, declared to the House of Lords in 1800 that he was accustomed to buying wool himself from nineteen counties, whilst his partner and agents made purchases in at least another fourteen.[4] On the farm or in the market squares he made his purchases, which he then carried away, by land or by water, to his head-quarters, a warehouse in the heart of the clothing district. Here the wool was cleaned, sorted, and classified according to its qualities and the uses to which it was to be put. Thence to the market stall, where the various clothiers came to purchase their supplies, large or small. Every manufacturing town had its market, where the manufacturer who could not journey to the East Riding to buy a hundred fleeces was able to procure his two or three stones of wool, the raw material for a week's work. The wool-stapler allowed a certain measure of credit, a facility of which most clothiers availed themselves.

' A wooll seller knows a wooll buyer ' is an old Yorkshire proverb, but if it was intended to indicate that the two were

[1] A paper, temp. Car. I (*D. S. P.*, vol. 515, f. 139), states the nature of the staplers' internal trade. They bought wool, sorted it into long or short, and then subdivided each kind into four or five qualities. Each class was then taken to the particular district where it was needed. ' And divers places, as in Yorkshire and at Oswestree, where there dwell many clothiers that make course cloth, rugs, course cottons and flannels, and use onely course sorts of wooll, buy these sorts of wooll of the staplers, ready sorted.'

[2] Defoe, *Complete Tradesman*, 1841 edition, ii. 188–9.

[3] *London Tradesman*, by R. Campbell (1757), pp. 199 and 340. The description given there reads as follows : ' He is the first Man into whose Hands that valuable Branch of our Trade, the Wool comes. He buys it up from the Farmer, and keeps large Warehouses in Town to receive it. He makes it up into several Sortments fit for the Manufacturers. It is a very profitable Branch, but cannot be enter'd upon with little Money.'

[4] *Minutes of Evidence before the House of Lords, relating to the Woollen Manufacture* (1800), p. 80. Another wool-stapler declared that he bought wool in thirteen counties. He made four journeys annually into nine counties, and an annual tour of four other counties ; p. 94.

matched for shrewdness it seems, like most proverbs, to be only partially true. Throughout the century there were numerous complaints that the buyer was being duped and deceived by the seller. To such a pitch did this rivalry of wits attain that widespread agitations were carried on in 1751–2, which brought about the passage of remedial legislation for the evils cited. A short extract from the petition of 1752 will best explain the whole story. The petitioners stated that ' in order to distinguish each grower's sheep feeding on common lands, it has been the ancient custom to put a mark of pitch or tar and other ingredients, capable of enduring the severities of the weather, upon some conspicuous part of the sheep ; but of late years they have in many places loaded the fleece . . . with such excessive quantities of marking stuff, in order to increase its weight, that the manufacture has been rendered universally difficult and often unprofitable ; that in order to make it workable the manufacturer is obliged to clip off with the mark as much wool as occasions a very great waste of that valuable commodity . . . and notwithstanding the greatest attention of the most careful manufacturers, the marking stuff is wrought into the goods of all sorts, which, when finished, are so spotted and stained thereby that their value and credit are greatly impaired at home and abroad.' The clothiers also complained ' that in all parts of the kingdom the wool-growers, in order to increase the weight and enhance the price of the wool, permit to be wound up, in the fleece, wool of inferior qualities, as tail wool, unwashed wool, lamb wool, etc., and also clay, stones, dung, sand, and other rubbish, to the inconceivable loss and deceit of the manufacturers, several of whom have found a total loss of one-fifteenth of the weight they bought ; . . . in truth they now find very few parcels of wool fairly wound and free from brands '.[1] The petitioners were unanimous in condemnation of such practices, and legislation at once made provision for the

---

[1] Petitions came from all parts of the country. See the list of towns in the previous chapter. Dyer also speaks of the practice of applying pitch. *The Fleece*, Book ii. 564 :

> Why will ye joy in common fields, where pitch
> Noxious to wool must stain your motley flock,
> To mark your property ? The mark dilates,
> Enters the flake depreciated, defiled,
> Unfit for beauteous tint.

punishment of offenders—a very desirable step when one considers the extent to which such frauds must have hindered a manufacture which knew little or nothing of the use of chemicals in washing and cleaning wool.[1]

Manufacture

We now follow the wool through the various processes, until it passes to the cloth market. Where the fleece had been bought whole and unsorted it was necessary to classify the locks, and set them aside, as long or short, good or inferior.

> In the same fleece, diversity of wool
> Grows intermingled, and excites the care
> Of curious skill, to sort the several kinds.
> Nimbly, with habitual speed,
> They sever lock from lock, and long from short,
> And soft and rigid pile in several heaps.[2]

The short wool was laid aside by those engaged in the worsted industry, and when augmented by the short fibres brought out in combing was sold to the woollen manufacturers, who used only short-staple wool.

After sorting the wool must be cleaned, and, if necessary, dyed, before being worked up into a thread. If the cloth was to be a 'mixed' (i. e. a dyed) fabric, the wool, after being washed, scoured, and cleared of dirt, burrs, twigs, &c., was dyed. The clothier had a small dyeing vat of lead, which sometimes stood outside his door, and occasionally was located in a 'dye house' attached to his cottage. Here the wool was dyed, frequently on primitive lines, and the resulting colour was often far from pleasant. Luccock waxed scornful over the methods and results of dyeing, and concluded his indictment as follows : 'But indeed what can we expect but faint, muddy, and uncertain colours, where wool is dyed, as is too much the custom in Yorkshire, without being scoured, in pans unwashed, and with materials mixed together upon a floor unswept, where a little before perhaps have been mixed ingredients calculated to produce a totally different tint '.[3] Not all wool was dyed,

---

[1] Before 1752, prosecutions are often recorded of fraudulent wool-dealers, e. g. *North Riding Sess. Rec.*, vii. 219, Thirske, 1709 : ' A Harriby yeoman for selling 160 fleeces of wool with certain tails and other deceptive locks.'

[2] Dyer, *op. cit.*, ii. 564.

[3] Luccock, *op. cit.*, p. 172. Luccock lived in Leeds, and knew the Yorkshire industry well.

for a large proportion of the wool was woven into white cloths, and consequently was not dyed until after the cloth had been made.[1]

The wool, whether white or dyed, was now sprinkled with oil and placed layer upon layer on the floor, each layer being sprinkled with oil; the whole mass was then tossed about, beaten with sticks, and thoroughly mixed up and permeated with the oil, so as to facilitate subsequent processes. Then came the distinction between the two kinds of wool—the short staple for woollens went to be carded, the long staple for worsteds to be combed. The carding was intended to work the wool into a fluffy mass of inseparable fibres, prior to spinning. Hand cards were used, and consisted of two boards fitted with handles, and covered on one side with wire teeth set in leather. A handful of the wool was placed between the boards, which were then brought close together, and worked about in every direction, especially in a circular motion. Thus the wool was mixed into a sheet of interlaced fibres, ready for spinning. Paul had invented some carding machinery in 1748, but the invention did not become generally adopted until improved by Lees and Arkwright in the 'seventies.

Wool-combing, as indicated in an earlier chapter, aimed at extricating the short fibres, laying the long ones in parallel lines, and clearing the wool of knots and foreign substances. The implements of the hand wool-comber were few and simple, consisting of

1. A pair of combs on handles. Each comb might contain from three to eight rows of teeth, which along with the handle formed an implement shaped like a T. The teeth in the outside row might be up to eleven inches in length, those in the inner rows becoming shorter with each row.

2. A post, to which one of the combs could be fixed on a peg or pad.

3. An iron comb-pot or stove, for heating the teeth of the comb and warming the wool. This heating was necessary to keep the fibres as soft, flexible, and elastic as possible, and the combs were constantly being reheated.

---

[1] The description of the processes is taken from Luccock, who is followed by James. Two admirable pamphlets on *Hand Card-making* and *Hand-combing* have been written by Mr. H. Ling Roth, of Bankfield Museum, Halifax.

The actual procedure differed from district to district, and there were many variations in the West Riding itself.[1] According to one account, the workman took a tress of wool about four ounces in weight, sprinkled it with oil, and rolled it in his hands to get all the filaments properly oiled. He then fastened a heated comb to the post, with the teeth in a horizontal position. Taking half the tress, he threw it on to the teeth, and pulled it through repeatedly, leaving a few fibres each time on the comb. When he had in this manner treated all the wool in his hands, he placed the loaded comb on or near the stove to warm while the second comb was similarly employed on the other half of the tress. The two combs were then taken by the handles and worked contrariwise through the wool, until one comb had taken it all on to its teeth. In some instances the comber sat on a low stool for this last process, working the combs on his knees : in others, one comb was fixed to the post. The long fibres were now gently pulled off the comb by hand, the short ones remaining on the butts of the teeth. A variation of this method was to throw the wool on to a comb attached to the post, and work it off on to the second comb, after which it was worked back on to the original comb. In the nineteenth century it was customary in the Bradford and Halifax area for combers to wash the wool after the first combing, and then repeat the whole process. The long fibres drawn from the comb by hand were called ' tops ' : the short ones which remained on the teeth were known as ' noils '. The former went to the worsted makers, the latter to the woollen.

Wool-combing was admitted to be the most unhealthy branch of the trade. The work was done near the charcoal stove, which filled the room with noxious fumes. One writer, reporting on the health of the industrial towns in 1845, gave a ghastly picture of the effects of wool-combing under domestic conditions. ' The workpeople are obliged to keep their windows open in all weathers, to prevent or to mitigate the evil effects of the gas. They are roasted to perspiration on one side, and often have a current of cold air rushing upon them from the window. They look pale

[1] For details of the various methods see James, *op. cit.*, pp. 249 et seq., or Burnley, *Wool and Wool-combing* (1889), pp. 88–90 ; the best description of the implements and their use is found in Roth, *Hand Wool-combing*, Halifax, 1909. This pamphlet of ten pages is profusely illustrated.

and cadaverous, few reaching fifty years of age. Their roasting employment and exposure to the gas gives them a desire for spirits and opiates.'[1] The writer on the woollen manufacture in Ure's *Dictionary of Arts, Manufactures, and Mines* (1861 edition) declared that hand-combing was far more severe labour than any carried on by machinery, because of the hot close atmosphere of the combing-room ; hence he wrote ' This is a task at which only robust men are engaged.'[2] Of course there was the open country, the fresh air, and the patch of ground outside. The comber was able to earn good wages if he worked regularly, but the work was hard, and the comber seldom did work regularly. He took occasional holidays, often drinking heavily ; he spent some time tending his garden,[3] or occasionally participated in a strike. But all these things did little to counteract the effects of the monotonous work and the charcoal fumes.

The wool, whether carded or combed, was now ready for spinning. This might be done by the wife and children of the small woollen clothier, or by the people living in the vicinity. But the entire population of the clothing area was insufficient for producing an adequate supply of yarn, and much of the wool was therefore taken far afield in Yorkshire and into the adjoining counties. James gives an instance of a clothier, residing at Otley, who put out his wool to be spun in Cheshire and North Derbyshire.[4] The manufacturers of Bradford and Halifax forwarded large quantities of raw material to Craven, the North Riding, and Lancashire. This carriage of wool from place to place was a prominent feature of the industry, and was inevitable so long as population was dispersed. The Otley manufacturer mentioned above bought his wool at York or Wakefield, and brought it 25 miles along the worst of roads to Askwith, near Otley. Here it was sorted, given out to be combed, and returned to the master's head-quarters : it then went to Cheshire to be spun, was returned to Askwith, and again handed out to be woven. Finally, the cloth went to Colne

---

[1] *Health of Towns Commission*, 1845. Report on cottage combers of Bradford ; Yorkshire section, p. 19.
[2] Ure, *op. cit.*, iii. 1045. See also Roth, *Hand Wool-combing*, p. 10.
[3] At Heaton, near Bradford, there were certain gardens to which the name of ' Wool-combers' Gardens ' still clung in the later nineteenth century.
[4] James, *op. cit.*, p. 292.

market to be sold. Yarn prepared in the Leeds and Bradford areas had formerly been sent to Norfolk; waste silk from London was washed, combed, and spun at Kendal, and then returned to be woven at Spitalfields. All this meant the employment of ' a prodigious number of people, horses, carts or wagons ', and a waste of time almost inconceivable. There can have been little speeding up in the old form of industry, when one man's business covered a whole county.

The wool was taken these long distances on the backs of pack-horses, and when it reached its destination was usually deposited with some agent, whose business it was to distribute the work over the countryside. The agent was sometimes a farmer or shopkeeper; but a great part of this distribution was apparently done by women, who augmented their earnings as spinners by the commission of one halfpenny per pound paid for putting out and collecting the wool.[1] When the spinning was being done by those who lived near the clothier, the spinner came to his employer's warehouse for the supply of wool. Spinning was done on the old distaff or on the single-thread spinning wheel. The former was still retained to some extent in East Anglia, but in the West Riding it had entirely disappeared, and the spinning wheel was a common feature in the equipment of almost every Yorkshire home. When the inventions of Wyatt and Paul were introduced about the middle of the century they met with some little favour, but until the 'nineties the bulk of the yarn for the Yorkshire looms was prepared by the spinning wheel. The work was largely carried on by the female members of the family or by the children. The employment of the youngest children was general, the parents being only too pleased to get their children to work, augmenting the family income by one or two shillings a week. Industrial schools and workhouses throughout the century devoted much of their time to teaching children the arts of ' scribbling ' or mixing wool,[2] and spinning.[3] Defoe, Young, and other writers noted

---

[1] James, *op. cit.*, pp. 311–12. See chap. xii, section on Worsted Committee, for notices of female distributing agents.

[2] Dodsley's *Description of Leeds* (1764); manuscript transcript in Leeds Reference Library.

[3] Poulson, *Beverlac*, p. 796. There were also in existence schools to which children went to be taught spinning.

with pleasure and satisfaction the prevalence of the practice of employing small children in these branches of the industry.

Around the spinning wheel has centred the Arcadian conception of eighteenth-century bliss ; but, like most popular opinions as to the charm of the ' good old times ', it must be taken with a great deal of caution. Southey spoke of ' contentment spinning at the cottage door ', and James had it on the authority of an old villager that the women and children of Bradford Vale used to flock on sunny days with their spinning wheels to some favourite pleasant spot, to pursue the labours of the day, though, James adds slily, ' these spinners in the sun were not free from the vice imputed to their grand-daughters of the modern tea-table '.[1] But, even assuming that the spinners at the cottage door or on the village green were the embodiment of contentment, and that fine sunny days were more frequent in the eighteenth century than they are to-day, the system was full of faults and imperfections, and open to one or two serious objections. In the first place, this employment of the housewife must have meant a grave neglect of domestic duties, or a very heavy additional demand upon her energies, if she was to be a wage-earner and also a housekeeper. Washing, baking, cleaning, &c., must have been relegated to odd moments and evenings, and the woman must have had even less opportunity for rest and recreation than she has to-day. To see what this meant, one has only to observe the state of affairs in the twentieth century in those households where the wife spends her days in the mill, and discharges her domestic duties before or after factory hours.

Secondly, the employment of young children was open to grave abuses. ' Scarcely anything above four years old, but its hands were sufficient for its own support ', said Defoe, and the part played by children in the eighteenth-century industry was quite important. The gross earnings of children under ten years of age must have been very considerable, and formed an integral part of the family income. But at what a cost ! We to-day know the price which has been paid in lives and health by the half-time system, and there is no reason to suppose that the employment of even younger children in the eighteenth century

[1] James, *op. cit.*, p. 289.

took a less heavy human toll. True, the work may have been light and the hours short, but even that is very doubtful. Yorkshiremen, either from thoughtlessness or necessity, have seldom spared their children, and one cannot doubt that many young workers were kept at tasks beyond their strength for long hours daily, to the ruining of their health and general physique.

The methods of spinning employed during the early part of the century were still primitive, and involved a great proportion of manual labour. Progress was slow, and the spinner could do little more than 1 lb. per day. Hence, although the industry was so widely scattered and every available person employed at the work, the supply of yarn was inadequate to meet the needs of the weavers. The proportion of spinners to weavers was now greater than in the sixteenth century,[1] due apparently to some acceleration in the speed of weaving. In 1715 it was stated that 7 combers and 25 weavers employed 250 spinners, i.e. 1 comber to 35 spinners and 1 weaver to 10 spinners.[2] Other estimates allowed 9 spinners to each weaver,[3] and even when spinning had been accelerated by the use of hand jennies in the latter part of the century the work of one weaver consumed the yarn produced by four spinners. The early figures may include a number of children, but even if this was so it would be very difficult for the clothiers to procure a steadily increasing supply of yarn as the industry grew in size. Old and young were employed, and yet the supply of yarn was inadequate. The scarcity was accentuated when the adoption of the flying shuttle made weaving so much more rapid, and thus the weaver was often compelled to remain idle for a day or two because he could not secure a supply of yarn. In these circumstances it was essential that some means should be devised for the acceleration of the process of spinning, and the first great inventions following Kay's shuttle were concerned with the spinning of yarn.

The supply of yarn was insufficient. Further, the quality of the produce varied considerably. The shopkeeper was not quite

[1] See Chapter III, section on Journeymen.
[2] *Great Britain's Glory*, by Haynes (1715), pp. 8–9.
[3] *The Weavers' True Case*, by a practical weaver, 1720 ; Smith's *Memoirs of Wool*, vol. ii.

the most suitable man for giving out work to the best spinners only, or for remonstrating with those who did faulty work. He would not offend the most incapable spinster by refusing to give her work, so long as she was a good customer at his counter. The employment of children was a cause of imperfect workmanship, and the clothier had to pay for the tuition of his future workpeople in uneven and badly spun threads. Also, it was wellnigh impossible to secure uniformity of yarn. The clothier asked for a definite standard when giving out the wool to be spun, but the tendency would be for each house and each spinner to vary a little in the thickness and firmness of the yarn ; some sent in ' hard twisted ', others ' soft twisted ', and it was very difficult to reduce the work to one standard.[1] Thus in irregularity, inadequacy, and inequality of supply the domestic system of spinning was rapidly becoming more and more unsuited to the needs of the times. It must vanish as soon as new possibilities were discovered, and hence we find that spinning was amongst the first processes to be absorbed in a factory system, where machinery and power could cope with the needs of the loom.

The yarn, when spun, was returned to the local centre, packed up, and forwarded to the clothier. Should he be catering for the looms of some southern field, the packs were dispatched to East Anglia, Gloucestershire, or elsewhere.[2] If the master utilized the yarn himself, he handed it out to his weavers, who wove it into a piece in his loom-shop or in their own homes. The small clothier gathered up the yarn produced for him by the labours of his family or neighbours, and set to work to weave the cloth with his own hands. The loom was prepared and the warp inserted in a very primitive manner, especially if we can accept Dyer's description as being at all representative :

> And now [the weaver] strains the warp
> Along the garden walk or highway side,
> Smoothing each thread ; now fits it in the loom
> And sits before the work.[3]

[1] *Reminiscences of an Octogenarian*, by Hall, printed in James, *op. cit.*, p. 312. To express it in technical terms, some spun to 16 hanks per pound, others to 24 hanks. When the manufacturer got his yarn back it had to be sorted, and the hard yarn used for warp, the soft for weft.

[2] The witnesses in 1806 referred to the sale of North Country yarn in Gloucestershire and other parts.   [3] Dyer, *op. cit.*, iii. 570.

At the beginning of the eighteenth century the loom was still comparatively simple in design. It was little more than a box-like framework, fitted with rollers, healds, and treadles. The village carpenter often served as loom constructor, though in the more populous clothing areas loom-makers were to be found. It was then placed in the loom-shop, if such a structure was attached to the house ; otherwise, it found a resting-place in the least inconvenient quarter of the home. Prior to the adoption of the flying shuttle, the weaving of narrow pieces was effected by passing the shuttle from hand to hand through the divided warp threads. This method had marked limitations and many faults. It was slow, clumsy, irregular, and required that the weaver should work leaning over the fabric, a position very detrimental to health. The weaving of broad cloths presented a still greater difficulty, since these pieces were of such a width as to render it impossible for one man to weave them. Dyer gives one of his most idyllic pen-pictures to a description of the method adopted.

> Or if the broader mantle be the task,
> He choses some companion to his toil.
> From side to side with amicable aim
> Each to the other darts the nimble bolt,
> While friendly converse, prompted by the work,
> Kindles improvement in the opening mind.[1]

The weaving was apparently merely an *obbligato* accompaniment to the elevation of two kindred spirits by mutual intercourse.

This slow and cumbrous procedure was ended by the adoption of Kay's ' flying shuttle '. Kay devised the idea of mounting the shuttle on four small wheels, which would enable it to run from side to side of the loom when knocked by hammers, of wood or leather, worked by cords held in the hand of the weaver. The new contrivance was slow in finding a place in the textile world. It was first made public in 1733,[2] and roused the fiercest enmity in East Anglia and Lancashire. It appears to have found a better reception on the eastern side of the Pennines, where it solved the difficulty of weaving broad cloths. Hence it seems that a number of Yorkshiremen began to make use of the invention, in a manner which drew from Kay the

---

[1] Dyer, *op. cit.*, iii. 570–1.   [2] Patent|no. 542, May 26, 1733.

following announcement in the *Leeds Mercury*, August 27, 1737 :

' Whereas John Kay of Bury . . . having obtained a patent for his new invented shuttle for weaving of broad cloths, and dyvers clothiers within the West Riding . . . have made use of the said shuttle without the lycense of the said John Kay, contrary to the prohibition in the said patent, This is to give notice that if any person will come to Mr. John Lazenby in Leeds, and lodge an information against a sufficient number of clothiers, &c.'

A reward was promised, and no divulgence was to be made of the informant's name. Whether or not the reward was claimed is unknown, but in the following year Kay came to Leeds and began a series of lawsuits against the offenders. The weavers refused to pay royalty, and formed a shuttle club which fought Kay, making the lawsuits so protracted that the inventor was ruined by legal expenses, and in 1745 he was compelled to flee from the town before the anger of his opponents.[1] From the evidence given in 1806 we learn that the flying shuttle was not really extensively used in Yorkshire until about 1760–70,[2] and many of the older men who appeared before the Parliamentary Committee in that year could remember the day when narrow cloths were woven by throwing the shuttle from hand to hand, and wider cloths required two men, or a man and a boy, to make them. Even when the improvement had been adopted, the loom was still limited in its scope. Its motions were heavy and cumbrous, as any one will quickly realize by examining and experimenting upon the few hand-looms which have survived. Fancy patterns could only be woven slowly and at great expense, and the rate of weaving ordinary cloths was far from rapid until later inventions had increased the speed at which the loom could work, strengthened the shuttle thread, and applied other than manual power.

The weaving suffered from frequent interruptions, due, in the first place, to a shortage of yarn. Then there were the breaks occasioned by taking the pieces to the clothier's head-quarters, the fulling mill, or the market, as well as those which occurred

---

[1] Swire Smith, *Manufacture of Textile Fabrics*, printed for private circulation, p. 4. See also Mantoux, *La Révolution industrielle* (1906), p. 199.

[2] *Reports*, 1806, iii, pp. 81, 128, 166.

in the harvest and haymaking seasons,[1] when men, women, and
children tramped away to the fields of the Vale of York, the
East Riding, Lincolnshire, and Nottinghamshire, to assist in
gathering in the harvest.

> Next from the slackened beam the woof unroll'd
> Near some clear gliding river, Aire or Stroud,
> Is by the noisy fulling mill received,
> Where tumbling waters turn enormous wheels,
> Where hammers, rising and descending, learn
> To imitate the industry of man.
> Oft the wet web is steeped, and often raised,
> Fast dripping, to the river's grassy banks,
> And sinewy arms of men, with full strained strength,
> Wring out the latent water. Then up hung
> On rugged tenters to the fervid sun,
> Its level surface reeking, it expands,
> Still brightening in each rigid discipline,
> And gathering worth.[2]

Such is Dyer's description of the next processes, milling or
fulling, and tentering. The piece, when taken from the loom,
was laid upon the floor, treated with various evil-smelling
liquids and pigments, and trampled under foot, in order to
remove the bareness of the web, and mat together the warp
and weft. The odour which emanated from the cloth after
receiving this treatment must have been revolting, for dung,
manure, &c., were often ingredients of the pigments. May in
1613 referred to 'the Scent of these Northern dozens',[3] and
Mr. Sykes in his history of Huddersfield remarks on the continuance of the practice in the eighteenth century.[4] The cloths
were then taken to the nearest fulling mill, in some cases a considerable distance away. Here the piece was 'scoured' with
fuller's earth, treated with soap, and beaten with heavy hammers
or 'stocks' (worked by a water wheel or horse gin), in order to
wash out the impurities, grease, &c., and thicken the fabric by
shrinking and 'felting' together the fibres of wool. It was
finally washed in the river, to get rid of the soap and fuller's
earth, and, after being measured and stamped by the inspector,

---

[1] Bigland, *Topogr. and Hist. Description of the County of York* (1812),
p. 612 ; also James, *op. cit.*, p. 312.

[2] Dyer, *op. cit.*, iii. 570.   [3] May, *op. cit.*, p. 21 et seq.

[4] Sykes, *Huddersfield and its Vicinity*, pp. 78–9.

was taken back home, or to some place where the clothier had the use of tenters.

Before leaving the topic of mills and milling, it might be appropriate to note a curious point which arose about 1739. During the second quarter of the century the output of cloth was increasing, and consequently the work of the fuller grew heavier. The clothiers were busy, and they kept the mill-men equally so. When time was so precious, it seemed a pity to waste it by relinquishing industrial pursuits on the Sabbath. The clothier's conscience might not allow him to weave on that day, and the journeyman would prefer to enjoy his weekly rest. But there was nothing to prevent the clothier from doing something, or rather from inducing some other person to do something for him. Hence it was represented to the Quarter Sessions at Pontefract in 1739 that ' it is, and for many years last past, hath been a common Practice to mill Narrow Cloth upon Sundays, and that the Clothmakers are now arrived to such a Scandalous and Shocking Degree of prophaning the Sabbath this way, that they even contrive to bring more cloths to be milled upon the Sunday than any other day, Whereby both Masters and Servants are guilty of a public Neglect of the Holy Duties of the day, and by certain Consequence are insensibly drawn into the Commission of all maner of Sin and Wickedness, To the great displeasure of Almighty God, the Scandal of the Kingdom, the Evil Example of their Neighbours, and the breach of all Laws, both divine and human '. For prevention of such enormities in future, it was ordered that ' no Millman of narrow woollen cloth shall wet, stamp, or put any cloth into his Mill after 12 of the Clock on Saturday Night, or before 12 on Sunday Night, on pain to forfeit his Salary ' for the milling of such cloths. The justices of the peace were requested to be very vigilant in the detection of offenders, and to punish all clothiers, or their servants, who should take cloths to the mill on Sunday, or indeed engage in any kind of textile occupation on that day.[1]

From the mill the cloth went to the tenter frame, on which the cloth was stretched, and its dimensions were increased by fixing one end and one side, and by fastening a movable beam to the other edge, as well as by pulling at the free end.

[1] Quarter Sessions Order Books, U, p. 141, Pontefract, May 1, 1739.

The cloth was attached to the beams by tenter-hooks, and then left for a day or two to dry and assimilate itself to its stretched proportions; after that it was ready for the market.   The piece would still be rough and unkempt; the white cloth would have to be dyed and finished before it was ready for the tailor, and the mixed woollen cloth had still some processes to undergo.   The worsted piece was not fulled at all, but it still required much attention after weaving before it was ready to be made into garments.

With the cloth ready for the market we leave the cottage system of manufacture.   We have followed the material through its various stages, and seen the family at work; but yet there is much that we do not know about the real nature of the workaday life of these people.   Thoresby's antiquarian writings do not give it us, and even Defoe's masterly pen left much unwritten. Perhaps the following extracts from a poem, written about 1730, will serve to give us a more intimate picture of family life and labour.   The poem is ' descriptive of the Manners of the Clothiers ',[1] and is written in a style at once intimate and colloquial.   The scene is situated ' some hundred yards from Leeds, crowded with . . . industrious breeds ' of merry clothiers, amongst whose ' greasy throng ' of workpeople the writer finds himself.   The day begins early with breakfast of oaten cakes (the famous ' Havercake '), milk, and porridge.   After which all get away to work,

> And through the Web the Shuttle throw.
> Thus they keep time with hand and feet
> From five at morn till eight at neet.[2]

Their wooden clogs, the whirr of the spinning wheel, and the constant chatter make a continuous hum throughout the day. Then, at eight in the evening, the workers are summoned by the housewife, and having washed themselves gather round the supper table.   Whilst the meal is in progress, the master addresses his family, apprentices, and journeymen.

> Lads, work hard I pray,
> Cloth mun be pearked next Market day.[3]

---

[1] The only copy of this poem which I have encountered is a manuscript copy in the Leeds Reference Library. It is bound up in a volume of Miscellanea, entitled ' Matters of Interest '.   [2] i.e. night.

[3] i.e. 'must be perched ', or examined to see that there are no holes or faults in the piece.

'And Tom mun go to-morn to t'spinners,
And Will mun seek about for t'swingers,
And Jack, tomorn by time be rising,
And go to t'sizing mill for sizing.[1]
And get your web and warping done
That ye may get it into t'loom.
Joe, go give my horse some corn,
For I design for t'Wolds tomorn.
So mind and clean my boots and shoon,
For I'll be up i' t'morn right soon.
Mary,—there's Wool—tak thee and dye it.

Here is an admirable picture of a master clothier employing
his own family and one or two others, probably apprentices, in
his own house, and a number of spinners in the neighbourhood.
He sets out for the Wolds to buy wool, but, before going, gives
detailed orders to his assistants, and instructs his wife Mary to
proceed with the dyeing of wool.   At this order Mary begins
to protest against being expected to do textile work as well as
housework, and we get from her lips the very objection which we
raised above against the employment of women in spinning, &c.

Mistress. So thou's setting me my wark.
I think I'd more need mend thy sark.[2]
Prithee, who mun sit at bobbin wheel,
And ne'er a cake at top o' th' creel,[3]
And me to bake and swing and blend,
And milk, and barns to school to send,
And dumplings for the lads to mak,
And yeast [4] to seek, and syk as that;
And washing up, morn, noon, and neet,
And bowls to scald and milk to fleet,
And barns to fetch again at neet.

To which forcible statement of objections the husband replies
in the strain of ' Business is business ' .

Master. When thou begins thou's never done !
Bessy and thee mun get up soon,
And stir about and get all done ;
For all things mun aside be laid,
When we want help about our trade.

[1] Sizing used to treat warp with, to strengthen it before putting into loom.
[2] Sark = shirt.
[3] Creel = the wooden framework hung near the roof, on which clothes and
cakes of oat bread were hung to dry.
[4] Yeast for baking, and probably for brewing herb beer and other drinks
which are still consumed in the Riding.   ' Syk ' = such.

Those last two lines sum up the whole situation, and against them further protest is useless. The wife therefore resignedly remarks :

> Why Bairn, we'll see what we can do,
> But we have both to wesh and brew,
> And shall want Malt, Hops, Soap, and Blue,
> And thou'll be most a week away,
> And I's hev t'wark folk to pay.

Master. Let paying for their wark alone,
> I'll pay 'em all when I come home.
> Keep t'lads at wark, and take this purse,
> And set down what thou dost disburse.

By this time supper is over, and the wife suggests to her husband,

> Come, let us go to Joe's,
> To talk and hear how matters goes.

As the two go out, other young people come in from neighbouring houses, and the merry party sits round the fire, drinking, smoking, laughing, and telling stories and jokes connected with the work of the day, its accidents and humours.

> Thus they do themselves well please
> With telling such like tales as these,
> Or passing of a merry joke,
> Till ten gives warning by the clock,
> Then up they start—to bed they run,
> Maister and Dame home being come.
> They sleep secure until the horn
> Calls 'em to work betimes i' th' morn.
> Ere clock strikes eight they're call'd to Breakfast
> And bowls of milk are brought in great haste.
> Good Water-Pudding,[1] as heart could wish
> With spoons stuck round an earthen dish.
> Maister gives orders to all in full,
> Sets out to t'Wolds to buy his wool,
> And while the good man is away,
> The neighbour wives all set a day
> To meet and drink a dish of tea
> With Dame while she is left a Widow.

And so the poem ends with a vivid picture of this ' At Home ', and the neighbouring women indulging that propensity which is known to-day as ' calling ', with the ' ca ' pronounced as in ' cat '.

---

[1] Probably oatmeal porridge.

The horn referred to a few lines from the end was an ante-cedent of the later whistle or ' buzzer '. Horn-blowing was practised at Bramley, Ossett, Yeadon, Otley, and probably in most places, and it seems to have been the custom to depute some individual to blow a horn vigorously in the village streets, to awaken the apprentices and journeymen. The horn was blown at five o'clock in summer and six in winter ; again, at eight in the evening, it gave the signal to cease work for the day. Even so late as 1860 one of the Otley mills called its employees to work by means of a horn blown in the streets near the mill.

During the second quarter of the nineteenth century, when the power-loom was ousting the hand-loom from the place of supremacy and the factory system was playing havoc with the old domestic organization, the lot of the hand-loom weavers was very hard. Their wages had gone down, unemployment was rife, and their day of grace seemed quite at an end. In these circumstances the hand-loom weavers looked back, with longing eyes, to the time when the factory was as yet unknown, and sighed for the ' good old times ' of the domestic system. To them, in their suffering, the eighteenth-century industrial world became idyllic, the very embodiment of perfect happiness and simplicity—Arcadia transplanted. This idea of the beauty and glory of the pre-factory system became generally accepted during last century, and many writers have sketched the domestic organization of industry in most glowing colours. Such an opinion, however, requires to be examined in the cold light of actual facts, so let us for a moment pause, and consider what were the chief points of advantage and disadvantage in the system which we have sketched in these chapters.

The employee was all in favour of the domestic system. He preferred to work in his own house, where there was an air of liberty and freedom from restraint and supervision. He could suit his work to his pleasure, he could enlist in addition the services of his family. William Child, for instance, resided at Wortley, and worked as a journeyman in his own home, where he had two hand-looms and a spinning jenny. Not only did he work, but his wife and six children were also pressed into service. His wife spun the yarn, the younger children wound it on to bobbins, and the eldest son, a cripple, occasionally did a little weaving on the second loom.[1] These two advantages are emphasized in the Report of the Commissioners on the Hand-Loom Industry in 1839–40. The commission remarked on the tenacity with which hand-loom workers still stuck to their trade, and stated in a very lucid manner the reasons for this forlorn clinging to a decaying industry. These reasons sum up the situation in the eighteenth century so well that they are worthy of citation : (1) Hand-loom work in the weaver's own cottage ' gratifies that innate love of independence which all more or less feel, by leaving the workman entirely master of his own time, and the sole guide of his actions. He can play or idle, as feeling or inclination leads him ; rise early or late, apply himself assiduously or carelessly as he pleases, and work up at any time by increased exertion hours previously sacrificed to indulgence or recreation. . . . There is scarcely another condition of any of our working population thus free from external control '. Undoubtedly this independence was a great asset to the workman. He could choose his own hours of labour, go from the loom-shop to his garden, and in harvest time tramp away to the fields and help to gather in the crops. (2) ' It concentrates the family under one roof, gives to each member of it a common interest, and leaves the children under the watchful eye of the parent.' [2] From many other sources one has this same advantage pointed out ; ' large families are no encumbrance ; all are set to work ', said Arthur Young,[3] and Radcliffe remarked that ' even the aged who retained the use of their eyes and limbs were able to earn their bread in some degree '.[4] Thus, as one journeyman bluntly expressed it in 1806, ' certainly we prefer having work in our homes ; . . . We can begin soon or late, we can do as we like in that respect, and those of us who have families have an opportunity in one way or another of training them up in some little thing '.[5]

The third advantage which has been urged in favour of the domestic system is its healthiness, its revelry in fresh air and

[1] *Reports*, 1806, iii. 102 et seq.
[2] *Hand-loom Commissioners' Report*, 1839, p. 604.
[3] A. Young, *Northern Tour*, iii. 250.
[4] Radcliffe, *Origin of Power-Loom Weaving*, p. 60.
[5] Evidence of W. Illingworth, 1806 *Reports*, vol. iii.

rural surroundings, which had their effects in producing a high
standard of national health, and a general increase in the average
length of life. Many instances of longevity are quoted. We
hear of fathers 140 years old accompanying sons aged 100 [1];
of a man in his ninetieth year marrying a wife who is already
a century old [2]; and Defoe declares of the Halifax district,
which he knew so well, that 'the people in general live long,
they enjoy good health, and under such circumstances, hard
labour is attended by good health'.[3] But it is dangerous to
base generalizations of longevity on these recorded instances.
One would require to see the birth certificates of these veterans,
and the very fact that their lengthy existence is commented
upon by contemporaries shows that they were the exception,
rather than a common feature of the world of that day. If,
however, one admits that there may have been a longer standard
of life and a higher degree of health, one must attribute it to
the whole manner of living, and not merely to the fact that
industry was carried on in the home rather than in the factory.
There was much in the cottage industry which was quite as
unhealthy as the conditions in the early factories. The cottage
itself violated many laws of hygiene, and was often low, dark,
damp, and ill-ventilated. The very presence of manufacturing
processes in or near the dwelling and sleeping apartments did
not add to the health-giving qualities of the domicile. The use
of oil and evil-smelling concoctions in the treatment of the
material, the mixing of the dye ingredients, and the boiling of
the dye-vat, all must have helped to render the atmosphere of
the cottage foul and unpleasant. The use of charcoal stoves
and the general conditions of combing stamped at least one
process as deadly, whilst the working of all the other branches
of manufacture must have been attended by a dirtiness of
dwelling and pollution of atmosphere quite equal to that of
the later mill-room. The cottage industry, in so far as it was
carried on in or adjoining the house, was unhealthy. What
really made for health was not that the work was done in the
cottage, but that the cottage was in the country. In the free
open expanse of countryside, in the possibility of alternating

[1] Defoe, *op. cit.*, iii. 145.   [2] *Annual Register*, 1762, p. 78.
[3] Defoe, iii. 137.

farming and industrial pursuits, in the enjoyment of the simplest
of diets, in the lack of great stress and bustle, and the absence
of working under high pressure were to be found the forces
which helped to counteract the influence of manufacturing conditions within the house, and gave the worker an opportunity of
renewing that strength which the circumstances of his occupation
tended to sap away.

One last merit has been occasionally attached to the domestic
system, especially by disciples of the school of Ruskin and
Morris. These men claim that the application of manual skill
and labour, such as was to be found in the cottage industry,
gave the workman an interest and pride in the work which he
was doing. The joy of creation and the gratification of seeing
the product of his labour gradually evolving, these were some
of the sentiments which are supposed to have chased through
the mind of the eighteenth-century weaver. But did the textile
worker ever feel these sensations? Was there much joy or
pleasure in working from 5 a.m. to 8 p.m. at a slow and cumbrous
hand-loom, making cheap cloth, every yard of which was like
every other yard? Was not this manual labour very monotonous, physically exhausting, and devoid of any variety and
pleasurable excitement? Had these men been carving gargoyles
or statues of saints for cathedrals, there might have been the
joy of craftsmanship and creative art in their work. But between
the production of artistic masterpieces, either in stone or metal-
work, and the manufacture of yard after yard of cheap kerseys
there is a great gulf fixed, and William Child, the weaver at
Wortley, found his work just as monotonous as does his modern
counterpart, except, of course, when he left his loom and went
away round the villages, persuading men to think as he thought
and join the union of which he was a shining light. The Industrial Revolution has been accused of having destroyed man's
joy in labour, and of depriving him of that pleasure which he is
supposed to have experienced from working in his own home,
at something which was entirely the work of his own hands.[1]
But the Industrial Revolution never destroyed any such joy
and pleasure in the textile industry, simply because they never
existed. The trivial round and common task of the eighteenth-

---

[1] This phrase is taken from Cole, *The World of Labour* (1913), p. 10.

century worker was drab and monotonous, and he would be intensely amused if he could realize the glamour which has been cast to-day over his dreary toil.

Such were the advantages from the workman's point of view, and many masters were quite willing to let the work be done in the men's homes rather than in their own shops. The weavers were paid at the same piece rate whether they were home workers or not, but masters felt that, human nature being what it was, it might be desirable to have one's employees under direct supervision. Thus in 1806 Mr. Walker, of Wortley, explained that he had his men working together as much as possible, ' on purpose to have [the work] near at hand, and to have it under our inspection every day, that we may see it spun to a proper length ' ; and he declared that cloth was generally ' more perfectly wrought and with less imperfections at home than abroad '.[1] In similar vein Mr. Atkinson, of Huddersfield, stated that he gathered his workpeople together ' principally to prevent embezzlement ; but if we meet with men we can depend on for honesty, we prefer having [the cloths] wove at their own houses '.[2] This feeling on the part of masters, that it might be preferable to gather one's workpeople together, had gained ground during the eighteenth century. With the expansion of the industry the need for better organization and consolidation became more pressing. The capitalist employer or the merchant was beginning to supervise the work, gauge the market, introduce new methods or new machinery, and supply large orders in a given space of time. But these things were very difficult, if not impossible, under the loose unregulated organization which existed in the domestic system. The liberty of the employee easily became licence ; we cannot ignore the persistent accusations of idleness, drunkenness, &c., which are encountered throughout the century, and though they may often be exaggerations they contain a substratum of truthful evidence that the weaver or comber had his seasons of lassitude and low pleasure, in which his own enjoyment caused delay and inconvenience to the master for whom he worked. Supervision of workmanship was impossible, the institution of regular standards of production could not be made, and the absence of the overseeing eye was responsible

[1] *Reports*, 1806, iii. 175 et seq.   [2] Ibid., iii. 220.

for that burning question of the embezzlement of material which will be dealt with in a later chapter.

The domestic system made it impossible to realize economy of supervision. It was equally impossible to effect any economy of time. In handing about the material from person to person, from place to place, from county to county, days and even weeks were wasted. Thirdly, there was the obvious obstacle to the introduction of new and large machinery into the cottage. The hand-jenny, when it became popular in the third quarter of the eighteenth century, did to some extent oust the spinning-wheel, being of such a size that it could be kept and worked in a room of the ordinary dwelling-house. Later inventions, which involved a larger machine or the use of power, were of no avail in the domestic workshop, and with their improvement and adoption the factory system grew apace. Thus, to sum up, the domestic system was to industry something of what the common field system was to agriculture. It fostered and preserved the small unit; it gave some measure of independence and freedom of action to the worker; it brought with it, as important con-comitants, conditions which worked for general physical well-being. But it was wasteful and uneconomical; it was conservative and antiquated; it was inadequate to meet growing demands, and to a great extent incapable of exerting itself to answer any sudden expansion in the market.

Such a system, loaded with difficulties and disadvantages, was sure to be outrun by any new order which could produce greater concentration and more efficient organization. This alternative was already in the field, in the congregation of work-people under one roof in the eighteenth-century factories. The modern factory system is based on the economy of the accumula-tion of machinery and the application of power; it embodies the use of capital, the congregation of workpeople, the division of labour, and the exercise of supervision. Each of these factors has great value in itself, but the major part of the economic advantage of the factory springs from the use of machinery capable of performing work quickly, and the use of power which can make the machinery go at a high speed. Until these ele-ments of speed became possible, the factory system did not possess any very great advantage over the cottage industry.

There would be the initial cost of acquiring a sufficiently large building, which would mean a considerable outlay of capital. Then the intending factory owner would have to encounter the objections of his workpeople, who preferred to carry on their occupation under their own roof. Even were such a factory established, its only merit would lie in the possibility of supervising the various processes, and this in itself did not seem to be a sufficient justification for any great expenditure in bringing the manufacture under factory conditions. Hence the factory remained a rarity until the end of the eighteenth century.

We must, however, note the instances in which certain elements of factory organization were being applied prior to the Industrial Revolution. The big clothiers around Leeds, with their dozen looms gathered into one room, had realized the advantage of employing men who worked together under personal supervision, and their loom-shops might be regarded as miniature factories, although the only power which was applied came from the hand or foot of the worker. Similarly there was the assembling of workpeople in the clothing farms west of Halifax, such as was described by Defoe : ' We saw the houses full of lusty fellows, some at the dye-vat, some at the loom, others dressing the cloth, the women and children carding or spinning, all employed, from the youngest to the oldest.' [1] These instances belong to what one might call the first phase in the development of the factory. The same machinery was used as in the cottages, the same power applied ; the only respect in which they can be regarded as factories lies in the assembling of workers, the division of labour, the slight accumulation of capital, and the exercise of supervision.

The adoption of water-power for working machinery brought the factory to its second stage. The use of the water-wheel for grinding logwood or corn and for working fulling stocks was common in preceding centuries. During the early part of the eighteenth century the possibilities of water-power were much more clearly realized, and quite large establishments were erected to utilize the latent force of the northern streams. The Derby silk mill, erected in 1719,[2] was amongst the first great factories in the modern sense of the word. Its machinery

[1] Defoe, op. cit., iii. 137.   [2] Bray's Tour (1783), p. 108.

was driven by a wonderful maze of gearings, in which, according to a contemporary writer, 26,586 wheels and 97,746 movements were all fed by one huge water-wheel.[1] The mill employed 200 hands, and turned out enormous quantities of silk yearly. This mill had its imitators, and there was a similar establishment at Sheffield, employing 152 hands, with its mechanism driven by a great water-wheel. Thoresby notices a mill in Leeds ' wherein, by the ingenious contrivance of Mr. John Atkinson, of Beeston, one water-wheel carries both the rape mill, a mill for grinding logwood, also a fulling stock . . . and a twisting mill with eighty bobbings '.[2] Similarly, a certain Mr. Joseph Stell converted a fulling mill at Keighley into a silk mill driven by water-power, where he wove tapes, ribbons, &c., until he came to an untimely end for counterfeiting coins, when his work perished with him.[3]

Charity, whether private or public, did something to establish instances of congregated industry and of the use of power and new machinery. Eleanor Scudamore died in 1698, and left £50 to be spent, at the discretion of the mayor and vicar of Leeds, for the use of the poor. They thereupon decided to employ the legacy in buying wool, tools, and implements for the manufacture of woollen cloth.[4] In the Leeds ' Workhouse ', set up by Alderman Sykes in 1629, the poor children were ' taught to mix woolls and perform other parts of that manufacture ',[5] and in Thoresby's time ' many poor girls and boys [were] taught to scribble, a new invention whereby different colours in the dyed wool are delicately mixed '.[6] In the similar institution at Beverley the poor were employed in work to which they were accustomed, spinning, knitting, &c.[7] Celia Fiennes [8] found at Malton (about 1696) ' an establishment by mine lord Ewer's coheiress ', who used the rooms of outbuildings and the gate-house of an old mansion ' for weaving and linning cloth, haveing sett up a manufactory for linnen which does employ many people '. Sixty years later Sir George Strickland made his

---

[1] Young, *Northern Tour*, i. 134; also Bray, *op. cit.*, p. 246.
[2] Thoresby, *Ducatus*, p. 79.   [3] *Keighley Past and Present*, p. 107.
[4] *Leeds Gen. Sess.*, ii. 18, April 19, 1699.
[5] Dodsley's *Description of Leeds*, 1764.   [6] Thoresby, *op. cit.*, p. 84.
[7] MSS. dated 1732, quoted by Poulson, *Beverlac*, p. 796.
[8] Celia Fiennes, *Through England on a Side-Saddle*, p. 74.

experiments in industrial charity on similar lines. He established a woollen manufactory at Boynton, four miles west of
Bridlington, which, says Young, ' deserves the greatest praise.
In this country the poor have no other employment than what
results from a most imperfect agriculture, consequently three-
fourths of the women and children are without employment. It
was this induced Sir George to found a building large enough
to contain on one side a row of looms of different sorts, and on
the other a large space for women and children to spin. The
undertaking was once carried so far as to employ 150 hands,
but the decay of the woollen exportation reduced them so much
that those now employed are, I believe, under a dozen.'[1] The
houses of correction in the West Riding were centres of woollen
industry, and here the inhabitants were compelled to spend
their time, not in picking oakum or breaking stones, but in
preparing yarn.[2] The Wakefield House had ' cards and spinning
wheels for the prisoners, for their use and employment ', and
similar institutions in other parts made like provision.[3]

But the finest description of a charitable mill comes from the
pen of Dyer, who certainly knew Yorkshire very well. In his
poem he has been bewailing the effects of thriftlessness and wild
intemperance in demoralizing and disorganizing industry. He
then expresses his sympathy with the maimed and genuine poor,
for whose sustenance he advocates ' houses of labour, seats of
kind restraint '. This is followed by an account of what was
evidently a highly organized charitable or poor law workhouse.

Behold in Calder's Vale . . .
A spacious dome for this fair purpose rise.
    By gentle steps
Upraised from room to room we slowly walk,
And view with wonder and with silent joy
The sprightly scene ; where many busy hands,
Where spoles, cards, wheels, and looms, with motion quick.
And ever murmuring sound th'unwonted sense
Wrap in surprise. With equal scale
Some deal abroad the well assorted fleece
These card the short, these comb the longer wool.

[1] Young, op. cit., ii. 7.
[2] Turner, Wakefield House of Correction, p. 70.
[3] Leeds Gen. Sess., ii. 291 (1705).

The next process, spinning, was performed by means of Paul's machine, which is described as follows :

We next are shown
A circular machine of new design,
In conic shape.   It draws and spins a thread
Without the tedious toil of needless hands.
A wheel invisible beneath the floor
To ev'ry member of th' harmonious frame
Gives necessary motion.   One, intent,
O'erlooks the work.

We have the dyer making colours ' to tinge the thirsty web ', and the other processes are described in detail. Thus Dyer sketches an establishment which seems to have been well organized and systematized on the lines of the modern factory.[1] From the lines in Dyer's poem we gather that similar ' mansions ' were to be found in many parts of the Riding.

These are all the instances which have been encountered of Yorkshire factories prior to the Industrial Revolution. Probably there were more than one is accustomed to suppose, but even then the sum total is only small.   The forces already analysed all combined to retard the growth of factory production, and to favour the survival of the old order. How long then did the cottage industrial system survive ?   The popular view is that the change was accomplished and that the domestic system had vanished before the end of the first third of the nineteenth century.   This is far from being correct, especially with regard to Yorkshire and its textile industry.   The migration to the town and the factory was a much slower process than we suppose it to have been, and was not complete at the middle of the century.   The cause of this slowness of decay was that the factory system was a long time in gaining an all-round advantage over the older method of production.   It required many improvements to make the eighteenth-century inventions really serviceable.   The new looms could throw the shuttle from side to side with much greater rapidity than the hand-loom had done.   This meant an increased strain upon the yarn which was used in the

[1] Dyer, *The Fleece*, iii. 571. The adoption of machinery in workhouses seem to have been more general than elsewhere. Espinasse, *Lancashire Worthies*, p. 313, says that some of Kay's inventions were lost to the world because of the riotous conduct of the operatives, and consigned to the workhouses of Leeds and Bristol.

shuttle, and therefore steps had to be taken for producing a stronger fibre. The worsted yarn fibre was naturally stronger than that of the woollen, and the power-loom therefore made more rapid progress in the worsted industry than in the neighbouring trade. And still the power-loom did not really capture the worsted industry till 1836 to 1845, as the following figures show :

Year.	No. of Worsted Power-looms in West Riding.
1836	2,768
1841	11,458
1843	16,870 [1]
1845	19,121 [2]

By 1845 the worsted hand-loom was practically a thing of the past, and the power-loom was now able to weave both plain and fancy goods. Similarly, combing did not really become a machine industry until the 'forties. The necessary machinery required much adaptation and improvement before it could produce finely combed wool. In 1838 the better qualities of wool were combed by hand, and only the coarser grades done by machinery. With the improvements made about 1840 hand-combing quickly vanished.

In the woollen industry, progress was still more slow. Carding, slubbing, and spinning passed into the mills between 1790 and 1825, and at the same time improved machinery was being devised for cloth finishing. But weaving still remained a task for the hand-loom ; the difficulty lay in the feebleness of the yarn, which was too weak to allow any great speed in the passage of the shuttle. This difficulty was especially marked where broad cloths were being woven, and when the power-loom was first introduced it went at no greater pace than the hand-loom. Hence the best pieces and the fancy woollen goods were woven much better and equally quickly by the hand-loom, and it required many improvements in both spinning and weaving before the power-loom could replace its predecessor. Thus the new-comer was scarcely known in the woollen industry until about 1832, and made very little progress during the next twenty years.[3] In the 'fifties we still find the cottage weaver clinging with marvellous tenacity to the homestead and

[1] *Reports*, 1844, xxviii. 559.   [2] *Reports*, 1845, xxv. 477.
[3] *Reports*, 1840, xxiii. 527–90.

hand-loom. Mr. Baines, in 1858, gave an analysis of the employees at Waterloo Mill, Pudsey, in which he showed that there
was no weaving whatever on the premises, whilst the cloth was
still sold ' in the balk ' or unfinished, and then dressed at Leeds.[1]

Number of hands engaged *on* the premises of the mill					136		
,,	,,	,,	*off*	,,	,,	167	{ 120 weavers / 7 warpers / 40 burlers
i.e. 167 worked in their own homes out of a total of					303		

The factory was still the centre where the wool was carded
and spun, or the cloth milled and finished. The women and
children worked at the mill, but the male weavers remained
in the loom-shop at home. 'Some years ago ', declared Baines,
' it was supposed that the great factories, by the power of capital,
the power of machinery, and the saving of time, must entirely
destroy the old system of domestic and village manufacture.
But they have not materially affected that system.' Probably, in
this utterance, the wish was father to the thought, for the words
were spoken just as the twilight was descending on the old
panorama. After 1851, and the great display of textile machinery
at the exhibition of that year, the hand-loom steadily lost its
hold upon the woollen trade. The number of power-looms
increased rapidly, the building of mills and the institution of
steam plant became general, and weaving, the last of the processes, eventually passed within the mill-gates. Old men tell of
the days when the loom stood in the homes of their childhood,
and a few survivals are still to be found. In the pattern-rooms
of our great mills, in a solitary cottage here and there on the
bleak stretches of the Pennines, on the ' Celtic Fringe ', and in
the corners of our museums the hand-loom and spinning-wheel
may still be seen. But they are the rare exceptions, reminders
of the once general rule. They have been swept into a back-
water, whilst the main stream of industry flows on, bearing on
its bosom the big factory and giant aggregation of capital,
beside which the cottage workshop and the small industrial
world we have been studying appear only as the most tiny of
toy boats.

[1] Baines, 1858, in Paper before British Association at Leeds. The lecture
is reprinted in *Yorkshire, Past and Present*, vol. ii.

CHAPTER XI

MERCHANTS, MARKETS, AND CLOTH HALLS

THE eighteenth-century towns, especially the smaller ones, functioned chiefly as trading centres. Such towns as Dent, Bedale, Skipton, Cawood, Aberford, and the like spent the greater part of the year in slumber, only awakening for the annual fairs or the more frequent market-days. In purely agricultural districts these periodical gatherings would be small and comparatively unimportant ; but in the industrial areas, where men had cloth to sell, and raw materials and provisions to buy, fairs and markets were as important as they were numerous.

So long as the Yorkshire trade in cloth was small, weekly markets for the sale of pieces were also small, and the cloth fairs, held periodically, once, twice, or thrice a year, were the most important centres for commerce in that commodity. In the early seventeenth century there were fifteen places in the Riding with charters for the holding of cloth fairs—Barnsley, Pontefract, Ripon, Lee Fair, and others. Here the cloth-makers brought their pieces on the appointed days, and met the merchants and factors. But with the growth of the industry those places which lay at the heart of the cloth district began to develop important weekly markets. This was the case with Wakefield, for during the middle years of the reign of Charles I that town sought to add to its commercial prestige by instituting a weekly cloth market. To this the inhabitants of the cloth-fair towns objected, and in 1640 the inhabitants of Barnsley and the other places sent a most urgent petition to Parliament, pleading that the weekly cloth market at Wakefield should be stopped, and only the fifteen cloth fairs allowed as in times past.[1] The petitioners failed to obtain redress for their grievances, and the weekly meeting at Wakefield became important, absorbing the

---

[1] *Hist. MSS. Comm.*, iv. 36. The following description of the town was given in 1628 : ' Wakefield now is the greatest markett and principal place of resorte of all sorts of Clothiers, Drapers, and other traffickers for Cloath in all these parts ' (*D. S. P., Chas. I*, xc. 54).

trade from neighbouring fairs and meeting the needs of the local clothiers. One fair which still exists underwent a marked change in consequence of the rise of the Wakefield market. The story is best told in the words of the petition of 1656 :

' There is a certaine ffaire comonly called Lee ffaire yearly kept at Baghill in ye said Parish [of West Ardsley] uppon two severall daies within less than a month of each, in ye time off Harvests W^ch ffairre formerly stood in Woollen Cloth. But since a Cloth Market hath beene setled in Wakefeild, there hath not for these many yeares beene any Cloth brought to the said ffairre. Soe that it is now utterly decayed and become a tumultuous meeting off the idle and loose persons of ye Country, where there is much Revelling and Drunkennesse, and hathe beene noted these many yeares to be a meetinge where there is usually more or lesse Bloodshed and some lives lost, and also most labourers and seruants hereabouts take occasion thereby to neglect ye Harvest. And as for the comodities brought thither, they are (except some few poore horses) only a few Pedling triffles, off wch ye Countrey may much Better, and with as much Conveniency, be supplyed every market day at Leedes or Wakefeild.' [1]

The petition was unsuccessful ; Lee Fair was neither suppressed nor revived as a cloth market, and to this day it carries on exchange in ' Pedling triffles ' and a few horses of doubtful age and breed.

In a similar manner the Leeds market grew in size and importance, so that it became one of the seven wonders of the north, which every tourist was bound to see. Leeds had grown to be the commercial centre of the woollen area, and as such it drew to itself the produce of a wide and busy field ; there were broad cloths and narrow cloths, white cloths and coloured cloths, and its market was therefore ' the life, not merely of the town alone, but of these parts of England '.[2]

In the seventeenth century the Leeds cloth market was held on the narrow bridge which spanned the Aire at the bottom of Briggate. Here it was open to the inclemencies of the weather, and exposed to the mists and cold damp atmosphere which arose from the river in the early morning. At the same time it was a great obstacle to passers by, and to vehicles coming into Leeds

---

[1] D. S. P., *Interregnum*, cxxvii. 20.   Petition of inhabitants of West Ardsley to J.P.'s of West Riding.   [2] Thoresby, *Ducatus*, p. 17.

from the south on market days. It was therefore removed in
June 1684, ' by order of the Mayor and Aldermen from off the
bridge to the broad street above, to prevent the inconveniency
from the cold air of the water in winter, and the trouble of carts
and carriages in summer '.[1] Briggate thus became the cloth
market, and here sales took place every Tuesday and Saturday,
until the erection of the Cloth Halls moved the centre of gravity
elsewhere.   Many eighteenth-century writers have described
the procedure of this open-air market, but none so well as Defoe,
whose account is vivid, and based on an intimate knowledge
of the method of exchange : ' The Cloth Market at Leeds ', says
Defoe, ' is chiefly to be admired as a prodigy of its kind, and
perhaps not to be equalled in the world. The market for serges
at Exeter is indeed a very wonderful thing, and the money
returned very great ; but it is there only once a week whereas
here it is every Tuesday and Saturday . . . Early in the morning,
trestles are placed in two rows in the street, sometimes two rows
on a side, across which boards are laid, which make a kind of
temporary counter on either side from one end of the street to
the other. The clothiers come early in the morning with their
cloth, and as few bring more than one piece (the market days
being so frequent), they go into the inns and public houses with
it and there set it down.'[2]   It requires a lively imagination to
picture the clothier setting out with, but often without, a horse,
in the very small hours of the morning, and tramping those
miles of execrable road to Leeds. The risks of assault on the
highway were scarcely less real than the risks of coming to
grief in a quagmire, a ditch, or a deep cart-rut. When at last
Leeds was reached about five o'clock, the clothier would need
something substantial to banish his hunger, and so he made
his way to the inns which lined Briggate. Here he ordered
a ' Clothier's twopennyworth ' or ' Brigg-shot ', which consisted
of ' a pot of ale, a noggin of pottage, and a trencher of boiled or
roast beef for two pence '.[3]

The stalls which were erected for the accommodation of the

---

[1] Thoresby, *Diary*, June 14, 1684.   [2] Defoe, *op. cit.*, iii. 117.
[3] Thoresby, *Ducatus*, p. 17, and Defoe, iii. 116. Harley, Earl of Oxford
(1725), ventured to suggest that the food was very inferior and declared that
' however trifling the price may appear for so many ingredients, yet so far
as I can conjecture it is a very dear bargain ' (*Portland MSS.*, vi. 140–1).

cloth were probably the property of the clothiers, or of some Leeds man who allowed the clothiers to use them on payment of a small fee. During the early years of the eighteenth century the innkeepers, who were so generous in providing big meals cheaply, began to attempt to get the stalls into their hands, especially those which stood in front of their own establishments. They then tried to compel clothiers who wished to use them either to patronize their inn profusely, or to pay an excessive fee for stallage. Discontent arose, and eventually the Corporation of Leeds had to take the matter in hand. In 1713 it issued the following declaration, which aimed at checking the efforts of the innkeeper, and also at minimizing the inconveniences which arose from the market taking place at such an early hour :

' Whereas there have beene severall complaints made to this Court of Great disturbances which have happened in the Cloath Market in Leeds Briggate (being a ffree Markett ffor all Sellers and Buyers of Cloath Resorting Thither), by [the Innkeepers] Ingrossing a pretended privilege of severall of the ffronts and placing their Stooles, Stees and Trussells of wood . . . and obleiging the Clothiers either to spend their Money profusely at the Houses or Inns to which the said pretended privileges belonged or to pay Extravagant rates for lyeing on theire Cloath, as aforesaid. And not only soe, But by the unreasonable time of Setting and Placeing the said Stooles, &c., which is frequently begun about 11 or 12 at night to the great disturbance of the Inhabitants lyeing neare. . . and to the great Hinderance of such who have occasion to pass along that way. For Remedy whereof, from Lady Day to Michaelmas no stall to be set up before 4 in the morning, and from Michaelmas to Lady Day not before 6 in the morning.'

Clothiers were not to set up their stalls before these hours, and no one was to pay any fee for the privilege of holding a stall, since all were to be equally free.[1]

At last the counters were erected, and, to continue Defoe's description,

' about six o'clock in summer and seven in winter, the clothiers all being come by that time, the market bell at the old chapel

---

[1] *Leeds Gen. Sess. Records,* ii. 678. A few days afterwards a number of men were indicted for attempting to hinder the market by claiming privileges for stalls, and by demanding fees.

by the bridge rings, upon which it would surprise a stranger to
see in how few minutes, without hurry, noise, or the least
disorder, the whole market is filled, and all the boards . . .
covered with cloth, as close as the pieces can lie longways, each
proprietor standing behind his own piece, who form a mercantile
regiment as it were, drawn up in a double line in as great order as
a military one. As soon as the bell has ceased ringing, the factors
and buyers enter the market, and walk up and down between
the rows as occasion directs. Some of them have their foreign
letters of orders, with patterns sealed on them, in their hands,
the colours of which they match by holding them to the cloths
they think they agree to. When they have fixed upon their
cloth, they lean over to the clothier, and by a whisper in the
fewest words imaginable the price is stated. One asks and the
other bids ; they agree or disagree in a moment. The reason
for this prudent silence is owing to the clothiers standing so near
to one another, for it is not reasonable that one trader should
know another's traffick. If a merchant has bidden a clothier
a price, and he will not take it, he may follow him to his house,
and tell him that he has considered it, and is willing to let him
have it. But they are not to make any new agreement for it,
so as to remove the market from the street to the merchant's
house. In a little less than an hour all the business is done, in
less than half an hour you will perceive the cloth begin to move
off, the clothier taking it upon his shoulder to remove it to the
merchant's house. About 8.30 o'clock the market bell rings
again, upon which the buyers immediately disappear. The
cloth is all sold, or if any remains it is generally carried back
to the inn. By nine the boards and trestles are removed, and
the streets are left at liberty for the market people of other
professions, linen drapers, shoemakers, hardwaremen, sellers of
wood vessels, wicker baskets, etc. . . . Thus you see 10 or 20,000
pounds' worth of cloth, and some times much more, bought and
sold in little more than an hour, the laws of the market being
the most strictly observed that I ever saw in any market in
England.'

When Harley passed through Leeds in 1725 he witnessed
a meeting of the cloth market, marked by all the above features.
There were about 2,000 persons in the market, ' who might
have dealings for £30,000 worth ' all concluded in half an hour,
' and yet all carried on with such hush and silence as if they
had all been bred in the school of Pythagoras. This they told us
was a very small market, many of the neighbouring traders having
been prevented from coming in by the floods and boisterousness

of the weather; at other times they have dealings here in the same space of time and with the same tranquillity for 50 to £60,000. Happy would it be for the family of the Moroses could they procure wives educated under this system.'[1] Such a market must have been an interesting sight. But the picturesqueness and the sense of quickness and silence did not prevent the market from suffering under many inconveniences. It was still open to the inclemencies of the Yorkshire climate, and also to the annoyance from street traffic. The former might be endured (thanks perhaps to the ' Brigg-shot ') so long as there was no rival afield which was providing greater facilities in the way of market·conditions. Thus the Briggate market was accepted as a natural institution, and as the only form of market, until the fear of competition brought the Leeds worthies to a realization of its faults. This awakening came at the end of the first decade of the eighteenth century.

The first sign of trouble came from Hightown, a hamlet situated almost in the very centre of the clothing district, about equidistant from Leeds, Huddersfield, Halifax, and Wakefield. Hightown was in especially close proximity to the white cloth area, and would therefore be an admirable site for a white cloth market. Early in 1709 Messrs. Green and Brooke, lords of the manor of Hightown, petitioned Queen Anne for powers to hold such a market every Monday, i. e. the day before the Leeds market. In reply to this request, the sheriff of the county was ordered to hold a court of inquiry, in order to discover whether there was need for such an additional market, and its possible effect on existing markets. After a great amount of evidence had been taken, the special jury which had been appointed to consider the matter decided ' that the erecting a market at High Town for white woollen cloth would be to the damage and prejudice of the sev'all markets of Leeds, Wakefield, Halifax, and Huddersfield '. Undeterred by this adverse decision, Green and Brooke renewed their petition, and evidently made out a strong case in support of their request. This importunity roused Leeds to strenuous opposition. The corporation, along with the leading clothiers and merchants, objected most strongly, declaring that whilst ' a competent number of

---

[1] Tour of Harley, Earl of Oxford, 1725 (*Portland MSS.*, vi. 140–1).

Markets are for the benefit of trade and commerce, So the unnecessary creation of new markets will divide, weaken, and destroy trade, and render small towns a nuisance to the public, as well as to one another '.[1]

Hightown was defeated, but Wakefield, the second rival, was more formidable. Wakefield had fought its way to the front, and its cloth market was now firmly established. The opening of the Aire and Calder Navigation had just given Wakefield excellent facilities for communication with other parts, and the town was becoming a most important commercial centre. The cloths made around Wakefield were generally broad white cloths, a type for which Leeds thought that it alone had the market. There had been constant disputes between the two places, chiefly with regard to tolls. The Leeds Corporation had supported its citizens in their refusal to pay toll to Wakefield, and intense commercial jealousy existed between the two market centres.[2] Leeds therefore was exceedingly annoyed when it learned in 1710 that Wakefield had erected a cloth hall, in which the pieces were to be sold instead of being exposed to the chances of the weather out in the street. This step caused Leeds to bestir itself, for if Wakefield was allowed to excel Leeds in its facilities for exchange, it would soon detach a large number of white-cloth manufacturers who were now coming to Leeds from Batley, Ossett, Dewsbury, and other places in the Calder valley. Leeds must checkmate the action of Wakefield by providing a similar hall, and so on August 14, 1710, Thoresby ' rode with the Mayor . . . and others to my lord Irwin's at Temple Newsam, about the erection of a hall for white cloths in Kirkgate, to prevent the damage to this town . . . of one lately erected at Wakefield, with design to engross the woollen trade '.[3] The excursion was most fruitful, for Irwin gave his enthusiastic support, and provided the site for the hall. Merchants and tradesmen contributed capital to the extent of £1,000, and as a result of these efforts ' a stately hall for white cloths ' was erected in Kirkgate, and opened in April 1711.

[1] Petition to Earl of Newcastle. Copy in MSS. of White Cloth Hall. Also *Portland MSS., Hist. MSS. Comm.*, ii. 209.

[2] See *Leeds Corp. Minutes*, i. 240 and 243. In 1687 the Corporation granted £50 to one man ' for defending the right of the Parish from payment of toll to Hull and Wakefield '. [3] Thoresby's *Diary*, ii. 65–6.

The building was not large; it was arranged round a quadrangular court, and its two storeys were filled with stalls, on which cloths were laid on market days. Here came the clothiers from the white cloth area of the county, and here for one or two hours every Tuesday afternoon the sales took place.[1]

But this first White Cloth Hall, glorying in its pillars and arches, and its cupola, pointed and gilded, soon became too small to answer the needs of the growing trade in undyed cloths. By the middle of the century the accommodation was quite inadequate, and in 1755 the second White Cloth Hall was opened. This new erection was situated on a piece of land south of Leeds Bridge, between Hunslet and Meadow Lane.[2] The building was much larger than its predecessor, and here for nearly twenty years the market found a home. Those years, however, comprised a period of rapid growth, and by the early 'seventies it had become obvious that still larger premises must be found if Leeds was to maintain its control over the trade in white cloths.

In 1774 such a step became more and more imperative because of the threatened rise of a rival, this time at Gomersal. The marketing accommodation at Leeds was inadequate, and many clothiers were doubtless unable to display their wares to advantage. Therefore certain influential gentlemen residing in and around Gomersal determined to take steps for the establishment of a rival hall at Gomersal Hill Top, about seven miles from Leeds. A piece of ground was given, and a considerable sum of money promised to defray the cost of the building. The leading clothiers of that very busy and flourishing area threw themselves with zest into the project, and persuaded or coerced their fellows to sign ' a bond obliging themselves not to expose their cloths in any other place than Gomersall '. All this roused the ire of Leeds ; the Cloth Hall trustees saw that the establishment at Gomersal would deprive the old market of much of its trade, whilst the Leeds merchants pictured to themselves the seven miles journey which they would have to make if they wished to draw upon the supplies of the Gomersal district. The trustees therefore attempted to frighten the audacious upstarts ;

[1] Thoresby's *Ducatus*, Addenda, p. 248, and *Diary*, April 22, 1711.
[2] Jackson's *Guide to Leeds* (1889), p. 143. Also ' Notes and Queries ', *Leeds Mercury Supplement*, no. 449.

they threatened proceedings at law, and offered assistance, pecuniary and legal, to those who would break the bond which they had signed. These fulminations were discounted by the open support which the Gomersal clothiers received from the local gentry; nothing could be more encouraging than the following letter, published in the newspapers of December 26, 1775 :

' GENTLEMEN,

' We, being fully desirous of promoting the Woollen Trade in the West Riding of Yorkshire, think it expedient to signify to you our entire approbation of your erection of a Hall at Gomersall, in order to establish your market there, and we recommend you to go on and complete your design with all possible expedition, being clearly of opinion that it will be of the greatest advantage to the industrious manufacturer, and also to the white cloth trade in general. Therefore we are determined to give all possible encouragement to so laudable an undertaking.

(Signed)   Sir GEORGE ARMITAGE, Sir THOMAS WENTWORTH, R. H. BEAUMONT, E. E. SAVILE, Sir JAMES IBBETSON,' and other manufacturing or landed chieftains of the West Riding.[1]

Spurred on by such encouragement, the Gomersal· clothiers completed their project and established a hall in defiance of the trustees at Leeds. In 1793 the *British Directory* remarks ' at Gomershall the clothiers have erected a large brick building for a Cloth Market, in hopes of bringing the merchants nearer home, and saving expense thereby. It was of course encouraged by the landowners, but it is doubtful whether it will answer.' [2] As a matter of fact, this hall never did get a firm grip on the trade, especially as improved means of communication made it more easy to use the market at Leeds. But in its inception in 1774 it gave Leeds a real fright, and was partly responsible for the taking of the next great step.

Whilst the trustees of the White Cloth Hall had been hurling their threats at Gomersal, the merchants of Leeds had turned their attention to more practical and satisfactory methods of

[1] *Leeds Mercury*, December 26, 1775.   [2] *Brit. Dir.*, iii. 325.

circumventing the new possible rival. This they did by providing the necessary improved accommodation at Leeds, and the erection of the third White Cloth Hall was almost entirely due to the initiative and energy of the merchants. This was only natural, for the new building must be of considerable size, and its cost would therefore be great. The merchants would benefit as much as the clothiers by such a provision, and the wealthy wholesale traders of Leeds were far more capable of raising £4,000 than were the manufacturers of the district. Hence the impetus and the necessary money came from the Dennisons, Bischoffs, Fountains, Wormalds, Smithsons, and other important Leeds merchant families.[1]

At a meeting of merchants held on September 10, 1774, it was resolved ' That a Subscription be forthwith opened for Erecting a Hall in Leeds, for the better accommodation of the White Clothiers ', and ten days later a similar meeting of merchants elicited promises to the extent of nearly £850. The trustees of the White Cloth Hall were invited to choose a committee to confer with a committee of merchants, and in their hands the scheme rapidly developed. An eloquent and persuasive circular, the postscript of which hinted that subscriptions might be of any amount from £10 to £50, was scattered broadcast to Yorkshire and London merchants, landowners, and all who were in the least interested in the welfare of Leeds. The response to this invitation was most encouraging, donations ranging from a guinea to £250 came from a great number of merchants, and the Leeds Corporation added £100 to the fund. By November the site had been decided upon. The building was to stand on a piece of land situate in the Calls, and known as the Tenter Ground. Viscount Irwin was the tenant for life of this land, which was held from him by the Committee for Pious Uses, on terms of copyhold, the revenue accruing to the Leeds Grammar

---

[1] The greater part of the information contained in the subsequent pages has been drawn from the MSS. of the White Cloth Hall Trustees, now in the possession of Mr. H. Greenwood-Teale, Atlas Chambers, Leeds. The writer wishes to acknowledge the courtesy and assistance which he received at the hands of Mr. Greenwood-Teale. The collection of MSS. is quite invaluable, and is a veritable mine of information concerning the textile industry of this period. For a more detailed history of the White Cloth Hall, see an article by the present writer in the Thoresby Soc. publications, *Miscellanea* (1913), vol. xxii, pt. ii.

School. The Committee of Merchants approached the copy-
holders, and in December 1774 an agreement was made whereby
the land and tenements should be transferred for the sum of
£300. A private Act had to be obtained before such a sale
could be legally recognized, but Irwin quickly carried this
through Parliament, and in March 1775 the plans were decided
upon and estimates invited. With such great expedition was
the work carried out that the hall was opened on October 17,
1775, thirteen months after the issue of the appeal for subscriptions—an undoubtedly remarkable achievement.

The building, part of which still remains, was much larger
than its predecessors. It was rectangular in shape, 99 yards by
70 yards, and was arranged round a quadrangle. The interior
was divided into five long streets, each with two rows of stands,
and contained in all 1,213 cloth-stands. These stalls could be
leased for life by paying 2s. 6d. per annum or a lump sum of
£1 10s. ; and eventually it became possible to acquire the freehold of a stall by paying the £1 10s. Such stalls were entirely
the property of the clothier, who could sell them, let them to
other clothiers at a rent, or bequeath them to others at his
death. Stall-owners were also liable to an annual levy ranging
from 6d. to 1s. 6d. to defray the cost of caretaking, sweeping,
cleaning, and repairs. Those who did not choose to purchase
or rent a stall could make use of the hall on payment of 3d. for
each cloth exposed for sale. With the boom in trade during
the next thirty years the value of the stalls increased rapidly,
so that stands which were purchased in 1775 for £1 10s. were
sold in 1806 for three to eight guineas, the price varying according to the situation in the hall.[1]

The establishment of this big market was almost entirely due
to the enterprise of the merchants of Leeds. They had subscribed the necessary capital, had carried through the legal
proceedings, and now that the hall was erected they called
upon their fellows to promise ' not to purchase, by themselves
or by their agents, any white cloth or coatings in any other
White Cloth Hall now erected, or to be erected within the West
Riding, except Huddersfield Market '.

The clothiers had played a comparatively insignificant part

[1] *A Walk through Leeds* (1806), p. 12.

in all these transactions, and the whole Cloth Hall estate had
been placed in trust in the hands of Darcy Molyneux, Joseph
Fountain, and Robert Green, three of the most prominent
merchants concerned in the venture. Now that all the preliminaries had been settled, and the new hall erected, prepara-
tions were made for handing over the establishment to the
clothiers, to be administered by them henceforth. In 1776,
therefore, negotiations took place, and at a joint meeting held
on October 21, 1776, the transfer was effected. The terms on
which the merchants surrendered their powers and possessions
were as follows : (1) That the clothiers should subscribe £1,000,
in order to pay off the deficit on the hall. The cost of land,
buildings, &c., had exceeded the amount of subscriptions by
£1,000, and the clothiers were therefore to saddle themselves
with that burden. This they did, and the money was at once
forthcoming. (2) That 'all persons who had exercised the
business of a broad white clothier, either for his own benefit, or
as a servant to others, for the space of five years, should be
deemed as duly qualified to purchase Stalls '. This clause seems
to have been somewhat vague, and subsequently was understood
to imply a five years' apprenticeship, instead of one of seven
years.

On these conditions, along with one or two others of minor
importance, the deed ' drawn up and settled by two learned
Councel, learned in the Law ', was signed, and the hall passed
into the hands of the clothiers, or rather of their representatives,
the trustees. Of these there were seventeen, chosen from the
white cloth districts, and each representing a certain constituency.
The distribution in 1802 was as follows :

Mirfield and Hopton .	. 2	Dewsbury, Soothill, Thorn-		
Hartshead and Clifton-on-		hill, and Ossett	.	. 2
Calder . . .	. 1	Alverthorpe	.	. 2
Cleckheaton, Wyke, Huns-		Idle, Bradford, and Bowl-		
worth, and Bierley.	. 1	ing . .	.	. 2
Liversedge . .	. 2	Kirkheaton	.	. 1
Heckmondwike	. 1	Batley and Morley .	.	1
Birstall and Gomersal	. 2			

The trustees were elected for three years. At the end of that
period, or whenever a vacancy occurred, a letter was sent to

some prominent clothier in the particular district, asking him
to convene a meeting of ' legal clothiers ', in order to nominate
and appoint ' a yongue man of the Most Respectabillity and
firstrate Character ', to serve as trustee for that area. The
meeting was held, and the person responsible for the arrangements then notified the trustees of the result in a letter, of
which the following is a fair specimen, so far as spelling is
concerned :

' 3 Augst 1814.
    ' Aat A meten Call at Cleckheaton it was unanmiseley a
greaded to That Wialam yeates is a pounted Truste for the
districket for Cleckton, And so forth for the white Cloth Hall at
Leed.'

The trustees met annually, on the first Monday in June, and
on other occasions when some special business called for their
attention. These annual meetings were often formal, and served
only as preludes to, and excuses for, the sumptuous banquets of
which we find detailed accounts in the cash books of the trustees.
At other times a great amount of business was transacted,
especially in the revision of by-laws, levying of dues, or alteration of policy. ' Good order without oppression ' was the end
the trustees were to keep in view, and under their strict rule
the hall prospered during the first forty years of its existence.

Meanwhile, what of the *coloured* cloth market ? The bi-
weekly meeting in Briggate had been somewhat relieved by the
transference of the white cloth trade to the hall, and probably
the absence of a rival coloured market had kept the makers of
these cloths satisfied with existing arrangements. There does
not seem to have been the least provision made for the sale
under cover of coloured cloths until the big hall was built in
what is now City Square.

In 1755 Leeds obtained an Improvement Act,[1] which gave
permission to effect several alterations in the thoroughfares of
the borough, and to widen Briggate. This proposed disturbance
of the street in which the cloth market was held helped to drive
the coloured cloth-makers to the decision to build a hall of their
own. They were further induced to take such a step by the
increased market fees which were charged in order to defray

---

[1] Statute 28 Geo. II, c. 41.

the cost of the street improvements. In 1756, therefore, the coloured cloth community eagerly discussed the situation. Local meetings were held, and general assemblies considered the project.[1] It was unanimously agreed to be desirable ' that a proper piece of ground shall be purchased in Leeds, and a convenient Hall or Building . . . thereon erected . . . for the purpose of lodging and exposing to sale of mixed broad woollen cloth '. A committee of fifteen clothiers was chosen, drawn from the various parts of the mixed cloth area ; the rank and file made their contributions, varying from £2 10s. to £7 10s., and paid the money into the hands of this executive, to be by them applied ' in the buying a proper piece of ground in Leeds, and in erecting thereon a Convenient Hall . . . to the Intent that the same shall be forever employed and made use of as a Common Hall for the Purpose of Lodging and Exposing to Sale of Mixt Broad Woollen Cloth, made and sold by the Mixt Broad Woollen Clothiers residing in the West Riding '. Armed with these powers, the trustees looked around for a site, and eventually secured a piece of the ' Park ' which is now divided between City Square and the Central Post Office. This land was part of the estate of Richard Wilson, and in selling the site for £420 Wilson made many stipulations. He retained the mineral rights, and demanded that if ever the buildings ceased to be utilized as a market for broad coloured woollen cloths, or were used for any other purpose whatever, both land and buildings should revert to himself or his successors. Wilson also extracted the promise that the buildings should not in any part exceed 24 feet in height, that no windows should be made on the south-eastern side, or stand out from the roof, without his express permission. A cottage might be built for a caretaker, provided that ' the occupier thereof shall be restrained from Keeping a Publick House for selling of ale or any other liquor, and from exercising . . . any Trade or Business on the Premises other than that of a Weaver of Woollen Goods '.[2] Having promised to abide by all these conditions, and paid their £420, the coloured Cloth Hall

---

[1] The various deeds of transfer for the Coloured Cloth Hall are in the hands of the Leeds Corporation. The writer's best thanks are due to Sir Robert Fox, Town Clerk, who kindly allowed him to examine the manuscripts.

[2] Deeds of Sale between Richard Wilson and Coloured Cloth Hall Trustees, May 1757.

trustees received the site for their market, a fine piece of land
120 yards by 66 yards. Contracts were given out to local
builders and the work began at once, so that in 1756 the hall
was ready for the transaction of business.[1] It was larger than
the White Cloth Hall of 1775, and its general arrangement will
be seen from the diagram below.[2]

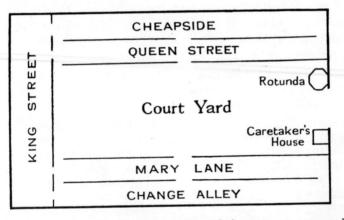

Each street was lined with stands, and there was accommodation for 1,770 stalls.[3] Each stall was 22 inches in width, and
was the freehold property of the clothier, whose name was
painted on the front. The clothier seems to have received
a stall for every £2 10s. which he subscribed, but no one held
more than three. Having paid this sum, no other charge was
made except an annual 6d. to defray general expenses. Towards
the end of the century the trade expanded considerably, and
there was a great demand for stalls. Hence those who wished
to sell could obtain from £8 to £15 per stall,[4] and in 1810 a second
storey was added to the north wing in order to provide a room
for the sale of certain kinds of ladies' dress goods. For permission
to make this extension the trustees paid Christopher Wilson
the sum of £250, and in return gained power to extend the hall
when necessary, to make windows wherever they pleased (even
on the south-eastern side), and to permit the sale of silks cottons,

---

[1] *Leedes Intelligencer*, April 19, 1757.
[2] Mayhall, *op. cit.*, i. 139. Also Macpherson, *Annals of Commerce*, iv,
app. iv ; also all maps of Leeds after 1760.
[3] *History of Leeds*, 1797, p. 6.
[4] *A Walk through Leeds*, 1806, p. 10.

worsted yarn, or any other kind of textile commodities, in addition to the orthodox coloured woollens.[1] By these exten-sions the number of stalls was increased, and in 1850 there were over 2,500 stands for the sale of cloth. Those men who did not own a stall were allowed to sell their cloth in the hall, paying 6d. for each piece.

Some time after the building of the main block a small octagonal structure was erected on the right-hand side of the gateway. This building, known as the ' Exchange ' or ' Rotunda ', served as the office and council chamber of the trustees, in whose hands the management of the property lay. There were fifteen trustees, one from each of the fifteen districts into which the coloured cloth area was divided.[2]

Leeds (3 districts) .	. 3	Dewsbury and Batley	. 1
Rawdon and Horsforth	. 1	Ossett and Horbury .	. 1
Idle and Eccleshill .	. 1	Calverley and Farsley	. 1
Armley . . .	. 1	Morley, Gildersome, and	
Yeadon and Guiseley	. 1	Churwell . .	. 1
Holbeck . . .	. 1	Pudsey and Stanningley	. 1
Bramley . . .	. 1	Hunslet . . .	. 1

Like their neighbours of the White Cloth Hall, these trustees were appointed every three years, and their powers of jurisdic-tion were very large. The transfer of stalls from one owner to another had to be registered by them ; they were to receive the income of the hall and control expenditure. They had power to draw up by-laws and ordinances, and levy fines on offenders. They watched over the interests of the industry, and were vigilant in enforcing the laws of the realm, whenever necessary. Sitting in the ' Rotunda ', they ordered the general affairs of the market, and acted as the fathers of the trade ; then at the end of the three years they straightened up their accounts, put all into order, and handed over books and property to the newly elected trustees.

The use of both halls was strictly limited to those who had served the ' full period of apprenticeship '.[3] At first this implied the seven years' term, but with the breakdown of apprentice-ship in the latter part of the century the trustees bowed to the

[1] *Leeds Dir.*, 1817. See also Deeds, July 2, 1790, and August 9, 1810.
[2] Deeds, January 14, 1757.
[3] See all descriptions of Halls, 1797–1809.

force of circumstances, and in January 1797 reduced the seven years to five.[1] This rule was rigorously enforced, and doubtless did much to maintain apprenticeship in the West Riding longer than it would otherwise have survived. The majority of the clothiers accepted the law, but there were many with cloth to sell who had not served the full term of apprenticeship. These men must find another home for their cloths, and thus there existed a market where the ' Irregulars ' sold their pieces. At first this market was in Meadow Lane, opposite the White Cloth Hall built in that part in 1755. Here, in the ' Potter's Field ', was a big room in which these men deposited their cloths, and here the merchants came as well as to the White and Coloured Halls.[2] In the early nineties this heretical market was moved to the ground floor of the Music Hall in Albion Street, where the cloths of the unapprenticed found a resting-place until they were sold. This third Cloth Hall caused great annoyance to the trustees of the orthodox markets, and many efforts were made to crush it. It became notorious as the home of the free, and was christened the ' Tom Paine Hall ' in honour of that apostle of individual liberty.[3] In 1803 the White Hall trustees determined to suppress this disreputable rival by a great stroke of policy. The Tom Paine Hall had been providing two markets per week, namely Tuesday and Saturday, whilst the White Cloth Hall had only a Tuesday market. The Saturday meeting was very popular, and was undoubtedly damaging the supremacy of the White Cloth Hall. In June 1803, therefore, the trustees asked for the opinion of their fellow clothiers as to the ' propriety or impropriety of holding a Saturday market in the aforesaid Cloth Hall ', and the decision was in favour of a bi-weekly market. Two years later the trustees agreed ' that the Manufacturers of the White Cloth who are in the habit of Manufacturing White Cloth only and attend the Opposition Market in Albion Street shall be permitted to come into the White Cloth Hall on condition that they be unanimous to come unitedly, and not be instrumental in forming an Opposition or Division at any time '. These two steps had a serious effect on the rival hall, and the suspension of the Apprenticeship Laws about the same time helped to remove the *raison d'être* of the

[1] 1806 *Reports*, iii. 13.   [2] Ibid., p. 200.   [3] Ibid., pp. 66 and 201.

Tom Paine market. In 1809 the number of men selling cloths there was only 260, and with the absolute abolition of the apprenticeship legislation all distinctions passed away, so that in 1817 this opposition cloth market was in the hands of wine and spirit merchants.[1]

The procedure of sale in the halls was very similar to that of the open-air market already described. On the mornings of market-days the clothiers brought their pieces to the halls. The horses, on the backs of which many clothiers brought their wares, were not to be left standing about in the Cloth Hall yard. Any horse found in the yard half an hour after the commencement of the market brought upon its master a fine of 1s.; hostlers must come and take all horses away, but boys were forbidden to perform this duty ' as Mischiefs frequently happen from their wantonly galloping the Horses in the street '.[2] The Mixed Cloth Hall opened first, but the early rising habits cultivated by the street market had been abandoned. The removal of the market indoors meant a postponement of the market hour in order to get adequate natural light. Therefore the opening hours of the Coloured Hall were 8.30 in summer, 9.0 in spring and autumn, and 9.30 in winter. At these hours the bell in the cupola was rung, after which the buyers paced the ' streets ' and inspected the cloths laid across the stalls. There was little noisy higgling, for both sides seemed to possess well-defined ideas as to how much they were prepared to give or take. The bargain was struck, and the piece carried off to the merchant's head-quarters. Meanwhile time had been flying, and at the end of an hour the bell rang again to inform the loiterers that they had now only a quarter of an hour's grace. When that quarter had elapsed, the bell rang once more for five minutes, by which time all transactions must have come to an end, or be abandoned. Any merchant or buyer of cloth who was found inside the gates of the hall yard when the bell ceased was fined 5s., with an additional fine of 5s. for every five minutes he still loitered. When the Mixed Cloth Hall had closed, that for white cloths was opened. The laws of sale were almost identical with those of the Coloured Hall, and all transactions must be carried through within an equally short space of time.

[1] *Leeds Dir.*, 1817, p. 29.   [2] Mixed Cloth Hall Orders, 1797.

Simplicity, dispatch, and absence of noisy bartering, such are the impressions one receives from all contemporary accounts of these markets ; but this simplicity was no hindrance to the discharge of great quantities of business. £20,000 to £30,000 worth of cloth changed hands in a busy market-day at the Coloured Hall alone, and during the hey-day of these halls an incredibly large volume of trade was carried on in that hour and twenty minutes.

In all this marketing the trustees kept strict watch over the halls and the stall-holders. In the early years of the trade no white clothier might have the use of more than two stalls, and no man was allowed to expose his wares on the stall of another clothier. Similarly, any person who offered for sale goods made by a clothier not free of the hall met with severe punishment. If a clothier fell into arrears with his yearly rent or his con-tributions to the upkeep of the hall, his stall was considered forfeit, and put up to auction, many stalls changing hands in this manner. The moral character of stall-holders was also placed under supervision. Any clothier guilty of felony, or convicted under the Worsted Acts, was deprived of the privilege of using the hall ; and at a special meeting in 1846 it was resolved that two men, 'having been convicted of Vagrancy under highly flagrant circumstances, leaving no doubt of their dishonest intentions, shall no longer be allowed to frequent this hall or expose any goods for sale therein '.[1]

One of the strangest rules of the White Cloth Hall was that which forbade stall-holders to expose any of their wares at any other market in Leeds. This rule referred not only to the Tom Paine Hall, but also to the Coloured Cloth Hall.[2] Such a stipula-tion did not impose any very great hardship so long as the clothiers confined their attention to white cloths, but by 1800 many of them were adding another string to their bow by making coloured fabrics as well as whites, and in some cases were deserting the white cloth manufacture entirely. But their trustees forbade them to trade in the Coloured Hall, and so many were in a dilemma. In 1810, therefore, the trustees

[1] All these aspects of regulation are to be found in the Orders issued by the trustees.

[2] e.g. 1816, clothier fined 5s. ' for exposing his cloth to sale in this and the Mixt Hall at the Same time '.

recognized the changed circumstances by allowing the sale of coloured cloths and fancy goods in a room which had recently been added to the White Cloth Hall, and in 1828 the whole of one of the ' streets ' in the building was devoted to the sale of such fabrics. The coloured goods invaded the market, and the White Cloth Hall became eventually a market for mixed cloths rather than whites.

The cloth halls were justly the pride of the city, alike in their size and the extent of their business. Distinguished visitors were taken to witness the working of the markets and observe the processes of sale. When the King of Denmark passed through Leeds in September 1768[1] he was not allowed to depart before he had been taken to see the sights of the Mixed Hall, and certain Austrian Archdukes honoured the halls with their presence in 1815. The buildings were also centres of social and political life before the days when the Town Hall, the Coliseum, and similar places had been erected. On December 4, 1786, Mr. Lunardi made a ' balloon ascent from the area of the White Cloth Hall amidst the plaudits of 30,000 spectators '.[2] In 1777 a suite of elegant assembly rooms was built over a part of the same hall, and opened on June 9 of that year ' with a minuet by Lady Effingham and Sir George Savile, Bart., when upwards of 220 of the nobility and gentry were present. . . . The appearance of the ladies and gentlemen was more brilliant than was ever remembered '.[3] Throughout the nineteenth century the hall yards were the scenes of many diversions provided by enterprising persons for the amusement of the citizens. Balloon ascents and displays of fireworks were very frequent ; pig-shows, horticultural exhibitions, circuses, &c., all found a home within the gates of the Cloth Hall yards, and the trustees drew no small revenue from these sources. At the same time these quadrangles formed admirable sites for open-air political demonstrations. The Coloured Cloth Hall yard was generally chosen, because of its spaciousness, and because the steps on the north-eastern side provided a suitable rostrum. Here every question of political moment was advocated to the vast crowds which flocked to listen. Catholic emancipation, the abolition of slavery,

[1] Mayhall, *op. cit.*, under date 1768.
[2] *Yorkshire Magazine*, 1786, p. 379.   [3] See *Leeds Mercury*, that date.

Free Trade, Parliamentary reform, household suffrage, education, &c., all were championed from the steps of the Cloth Hall
yard. Here Wilberforce and Brougham delivered weighty utterances, here Cobden denounced the Crimean War,[1] and here at
the last great meeting, in 1881, Mr. Gladstone held a gigantic
audience spellbound with one of his orations on foreign and
colonial policy.[2]

The Cloth Halls of Leeds were by no means the only ones in
Yorkshire, nor were they even the first in the county. Bentley,
in 1708, speaks of a ' large and spacious hall ', erected by Lord
Irwin at Halifax, ' where the weavers and buyers do weekly
meet. . . . The sales are so great that the lord's collector often
gets as much as thirty to forty shillings at the rate of a penny
per piece '.[3] These were undyed pieces, which were sold in
a building provided by the lord of the manor, who received a toll
on each cloth. The hall was opened by the ringing of a bell,
and, in order to prevent forestalling, a penalty of 39s. 11d. was
levied on any person who even asked the price of a piece of
cloth before the bell rang, the fines being distributed amongst
the poor of the town in which the offender lived.[4] As the Halifax
industry expanded this hall became too small, and much cloth,
especially coloured cloth, had to seek a market in the Butchers'
Shambles. At a meeting of manufacturers in April 1774 it was
agreed that ' a Hall, erected in some convenient place in the
town, . . . would be of great public utility '.[5] This resolution
was speedily acted upon, and a scheme for a big building drawn
up. The site was offered as a gift by Mr. Caygill, and, after
a long and bitter dispute amongst the manufacturers, finally
accepted.[6] The hall was completed by December 1778, and
opened on January 2, 1779, amid great jubilation and a display
of fireworks.[7] The building was erected on the slope of a hill,
and therefore contained three storeys in the lower part and
two on the higher ground. It was built around a quadrangle,
measured 112 yards by 100 yards, and cost nearly £10,000.

[1] *Leeds Mercury Supplement*, May 3, 1879.
[2] Morley's *Life of Gladstone*, iii. 59–61.
[3] *Halifax and its Gibbet Law placed in a New Light*, by Henry Bentley, p. 9.
[4] *Halifax and its Gibbet Law placed in a True Light*, by S. Midgley (1761),
pp. 9–10.   [5] *Leeds Mercury*, April 5, 1774.
[6] *Yorkshire Coiners*, pp. 207–19.
[7] *Leeds Mercury*, December 30, 1771. See advertisements, 1776 to 1778.

It differed from the Leeds halls in that it did not consist of streets of stalls. Instead of that arrangement, there were 315 closets or apartments. Each of these rooms was quite separate and private. They were taken up by clothiers for about £28 each, and here the pieces of cloth were kept, only to be brought out for the weekly market, which was held from ten to twelve every Saturday morning. Instead of merely owning a stall, the Halifax clothier had a private room, in which his unsold stuffs could be left until next market-day.

During the last twenty years of the century the Halifax Hall prospered greatly. In 1787 only 22 rooms were unoccupied; the remainder were in the hands of men who hailed from Halifax, and also from the wide expanse which lay north and west of the town, Burnley, Bingley, Colne, Haworth, Keighley, Pendle, Skipton, &c., as well as Bradford and other places to the east. From this widely scattered area came woollens and worsteds, and in 1805 cotton goods were admitted. Merchants from Leeds, Hull, and York, and middlemen who bought for foreign patrons came to the Halifax market, and a very large trade was carried on, until the growth of Bradford and the decay of this system of exchange deprived the hall of its trade. It sank from its former usage about the middle of the nineteenth century.

Bradford was comparatively late in obtaining a Piece Hall.[1] This was because the worsted manufacturers were on a more capitalistic basis than their woollen *confrères*; there were fewer of them, their individual stocks were larger, and also, from the beginning, there was a great amount of direct dealing with the merchant or the consumer, and much working to order, without the cloth passing through the open market. Still there did exist a worsted market in Bradford, and as the industry expanded this meeting of merchants and makers became more important. The arrangements for the market were very inconvenient, especially to the merchants. Those worsted makers who lived in Bradford had piece rooms at their own houses, but those who came from the outlying parts had cubicles in a large room at the White Lion Inn, in Kirkgate, where they exposed their

---

[1] Housman, *Topographical Description of . . . the Western Part of the West Riding* (1800), p. 193, stated that it was reckoned that £50,000 worth of cloths were exposed for sale at one time. The building still stands, and is used by various traders.

goods for sale on market day, and locked up what they did not sell till the following week. Such a system was most unsatisfactory. The market was scattered about in the piece rooms of the clothiers and in the room at the White Lion, and thus there was a great waste of time in passing from one place to another. The growing industry was seriously handicapped by such inadequate market provision. Meetings were held, at which it was decided to erect a hall, and in 1773 the building was opened.[1] The hall was on the same principle as the later Halifax Hall, and contained at first 100 apartments, each with a show board in front of it, on which the cloth was placed during the hours of sale. But this first building soon became too small, and in 1780 an extension was opened, containing accommodation for another 158 holders. The hall was essentially for the sale of worsted, but provision was made by which yarn could be sold at the conclusion of the cloth market. The market commenced at ten o'clock each Thursday morning with the ringing of a bell. Every person who sold goods either before that hour or after 11.30, when the market closed, was fined 5s. Further, if any person was found exposing goods for sale which were not his own property or the property of some fellow occupier, he was severely punished. Any manufacturer behaving himself in a rude or disorderly manner, so as to give public offence, was expelled from the hall and deprived of participation in its privileges. The establishment flourished during the early part of the nineteenth century, but by 1850 trading transactions were generally carried on in other quarters.[2]

There were other Cloth Halls at Wakefield, Huddersfield, and Colne. Though Colne lay on the Lancashire side of the border, it fed very largely on the industry of the Yorkshire slopes, Craven, and Upper Wharfedale. Eventually its trade was absorbed by Bradford, and the little town lost most of its commercial importance.[3] Huddersfield had obtained a charter for a market in 1671, and the cloth was exposed for sale on the

---

[1] See advertisements, *Leeds Mercury*, 1772–3. Also *Old History of Bradford*, (1776), p. 77. Also *Bradford Antiquary*, i. 135, for article on the Bradford Piece Hall.

[2] Rules and Orders to be observed by the Merchants, Buyers of Goods, and Occupiers of Stands in the Manufacturers' Hall in Bradford '; poster in Bradford Reference Library. [3] James, *op. cit.*, p. 632.

walls of the churchyard. The town made great progress during
the eighteenth century, and a hall became necessary. The need
was supplied by the chief Huddersfield family, when in 1766
a large circular building was erected at the expense of Sir John
Ramsden. It was enlarged in 1780, and about 600 manufacturers brought their cloths here to be sold. The hall was the
property of the Ramsden family, who administered the affairs
of the market without the assistance or interference of trustees.
No stipulations were made as to apprenticeship, and any one
might use the hall, provided he paid a certain toll on each
cloth.[1] Yorkshiremen from the Pennine valleys sold their wares
there, and it was quite a common sight to see clothiers from
the neighbouring parts of Cheshire, Derbyshire, and Lancashire
offering their goods for sale at the Huddersfield market.[2]

As for Wakefield, we have already seen the fear caused in
the breast of Leeds by the erection of a Cloth Hall at Wakefield
in 1710. This hall met the requirements of the local clothiers
for half a century, but in 1766 the ' Tammy Hall ' was erected
for the sale of that type of worsted, and here a considerable
trade was carried on every Friday.[3]

Such was the method of marketing the cloth. From the hand-
looms of the scattered cottages came the pieces, rough and
unfinished. In the covered market buyer and seller met, and
within strictly defined limits of time concluded their bargain.
We have observed in some detail the character of the seller.
Who was the buyer ? It now becomes necessary to analyse
more closely the composition of the mass of purchasers which
thronged the halls and cloth markets. First, there was the
small buyer, the tailor or shopkeeper, who purchased one or
two pieces for retailing in his own shop. There was also the
pedlar, getting in his small stock of wares, prior to making his
regular and extensive itinerary. But these men were in the great
minority, and were insignificant when compared with the larger
purchasers, who were the most important figures in these market

---

[1] Sykes, *Huddersfield and its Vicinity*, pp. 216, 246, and 279.

[2] See Mayhall, *op. cit.*, i. 146. Also Sykes, *op. cit.* Also *Reports*, 1806,
iii. 221. Also Allen, *History of the County of York*.

[3] Housman, *op. cit.*, p. 183 ; Allen, v. 460. The Tammy Hall had fallen into
disuse by 1830. Mayhall, i. 145. See Leeds newspapers, April 1765 ; *Leeds
Mercury*, December 5, 1775.

transactions. These purchasers fall under two headings, merchants and agents. The merchants might be engaged in either
home or foreign trade. There was a large class of home merchants who bought in the Leeds market in order to sell wholesale
throughout England. Defoe gives an admirable description of
this body of men. After pointing out that the Leeds goods
are everywhere utilized ' for clothing the ordinary people who
cannot go to the price of the fine cloths made in the West of
England ', he states ' there are for this purpose a set of travelling
merchants in Leeds who go all over England with droves of
pack-horses to all the fairs and market towns over the whole
island, I think I may say none excepted. Here they supply not
the common people by retail, which would denominate them
pedlars indeed, but they supply the shops by wholesale and
whole pieces, and not only so, but give large credit, to show
that they are really travelling merchants, and as such they sell
a very large quantity of goods. It is ordinary for one of these
men to carry £1,000 value of cloth with him at a time, and
having sold it at the fairs or towns where they go, to send their
horses back for as much more, and this very often in the summer,
for they choose to travel in the summer, and perhaps towards
the winter, though as little in winter as they can, because of the
badness of the roads '.[1]

Next, there came the foreign merchant, who traded with
various parts of Europe, the Mediterranean, and North America.
The pioneer companies had broken down, and there was now a great
measure of freedom for merchants, which enabled many men to
enter into foreign trade who might have been excluded under the
regulations of the Merchant Adventurers and Eastland Merchants.

Along with the merchant there was the factor or agent, the
middleman, a very important figure in the organization of the
cloth trade. The factor purchased cloth for merchants whose
head-quarters might be in Yorkshire, London, some other part
of England, or abroad. In the Yorkshire newspapers of the
eighteenth century there are numerous advertisements similar
to the following :

(*Leedes Intelligencer*, July 16th, 1782). ' To Manufacturers
and Others. A person at this Time wants to engage with an

---

[1] Defoe, *op. cit.*, iii. 119.

agent, who has a competent Knowledge in the different Articles manufactured at or near Leedes, to purchase goods on the best Terms : whose character must be unexceptionable, as Two or Three Thousand Pounds will be in his Hands for that Purpose. A commission equal to the Attention in this Business will be allowed : any Person capable of executing the above properly addressing a line for X Z, No. 16, Lombard Str., London, (Post Paid), will be duly regarded.'

In like manner, merchants residing in Holland, Hamburg, and other parts of Europe retained the services of factors, through whom they made large purchases in the markets of the West Riding. Concerning factors Defoe remarks that they ' are not only many in number, but some are very considerable in their dealings, and correspond with the farthest provinces in Germany',[1] and he gives an instance of a factor who purchased kerseys in Halifax market to the extent of £60,000 annually, all of which cloths were then dispatched to the middleman's patrons residing in Holland and Hamburg.[2]

Such a man was Joseph Holroyd, of Soyland.[3] He was a factor engaged in purchasing cloths for English and foreign clients. Amongst his customers were a few London merchants, but the greater part of his trade was with Dutchmen, resident in Rotterdam and Amsterdam, e.g. John d'Orville, Livinus de Dorpere, Ludovicus de Wulf, Peter Deynoote, Hermanus Struys, and others. He kept these men well informed as to the state of the market, sending a list of current prices every fortnight or three weeks, and in 1706 he paid a visit to Holland, strengthening his position with old patrons, and seeking new ones. From them he received standing instructions to purchase a certain number of cloths annually, or obtained isolated orders from time to time. He then purchased the necessary pieces from the clothiers of the Halifax area, dispatched them to his masters, and received for his services a commission, generally amounting to $1\frac{1}{2}$ per cent. The financial arrangements were carried on through the medium of bills of exchange, and in the course of a year Holroyd seems to have had a turnover of at least £30,000. Acting as middleman was no easy task, and Holroyd often found himself between two

---

[1] Defoe, *op. cit.* (1748 edition), iii. 120.   [2] Ibid. (1724 edition), iii. 106.
[3] See *Letter Books of Joseph Holroyd and Sam Hill*, edited by the present writer (Halifax, 1914), *passim*.

millstones. On the one hand the patron fixed a maximum
price, and ordered the factor to pay no more than say 30s. for
a certain kind of kersey. On the other hand the clothiers had
their minimum price of say 32s. for the same type of cloth, and
firmly refused to pass below that figure. Holroyd therefore
frequently found himself in a dilemma, and when he ventured
to exceed the maximum allowed by his master he called on his
head the most scathing vituperation. Nor was this the only
kind of difficulty. Cloths were often delayed by bad weather,
which prevented the pieces, hung on the tenters, from drying,
and so many cloths were still unready long after the invoice
had been dispatched and the ships had sailed. Further, shipping
at the beginning of the eighteenth century was still unsafe,
unless accompanied by a convoy, and even the presence of protecting vessels did not safeguard the cloth ships from stormy
seas in winter. Shipping was therefore still limited; it was
unwise to go without a convoy, and it was courting disaster to
set sail in winter time. During the winter months the market
was asleep, and the factor had to be content with laying in
a store of cloths ready for the spring sailings. But in spite of
these difficulties the factor was an indispensable part of the
commercial machine, and this class of middlemen became both
numerous and wealthy during the century.

These were the men who made the swift bargains with the
clothiers in the halls. When the purchaser decided to take
a cloth, he agreed to a price based on a hasty examination of
the quality of the piece and determined by the length and breadth
as stated on the leaden seal fixed to the end of the cloth. The
clothier then carried his fabric to the merchant's home or warehouse, where it was carefully measured and examined, deductions
being made for any deficiency in length or flaw in quality.
Then the clothier received the whole or a part of the revised
price; if he did not obtain the full amount, he took a bill of
credit, but the smaller clothiers preferred the cash payment, as
they could not afford to build up a store of credit notes.[1] If
the clothier had two pieces for sale, he brought one to the hall,
and usually the merchant who purchased this one sent him to
fetch the second.

[1] Defoe, *op. cit.*, iii. 119; also *Reports*, 1821, vi. 486.

The cloth hall system of marketing cloth was especially suit-able for an industry carried on by a host of small manufacturers. So long as the makers of cloth were many, and their individual output small, it was highly desirable in the interests of clothier and merchant alike that a public market of this type should be organized, so that exchange could take place regularly and frequently, with the maximum of advantage to both sides. Therefore, so long as the small clothier survived, so long did the cloth halls continue to offer him a ground on which to meet the merchant or factor.   But during the eighteenth century other methods of exchange were growing up which destroyed the need for a public market, and eventually superseded the .cloth halls.

In the first place, there came to be more working to order. A merchant or factor desired a number of cloths of a certain quality and size. He would give his specifications to some clothier, who then set to work to produce the required number of cloths according to the data supplied by the purchaser.   Or, on the other hand, the clothier brought one cloth to the market ; it attracted the attention of some merchant, who purchased it, and gave an order for more cloths of the same kind. These subsequent pieces never came into the market, and eventually the clothier would be so busily employed in working to order that he had no further need of the cloth market. In the worsted industry an enormous amount of trade was carried on directly and privately between merchants and clothiers. The manu-facturer was generally a large producer, and could take up big orders. Thus the London merchants frequently advertised in the Yorkshire papers for worsted manufacturers who were willing and able to supply them direct with regular stocks of worsted goods, or for agents who would get together these supplies for them. Witness the two following advertisements, which are typical descriptions of the arrangements by which the halls were being superseded.

(*Leedes Intelligencer*, Nov. 12, 1782). ' Tammies, Shalloons, and Callimancoes. Wanted a quantity of the above goods to be delivered in London weekly.—Any person capable of supply-ing the Same, whether as agent or manufacturer, on the most moderate terms should write to J. B., London Bridge Coffee House.'

(Same issue). ' Wanted to settle a Correspondence in the North of England with a person of repute, capable of supplying with a quantity of Shalloons and Tammies and other articles, in the Grease, weekly or monthly, on the most moderate Terms. As the person addressing this wants a considerable quantity of these articles, he wishes that none but responsible characters will apply. [Address London].

' N.B. The Advertiser has no objection to treat with a Person as Agent.'

In these two advertisements we see the nature of the tendency which had become more and more marked during the eighteenth century, namely the desire on the part of the absentee mer-chants to make sure of a large and steady supply of the kind of goods which they required. If possible, that supply was to be obtained direct from the producer, and in the worsted industry the predominance of large manufacturers made this direct connexion between producer and merchant possible. In the woollen industry, with its multitude of small masters, the merchant could not trouble to enter into contracts with a great number of small manufacturers, so he left that work to the factor; the latter, being in the industrial field, could make the necessary agreements, and get together his large supplies for the merchant by giving orders to the small clothiers around him.

That these methods were being practised long before the introduction of the factory system is seen clearly in the letters of Holroyd and Hill. Holroyd, as a factor, was buying many cloths in Halifax market in 1706. But he also secured great quantities of wares which had never been near the Cloth Hall. He used to call on the clothiers in their houses or workshops, and there bought pieces which they had ready, or gave them orders to make a certain number of cloths for him according to some definite specifications, and for some fixed price. From his correspondence we gather the impression that this private buying was more important than his purchasing in the market. Sam Hill was a clothier, actually engaged in the manufacture of kerseys, bays, and shalloons, and working on a fairly large scale. The greater part of his wares were made in accordance with the orders of his patrons, merchants of London and Holland. From these men he received isolated demands, or was com-missioned to send a certain number of pieces each month or

each year. In one of his letters he states that most gentlemen
he serves have agreed to take a certain quantity each year,
and fix the months in which they require them, or the number
they require each month ; in another epistle he says to one of
his best foreign customers, ' I shall be very glad [to know] what
Kerseys you think you'll want this Year, y^t I may forbeare
engageing too far, and leave myself able to serve you with what
you want '.[1] The price at which the cloths were sold when
ready varied according to the prevailing market rate, and so
merchants received their goods at market price, without having
to go into the market to secure them. Hill had connexions
with a great number of merchants, and was so well supplied
with orders at the time the letters were written that he had no
time to spare to supply new customers, much less place any
cloths on the public market. In his experiments in worsted-
making he solicited his patrons to take a few of his shalloons
and try to dispose of them ; but this branch of his work was
small compared with the amount of woollen cloths which he
made to order.

The clothiers with whom Holroyd dealt were on the whole
a sturdy set of fellows, who retained much of their independence
in the face of the encroachment of the factor and the system of
working to order. In 1706 the public market was still the great
centre of exchange, and the producers were largely free from the
thraldom of the mercantile class. Thirty years later Hill's
strength of character enabled him to stand erect and independent,
in spite of the fact that he was the servant of a number of
merchants. But in the rise of these new methods of marketing
there was a possibility that the merchants would gain control
over the manufacturers and the latter become in name and in
fact the servants of the wholesale dealers. This possibility
became a reality before the end of the century, when many
merchants gained absolute control over production by becoming
manufacturers themselves. Merchant and maker became united
in the same person, the gulf was bridged, and the wholesale
seller of cloths began to employ weavers and spinners to manufacture his pieces. This development was probably most marked
in the worsted industry, where a man would employ wool-

---

[1] See *Letter Books of Joseph Holroyd and Sam Hill*, nos. 110 and 113.

combers, spinners, and weavers, and sell the yarn or the pieces
himself. In the woollen industry the absorption was slower,
and did not become a predominant feature of industrial organization until after the Industrial Revolution. But in the years
from 1790 onwards there were constant complaints from the
domestic clothiers that the merchants were becoming manufacturers, and so were ruining the small independent men.[1] In
1794 a Bill was submitted to the House of Commons, to give
the Cloth Hall trustees power to make by-laws with a view to
preventing this trespass on the part of the merchants. The Bill
was dropped,[2] and the merchants gradually gained a firmer hold
on the industry. The large woollen merchant who lived in
Yorkshire was by this time a strange mixture. He had looms
in his own establishment, and employed other weavers who
worked in their own homes; he gave orders to independent
clothiers to make cloth for him according to specification; at
the same time he visited the cloth halls, and bought in the open
market. Thus he drew his pieces from three sources of supply,
and whilst he could not yet afford to dispense with the cloth
market, he was obtaining an increasing proportion of his wares
through private channels.[3]

The inevitable consequences of these developments were not
fully apparent until well into the nineteenth century, though even
before 1820 there was a diminution in the number of stand-
holders in the cloth halls, and many stalls were vacant. So
much was this the case that, when in 1818 the Leeds Corporation
sought to acquire the White Cloth Hall to serve as a cattle
market, the trustees of that hall gave the suggestion very
serious consideration. They were willing to abandon the building, provided the white clothiers could be given accommodation
in the Mixed Cloth Hall. The trustees of the latter market were
approached, and offered 900 stands, but on such exorbitant
terms that the negotiations were abandoned. During the next
thirty years the importance of the halls steadily declined.
True, clothiers still came there with their wares, but these men
were giants compared with the 3,000 men who had found

---

[1] *Reports*, 1806, iii. 16. [2] *House of Commons Journals*, xlix. 275 et seq.
[3] e.g. Mr. L. Atkinson, of Huddersfield, merchant (*Reports*, 1806, iii. 220).
For the story of the decline of the Leeds White Cloth Hall, see Thoresby
Soc. publications, 1913; article on White Cloth Hall, by present writer.

a market there in the palmy days of the eighteenth century. The Coloured Cloth Hall contained its 2,526 stalls, which were held by only 680 persons, who possessed any number from two up to forty, and were in many cases quite large manufacturers. The White Cloth Hall had changed in character, by reason of the growing practice of making dyed in place of white cloths, and more coloured fabrics were sold there than whites. In 1848 some of its 1,237 stands were unoccupied, and the rest were registered in the names of 456 owners. Of these, 256 no longer frequented the market, and many clothiers owned as many as 20 or 25 stands. A stall could now be purchased for less than 10s., and when any stands were put up for sale by auction, because of the arrears of the owner, they seldom brought in more than 5s. or 6s.

By the middle of the century the growth of warehouses and the other changes in the methods of marketing cloth were cutting the ground from under the feet of the cloth halls. Still the halls survived, and a few merchants and manufacturers were to be found there on market days. The White Cloth Hall, standing in the Calls, presented a barrier to the extension of the North Eastern Railway into the heart of Leeds, and in 1868 the railway company was obliged to build a new hall before it could demolish part of the old establishment. The new building, erected in King Street at a cost of about £20,000, was never fully occupied, and before 1890 the cloth market there had lapsed. The building occupied a valuable site in the business heart of the town, and in 1896 therefore the whole concern was wound up. In that year purchasers were found for the estate, and the trustees received a cheque for £40,000. After providing an annuity for the hall-keeper, the money was shared out to all stall-holders, and worked out at about £30 per stall, a figure eminently satisfactory to those who had purchased the same for a few shillings. The building was demolished shortly afterwards, and a palatial hotel now occupies the site. The old hall of 1775, however, still survives, behind the Corn Exchange— a broken relic, low, squat, and dirty, with the cupola still aloft over what was once the gateway. The railway ploughs through the middle, and the building is divided up into warehouses, in which are kept all manner of commodities—except cloth. Few people who pass that way are aware that this grimy building was once the scene of great activity and vast exchange, and only by the name of the street do we realize that here was formerly one of the two great valves by which the produce of the West Riding was passed through the arteries of commerce of the world.

The fate of the Coloured Cloth Hall was even more complete, for the whole of the old building was swept away, and no vestige remains. The hall bulged out into what is now City Square, and the meeting of many ways at that point caused chronic congestion of traffic. In the 'eighties many complaints were made concerning the thoroughfare at this point, and the *Yorkshire Post* echoed the opinion of many when, in 1888, it declared that Leeds was ' choked in its very centre by a congestion of unsightly buildings which would not have been tolerated for a year in boroughs of far less pretensions '. The municipal authorities wished to acquire part of the site, in order to effect street improvements, whilst the postal authorities were in search of a piece of land on which they could erect the Central Post Office. From 1870 onwards, therefore, the Corporation made several attempts to purchase the whole Cloth Hall estate. For a time they encountered opposition from those who still used the market, and who thought that the closing of the hall would be ' a taking and destruction of their property, which would be a hurt to trade, and a most unnecessary and unjust interference with their property, rights, and interests '. Gradually the trustees adopted a more conciliatory attitude, and were willing to get rid of an institution which had ceased to have any commercial importance. In 1885 the ' Leeds Coloured Cloth Hall Act ' gave the trustees power to sell the site and buildings, and negotiations were opened with the Corporation. These proceedings were impeded by the question of the price to be paid by the borough. Eventually terms were arranged, and on April 1, 1889, the representatives of both parties met, and the necessary documents were signed. For the sum of £66,000 the Corporation received about two acres of land and the whole of the buildings, with absolute power to treat the property as it thought best. After the transaction of this business, and after the Town Clerk had handed over the cheque for £66,000, the trustees entertained the Corporation to luncheon, at which the chairman of the trustees handed round copies of a black-edged card, inscribed as follows :

IN MEMORIAM.
Mixed Cloth Hall,
Better Known as the
Coloured Cloth Hall, Leeds.
Erected 1758.   Fatum exitus 1889.

That was almost the end of the story. The money received was divided between the stall-holders and the reversioners, heirs of Richard Wilson, who had sold the land in 1756. Evidently the reversioners claimed the lion's share of the spoils, for the clothiers received only £4 15s. for each stand they owned, which cannot explain the destination of more than £12,000 out of the £66,000. As to the building, the Corporation began to demolish it at once, in order to make the necessary road improvements ; part of the estate was then handed over to the Postmaster-General, and on it the present Central Post Office was erected.[1]

We have wandered far away from the eighteenth century and its methods of marketing ; but the story of these cloth halls is interesting, and it seemed desirable to devote a few words to the decline of the public markets. We must now get back to our proper period, and pick up the thread where we dropped it, with the cloth delivered by its maker at the house of the merchant or factor.

The piece had now to be finished, and, in the case of white cloths, to be dyed. There had been a great improvement in the art of cloth-finishing since the days of Cockayne's experiment. The sojourn of Englishmen in Holland and the immigration of Dutch workers and merchants to England did something to raise the standard of English dyeing ; London and Coventry became noted as dyeing and finishing centres, and ' Coventry true blue ' was soon a classic amongst colours. In the north, improvement was equally rapid. In 1678–9 Thoresby went to

[1] For many facts concerning the later history of the Coloured Cloth Hall the writer is indebted to Mr. Milner, solicitor, Albion Street, Leeds, who kindly placed at his disposal a number of documents concerning the winding up of the hall. The various deeds of transfer are in the possession of the Corporation, but there is reason to fear that the minute books, accounts, and all the other valuable papers which must have accumulated in the course of over a century have been destroyed. See also Leeds Newspapers, 1889–90.

Holland to learn the art of fulling, dyeing, and finishing of cloth, as practised there,[1] and this trip was part of the recognized scheme of training. During the eighteenth century, therefore, the finishing of cloths at home was a general feature of the trade, and few pieces went abroad to receive their final treatment. Within Leeds itself, and also scattered up and down the county, establishments were to be found at work, dyeing, preparing dyeing materials, raising the nap on cloth, shearing, dressing, and performing all the processes necessary for the completion of the perfect piece. These finishing mills might be the property of some independent master who was neither clothier nor merchant, and who performed the work for merchants, receiving a fixed rate per piece ; but it was now a very common arrangement for merchants to possess their own finishing [2] establishments, and so free themselves from dependence on another man.

The processes of finishing were primitive and the results far from superfine. Approximation to the required colour in dyeing seems to have been all that could be obtained, and any new tint was discovered rather by accident than as a result of scientific research. The nap was raised by means of teazles, and then the shearing, which was done in order to remove the inequalities of the nap surface, was performed with hand-shears, which were generally large, heavy, and cumbrous. The piece was then again tentered to its final dimensions and left to dry.

A piece of cloth stretched on its tenter frame was a great temptation to those persons whose honesty was not above suspicion, and clothiers and finishers were much disquieted in consequence of the ease with which cloth could be stolen whilst left out in the open. A newspaper letter dated November 28, 1774, complains of ' the frequent and almost daily robberies committed in this parish [Halifax], and that stealing pieces from the tenters is almost daily practised, by which the persons [employed] in that necessary branch of business are greatly distressed. . . . They cannot take off their goods every night without doing them visible damage, and so are forced either to watch them all night in the cold, or run the dreadful hazard of losing in a single hour the profits of the labours of many months '.[3]

---

[1] Thoresby's *Diary*, July 4, 1678, and onwards.
[2] *Reports*, 1806, iii, p. 9.   [3] *Leeds Mercury*, November 28, 1774.

The danger was not confined to the bleak uplands around
Halifax; witness the following notices from the *Leedes Intelligencer* .

December 31, 1754 : ' In the night betwixt the 26th and the
27th, five yards of cloth were cut off the tenters of Mr. John
Darnton, dresser to Sir Henry Ibbetson, Bart.'
January 7, 1755 : ' Last Saturday night two yards of cloth
were cut from the tenters of Robert Wainman, dresser to Mr.
Blaydes.'
January 7, 1755 : ' In the night of the 1st instant, five yards
of colou'd cloth were cut off the tenters of Joseph Tate, dresser
to Mr. Bischoff.'

And so throughout the century, especially during winter
and times of bad trade, the purloining of cloth went on. The
writer of the letter quoted above may have meant that whole
pieces were spirited away, but the risk attendant upon such
a proceeding would be very great, and in the towns the prowler
was evidently content with his four or five yards, which could
be easily carried away and hidden. The offence was one of
respectable antiquity, and early Halifax offenders received
summary treatment. Here the cloth-stealer, along with other
kinds of thieves, was a common figure in the sixteenth century,
and it was the custom to condemn any one convicted of this
offence to be put to death at once by being guillotined. The
framework for this instrument of death stood on a large square
stone, which was recently unearthed ; the axe-head was released
by pulling out a wedge or catch, and fell down a groove in
a manner so well known to the French at a later day. This
custom of beheading thieves had survived in Halifax alone, long
after it had fallen into disuse in other parts of the country. Up
to the middle of the seventeenth century the Gibbet Law was
no mere dead letter, the machine no antique ornament; the
names of men and women alike appear in the list of victims,
and this practice earned for Halifax a place of honour in the
Beggars' Litany.

From Hell, Hull, and Halifax,
Good Lord, deliver us ! [1]

[1] For a discussion of the legal and other aspects of the Halifax Gibbet,
see the article on that subject by Mr. J. Lister, in Ling Roth, *Yorkshire
Coiners*. Also any history of Halifax.

This grim method of upholding the eighth commandment was
not generally adopted, and was abandoned in Halifax after
about 1650, cloth thieves being punished like other culprits by
imprisonment or transportation.   In 1742 legislation made
a special effort to eradicate the evil.   In an Act passed in this
year it was pointed out that ' clothiers and others concerned
in the woollen manufacture are under a necessity of letting
their cloth or other woollen goods remain upon the rack or
tenters, as also of suffering their wool to lie exposed in the night
time, in order the better to dry and prepare the same ; whereby
their said goods are more frequently liable to be stolen by wicked
and evil-designing persons who are encouraged in their wickedness by the difficulty of proving the identity of the goods
stolen '.[1]   The statute therefore gave clothiers power to enlist
the services of the justices of the peace in the search for stolen
wares.   The magistrates were to grant power to search the
premises of any suspected person, and if the search revealed
the existence of any fabrics for which the suspect could not
give a satisfactory explanation, the culprit was liable to a term
of imprisonment for the first two offences, and transportation
on the third conviction.   Here was another of those many Acts
which make little difference to the world they wish to reform.
The Act was drawn up, but no machinery was provided to
enforce its clauses with any stringency.   The whole of Leeds
was guarded by ten constables ;[2] there was practically no
lighting, and a general deadly stillness brooded over the tenter-
close by night.   We fail entirely to realize the thick darkness
and loneliness of an eighteenth-century town ; the marvellous
feature is not that any one should have escaped, but that any
should be caught.   It was such an easy task stealing in those
days : such a difficult task trying to prevent it, or detect the
thief.

At last the cloth was ready for dispatch.   It was handed over
to the merchants or factors who were to take it to other parts
of England, or was given into the hands of the carriers and
shippers, who would convey it to its destination at home or
abroad.   And so the material takes to the road once more, after
the many peregrinations in its progress from raw wool to finished

[1] 15 Geo. II, c. 27.   [2] *Directory of Leeds,* 1797.

cloth.   In sketching these numerous wanderings we have had
no time to stay and consider the nature of the roads or waterways along which the wool and cloth were carried.   Let us therefore conclude this chapter with a short survey of the condition
of the means of communication in Yorkshire during the eighteenth century.   In an economic organization such as we have
been studying, it is difficult to over-estimate the importance of
the means of communication.   On their excellence depends the
quick and easy transit of materials, raw or finished, from place
to place ; by their unkempt condition, every aspect of industry
is 'sore let and hindered'.   A bad main road or a shallow rapid
river may be as effectual a check to the transfer of produce as
the strictest legal prohibition, or the most rigorous system of
police.

All records [1] contribute to prove that the roads of the north
country had, in the early part of the eighteenth century, plumbed
the uttermost depths of disrepair.   Tudor legislation, with its
demand for statute labour on the highways, had been almost
ineffective, and such work as was done upon the roads was of
a perfunctory character, leaving the last state as bad as the
first.   Thus, in spite of the constant efforts of the local justices,
the roads of England in 1700 were nearly all bad.   Thoresby's
Diary is illuminating on this topic.   Now he loses his way between
Doncaster and York ; [2] at another time the roads are impassable
by reason of the floods, and he is compelled to ride across fields
with the water up' to his saddle skirts ; [3] again he finds the
northern roads a frozen quagmire, ' full of snow, and which was
worse, on a continuous ice almost, the melted snow being frozen
again, that made it dangerous and very troublesome, so that
I was more fatigued with this last twenty miles than with all
the journey besides.' [4]   Defoe bears out these statements in
his remarks on many Yorkshire highways, e. g. ' the roads to
Halifax used to be very bad, and except at the west end, almost
inaccessible '.[5]

From about 1727 onwards came the turnpike era, and some

---

[1] The records of the J.P.'s for the West and North Riding are full of orders
concerning the repair of roads.   For the whole history of roads during modern
times see S. and B. Webb, *The Story of the King's Highway* (1913).

[2] Thoresby, *Diary*, August 3, 1712.   [3] Ibid., May 17, 1695.

[4] Ibid., February 17, 1709.   [5] Defoe, *op. cit.*, 1762 edition, iii. 143.

of the highways were taken in hand by the turnpike trusts. But
the general improvement was very slight, even on the main
thoroughfares, whilst the parish roads remained in their ' state
of nature '.[1] The most entertaining pages of Arthur Young
are those in which he hurls his fierce indictments against the
northern highways. Perhaps he exaggerated at times, and his
attacks on backward rural economy inspired a similar tirade
against the roads of these counties. But his general statements
are borne out by other writers, and make one wonder how travel
of any kind was possible. Young speaks of roads which are
' execrably bad ', ' very stony and full of holes ' ; [2] the highway
through Wakefield was so bad ' that it ought to be indicted ',
and the main road between Wakefield and Leeds was ' stony
and ill-made ', in spite of the fact that it was a turnpike. The
road to Askrig was ' only fit for a goat to travel ', and the way
to Darlington was along a track ' sufficient to dislocate one's
bones '.[3]

On the other hand, some roads were just as good. All in the
Vale of York and in the East Riding attained the standard of
' excellent ', whilst on the estates of the more progressive
gentleman-farmers an almost perfect network of roads was to
be found. But, on the whole, the verdict was bad. Later
writers [4] support this general contention, and from a survey
of the whole evidence we obtain a vivid picture of the chief
faults which were to be found on most of the land routes.
Firstly, there was a lack of definition about the less frequented
roads. Many went over commons or through wooded districts,
and there were few hedges or fences to mark out the bounds of
the highway. The number of confusing cross-roads was legion,
and there was scarcely any provision of finger-posts or milestones until about the middle of the eighteenth century. Hence
we have Thoresby losing himself in his own county ; [5] we have
a road from Pickering to Whitby on which no traveller dared
to venture without a guide ; [6] we hear of people lost on the
Pennines, not knowing which cart track was His Majesty's

---

[1] Bigland, op. cit., p. 326.   [2] Young, Northern Tour, i. 132.
[3] See Young's section on Roads, in Northern Tour, iv. 574-7.
[4] Other observers who make remarks on the Yorkshire roads are Marshall
(1788), Housman (1800), Dayes (1805), Cooke (1812), Bigland (1812).
[5] Thoresby, Diary, August 3, 1712.   [6] Bigland, op. cit., p. 326.

highway ; [1] and it is recorded that he was thought a wise man
who could find his way through the Forest of Knaresborough
without expert assistance. The road itself was generally narrow.
If it ran through wooded regions, hedges or trees hung over both
sides, not only shutting out the light but interfering directly
with the progress of travellers, especially those on horseback.[2]
The road surface might be either concave or convex, according
to the amount and nature of the repairs which it received. In
the former case, water stood in pools during the wet seasons,
froze in winter, and perpetuated a quagmire during the greater
part of the year. When material had been piled on to the
middle of the road, all traffic, heavy or light, stuck to this
central elevation, making wheel ruts and horse paths, from
which no one cared to stray for fear of toppling over into the
ditches.[3]

Much of the inefficiency of the roads was due to the manner
in which they were repaired. No one as yet knew the art of
road-making, and there was a general ignorance as to the best
methods of preparing and maintaining a durable road surface.
The use of ' metal ' was still unknown, and any material which
happened to be at hand was used, regardless of its suitability.
Marshall[4] and Cooke[5] complain of the practice in vogue in
parts of the East Riding of spreading gravel over soft clay soil,
which became hard and firm when dry, but in winter sank into
the mire, and only accentuated the heaviness of the path.
They also remark on the use of earth,[6] obtained from the ditches ;
such a mad practice could have only one result, in adding
to the quantity of mud through which the traveller had to
wade. In the West Riding freestone[7] was used, being near at
hand and cheap ; but this stone quickly broke up under the
pressure of the constant traffic on the arterial roads, and became
little better than mud and sand. The roads about Sheffield
were re-surfaced by using the cinders and refuse from the
forges.[8]

[1] Housman, *op. cit.*, pp. 138–40.
[2] Marshall, *Rural Economy of Yorkshire*, i. 192.
[3] Whitaker, *Loidis and Elmete*, i. 186–7.   [4] Marshall, *op. cit.*, i. 180–1.
[5] Cooke, *Topogr. Description of Yorkshire* (1812), p. 89.
[6] Marshall, *op. cit.*, i. 186.   [7] Housman, *op. cit.*, p. 140.
[8] Dayes, *op. cit.*, p. 18.

One redeeming feature was to be found on some roads in the provision of a causeway or flagged footpath down the middle or side of the road. These ' causeys ' were used alike by pedestrians and horse traffic, ' a practice only to be excused by the peculiar badness of the main road '.[1] Along them came the string of pack-horses, the merchant on his way from place to place, and the clothier carrying his raw materials or pieces. The paths were often rough and broken.[2] The heavy use to which they were put rendered them irregular in surface : there were frequent breaks in the causeway, and from the slipperiness of the stones in winter and the irregularity of the surface there was often as much danger to the night traveller as upon the road itself.

Another saving grace enjoyed by Yorkshire was its supply of bridges. Defoe constantly refers to the abundance of large stone bridges at Harewood, Ripon, Doncaster, Sheffield, and elsewhere.[3] Between these great erections and the narrow single-arched pack-horse bridges came every variety of provision for crossing the numerous streams. Stone was cheap in the West Riding, and so the supply of bridges was at least equal to that in any other part of the kingdom.

Up to the time of the turnpikes the roads were repaired by statute labour, the inhabitants of each neighbourhood working a certain number of days yearly on the roads under the supervision of the surveyor of the highways. This system, which looked excellent on paper, seems in practice to have been a complete failure. The labour was evaded as much as possible, or done in a most perfunctory manner, leaving the road scarcely any better for the treatment.

With the growth of the turnpike movement there was a gradual though slow improvement in the means of land transit. From about 1740 onwards Turnpike Acts showered on Yorkshire, and by 1760 that network of roads, so well known to motorists and cyclists to-day, had been woven. The early efforts, however, did not remove the grievances of which travellers complained, and supplementary Acts had to confess in their preambles that the turnpikes already established were ' still in a ruinous

---

[1] Housman, *op. cit.*, p. 14, and Cooke, *op. cit.*, p. 62.

[2] See *North Riding Sess. Rec.*, vols. vii–ix, *passim*. Also Housman, *op. cit.*, p. 160.

[3] Defoe, *op. cit.*, iii. 122, and *passim*. At Ripon there was a bridge with seven arches.

condition, very dangerous to passengers, and in the winter season almost impassable '.[1] Young's wrath was often aroused against the main turnpikes, whilst Bigland and other writers of the early nineteenth century lamented the wretched surface conditions which still existed on most of the popular highways. The reasons are not difficult to find. The turnpikes were in the hands of large bodies of trustees, including lords, gentry, clergy, merchants, &c., men from almost every walk of life. These men were not paid for their services, and could not be expected to give full, serious, or expert attention to the welfare of the road. Their interest was only general, and their attendance at meetings so casual that nine was the quorum usually fixed by the Acts as being necessary for the transaction of business. Such a loose central body was of little value, and much of the real work must have been left to the surveyors and toll-collectors. But these men were often quite ignorant of the best principles of road-making; they had no thorough plan for constructing a good permanent way, and, even if they had, there was no supply of proper material available. The surveyor had no guiding principles to direct him in his work. He had no notion of winding a road up a hill, but confronted the summit, and attempted to go straight over the crest rather than round it.[2] Further, the lack of suitable material was a great impediment, and the surveyor therefore used such stone as was nearest to hand, regardless of its qualities for road surface purposes. It required a Blind Jack of Knaresborough, a Telford, or a Macadam to reveal the economy of getting good material, even though the expense might seem to transgress the bounds of common sense. Hence it was not until the nineteenth century that the revolution in highway communication became at all complete, and this was just at a time when improvements in the steam engine were making the railway an accomplished fact.

Along roads such as we have seen above, progress was necessarily slow, and means of transit were primitive. Wagons were seldom used in the hilly districts,[3] and in the Vale of York

[1] e.g. 24 Geo. II, c. 22, Act for improving Selby to Leeds road.
[2] ' The engineers of those days used a corkscrew oft enough, but they had not learnt a lesson in roadmaking from it ' (Sykes, *Huddersfield and its Vicinity*, p. 262).   [3] Young, *op. cit.*, ii. 113.

and the agricultural areas haulage was done largely by oxen, which were more sure-footed than horses on the muddy roads and slippery hill-slopes.[1] For heavy and more extended transit, however, the horse was the favourite animal, and it was largely by means of the horse alone that land carriage was effected in the clothing areas, until improvements made possible the use of carts, wagons, coaches, and other wheeled vehicles. The string of pack-horses was to be seen on every road : they were the carriers of raw material, finished goods, food-stuffs, books, letters, and even passengers. The goods were packed up in hampers or bags, which were slung across the backs of the horses ; letters and travellers were handed over into the custody of the carriers, and away went the long procession over the rough road to its many destinations. These beasts of burden did not need a well-paved broad highway ; the mere country lane or narrow bridle path sufficed. If there should be a ' causey ', the horses stuck tenaciously to it, and many a dogged encounter took place when two such packs met. The horses could cross fords, and make use of the frail pack-horse bridges which would instantly have collapsed under the weight of a cart or wagon. The first horse carried a bell attached to its collar, the tinkling of which was of no small value on dark nights. In every town was the ' Pack Horse Inn ', with extensive stables in which the horses were housed when night came down.[2] All sizes of contingents, from the large pack of thirty or forty horses to the solitary steed of the small manufacturer, were to be seen moving to and from market, laden with produce or with the food for future labour. ' In winter ', says Whitaker, ' the distant markets never ceased to be frequented. On horseback, before daybreak and long after nightfall, the hardy sons of trade pursued their object with the spirit and intrepidity of a fox-chase, and the boldest of their country neighbours had no reason to despise their horsemanship or their courage. Sloughs, darkness, and broken causeways certainly presented a field of action no less perilous than hedges and five-barred gates.' [3]

Nor were the sloughs and broken causeways or the over-

---

[1] Ibid., i. 163, and Marshall, *op. cit.*, i. 260 et seq.
[2] One inn at Huddersfield had accommodation for 100 horses (Sykes, p. 247).
[3] Whitaker, *op. cit.*, p. 81.

D d

flowing river the only dangers. To the ne'er-do-well, or the
man who was ' down on his luck ', there was something terribly
tempting in the thought of the dark night, the lonely road, and
the solitary traveller returning from market with his money in
his pocket, or his ' £1,000 of cloth ' on the backs of his horses.
The eighteenth-century newspapers are therefore full of accounts
of highway robberies, in which unfortunate clothiers or merchants were compelled to stand and deliver.[1] Woe betide the
man who made attempt at resistance ; there was short shrift
for him, and many entries bear witness to the revolting cruelty
with which the sword was used, the pistol fired, and the hapless
traveller left a mangled wreck by the wayside. Few men,
therefore, set out on a journey unprepared for what the fate of
the road and the fortune of night might bring their way.

Whilst land transit was bad up to about 1775 or 1800, internal
water communication was little better. In their natural condition, the many rivers which flowed through the clothing area
were of little use. The upper waters were generally too shallow
or rapid ; their banks had not been strengthened, and every
severe storm or prolonged rain brought extensive floods, which
washed away bridges and spread ruin and disaster over the
adjacent lands.[2] On the lower levels the streams wound along
with serpentine grace ; the course was shallow, and the water
choked with weeds, stones, or overhanging trees, with small
waterfalls and weirs occurring in places. Navigation along such
streams was impossible except with small craft and for short
distances, and any really extensive use of the rivers could only
be made by drastic removal of these impediments.

The canal did not appear in Yorkshire until about 1770, but
during the reign of William III steps were taken to render the
Aire and Calder navigable.[3] The improvement of the facilities
afforded by these two streams brought about a large increase

---

[1] e.g. *Leedes Intelligencer*, November 12, 1754 : ' On Tuesday last, betwixt
the hours of 5 and 6, as one Craven, a cloth maker, who lives at Horbury,
was returning from Leedes Market, he was stopped on Rothwell Hague by
two men on horseback, one of which brandishing a sword before his face and
demanding his money took from him 2 gns. in gold and 2s. 6d. in silver.'

[2] *North and West Riding Sess. Rec., passim* ; Bigland, *op. cit.*, p. 81. Also
Mayhall for frequent accounts of floods.

[3] Statute 10–11 Will. III, c. 19, granted power to improve navigation of
these rivers.

in the amount of river traffic ; Wakefield and Leeds benefited greatly, whilst the extension of the Calder navigation to Halifax in 1740,[1] and to Sowerby Bridge in 1758–60, brought that important kersey-making area into water communication with the sea.[2]   All this was a great asset to the textile industry. The cost of carriage was reduced, coal, iron, and building materials were obtained more cheaply and quickly ; wool, logwood, and oil were brought up-stream ; an easy outlet was afforded by which cloth, &c., could be sent down to Hull, and thence to home and foreign markets.   The increased facilities for obtaining food supplies were no less valuable, and this led to the establishment of large depots for food-stuffs, partly at Leeds, but especially at Wakefield, which now became a still more important market for wool, corn, coal, and all the various commodities needed by the Riding.

Next came the canal era.   As early as 1764[3] plans were being drawn up for a scheme of canals in the county, and John Hustler urged the need for a waterway which would link up the Irish Sea and the Humber mouth.   Meetings were held in 1766,[4] and the scheme gradually matured.   By 1770 all preliminaries had been settled, an Act of Parliament obtained,[5] and the work of excavation begun.   Progress was fairly rapid at first, and by 1777 thirty-three miles, from Leeds to beyond Skipton, were open for trade, whilst a similar length had been made on the Lancashire side.   But the cost had already exceeded £300,000, whereas the estimated cost of the whole undertaking had been only £260,000.   Lack of funds and differences of opinion concerning the route for the remaining fifty miles caused a suspension of operations, but in 1790 work was resumed, and the canal eventually completed in 1816, at a cost of nearly one and a quarter millions.[6]

This waterway was the most important of the northern canals.   Bradford was linked up to it by a short canal opened

---

[1] Defoe (later editions), iii. 122, 146.
[2] 31 Geo. II, c. 72.   Destroyed by floods, but repaired in 1769.
[3] The *York Courant* had taken up the idea in 1764.   Also pamphlet written by Hustler.   See admirable article by Killick, on the ' Early History of the Leeds and Liverpool Canal ', in the *Bradford Antiquary*, vol. iii.
[4] *Leedes Intelligencer*, July 2, 1766.   [5] 10 Geo. III, c. 114.
[6] Priestley, *History of Inland Communication* (1831), p. 424.
[7] Ibid., p. 427.

in 1774,[1] and three other waterways provided continuous passage between Yorkshire and the counties west of the Pennines.[2] All these routes helped in the development of commerce in the county, and assisted in the rapid expansion of the industry during the subsequent half century. By 1830 Yorkshire manufacturers and merchants had at their disposal an admirable system of highways and waterways, but the next thirty years were to witness the provision of a network of railways which destroyed much of the commercial importance of road and canal. This wealth of means of transit presents a marked contrast to the position of the clothier and merchant a century previous. There is much to admire in the picture of these eighteenth-century Yorkshiremen, toiling away amid all manner of difficulties, fighting the storms and floundering in the mud. That weekly journey of the clothier to market, or the regular itinerary of the merchant, was no easy task, and these men were ready to endure much and to risk much in the pursuit of their trade.

[1] *Old History of Bradford* (1776), pp. 13–14.
[2] These routes were (1) canal from Calder and Hebble Navigation over to Rochdale ; (2) Trent and Mersey Canal ; (3) canal from Calder to Huddersfield, thence over Pennines to Oldham, where a canal had been made to Ashton and Manchester. The Pennine canal was made in 1794.

CHAPTER XII

THE STATE AND INDUSTRIAL MORALITY IN THE EIGHTEENTH CENTURY

In chapters iv and vii we have seen the comparative failure of all attempts to regulate effectively the cloth industry. Tudor legislation, which fixed lengths, breadths, and weights, had been of little avail to check frauds and deceits; the ulnager had disappeared in the early part of the eighteenth century; finally, the Stuart corporations had failed entirely to maintain high standards of workmanship, and were either dead or in a state of impotence by the accession of Anne.

These persistent failures did not dissuade the Government from attempting once more to establish efficient machinery of supervision, and the statute book of the eighteenth century is loaded with legislation which aimed at producing a higher moral tone in industrial life. Some of this legislation affected all parts of the country, but the reputation of the Yorkshire industry was as lamentable as its importance was great, and many acts were passed during the first three quarters of the eighteenth century to deal with the West Riding alone.

The Act of 1623 which had been operative throughout the seventeenth century had fixed definite lengths, breadths, and weights for various kinds of cloths. This legislation, reinforced by the ordinances of companies and corporations, had survived to some extent up to the end of the seventeenth century; but by that time it had become patent that the Stuart machinery had broken down, and that new regulations must be made in the light of changed conditions. Excessive tentering and stretching of cloth was still as common as ever, and the old maximum legal sizes had long since been exceeded, so that, as Thoresby [1] pointed out, the Northern Dozens might now be of any length up to 60 yards. Some of this length was fictitious, being due to the extent to which the cloth had been tentered; there was a lead tag on the end of each cloth stating the inflated dimensions

[1] Thoresby, *Ducatus*, p. 78.

of the piece, but when the merchant bought the cloth and took it to be finished he found that it shrank when immersed in water.

The complaints concerning these cloths grew very loud in 1708, when petitions were sent to the House of Commons, asking for strong statutory interference.[1] A Bill, backed by Thoresby[2] and many of the leading inhabitants of the Riding, was placed before Parliament and rushed through all its stages, becoming law in 1708, as ' an Act for the better ascertaining the lengths and breadths of Woollen Cloths made in the County of York '.[3] Briefly, this Act fixed minimum breadths and maximum lengths ; broad cloths were to be at least $5\frac{1}{2}$ quarters in breadth, and whole broad cloths not more than 46 yards in length. These measurements were to be the limits of the cloth when it was thoroughly wet and had therefore shrunk to its minimum size. Hence the fuller, when he had the cloth immersed, was to measure the piece, and stamp its dimensions on a seal of lead, which was then riveted to the end of the fabric. He was to charge the clothier a penny for this work and for the seal, and if any fuller neglected to perform his duty he was liable to a fine of 20s. Then, with the real minimum size of the cloth stated on the seal, it would not be wise for the clothier to stretch it unduly, since the merchant would be able to gauge the real value of the cloth from the seal affixed by the fuller. But, lest any one should still blindly persist in stretching more than 4 inches per yard of breadth, or more than 1 yard in 20 yards of length, offenders were declared to be liable to heavy fines, half of which went to the informer and half to the poor of the parish in which the culprit lived. One last clause is of interest. Parliament had realized that it was of little use issuing legislation against clothiers, if that legislation was to be administered by justices of the peace who were themselves clothiers or men actually interested in the trade. Therefore any indictments for the infringement of this Act were to be brought only before justices who were neither merchants nor makers of woollens.

This Act, with its demand that the fuller would stamp the

[1] See Petition from Huddersfield, *House of Commons' Journals*, xvi. 142.
[2] Thoresby's *Diary*, January 1709.
[3] 7 Anne, c. 13. This Act went through its Committee stage in one day, without any amendment (Stowe MSS. 748, f. 79).

cloth, might have been effective had there been any adequate provision to ensure that the fullers were really doing their duty. But this was not the case; the system of searching by officials elected at the Quarter Sessions had fallen into abeyance, and, whilst there was some attempt to enforce legislation in Leeds, the fullers who were dotted up and down the country had little to fear from the vigilance of searchers. Hence the fuller stamped the cloth according to the wishes of the clothier, rather than in accord with its true dimensions when in the water. The old evils therefore continued, and in April 1723 the justices at the Pontefract Quarter Sessions appointed a committee to inquire into the frauds prevalent in the Riding.[1] This committee, which consisted of gentlemen, merchants, and clothiers, found that the laws were defective, and therefore appealed to Parliament for more effective legislation to prevent such misdoings. There was much opposition to such measures, on the ground that all statutes of this type had been futile and useless and that the Government ought not to attempt to interfere further with the trade.[2] In these inquiries before the justices and before Parliament a quaint story was circulated, apparently for the first time,[3] and it so struck the imagination of those who heard it that it passed into the ranks of the local legends, and was reproduced as authentic on many subsequent occasions. The story came from a merchant engaged in the trade with Russia, who had supplied Yorkshire cloths to the Russian army. The rough heavy fabrics in which he dealt were admirably suited to military wear, and many Leeds clothiers and merchants were engaged in supplying the needs of the Russian and other armies. But the cloth was all more or less deceptive, excessively stretched, and certain to shrink on its first encounter with water. It appears that the Russian army had just obtained a new uniform, and the whole of the troops, clad in these new garments made of Yorkshire cloth, turned out one fine day to be reviewed by their sovereign. Just as the regiments were lined up, ready for inspection, the sky became cloudy and a short, sharp shower of rain came down, wetting the new apparel. The effect was

[1] *House of Commons' Journals*, xx. 365.
[2] Ibid., p. 423; also 246 et seq.
[3] Add. MSS. 33344, f. 19: 'The Case of the Yorkshire Clothiers' (1730 ?)

almost instantaneous, for the foul Yorkshire cloth at once shrank very considerably, so that the garments went all awry. The sleeves became too short, and the pockets crept up towards the men's arm-pits. This episode brought so much discredit upon English fabrics that the Russian Government imposed heavy duties on all further importations, and set to work to manufacture its own pieces. The story was evidently raked up again about 1760 ; [1] it was repeated in 1790, when one finds it recited at great length, and with many embellishments for the benefit of French readers, in the *Moniteur* of July 1790.[2] It seems to have appeared again in 1816, and is finally told in a volume entitled *Data and Postulates*, published in 1852. Here the narrative is admirably expanded, garnished, decorated with great wealth of detail, and recounted with real literary exuberance.

But to return to the committee of 1723. The objections urged against further legislation were overriden and a comprehensive statute issued in 1725. This Act[3] really attempted to establish proper regulations, and also to set up machinery of supervision to ensure that the Act was efficiently administered ; but it concerned itself with broad cloths only, and for some years to come narrow cloths were left untouched.

The provisions of this Act were briefly as follows :

1. The clothier was to weave or sew his name and address at the end of all his pieces, under pain of being fined £5.

2. Maximum lengths and minimum breadths were fixed for cloths, and these dimensions were to be complied with by pieces when they had been thoroughly washed, scoured, and fully milled. A fine of 20s. was imposed on every yard by which a cloth exceeded the stipulated length.

3. The fuller was again commandeered to attest the quantity of the cloth. Every fuller was required to take an oath before the justices that he would well and truly measure all cloths before they left his hands, and fix at each end of every piece a seal of lead, on which were stamped his own name and the

---

[1] *Reports* 1806, iii. 373.
[2] *Moniteur*, no. 191, Samedi, 10 juillet 1790, v. 77. Despatch ' de Leeds, le sept juin '. For the full story see *Tricks of the Trade*, by the present writer, Thoresby Soc., vol. xxii, pt. iii (1914).
[3] Statute 11 Geo. I, c. 24.

size of the piece. He was then to enter in a register full particulars of each broad cloth which he milled, and, finally, he was to charge the clothier 2d., one penny of which went to the Treasurer of the West Riding, the remaining penny being his own recompense for his trouble, as well as a payment for the seals. If he failed in these duties, or made out the seals falsely, he was liable to a fine of £5.

4. Thanks to the above provision it was hoped that frauds might vanish at once, and confidence be restored to the buyers of Yorkshire cloths. But in case the merchant, having purchased any piece, felt dubious as to the accuracy of the statements made on the seal, he could, within six days of purchase, have the cloth immersed, in the presence of the clothier; if, after four hours' immersion, the measurements differed from those recorded on the seal, the merchant could demand a reduction of one-sixth of the price of the piece, the clothier being allowed to compensate himself for this loss by claiming the same amount from the fuller.

5. Finally, in the finishing of cloth by the dresser, all parts of the cloth were to be finished and dressed evenly, 'not only at the sides and edges next to the list (as hath of late years been the custom) but also in the middle from end to end'. After which the cloth-dresser was to add a seal containing his name at the end of each piece

Thus labelled by clothier, fuller, and finisher, it was hoped that the cloth would at last be of good repute. But most of these provisions were similar to those of previous enactments, and so it might be expected that the pious aspirations which brought them into being would have ended in smoke, as in previous attempts. Such, however, was not to be the fate of this Act, for its most important feature was the stress laid upon the provision of machinery to enforce these regulations. Each year the justices of the peace were to choose as many men of good character as they thought necessary, to be searchers for the following year, and were to pay these men a salary not exceeding £15 per annum, this money being taken out of the pennies forwarded by the fullers to the Treasurer of the West Riding. Thus the clothiers, in paying their 2d. per cloth, provided 1d. towards the salaries of the inspectors who were to make them honest men. These searchers were given full power to enter any mill where cloth was being fulled, and, if they wished, to measure any cloth found there. Also they might examine the register of cloth kept by the fuller, and had power to bring any offender to justice. Lastly, they might enter any house, shop, outhouse, tenter ground, or warehouse, to search for any cloth which infringed the various clauses of the Act; any person resisting them was fined £10, and any fraud discovered meant a penalty of £5.

This Act, renewed in 1733 and 1741,[1] remained in force until 1764 or 1765. Each April the justices of the peace at Pontefract Quarter Sessions [2] appointed a number of broad cloth searchers for the following year, and gave to each of these men a special district to supervise. The number appointed was generally between 11 and 15, and each inspector received a salary of £12 to £14. The renewal of the Act in 1741 allowed 3d. to be charged on each cloth, 2d. of which came to the Treasurer. Hence, with a growing industry, and with more than doubled revenue, the small band of searchers could be made into a legion,[3] scattered further afield, and more able to give attention to the outlying mills. For the broad cloth area 25 searchers were appointed, with salaries varying from £5 to £15. Eight searchers, with salaries of £1 to £3, were appointed to supervise those parts of the narrow cloth area where some few broad cloths were milled (i.e. around Halifax), and six men were given the sole duty of inspecting the tenters of the whole district, in order to see that cloth hung out on these frames fulfilled the legal demands. In fact, the total salaries paid amounted to about £360 annually. The men were to examine the pieces and test the accuracy of the seals, they were to see that the fuller kept his register properly, and, by haunting their district as much as possible, were to strive to uphold honesty according to the tenor of the cloth laws.

These Acts were confined to the broad cloth industry only, and therefore applied almost entirely to the area within a radius of 10 miles south and west of Leeds. Meanwhile, the narrow cloths, the kerseys, &c., manufactured around Halifax, Hudders-

---

[1] Statute 7 Geo. II, c. 25, and 14 Geo. II, c. 35.

[2] See Quarter Sess. Records, annually, eighteenth century, e. g. 1733, three searchers for Wakefield, two for Dewsbury, six for Leeds, two for Birstal, two for Yeadon, one for Arthington, two for Liversedge and Calder.

[3] Quarter Sess. Order Book, U, p. 245.

field, and the Calder valley generally were escaping scot free, because the laws concerning them had fallen into abeyance. There was no appointment of narrow cloth searchers at the Quarter Sessions, and the clothiers therefore tentered and stretched their pieces to suit their own pleasure. This must now be stopped, and the statute of 1738 brought the narrow cloth industry under a control similar to that of the broad cloth trade. This Act profited by the failings demonstrated in the administration of the sister Act, and more efficient rules were drawn up than were in force in the broad cloth industry. In the first place, the statute abandoned all attempts to fix standards of length and breadth, and allowed clothiers to make pieces of any dimensions they pleased. This was a great concession, and probably did much to remedy fraudulent work, for if legal standards were demanded any cloth which did not approximate to such dimensions could be made to do so by a little extra tentering. Therefore the relinquishing of fixed measurements removed one of the prime causes of over-stretching. Secondly, the weaver was to set his initials at the head of his pieces, and every piece was to be measured by the fuller and also by the searcher. The fuller put a seal at one end, containing his name and the length and breadth, as measured by him ; the searcher put a seal at the other end, stating the dimensions as he found them. Then fuller and searcher entered full particulars of each piece in books which they both kept for that purpose, and only when the piece had been sealed by the searcher could it depart from the mill. This was a great advance on the arrangement for the broad cloth industry, in which the searcher did not seal the pieces, but examined only those which happened to be in the mill when he called. Here in the narrow cloth mills every piece had to be searched by him, and any cloth which left the premises before obtaining his approval brought upon its owner or upon the fuller a fine of £5.

Such onerous duties on the part of the searcher necessitated his being in constant attendance at the mills, and therefore the area allotted to each man was small. In 1738 twenty-two searchers [1] were chosen ; some of them had jurisdiction over one

[1] The searchers were men of good character and repute, men who had served an apprenticeship to the trade of making narrow cloths, and were

mill, at a salary of £2, whilst others supervised four mills, a task which involved a considerable amount of walking, and were therefore paid about £14 per annum. With such limited areas, the searchers were ordered to ' attend at the several mills, tenter grounds, and places under their charges twice every day at least, i.e. once in the morning and once in the afternoon '. In this way the fullers of the Holm and Calder rivers and the various becks of the Pennine district were watched. The clothier brought his piece ; it was fulled and scoured, measured and sealed by fuller and searcher, and only then could it depart. On taking it away, the clothier had to pay 2d. to the fuller, 1¼d. of which went to the Treasurer of the West Riding to defray the cost of inspection.

As far as we can gather, these Acts were administered with a large amount of earnestness, and were probably as successful in achieving their aim as any such Acts ever were. The Act of 1725, regulating the broad cloth industry, met with considerable opposition at first. Clothiers refused to pay the fines inflicted upon them, and in many cases the justices of the peace reversed decisions which had been made previously. These difficulties, however, were gradually overcome, and the clauses of the Act more generally obeyed. In 1756 there were 48 broad cloth searchers [1] and 31 for narrow cloths.[2] But that these men rigorously administered the full and strict letter of the law it is impossible to suppose. They were men who did the work of searching as a by-occupation, and so their duties would be neglected when the pressure of other business was at all great. This was especially the case with the narrow cloth searchers, who were expected to break off their ordinary occupations twice a day, in order to go and examine cloths at the mill or mills under their charge. Fullers therefore often had reason to complain that pieces were delayed in their hands, awaiting the tardy visit of the searchers,[3] and in 1743 a surveyor was appointed to travel round the Riding and see that the searchers carried

---

therefore generally clothiers who took up the searching as an extra means of livelihood (11 Geo. II, c. 28). Alehouse-keepers or those in charge of ' tipling houses ' could not become searchers (Quarter Sess. Order Books, Y, p. 61. Also U, pp. 97–9, and *passim*).

[1] Order Books, Y, p. 172.   [2] Ibid., p. 60.

[3] e.g. complaint that searchers are neglecting duty (Order Books, U, p. 235).

out their duties with promptitude.[1] By the sixties the Acts had broken down, especially in this respect, and one witness giving evidence in 1765 declared that ' the searchers very seldom attend at the mill, but leave the miller to stamp [the cloth] himself, because the salaries allowed them are not adequate '.[2] Thus many cloths were milled without the searcher ever seeing them ; the fuller registered only those cloths which the searcher saw, and many were therefore never registered at all. Hence the figures published annually as to the number of cloths milled in the West Riding were probably always too low.

Further, the searchers were often men who had been brought up in the cloth industry, and who knew all its needs and its difficulties. Such men would not be likely to enforce too zealously laws which affected themselves as well as their fellows, and so doubtless there was much harmless collusion between searcher, clothier, and fuller, by which the arm of the law was tacitly evaded.

Lastly, the conditions of the broad cloth Acts almost compelled some faking and excessive tentering of the pieces. The law set up certain standards for these cloths ; the broad fabric must not be less than $5\frac{1}{2}$ quarters (i.e. 1 yard $13\frac{1}{2}$ inches) in width. Now when a clothier took a piece to the fuller he did not know exactly how much the cloth was likely to decrease in width when immersed in water. The shrinkage depended upon the nature of the wool, the fineness of the spinning, the quality of the weaving, &c. Hence when the cloth had been watered, it might be of adequate width, or it might be too narrow. In the latter case, there would be a hurried conversation between the clothier and the fuller, and the stamping of a false breadth on the seal ; and when the cloth was taken home it would be stretched until it attained the standard width. Thus the establishment of a standard encouraged the excessive tentering of cloths ; as one witness declared, ' if there was not any standard, cloth would come into the market better both in breadth and quality, as the cloth would be truly stamped, which would be a means of preventing the clothiers stretching the

---

[1] Ibid., Y, p. 144.
[2] *House of Commons' Journals*, xxx. 263. Evidence before Select Committee on West Riding Cloth Laws.

cloth as much as they do at present, because when it is under the standard they stretch it in order to avoid the penalties '.[1]

A comparison of the two Acts shows that, whilst the narrow cloths were allowed the greater liberty, the provision made for the searching of these cloths was much more thorough than was that for the broads. Hence, whilst the narrow cloth Act remained in force so long as cloths were inspected and sealed, the broad cloth Act had fallen into disuse by the sixties of the eighteenth century. In those parts of the Riding where it had been enforced trade had left the local fulling mills and migrated to more easy-going districts, or fled across the boundaries, taking the pieces to be finished in those counties to which the Act did not extend. Even so early as 1731 the Yorkshire justices asked that the broad cloth Act might be extended to the neighbouring Ridings and counties, so as to equalize competitive conditions,[2] and in 1765 it was stated that much Yorkshire cloth was taken to be finished in Lancashire, because that county was outside the scope of the searchers' jurisdiction. During 1764–5 many petitions came from the West Riding, asking for a thorough renovation of the broad cloth laws, and for a readjustment to meet the real needs of the situation. A Select Committee of the House of Commons inquired into the matter, and eventually the Act of 1765 was passed, ' for repealing several laws relating to the manufacture of woollen cloth in the County of York, and also so much of several other laws as prescribes particular standards of width and length to such woollen cloths, and for substituting other regulations of the cloth trade within the West Riding . . . for preventing frauds in certifying the contents of the cloth, and for preserving the credit of the said manufacture at foreign markets '.[3] An ambitious title for a very full and complicated Act.

This statute was about the last of its kind, and it certainly wound up the series in a blaze of legislative and administrative glory. The Act repealed all its predecessors, which had been ' found by experience not to be effectual for the preventing the frauds, abuses and deceits ' practised in the broad cloth industry. This meant the abolition of all legal standards of dimensions,

---

[1] *House of Commons' Journal*, xxx. 263.
[2] Quarter Sess. Order Books, S, p. 189.   [3] 5 Geo. III, c. 51.

and cloth henceforth might be of any length, breadth, or weight. Further, the justices of the peace, who must not be dealers in cloth or occupiers of fulling-mills, were ordered to choose annually a sufficient number of searchers, men of good character, who followed or had been brought up in the trade. These officials were to be the measurers and sealers of all broad fabrics. Henceforth the fuller did not seal and stamp the cloth ; that task was taken out of his hands, and given entirely to the searcher. Every piece had to pass under his inspection, and no cloth could leave the mill until he had stamped upon its seal the correct length and breadth. When the seal had been affixed and the necessary fee paid, the clothier might take away his piece, and, after measuring it to see that the first seal was correct, could tenter it as he pleased. Also the clothier was compelled to weave or sew into one end his name and address in full. This last clause was responsible for a number of amusing cases during the first twelve months that the Act was in operation, for many clothiers innocently and ignorantly used abbreviations, or mis-spelt their names and addresses ; some worthy informer, on the alert to earn an informer's share of the fines, dragged these men before the court, where they were convicted ' for false spelling or abbreviating their names and place of abode '. Therefore in the following year an amending Act was passed, one of the clauses of which allowed the clothiers ' to use some common or known usual abbreviation '.

The measuring and sealing of cloths was now placed entirely in the charge of the searchers. This Act was remarkable for the variety of officials which it created. The searchers did the actual sealing at the mill, but in addition there were inspectors, whose duty lay in visiting the workshops, tenters, warehouses, &c., where cloths were tentered and dressed, to see that all cloths were sealed and not excessively stretched. Finally there were supervisors, inspectors-in-chief, who went round to both fulling-mills and dressing establishments, to ensure that searchers and inspectors were discharging their duties.

With this threefold provision of officers, with the liberty to make cloths of any dimensions, with the insistence upon each cloth being sealed by the searcher, and with a superior officer to detect any carelessness or sloth on the part of the searchers,

it might be expected that at last the machinery of supervision
had reached perfection, and would work harmoniously and
efficiently for ever. Each July at the Bradford Quarter Sessions [1]
the officers were chosen for the following year, and their salaries
fixed. In 1777 there were 46 searchers with salaries up to £24
each, 17 inspectors with stipends up to £25, and 4 supervisors
who received up to £80 each. For a time these men did their
work with the exemplary thoroughness attributed to new
brooms, and a witness in 1806 remarked that ' when the Act
was first obtained we saw them [the inspectors] once, twice, or
some times three times a day examining our tenters '.[2] The
searchers' work was discharged the most effectively, because it
involved the collecting of the fees out of which all the officers
were paid. But gradually there came a decline in the vigour
with which the Act was administered, and the evidence given
in 1806 indicated that the machinery was practically at a standstill by that date. One witness remarked that the stamping
was being done in a slipshod manner, and the inspectors very
seldom troubled to examine tenters. ' I suppose ', he stated,
' they like to do their business with as little trouble as possible,
and unless we send for them we never see them. We go on with
our own business without the inspector. We think we know
how to stretch the cloth better than him. We do not trouble
our heads about it, unless sometimes, when we are apprehensive
of a dispute between us and the clothiers, and then we send for
him.'[3] Another Yorkshireman stated ' I have no means of
knowing what the searcher does, but if they do their business
no better than the inspector and supervisor does, they do it
very ill indeed. . . . I think we do not see [the inspectors] twice
in a year, unless we send for them.'[4] The searcher had become
equally useless as a check on tentering or as an authority on the
length of a piece. His task was now chiefly to collect the fees,
and keep the register of the number of cloths ; and as a longer
cloth meant a larger fee, there would be no very scrupulous
measurement of the pieces. Thus the merchants who gave
evidence were unanimous in their disregard of the statement of
dimensions made on the searcher's seal. ' In no instance do

[1] Quarter Sess. Records, Bradford, July 1777 ; Order Books, FF, p. 9.
[2] *Reports*, 1806, iii. 157.   [3] Ibid., p. 155.   [4] Ibid., pp. 155–7.

they depend upon the stamper's mark ',[1] declared one man, and others pointed out that they never took any notice of the seal, but always had the cloth measured in their own warehouse, before payment was made.[2]   Finally, many merchants agreed that the cloths which they bought unsealed from other counties were often superior in quality to those which were purchased sealed in the West Riding ; and the conclusion was that the system should either be abandoned entirely, or enforced strictly, in which latter case it might perhaps be beneficial.[3]   In 1821 a committee inquired into the working of these cloth laws. It found that they were not in the least fulfilling the purposes for which they were promulgated, and therefore advised the dis-continuance of all such provisions.[4]   Parliament acted upon these suggestions, repealed all the acts which had been framed in the previous century, and the whole system of searching at once lapsed.

The disappearance of the searcher marks the end of centuries of attempts to regulate the quality of cloth. From the Assize of Measures (1197), and probably before that time, down to the early part of last century the State had been concerned with cloth, either as a source of revenue, or as an important com-modity of commerce, or both. It had struggled to bring cloths to a few standard sizes, so as to simplify the assessment of taxation. It had attempted to fix legal dimensions, to forbid or limit processes and the application of utensils, in its desire to maintain a high quality in English cloths. In these efforts it had been baffled by the growing variety of fabrics, by the fundamental qualities of the materials, by the commercial necessities of cloth-makers and dealers, and by the dispersed nature of the industry. In our own days attempts to regulate the conditions of labour by Factory Acts, Trade Boards, &c., are subject to grave limitations and difficulties in enforcing the law. These difficulties would be infinitely greater if we essayed to regulate, not conditions of labour, but quality of goods. Therefore the task of supervising a scattered industry, working on unscientific lines in days of deficient communications, must have been almost superhuman. The State adopted the best

[1] Ibid., p. 155.   [2] Ibid., pp. 154, 183, &c.
[3] Ibid., p. 155.   [4] Ibid., 1821, vi. 437 et seq.

line of attack by placing the administration of the statutes in the hands of local authorities; but this had its many disadvantages, and so all attempts to interfere with the quality of the goods which the clothier offered for sale were entirely abandoned. The policy of *laissez-faire* triumphed, and the sole guide in all future transactions was *caveat emptor*.

The Worsted Committee

One other aspect of industrial regulation remains to be considered, and here we come in contact with an institution established in the eighteenth century, which, after many vicissitudes, still exists in a state of comparative health and vigour. The Worsted Committee was inaugurated in order to safeguard the interests of the worsted master in the domestic system of the eighteenth century; and, though the domestic system has vanished, the officers of that committee still continue the work of preventing frauds and embezzlements on the part of employees.

The domestic system lent itself easily to those practices which arise from lack of supervision. When raw materials were handed out to a workman, and work was done out of sight of the master, it was not difficult for the employee to practise any number of fraudulent tricks on his employer. Embezzlement of material, exchange of poor wool for good, the wetting of wool in order to make it weigh heavier, imperfect or inaccurate spinning, &c., all these things might be practised with a fair chance of success, since the eye of the master or foreman was not ever on the workman. Further, when a master gave out work to be done he often had to wait a long time before he got back the material. The employee worked when he felt disposed, and often neglected work entrusted to him, with the result that the weavers and those dependent upon combers and spinners were often unemployed, by reason of the laziness of those who were preparing the yarn.

These difficulties, though not absent from the woollen industry, were very present to the worsted clothiers of the West Riding. Here there was a stronger capitalistic organization on the one hand, and a keen sense of solidarity of labour on the other. If the master dared to punish an offending workman, either for fraud or neglect, he generally called upon his head the wrath of

the labouring classes in his locality, and might suffer severely
for his temerity.

To protect employers, the State had long been attempting to
prevent workpeople from making free with their masters' goods.
As early as 1610 all spinsters ' embezilling or detaining any wooll '
were sentenced either to make full satisfaction, be whipped, or
put in the stocks by the constables.[1] Nearly a century later [2]
legislation made another effort, when an Act of 1702 declared
that 'frauds are daily committed by persons employed in woollen,
linen, cotton, and iron manufactures, by embezzling materials
with which they are entrusted ', and heavy penalties were laid
down for such offences. This Act was occasionally amended,[3]
and at times actually enforced, as for instance in August 1764,
when ' Lydia Longbottom, of Bingley, was publickly whipt
thro' the market at Wakefield, for reeling false and short yarn
. . . the town bailiff carrying a reel before her '.[4]

But this constant issue of legislation was of little avail,
because there was no provision for the actual administration of
the law, other than through the ordinary channels of justice.
If a constable found an instance of embezzlement or the like,
he might take the culprit before the court, or if a master detected
one of his employees he might follow the same course. The
constable, however, had abundance of other matters which
needed his attention, and could give very little time to running
down fraudulent workpeople ; and the master shrank from
putting the law into operation, because he feared the reprisals
of his workfolk. Hence, the isolated master was baffled, and
the law of no effect. During the seventies the situation became
critical. ' Woolcombers embezzled their masters' yarn, spinners
reeled false or short yarn, and in case a master tried to put the
law into force such a combination existed amongst his workpeople that he could obtain no blacklegs, and his own person
and property were endangered.' [5] Against this organized labour
the individual master was powerless. Therefore it needed some
similar organization amongst the masters, some fearless, united,
and permanent institution, which would boldly search out and

[1] Statute 7 Jas. I, c. 7.   [2] 1 Anne, stat. ii, c. 22.
[3] 13 Geo. II, c. 8 ; 22 Geo. II, c. 27 ; 14 Geo. III, c. 44.
[4] *Leedes Intelligencer*, August 17, 1764.   [5] James, *op. cit.*, pp. 202-3.

bring to court all cases of fraud, and so ensure that the Acts were more than mere dead letters. This need for an employers' union or association rapidly became more and more apparent, and in about 1775 an informal organization was established, which gathered contributions from voluntary subscribers, and used these funds to employ inspectors who were to safeguard the interests of the worsted masters. This initial step was attended with success, and the employers began to seek further powers, and to gain legal sanction for their association. Eloquent petitions informed Parliament of the grievous state of affairs in the West Riding : the worsted clothiers showed that the laws were entirely neglected and overlooked, and that the only remedy lay in establishing a committee of masters and a permanent inspectorate, to see that the statutory provisions were enforced.[1] The representations of the Yorkshiremen were strengthened by similar statements from the masters of Lancashire and Cheshire, counties in which large quantities of raw wool were combed and spun ; and thus the North put forward a very strong case. Parliament acceded to the request, and the Worsted Act of 1777 established on a legal basis that organization of masters which still exists as the Worsted Committee of the Counties of York, Lancaster, and Chester.[2] Once the northern masters had obtained their weapon of defence, those in other parts of the country sought similar protection. In 1784 Suffolk was granted power to establish a committee ;[3] in the following year the worsted masters of Bedfordshire, Huntingdon, Northampton, Leicestershire, Rutland, Lincolnshire, and the Isle of Ely formed a similar organization,[4] and in 1790 Norfolk and Norwich set up a Worsted Committee.[5] Thus the State recognized four bodies similar in many respects to the corporations of the seventeenth century, the aim of which was to promote the welfare of the masters, and to provide special machinery for the administration of a certain type of legislation. When these institutions were erected, three out of the four districts were already losing their textile industries, so that the northern Worsted Committee was really the only one to achieve any importance.

---

[1] *House of Commons Journals*, xxxvi. 85, et seq.   [2] 17 Geo. III, c. 11.
[3] 24 Geo. III, c. 3.   [4] 25 Geo. III, c. 40.   [5] 31 Geo. III, c. 56.

The preamble to the Worsted Act states the reason for the establishment of the committee. It refers to the various laws passed against embezzlement and falsehood in the preparation of yarn, but states that ' the good purpose of the laws has been greatly frustrated, from the manufacturers . . . being unwilling to expose themselves singly to the loss attending the resentment of the spinners and workpeople by prosecuting them for offences against the said Acts ; . . . and this important branch of the woollen manufacture will be greatly prejudiced thereby, unless the manufacturers are enabled jointly to carry these laws into effectual execution, which cannot be done without the aid of Parliament '. Therefore it was ordered that a general meeting of the manufacturers of combing wool, worsted yarn, and worsted goods in the counties of York, Lancaster, and Chester should be held immediately at Halifax, due notice having been given in all the local newspapers. At this meeting the committee was to be elected, composed as follows : The Yorkshire manufacturers were to elect 18 representatives, whilst those of Lancashire and Cheshire jointly were to choose 9 persons. These 27 men were to constitute the committee by which the Worsted Acts were to be enforced. They were to meet quarterly, in order to report progress and discuss policy. Above all, they were to watch over the work of the worsted inspectors. These officials, of whom there must be at least two, were to be nominated by the committee, and recommended to the justices of the peace, who at quarter sessions licensed them to act in accordance with the powers granted by the statute. The inspectors were then given definite areas, and each in his respective district was ' to use all due diligence and industry for the convicting and bringing to justice of all offenders '. They were from time to time to inspect the reels of spinners, and whenever they found any breach of law were to lodge information against the offender, and carry on the prosecution of the culprit.

Further, one of the most fruitful centres of fraud would be the home or storehouse of those agents who received the wool, and then gave it out to be spun. These distributors of the raw material might practise many deceits and embezzlements, and it was necessary, therefore, that the inspectors should have power to keep them under supervision. The statute granted that the inspectors could demand entrance, at all reasonable times, into the dwelling-house, shop, or outhouse of any agent or other person employed to put wool out to be spun, to inspect the yarn in the stock of such agent, and to bring to justice any who offended in such particulars. Any inspector failing in his duty, or guilty of screening an offender, was to be discharged from his office, and placed for a month in the House of Correction. For the guidance of these inspectors, the Act then stated the nature of offences and their consequent penalties. A standard for reeling was fixed and a scale of punishment laid down for false reeling, for embezzling or disposing of materials entrusted to a person to be spun, and for the refusal by agents to allow inspectors to examine their stock. A further Act in the same year[1] revised all the previous statutes concerning misdemeanours, and gave the inspectors further grounds for action. Persons found buying or receiving goods which they knew to be stolen, and persons pawning or selling such materials were to be severely punished. If the inspectors or any one else suspected a person of having in his possession goods which he ought not to have, they were to make complaint to the justices of the peace, who then granted a warrant for the search of the premises of the suspect. The search took place, and if any suspicious goods were found the accused was taken before the justices. If he could not give a satisfactory account as to how he came by the same, he was deemed guilty, and punished, although no evidence had been given to show who was the owner of such materials. The *onus probandi* lay with the defendant. The goods found in his possession spoke against him, and he was a guilty man until he proved himself innocent.

Lastly, this Act gave the master increased power over his workmen, even though the latter did not work under the employer's roof. An Act of 1749 had allowed a man twenty-one days in which to complete and return work entrusted to him.[2] This period of time had proved unsatisfactory, and was obviously too long. Therefore the Act of 1777 reduced it to eight days, and declared that any workmen who did not return the material, properly worked up, within that time would be liable to the same punishment as for purloining and embezzling. Masters

---

[1] 17 Geo. III, c. 56.   [2] 22 Geo. II, c. 27.

were granted power of entrance into the shops and outhouses of any persons employed by them, in order to see that their work was being done properly; and finally, protection was granted to the tools, dye-stuffs, &c., which masters gave out to their employees. Thus the sphere of interference was very large, and the master, or the Worsted Committee inspector as his representative, was given wide powers of supervision in order to enforce the law.

The Worsted Committee, therefore, was to be an organization of masters, protecting materials in the hands of the domestic workers, and the inspectors were to act as an industrial police force, sanctioned by law, and licensed by the justices of the peace. But such a task needed a comparatively large number of inspectors; it needed money. Whence were the funds to be obtained? Before the passing of the Act, the salaries of one or two inspectors had been provided by voluntary subscriptions, but now, with a salaries bill of about £400 per annum, the worsted clothiers could not be expected to contribute so large a sum. There was nothing in the Act to allow the committee to levy contributions, and so the revenue must come from another source. There was at this time a duty on all soap used in England; it amounted to $1\frac{1}{4}d.$ per pound on all imported soap, and $\frac{1}{2}d.$ per pound on English soap,[1] and had been levied all through the eighteenth century. Such a tax would have been a heavy burden on the textile industry, where large quantities of soap were used in washing, scouring, and cleaning the wool before it was worked up. One pound of soap was required for every ten pounds of wool, and thus the accumulated duty on a year's work would be a considerable sum and a heavy imposition on the industry. A drawback, amounting to one-third the duty, was therefore granted on all soap used for textile purposes;[2] from time to time the clothier made a statement as to the amount of soap he had utilized in cleaning wool, and then received back one-third of the duty which he had paid on that quantity of soap. All masters who prepared their wool for weaving were affected by this drawback, but at the same time all were to benefit by the activities of the worsted inspectors.

[1] Statutes 10 Anne, c. 19 : 12 Anne, stat. ii., c. 9.
[2] 10 Anne, c. 19, § 29.

Therefore let the cost of the police system be defrayed out of the drawback which the clothiers received. This was the arrangement established by the Worsted Act. When a clothier was receiving his drawback, twopence out of each shilling was deducted from it, and these twopenny levies were forwarded to the Treasurer of the West Riding, who then provided the necessary money for salaries. Thus by an impost on the soap drawback the Worsted Committee was to be financed.

Granted these powers, the worsted masters promptly set to work to erect the machinery for the protection of their interests. The general meeting was held at the Talbot Inn, Halifax, on June 9, 1777, and the 27 members of the committee were chosen, representing the various parts of the three counties. Thus six committeemen were chosen by the Halifax area, four by those attending the Bradford market, two by Leeds, one by Ripon and North Yorkshire, whilst the Lancashire and Cheshire members were distributed in similar manner. The names of these first committeemen are those of famous cloth-making or cloth-selling families—Holden, Currer, Fielden, Garnett, Clapham, &c. Mr. John Hustler, the energetic Bradfordian, who had been largely responsible for the institution of the committee, became the first chairman.[1]

The first committee was chosen by a general meeting of all the worsted manufacturers of the three counties. But with that election the share of the ordinary clothier in the management of the committee practically ended. At times the committee would call a general meeting to support or oppose some piece of prospective legislation; the deduction from his drawback reminded the clothier of the existence of the committee, whilst the periodical visits of the inspector and reports of prosecutions kept the activities of the Worsted Committee well in the public eye. But as to the policy or government of the body the rank and file could say nothing; the committee was in practice, if not in theory, a close oligarchy. If it mismanaged affairs and neglected its duty, the general body of clothiers could meet and depose it from office, electing a new committee

---

[1] The information for this section has been obtained from the Minute Books of the Worsted Committee, in the hands of Messrs. Mumford & Johnson, solicitors, Bradford, to whom the writer wishes to express his gratitude.

in its place. But such things never happened, and the committee remained autocratic and all-powerful. Its first members
were elected for life, or for so long as they engaged in industry,
and on the retirement or death of a member the committee
elected his successor.   If a member retired from business or
absented himself from the quarterly meetings of the committee
for the space of a year, he was deemed to have vacated his
position [1] and another person chosen to take his place.   The
committee met four times a year, three of which assemblies were
in Yorkshire, the remaining one in Lancashire or Cheshire.
Hence the committee met most frequently at Bradford and
Halifax, though Leeds, Luddenden, Hebden Bridge, Wakefield,
Keighley, Liverpool, Manchester, Burnley, and Colne were
amongst the meeting-places of the quarterly council. Mileage
and other expenses were allowed to all who attended the meetings.[2]
Any one guilty of unpunctuality was fined 1s. for each hour
he was late, and 2s. 6d. if he failed to put in an appearance ; [3]
in 1782 it was ordered ' that no person, after having his name
entered as present, shall absent himself from the business of the
Committee for the space of fifteen minutes, betwixt 11 and
2 o'clock, without leave of the Chairman or the Committee first
obtained, under the penalty of receiving no money, either for
his day's attendance, or for his Expenses '.[4]

The chief task of the committee was the appointment and
control of its inspectors. At its first meeting the worsted area
was divided into six districts, of which four were in Yorkshire.
For each of these an inspector was appointed at a salary of £50,
to be paid out of the soap money, whilst the seventh official
was appointed to ' make a general inspection and give his
Assistance and Information to the other six Inspectors '.[5] The
payment to these men was sufficiently large to provide them
with an adequate livelihood, and so they were forbidden to take
up any other work. As the initial order declared, ' The Inspectors

[1] September 27, 1779 : ' Mr. Richard Brown, one of this Committee having
declined being a Manufacturer, and wilfully absented himself from the
quarterly meetings of this Committee for the space of one year ', his place
was therefore filled.

[2] 10s. 6d. per day and 7s. 6d. for travelling were the grants made to those
who attended the meetings. See Minutes, September 23, 1782.

[3] Minutes, July 22, 1778.   [4] September 23, 1782.

[5] June 23, 1777.

shall devote their whole time in that Employ, and shall not be concerned or employed in any other Business whatsoever, and . . . no part of the Family of such Inspectors shall be employed as putters out of Wool to spin '. These inspectors were not technically appointed by the committee ; the committee's business was to find suitable men, and to recommend them to the justices of the peace, who then formally licensed them.[1] This was the result of the curious status of the committee. It was a body established by law, constituted of master manufacturers, and administering laws by the motive of self-interest far more efficiently than they could have been operated through the ordinary channels. Hence that strange alliance between a sectional industrial society and the regular machinery of justice. The inspector, when appointed, became subject to the control of the committee, and held his post so long as he gave satisfaction to his master. Each inspector was placed under the special tutelage of a member of the committee, to whom he had to submit weekly reports, and from whom he obtained orders and supplies of money. If he neglected his duty, this member brought the offence before the whole committee. Some inspectors held their posts for the whole of their lives, as in the case of William Shepherd, who served the committee from 1785 until his death in 1828. Others held office only a very short period, being dismissed quickly for neglect of duty, drunkenness, misbehaviour, screening offenders, mismanaging financial matters, or for ' being incapable of keeping proper accounts ' after being repeatedly instructed in the art of book-keeping.[2]

With such equipment, the Worsted Committee set to work to enforce the laws against fraud, theft, and general industrial immorality amongst the workpeople. The first inspectors were approved at the July Quarter Sessions, 1777, and soon the West Riding began to be inundated with handbills and newspaper announcements. The wicked world was immediately to be cleansed and purged by the committee and its seven stalwart inspectors. Witness the stern fearlessness behind the following

---

[1] Quarter Sessions Books, FF, p. 6.

[2] Minutes, June 23, 1783. Also September 24, 1792 : ' It appearing to this meeting that Henry Parkinson, an inspector, has Misbehaved in his office, by being negligent, and particularly being in liquor when he attended the justices at Otley ', therefore he was discharged.

manifesto, which appeared in the *Leeds Mercury* of August 19, 1777 :

' The Committee of manufacturers of combing wool have nominated [seven persons here named] to be inspectors for preventing frauds and abuses committed by persons employed in the manufactures of combing wool, worsted yarn, etc., . . . and do hereby give notice, by virtue of an Act passed last Session, and forewarn all spinners who shall be guilty of reeling false or upon false reel that they will be prosecuted and punished by the said inspectors, as the law directs, without any favour or partiality. They likewise give notice to all agents or persons hired or employed to put out wool to be spun into worsted, that by the said Act such agents are liable to pay a penalty of five shillings for every parcel of yarn made up which is short weight, and which is false or short reeled, unless they produce and do give in evidence what person was the reeler of such yarn, so that he or she may be lawfully convicted ; for which purpose it will be expected that the putters-out ticket their yarn.'

The committee set to work in earnest, but its early efforts were not all crowned with success. In the first place, there was trouble with the inspectors, who did not always discharge their duties with the desired efficiency, or prove themselves burning enthusiasts. Of the seven inspectors appointed in 1777, three had been discharged and two had resigned before the summer of 1779, and the committee had much difficulty in securing satisfactory men. The inspectors were paid their wages, but were granted nothing towards their expenses. Hence, when they discovered a culprit, they had to defray their own costs, and reimburse themselves by the share of the fine which came to them as informers. Thus the inspector's task was at times most unenviable, for he had all the expense of bringing an offender to court, and then had to depend on winning his case in order to regain the money outlaid. In such circumstances it was only natural that he should overlook the offences of those who would be unable to pay the fines, and devote his attention to the more wealthy artisans and agents. This miscarriage of justice became notorious in 1784, whereupon the committee declared that the ' Inspectors neglect to prosecute embezzlers and buyers of embezzled materials when they think they can receive no advantage, and that they are too eager in prosecuting such persons as they think will pay the pecuniary penalties inflicted for such offence '.[1]   It was therefore ordered that the committee should in future defray the expense of all prosecutions, and that all money received by inspectors in their capacity as informers should be handed over at once to the treasurer of the committee, to be distributed to various charitable organizations.   Thus a big incentive to favouritism and partiality was removed, and the committee thereby did much to ' render the Inspectors more respectable and independent prosecutors '.[2] Gradually satisfactory men were found, the number of discharges became smaller, and the inspectorate reached a state approaching efficiency.

The second obstacle with which the committee had to deal was the ignorance, apathy, or actual hostility of the magistrates. The worsted industry covered a wide area, in much of which agriculture was the predominant industry, and the production of yarn merely a by-occupation.   In these parts the justices could not be expected to be conversant with all the details of complicated textile legislation.   Many cases which were brought forward by the inspectors were dismissed by magistrates who did not know the nature of the Worsted Acts, and the committee was constantly printing digests of the law, handbills, &c., or sending deputations[3] to explain to these benighted justices the wonders of the statutes.   But knowledge, when it came, did not convince the local authorities of the error of their ways. Doubtless they objected to being taught their duty by an upstart industrial organization, and did not intend to obey the behests of John Hustler and his minions.   Hence the minutes of the committee are sprinkled with instances of conflicts between the committee and the justices of the peace who presided over the more outlying districts.   In the heart of the worsted area justice was served out in full measure, but in the agricultural regions the magistrates were always ready to snap their fingers at the fussy cloth-makers.   Thus in December 1777 the Recorder of Pontefract, along with other justices, complained that the inspectors were being too severe in their prosecution of the spinners, and asked for greater leniency towards offenders.[4]   In

[1] Minutes, April 6, 1784.   [2] Ibid.
[3] e.g. the chairman, the clerk, and another member were sent in June 1779 to explain the Act to two justices of the peace in Bedale.
[4] Minutes, January 5, 1778.

the following year some Lancashire magistrates refused to hear the evidence of an inspector, and discharged the defendant, much to the disgust of the committee who at once entered upon a dignified correspondence with the offending justices. The committee stated that ' they was hurt at the Conduct of the Justices, . . . that they would give up the matter for this time, and hoped for the future that the justices ' would administer the Act properly.[1] The Mayor of Doncaster was the most stubborn opponent of the committee, and the two were per-petually at war. In September 1784 [2] the committee threatened King's Bench proceedings against him, for refusing to hear certain cases of false reeling. In the same year he allowed women to escape from the district without having paid their fines, at which the committee wrote that they ' think them-selves very ungentilly Treated, and demand a Specific Answer from himself for such extraordinary behaviour '.

What happened to the mayor we do not know, for the matter is not mentioned again ; but the whole attitude of these country magistrates is seen at its best in the action of the justices of Richmond in 1801. On this occasion, the inspector had brought certain women, charged with unduly neglecting their work, before the magistrates. Still, ' although the offence was com-pletely proved before the Magistrates, they refused to convict [the women], alledging that the Act of Parliament was arbitrary and not fit to be put into execution '. The inspector asked for reasons, but the magistrates declined to give any ; thereupon the committee, donning its best style of injured dignity, declared that ' the justices . . . must do their duty in administering the law. . . . It is no excuse for a Magistrate to say that the Law is arbitrary and therefore not fit to be executed, . . . and the magistrates' decision has caused considerable surprise and regret.' If, therefore, the justices still refuse to give adequate reason for their contempt of the law, ' the Committee feel them-selves under the disagreeable necessity . . . to direct an informa-tion·to be filed against the magistrates, or to take such steps as counsel shall advise '.[3] And there, so far as the minute books

[1] Ibid., January 4, 1779, and March 29, 1779.
[2] Ibid., September 27, 1784 ; January 3, 1785.
[3] Ibid., June 22, 1801.

are concerned, the matter seems to have ended. Still, in spite of these obstacles, the Worsted Committee undoubtedly succeeded in a great measure in achieving the aims which it sought to attain. The constant circulation of handbills and the advertisements in the local papers made people aware of the main features of the Act, and the inspectors often succeeded in finding many cases of deceit. If one turns to almost any copy of the Leeds newspapers from 1777 to the end of the century, one encounters instances of prosecutions. For instance, the following,[1] in a little over a month :

January 10, 1782 : Four women of Wakefield and one of West Ardsley were fined 5s. each for reeling false or short yarn.

January 28, 1782 : Mary Leach, of Cullingworth, was fined £20 for receiving a quantity of purloined or embezzled worsted yarn.

February 19, 1782 : Twenty-five women indicted for reeling false and short yarn. One was fined 40s., this being a second offence, and a man for a third offence was ordered to be ' committed to the House of Correction for one month, and to be publickly whipt at Colne upon a Market Day.

It is surprising to find so many women figuring in the lists, but this is due to the fact that spinning and reeling were done chiefly by women, who also acted as distributing agents, receiving the wool from the clothier, and handing it out to be spun by neighbours. Such agents were compelled to examine all yarn returned to them, and to take note of any which was falsely worked. If they failed in this, they themselves were liable to a fine, and thus we find a certain woman at Heptonstall fined 10s. for refusing to discover who reeled two pounds of short yarn.[2] All these cases were brought before the justices by the worsted inspectors, and the courts were regularly employed attending to such offences.

Another aspect of the Worsted Acts was also given attention—namely, the punishment for neglect of work. Eight days were allowed for the fulfilment of any task entrusted to an employee. If at the end of that time the material was not returned, the employer informed the inspector, who at once called on the offender, or sent him an official note, and instituted proceedings unless the goods were at once returned to their owner. The

---

[1] *Leedes Intelligencer,* under these dates.   [2] Ibid., January 8, 1782.

punishment for this offence was incarceration, and many culprits, chiefly women, were committed to the House of Correction for a month, under conviction of having neglected the performance of their duties for eight days. This preponderance of female culprits makes one wonder if the men were especially law-abiding, or if the ' solidarity of labour ' which had frightened the masters at an earlier date was also instrumental in causing the inspectors to wink at male offenders, whilst taking advantage of the disorganization of the women to pounce upon female transgressors. There is no conclusive answer to this query, but, from a perusal of the offences recorded in the newspapers, one certainly gets the impression that the law was invoked against women and very seldom against men.

The Worsted Committee was established to discharge the above definite functions and administer the Worsted Acts ; but the committee consisted of a number of influential and energetic cloth magnates, and therefore it was only natural that it should concern itself with the whole of the wide field of economic life. Anything which affected the worsted industry was a fit and proper subject for the committee's attention. Hence we find in its minute books brief references to the many economic movements which were on foot at this time, and few matters of importance escaped the committee's notice. In the first place, it is gratifying to find that whilst the committee was primarily an association of employers, bent on administer-ing laws favourable to masters, it did not neglect the interests of the workmen. Various laws during the century forbade the payment of wages in truck, and the committee frequently issued notices drawing the attention of masters to this provision. Occasionally an inspector brought a master before the courts for paying a workman in goods instead of in money,[1] and when, in times of depression, work and wages were scarce, the com-mittee did its best to ensure that truck payments should, if possible, be prevented.[2] In its treatment of its inspectors, the committee strikes at least one happy note when, in 1796, ' on account of the present temporarily high price of provisions and

---

[1] e.g. September 27, 1784, when Wm. Smith of Leeds, dyer, was convicted of having paid in truck.
[2] April 12, 1802, 1,000 handbills issued concerning truck.

other necessaries of life ', it was resolved ' that the Salaries of
the Inspectors be advanced £5 per annum in addition of their
present salaries of £50 ', this to continue so long as the committee thought proper and necessary.[1] But, whilst safeguarding
the workmen from truck, the committee also attempted to
suppress combinations of labour such as might induce the
employees to seek higher wages for themselves. The committee
itself might be regarded in its general nature as a masters'
union, instituted for the protection and advancement of the
employers' welfare. But at the same time any workmen's
union was forbidden by law, and although some kind of organization certainly did exist, the Worsted Committee did its best to
stamp out all such unions of labour. In 1791 it prosecuted
certain Halifax wool-combers[2] for having conspired to raise
their wages, and in the following year it expressed the opinion
that friendly societies, if allowed to grow up, would ' have a prejudiciall tendency by enabling the members thereof to form
illegal Combinations '.[3] Thus, though the committee sought the
welfare of man as well as master, the journeyman must not
attempt to better himself by corporate action. He must refrain
from union with his fellows, and be content with the individual
bargaining and free contract between himself and his master.

Secondly, the committee paid special attention to all matters
concerning the wool supply. When the Lincolnshire wool-
growers sought permission to export their surplus wool, the
Worsted Committee was loud in its objections, and spent eighty
guineas in opposing the application.[4] In 1787 similar support
was given to the Act strengthening the prohibition on the
exportation of wool, and one hundred guineas were taken from
the funds to meet the cost of procuring that statute. Then,
when the Act was actually passed, the committee flooded Yorkshire with notices quoting its clauses, and joined with the Leeds
Cloth Halls trustees in prosecuting Mr. Hainsworth, the Leeds
merchant, who attempted to smuggle wool abroad. In fact,
during this and later agitations, the committee spent vast
sums of money on the anti-smuggling crusade.[5] At the same
time, the exportation of machinery and cloth-making imple-

---

[1] June 20, 1796.   [2] Minutes, January 3, 1791.   [3] Ibid., April 2, 1792.
[4] See Minutes, 1781–2.   [5] Ibid., all 1789.

ments was closely watched, and the activities of the committee
were largely responsible for obtaining the Act of 1780–1 which
prevented the exportation of utensils used in the woollen manufacture.[1] When this Act was passed offenders were brought to
justice by the committee for attempting to export the actual
implements or plans of the same.[2] Wherever any project was
being discussed the voice of the Worsted Committee was heard,
and in all parliamentary and legal matters which touched the
welfare of the Yorkshire cloth trade the employers' committee
would fearlessly put forward its own point of view.

Thirdly, the committee attempted to foster the mechanical
arts, and to encourage all inventions which might conduce to
the welfare of the industry. When a local inventor had materia-
lized some new idea, he would show it to the Worsted Committee,
and if it was regarded as being a valuable discovery the inventor
would be rewarded—under conditions. Thus, in 1779, a certain
Mr. Mordaunt reported to the committee that he had discovered
a more expeditious way of spinning wool ; but the invention
does not seem to have gained the approval of the committee,
for we hear nothing further about it. In 1785, however, an
important innovation was brought before the committee. This
consisted of an improved method of washing wool, which would
perform that task more quickly and thoroughly than the older
methods were able to do. The inventor, James Hartley, who
lived near Gisburn, offered to give a demonstration to the committee, and disclose the details fully to them if they cared to
pay for the knowledge. A deputation of six was ordered to wait
upon Hartley, examine his process, and make a report to a special
meeting of the members. The verdict expressed was entirely
favourable ; the deputation thought Hartley's discovery a great
improvement on existing methods, and declared that it would
be of public utility. The committee therefore decided to give
Hartley £100, on condition that he revealed every detail of his
improved process to them ; and in June 1785 the last instal-
ment was paid, Hartley having satisfactorily surrendered his

---

[1] Minutes, September 24, 1781.
[2] Ibid., also September 23, 1793. In February 1787 the committee resolved
that ' the permitting any tools or implements used in the woollen manufacture
to be exported will be very detrimental and highly injurious to the Trade of
the Kingdom '.

discovery to the committee.[1] Thus, in the advancement of technological knowledge, the Worsted Committee kept an open eye and an open purse for those who made some contribution towards industrial skill.

Lastly, the committee figured in some small degree as a philanthropic agency, supporting the cause of charity and education. As we noted above, the inspectors received the informer's share of all fines levied upon their victims, but the Worsted Committee insisted that these moneys should be immediately handed over to itself. This order was made in April 1784, and at once informer's money began to flow into the special fund set aside for it. Here it remained until a substantial sum had accumulated, when it was distributed to local philanthropic or educational institutions. The chief places to receive support were the General Infirmaries of Leeds and Manchester, which in 1787, for instance, received contributions of twenty guineas and ten guineas respectively.[2] In fact, by 1796 the committee had paid such sums into the coffers of these hospitals that it claimed the right to recommend patients for admission, and the members of the committee were informed that if they were desirous of recommending any ' distressed objects ', they were to write to the Clerk of the Committee, and obtain the necessary formal approval from him.[3] At the same time, occasional grants were made in support of local Sunday schools. In 1791 the sum of £4 11s. 3d. was handed over to the Sunday schools of Northowram, near Halifax,[4] and in the following year the sum of £10, received by an inspector as informer's money, was given to a very deserving school in another part of the Riding.[5]

Such were the varied activities of the Worsted Committee. They touched almost every side of economic and political life, and no issue relevant to the industrial welfare of the county was allowed to pass unattended. Existing legislation was enforced on masters and men alike, suggested laws were supported or opposed, and new ideas in textile procedure were welcomed. In its character the committee contained something of a seventeenth-century corporation, something of a chamber of commerce, something of an employers' federation or union :

[1] Minutes, January to June 1785.   [2] Minutes, December 31, 1787.
[3] Ibid., March 21, 1796, and June 1797.
[4] Ibid., September 26, 1791.   [5] Ibid., June 20, 1792.

in the methods of its officers it bore some resemblance to the
Royal Society for the Prevention of Cruelty to Children.   It was
a strange institution, and perhaps the strangest thing about it is
the fact that it still exists.   The Worsted Committee is now
a comparatively flourishing body, which administers those
clauses of the eighteenth-century Worsted Acts which are still
operative.   Between the prosperous condition of the eighteenth
century and that of to-day there is a long story of many narrow
escapes from extinction, into which we cannot enter at any
length ; but let us briefly note the outstanding events in the
committee's history during the last century.

    The *raison d'être* of the Worsted Committee lay in the domestic
system of industry, by which goods were worked up free from
constant or detailed supervision. So long as the preparation of
yarn was carried on in the cottages, so long would it be necessary
for the inspectors to go round, attempting to check frauds and
thefts amongst the workpeople.   But, when spinning machinery
began to be congregated in factories, and spinning became
a factory process, the merchant could more effectually watch his
spinners, and guard against wrongdoing.   When this took place,
the worsted inspector was deprived of the chief of his functions,
for it had been in the spinning and reeling of yarn that his police
duties were most necessary.   When wool was not sent out to
agents to be distributed by them, it was no longer possible to
defraud the owner by substituting inferior wool, and when all
the spinning and reeling was performed on standard machines
under the eye of an overlooker it was difficult for the operative
to transgress as in former days. This change took place in the
last years of the eighteenth and the early years of the nineteenth
centuries, and with it came a contemporaneous decline in the
demands on the energies of the inspectors.   In September 1801
the committee decided that ' from the very great decrease of
spinning at home' five inspectors would be sufficient to carry
out the duties of the committee, and therefore discharged two
of its staff.[1]   In 1804 the number was reduced to four,[2] and in
1807 the committee ordered ' that in consequence of the resignation of John Sutcliffe, Inspector, and of the great decrease of
hand-spinning, that there is no occasion for a succession, but

[1] Minutes, September 28, 1801.   [2] Ibid., March 26, 1804.

F f 2

that a new division of the districts be made out ', and the number of inspectors thus came down to three.[1]

With this reduced staff the committee continued its activities for the next half century. It still drew its income from the drawback on soap, and, with the expansion of the West Riding industry, the amount of this drawback increased rapidly. The committee was quite wealthy, and at times was at a loss how to dispose of its funds. In 1820[2] the mileage grant for committee-men was raised from 6d. to 2s. per mile, and in 1821[3] it was ordered that ' each member of the Committee be paid the sum of two guineas for his attendance at each meeting, exclusive of travelling expenses '. At the same time, whilst any slackness on the part of inspectors was severely penalized, faithful servants were treated most generously, with pensions on their retirement, and grants to their widows on their deaths. Thus in 1849 an aged inspector was given twenty guineas on his retirement,[4] and in the previous year, on the death of another inspector, ' after a painful and expensive illness ', the committee resolved that ' a gratuity of thirty guineas be paid to his widow, as a mark of approbation '.[5]

This wealth, however, was not to continue much longer. Throughout the early part of the nineteenth century chancellors of the exchequer had tried to abolish the drawback on soap. On such occasions the Worsted Committee made strong protests, which usually resulted in the continuance of the exemption, and therefore of the committee's income. With the reform of the financial system during the 'forties and 'fifties it was inevitable that the soap duty should be removed, and the step was eventu-ally taken by Mr. Gladstone in 1853.[6] This cut off the com-mittee's source of revenue at one blow, and left the members in a state of perplexity. The committee at once began to take stock of its position, dismissed three inspectors, and appointed a sub-committee to inquire into the financial situation and give advice as to the future. The sub-committee urged that the efficiency of the committee should be maintained as long as the funds lasted. Economies were to be effected by stopping all mileage and attendance allowance, by retaining only one in-

---

[1] Minutes, September 28, 1807
[2] Ibid., June 18, 1820.
[3] Ibid., September 24, 1821.
[4] Ibid., September 24, 1849.
[5] Ibid., September 25, 1848.
[6] Ibid., June 20, 1853.

spector, by reducing the clerk's salary from £40 to £20, and by drastically curtailing the printing bill.[1] This report was accepted, and the committee lived on. But it was a precarious existence ; in place of the 18 or 20 members who had attended the meetings prior to 1853, the attendance now fell to ten, six, four, two, and at times the secretary was the only person to make an appearance.[2] The funds of the committee were invested in canal shares, scarcely a profitable source of income. All efforts on the part of the surviving members failed to enlist the interest and financial support of the worsted masters, and for nearly twenty years the outlook for the organization was very gloomy, so much so that at times it seemed almost desirable to commit suicide. After 1870 the energetic appeals of the committee brought about a revival of interest. Manufacturers began to see that the growth of factory production had not entirely removed the possibilities of fraud and theft, and that there was still need for a police organization such as the Worsted Committee. Subscriptions began to trickle in, and from that time onward the committee received considerable support. In 1889 an attempt to repeal the Worsted Acts was defeated, thanks to the strong opposition of the committee. Hence the organization still lives. It receives subscriptions from about 360 firms, chiefly located around Bradford, Halifax, and Keighley, and meets quarterly to transact any business which may require attention. Its two inspectors discharge the same duties as did their predecessors over a century ago. They seek out cases of purloining, embezzling, stealing, pawning, or selling of yarn, and bring to punishment those who buy such stolen material as well as those who sell. They visit railway warehouses, and try to identify unclaimed worsted materials which may be lying there ; and in every possible way they strive to protect the masters from theft and loss. The number of the offences which they discover is not very great, and, to an outsider, scarcely seems to justify the continuance of the institution. But evidently the heads of the worsted industry hold a different opinion, and so the committee, having emerged from the shadow of the 'sixties, will probably continue its existence until the perfect man is evolved, on which distant day lawyers, magistrates, and worsted inspectors may find their occupations gone.

[1] Minutes, September 26, 1853.   [2] Ibid. See list of attendances, 1853–70.

BIBLIOGRAPHY

1. MANUSCRIPTS

Record Office

State Papers, Henry VIII to Edward VI.
Domestic State Papers, Mary to William III.
Entry Books, especially *temp*. Chas. II. Also Docquet Books.
Order Books of Council of State, especially Interregnum and Chas. II.
Treasury Papers and Books, Stuart period.
Home Office Papers, especially 1700–60.
Ancient Petitions, especially nos. 5371, 7485, 7486, 10673, and 11890.
Exchequer Depositions by Commission, 1613, 1638, and 1676. For detailed
references, see footnotes to Chapter VI.
Ulnage Accounts, in Exchequer MSS. (Exch. K.R. Accounts, bundles 339–47).
Patent Rolls.
Close Rolls.

British Museum

Cotton MSS., especially Titus, B. i, f. 279 ; Galba, E. i, ff. 284–6, 320–2, 399.
Harleian MSS., especially 306, ff. 26–8 ; 433, ff. 159 b and 187 b ; 1327,
ff. 7 & 9 b.
Stowe MSS., especially 354, ff. 63–5 ; 554, f. 45 ; 746, ff. 110, 128, 136, 138 ;
748, f. 79.
Sloane MSS., especially 817, f. 21.
Lansdowne MSS., especially Burghley Papers, 110, f. 65.
Coke MSS., especially i, f. 465.
Additional MSS., especially 21427 *passim* (*Baynes Correspondence*, vol. xi) ;
also 15873, f. 70 ; 32863, ff. 259–60 ; 33344, ff. 1963 et seq. ; 34324,
ff. 8–10, 14, 201, 203, 213 ; 34727, f. 29 ; 35670, ff. 146 et seq. ; 36996, f. 58.

Yorkshire MSS.

West Riding Sessions Records. These commence at 1638, and continue
from that date in an unbroken series. There are about fifty volumes
of Order Books, recording the orders made by the justices of the peace ;
also there are a similar number of Indictment Books, beginning 1637,
and written in Latin until 1732, the Commonwealth period alone excepted.
The Sessions Rolls, which begin with 1669, are fragmentary at first. All
these manuscripts are in the charge of Mr. Vibart Dixon, Clerk of the
Peace, County Hall, Wakefield, who kindly allowed me to examine them
at my leisure.

Leeds Corporation MSS. These consist of the Minute Book of the Corporation from 1661 to the present day. The Corporation also has in its
possession the various deeds of transfer concerning the Coloured Cloth
Hall. All are housed in the Town Hall, Leeds.

Leeds Sessions Records. These are Order Books similar to those of the West
Riding, and cover part of the seventeenth and the whole of the eighteenth
century. They are in the custody of the Clerk of the Peace, Mr. Leake,
Basinghall Street, Leeds.

York Municipal Records. The stock of manuscripts in the Gildhall, York,
is enormous, but access to these papers is very difficult. There are a few

volumes containing ordinances (1607 and 1629) and accounts (three vols.) of the Weavers' Company : also various articles of agreement between York and weavers who came there to teach the poor the textile trade in the seventeenth century (1655 and 1698) ; the Corporation Minute Books (House Books) contain frequent references to textile work, many transcripts of which Dr. M. Sellers kindly placed at my disposal.

Leeds White Cloth Hall MSS. These comprise a large collection of letters, minute books, posters, account books, Blue Books, &c., relating to the white cloth trade and its market during the eighteenth and nineteenth centuries. They are in the keeping of Mr. H. Greenwood-Teale, Atlas Chambers, Leeds.

Worsted Committee MSS. A number of minute books, dated from 1777 to the present day : in the charge of Messrs. Mumford and Johnson, solicitors, Bradford.

Bradford Manor Court Rolls, Edward III to Henry V. A transcription (four vols.) is in the Bradford Reference Library.

Letter Books of Joseph Holroyd and Sam Hill, 1706 and 1738. These two fragments are in the Bankfield Museum, Halifax ; extracts from them have been published, edited by the present writer (*Bankfield Museum Notes*, Second Series, no. 3. King, Halifax, 1914).

Isolated MSS., such as apprenticeship indentures, inventories, wills, deeds, account books, letters, &c., are to be found in many places. Mr. J. Lister of Halifax kindly lent me transcripts of many such documents, or the actual documents themselves : others are in the Thoresby Society Library, including one or two important petitions (in Cookson MSS.), figures concerning the population of Leeds, a list of Leeds aldermen in the seventeenth century ; the poem quoted in Chapter X is in manuscript form in the Leeds Reference Library, and the Bradford Reference Library has in its possession a number of stray manuscripts relating to the local industry.

2. PRINTED RECORDS

Statutes of the Realm : also *Statutes at Large.*
Rymer's *Foedera* (original edition in 20 vols., and also Record edition).
Ordinances of the Privy Council, 1558 to 1603.
House of Commons Journals.
Rotuli Parliamentorum (Record Commission).
House of Lords Journals.
Historical Manuscripts Commission, especially the following volumes :
   Beverley Corporation, Dartmouth, Graham, House of Lords, Kenyon, Kendal Corporation, Middleton, Portland, Salisbury, Stewart ; also Order Book of the Justices of the North Riding (vol. ix of Report).

Rolls Series, especially the following :
   Chron. Melsae (Meaux Abbey).
   Chronicle of Symeon of Durham.
   Chronica, Roger de Hoveden.
   Chronica Maiora, Matthew Paris.
   Liber Custumarum, in *Munimenta Gildhallae.*
   Materials for a History of Henry VII.
   Registrum Palatinum Dunelm.

Surtees Society publications generally. The most valuable for our subject are :
   Vols. 2, 38, 112, 116, 121. *North Country Wills and Inventories.*
   Vol. 3. *Towneley Mysteries.*
   Vols. 4, 30, 45, 53, 79, 106. *Testamenta Eboracensia.*

Vol. 17. *Life and Correspondence of Matthew Hutton, Archbishop of York.*
Vol. 33. Best, H. *Rural Economy of Yorkshire in 1641.*
Vol. 49. *Kirkby's Inquest, 1284–5.*
Vol. 65. *Yorkshire Diaries* (seventeenth and eighteenth centuries).
Vol. 77. Priestley Memoirs, in *North Country Diaries.*
Vols. 91–2. *Report of Chantry Commissioners on Chantries, Gilds, &c., in the County of York.*
Vols. 93 and 101. *Extracts from the Records of the Merchant Adventurers of Newcastle-on-Tyne.*
Vol. 94. *Pedes Finium Ebor', regnante Iohanne* (1199–1214).
Vols. 96 and 102. *Register of the Freemen of York, 1272–1759.*
Vols. 118 and 124. *North Country Diaries* (1630–1790).
Vol. 120. *York Memorandum Book*, vol. i. Vol. ii not yet to hand in Australia.

Yorkshire Archaeological and Topographical Society : *Record Series.*

Vol. 3. *West Riding Sessions Records*, 1597–1602.
Vols. 4, 6, 11, 14, 19, &c. *Yorkshire Wills and Registers of Wills.*
Vols. 12, 23, 31, 37. *Inquisitions* (thirteenth and fourteenth centuries).
Vols. 15, 16, 21, 25. *Lay Subsidies* (thirteenth and fourteenth centuries).
Vol. 44. *Assize Roll, temp. Henry III.*
Vols. 29 and 36. *Court Rolls of the Manor of Wakefield, 1272–1327.*
Poll Tax Returns for the West Riding, ed. Lister, have also been published by the same Society.
Poll Tax Returns for East Riding, in *Yorkshire Archaeol. Journal*, vol. xx.

Thoresby Society publications, *passim* ; especially the following vols. :

Vols. 1, 3, 7, 10, 13, 20, 23, 25. *Leeds Parish Church Registers*, 1572–1757.
Vols. 2, 4, 9, 11, 15, 22. *Miscellanea*, containing reprints of occasional manuscripts referring to the local textile trade.
Vol. 6. *Calverley Charters.*
Vol. 8. *Coucher Book of Kirkstall Abbey.*
Vols. 1, 19, 22, 24, contain numbers of Leeds and District wills.

Various volumes.

Acts and Ordinances of the Eastland Merchants, ed. M. Sellers, Camden Society, 3rd series, vol. 11.
Bland, Brown, and Tawney. *English Economic History, Select Documents* (1914).
Booke of Entries of the Pontefract Corporation, 1653–1726 (1882).
Cartwright, J. J. *Chapters in the History of Yorkshire, being a collection of original letters, papers, &c., illustrating the state of that county in the reigns of Elizabeth, James I, and Charles I* (Wakefield, 1872).
Clay, J. W. *Halifax Wills (fourteenth to sixteenth centuries)*, 2 vols., n.d.
Davies. *Extracts from the Municipal Records of York* (1843).
English History Source Books, no. 1, ed. by Wallis (Bell, 1913).
Farrer. *Early Yorkshire Charters*, vol. i (1914).
Hamilton, A. H. A. *Quarter Sessions Records, from Queen Elizabeth to Queen Anne* (1878).
Hundred Rolls (Record Commission).
Leach, *Beverley Town Documents* (Selden Soc., vol. xiv).
Life of Marmaduke Rawdon (Camden Soc., vol. lxxxv).
Little Red Book of Bristol (2 vols., 1900).
North Riding Quarter Sessions Records, ed. J. C. Atkinson, 9 vols. (1883 et seq.).
Pipe Roll, 31 Hen. I (Record Commission).
Pipe Rolls, 5–29 Hen. II (Pipe Rolls Society).

Survey of Manor of Bradford, 15 Ed. III (in *Bradford Antiquarian*, vol. ii, pp. 137–8).
Thoresby's Diary, 1677–1724, ed. by Hunter, 2 vols. (1830).
Toulmin Smith, L. *York Mystery Plays* (1885).

3. PARLIAMENTARY REPORTS

Reports on Smuggling of Wool, 1786. *General Collected Reports*, vol. xxxviii, nos. 82–5, 87.
Report of the Committee on the petitions of the woolcombers. *House of Commons Journals*, xlix. 322.
Report of House of Lords Inquiry concerning the Wool Trade, 1800. Copy in Leeds Reference Library.
Report of Select Committee on petitions of merchants and manufacturers in the woollen manufacture of Yorkshire. *Reports*, 1802–3, vol. v.
Report of Select Committee appointed to consider the state of the woollen manufacture in England, 1806. *Reports*, 1806, vol. iii.
Report of Committee on Cloth Stamping Laws, 1821. *Reports*, 1821, vol. vi.
Census Reports, 1831, 1841, 1851.
Reports, various, on condition of hand-loom weavers. *Reports*, 1835, xiii ;. 1839, xlii ; 1840, xxiii and xxiv.
Factory Inspectors' Reports, 1840–5.
Poor Law Commission, 1834. *Reports*, 1834, xxvii and xxviii.
Health of Towns Commission, 1845. *Reports*, 1845, xviii. The Yorkshire section was printed separately ; a copy is in the Bradford Reference Library.

4. CONTEMPORARY LITERATURE

(a) *General*

Aikin. *England Delineated* (1809) ; *England Described* (1818).
Anderson. *History of Commerce* (1764).
Annals of Agriculture (1790–1804).
Annual Register.
British Directory, 1790–3, 5 vols.
Britannia Linguens, or a Discourse of Trade (1680).
Camden. *Britannia* (1789 edition).
Campbell, R. *The London Tradesman* (1757).
Carter, W. *England's Interest by Trade Asserted* (1671).
Chamberlayne. *The State of England* (1737).
Child, Sir Josiah. *A New Discourse of Trade* (1720 ?).
Chronicon Rusticum Commerciale, or Memoirs of Wool ; a series of extracts from seventeenth and eighteenth-century pamphlets by various writers, dealing chiefly with the wool and cloth trade ; compiled by J. Smith, 2 vols. (1747).
Defoe, *Tour through Great Britain*, many editions, 1724, 1748, 1762, 3 vols.
—— *Complete Tradesman* (1737 ?), 1841 edition, 2 vols.
Dodsley's *Road Book* (1756).
Dyer. *The Fleece* (1757) (English Poets Series).
Eden. *State of the Poor* (1797), 3 vols.
Fiennes, Celia. *Through England on a Side-Saddle in the Time of William and Mary* (Intro. by Hon. Mrs. Griffiths, 1888).
Fuller, T. *Church History of Britain* (1655 and 1845 editions).
—— *Worthies of England* (1811 edition), 2 vols.
Gee. *Trade and Navigation of England Considered* (1739).
Gentleman's Magazine, 1731 onwards.

Haynes, J. *Great Britain's Glory* (1715).
—— *A view of the present state of the clothing trade in England* (1706).
Laurence. *The Duty of a Steward to his Lord* (1727).
Leland. *The Itinerary of John Leland* (1745 edition), 7 vols.
Luccock. *Observations on British Wool* (1800).
Macpherson. *Annals of Commerce* (1805), 4 vols.
May, J. *A Declaration of the Estate of Clothing now used within this Realm* (1613).
Observations on British Wooll and the Manufacture of it, by a Northamptonshire Manufacturer (1738).
Pamphlets on Wool, in Brit. Mus., 712. g. 16. Contains all the important pamphlets of the seventeenth and eighteenth centuries, especially *The Golden Fleece*, by W. S., gentleman (1656) ; *The Weavers' True Case*, by a practical weaver (1720) ; *England's Glory by Foreign Trade*, by a true lover of his country (1669).
Pennant. *Tour through Scotland* (1770), 3 vols.
Pococke. *The Travels thro' England of Richard Pococke*, 1750 and following years (Camden Soc. publications, vols. 42–4).
Radcliffe. *Origin of Power-Loom Weaving* (1828).
Smith, Adam. *Wealth of Nations* (Routledge edition, 1903).
Wheeler. *A Treatise of Commerce* (1601).
Young, A. *A Six Months' Tour through the North of England* (1771), 4 vols.
—— *A Farmer's Tour through the East of England* (1771), 4 vols.
—— *Travels through France* (1794 edition), 2 vols.

(b) *Local*

A Cordial Drop, being the substance of a conversation between a master and journeyman in a large manufacturing town in Yorkshire, 1792 ? (Brit. Mus. 554. g. 31 (2)).
A History of Leeds, compiled from various authors by Wright (1797).
A Walk through Leeds (1806).
Bentley. *Halifax and its Gibbet Law* (1708).
Bigland. *Topographical and Historical Description of the County of York* (1812).
Boothroyd. *History of Pontefract* (1807).
Bray. *Sketch of a Tour into Derbyshire and Yorkshire* (1777).
Charnock. *Essay on Farming of the West Riding* (*Royal. Soc. Journal*, ix).
Cooke. *Topographical Description of Yorkshire* (1812).
Dayes. *An Excursion through the Principal Parts of Derbyshire and Yorkshire* (1805).
Description of Leeds, printed by Dodsley (London, 1764. Transcript in Leeds Reference Library).
Drake. *Eboracum* (1737).
Gent. *The Antient and Modern History of the Famous City of York* (1730).
Hadley. *A New History of Kingston-upon-Hull* (1788).
Housman. *Topographical Description of . . . a Part of the West Riding* (1800).
Langdale. *Topographical Dictionary of Yorkshire* (1822).
Leedes Intelligencer, 1754 onwards.
Leeds Directories, numerous from 1797 onwards ; especially 1797, 1798, 1809, 1817.
Leeds Guides, various dates, especially 1806, 1808.
Leeds Mercury ; files from 1737 onwards in Leeds Reference Library ; see extracts from 1721–37 in Thoresby Soc. publications, xxii and xxiv.
Marshall. *Rural Economy of Yorkshire* (1788), 2 vols.
Matters of Interest, a volume of odds and ends, 1720–1850, in Leeds Reference Library.

Maude. *Verbeia, or Wharfedale* ; a poem descriptive of that part of Yorkshire (1782).
Midgley. *Halifax and its Gibbet Law placed in a true light* (1761).
Northern Star, or Yorkshire Magazine, 3 vols., 1817–18.
Plain Reasons addressed to the People of Great Britain against the intended Petition to Parliament for leave to export wool, 1782.
Poulson. *Beverlac* (1829), 2 vols.
The Case of the Narrow Clothiers and other Woollen Manufacturers in the West Riding of the County of York, 1732 ; Brit. Mus. 357. c. 1. (59).
The Old History of Bradford (1776).
Thoresby. *Ducatus Leodiensis* (1715) ; ed. by Whitaker (1816).
To the King's Majestie, the Humble Petition of the Clothiers of Leeds for redress of Grievances affecting their Trade, 1642 ; Brit. Mus., E. 144 (6).
Watson. *History and Topography of Halifax* (1775).
Whitaker. *Loidis and Elmete* (1816).
Wright. *The Antiquities of the Town of Halifax* (1738).
York Courant, 1764 onwards.
Yorkshire Magazine, 1786–7.

5. PRINTED WORKS

(a) *General*

Abram, A. *Social Life in England in the Fifteenth Century* (1909).
Ashley, W. J. *An Introduction to English Economic History and Theory* (4th edition, 1909).
Ashley, W. J. *The Early History of the English Woollen Industry* (1887).
—— *The Economic Organisation of England* (1914).
Baines, E. 'An Account of the Woollen Manufacture of England' (Brit. Assoc. Lecture at Leeds, 1858, printed in *Yorkshire, Past and Present*, 1870).
Bateson, M. Review of 'Beverley Town Documents' (*Eng. Hist. Rev.*, xvi).
Bischoff, J. *Comprehensive History of the Woollen and Worsted Manufactures*, 2 vols. (1842).
Bonwick, J. *Romance of the Wool Trade* (1894).
Burnley, J. *History of Wool and Wool-combing* (1889).
Clapham, J. H. 'Economic Change' (*Cambridge Mod. Hist.*, vol. x).
—— *Woollen and Worsted Industries* (1907).
Clarendon. *History of the Great Rebellion* (1888 edition, Oxford).
Cole, G. H. D. *The World of Labour* (1913).
Cooke, A. M. 'The Cistercian Settlement in England' (*Eng. Hist. Rev.*, viii).
Cooke Taylor, T. *The Modern Factory System* (1891).
Cunningham. *Growth of English Industry and Commerce* (1907 and 1910).
Dechesne, L. *L'évolution économique et sociale de l'industrie de la laine en Angleterre* (Paris, 1900).
De Gibbins, H. B. *Industry in England* (1897).
—— *Industrial History of England* (1910 edition).
Dixon. *Florentine Wool Trade* (Trans. Royal Hist. Soc., New Series, vol. xii).
Dodd, A. F. *Early English Social History* (Bell, 1913).
Dodd, G. *Textile Manufactures of Great Britain* (1844).
Durham. *Relations of the Crown to Trade under James I* (Trans. Royal Hist. Soc., New Series, xiii).
Espinasse, F. *Lancashire Worthies* (1874–7).
Forbes, H. *History of the Worsted Manufacture in England* (1851 Exhibition Lectures, vol. ii, pp. 301–31).
Gardiner, S. R. *History of England, 1604–42* (1883).
Green, Mrs. J. R. *Town Life in the Fifteenth Century* (1894).
Gross, C. *The Gild Merchant* (1890).

Guiseppi. *Alien Merchants in England*; trans. R. Hist. Soc., n.s., vol. ix.
Hasbach. *History of the English Agricultural Labourer* (1908).
Hirst, W. *History of the Woollen Trade during the past sixty years* (1844).
Hobson, J. A. *Evolution of Modern Capitalism* (1906).
James, J. *History of the Worsted Manufacture in England* (1857).
Lambert. *Two Thousand Years of Gild Life* (1891).
Law, A. *The English Nouveaux-Riches of the Fourteenth Century* (Trans. Royal Hist. Soc., New Series, vol. ix).
Leonard, E. M. *Early History of English Poor Relief* (1900).
Lingelbach. *The Merchant Adventurers of England* (Philadelphia, 1902).
Lipson, E. *An Introduction to the Economic History of England in the Middle Ages* (1915).
Lohmann, F. *Die staatliche Regelung der englischen Wollindustrie, vom xv. bis zum xviii. Jahrhundert* (1900).
Madox. *The History and Antiquities of the Exchequer* (1711).
Mantoux. *La Révolution industrielle au XVIIIᵉ siècle* (1906).
McCulloch. *Commercial Directory* (1839).
McLaren, W. S. B. *Spinning Woollen and Worsted* (1884).
Morley, J. *Walpole* (1899).
—— *Life of Gladstone* (1903).
Price, L. L.: *Money and its Relation to Prices* (1909 edition).
Priestley, J. *Hist. Account of Navigable Rivers, Canals, &c., throughout Great Britain* (1831).
Ramsay. *Lancaster and York* (1892).
Rogers, J. E. T. *History of Agriculture and Prices* (1886–7).
Salzmann, H. *English Industries in the Middle Ages* (1913).
Samuel Bros. *Wool and Woollen Manufactures of Great Britain : a Historical Sketch* (1859).
Schanz, G. *Englische Handelspolitik gegen Ende des Mittelalters* (1881).
Seebohm, F. 'The Black Death' (*Fortnightly Review*, 1865).
Sydney. *England in the Eighteenth Century* (1891).
Tawney, R. H. 'The Assessment of Wages in England by the Justices of the Peace (*Vierteljahrschrift für Social- und Wirtschaftsgeschichte*, 1913).
Toynbee, A. *The Industrial Revolution of the Eighteenth Century in England,* (1908 edition).
Unwin, G. *Industrial Organisation in the Sixteenth and Seventeenth Centuries* (1904).
—— *The Gilds and Companies of London* (1908).
Ure, A. *Philosophy of Manufactures* (1835).
—— *Dictionary of Arts, Manufactures, and Mines* (1861 edition).
Webb, S. and B. *History of Trade Unionism* (1902).
—— *History of Local Government : the Manor and the Borough* (1906).
—— *The Story of the King's Highway* (1913).
Westerfield, R. B. *The Middleman in English Business, particularly between 1660 and 1760* (1915).
Wood, Trueman. *Industrial England in the Eighteenth Century* (1911).

(b) *Local*

Allen. *History of Yorkshire*, 6 vols. (1828).
Atkinson. *Ralph Thoresby, His Town and Times*, 2 vols. (1891).
Baines, T. *Yorkshire, Past and Present*, 4 vols. (1870).
Beddoe. 'Ethnology of the West Riding' (*Yorks. Archaeol. and Topogr. Journal*, vol. xix).
Bradford Antiquary, 4 vols. (1884–97).
Clapham, J. H. 'Industrial Organisation of the Yorkshire Woollen and Worsted Industries' (*Economic Journal*, xvi (1906)).

Clapham, J. H. 'The Transference of the Worsted Industry from East Anglia to the West Riding' (*Economic Journal*, 1910).

Colman. *History of Barwick-in-Elmet* (Thoresby Soc., vol. xvii (1907)).

Cook. *Historical Notes on Beverley* (1880).

Cropper, An Old Leeds. *Old Leeds, Its Bygones and Celebrities* (1868).

Dawson. *Loose Leaves from Craven History* (1891).

Fletcher, J. S. *Picturesque History of Yorkshire*, 6 vols. (no date).

Halifax Antiquarian Society Reports (1900 onwards).

Heaton, H. 'The Assessment of Wages in the West Riding of Yorkshire in the Seventeenth and Eighteenth Centuries (*Economic Journal*, 1914).

—— *The Leeds White Cloth Hall* (Thoresby Soc., vol. xxii (1913)).

—— *Tricks of the Trade* (Thoresby Soc., xxii, part iii (1914)).

Hewart, B. 'The Cloth Industry in the North of England in the Sixteenth and Seventeenth Centuries' (*Economic Journal*, 1900).

Hodgson. *Textile Manufacture . . . in Keighley* (1878).

Holroyd. *Collectanea Bradfordiana* (1873).

Ibbetson's *Directory of Bradford* (1845).

Jackson. *History of Barnsley* (1858).

—— *Guide to Leeds* (1889).

James, J. *History and Topography of Bradford* (1841 and 1866 editions).

Keighley and Holmes. *Keighley, Past and Present* (1858).

Law, M. C. D. *The Story of Bradford* (1913).

Lister, J. 'Halifax in the Days of Henry VIII' (*Halifax Almanack*, 1913).

—— 'Notes on the Early History of the Woollen Trade in Bradford and Halifax' (*Bradford Antiquary*, vol. ii).

Lister, J., and Ogden. *Poll Tax Returns for the Parish of Halifax*.

Mayhall, J. *Annals of Yorkshire*, 3 vols. (1870).

Murray's *Handbook to Yorkshire* (1904).

Notes and Queries (*Leeds Mercury Supplement*, 1890 onwards).

Old Yorkshire, ed. Smith, 8 vols. (1881–91).

—— ed. Wheater, 1 vol. (1885).

Parsons, E. *History and Description of the Manufacturing Districts of the West Riding*, 2 vols. (1834).

Price, A. C. *Leeds and its Neighbourhood* (1909).

Raine, Canon. *History of York* (Historic Towns Series, 1893).

Robinson. *Relics of Old Leeds* (1906).

Roth, H. Ling. 'Hand Card-making' (*Bankfield Museum Notes*, 1st series, xi).

—— 'Hand-combing' (*Bankfield Museum Notes*, 1st series, vi).

—— 'Bishop Blaize, Saint, Martyr, and Woolcombers' Patron' (*Bankfield Museum Notes*, 2nd series, vi).

—— *Yorkshire Coiners* (1906).

Schroeder, H. *Annals of Yorkshire*, 2 vols. (1851).

Sellers, M. Chapters on 'Economic History' and 'Textile Industries', in *Victoria County History of Yorkshire*, vols. ii and iii (1913).

—— 'The Merchant Adventurers of York' (*Brit. Association Handbook*, York, 1906).

—— *The Merchant Adventurers of York* (pamphlet, 1913).

—— 'York in the Sixteenth Century' (*Eng. Hist. Rev.*, vol. xvi).

Smith, W. *Rambles round Morley* (1866).

Sykes, D. F. E. *Huddersfield and its Vicinity* (1898).

Travis, J. *Notes, Historical and Biographical, of Todmorden and District* (1896).

Turner, J. Horsfall. *Shipley, Idle, and District* (n.d.).

—— *The Wakefield House of Correction* (n.d.).

Wardell, J. *Municipal History of Leeds* (1848).

Wilson. *History of Bramley Parish* (1860).

INDEX

PRINTED IN GREAT BRITAIN
AT THE UNIVERSITY PRESS, OXFORD
BY VIVIAN RIDLER
PRINTER TO THE UNIVERSITY